SOUL OF THE WORLD

The man in the red coat shot a look up the street toward their approach, and the sailors she'd been following broke in terror.

It was all she could do to dive out of their way, a stampede fleeing as fast as their legs could carry them, tripping over each other in a mad rush. And no denying the source. Even from a distance she could see the man in the red coat nod in satisfaction, then bark an order to the men unloading the warehouse in front of him.

What under the Gods? He hadn't made a threatening gesture, or brandished a weapon that she could see. If it was a leyline binding, it was like no binding she'd seen. He'd sent a troop of sailors running like… well, like the soldiers who had come before them, and with no more than a glance.

She picked herself up, still shrouded by *Faith*, and felt half an urge to find the city watch herself. Still, whatever he'd done to the sailors, it hadn't affected her. Perhaps she could get closer, enough to see the contents of the crates his men were unloading.

He turned again, frowning as he stared right at her.

By David Mealing

The Ascension Cycle
Soul of the World
Blood of the Gods

SOUL OF THE WORLD

The Ascension Cycle:
Book One

DAVID MEALING

www.orbitbooks.net

ORBIT

First published in Great Britain in 2017 by Orbit
This paperback edition published in 2018 by Orbit

1 3 5 7 9 10 8 6 4 2

Maps by Tim Paul

Excerpt from *Mageborn* by Stephen Aryan

All characters and events in this publication, other than those clearly in the public domain, are fictitious and any resemblance to real persons, living or dead, is purely coincidental.

A CIP catalogue record for this book is available from the British Library.

ISBN 978-0-356-50894-8

Printed and bound by CPI Group (UK) Ltd, Croydon CR0 4YY

Papers used by Orbit are from well-managed forests and other responsible sources.

Orbit
An imprint of
Little, Brown Book Group
Carmelite House
50 Victoria Embankment
London EC4Y 0DZ

An Hachette UK Company
www.hachette.co.uk

www.orbitbooks.net

For Lindsay

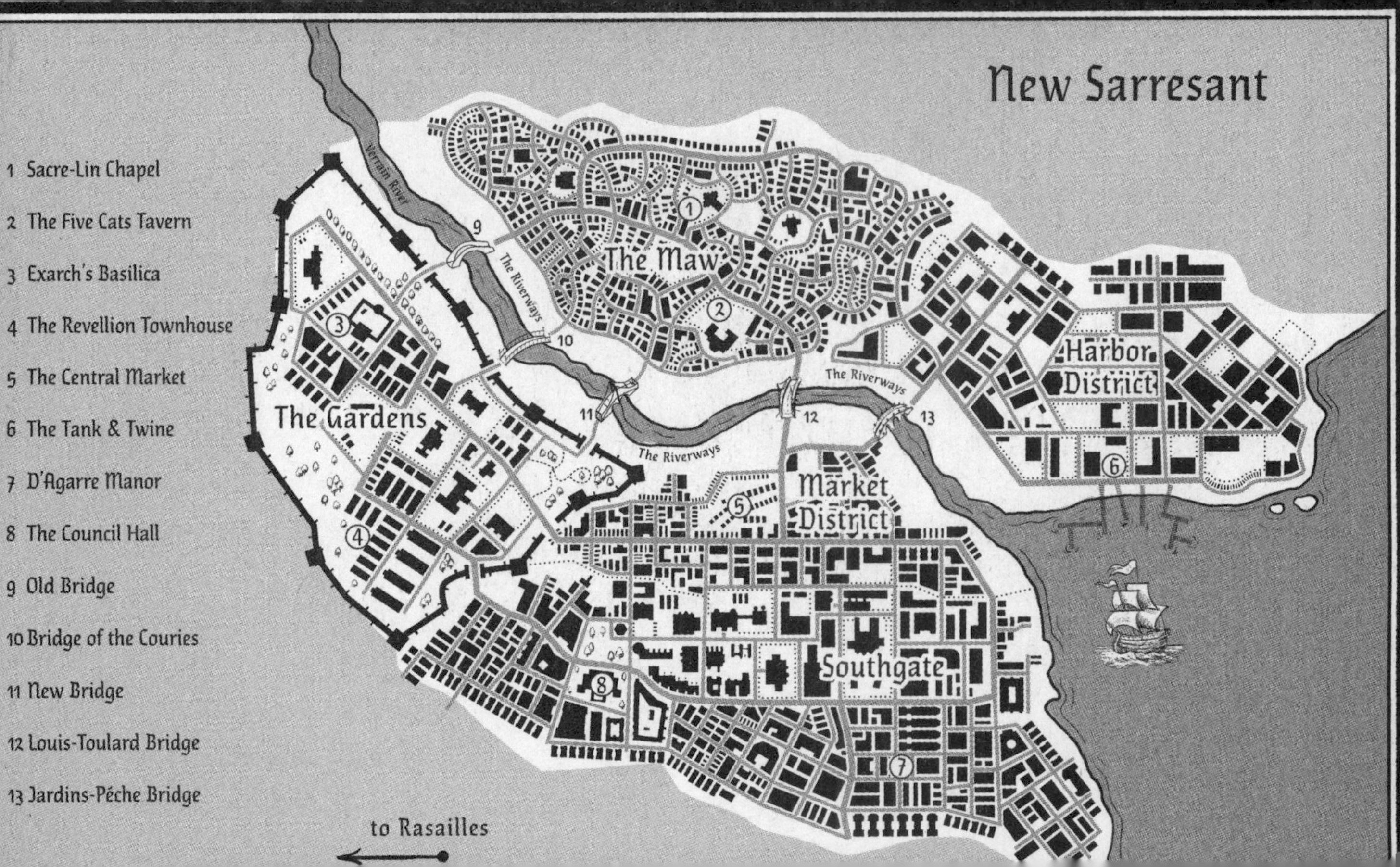
New Sarresant
1 Sacre-Lin Chapel
2 The Five Cats Tavern
3 Exarch's Basilica
4 The Revellion Townhouse
5 The Central Market
6 The Tank & Twine
7 D'Agarre Manor
8 The Council Hall
9 Old Bridge
10 Bridge of the Couries
11 New Bridge
12 Louis-Toulard Bridge
13 Jardins-Péche Bridge
The Maw
The Gardens
Harbor District
Market District
Southgate
The Riverways
The Riverways
The Riverways
Verrain River
to Rasailles

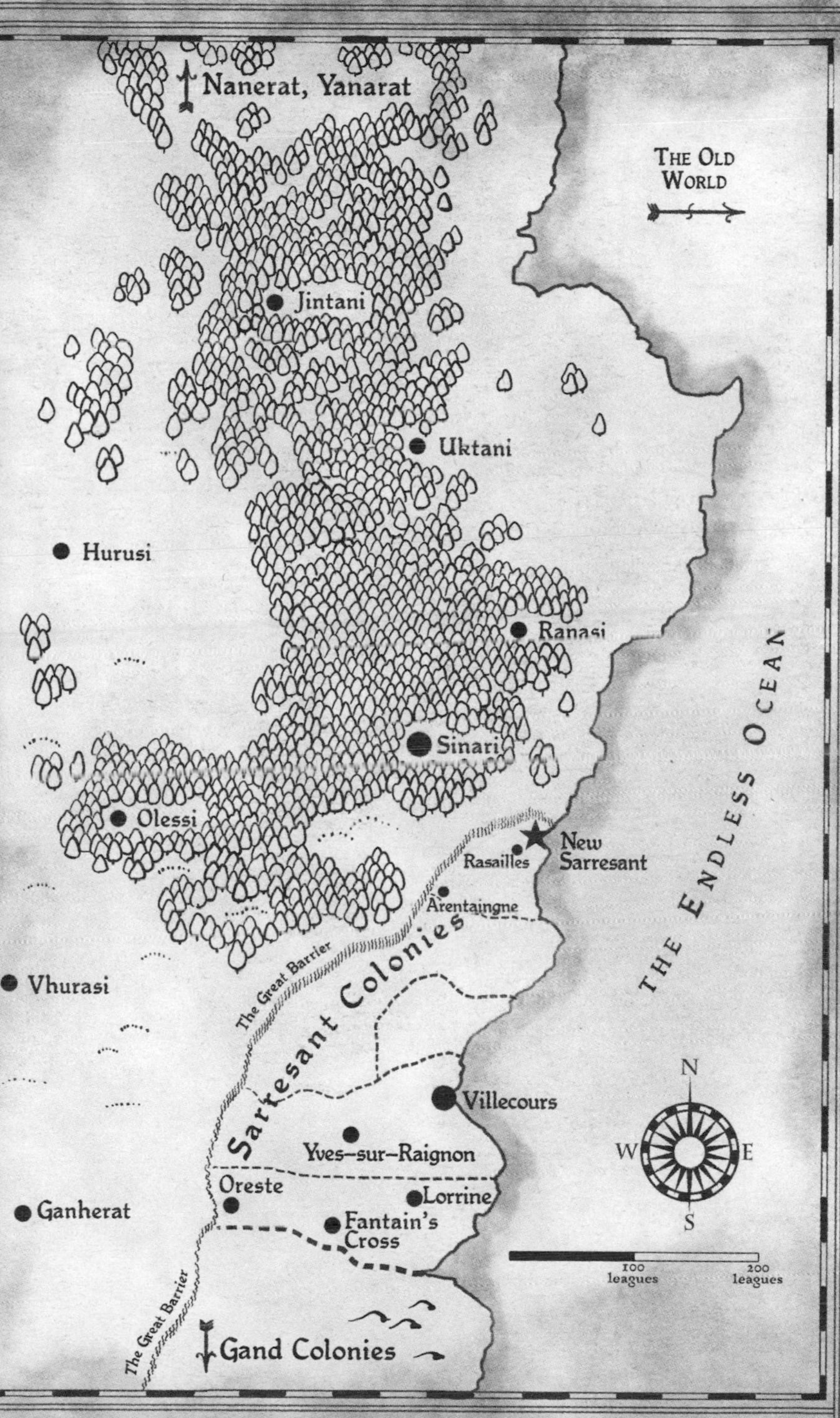
Nanerat, Yanarat
The Old World
Jintani
Uktani
Hurusi
Ranasi
Sinari
Olessi
New Sarresant
Rasailles
Arentaingne
The Endless Ocean
The Great Barrier
Sarresant Colonies
Vhurasi
Villecours
Yves-sur-Raignon
Oreste
Lorrine
Ganherat
Fantain's Cross
N
W
E
S
100 leagues
200 leagues
The Great Barrier
Gand Colonies

PART 1: SPRING

SEASON OF THE ORACLE

1

SARINE

Fontcadeu Green
The Royal Palace, Rasailles

"Throw!" came the command from the green.

A bushel of fresh-cut blossoms sailed into the air, chased by darts and the tittering laughter of lookers-on throughout the gardens.

It took quick work with her charcoals to capture the flowing lines as they moved, all feathers and flares. Ostentatious dress was the fashion this spring; her drab grays and browns would have stood out as quite peculiar had the young nobles taken notice of her as she worked.

Just as well they didn't. Her leyline connection to a source of *Faith* beneath the palace chapel saw to that.

Sarine smirked, imagining the commotion were she to sever her bindings, to appear plain as day sitting in the middle of the green. Rasailles was a short journey southwest of New Sarresant but may as well have been half a world apart. A public park, but no mistaking for whom among the public the green was intended. The guardsmen ringing the receiving ground made clear the requirement for a certain pedigree, or at least a certain display of wealth, and she fell far short of either.

She gave her leyline tethers a quick mental check, pleased to find them holding strong. No sense being careless. It was a risk coming here, but Zi seemed to relish these trips, and sketches of the nobles were among the easiest to sell. Zi had only just materialized in front of her, stretching like a cat. He made a show of it, arching his back, blue and purple iridescent scales glittering as he twisted in the sun.

She paused midway through reaching into her pack for a fresh sheet of paper, offering him a slow clap. Zi snorted and cozied up to her feet.

It's cold. Zi's voice sounded in her head. *I'll take all the sunlight I can get.*

"Yes, but still, quite a show," she said in a hushed voice, satisfied none of the nobles were close enough to hear.

What game is it today?

"The new one. With the flowers and darts. Difficult to follow, but I believe Lord Revellion is winning."

Mmm.

A warm glow radiated through her mind. Zi was pleased. And so for that matter were the young ladies watching Lord Revellion saunter up to take his turn at the line. She returned to a cross-legged pose, beginning a quick sketch of the nobles' repartee, aiming to capture Lord Revellion's simple confidence as he charmed the ladies on the green. He was the picture of an eligible Sarresant noble: crisp-fitting blue cavalry uniform, free-flowing coal-black hair, and neatly chiseled features, enough to remind her that life was not fair. Not that a child raised on the streets of the Maw needed reminding on that point.

He called to a group of young men nearby, the ones holding the flowers. They gathered their baskets, preparing to heave, and Revellion turned, flourishing the darts he held in each hand, earning himself titters and giggles from the fops on the green. She worked to capture the moment, her charcoal pen tracing the lines of his coat as he stepped forward, ready to throw. Quick strokes for his hair, pushed back by the breeze. One simple line to suggest the concentrated poise in his face.

The crowd gasped and cheered as the flowers were tossed. Lord Revellion sprang like a cat, snapping his darts one by one in quick succession. *Thunk. Thunk. Thunk. Thunk.* More cheering. Even at this distance it was clear he had hit more than he missed, a rare enough feat for this game.

You like this one, the voice in her head sounded. Zi uncoiled, his scales flashing a burnished gold before returning to blue and purple. He cocked his head up toward her with an inquisitive look. *You could help him win, you know.*

"Hush. He does fine without my help."

She darted glances back and forth between her sketch paper and the green, trying to include as much detail as she could. The patterns of the blankets spread for the ladies as they reclined on the grass, the carefree way they laughed. Their practiced movements as they sampled fruits and cheeses, and the bowed heads of servants holding the trays on bended knees. The black charcoal medium wouldn't capture the vibrant colors of the flowers, but she could do their forms justice, soft petals scattering to the wind as they were tossed into the air.

It was more detail than was required to sell her sketches. But details made it real, for her as much as her customers. If she hadn't seen and drawn them from life, she might never have believed such abundance possible: dances in the grass, food and wine at a snap of their fingers, a practiced poise in every movement. She gave a bitter laugh, imagining the absurdity of practicing sipping your wine just so, the better to project the perfect image of a highborn lady.

Zi nibbled her toe, startling her. *They live the only lives they know,* he thought to her. His scales had taken on a deep green hue.

She frowned. She was never quite sure whether he could actually read her thoughts.

"Maybe," she said after a moment. "But it wouldn't kill them to share some of those grapes and cheeses once in a while."

She gave the sketch a last look. A decent likeness; it might fetch a half mark, perhaps, from the right buyer. She reached into her pack for a jar of sediment, applying the yellow flakes with care to avoid smudging her work. When it was done she set the paper on the grass, reclining on her hands to watch another round of darts. The next thrower fared poorly, landing only a single *thunk*. Groans from some of the onlookers, but just as many whoops and cheers. It appeared Revellion had won. The young lord pranced forward to take a deep bow, earning polite applause from across the green as servants dashed out to collect the darts and flowers for another round.

She retrieved the sketch, sliding it into her pack and withdrawing a fresh sheet. This time she'd sketch the ladies, perhaps, a show of the latest fashions for—

She froze.

Across the green a trio of men made way toward her, drawing curious eyes from the nobles as they crossed the gardens. The three of them stood out among the nobles' finery as sure as she would have done: two men in the blue and gold leather of the palace guard, one in simple brown robes. A priest.

Not all among the priesthood could touch the leylines, but she wouldn't have wagered a copper against this one having the talent, even if she wasn't close enough to see the scars on the backs of his hands to confirm it. Binder's marks, the by-product of the test administered to every child the crown could get its hands on. If this priest had the gift, he could follow her tethers whether he could see her or no.

She scrambled to return the fresh page and stow her charcoals, slinging the pack on her shoulder and springing to her feet.

Time to go? Zi asked in her thoughts.

She didn't bother to answer. Zi would keep up. At the edge of the green, the guardsmen patrolling the outer gardens turned to watch the priest and his fellows closing in. Damn. Her *Faith* would hold long enough to get her over the wall, but there wouldn't be any stores to draw on once she left the green. She'd been hoping for another hour at least, time for half a dozen more sketches and another round of games. Instead there was a damned priest on watch. She'd be lucky to escape with no more than a chase through the woods, and thank the Gods they didn't seem to have hounds or horses in tow to investigate her errant binding.

Better to move quickly, no?

She slowed mid-stride. "Zi, you know I hate—"

Shh.

Zi appeared a few paces ahead of her, his scales flushed a deep, sour red, the color of bottled wine. Without further warning her heart leapt in her chest, a red haze coloring her vision. Blood seemed to pound in her ears. Her muscles surged with raw energy, carrying her forward with a springing step that left the priest and his guardsmen behind as if they were mired in tar.

Her stomach roiled, but she made for the wall as fast as her feet could carry her. Zi was right, even if his gifts made her want to sick up the bread she'd scrounged for breakfast. The sooner she could get over the wall, the sooner she could drop her *Faith* tether and stop the priest tracking her binding. Maybe he'd think it no more than a curiosity, an errant cloud of ley-energy mistaken for something more.

She reached the vines and propelled herself up the wall in a smooth motion, vaulting the top and landing with a cat's poise on the far side. *Faith* released as soon as she hit the ground, but she kept running until her heartbeat calmed, and the red haze faded from her sight.

The sounds and smells of the city reached her before the trees cleared enough to see it. A minor miracle for there to be trees at all; the northern and southern reaches had been cut to grassland, from the trade roads to the Great Barrier between the colonies and the wildlands beyond. But the Duc-Governor had ordered a wood maintained around the palace at Rasailles, and so the axes looked elsewhere for their fodder. It made for peaceful walks, when she wasn't waiting for priests and guards to swoop down looking for signs she'd been trespassing on the green.

She'd spent the better part of the way back in relative safety. Zi's gifts were strong, and thank the Gods they didn't seem to register on the leylines. The priest gave up the chase with time enough for her to ponder the morning's games: the decadence, a hidden world of wealth and beauty, all of it a stark contrast to the sullen eyes and sunken faces of the cityfolk. Her uncle would tell her it was part of the Gods' plan, all the usual Trithetic dogma. A hard story to swallow, watching the nobles eating, laughing, and playing at their games when half the city couldn't be certain where they'd find tomorrow's meals. This was supposed to be a land of promise, a land of freedom and purpose—a New World. Remembering the opulence of Rasailles palace, it looked a lot like the old one to her. Not that she'd ever been across the sea, or anywhere in the colonies but here in New Sarresant. Still.

There was a certain allure to it, though.

It kept her coming back, and kept her patrons buying sketches whenever she set up shop in the markets. The fashions, the finery, the dream of something otherworldly almost close enough to touch. And Lord Revellion. She had to admit he was handsome, even far away. He seemed so confident, so prepared for the life he lived. What would he think of her? One thing to use her gifts and skulk her way onto the green, but that was a pale shadow of a real invitation. And that was where she fell short. Her gifts set her apart, but underneath it all she was still *her*. Not for the first time she wondered if that was enough. Could it be? Could it be enough to end up somewhere like Rasailles, with someone like Lord Revellion?

Zi pecked at her neck as he settled onto her shoulder, giving her a start. She smiled when she recovered, flicking his head.

We approach.

"Yes. Though I'm not sure I should take you to the market after you shushed me back there."

Don't sulk. It was for your protection.

"Oh, of course," she said. "Still, Uncle could doubtless use my help in the chapel, and it *is* almost midday..."

Zi raised his head sharply, his eyes flaring like a pair of hot pokers, scales flushed to match.

"Okay, okay, the market it is."

Zi cocked his head as if to confirm she was serious, then nestled down for a nap as she walked. She kept a brisk pace, taking care to avoid prying eyes that might be wondering what a lone girl was doing coming in from the woods. Soon she was back among the crowds of Southgate district, making her way toward the markets at the center of the city. Zi flushed a deep blue as she walked past the bustle of city life, weaving through the press.

Back on the cobblestone streets of New Sarresant, the lush greens and floral brightness of the royal gardens seemed like another world, foreign and strange. This was home: the sullen grays, worn wooden and brick buildings, the downcast eyes of the cityfolk as they went about the day's business. Here a gilded coach drew eyes and whispers, and not always from a place as benign as envy. She knew better than to court the attention of that sort—the hot-eyed men who glared at the nobles' backs, so long as no city watch could see.

She held her pack close, shoving past a pair of rough-looking pedestrians who'd stopped in the middle of the crowd. They gave her a dark look, and Zi raised himself up on her shoulders, giving them a snort. She rolled her eyes, as much for his bravado as theirs. Sometimes it was a good thing she was the only one who could see Zi.

As she approached the city center, she had to shove her way past another pocket of lookers-on, then another. Finally the press became too heavy and she came to a halt just outside the central square. A low rumble of whispers rolled through the crowds ahead, enough for her to know what was going on.

An execution.

She retreated a few paces, listening to the exchanges in the crowd. Not just one execution—three. Deserters from the army, which made them traitors, given the crown had declared war on the Gandsmen two seasons past. A glorious affair, meant to check a tyrant's expansion, or so they'd proclaimed in the colonial papers. All it meant in her quarters of the city was food carts diverted southward, when the Gods knew there was little enough to spare.

Voices buzzed behind her as she ducked down an alley, with a glance up and down the street to ensure she was alone. Zi swelled up, his scales pulsing as his head darted about, eyes wide and hungering.

"What do you think?" she whispered to him. "Want to have a look?"

Yes. The thought dripped with anticipation.

Well, that settled that. But this time it was her choice to empower herself, and she'd do it without Zi making her heart beat in her throat.

She took a deep breath, sliding her eyes shut.

In the darkness behind her eyelids, lines of power emanated from the ground in all directions, a grid of interconnecting strands of light. Colors and shapes surrounded the lines, fed by energy from the shops, the houses, the people of the city. Overwhelmingly she saw the green pods of *Life*, abundant wherever people lived and worked. But at the edge of her vision she saw the red motes of *Body*, a relic of a bar fight or something of that sort. And, in the center of the city square, a shallow pool of *Faith*. Nothing like an execution to bring out belief and hope in the Gods and the unknown.

She opened herself to the leylines, binding strands of light between her body and the sources of the energy she needed.

Her eyes snapped open as *Body* energy surged through her. Her muscles became more responsive, her pack light as a feather. At the same time, she twisted a *Faith* tether around herself, fading from view.

By reflex she checked her stores. Plenty of *Faith*. Not much *Body*. She'd have to be quick. She took a step back, then bounded forward, leaping onto the side of the building. She twisted away as she kicked off the wall, spiraling out toward the roof's overhang. Grabbing hold of the edge, she vaulted herself up onto the top of the tavern in one smooth motion.

Very nice, Zi thought to her. She bowed her head in a flourish, ignoring his sarcasm.

Now, can we go?

Urgency flooded her mind. Best not to keep Zi waiting when he got like this. She let *Body* dissipate but maintained her shroud of *Faith* as she walked along the roof of the tavern. Reaching the edge, she lowered herself to have a seat atop a window's overhang as she looked down into the square. With luck she'd avoid catching the attention of any more priests or other binders in the area, and that meant she'd have the best seat in the house for these grisly proceedings.

She set her pack down beside her and pulled out her sketching materials. Might as well make a few silvers for her time.

2

ERRIS

14th Light Cavalry
Gand Territory

"Over there, you see it?" one of her lance-corporals whispered.

"There, in front of the trees." A soldier beside him pointed.

More excited whispers.

Erris snapped her fist up, signaling quiet in the ranks. She saw it. At the base of the forested hill she'd managed to sneak her men up during the night: a faint shimmer in the air, facing away from her soldiers, toward where she'd camped the night before. It meant the enemy had a binder skilled enough with *Shelter* to weave a shield against her attack.

And it meant their commander was a fool.

This flanking maneuver was far from her finest work. Simple. A child should have seen it. Anger flared, to think those poor soldiers at the base of the hill had to suffer under the command of an imbecile. Well, they wouldn't have to suffer much longer.

"Draw sabers," she whispered. "One volley with sidearms, then give them steel. Keep it quiet. Pass the order."

Her command flew from soldier to soldier down their line, accompanied by the muted *shink* of cavalry sabers. She signaled to the horse-sergeants to stay in the rear with their mounts. The hill's sloped angle and thick foliage wouldn't allow a charge on horseback. Was that why the enemy commander was such a buffoon? Was he one of those who thought cavalry must stay mounted, that putting his soldiers' backs to terrain impassable to horse rendered them impervious to her attack?

She spat.

A raised saber served to give the order, and she wheeled it forward to indicate a charge. As one her men surged over the brush and rocks they'd hidden behind.

A light rain began to fall, mixing with blood and gunfire as the sounds of battle rang through the trees.

"Hold still, damn you," one of her sergeants cursed. "The brigade-colonel is on her way."

"She's arrived, Sergeant," Erris replied, dropping to a knee. The soldier being held down by his squad commander stared through them both as he moaned. Young. Fresh-faced and clean-shaven, with eyes like saucer plates, filled with the horror of coming face-to-face with death for the first time.

The sergeant edged forward to make room for her at the boy's side, losing his grip on an arm. She had to duck backward to avoid being taken across the side of her face as the wounded soldier flailed.

"Easy, son," she said, moving to place her hands on his chest as she pulled off her gloves, exposing the binder's marks on the backs of her hands. "I've seen worse than you this morning." She had. The boy's wound was among the least severe to be judged worthy of her attention. A musket ball that, from the thin streams of blood, had missed his major arteries. He might have been fine in due time without her, though Gods be damned if she'd let her men roll the dice and recover without her intervention.

The boy seemed not to hear, his rapid breathing punctuated by gasps and unintelligible muttering. She inhaled deep, closing her eyes. The green pods of *Life* energy were abundant in the wild, pooling in clouds beneath the elms and oaks, where fallen leaves and broken brush gave refuge to wildlife hiding from the sounds of battle. She tethered a strand between the boy and one of the nearby leylines. Not half so effective as if he could hold a binding on his own, and the barest sliver of what a fullbinder like Erris could do. But it would suffice.

"There you go," she said. "Easy." The boy sucked in air as energy coursed through him, giving his body strength to deal with the pain. For the first time since her arrival his eyes came into focus. He was one of the new recruits, freshly conscripted from the southern colonies before they crossed the Gand border. Seventeen if he was a day, tempted by the glory of honorable battle against the enemies of the crown. Six months ago he might have had a season's training, drilling under the watchful eye of foul-mouthed instructors, before they put him in the saddle. But they were at war now, and the army took what it could get.

"Thank you," the boy whispered hoarsely.

"You'll be fine, son." She patted his shoulder as she stood. "Listen to your squad commander and you'll be riding again within a day or two." He sputtered a cough, nodding as he closed his eyes.

The sergeant laid the boy down and rose to his feet with a hasty salute, fist to chest.

"Thank you, sir," he said. "Shudder to think what we'd do without you."

"Feed the worms, I expect, Sergeant," she said with a smile, eliciting a nervous laugh from the man. A fullbinder with Erris's strength was a rare thing. The medics did their best with the supplies available to the army, but her gifts had kept the 14th Light Cavalry on its horses throughout this campaign, and her men knew it as well as she did.

She returned the sergeant's salute and left him to tend to his squad. One never got used to the smell of blood on this scale, the sounds men made as they lay dying. Lines of prisoners marched beside her, prodded by saber or carbine toward the field where her men had started to gather, away from the carnage of the fight. A skirmish, really. Two brigades colliding away from the trade roads. Little chance of any glory, or of seeing the battle named in the colonial papers. Such was the lot of the cavalry. Men with noble titles and fat purses declared wars for the glory of king and country, and her men did most of the dying, far away from medals, in backwoods and countryside left untouched in better times.

Six months, now, since the crown had declared its war on Gand, and expected its colonies across the sea to follow suit. A means to check the enemy's expansion, according to the pamphlets circulated to justify the invasion, though Gand had not been alone in its drive to empire. Conquest and colonies brought the great powers gold and trade, but more important, discoveries of new bindings. The academics had argued larger claims of territory led to a stronger leyline grid, able to retain a broader spectrum of energies and bolster the gifts of those who could tether them. It had proven true enough, even in her lifetime. The Thellan War, five years before, had resulted in a select few of Sarresant's binders gaining access to *Entropy*. No way of telling what a successful campaign against Gand would bring. And not her place to speculate. It was for men two hundred leagues north, in the palaces and manors of New Sarresant, Rasailles, and Villecours, or two thousand leagues across the sea, to dream up reasons to fight. Enough for her that the red-coated soldiers wanted her men dead, and it took killing them to keep her boys alive.

Her aide stood a few paces up the hill, waiting for her to finish reviewing the wounded. Sadrelle was a good man, a veteran of the autumn campaign who'd proven himself as a scout. Newly promoted to his lieutenant's stripe, but that was the way of things during war. Her last aide had run afoul of a Gand sharpshooter, so now she had Sadrelle.

He made a salute as he fell into step beside her.

"Sir. Lance-Captain d'Guile has the prisoner you asked for. And the medics sent the bill."

"How bad is it?"

"Fourteen dead. Six more critical beyond your aid. Thirty-six wounded and recovering."

She cursed under her breath. A light toll, considering the forces had been almost evenly matched. But even a light toll weighed heavy on her shoulders. The soldiers trusted her with their lives; every mistake was paid in blood. Twenty dead, or would be soon enough.

"Thank you, Aide-Lieutenant. See to it the supply wagons arrive on the double. I need our wounded ready to travel within the half hour."

"I've already sent word, sir."

"Good."

They walked on in silence, making their way back to the impromptu command post where her officers had placed her flag. Let the men see her, poised and outwardly confident, the very image of a brigade-colonel in her moment of victory. Inside her stomach roiled. Five hundred and seventeen souls in the 14th now. The Nameless take the butcher and his bills.

At the base of the hill, a double line of empty-saddled horses trotted into view. The horse-sergeants must have led them around the back of the approach as soon as she gave the order to charge. A confident move, approaching hubris. What if it had been a trap? She made a mental note to dress the handlers down that evening. She was not infallible as a commander, no matter what her men liked to think.

The men around the command post saluted her approach, all save a slumped figure at their center.

"What do we have, Lance-Captain?" she asked. Lance-Captain d'Guile had command of one of her four fighting companies, five hundred horse at full strength, though the 14th hadn't been close to full strength in some time.

"A lieutenant, sir. Second in command of a company of infantry. Says they were with the Second Army, under Duke Dunweir."

She raised an eyebrow. A lieutenant, the highest-ranking officer among those who hadn't fled or been slain in the fighting. And 2nd Army. That was damned curious. The prisoner had lines under his eyes, dust smeared in ink-black patches on his skin as only a forced march could do. He'd been driven hard, perhaps a week or more of dawn-to-dusk marches without the benefit of a horse or a binder to spell his fatigue. What was the Gand 2nd Army doing so far north?

"Let's see what he has to say." She nodded to Sadrelle, who among his other talents had a near-perfect command of the Gand tongue. Her own ability with the language was not poor, but it wouldn't do to have a Sarresant commander stutter over simple questions when interrogating a prisoner. "Ask him to repeat his rank and designation, for my sake."

Sadrelle relayed her question in the harsh, chopped speech of the Gandsmen and the prisoner raised his head, looking her in the eyes as he responded. She gave the lieutenant full marks for bravery. Enemy he may be, but this man was no coward.

"Lieutenant Alistair Radford," the prisoner said in the Gand tongue, voice straining with a mix of pride, fatigue, and resignation. "Second to Major Stuart, third company of Colonel Hansus's regiment, Second Army under his excellency the Duke of Dunweir."

"And what were your orders on this march, Lieutenant? Why was your regiment split from the main body of the Second Army?" Sadrelle relayed the message.

The prisoner stared at her.

She held his gaze, maintaining calm in her eyes as she spoke. "Tell the lieutenant his cooperation will determine whether he dines with Colonel Hansus in a fortnight or I put him and his fellow soldiers to the sword. He knows a cavalry unit isn't going to march prisoners behind our supply wagons."

Silence hung in the air after Sadrelle finished the translation. At last, the prisoner spoke. "Colonel Hansus is dead," he said bitterly. "I stood beside him as he fell."

She dropped to a knee and replied in Gand tongue herself. "Then you know what to do. Your men need you. Don't fail them."

The prisoner held his silence for a few more moments, then hung his head as he began to talk.

Half an hour later, she sat astride Jiri, issuing her final commands before they moved. A blessing from the Gods to be with her mount once more. Jiri whickered, bobbing her head up and down, and she patted the white mare's neck in a calming gesture. Just as Erris worried for her soldiers, she knew Jiri worried for her. They were a pair; such was the nature of the bondsteed's training, though no few of the prisoners cast dubious glances toward the figure she cut on Jiri's back. Erris was not a tall woman, nor thickly built. Her blue cavalry uniform had to be specially sized for her frame, as did the long steel saber she wore on her belt. Jiri on the other hand would never be mistaken for anything other than what she was. Nineteen hands high and finely muscled despite her size, Jiri towered over any other horse on the 14th's rope lines. Her training as a bondsteed—the formal name for mounts accustomed to bindings from their riders—only added to a strength and grace that would have made her an armored charger a few centuries before.

Erris maintained a simple binding of *Life* energy to keep their senses sharp. Her men had made quick work of preparing for the day's ride, and if the weather permitted they would cover thirty leagues before sundown. A hard ride made harder for having started the day with bloodshed, and another fifty leagues tomorrow, Gods and the weather permitting. Enough to reach the main body of the Sarresant army, to deliver the prisoner's information with time to act, if the bloody fools at high command took it for what it was.

The captured subcommander of an infantry company couldn't know the gravity of what he'd revealed. But if Duke Dunweir's 2nd Army was committed to a march into the Sarresant colonies, it could only mean the Gandsmen were trying a desperate gambit, leveraging their superior numbers for a hammer strike at New Sarresant itself. A gambit that might have gone undetected if Colonel Hansus's regiment hadn't taken the wrong fork two days past and stumbled into her patrol sweep.

Dumb luck. Or a trap. She couldn't rule out either, in the military. Amusing just how thin the line could be between genius and idiocy.

She nudged Jiri forward with her knees, riding to the front of the column.

"Sure we can't talk you out of this, sir?" d'Guile asked, a wry grin on his face.

She heeled Jiri to a stop beside them. "No, Captain; the order stands. You are to ride for the main body of the army in all haste. Relay what we've learned to high command. I'll be along within a few days to confirm with a visual report."

Lance-Captain Pourrain coughed politely beside her. "Colonel, with respect, didn't Vicomte-General Carailles reprimand you quite severely the last time you led a squad to do reconnaissance?" Pourrain was her most veteran commander, a former enlisted soldier who'd been promoted to a captaincy despite having never attended an academy. He kept his expression level, but she knew him well enough to recognize the dry humor behind his comment. Vicomte-General Carailles could bugger himself on the Exarch's longblade for all she cared what the man thought of her command performance, or her personal risk-taking.

All four of the lance-captains chuckled.

"Take care of yourself, sir," Lance-Captain d'Guile said.

"And you take care of the men," she said. "D'Guile, you have the Fourteenth until I return."

He saluted, followed by the other three captains. She saluted back, dismissing them.

The 14th Light Cavalry split into two columns. One long, sinuous line of horse and wagons followed behind d'Guile's banner as it turned northward, back toward the Sarresant border. The other, a squad of six led by the brigade commander, turned east toward the last reported position of the enemy army.

3

SARINE

Sacre-Lin Chapel
Maw District, New Sarresant

Rays of purple and orange streamed through the chapel's stained glass, making a mask of bright color over her eyes. She might have appreciated it more had she not been soaring over a field of freshly bloomed flowers, taking in the spring scents as she glided on a soft breeze. Or something like that. The dream haze faded and she sat up with a long stretch and a yawn.

Her loft at the top of the chapel was small, an alcove made for the glass workers to tend to the stained-glass relief that dominated the central nave. Three panes of glass in rectangular slats, depicting each of the three Trithetic Gods: two smaller panes depicting the Oracle and the Veil, with a centerpiece showing the stern, armored figure of the Exarch. She offered a quick prayer of thanks to all three as she rose from her makeshift mattress of piled blankets. Her devotion to the virtuous paths had never been as sincere as her adoptive uncle might have liked, but she had a warm place to sleep now, and plenty of space to display her sketches. Being awoken by sunlight through a stained-glass masterwork was a far sight better than feral cats scratching at her, hoping she'd died in the night and gifted them an easy meal. Or worse. The Maw district was not a kind place. Whatever perverse notion inspired the priests to build a chapel in the slums she could hardly fathom. It saw little enough use, for all the love her uncle put toward its upkeep.

He was up already, sanding away at one of the wooden benches facing the dais below. She knelt beside the wooden divider at the edge of her loft, folding her arms and resting her head on her hands as she watched him work. Father Thibeaux wasn't truly a blood relative, just an old priest with a soft temperament who had taken pity on a girl in need.

He is kind, Zi thought to her. He phrased it delicately, as if the concept of kindness needed to be handled with care.

"Yes, he is," she said in the soft whisper she always used when talking to Zi in the chapel. "Having second thoughts about letting me tell him about you?"

That would be unwise.

She sighed, looking over the divider, watching her uncle work until he noticed her, looking up with a smile. His thick gray mustaches and long eyebrows exaggerated his every facial expression, and this was a welcome one. The priest's robes he wore were old but well mended, long brown wool with a single line of buttons running from the top of his neck to below his waist. Only the pink marks on the backs of his hands unnerved her, a sign of what would happen to her if she ever ran afoul of the priests, or the city watch.

Binder's marks. The product of the test administered to every child in the realm, the sign of duty owed the crown for permission to touch the sacred lines of power. Twenty years' service, or a lordly sum of gold paid to the King for a writ of pardon, and the blue and gold tattoos that came with it—such was the price for the gift of magic. The same gift she had, yet her hands were smooth and clean, and she meant to see they stayed that way. For reasons he had never disclosed, Father Thibeaux had helped to shield her from his fellow priests since he'd first taken her in from the streets.

"Good to see you awake, child," he called up to her. "Fancy giving me a hand with the benches before you head out for the day?"

"Of course, uncle." No sense dwelling on unpleasantness. She wasn't like to be caught by the watch in the middle of the chapel.

She finished dressing and gathered her sketching materials into her pack. Yesterday's sketches she left behind, the elegant lines of the nobles laughing on the green and the gore of the young soldiers separated from their heads in the public square. Not that there wouldn't be demand for those in the market—if anything, selling both sets alongside one another would speak to the city's mood. But that was precisely the point. Juxtaposing the nobles' frivolities against their execution of peach-faced youths could land her in a cold chamber in a guardhouse somewhere. Wiser to let tensions subside for a few days.

She climbed down the ladder into the main hall of the chapel, setting her pack down before grabbing a cloth and kneeling to work on the front row of benches.

"So," her uncle asked as he stooped over the bench he was scouring. "What's today's adventure?"

"The Harbor," she replied. "They're expecting the *Queen Allisée* to arrive shortly after the morning tide."

"The warship?" he asked, harrumphing when she nodded. "Too much warmongering lately. You'll take care down at the Harbor, yes? Rough types there, sailors and the like."

"I'll be careful, uncle. The docks aren't dangerous with all the soldiers about."

He paused a moment, then cleared his throat as he always did before he recited scripture. "Vigilance. Third virtue of the Exarch. Sixth verse."

He was testing her. "*Second* virtue of the Exarch. Sixth verse. 'The threatening blade is wielded by those under the veil.'"

He nodded, satisfied. "And what are we to make of the sixth verse?"

"Look for danger where we least expect it," she said. She'd recently reread this passage in the holy books, the grand stories supposedly left behind from a time when the Gods walked the earth, imparting their wisdom as they fought battles against their ancient enemy. Whatever she made of the lessons within, the holy books were the only writing she had at hand. It wouldn't do to squander her uncle's lessons by letting her mind go dull.

He nodded again. "That is one interpretation, and the common one in Sarresant," he said, his eyes alight with interest. "Would you believe the Thellan translation ascribes that passage to the virtues of the Veil instead? They interpret it to mean that those loyal to her virtues are the most threatening of warriors."

She listened as he weaved an impromptu sermon. It was a shame they got so few parishioners here in the Maw. Her uncle had a gift. Not for the first time she silently questioned why a priest with his ability for rhetoric and analysis had been content with such a small piece of the ecclesiastical pie. In all the years he'd been in charge of the Sacre-Lin, he'd never so much as asked for another priest to help him maintain the place, as far as she knew.

He was wrapping up as they finished scouring the last two benches in the center of the chapel, when his tone shifted, growing somber.

"Sarine, you must take care out there," he said, meeting her eyes with a look of concern.

"Uncle…?"

"I'm serious, child. These are dangerous times, especially so for you. Imagining you up on the headsman's block, facing down one of those guillotines…it's more than an old man can stomach." His eyes had reddened, his cheeks flushed. What was this? It was true they'd been executing lawbreakers with more zeal than normal lately, but she had her gifts. He should know; he'd trained her himself, at least with the basics of her binding abilities. And yes, it wasn't exactly legal for her to do what she did without a sanction from the crown, but he'd always been confident in her skills before.

"Uncle, I am careful."

He nodded, wiping his eyes. "I know, I know. I've taught you what little I can, though it may damn my soul, but even with your talent there are dangers. I don't fear for my head, but you, I could not stand the thought…"

She moved over and slid her arms around him.

"Thank you, child," he said. "Only, promise me you will keep yourself safe."

"I promise."

"Oracle's tits, girl, watch where you're going!" a voice yelled down from a second-floor balcony. The crate that had slipped loose from their winched ropes and crashed to the ground had missed her by inches, though the worker's shouting did a fine job of clearing the shock from her mind.

"Did your mother teach you to tie that knot, you wine-limp son of a whore?" she shouted back. The rope puller dismissed her with an obscene gesture as a pair of warehouse men rushed to the street to gather the crate's contents and clean up the mess. Zi trundled behind her, his legs pumping to keep pace as he swiveled his head around, drinking in the scene. His scales seemed to be fighting a battle over whether to be a deep emerald green or a dark crimson. Zi loved coming here, though Sarine found it too frenetic without a good vantage point from which to observe.

It was toward just such a point she strode, a neatly stacked tower of barrels and crates that would take the customs men several hours to clear, given the throng of activity surrounding the *Queen Allisée*. Plenty of time for her to sketch the day's events.

She edged around the crowds, staying close to the warehouses lining the harbor. Soldiers and seamen wandered the waterfront with hungry eyes, having set foot on dry land for the first time in a month or more. She had no illusions what they hungered for. More than a few pointed at her in her slim-fitting trousers and coat, making ribald asides to their companions. She ignored them, climbing the crates as quick as she could. Gods knew the brothels of New Sarresant celebrated every ship that made anchor in the city's deep harbor. Plenty of such ships today, though none of them half so grand as the triple-decked man-o'-war that had pride of place beside the city's longest dock. Sarine settled in atop a large crate, making space for her pack as she fetched out her sketching materials. The docks could be an irritating mass of even more irritating people, but she loved to sketch the ships. So many lines, like a puzzle of ropework to unravel with her charcoals. She got to work on the *Queen Allisée*, relishing every stroke of the ship's majesty as it lolled back and forth with the tide.

Zi draped himself atop a barrel beneath her as she worked, regarding the teeming mass of people below. Every so often he paused and perked up his head with interest as something caught his attention, a dustup or shouting match or something of the kind. Zi was the best sort of companion. He required little more than a good observation spot, and he gave her the space she needed to concentrate on her work.

And without him she never would have survived the Maw.

She suppressed a shudder at that thought, her mind straying to memories she would as soon forget.

Yellow.

She frowned.

"Zi, what does that mean?"

Yellow. Nearby.

She rested her charcoal on the leg of her trousers, panning a look across the harbor for a sign to indicate his meaning. Nothing more than business as usual: fishmongers hawking wares, dockworkers loading or unloading crates, sailors looking to get drunk no matter the time of day. Almost she said as much, when a pair of blue-coated soldiers came around a winding street at the southern end of the docks, running as if they'd been set afire, threatening to trample anyone between them and wherever they intended to go.

She wasn't the only one to have noticed. It was one thing for children or less-than-savory types to go running through the streets in the middle of the day. Even from atop her stack of crates it was clear the soldiers were panicked, setting pretense aside in a desperate rush to get far away from whatever put them to retreat.

The harbor's buzz fell quiet as more heads turned to watch the soldiers run.

"Stop there," came a deafening bellow, loud enough to hear it even half a harbor away. "You lads, hold fast."

She couldn't see the source of the commands, but they'd fallen on deaf ears. The soldiers kept at their run, leaving behind a wake of gossip and speculation in the Harbor crowds milling beneath her crates.

"What was that, Zi?" She craned her neck down toward the harbor. "What was that you said about 'yellow'?"

It was Yellow, he replied.

Zi lay back down on the crate beside her, appearing more interested in the buzzing of the crowd than the soldiers' strange flight. She frowned again, preparing to press the issue, when a squad of sailors trotted down the waterfront toward where the soldiers had come running. She spared another look at Zi, then shook her head and began gathering up her materials.

Going so soon?

"Going to chance a look at whatever's happening down there," she said. "Since it doesn't appear you're going to be any help."

He let out a long yawn, uncoiling his back as he stretched.

"Well?" she asked.

Fine by me.

That was something. Zi wouldn't let her walk unaware into danger. The soldiers' display would be on the tongues of half the commonfolk in the Harbor by now, and well on the way inland before suppertime. A sketch or two of whatever had sparked this news would draw more than its share of eyes in the market. She secured her pack and made her way back down to the street just in time for the squad of sailors to pass by the base of her crates. For once they spared no attention for her as they made their way toward whatever had sent the first group of soldiers running for their lives.

She closed her eyes and shifted her vision to the leylines, finding an ample reserve of *Faith* beneath the ships rolling on mooring lines with the tide. Most such stores would fade after a few days at port, but the warship's flotilla was fresh enough to retain whatever belief sustained its sailors on the long trek across the ocean, and that meant *Faith* for her. She made the tether, fading from view as she fell into step behind the men.

At first the street seemed normal enough. The southern part of the harbor was less trafficked than the northern end, but it had the usual assortment of shops, taprooms, loading docks, and wide warehouse doors facing the street. It took a dozen paces before she noticed the street was not just quiet—it was silent. Especially in light of the *Queen Allisée*'s arrival, that was unheard of for the midmorning harbor. As far as she looked up and down the waterfront, not a soul stirred, save a small knot of what looked like dockworkers fussing over some crates they carried from a warehouse to load a wagon facing inland toward the Riverways. Nothing out of the ordinary there, except they appeared to be supervised by a man in a finely embroidered red coat half again too richly dyed for a dockside quartermaster.

The sailors marching ahead of her seemed to follow the same line of reasoning, shifting course toward the workers and their red-coated master. She followed behind at a healthy distance, maintaining the cloak of *Faith* bound through the leylines in the north side of the harbor.

The man in the red coat shot a look up the street toward their approach, and the sailors she'd been following broke in terror.

It was all she could do to dive out of their way, a stampede fleeing as fast as their legs could carry them, tripping over each other in a mad rush. And no denying the source. Even from a distance she could see the man in the red coat nod in satisfaction, then bark an order to the men unloading the warehouse in front of him.

What under the Gods? He hadn't made a threatening gesture, or brandished a weapon that she could see. If it was a leyline binding, it was like no binding she'd seen. He'd sent a troop of sailors running like... well, like the soldiers who had come before them, and with no more than a glance.

She picked herself up, still shrouded by *Faith*, and felt half an urge to find the city watch herself. Still, whatever he'd done to the sailors, it hadn't affected her. Perhaps she could get closer, enough to see the contents of the crates his men were unloading.

He turned again, frowning as he stared right at her.

Red, Zi thought to her. And then, *Yellow*.

She froze, expecting him to approach, or bark an order, or raise a weapon. Instead he shook his head, laughing to himself as he returned his attention to his men's thievery.

Close. Even if he were a binder, he wouldn't be able to see her behind *Faith*, only trace the pattern of her connection. Too much to risk, though. Whatever they were doing, she'd seen enough.

She backed away, a knot of curiosity still lodged in her throat as she made way back toward the northern harbor.

4

ARAK'JUR

Ipek'a Hunting Grounds
Sinari Land

An ethereal nimbus surrounded him as he called upon the spirit of *anahret.*

Anahret was small; a child or a woman might mistake one for a common lizard. The eyes were the difference. Instead of the normal iris-and-pupil of a common reptile, *anahret*'s sockets were filled with pools of black mist. A trail of vapor marked their movements, thin wisps when they turned to track their prey. Easy to miss, and costly. The bite of *anahret* was death.

He knew them well, understood what it was to wear their skin. A gift earned by slaying one of their kind, beseeching the spirit that answered when it fell. A wave of cold washed over him as the spirit granted its power, and his heart stopped, his lungs slowing until he no longer felt the need to breathe. It was in this state *anahret* lay in wait beside feeding grounds and watering holes. The creatures could remain motionless for days, until prey approached. He needed that patience now, so close to the end of his hunt.

Nearby, a copse of bushes rustled as a pair of birds took flight. Otherwise the forest was quiet, breeze rattling branches, shaking loose a bough of leaves from a nearby elm. Arak'Jur lay beside a boulder, covered in dirt and fallen leaves, with a vantage to spot the approaches to the stream winding through the wood below.

Any moment, she would call again.

A trumpet blast thundered through the wood, the bone-chilling screech of a female *ipek'a.* This female was a magnificent creature, nine feet tall, long crimson feathers bristling off her back like a rack of deadly spikes. One could tell how recently an *ipek'a* had made a kill by the hue of its plumage. Whelps and males, smaller and less aggressive than the females, were white, or a light shade of pink. The females were darker and richer. This one was a deep, lustrous red. The color of fresh blood.

He couldn't see her as she sounded, but he'd been shadowing her pack for three days. They'd stopped to weather the storm on the horizon, black thunderclouds sweeping in with the evening breeze. Smart creatures. The cave they'd found could as easily have been chosen by men for its defensible position and easy access to fresh water. This storm was precisely what he needed. On the move, the pack would never have relaxed their guard around water. For his plan to work he needed one of their young to venture out alone.

At the base of the incline, a brown elk stepped from behind a bush, keeping its head down as it strode toward the running waters of the stream. The *ipek'a*'s screech had passed, and the elk must have thought it safe to sate its thirst. So near a pack of *ipek'a* the creature's instinct served him poorly. The elk reached the stream and lowered its head, lapping at the cool fresh water.

A flurry of crimson streaked into view, and the elk scarce had time to cry out before a scything claw took it in the throat. Blood and fur spattered across dried leaves as the elk's cry became a gurgling noise, halfway between a scream and a whimper. And there she was. *Ipek'a.* She arched her long neck into the air as the roots of her feathers darkened, as if each feather drank a sip of blood from the flesh of her kill. She let out a triumphant snort, leaning down to extract a bloody clump of flesh in her powerful jaws. The *ipek'a* had inverted joints and enormous musculature in their hind legs. They did not run at their prey. They leapt. No telltale vibrations in the ground or crashing through underbrush. When an *ipek'a* committed to a kill, it was silent, swift death from above.

Sated by the first taste of her prey, the female clamped her razor-sharp teeth around the elk's neck, bobbing up and down as she dragged her prey back toward their cave.

Arak'Jur lay alongside the boulder as the storm hit, covering the area with rain and thunder through the night.

As guardian, he had been given a sacred charge. He was a hunter, yes, but also a protector. Long ago, his ancestors had hidden behind walls of stone, living on barren lands atop steep mountain slopes in fear of great beasts like *ipek'a* and *anahret*. His people had rich lands now. The legacy of the first men who dared to venture into the wild, to listen to the will of the spirits they found there. The first tribesmen. Now his people thrived; the tribe's shaman saw glimpses of things-to-come, revealing great beasts near enough to threaten their people, and he hunted them. Such was the great pact of the tribes. Spirits of things-to-come, to guide the shamans and whisper their will to their people; spirits of the land, to empower the women in their secret councils; and spirits of beasts, whose gifts Arak'Jur wielded to keep his people safe.

The morning brought no respite from the storm. But it did provide an opening.

Two of the whelpling *ipek'a* emerged from the cave, feathers white and dripping from the rain beaded across their long necks and thin bodies. They made their way down the slope toward the running stream below. It was difficult to see them as the lethal predators they were, wobbling and swaying, uneasy on their child's legs. One of the males kept a lazy eye on the younglings, hovering near the cave entrance, but the massive female was nowhere in sight. Such was the difficulty of being a protector. All creatures, great and small, had to sleep, in time.

After waiting so long, the last moments stretched on and on. One more step. Another. And *there*. They were too far to turn back. Still the young *ipek'a* marched on, oblivious to their fates. They arrived at the stream, lowering their heads to drink.

He struck.

He asked aid from the spirits of *una're* and *mareh'et*, and a pale nimbus surrounded him in the form of both spirits as they blessed him with their gifts. Crackling energy surged across his hands, blessed by the lightning-empowered strikes of the Great Bear's claws. He leapt with otherworldly speed and agility, with the grace of the Great Cat.

He soared down the slope, landing with adroit precision between the two beasts as they drank from the stream. The larger of the two *ipek'a* turned toward him, and he landed a crushing blow to its throat, wrapping his fist around its windpipe, electrical energy crackling and surging into his prey. The creature's flesh hissed and popped, black streaks scoring beneath its feathers. Surprise had only just reached its eyes when it died, irises rolling back up into its skull as its legs buckled and slumped to the ground.

He was already on the smaller one, leaping into the air and kicking down with the force of the Great Bear. The creature began a screech, a juvenile imitation of its mother's cry, fraying into a desperate howl as its leg snapped.

Satisfied, he darted beside a nearby elm and invoked the spirit of the *juna'ren*. An image of the tiny amphibian shimmered around him, and his naked skin and hide leggings blended into the browns and bark patterns of the tree at his back. It was not a perfect camouflage, but it would serve.

The younger and smaller *ipek'a* whelpling lay whining on the ground beside its dead sibling. It began and choked off screeches in a pitiful rhythm, interrupted by pain as it put weight on its shattered leg. The rest of the pack came flooding out of the cave in a panicked rush of feathers and cries of alarm, led by the alpha female. There was no force in nature stronger than a mother hearing the cry of a child. Arak'Jur stood as still as he could manage without the blessing of *anahret*—too soon to ask for its blessing again—waiting as his heart pounded. The keen senses of an alpha female *ipek'a* should never be fooled by a ruse as simple as the gift of the *juna'ren*. But all her attention was focused on the wounded infant, on doing everything in her power to protect it, to heal it, to make the world right again.

She rushed to its side, leaning down to nudge her child with her narrow snout. In a moment, her nurturing instinct would be replaced with fury, an insatiable desire for revenge. But he had this one, short window to act. And he took it.

A nimbus of the *valak'ar* surrounded him, the image of a serpent uncoiled to its full height. Only a single *valak'ar* had ever come near Sinari land, thank the spirits. The wraith-snake was a ghost given form, able to pass through stone, clay, or flesh to deliver its deadly bite straight to the heart of its victims. Its wispy hide was proof against any weapon, save at the moment it struck for the kill. The *valak'ar* that came to the Sinari village had killed Arak'Mul, the former guardian, and countless others. In slaying it, Arak'Jur had become guardian, chosen by the spirits to take the *Arak* name, to hunt the beasts in the shamans' visions for the protection of his tribe.

Wrapped in the power of the terrible serpent, his fist passed through the female's coat of feathers, through her thick outer hide, through the bone and sinew that encased her powerful heart. With a touch, he delivered a stroke of blight directly into her blood, and she died.

Her proud red feathers went black, sick and warped. Her flesh hissed as it stretched taut, snapping away from her muscles, leaking green mucous into steaming pools in the dirt. The other *ipek'a* reacted in force, swarming toward him in a rage, but he'd already sunk to his knees, rain streaming over his uplifted face in muddy streaks. His eyes had gone white.

A calming force settled over the creatures. Instinctively they recognized what had happened here. They were in the presence of the spirits. And even the most savage beast in nature knew to respect that power.

YOU KILLED HER.

The voice was assertive, proud, shocked.

I did, he thought back to it.

SHE WAS STRONG.

Yes, he agreed.

AND YET YOU BESTED HER. A MAN.

He thought nothing in return, letting silence fill his mind. Reverence settled between them, as though he was watched by unseen eyes, weighed against some standard he could not comprehend.

YOU HAVE STRENGTH, the voice announced, a grudging admission.

Thank you, Great Spirit, he thought back to it, trying to hide his relief. Even here, after stalking and slaying the beast, acceptance was no sure thing. The spirits of each great beast mirrored and perfected the traits of their scions; *mareh'et* was capricious, *anahret* stoic and reserved. He could not be sure how best to gain their favor until he faced them, and came to understand what it meant to wear their skins.

IT IS GOOD FOR MEN TO GAIN STRENGTH. THE GODDESS WILL HAVE NEED OF YOU, IN TIMES TO COME. ARE YOU HER CHOSEN? WILL YOU BE HER VOICE?

Always they asked this. He didn't know what it meant.

No, Great Spirit, he replied. *I seek only your gift, the gift of* ipek'a, *to protect my people.*

A SIMPLE REQUEST.

He waited, saying nothing as the spirit contemplated.

The moments stretched on until the voice thundered inside his head once more.

GRANTED.

He felt a wave of energy rush through him, from the top of his head through his chest, to the tips of his fingers and the soles of his feet. For a moment, he saw through the alpha female's eyes, and felt for himself what it was to be *ipek'a.* He raced across the grassy plains, leaping into the sky, crashing with thunderous force on unsuspecting prey. He was unstoppable, a blizzard of raking claws. He was a sower of terror, the leader of his pack, a hunter without peer. He preened and relished the envy of the other hunters, displaying the blood-red feathers that signified his prowess and deadly skill. He was *ipek'a,* proudest of all hunters, and he bore the mark of a thousand kills in his flesh, displayed for all to see.

In time, the visions faded.

Thank you, Great Spirit, he thought with reverence.

REMEMBER HER.

The voice echoed through his head, and his senses slid back into his body.

He rose to his feet. Bite marks and exposed bone covered the bodies of the whelps, sign of carrion-eaters come for an easy meal, though the sickly corpse of the matron had not been touched. The rest of the pack was gone.

He looked up to a cloudy blue sky, vestiges of the storm still hanging in the breeze.

"I will," he said softly.

Past time to head home. He began to walk.

5

ERRIS

Approaching a Picket Line
Northwest of Durington, Gand Territory

They'd ridden hard for three days.

Even Jiri was coated with sweat. Maintaining leyline connections so close to the enemy columns was an unnecessary risk, and so both rider and mount made do with their natural stamina. Only at the end of a day's ride would she use a binding to refresh her and her five companions. Short bursts were more difficult to detect, and even a temporary surge of *Life* or *Body* energy was a welcome respite from the rigors of hard travel.

They'd learned what they could, trailing behind the enemy's march. All three Gand armies had come together, a combined force upward of seventy thousand men under a single command. She wanted another count from the east to be sure of exact numbers and unit positioning, but she had enough to understand the layout of their forces. The Gandsmen drove north like a spear pointed straight at the heart of the Sarresant colonies. Their intent was clear. Only one piece of the puzzle continued to elude her.

Who was in command?

Something had changed during the winter months, when both sides had hunkered down to endure the harsh cold and biting storms of the season of the Veil. She'd seen enough action to know a change of command when she saw one. This was a different army than the one she'd danced circles around last autumn, in the deep woods of the Gand colonies. She needed to know. She needed the name of the commander who dared such a bold move, when every other Gand officer seemed mired in caution and reserve. But first, she needed some uniforms.

Her company rode two abreast on a winding hunters' track through the forest outside Duringston. It was twilight now, a wet breeze on the air promising storms coming in from the north. Soon night would settle on the small Gand town. Generals and high commanders could never resist a warm, dry bed when they called a halt with civilization nearby; she knew she'd find her answers there. In more peaceful times, Duringston oversaw a healthy clip of trade between New Sarresant and the Gand colonies farther south. Now its forges and foundries sang into the late hours, churning out arms to equip her enemies.

She rode at the head of the pack alongside Aide-Lieutenant Sadrelle, with Horsemen d'Fer and Irond behind a horse length, and Horseman l'Orai and Sergeant Fessac bringing up the rear. Apart from their sabers, pistols, and carbines they might have been common riders—the civilian clothes they'd procured gave service to the lie that they were Gand scouts come home from a sortie behind enemy lines. They rode at an easy pace, relaxed with no outward sign of caution or concern. This was what a squad of scouts looked like returning to camp; the six of them had done it enough to pull off the act convincingly.

An infantryman stepped out from behind a tree fifty paces ahead, raising his musket to block the way. He had the look of a raw recruit for all his gray beard bespoke advanced age, a nervous twang in his voice as he called out to the approaching patrol. He was right to be unsettled. Picket duty was a dreaded assignment. The picketmen were the feelers of the army, first to know when enemies approached, first to die when enemy scouts came too close.

"Ho there," the soldier called in the Gand tongue. "Who approaches?"

"Westerly patrol returning," Sadrelle called back. Gods bless him and his perfectly accented Gand. "Twenty-Second Scouting Company, Fourth Brigade under Colonel Devon."

Doing her best to look unconcerned, Erris held aloft a rolled parchment she'd sealed with red wax that morning for precisely this purpose. The paper was blank. A stage prop to string along the hope that this was all legitimate, that her group posed no danger.

She dismounted, blinking to shift her vision to the leylines. She saw none of the telltale white tethers that would suggest the presence of enemy binders, though it was no guarantee. It was common practice to post *Life* binders as scouts, for the same reason she watched the leylines now. Enemy soldiers would feed green pods of *Life* into the leystream with their presence—difficult to get an exact count, but better than nothing. She turned back to her men and spoke softly.

"Two on the left flank, four maybe more on the right."

She left Jiri behind, walking forward alone, holding the parchment in front of her like a gift. At the corner of her eye she saw one of the old man's fellows, pressed up against an oak tree to the left of the path, trying to stay out of sight. She ignored him, holding the paper out for the first soldier as she calculated her angle of attack. The old man planted the butt of his musket in the dirt and furrowed his brow, reaching out to grab the paper from her, thumbing the edge of the wax.

Her eyes snapped shut, and she found a small mote of red *Body* energy. She bound a tether into herself, and her muscles surged with speed and power. Lightning-quick, she drew her saber, sweeping it up from the scabbard in an arcing cut that took the picketman across the face. Blood gushed from the wound as he fell, but she was already moving. She let the saber's momentum carry her, spinning into the air and kicking off from the corpse, sending her soaring toward the second picketman behind the tree. The blade continued its arc as she delivered a cut to the side of the second picketman's head, his eyes barely given time to widen before his head slammed into the tree like a jar of fresh-packed jelly. A spray of thick, dark blood splattered across her as she landed.

Startled cries went up around her, and shots rang out as her men opened fire. She whirled in time for a strand of inky *Death* to blur into her vision, sliding toward her, threatening to snap her *Body* tether. Gods damn it; the bloody picketmen had a binder after all, and a *Death* binder to boot. She cursed as the *Death* binding touched her, draining her speed as if she hadn't made the *Body* tether at all.

The *Death* tether vanished abruptly before she could trace the connection. It took a heartbeat of confusion before she understood. The shooting had stopped. The fight was done.

Sadrelle dismounted, cracking his pistol open to reload while d'Fer and Irond shouldered their carbines. L'Orai and Fessac were on foot already, approaching her as the smoke from the exchange trailed up through the trees.

"Fine blade-work, sir," Sadrelle said.

"They had a Gods-damned *Death* binder," she said, pausing to wipe the edge of her saber with a rag. "No one wounded?"

"No, sir," came the reply from her men.

She sheathed her saber and they set to work. Another round of bangs and smoke filled the clearing as she and Fessac delivered coups de grâce to the wounded while l'Orai and Sadrelle worked to strip their uniforms, piling the bodies a short distance away from the path. They'd be discovered in due time. But by then she and her squad would be riding north, Gods willing.

"Nothing in your size, sir," Irond said as he pulled the last of the red coats from the dead soldiers.

"They trained you in sewing at the convent, didn't they?" she barked back. "Let's have some alterations, on the double now."

The rest of the men laughed as Irond waved her away, still grinning.

Piling the usable tunics, breeches, and coats revealed a stroke of luck: They had enough to make do without ambushing any more picketmen. Their civilian clothes they piled with the bodies, all save her doeskin leather gloves. No suitable replacement for those among the dead, and the scars of the binder's marks perforated into the backs of her hands would call the worst sorts of attention if she went without. Better to chance a pair of non-standard-issue gloves she might have won at dice or cards than go about displaying that sort of sign.

"Well," d'Fer said as he finished putting on a dead soldier's red tunic. "I suppose I look like a Gandsman now." He gestured to the holes in the fabric of his tunic, caked with fresh blood where their shots had struck home. She bit back a laugh. Blood on a uniform was common enough, and with luck they wouldn't need to get close enough to other soldiers to trigger suspicions. Well, five of them wouldn't. They'd saved the most pristine of the uniforms for Sadrelle.

"Aide-Lieutenant," she called to him. "Don't spend more time than you have to, and don't get any ideas about assassinating generals while you're in there."

He feigned a look of devastation, then smiled. "Don't worry, sir. Intelligence gathering, no more."

She gave him a long look for emphasis as she climbed back into Jiri's saddle, then nudged her mount forward. With luck, these uniforms would let them pass through the enemy's lines, saving half a day that otherwise would have been spent riding around to the east. Sadrelle should be able to get the name of their new commander and some fresh details on the rest of their command structure to boot. Not the most elegant mission she'd ever led, but the 14th had its reputation for a reason.

The six riders split as they descended into the outskirts of the town. She'd drawn a rough map, dividing the camp into sections. Sadrelle had Duringston itself, the most dangerous assignment by far. To herself she assigned the second-most dangerous area: the highlands overlooking the roads to the east. The hills were steep and rocky, but they commanded the town. Hold those and you could harry an enemy whether they chose to retreat or engage. It was likely to be fortified, but she would deal with that when the time came; it was worth the risk to gain a vantage above the rest of the encampments. Even if, Oracle forbid, one of her men failed to return, her report would have the necessary basics. They were to regroup in the woods to the northeast after the next day's march began, using the cover of the morning's scout patrols to slip away from the main body of the enemy army.

Not for the first time, she questioned whether it wouldn't have been wiser to ride a less distinctive mount on these missions. Jiri snorted, and Erris leaned into her, stroking her neck. Never. She couldn't imagine trusting another horse. There were plenty of oddities in an army encampment. So long as she rode with purpose, exuding the confidence of belonging and the mild irritation of being on important business, she could bypass all but the most alert of their sentries. She rode past one now, muttering in the Gand tongue under her breath, a jumble of words meant to sound like cursing her superior officer. The sentry's cloak stirred as if he made to rise from his seat by the coals of the brazier, but instead he nodded to her as she passed, earning a nod from her in return. She would have liked to think it would not be so easy to navigate a Sarresant army camp like this, but she knew better. Even the best soldiers could be lulled into complacency by the illusion of the familiar.

Within the hour she'd made it past a half-dozen such sentries, slipping through the city's outskirts into the fields beneath the highlands. Here her tactics changed. Cutting across the grass by herself under a cloak of nightfall would be construed as skulking—the very thing to set sentries abuzz with a need to investigate. Instead she took on the slumped, plodding gait of an exhausted soldier delivering a message far away from the watchful eye of anyone important. Tired grunts sufficed for greeting when she passed the occasional soldier or wagoneer on the dirt roads winding through the fields, other men and women at the exact business to which she pretended. Slow going, but in time she found herself trekking up the steep inclines of the large hill overlooking the town.

She found a secluded area and set Jiri to watch for anyone approaching while she worked. The relative emptiness of the highlands confirmed one thing for her: Whoever the new commander was, their genius did not extend far down the chain of command. Any commander worth their rank should have seen the strategic value of this hill and taken the time to station at least a regiment's strength atop it. Yes, it meant backbreaking work moving the rocks into makeshift fortifications, but a position like that would be worth ten times the number of men on level ground if battle found them while they camped. Of course, the Sarresant army was a week's march to the north, so why expend the effort? Except that was the point. A good commander knew to be prepared for the impossible.

She got to work, tethering a *Life* binding to enhance her vision as she counted the tents in the night. Her ability to bind three leyline energies—*Life* to enhance her senses and heal wounds, *Body* to enhance her strength and speed, and *Death* to sever enemy bindings—counted her among the most gifted binders in the army, an asset as valuable as any battery of artillery, any company of horse. According to the ancient histories, fullbinders were said to be able to handle every type of energy, but those were foolish myths taught by priests to cow civilians into obedience. Only in her lifetime had the army had more than a handful of men or women who could handle more than two bindings with any strength. Scholars claimed the talent would grow among their people as they expanded the territory under the crown's control, whether from conquest or colonies across the seas. As likely a justification for war as any, she supposed, and more than a soldier needed. She did her duty, as a trained weapon of the crown.

She made careful note of the troop composition as she worked, whether infantry, cavalry, sharpshooters, or specialists. The layout of the camps suggested the order in which the columns would march, which in turn suggested which units would deploy first when they took the field. Much could change in the intervening days, but it was vital to report everything she could. The smallest edge could prove decisive in the battles to come.

She worked through the night, until the first rays of sunlight cut through the openings in the cloud cover. The rains would be heavy today, judging from the black thunderheads rolling in on the morning winds from the north. From the look of it the enemy's march today would be miserable. Already they were striking tents, sounding the reveille, beating to assembly. Past time for her to go. She clicked her tongue to summon Jiri, gathering her papers into one of the saddlebags, then rose to her feet to cast one last look down at the assembled enemy army. Ants, with the anthill kicked. The damage she and her men had done tonight would not be felt for days, but the cut was there, whether they saw it or no.

She reached level ground quickly, traversing in broad swathes, left and right. Once again she encountered soldiers and horsemen on the dirt tracks surrounding the town, but no sentries this time. The vigilance of an army at rest melted away like so many candles in the light of day, every soldier scurrying about with purpose. She adopted the same air and blended in without side looks from her adopted fellows.

She'd almost reached the woods when a commotion from behind drew her attention.

The sight struck her like a punch to the gut. Even at this distance, she recognized Horseman Irond as he drove his stallion in a fury, a squad of mounted Gandsmen in fast pursuit. Irond wheeled to the right through the open field, spurring his mount to leap over a wooden split-rail fence before he pivoted again, this time to the left. The riders at his heels weren't half so skilled. They didn't have to be. Irond's mount was in shock, its mouth frothing and its eyes peeled wide. Streaks of blood ran down the beast's flank, signs of pistol or musket shot struck home, and it was only a matter of time until the stallion collapsed. Irond gave the animal its head, racing over the open field in the direction of the same thick forest she and Jiri plodded toward along the dirt road.

He'd never make it.

She gritted her teeth, knuckles white on Jiri's reins as she watched. She'd trained Irond well. He knew what he had to do.

Irond leapt from his saddle as the stallion buckled beneath him, its reserves exhausted. He rolled to his feet, taking up a defensive posture, his saber out, glinting in the sunlight breaching through the gathering clouds. Taking their time now, the Gandsmen slowed their mounts and spread a half circle around him. Hounds with the fox in their sights. The rest of the soldiers traveling on the dirt road had all stopped to watch the action, a bit of unexpected entertainment to liven their morning duty.

Irond backed away as his pursuers approached, their pistols cocked and leveled. Irond's stallion had collapsed in a heap, its death throes echoing across the grass in stomach-wrenching screeches. The first shots went off and Irond spun, diving behind the dying animal. His pursuers missed the mark, eliciting another wave of shrieks as their pistol shot peppered the stallion's hide. Frustrated, the enemy cavalrymen holstered their guns, drew sabers, and charged.

This was it. This was what he needed. The thunder of their charge shook the ground, accompanied by the cries of the riders and the onlookers who cheered them on. The enemy raised their blades, and with a single, smooth motion Irond stepped from the cover he had taken behind his dying mount. He stood, feet level, saber in an overhead guard to meet their attack as they closed on him from both sides. In the moment before impact he lowered his blade, stepping into their path. A lethal cut from the first rider opened his chest. The second rider trampled him into the dirt.

Good man. A wise enemy would have wounded him, taken him prisoner, and gotten answers. There, in a heap of broken flesh amid the long grass, Horseman Irond had done his duty.

Fessac and l'Orai had watched the grisly scene from the safety of the woods. D'Fer arrived some time later, and they had to tell him the news. They each shone with pride, recounting their fellow's last flight, sharing their best and worst memories of him as they passed the time waiting for Sadrelle.

Two hours later, the four of them could wait no longer, and they rode.

6

ARAK'JUR

The Guardian's Tent
Sinari Village

He took her roughly from behind.

Llanara let loose the breath she'd been holding as his motion slowed and stopped. His head cleared, and he pulled himself out of her as she collapsed onto his bed.

She was his, but she was not his wife. *Rhealla. Forgive me.*

He winced as he stood, reaching down to pull up his leggings.

"Are you going, then?" she asked, breathless from their mutual exertion. "A trip with the men would be good for you."

He shook his head. "They do not need me for simple trade. I'd thought to speak with the shaman after the ceremony."

She turned to regard him, a thoughtful look wrinkling the smoothness of her young face. She was a beauty. Llanara. Fierce like the *mareh'et*, terrible to behold when her wrath was stirred, with claws as sharp as the Great Cat's. She had a vibrance he thought gone from his life forever. He did not deserve a woman like Llanara, and if his will were stronger he might have turned her away. Youth deserved youth, not a man burdened with his memories.

"Arak'Jur," she said. "You will need to choose eventually, you know." She rolled over, exposing the curve of her backside to him, flashing him a smile as she stretched over the full length of his bed of long grasses. "You give me your seed, am I not worthy of your tent?" The look on her face was playful, though her words were solemn.

"Llanara," he said as formally as she had, enunciating every syllable of her name. "You are young, and I can forgive your poor choices. The elders would not be so understanding, if you sought to pledge to a man such as me."

She laughed, a rich sound that brought color to the browns and grays of his tent. "May I at least accompany you to the ceremony?"

"I will allow it," he said formally again, eliciting another laugh.

She stood, teasing him again with the sight of her body as she twisted, putting on her hide leggings and woven tunic. He took her arm, and they closed the flap of his tent behind them as they walked the pathway into the heart of the village.

The village woke around them as they walked, gestures of greeting and nods of respect as elders, children, men, and women started their days. Smells of smoking elk meat and simmering maize drifted from the cookfires at the village center, preparation for the feast that would see the traders off to meet with the fair-skins of New Sarresant at the opening of their barrier. Hides, beads, woodcarvings, and woven blankets traded for steel, fishhooks, muskets, iron pots, knives, and axes for woodchopping. The fair-skins' arrival had brought wealth, an end to the old war between the Sinari and the coastal tribes of the Tanari, and a profitable relationship in the years since, even after the fair-skins' barrier went up to claim their fallen enemies' land. He knew their barrier ran far to the south, unbroken for many moons' journey, and that not all the tribes living along it had been so welcoming of their newfound neighbors. But the Sinari had prospered more than most tribes from trade.

"Tell me, my guardian," Llanara said, draping his title in playful mockery as they walked. "Will you join the shaman in blessing the traders before they go?"

"They do not need my blessing, Llanara. I am no *Sa'Shem*."

"You could be."

He said nothing to that. This was her game, and he let her play it. Instead he turned toward the village center, watching as the men piled hides to be counted, awaiting the shaman's blessing on their exchange. He kept silent, and she stood beside him, letting him feel her presence.

At once she spoke. Brazen, bold, without fear. "Will you ask the shaman to find you an apprentice?"

He frowned. She had never asked him this, never directly. He could not pledge blood-oath to her so long as he was *Arak*, guardian of the tribe. And there could be no new guardian until he had time to train an *Ilek*, an apprentice many whispered was long overdue.

He took his time in answering, framing the words carefully in his mind. It was time he tell her the truth. Her boldness deserved a bold reply. But when he spoke, it was in a whisper.

"Ka'Vos never saw the coming of the *valak'ar* to our lands, Llanara. He had no vision of my slaying it, no vision of Arak'Mul's death. Perhaps the spirits never intended me to be guardian. If I ask the shaman to look, do you know what he will see?"

She sucked in a breath. The coming of a tribe's guardian was a thing foreseen by the shamans; for Arak'Jur to have come upon his power unbidden was a dire omen. If it were known his guardianship had not been foretold, it would cast doubt on the status of their tribe. It might even betoken a curse—the threat of the spirits' withdrawal, leaving them unprotected against the ravages of the wild.

Llanara said nothing, only stood beside him, watching the men continue their preparations.

She wanted more than just the blood-oath that would make her his wife. She wanted him to give up the mantle of guardian, to seek greater status as *Sa'Shem*, chief, or as warleader, *Vas'Khan*. The Sinari, like the rest of the northern tribes, were led by councils of elders in times of peace, with each voice speaking freely, inviting others to weigh and consider arguments by merit rather than the station of the speaker. But other tribes' shamans had seen omens, had spoken of blood, fire, a hunger for war. Other tribes' hunters had shed their Valak names, taking up the mantles of *Venari*, the warrior, and *Vas'Khan*.

The Sinari shaman was silent.

Ka'Vos saw the coming of great beasts; in this his gift continued. But not for the first time Arak'Jur wondered whether Ka'Vos had lost some part of his magic, the deep connection to the spirits of things-to-come. It was a blasphemous thought, a frightening thought. That did not make it untrue.

"Have I frightened you, Llanara?"

"Yes."

"This is why you belong with a younger man, with simpler troubles."

She shot him a hot look, but did not stir. She stood by his side, contemplating the truth he had revealed. As a woman, she was no hunter, but she had strength just the same. For all the heat in her blood, her mind was quicker than his, when she stopped to consider.

Finally, she spoke. "If you did not need the shaman's blessing to become guardian, you do not need a vision to find your apprentice."

He sighed. It was a typical answer, the sort he expected from her. "You would have me ask Ka'Vos to lie?"

"Do you need ask Ka'Vos for anything?"

She stared him down, defiant. "Llanara . . ." he began. She waited for him to finish.

"It is more complicated than that," he said finally.

At this, their exchange was broken up by a group of young men who'd noticed the guardian and his woman. They beckoned, welcoming him and Llanara to help with the preparations for the ceremony. He was pleased to do so, pleased for the simple distraction of physical work. He helped to hang the hides, the cords strung with bone, the racks of elk antlers and beaver tails they'd claimed in seasons past. Llanara let him go, with a look in her eyes promising further discussion when next they were alone. She saw to the women's work, the mixing of the *echtaka*, the decorative paint the hunters wore, and of the dried meats, fruits, and ground maize the men would carry for sustenance.

The other men cheered him on when, at their urging, he invoked the spirit of the *una're*, the Great Bear, and called for strength. With the beast spirit's magic he hoisted a pole alone, doing the work of six men. It was vulgar to use his gifts for such, but it brought heart to the men, and the Great Bear was more understanding than most when it came to the ties of loyalty.

Ka'Vos emerged when their preparations were complete, as if the spirits had whispered to the shaman the precise moment for his arrival. He and his apprentice, Ilek'Inari, passed like a chill wind through the crowd, cloaked in the furs of elder beasts, their faces painted with black stripes, eyes glazed with visions of the spirits. The women backed away as the shamans took their places, gathering for rituals of their own. Llanara caught his eyes as she left, and he did not miss the heat she directed toward him, and toward the shaman standing at the center of the grounds, before she vanished from his sight.

"Men of the Sinari," Ka'Vos intoned when the women had gone. "You seek to travel south and east, to trade with the fair-skinned men and women who are no sons and daughters of these lands."

The crowd murmured its assent, until one voice emerged to speak on their behalf. Valak'Anor, a young man who bore the *Valak* name, a master hunter, though he was freshly come to it. "Honored shaman," Valak'Anor replied. "We do. Our pelts and fish, exchanged for goods of metal and woven cloth. Honed edges, to tame the trees, and fabrics to tame the wind and cold. By trade we are made strong, if the spirits will it so."

"You are wise to consult the spirits in this exchange," Ka'Vos said with a slow nod. "Do not forget our people once lived as the fair-skins do: hidden behind walls, afraid to spread ourselves and claim the bounty of these lands. Listen, and remember. Remember the first tribes, the first *Ka*, who found the spirits and learned to heed their call. On a day not quite so different from this, in a time long ago, in a faraway place we once called home."

Arak'Jur smiled as Ka'Vos told the tale. He'd heard its like before—every man of the Sinari had, in gatherings such as this, the private histories of their people preserved in the wisdom of the shaman's tellings. By the end, the exuberance of the gathering had been replaced by somber reflection, a note of wisdom that suited Arak'Jur's mood.

The women returned shortly after, and the traders said their farewells, lashing furs and leather bags to their horses, bound for the edge of Sinari land. They would make their trades with the fair-skins and some would continue on, to the Ranasi tribe in the north, and the Olessi in the west. Goods would be traded between each neighbor in turn, before the men returned to the village, gathering more goods in advance of the next opening in the fair-skins' barrier.

Llanara was not among the women who returned to see the hunters and traders off, and so he was left alone with the shaman beneath the totems of the gathering place. Ilek'Inari moved to clean and retire the implements of their ceremony while Ka'Vos approached him, meeting his eyes with a familiar nod.

"Arak'Jur," the shaman said, sounding winded, tired, now that he was finished speaking on behalf of the spirits. Ka'Vos's hair had long since gone to gray, his skin tough and creased with the lines of age.

"Ka'Vos," he said, returning the nod of respect. In his time as shaman

Ka'Vos had presided over generations of peace with their neighbors, good harvests, and bountiful births. It was not so easy to disregard a lifetime of service, whatever Llanara wanted to think.

"Walk with me," the shaman said. Arak'Jur complied, settling into an easy stride beside the old man's long walking staff.

"I have seen a vision," Ka'Vos said quietly. "But I do not know what it means."

Arak'Jur turned, eyebrows perked with interest. "Would you speak of it with me?"

"Yes. A scaled creature, in the company of a fair-skin. It drank deep from us, filling itself, but with the blood of our enemies as much as from our strength. And then it vanished."

"A troubling vision," Arak'Jur offered. "Could it be another great beast, so soon after *ipek'a*?"

Ka'Vos clutched tight to his staff as they walked, but kept his eyes forward, focused on the path ahead. "The land has teemed with them of late. But I do not think so. This creature was different."

Arak'Jur slowed, eyeing Ka'Vos as the old man paced beside him, waiting for more. The shaman looked fragile, the gray in his hair seeming to echo the lines beneath his eyes, the creases in his skin.

"What of the fair-skin?" Arak'Jur asked when the shaman did not continue. "Is the creature some sign of their magic? A warning from the spirits of things-to-come?"

Ka'Vos shook his head. "I cannot be sure. The creature drank from us, but from our enemies as well, enemies come from a great distance. And the fair-skins have not stirred from behind their barrier since the destruction of the Tanari."

Arak'Jur nodded. He knew the stories. The Sinari people had fought great wars against the Tanari tribes for generations, in the time of his grandfather's grandfather's grandfather. Much blood had been shed on both sides, until the fair-skins arrived from across the sea. The strange foreigners had made useful allies, but when the war was done they erected their barrier and multiplied behind it, building cities of iron and stone on lands that had belonged to the Tanari, and to still more tribes, extending far to the south. The fair-skins were many now, but few among them dared to leave the lands they'd claimed—they had no shamans, no guardians to protect them from the great beasts of the wild.

"Perhaps these are the visions the other tribes' shamans have seen," he said.

"Perhaps. But our bonds with our fellows are not so strong as they once were. I fear it, Arak'Jur. I fear if war comes, it will not be so easy to divine our enemies, even with the spirits' guidance."

The silence stretched on as they walked the winding paths through the woods near the village. Each of them deep in his thoughts, considering the implications of what Ka'Vos had seen.

Until Ka'Vos froze mid-stride in the center of the path.

"What?" Arak'Jur asked. "What is it?"

"He comes." Ka'Vos's voice was cold, pained.

"Who?"

"The fair-skin. The scaled beast. They come now!"

With wide eyes, Arak'Jur turned and ran back toward the village.

Arak'Jur rushed into the clearing, where a strange man stood at the head of the path, alone, as if waiting to be greeted. He wore a red coat, bright like the sun at the height of the season of fire, a hue so bright it shone despite the overcast skies. Light hair to go with his light skin, and pale blue eyes like none Arak'Jur had ever seen on a tribesman.

The rest of the tribe had withdrawn into the village at the fair-skin's coming. Without the hunters and traders present they were ill-equipped to deal with a threat. Better to wait for their guardian to handle this strange newcomer. Only Llanara had stood her ground, curse her for a fool. She stood in the center of the gathering place, watching the strange man with an intense gaze. Yet neither moved. For all her bravery, she was not fool enough to approach the man unbidden. And the fair-skin seemed content to wait.

Arak'Jur was not. He strode toward the man and raised his hand, calling a cautious greeting in the fair-skins' tongue. He'd learned enough to make himself understood, when the hunters met with the fair-skins at the openings of their barrier, though he would not trust his words to settle matters of import. Perhaps it would be enough to learn why the man had come.

Yet when the red-coated man replied, he spoke the tribes' tongue perfectly, without accent or inflection. Odd. Perhaps the man was a trader, accustomed to dealing with his people. But even among their traders, he had never heard of a fair-skin brave enough to approach a village without escort.

"Hello, guardian of the Sinari," the man said. "My name is Reyne d'Agarre, and I bear an offering of peace to you and your people. Peace, and power."

The man nodded to something unseen beside him, and a crystalline serpent materialized, as if from thin air. Its scales were flushed a deep blue, and it craned its head to look him directly in the eyes.

A voice sounded inside his head, strange and foreign.

Peace, and power. The power to protect your people, Arak'Jur.

7

SARINE

The Five Cats Tavern
Maw District, New Sarresant

The bustle of men storming into the tavern made her flinch by instinct, though thankfully not enough to have her reaching for *Faith*.

She sat alone at a table opposite the main door, the flaking crust of a meat pie decorating a pewter plate in front of her. A treat and a delicacy, given each pie cost a full silver mark since the onset of the war. But Madame Guillon made the best pastries in the Maw, even if she did it with scraps left from the supply wagons before they headed south. And the woman ran a clean tavern, brooking little in the way of nonsense from the district's citizens. It had always been a safe place when she'd needed one, even as a child, and all the more so now with the coin from her uncle's stipend in a bag hidden in the bottom of her otherwise empty pack. She was tasked with finding foodstuffs for the chapel's kitchen, and made it a point to delight her uncle with better fare than bread and cabbage when she could.

"There's been another theft," the men were saying, passing rumors as they crowded round a table at the center of the room. "In the Market district."

Only a handful of patrons other than herself had occupied the taproom prior to the men's entrance, but the commotion drew every eye, hers included. Better if she went unnoticed by anyone, especially when she had coin. But she caught sight of the object of the men's exclamations—a rag linen newspaper, brandished like a torch—and she couldn't help but crane to try to hear them read its contents.

"Two days past," a man at the center of the group read aloud to his fellows, most of whom doubtless couldn't have read it themselves. "A store of supplies intended for the army reported missing after a commotion with the city watch. Four constables upbraided for dereliction of duty, seen fleeing their posts prior to the robbery of three hundred pounds salt pork, forty-eight muskets, and six casks of beer intended for delivery to the southern front."

"What's this then?" Madame Guillon, the proprietress of the tavern, joined in over top of the men as she strode in from the kitchens.

"Another theft, mum," one of the men said.

"I know where they can deliver those casks of beer," another man said.

"And I know where they got them," Madame Guillon spat. "Raiding our larders, for the benefit of the crown's soldiers. A tax, and I call it theft. Can't steal what's already stolen."

Murmured agreement passed among the men before they moved on to the next piece of news, a murder reported on the deck of the *Fleur-Gascon.* Sarine didn't listen. Four constables of the watch charged with dereliction of duty, running in fear from their posts. And then a robbery. She'd seen the same scene play out in the Harbor, overseen by the man in the red coat. A chill passed down her spine as she remembered the look in his eyes when he'd stared at her, even shrouded behind her *Faith* tethers.

A half bushel of carrots dropped to the table across from her plate and Madame Guillon slid into the seat opposite her.

"This is all I can spare, even for Father Thibeaux's charity," Madame Guillon said. "It's been a hard winter, and no sign of getting any easier now the snows are gone."

Sarine reached for the carrots, quickly stuffing them into her pack, though more than one of the men listening to the day's paper caught a glance before she got them out of sight.

"Thank you," she said. "Everything helps. Uncle will include you in his prayers, I'm sure."

"I'd as soon he urge his congregation to drink from my taps, if there are any left who can afford it. And it's eight silver pennies this time."

"Eight?" That was more than double what she'd paid for half again as many carrots not two weeks prior.

Madame Guillon held up a hand to forestall the argument she had to know was coming. "It's eight or nothing. The Duc-Governor's quartermasters are bleeding me dry, me and every farmer in riding distance of the city. High time we chop the forests, or push out the barrier, take some more land from the savages. But until we do, you pay what I pay. Not an ounce of profit in it, I swear on the Veil's truth."

Sarine frowned, but fished up the coins just the same. Madame Guillon wasn't one to slight the Gods. But if the army was seizing goods at the rate Madame Guillon claimed, her excursion today would be less fruitful than she'd hoped. At this rate she'd need to sell twenty sketches a week just to pay for their meals, over and above the stipend they got from the Basilica.

So it had been, and growing worse in the months since the crown had declared its war on Gand. Though the wines and cheeses never seemed in short supply on the palace green, or in the townhouses and salons of the Gardens district, she was sure. The nobles had to expect the people to lash out, to organize thefts of precisely the sort executed by the man in the red coat. The papers had made no mention of him in the Harbor, nor again in today's news of the panicked watchmen in the Market district. But it sounded too similar not to be the same man. Curiosity once again gnawed at her, the same as hunger would if prices kept driving themselves northward. Perhaps they'd all be thieves before the end.

"Our thanks, again," she said after Madame Guillon had taken her coin.

"And mine," Madame Guillon replied. "Take care of yourself, child. And give my blessings to your uncle."

She collected her pack, bowing as she licked the last scraps of her meat pie from her fingers. The men at the center of the common room were reading a story about an accident at a Southgate munitions factory—six workers dead, and half a warehouse burned beyond repair—but two of them had taken notice of her, first when Madame Guillon delivered the carrots, and then again, just as intently, when she'd produced the coin to pay for them. A quick check of the leylines showed *Body* aplenty, and *Faith*, as there always was near the Five Cats. She could escape their attentions easily enough, if it came to it. The Maw was never a kind place, but she hoped it hadn't yet descended to assault and theft in the light of midday.

Thankfully the men didn't follow, or if they did they waited too long, and she pushed through the doors and vanished into the crowds lining the streets outside the tavern.

A makeshift farmers' market made for the second stop of the day. No more than a city block lined with wagons of foodstuffs deemed unworthy of the Gardens or Southgate—else why cross the river to sell them in the Maw—but she could ofttimes find surprises nestled among the bags and bushels in the farmers' carts. Today she'd managed three cabbage heads and a half-rotten onion to go along with Madame Guillon's carrots, and reckoned the lot a treasure weighed against the empty bags of too many in the crowd, stalking between carts seeking food they could afford.

"Corn heads and bean sprouts!" a farmer was shouting, and Sarine shook her head as she passed him by. From the look of it his corn had already been picked over by wild birds, and his sprouts were more grass than anything edible.

She passed two wagoneers packing up empty carts, preparing to hitch mules and leave their spots along the thoroughfare, before a basket of red apples caught her eye.

"How much?" she asked over the din, shouting and pointing to make herself heard.

The farmer eyed her with a squint before replying. "Two silver coins apiece. No worms; fresh picked."

"Two silvers? Each? I could have your wagon for half your basket. That's—"

Green.

A chill passed through her as Zi's voice sounded in her head.

"Bugger off, girl." The farmer waved her away. "They cost what they cost."

She glanced up the street, toward a swelling crowd that would have betokened no more than well-stocked carts at that end of the market if not for Zi's cryptic thought.

"What does that mean, Zi? '*Green.*' Is that related to what you saw in the Harbor?"

"I said bugger off, girl!" the farmer bellowed, gesturing for her to move along.

That was Yellow, Zi replied as she moved toward the crowd. *This is Green.*

She frowned, as much for her companion's sake as the commotion at the far end of the street. Last time she'd followed that sort of prompting it had ended with her almost trampled by fleeing sailors and a glimpse of the man in the red coat stealing crates from a warehouse. The same man who had to have been behind the theft she'd heard reported in the daily papers.

Prudence suggested she take her pack and head back to the Sacre-Lin. But curiosity had lingered in her mind since the Harbor. There she'd been alone on the street; if the man in the red coat was a binder—or had binders with him—he could have traced her tethers in an eyeblink. Here she'd be safe, hidden in the crowd. If it was him at all. She'd never heard Zi give a color as a warning before, but twice in as many weeks was too much to give to chance.

She moved around the press, keeping her pack clutched tight for the sake of pickpockets no doubt working the street. Men and women packed the way ahead of her, those on the periphery drawn by the presence of the crowd itself, as she had been, craning their necks and passing questions as to what was going on. She wouldn't get close trying to wade through their number. Instead she ducked down an alley, found the familiar red motes of *Body* and white clouds of *Faith,* and scrambled up an iron gate adjoining the roof of a block of shops until she had a vantage overlooking the whole of the square.

As she looked down on it, the crowd was thicker than she'd imagined, running the length of two city blocks at least, extending past the farmers' market and spilling into side streets in every direction. But it seemed to be centered on a wagon surrounded by a circle of clear space, two streets ahead.

A running leap bridged the gap between the roof she'd scrambled up and the next one, and she caught sight of the man in the red coat.

It was him, sure as her uncle's sermons.

Standing at the heart of the crowd, with men in plain clothes surrounding him, handing some sort of parcels to those who approached. Yet for all the buzz of whispers and jostling on the streets around his crates, those who reached him seemed docile, orderly, willing to wait their turn. They came forward one at a time or in pairs, received whatever it was they were being handed, then spoke with the man in the red coat, bowing and genuflecting as though he were a priest offering blessings of kindness and salvation.

No, not blessings. And not parcels. He was handing them slabs of meat and loaves of bread.

Her jaw pried itself open at the sight of it. Gold marks—*hundreds* of gold marks' worth of food, at a time when silver bought rotten vegetables and brass bought dirt and shoe leather. And the people clustered around his wagon—Maw folk, the sort who would split your skull for a half-empty purse if they thought no one would see—shuffled forward like lambs, accepting their gifts and moving on without comment from those still waiting to approach. Women and children, even street children in rags and filth, carried treasures past men who could kill them with little more than a square kick to the ribs. She'd dodged men like that for years before her uncle had taken her in. And no one had ever handed her a loaf of bread and slab of pork.

Green, Zi said again. And then, a moment later, *Yellow.*

She stared, her companion's voice almost beneath her notice.

"I don't understand, Zi. How is he doing this?"

Force, against their nature. They respond to sympathy.

"What does that mean? He's doing something to keep them calm?"

Zi appeared at the lip of the roof, lolling his head over the side as his scales flushed green and white. It might have been a nod; it might have been silence. Gods but he could be infuriating.

In spite of Zi, her pack felt suddenly empty, weighed against the prizes being given out below. Did she dare join the throng, to try to secure a parcel for herself? Her uncle would be beside himself if she came back with that sort of bounty, but then again the district would have less need for the Sacre-Lin's charity in coming days than it ever had before. A gnawing feeling suggested she should want nothing to do with whatever was going on in the square, but the rest of her—

Thunder sounded from a block on the opposite side of the square. A guttural roar, ringing from the sides of buildings, that gave way to screams.

She pivoted around, but saw nothing to indicate the source, only the crowd rippling in on itself. Smoke rose from an intersection one block south of her place atop the roof as that street cleared, leaving a handful of figures huddled on the ground, with a few more standing stock-still, staring, frozen while their fellows ran.

It took another instant—and the emergence of blue-uniformed city watchmen through the haze of the smoke—before she understood. That hadn't been thunder; it was gunfire.

"Thieves!" one of the watchmen shouted, bellowing loud enough to be heard above the screams. "Return the goods you've stolen or face the crown's justice!"

She checked her *Faith* tether by reflex, walking to the edge of the roof as though a few paces might make the difference in understanding what was going on. The city watch were ruthless at times, but she'd never seen them fire into a crowd of unarmed citizens. A glance toward the center revealed the man in the red coat hadn't moved, as though he'd either expected this attack or wasn't fazed by watchmen leveling pistols at the people he'd been trying to feed. Already men lay dying in the street, and women, and…

The sight of a child frozen in place at the center of the southbound street almost started her forward off the edge of the roof. A small boy, with a slab of pork under one arm and a loaf of bread under the other. Most of the rest of the street had cleared, but the boy stood in place, directly in the watchmen's path.

Instinct told her to run, to use her *Faith* and every other gift at her disposal to leap down and disappear among the winding streets of the Maw. But that boy could have been her, years ago. With *Body*, and Zi's red haze, she could reach him in time to spirit him away. No one else was moving toward him, only the inexorable tide of the city watch.

She released *Faith* and made the tether for *Body* as she leapt from the roof's overhang, trusting to her added strength to absorb the shock of landing. Better for staying hidden if she'd maintained the *Faith* tether, but the crowd couldn't move aside to let her through if they didn't know she was coming. And she had to be quick.

"Zi, I need you!" she cried as she shoved against the current of the crowd. Her companion answered with the familiar rush of blood, a red haze coloring her vision as her muscles sang with energy.

The crowd froze around her.

One moment they'd been running away from the southbound street where the watch had unleashed their pistols. The next they were deathly quiet, every man and woman stopped, wearing blank looks as though they couldn't remember why they'd been running for their lives.

She shoved through the crowd anyway, breaking through the last of them in time to see the boy still trembling, standing in place. But the watchmen had frozen, too, all their bluster and shouting replaced by aimless stares set against the backdrop of their pistol smoke.

Green, Zi thought to her.

"Stop!" a man's voice shouted from behind. "In the name of the Gods themselves, whoever you are, stop at once!"

She reached the boy, turning his shoulders only to find the crowd's puzzled stare mirrored on his face. If he'd been panicked before, he hid it now behind confusion and wonderment. What under the Gods was going on?

She turned toward the square and saw the man who was shouting at her. The man in the red coat, barreling toward her through the fissure she'd cut through the crowd.

Fear bloomed like ice poured down her spine.

Faith came easily, white clouds tethered from the leylines beneath where the man in the red coat had given out his gifts, and she ran.

8

ERRIS

1st Division Command Tent
Sarresant Territory, Near Yves-sur-Raignon

She stood at parade rest. Her arm ached, joints as stiff as they would have been after a hard day's ride. Daylight had lit the camp when she'd arrived; lanterns and candles lit it now. Four hours, at least, spent waiting on the pleasure of his lordship, the Vicomte-General Carailles.

Around her the camp swarmed with activity despite the late hour, a bustle of couriers and commanders. It fell to the cavalry to collect the scouting reports that drove the army's movements, but it was the aides' province to deliver them, issuing the orders that moved tens of thousands of soldiers on little more than her word and the best guesses of the army's highest-ranking generals. A single cavalry brigade could do little more than the 14th had done to prepare for what lay ahead, and high command's response had been swift, ordering all three corps to dig into the hills around Yves-sur-Raignon, a rich town responsible for much of the colonies' textile production. The vast fields of cotton and flocks of sheep pastured in her rolling hills would prove tempting for the Gand armies on their northward march, and those same hills sheltered them now as the Sarresant army built stone walls on the heights and stockpiled ammunition for a protracted fight. It was a predictable defensive maneuver, the kind of tactic that had served them well during the autumn campaign.

On another day, she might have trusted the enemy to be stupid enough to take the bait. But this new enemy general, whoever they were…

Damn Sadrelle. Damn him into the arms of the Nameless. She needed to know what they faced. She knew the record of most of the Gand senior officers, and certainly every notable division and corps commander in their armies; she knew General Chamberlain's preference for artillery, General Abrams's tendency to ignore his flanks, General Cadwallader's overreliance on scouting maneuvers. Whichever of them had the command would inform the best response to this surprise march, would tell her where to look to find weaknesses to exploit. And instead she was blind. Two days now since she'd returned to camp. It wasn't beyond hope that Sadrelle had survived and might still be bringing her the information she needed, but every passing hour made it less likely.

She gave an inward sigh. At least she'd made it two days before the inevitable dressing-down from the vicomte-general. It was not above her commanding officer to use every available means to send a message to her about where exactly she stood in the chain of command. Four hours was excessive, though, even for him.

She wondered idly how much more effective the army would be if the "General" mattered more than the "Vicomte" in her commanding officer's title. Try as she might, it was unlikely a lowborn like her would ever be promoted to the flag. Especially not if she kept up her habit of provoking meetings like this one.

"Brigade-Colonel Erris d'Arrent?" a nasal voice piped up.

Finally.

"Here." She saluted, fist to chest.

"Yes. Right. The vicomte-general will see you at once." He held the tent flap open for her.

She entered.

The inside of the tent was opulent by military standards. A carved oak desk dominated the space, and she felt a pang of empathy for the poor beasts that had to cart the thing between encampments. Sardian rugs crisscrossed the dirt and grass on the floor, and tapestries from Thellan hung from the tent's cross frames, depicting various scenes from their history. A pair of carved chairs in the Sarresant-Valcours style sat in front of the desk, cushions sewn with patterns of blue and gold. Atop the desk neatly organized stacks of paper and maps gave the impression that hard work was being done here, never mind the other comforts.

And seated in a thickly cushioned chaise behind the desk: the vicomte-general.

Carailles was not thin, nor was he excessively fat. He had the look of a man who had once been a soldier but had long since graduated to command.

"Brigade-Colonel Erris d'Arrent," he said gruffly. "Commander, Fourteenth Light Cavalry."

"Sir, reporting as you requested, sir."

"Brigade-Colonel, do you think me a fool?"

Yes. "Sir, no, sir."

"I ask because you seem to enjoy disobeying my orders."

She said nothing, waiting for him to continue his soliloquy.

"Brigade-Colonel?" he went on. "You do recall me ordering you not to go off on any more scouting patrols as if you were a conscripted farmhand with something to prove, yes? I gave you this order directly, and you know damned well the directive came from Duc-General Cherrain himself. And what did you do? On your next Gods-damned patrol, you rode off, risking vital military assets without authorization. Well? Explain yourself, Brigade-Colonel."

"Sir, I judged the information we collected shadowing the enemy's west flank to be insufficient for planning a defense against their northbound march. I ordered Lance-Captain d'Guile to take command of the Fourteenth and deliver the westerly report while I took command of a smaller team for espionage against the enemy's east flank."

"Gods damn you, d'Arrent!" She snapped back to attention. "You are a fullbinder; you are not to be risked for a Gods-damned scouting report."

"Sir, I command a cavalry brigade." It was an insubordinate remark. She knew it as well as he did. His eyes widened in anger and he stood from his chair, gripping the edge of his desk.

"You suggest I reassign you to the infantry? Have you tethering leylines to keep latrines clean and cookfires lit? Is that the extent of your worth, Brigade-Colonel?"

"Sir, no, sir."

"You try my patience."

She said nothing, arms rigid at her side.

"As it happens," he said with a snarl, "you will not command a cavalry brigade for this battle."

Her jaw clenched. He looked at her with contempt, holding the silence.

At last he spoke, his words dripping with venom. "Field-Major d'Ellain and Brigade-Colonel Savasse have taken ill with the spotted fever. You will have d'Ellain's artillery and the Ninth Infantry, in addition to the Fourteenth Light Cavalry. The division's left wing is yours. We march at dawn. See to your command and get out of my sight, Brigade-Colonel. Dismissed."

She saluted and wheeled about, the corners of her mouth fighting to turn up in a smile.

Perhaps Carailles was not a *complete* fool.

"Sir, Field-Captain Regalle for you, arriving within the quarter hour."

"Very good, Lieutenant. See him in at once when he arrives." She saluted to dismiss the aide from her tent. Contrary to the vicomte-general's example, her living space was sparsely decorated. A simple rug from her home province of l'Allcourt in the southern colonies, with a pair of small wooden tables covered by maps she'd requisitioned from the division stores. The maps had already been marked up with notes from the patrols she had sent to canvass the area around Yves-sur-Raignon. She'd had another report from the scouting parties before Carailles's summons. The area around the town was a good defensive position. Too good. A wise enemy commander would disregard their fortifications and bypass Yves-sur-Raignon, taking the eastern route toward the coast. It was harder going without the benefit of the colonial trade roads, but it was what she would have done. Assaulting an entrenched enemy in these hills was suicide. Not that the Gand armies hadn't made suicidal decisions in the past, but this new commander of theirs was a different breed.

Settling in, she got to work on a battle plan for her fledgling command. Two and a half brigades. Almost a division command, in wartime. At full strength she would have had nearly seven thousand men, though they couldn't number more than half that at present;

she'd have the count from their reports soon enough. Vicomte-General Carailles's 1st Division was to be at the left flank of the Sarresant army, as far east as their troops extended. And she had the left wing of the division. If the enemy general did in fact swing around them to the east, she would be the best positioned to harry of all the commanders in the army. Carailles's battle plan called for extensive fortifications on hillsides near the colonial road, and she had already given the order to be sure her troops could execute a basic version of that plan.

But she had a better one.

After a time, her aide returned, folding aside the tent flap that served as a makeshift door.

"Field-Captain Regalle, sir, if it please you."

"Very good, Lieutenant, send him in."

A moment later, Regalle entered her tent, saluting fist to chest.

"So, Regalle," she said, returning his salute, "it seems they gave you the battery."

"Yes, sir," he replied. "They did indeed, so long as the spotted fever has the major vomiting his lunch into his bedpan."

She grinned. She didn't make it a point to be on familiar terms with every artillery captain in the army, but she knew every fullbinder. Anchard Regalle could bind *Death* and *Mind. Death* was a necessary defense for any unit, giving him the ability to disrupt enemy bindings if any came too close to his battery. But it was *Mind* that made d'Ellain's artillery among the most feared guns in the army. Its simplest use, to send out copies of its wielder, was useful enough in a mêlée, but the scholars had discovered another technique in recent years, letting Regalle and other *Mind* binders project their senses to a forward point on the battlefield. With *Mind,* Regalle could serve as his own forward spotter, adjusting the trajectory of his guns with near-perfect precision, firing blind over hills or through the smoke clouds of musket shot.

"I'll put your boys to good work, Captain. You acquitted yourselves well at Ansfield. Fine gunnery work as I recall it."

"Thank you, sir." He held out a parchment, which she accepted, cracking the wax seal. "The field-major sends his compliments, and bids you accept his reports on our strength and disposition."

"Very good," she said, scanning the report. "Thirty-seven guns and crews fit for combat. Good." She nodded, then looked to the field-captain questioningly. "How much pull do you have with the quartermasters? Any owed favors? We need to increase stocks from sixty shots per gun up to eighty, at least, before we're engaged."

His eyebrows raised. "I can call in a debt or two, sir."

"Very good."

Her tent flap opened again and her aide ducked his head inside.

"Rider for you, sir," the lieutenant said. "Arriving shortly."

"Another courier from Carailles? Very well, have them wait with you after they clear sentries. The field-captain and I will conclude shortly."

"Yes, sir." He saluted and she dismissed him, walking back over to her tables.

"Now," she said, turning to the maps of the hills to the south of Yves-sur-Raignon, "let me show you our primary plan, if the enemy approaches from the south."

"Our primary plan, sir?"

She gave him a wry look. "You didn't think I'd have only one, did you?"

He smiled, and she continued. "Your first battery will be deployed here, on the heights." She pointed, tracing the line of their position.

"No cavalry at the base to screen for us, sir?"

"No. I want your men to be given the order to look disorderly, as if they'd just arrived in their position. Maintain that façade without pause; do not assume their scouts aren't watching."

He nodded, looking at the map intently.

"I'll have d'Guile's company positioned here"—she traced it—"behind the hill, out of sight. Have runners standing by to signal him when the enemy approaches. When the enemy is committed to the charge—and charge they will, seeing unprotected artillery—you give the signal and raise arms. D'Guile will ride around and break them with a charge of our own, if they don't break from your barrages while they scale the heights."

"Very good, sir. Do we have a fallback if the enemy advances with more numbers than we can hold?"

"Yes, here, along this switchback trail, to the northeast."

Her tent flap opened again, and her aide once more ducked his head inside. "Rider for you, sir," he said.

"I told you to have them attend outside the tent, Lieutenant."

"Yes, sir, but—" the aide started.

"—he thinks you'll want to receive this rider immediately," a voice said as the tent flap pulled farther aside, admitting the newcomer.

Lieutenant Sadrelle.

"You tried to kill their commander, didn't you?" she snapped as soon as they were alone.

Sadrelle seemed taken aback by the question, feigning a moment of protest before he took a seat beside her table, relaxing into a wide grin.

"Bloody fool," she said.

"Sir, in my defense you'd have done the same. They hadn't even posted a guard at—"

"Did I not stress enough the importance of completing your mission? Did I not specifically say '*no assassinations*'?"

He fell quiet, perhaps sensing the severity of her mood. "Sir, yes, sir."

She sighed.

"Too much to hope you succeeded?"

He shook his head, remaining silent.

"Well, out with it then. Details. What under the Nameless happened back there?"

"Alrich of Haddingston," he said. "That's their new commander. I had his name from one of their quartermasters."

She frowned, searching her memory. That was a commoner's name. Haddingston was a milling town far to the south, in the high country of the Gand colonies. So, a native of the New World, not an import from their homeland across the sea. Yet it wasn't a name she recognized from any of the prominent army postings or division commands.

"I've never heard of him," she admitted finally.

"No one had heard of him, sir. But they speak his name like a priest paying homage to the Exarch. They say his eyes glow gold and he can talk to the Gods."

She snorted a laugh.

"Sir . . ." He gave her a pained look.

"You can't be serious?"

"I thought it nonsense, too, of course, sir. But I saw his eyes glowing gold, sure as I see you now. He saw straight through to where I'd hidden myself in his sleeping chambers while he was away. Was all I could do to dive through a window and get myself back to the camp."

She studied him, waiting for sign of a joke, inappropriate as it would have been. But no. Sadrelle was not the sort to spin fables for attention.

"Some new use for a *Body* binding, perhaps? Or *Shelter*? An illusion conjured up as a pretense to justify promoting an unknown?"

"Perhaps, sir."

She drew in a deep breath, glancing back down at the maps of the coast in front of her. Alrich of Haddingston. And a new binding, one the scholars of Sarresant had not yet divined for their army's use. The very thing the nobles and politicians had feared, and the reason for Sarresant's preemptive invasion of Gand: a new binding, a result of Gand's expansion, while Sarresant had only just secured *Entropy* for itself. No telling what the binding might be, or how decisive it would be in the field.

Well, whatever else they faced, it was clear enough the enemy's new general was a master tactician. And in command of the entirety of the Gand armies. She'd have to go over her plans again in light of the new information, line by line.

"I'll read the rest of the details in your report, Lieutenant. Unless there's more news from their command tents?"

"No, sir. No other changes in their command."

"Very good. Dismissed then," she said. "It's good to have you back."

"Thank you, sir," he said, rising to salute.

She returned it.

"And Sadrelle, you're on latrine duty until further notice. We have orders for a reason."

He grimaced. "Yes, sir."

"Dismissed, Lieutenant."

9

ARAK'JUR

Steam Tents
Sinari Village

The rocks at the center of the tent hissed as Llanara poured another cup of water over them. As the youngest in attendance, the duty of maintaining the steam fell to her. It was not a task to which he was accustomed to seeing her perform, here in the elders' tent. A rare thing to have one so young invited to council. But this was no time to be in thrall to tradition.

Arak'Jur sat cross-legged on a woven mat beside the fire. A proud place, opposite Ka'Vos, who sat on another mat with his apprentice, Ilek'Inari, beside him. Ghella, a gray-haired matron, had the third and final place of honor. The elders were nominally equals, but the tribe gave due reverence to the threefold kinds of spirits—of land, beasts, and things-to-come—by honoring the foremost wielder of each among their number. The rest of the elders sat ringed around the fire. Already they'd deliberated for an hour, their naked bodies glistening with a sheen of sweat. The steam from the heated rocks had to be tended judiciously, and it had been. In this, as with all other tasks to which she applied herself, Llanara was exceptional.

If only she had not chosen to argue in favor of accepting the stranger's offer.

"It seems to me," Llanara said as she sat back down, naked and cross-legged on her mat, "we are in no place to reject an offer of new magic, when it has proven itself against the fair-skins' barrier."

"You assume the stranger told us true." That was Hanat'Sol, the master leatherworker, who had emerged as one of the leading voices against the stranger. "We have no proof he passed through their barrier on his own; he may have come through with their priests' aid, before the traders reached the opening."

Llanara nodded, seeming to consider. "An easily testable claim. We can ask he demonstrate it for us, as part of our agreement."

Uncomfortable looks passed around the assembled elders. She was right, of course, and Hanat'Sol had given her the opening to suggest an opportunity to verify at least that part of the stranger's story. A small victory for her.

"And if it proves true?" Ghella asked from the place beside him. "If we gain a magic capable of piercing the fair-skins' barrier, what would we do with it? We have lived at peace for generations. Are we fool enough to contemplate war? Think of the Tanari."

Llanara leaned forward. "Are we safer, for not having the option?"

Murmurs sparked around the tent, and Llanara raised a hand, quelling them before she continued.

"I do not propose we consider war. But we have the gift of these lands precisely because a gathering of elders once sat, as we do now, and embraced the possibilities of an unknown magic. Are we so afraid of the fair-skins that we would reject an offering of power, one that might decide the course of our people's future?"

"The hunters agree," Valak'Anor said. "We have lived at peace with the fair-skins, but we have all of us heard stories, of stolen lands and war between the fair-skins and the tribes to the south. Would we cast aside a tool our enemy left behind because it had touched his hand? We have the wisdom of the spirits of things-to-come to guide us. They would not lead us into folly."

Llanara met Arak'Jur's eyes.

Arak'Jur cleared his throat. "Ka'Vos will speak for this."

The shaman lifted his head, as if he stirred from a long rest.

Ka'Vos looked around the tent, pausing before he spoke. "This fair-skin magic is strange to us. It is strange to the spirits of things-to-come as well. Perhaps they cannot foresee what its use will bring."

"Tell me, honored shaman," Llanara said. "Do you foresee a lasting peace? Will the Sinari prosper, while other tribes' shamans see visions of war?"

She locked eyes with Ka'Vos, who stayed calm, unblinking, silent. Her gaze was full of fire.

"These are uncertain times," Llanara continued. "If the spirits of things-to-come cannot foresee a lasting peace, perhaps we should embrace possibilities that lay beyond their vision."

Uneasy voices stirred throughout the tent.

"Are you so quick to risk bringing down a curse?" Ghella asked coldly.

"Are you so sure we are not cursed already?"

The tent, already sweltering, turned fiery hot. Arak'Jur raised his hand to quell the muttered outrage.

"Llanara speaks wisdom," he said. Eyes across the tent turned to him with a mix of curiosity and shock. "We must consider her words."

When the tent flaps lifted, a great cloud of steam billowed into the night air. Blankets were draped over the elders as they emerged into the cold, their fragile bodies swaying from the strain of sitting so long in the heat. Llanara strode out of the tent, head held high, beads of sweat covering her naked skin. He emerged a pace behind her, his body slick and glistening, with no need for a blanket to ward off the cold—part of the beast spirits' gift, given when he first slew a great beast to mark himself a guardian, his skin made proof against the elements, tougher and stronger than ordinary men's. Llanara turned to wait for him, moving to take his arm as they walked together.

Neither of them spoke as they made their way through the village. He was not surprised she declined to cover herself as they walked. It was her right, and she had acquitted herself well in her first council meeting. The glow surrounding her no doubt reflected an inner warmth; he recalled similar feelings many a time from his younger days. After a vigorous debate, one seldom needed any shelter from the cold beyond one's own zeal.

All the more so since she had won.

Not a complete victory, but she was wise enough to see it for what it was. A handful of youths would be granted leave to accept Reyne d'Agarre's offer, to submit themselves for testing to see if they could learn his strange serpent's magic when he returned as promised, at the turning of the new moon. It was less than testing the entire village as Reyne d'Agarre requested, but far more than the elders had believed themselves ready to concede. Llanara had argued well. If his support lent her aid in securing consent, it was only to shorten the time it took to reach the inevitable conclusion. Long council meetings in the steam tents took their toll on the elders.

When they reached his tent, she stopped, showing him the fire in her eyes. He took her by the arms, carrying her naked skin against his, and granted her the fruits of her victory.

After, they lay together atop his bed, limbs entwined and slick with sweat. She turned and gave him an easy look, holding his gaze. Her eyes were a deep brown, full of promise, the color of weathered oak. He saw youth, pleasure, contentment. And the rest of her plan, writ plain behind her smile.

"You mean to submit yourself as one of those to be tested," he said.

She nodded. "I do."

It was not what had been negotiated. But he knew none would speak against it.

He said nothing, lying on his back looking up at the peak of his tent. She raked her fingers through the hair on his chest, thick and black.

"I would be your apprentice, you know, if you would have me."

He laughed. "As well ask me to learn this new magic from Reyne d'Agarre. Women cannot converse with the beast spirits. You know this."

"Have any tried, I wonder?"

He gave her a stern look. "Llanara, I will not countenance this sort of talk."

She laughed, scratching harder with her nails on his chest, causing him to wince. "I know, Arak'Jur. I will be content with what I have."

He nodded, reaching around her shoulder to draw her into his embrace. She nestled into him and closed her eyes, still wearing a contented smile.

When morning came, Llanara drew a crowd of excited youths who'd heard the outcome of the council's deliberations. None were so obvious as to hover beside Arak'Jur's tent, though they made sure they had reason to be there. Seeds to gather from bushes at the edge of the forest. A spear lesson in a nearby clearing. When he and Llanara dressed themselves and left the tent, the youths converged.

His heart warmed to see it. She looked to him from their midst as they surrounded her, questions coming from all sides. Her eyes were wide with excitement, and unless he missed his guess, a touch of panic. Well, it was natural to question oneself when first given real responsibility. She would bear it, and thrive.

He stepped aside, leaving her to field the young ones' questions. This new path Llanara had forged made him uneasy, but he was not so old and set in his ways he could not recognize wisdom for what it was. A new line of magic was a mighty gift. The Sinari could not afford to disdain such things, no matter their source. He did not fear the fair-skins; without shamans and guardians of their own, they could not survive in the wilds, could not fight a war against his people and hope to win. Valak'Anor had spoken true, in the steam tent, that the fair-skins had gone to war against southern tribes, trying to carve out more land to place behind their barrier. But those wars had never lasted longer than it took for the great beasts to push the fair-skins back behind their walls. They were a weak people, whatever their gifts of steel and iron.

No, if the elders were right, the threat of war came from the other tribes, loath as he was to consider it. Trade had made the Sinari wealthy, and though they did much to spread that wealth in turn to their neighbors, he knew well enough that avarice could fester like disease, even among friends.

He made his way through the village to a cluster of tents behind the cookfires. Here the last of the meat from the beasts slain for trade was being smoked for storage, its savory smell lingering in the air. The traders' return had been less jubilant than he'd hoped, owing to the visit from the stranger. He worried Reyne d'Agarre's promises would pull on the hearts of the young men, dimming their yearning for trade, and the hunt, replacing it with promises of strange magics, dreams of war. The Sinari had not made war for generations. It took an older man, a man who had once made a child, to understand the horrors of setting peace aside.

Was this a time for youth? Llanara's easy confidence was a thing lost to him. Perhaps it was better for the elders to step back and let passion guide the tribe's course. For generations the Sinari had prospered, choosing peace and trade in the shadow of the fair-skins' Great Barrier. No longer, it seemed. Yet on the matter of war the spirits of things-to-come remained quiet, offering none of the guidance for which his people grew ever more desperate.

His thoughts turned to Ka'Vos, and to his apprentice. Perhaps if the master could not get an answer, then Ilek'Inari could. Ilek'Inari's training was nearly complete; the time drew near when he would be an apprentice no longer. He would be Ka'Inari soon, a new vessel for the visions of the spirits of things-to-come. Ilek'Inari was a young man, and though the path to become shaman was long and difficult, by all accounts Ilek'Inari had borne it with strength and perseverance. Ka'Vos was rightly proud. Already the apprentice worked to gather the implements he would use to complete his rites of initiation. The exact materials were a closely guarded secret, but Arak'Jur knew the preparation had begun. It was customary for the tribe's guardian to protect the apprentice when they ventured into the wild to complete their tests, and he was sure the call would come soon, by season's end, if the shamans' spirits were good.

He suspected Ilek'Inari was gathering his materials now, struggling to strip the carcass of an elk before the women went to work preserving its meat. Arak'Jur smiled ruefully at the sight. Had he been called to prepare materials for a ritual that required elk antler, it would not have occurred to him to do anything other than hunt the elk himself.

"Do you need help, Ilek'Inari?" he asked.

"Guardian!" The young man's voice escaped in a startled rush. "Yes, if you are not busy." He gestured with a shrug of frustration toward the rack of half-formed antlers protruding from the beast's skull.

"Let me."

Arak'Jur reached down, calling on the spirit of the *mareh'et*, the Great Cat, whose claws sheared through bone as easily as flesh. A nimbus of fur and claw surrounded him, then faded. The antlers came free.

"Thank you, honored guardian," Ilek'Inari said, sheathing his bone knife.

Arak'Jur waved a hand dismissively, then reached to help the apprentice shaman to his feet.

"I wondered if you might share your thoughts on last night's council," he said as Ilek'Inari stood, patting his fur-lined breeches to shake off the dirt from kneeling beside the elk.

"Llanara spoke well," Ilek'Inari replied. "If the spirits willed us to a different course, they might have blessed the tongues of the elders who argued against her."

Arak'Jur nodded.

The younger man continued. "My master had a vision of his coming, the stranger."

"Yes. He told me, before the fair-skin arrived."

"It made Ka'Vos uneasy, but the vision did not warn against the stranger, or what he brings. It seems to me the council made the right decision. Oftentimes the spirits of things-to-come work through us, through the shamans, but it need not always be so."

"Would you have made the same decision, if it fell to you alone?"

"If I were chief? Spirits save us, guardian, I would as soon not contemplate visions so dire. The world is dark enough as it is."

Arak'Jur smiled. "In truth, though, where did your heart lay, at the end?"

"As I said, Llanara spoke well. I am troubled by the unknown, but I trust in the spirits of things-to-come. They have guided us well, for a great many generations, and I believe we follow them in this." A moment of quiet, then the apprentice shaman went on. "What about you, guardian? You named it wisdom, and I think you convinced more than a few to pay her heed."

"Perhaps you are right, and I was guided by the shamans' spirits."

"That is not an answer," Ilek'Inari said, and Arak'Jur bowed his head to acknowledge it.

"You will make your journey soon," Arak'Jur said.

"I will. Though I have much to learn from Ka'Vos. Last night I had a vision of *mareh'et* passing through our lands. But when I awoke and asked Ka'Vos to look, he saw nothing, and I could not find it again."

"Just as well," Arak'Jur said. "A terrible thing, for a *mareh'et* to stalk our people."

Ilek'Inari nodded, and seemed content to leave it there, gathering the materials he'd come for and offering a respectful bow.

Arak'Jur watched him go. A chill passed through him, though he took care to give no outward sign. No great thing, for an apprentice shaman's visions to err. And if Ilek'Inari and Ka'Vos both failed to see a beast, it surely meant the tribe was safe. Yet he could not dismiss a sliver of doubt, stuck in his side like a thorn ripped from a noxious weed.

10

SARINE

Central Square
Market District, New Sarresant

She'd arrived at the central square early that morning, as she always did when she had sketches to display. It had been days since the madness in the Maw, since her strange encounter with the man in the red coat and the chaos that had followed. The city's papers had called it a riot, exonerating the city watch for their part in the violence and condemning the Maw citizens for theft and bedlam. She knew the truth, as did every man and woman who had seen it firsthand. Whatever else he'd done, the man in the red coat had distributed a king's share of food among the poor, and the watch had paid for it by firing their pistols into the crowd. The lies printed in the papers stirred anger that was already simmering among the city's people, making for hushed grumblings in the Maw's taprooms, and giving her uncle fits at the thought of venturing outside the chapel. But her sketches sold best when they reflected the goings-on in the city, and she could only resketch the main reliefs of the Sacre-Lin so many times before she needed a few hours' escape. Today it meant a spread along the walkways in the central markets, close enough to need to shield her sketches from the spray of the fountains near the river's edge.

"Ooh, daddy, daddy, the ship! I want the ship!" a shrill voice cried, wagging a sausage-shaped finger in the direction of her sketches.

She put on her most humble smile, the one that played best with the nobles and the wealthy, and rose from her cross-legged pose, affecting a reasonable facsimile of a curtsy toward her newest patron. The child, no more than ten, was bedecked in ribbons and silks, with a plump figure suggesting her household had weathered rather well the austerity of a country at war. Her father made a gesture to one of their servants, checking the timepiece he pulled from his hip pocket with a look equal parts boredom and exasperation. A pair of porters rounded out their entourage, already loaded with parcels and trinkets from the day's affairs.

The servant pointed to one of her sketches of the *Queen Allisée*. "How much?" he asked in a gruff voice.

She bowed her head gracefully. Ten times the normal price ought to do it.

"A silver mark, sir. Not a print or a wood press. Drawn by hand on the day the ship arrived in the harbor, if it pleases her ladyship." This she said with a nod toward the child, who had already turned her attention to devouring an apple pastry as she stood waiting beside her father.

The servant sighed and reached into a pouch at his belt for the coin. Had it been earlier in the day she expected he would have haggled. As it was, his little mistress's wrath proved too fearsome to be risked. Smiling, Sarine pocketed the payment, rolled the parchment into a tight tube, and wrapped it with a piece of twine tied in a simple bow knot. She handed it over with another curtsy and watched them go, sauntering down the street at the child's pace.

She sat back down on the hot stones, reclining against the embankment behind her. Did the nobles notice, she wondered, the stares following them as they walked? Their world had an undeniable beauty to it, an allure she had indulged in often enough for it to be a permanent fixture in her idle bouts of fancy. But half the city was starving, and the rest close enough to shave with the difference. Like as not the nobles thought the stares that followed them were envy, if they noticed them at all, and the commonfolk knew better than to show anything more. Here in the market, the best way to an easy coin was deference, and respect.

Zi lay on his back, his scales glinting bright green in the midday sun. He seemed to struggle to find the right angle before relaxing and letting his body uncoil across the pavement stones. Frustrating that he refused to allow her to sketch him. A glint of mischief in her eye, she turned to a blank page in front of her, set one of her charcoals to the paper, and—

Don't.

His gemstone eyes were locked on to her, a flush of red creeping into the scales around his long face.

"Only playing with you, Zi."

Sketch them instead.

She turned to look, finding a pair of blue-uniformed city watchmen making their way through the crowd. Her stomach sank, remembering the thundercracks and blood from the Maw. It appeared these two were beelining for a street vendor, a thin man in spectacles with a crate lying open atop a blanket he'd spread on the ground. A pamphleteer, though this one hadn't been hawking his text with the wordsmiths' usual fervor. She hadn't noticed him, or hadn't paid especial attention anyway. Now she craned her neck to see, along with the rest of the street's occupants.

At first the watchmen stopped and spoke to the pamphleteer, and the man nodded as if in response to a question. She gasped along with the rest of the crowd when they struck him, leather-clad fists taking the man by surprise. He spit blood, eliciting a horrified shriek from passersby as they scrambled out of the way. The watchmen struck again, and the pamphleteer crumpled into a ball atop his blanket. His spectacles clattered onto the stone as one of the watchmen continued yelling curses at him. The other turned his attention to the man's crate, giving it a swift kick, splintering the wood and scattering straw and paper into the street. He called out, his voice ringing above the now deathly silent market.

"Fantiere's filth is banned, by order of the Duc-Governor." He gave the crate another kick. "Possession of banned texts will result in arrest and detainment."

The first watchman pulled the street vendor to his feet, holding him up while he clapped iron manacles around the man's wrists. Together they shambled away toward the guardhouse at the district boundary. The other watchman trailed behind them, picking up the ruined crate, made all the more difficult to carry by having destroyed it for the sake of spectacle. A cloak of silence hung over the street's occupants until the ignoble procession disappeared from view.

And then the market erupted.

Some fled the scene, eager to be away from the violence hanging in the air. Others set to gossip, sharing what they'd seen with each other and newcomers alike. Many, many more inquired as to the contents of the now-forbidden crate. She managed to catch the title in a hurried exchange as a pair of would-be readers rushed past her display: *Treatise on the Virtues*, by Jaquin Fantiere. It sounded like a religious text, though she suspected from the reaction she'd just witnessed that it was not.

"Here," a man said in a flat voice, handing her a sheaf of paper. She blinked in surprise.

"What? Who are you?" she stammered, accepting the proffered document by reflex. The man was a common citizen by the look of him, dressed in simple attire. "What is this?"

The man made no reply, only turned and walked down the street.

It seemed like you wanted to read it.

"Zi!" she exclaimed, her eyes darting to the title of the pamphlet in her hand. Sure enough, *Treatise on the Virtues.* She wheeled around and stuffed it into her pack, glaring at her companion. He'd done something to provoke the man, clear enough, but asking after Zi's gifts was like trying to squeeze rain from a bank of morning fog. He'd never told her anything about what he could do, and said as much now, lowering his head to lie flat on the stones, his scales a mix of green and purple as he took in the goings-on around them.

Her heart thrummed as she glanced about, expecting someone to have noticed the odd exchange. A few moments passed before the street settled back into a semblance of normalcy. If anyone had noticed, they gave no sign, though that was no guarantee.

"This is lovely, dear, did you do this yourself?"

The voice startled her back to the moment. A woman looked up at her, lines on her face creasing around a smile.

"Yes, it's a drawing of the Sacre-Lin chapel," she said. "The main relief. I have a dozen or so, in different angles." She gestured to a few more of her sketches, displayed in rows along the edge of the street.

"Lovely." The woman paced a few steps, admiring them.

"A copper penny if you fancy any in particular."

The woman considered for a few more moments before selecting one of the drawings of the chapel's smallest glass window. The Oracle's stern gaze rose from the page, charcoals capturing the distant look in the

Goddess's milky-white eyes. She accepted the woman's coin with thanks, and a blessing.

By now the market had returned to its business in full, only a low hum of rumors suggesting the earlier excitement. She supposed that was how the people of the city bore it, living their lives in the shadow of the powerful: hope you escaped notice and make the best of whatever good fortune came your way. There was a certain virtue in that. The Exarch may extoll them to courage, vigilance, adherence to duty, but the Commoner preached keeping one's head down. She laughed to herself at her private blasphemy. Her uncle would not appreciate her inventing new Gods, nor ascribing them virtues mocking the paths of Tritheticism. But what use were the virtues of heroic Gods, inspiring men and women to mighty deeds, when one's most pressing concerns were scraping together enough coin to buy food and hoping the city watch didn't take an interest in your affairs?

Her stomach twisted at the thought, recalling the contents of her pack. At least if it came to it, she had her gifts, and Zi's. The combination had always been enough to keep her safe, to escape the notice of the watch, the priesthood, and the darker sorts, the toughs and street gangs she'd avoided growing up on the streets of the Maw.

"I knew it must be you," a voice said from behind. "Please, don't run."

She turned and found herself face-to-face with the man in the red coat.

"Please," the man repeated, holding his hands upraised and empty.

Words went dry in her throat. It was the same man she'd seen in the Harbor, and again in the Maw, of a surety. Middling height, on the old side of young, with the beginnings of creases in his skin but no wrinkles or gray in his hair. His red coat was every bit as fine as it had looked from a distance, with the sort of embroidery and rich velvet one paid for in gold, not silver. He wore a long, sheathed knife on his belt rather than the dueling sword favored by some among the noblemen, but otherwise she would have considered him right at home among the denizens of the Gardens, or perhaps the wealthiest merchants of Southgate.

Green, came the thought from Zi.

She frowned, which by itself seemed to elicit a look of surprise from the man. He recovered quickly, offering her an easy smile, the sort certain types of men practiced alone with a mirror before they used it in public.

"Who..." she began, then started again. "What are you doing here?"

"You're an artist," he said, looking over her sketches.

"I am," she said, though instinct carried her a step forward, to interpose herself between him and her drawings. She'd seen this man scatter guardsmen like alley cats, thieving crates of goods from the Harbor and doing something to freeze half a city block of citizens and city watchmen in the Maw. He was dangerous, to say the least, whatever his proclivities for charity. If not for her sketches she might have run, same as she did before. But he took his time, as though he were no more threatening than any other customer perusing her work, as though she were any of a dozen vendors on the street.

"Such detail." The man paused in front of one of her portraits of the ships in the harbor. "Tell me, these sketches, you did them from life, from observation?"

"Yes," she replied, still on her guard.

"Do you always work from life?" he asked nonchalantly, thumbing through some more. She nodded.

Then he picked up a sketch of the nobles lounging on the Rasailles green.

"W-when I can."

"Of course. These really are exceptional. Such a gift."

"My lord, what is it exactly you want?"

He picked up one of the portraits, a sketch of the building where the Council-General, the elected assembly for the commonfolk, met to do whatever it was they did, ostensibly on behalf of the citizens of the colonies.

"I'll take this one. And I'm no lord, merely one of the fools who sit on this council." He made a slight gesture with the portrait to indicate his meaning. "This is a wonderful rendition of the council halls."

She opened her mouth to speak, then closed it when he reached into his purse and produced a gold mark.

"Yours, as a token of good faith. For the portrait, and your name."

Suspicion flared as she looked between him and his gold.

"I saw you," she said. "In the Maw."

"Yes. And I promise you, I bear you no ill will. Quite the opposite, in fact."

"I also saw you in the Harbor, the day the *Queen Allisée* arrived in port."

That gave him pause, his smile slipping for a moment.

"So," he said. "It seems we already know some measure of each other's secrets."

Fear coursed through her. Did he mean he knew about her *Faith*? If he meant to threaten her, she knew damned well the magistrates would take a wealthy man at his word, no matter how absurd the claim. But he raised a hand in a calming gesture before he spoke.

"I assure you, whatever you think I am about, you will not find my message amiss." He brandished the coin again. "Instead of suspicion, let this be the start of trust between us."

"A gold mark, for the sketch, and my name?"

He nodded. "And a chance to speak further. That's all I ask."

"Sarine, then." She reached to take the gold from his hand. "My name is Sarine."

"A great pleasure to meet you, Sarine. My name is Reyne d'Agarre."

At that moment another pair of city watchmen trotted into view at the end of the square, and d'Agarre grimaced. "This is a poor place for further conversation." He tucked the rolled-up parchment into his belt pouch. "I'll send an invitation to my salon. We can speak there, and come to a better mutual understanding."

She frowned. She wasn't about to refuse a gold mark, but neither would she betray her uncle's trust by telling a stranger in the market where to send his invitation. Yet he didn't give her a chance to reply, striding away as he called back to her.

"Watch for my letter. We will meet again."

11

ERRIS

The Battle of Villecours, Left Flank
Sarresant Territory, Near the Coast

Hold, men!" she cried, wheeling her saber above her head. "Hold the line! Hold for Sarresant!"

Beside her, musket shots streaked through the meager protection of a guttering *Shelter* binding. Men fell. The smell of blood mixed with the screams of the dying. And still the enemy approached.

She'd started the day's action with the first company of Field-Captain Regalle's artillery but had long since committed herself to plugging gaps in the lines of the 9th Infantry. They protected the Sarresant army's left flank, and the enemy was probing them, testing for weaknesses. They had fought for the better part of the morning, hotly engaged for the last hour.

A column of enemy muskets advanced past the safety of their makeshift fortification, trotting forward onto the deadly ground between their lines. Ox shit on a plate. These were fresh troops, and her right flank was already engaged. Had the enemy already committed reserves to this attack? How many of the Gods-damned Gandsmen were there on this battlefield?

"Hold, men," she called once more. "Prepare for action. Hold fire until they're on us."

The men beside her went through the steps to reload with practiced efficiency. Tear the cartridge, pour the powder and ball, ram it down the barrel, set the cap, cock the hammer. A good soldier could fire three shots per minute. A far cry from the six-shot revolvers carried by the officers, but accurate to five hundred paces or more on a clear day, whereas her pistol was good for close-up work and little else.

She turned and called another order over her shoulder. "Sights to three hundred paces."

The infantry captains took up her order, repeating the command up and down the line. The sharpshooters, men who had earned four and five stripes on their sleeves, stood twenty paces up the hill behind them. She'd committed the rest of her reserve to filling the lines. She trusted the sharpshooters to fire through the line, in spite of the risk of hitting their own. It was an edge, and she needed every advantage on offer.

Cannon fire whistled overhead as the enemy came into range. Gand soldiers howled and collapsed, but still they pressed on, a seemingly endless wave of red coats closing across the open field.

"Volley at three hundred paces," she called out, waiting for the enemy line to approach. Twenty more paces. Ten. "Fire."

A rippling thundercrack went off along her line, ringing a high-pitched whine in her ears. At this range Sarresant soldiers were deadly accurate, and through the musket smoke the front rank of the Gandsmen fell as if they had choreographed it for a dance. Still they came. Gods damn it, there were so many.

"Reload," came the order from her officers.

She made a quick estimate of the numbers on the opposite side of the field as she watched the outline of enemy soldiers advancing through the fog of her volley. She'd take a single Sarresant marksman over a half dozen of their counterparts from Gand, but those were about the odds they faced today, if she had to guess. At least the odds that were left to them after the morning's disastrous charge into the enemy center. Gods-damned virgin-blooded fool, whoever ordered that massacre. She held now along the left flank to try to provide cover as the Sarresant army retreated and regrouped. At least those were the orders high command sent by courier two hours past. She had other ideas. But for now, her position was being charged by at least a regiment of fresh reserves.

"Second volley," she called. "Fire."

Another belch of smoke and flame, and another rank of Gandsmen fell to decorate the grass. This time they were close enough to hear the screams. Two hundred paces. Closer. The enemy stopped to drop to a knee and send a volley into her line, musket shot knifing through the air around her as men screamed and fell.

She called another order over the top of the chaos. "Bayonets!"

The call was repeated, accompanied by the *shink* of metal being drawn and affixed to the barrels of their guns. From the look of it the Gandsmen were reloading to prepare another volley. Good. No better time to strike than when the enemy would be distracted ramming powder down their barrels.

"Charge!"

She bared her teeth, letting loose a battle cry picked up by her soldiers as they rose from behind their fortifications and swept toward the enemy line. A few stray shots rang out from enemy soldiers who'd been quick to reload. But no concentrated fire, and if she was lucky, little time for them to aim. Roars came from behind as Regalle's heavy guns spat out their last shots before her charge impacted the enemy line.

One hundred paces. Fifty. Close enough she could see fear in the Gandsmen's eyes, facing down hundreds of screaming-mad Sarresant soldiers led by a commander who'd decided an old-fashioned mêlée was preferable to letting them threaten to sweep past her flank.

The lines collided.

Tethering *Body* and *Life*, Erris tore through the enemy's front rank in a flurry of blood and steel. She danced ahead of the bayonet palisade, ducking as a pair of fresh-faced Gand soldiers lunged at her together. One of them she parried with her saber, shoving herself backward behind the other one's guard. She channeled leyline energy, punching the second soldier in the mouth. Without the binding she might have broken some teeth. With it she caved his skull in around her fist, soaking her forearm in blood. In the same motion she shoved off the second soldier's body and spun toward the first, landing a deep cut, dropping him where he stood.

She went to work, an elegant dance from soldier to soldier. Her steel flashed around their bayoneted rifles, almost too fast to see. A cry went up in the Gand tongue: "Fullbinder! Fullbinder!" The least of their worries. She couldn't maintain bindings at this strength for long without tiring, but she didn't have to. As planned, the ground started to rumble shortly after the infantry lines entangled.

The cavalry had arrived.

A simple hammer-and-anvil technique, her infantrymen taking on airs of a desperate unit on its last legs, spread thin, making a show of plugging the lines with reserves. First bait the enemy into coming close enough for a charge, then the cavalry of the 14th could wheel around and trample their back line. The fresh reserves complicated things, but she'd overestimated enemy morale. They broke easily enough.

The Gandsmen scattered, making for the hills across the sparsely wooded grasslands where the forest broke to the east. Like as not they would re-form and return to the battlefield in time. By then she would have long since executed her plan.

"Excellent to see you hale and whole, sir," Lance-Captain Pourrain called down to her with a salute, one of his horsemen trotting up beside them holding Jiri's reins.

"Let's hope Vicomte-General Carailles is worth more than his usual tepid shit today," she said, grinning as she swung up into the saddle. "Nice work on the approach there; using the sun's glare was fine thinking."

Pourrain bowed his head, acknowledging the praise.

She patted Jiri's neck, her mount in good spirits to have her rider once more. On a lark, she channeled a quick binding of *Life* into Jiri, eliciting a soft whicker. Ah, but it felt good to be whole again.

"Let's send another rider to the general," she said. "There's more bloody work to be done, but all of this is for naught if he isn't in position by the time we arrive."

"Very good, sir." Pourrain gave another salute, riding to carry out her orders.

They were moving again, infantry in tight ranks at a double-time march behind the cavalry. It was no easy feat, maneuvering so many men and horses into the tree line, but she trusted her unit commanders. By now the main body of the enemy army would be pressing forward to harry the shattered lines of the Sarresant forces. Discipline or no, she'd never known men in the grip of battle lust to give up a chase easily. No matter that the Gandsmen's right flank had faltered and they had no presence in the trees along the eastern line of battle. If the Gods willed it, a few advance scouts were all that stood between her and a covered approach to the Gand reserves. And, unless she missed her guess, the enemy's command tents.

The preparations at Yves-sur-Raignon had been a disaster. Three days' fortification and the enemy ignored them with a march along the eastern route toward the coast, exactly as she'd predicted. By the time the lords-general realized the enemy intended to avoid their little trap, the Gandsmen were halfway to Villecours. An admirable turning of the tides. For nigh on three seasons now, the Sarresant army had fought a defensive campaign despite operating in Gand territory, using just such tactics as the enemy now deployed against them. Maneuver in the open, refusing to commit to an engagement until you placed yourself in between the enemy and some important strategic objective. Then dig in and force them to attack over unfavorable ground. Simple, but effective. And now the enemy had cut them off from the port city of Villecours, second in importance only to New Sarresant itself here in the New World.

Unthinkable, to lose Villecours. But that was precisely what they faced with the enemy led by this new commander. Alrich of Haddingston, who could talk to the Gods. No time now to worry over the unknown. If her plan worked it wouldn't matter whom or what the enemy commander could talk to.

The birds chirped a greeting as her men tracked through the woods, a column of horses and infantry four abreast. Their lines weaved through the foliage, staying tightly together, as she'd ordered. They would engage as soon as they arrived if Vicomte-General Carailles was in position when he received the signal. For all the general's bluster in the command tent, he knew to trust her scouting reports and deployment "recommendations" during an engagement. She Gods-damned hoped he did anyway. They'd never crack the Gand reserves without a distraction.

"We're in position, sir," Lance-Captain d'Guile said with a salute as she approached the tree line.

"Very good, Captain. How are the battle lines disposed?"

D'Guile gave her a grim look, which she took as answer enough. She nudged Jiri forward and withdrew a spyglass from her saddlebag, surveying the plains where the main action had commenced earlier that morning.

Gods take them all. Had the Gandsmen kept half their army in reserve?

Ten thousand men if there were a hundred, arrayed in neatly divided lines beneath a row of low hills. Infantry, almost all, muskets sprouting from their shoulders like weeds in a flower bed. She'd guessed the disposition of the enemy line from studying the maps, and gotten their placement right, if not their numbers. Carailles's men—the remainder of Sarresant's 1st Division—were in place near the base of the hills, and hers were here, hidden in the trees. A swarm of red coats between them was a ripe apple tucked between their jaws, if swallowing it didn't burst their bellies in the attempt.

She gave the order to raise the signal. Flags went up under the cover of trees, angled so the vicomte-general's men could see, and the Gand army could not. And now they waited.

As she had "recommended," Carailles's soldiers had approached in the open, giving the enemy reserves plenty of time to deploy to meet them. All that remained was for Vicomte-General Carailles to order the charge, to pull as many as possible away from the center, where, sure enough, she could see the banners of their command tents. With the reserves committed to action, her men could sweep around, striking at the very heart of the enemy's command.

Time stretched on, moments sliding toward minutes. What was he waiting for? She ordered the signal flown again, and it was. *Go, you sack of pig shit. Attack!*

Her heart sank.

He wasn't going to give the order.

The lines wavered, a deadly game of waiting for the other side to cross the threshold where engagement was an inevitability. Any moment now, Carailles's courage would wilt into an order to retreat, rather than attack. It was coming. She could see it, sense it, feel it coming like an oily sickness spreading over her skin.

She couldn't let it happen. Her men were exposed; safe for now behind the cover of the tree line, but positioned like a wedge between the main lines and the enemy's reserve. Without the distraction of Carailles's attack to screen her movements, the enemy would have ample time to collapse, squeezing her brigades like a grape in a winepress. She had to act. She needed to do something to save her men, to save the battle and any hope of victory.

In the distance, she saw a glimmer of gold in the center of Carailles's lines. A shining light like a beacon, beaming from where his soldiers sat in the open field. It was as if a leyline had overflowed onto the battlefield, leaking energy into her normal vision.

She'd never seen anything like it.

Guided by instinct, she slid her eyes shut, and it was there: an unfamiliar pattern of leyline energy, gold light pulsing like a beating heart, bright enough to overshadow the twisting grid of lines beneath the earth. She bound it, tethering herself to the source in one smooth motion.

Her eyes slid into another body.

"What should we do, Vicomte-General?" came a whining voice at her side. "Shall I give the order to fall back?"

"No." She heard herself say it, but the voice coming from her throat was deep and baritone, a man's voice. She squinted, the battlefield in front of her coming into focus. The same flags, the same lines of soldiers, but from another vantage, as if she had leapt across the field.

She said it again. "No."

"Sir?" the aide asked, full of bewilderment. "Sir, your eyes—"

"We attack," she said. "Attack! Order the charge! Do it now!"

As soon as she said it, the strange golden binding slipped away from her, and she felt her vision settle back into her own familiar form, resting atop Jiri's saddle.

Her senses snapped into place together, an overload of sensation all at once. What had happened to her? The golden light...

"There! They're attacking, sir!" Lance-Captain d'Guile pointed. Battle cries echoed across the plain as the two lines charged toward each other.

"That's our signal." Fog cleared from her mind at the sight. "Attack! Charge!"

Her soldiers flowed out of the forest, an arrow of men and horse pointed straight at the enemy command tents.

She tethered full-strength *Body* and *Life* bindings through herself and Jiri, holding a *Death* tether at the ready to slice through any defenses from the enemy line. The reins went slack in her hands, and she let Jiri fly. The rest of her cavalry surged in a storm of hooves, but Jiri danced on water, carrying her ahead of them in a furious dash. Let the men see her, let them take heart as their commander streaked ahead, her saber held aloft and glinting in the midmorning sun.

Across the plain they'd already been noticed. Companies of the enemy's reserve were trying to split off from their skirmish with Carailles's 1st Division, where the vicomte-general's men tied them down. A pittance of defenders had been left around the command tents, and it was to them she turned her full attention.

Her saber streaked, flashes of cold steel empowered by *Body* striking down the frontline soldiers as Jiri crashed through them like a bolt of white lightning. Her *Death* binding sliced through a feeble attempt to block her path with *Shelter*, and she crashed into their camp. Jiri reacted with impossible agility, leaping tents, cookfires, and sentries alike as they struck deep, searching for Major General Alrich of Haddingston. A swarm of enemy soldiers trailed behind them, unsure whether to chase after her intrusion or turn to meet the horde bearing down upon their camp in her wake.

There. The command tent. Jiri saw it the moment she did, changing direction, racing with the full power of her long stride.

Heartbeats before they arrived, a man lifted the tent flap and looked out. A man in a general's uniform, his eyes awash with golden light.

Jiri trampled the tent, but not before her saber took the enemy general across the face. Blood coated the end of her blade as she completed her follow-through, trailing droplets scattering to the wind. The enemy commander never even raised a weapon, made no defensive posture. Had he even been trained to combat?

Together, mount and rider thundered through the remainder of the camp, turning to survey the rest of the engagement.

Her men continued to swarm over the defenders in the tents, but the enemy soldiers had broken. There was a bond between men and their commander, unspoken but real, and she'd snapped it. The Gandsmen knew it, sure as sunrise, watching her forces swarm through the command tents. And knowing what he'd meant to them, how their fortunes had changed under his command, the Gand soldiers reacted with a mix of violent rage and despair. Both enemies of discipline. Even so, the Gandsmen had the advantage of numbers. This battle was not over yet.

Spurring Jiri back toward her lines, she called out the order to withdraw.

12

ARAK'JUR

Searching for Ka'Ana'Tyat
Sinari Land

He was fairly certain Ilek'Inari was lost.

Not that he doubted the apprentice's gift; with Ka'Vos's help, the shaman and the apprentice had divined the location of the meeting to which they now traveled. But Ilek'Inari had no head for woodcraft. They walked from tree to tree, glade to glade, until the sun rose high and shadows stretched across the forest floor. The Ranasi guardian and his charge would long since have arrived, and Arak'Doren would not be kind to Ilek'Inari when they finally did the same. Just as well. His own good humor had departed some time ago.

"Here, honored guardian, this mark, I have seen it!" Ilek'Inari gestured to a gash in the side of an oak tree, three broad cuts. A bear had hunted here.

"As you say." He inclined his head out of respect, walking behind as they changed directions again. Ilek'Inari took long strides, shifting the packs he carried from shoulder to shoulder. Perhaps they were getting close at last.

Ka'Vos had declared the signs favorable—no great beasts near Sinari lands—and so Arak'Jur had been sent to accompany the apprentice on the final step of his journey. The Ranasi, their neighbors to the north, would also send a woman to complete the ritual. A fine omen, a chance to demonstrate to their neighbors that the Sinari still held the spirits' favor.

"Yes, this is it!" Ilek'Inari exclaimed, calling back over his shoulder. "Two more hills and they will be there, where a stream is divided by a white rock."

He grunted in reply.

They paced up a slope before descending into a narrow valley where, as promised, he heard the rush of running waters. A strange thing, the gift of the shamans. The guardians' magic was simple, a blessing granted by the spirits of slain great beasts. To see far-off places or glimpses of what-might-be—these were things he did not understand, any more than he understood the secrets of the women's magic, tied to the third kind of spirits, the spirits of sacred places and the land. Journeys to escort the shamans and the spirit-touched among the women were as close as guardians came to such mysteries.

He smiled, raising a hand in greeting. Oh, he had been right. Arak'Doren was not pleased.

"Brother," he called to the figures beside the white rock at the center of the stream. "Honored sister."

Arak'Doren scowled as he rose to his feet, gray-haired and leather-skinned, though he was strong and lean, with no sign of slowing from his age. Ilek'Inari earned a glare when the apprentice tried to make a similar greeting. The woman was not so sour, welcoming them both with a formal bow. He didn't recognize her, though she was young, scarce older than Llanara, which made her young indeed to be making one of the women's journeys. The subtleties of the women's ways were beyond his understanding, but he'd accompanied enough of the neighboring tribeswomen to recognize her youth as exceptional. Arak'Doren spoke to introduce her: Corenna, daughter of Ka'Hinari, the Ranasi shaman.

She was garbed in the women's ceremonial dress, white fur sewn around cured hides dyed white and bound in a tight wrap, with long skirts to match. Her face was painted white, save for a single blue line running from her hairline to her chin. Leather cords threaded with feathers completed the garb, binding her black hair back in a tight braid.

He and Arak'Doren left their charges to their ritual gifts and tokens, walking a few paces to make their own exchange.

"It is good to see you, brother," he said. It took a fellow guardian to understand the life they led. It was not an affectation, to name him brother.

"It would have been good to see you yesterday," Arak'Doren said, but they grasped forearms just the same. "So that's the new Sinari shaman, then?"

"It is. Ilek'Inari is a good man."

Arak'Doren grunted, eyeing their charges as Ilek'Inari and Corenna spoke their ritual parts to one another.

"Though," Arak'Jur added, "he is not the best, when it comes to the wild."

Arak'Doren laughed. "No, no he is not. Best hope Ka'Vos lives another generation, my friend. This one will have you warding in Hurusi territory when the *juna'ren* is hiding in your water stores."

Arak'Jur smiled.

"Watch over Corenna," Arak'Doren said. "She is precious to the Ranasi."

"She has my full protection." This was a sacred trust, between tribes. Ranasi women came to him for their journeys, and Sinari women came to Arak'Doren for theirs. Wars had started over guardians failing their charges. But a successful journey was a thing to celebrate for both tribes.

"These are clouded times," Arak'Doren said. "It is good for the Sinari to gain another shaman."

"Yes," he agreed, cautiously. "Ka'Hinari's visions have not changed?"

Arak'Doren shook his head. "They have not. We fear what they betoken. Death. Fire."

"Perhaps this journey will mark an end to such things. The spirits have changed their paths before."

"I hope it will be so, brother."

Their charges had finished their ceremony. Seeing it, he embraced his counterpart once more.

"Safe journeys, guardian."

"To you as well. Blessings, Arak'Jur."

Once again, Ilek'Inari led the way through the trees. The bear they sought had left sign, back the way they'd come. Yet another omen of the spirits' favor. His heart had warmed in reverence for the spirits when

Corenna revealed Bear would be the totem for their journey. Ilek'Inari's had, too, he was sure, after being reminded they'd seen bear sign on the way to the meeting.

Corenna kept a good pace for all she wore the long skirts of the women's ceremonial dress. She answered his questions about the Ranasi with deference, showing proper respect for another tribe's guardian. It was not her first journey, nor even her first journey outside Ranasi lands; she had ventured into neighboring Olessi land, and had once spent two moons traveling to the lands of the Yanarat, in the icy reaches of the North. A curious woman. She was of an age with Llanara and had already made more journeys than any grandmother of the Sinari. Perhaps he should speak with Ka'Vos about urging the spirit-touched among their women to hone their talents. It was a time for such things, little as they would appreciate wisdom coming from the men.

Like himself, Corenna was unencumbered. It fell to the shaman's apprentice to carry her provisions on the journey, as well as the implements for the apprentice's own ritual. Ilek'Inari bore it in good spirits, with an infectious humor that passed the hours in easy conversation.

"Almost, you make me wish the guardians had pilgrimages of their own, honored sister," Arak'Jur said.

Corenna favored him with a smile. "It is true, guardian. My father saw visions of a new sacred site on Yanarat lands, hidden across an icy channel. I thought Arak'Uro would let me go on alone, but he dove into the ice."

He boomed a laugh. "Do not underestimate our pride."

"The Yanarat shaman had no notion the sacred site existed?" Ilek'Inari asked over his shoulder.

"None. My father's gift is powerful, but the spirits do not reveal everything to the shamans, especially where women's secrets are concerned." She smiled. "Yet even the Yanarat women had no knowledge of this place. We were the first to learn its secrets."

"It was covered over in ice, then?" Ilek'Inari asked.

"It was. Blessings to the guardians for their talents. Arak'Uro made short work of it, with what help I could provide."

Arak'Jur nodded approval. "A mighty thing, such a well-kept secret of the land."

"Oh, we were not through to it yet. Tell me, Arak'Jur, have you heard of the *sre'ghaus*?" When he shook his head no, she went on. "Neither had Arak'Uro. And whatever shrouded the sacred site from the Yanarat shaman, it seemed had hidden the *sre'ghaus* as well."

Now he listened with rapt interest. A new great beast, the third such reported in as many turnings of the seasons. Vital for the guardians to share and learn what they could, before the shamans saw a new beast approach the tribe's lands.

"They are small creatures," she continued. "Like beetles. But they move together, as if by a single mind. And when slain, they dissemble into mist, then re-form before your eyes."

"How do you keep them dead?" Ilek'Inari asked.

She shrugged. "We never found the way. Arak'Uro fought them for a time while I completed the ritual, and we left."

A fine story. He would have to send word to Arak'Uro and plead for wisdom on dealing with these *sre'ghaus*, spirits send they stayed far away from Sinari lands during his lifetime.

He motioned the other two to silence as they crested the hill. This was the place, a few hours' walk from where the white rock forked the stream. Ilek'Inari had described his vision, and the cave up ahead—a simple recess into stone—matched it exactly. Inwardly he felt a wave of relief to be spared another long journey. This was not Ka'Ana'Tyat, the sacred place where Corenna and Ilek'Inari would make their communion with the spirits, but it was the first step toward that path. Each time he had visited a sacred place, the woman in his keeping had been tasked with slaying a beast as an offering to the spirits.

Corenna turned to him, expectant.

"Honored sister." He bowed to her. "This is your task. I will safeguard you, should your magic fail."

She nodded, striding toward the mouth of the cave, stopping to plant her feet as she faced the opening ahead. Her eyes glazed over, the deep blue of a winter storm, and when she raised her hands the wind began to stir. A breeze at first, then an icy gale. It swept into the cave, a torrent of frost that had no place beneath a clear blue sky. A low roar sounded from within.

She held her arms in place, and the storm continued.

A silhouette appeared, pacing side to side to shelter itself from the buffeting cold. It roared again as it stepped into the light, this time a thunderous echo ringing through the trees. The bear locked its eyes on Corenna, and Arak'Jur watched as the beast lowered its head and charged.

With a smooth motion, Corenna drew one hand back and snapped the other forward. A lance of ice sprang from her fingers, impaling the bear through the crown of its skull. It slumped to the ground, skidding toward her with a crunch as it rolled over the frost that had settled from the storm. The winds faded.

She made a formal bow to the bear, and another to him and Ilek'Inari. Her eyes returned to normal.

"A mighty gift indeed, honored sister," he said.

"It was well worth the trouble. I hope Arak'Uro agrees. He was shivering for hours after his dip in the ice."

She stepped back as he laughed, and Ilek'Inari went to his knees, unsheathing his bone knife to pry the bear's teeth loose from its jaw.

A fine thing. He'd seen such displays before, but never so smoothly done. Arak'Doren spoke true when he said Corenna was precious to the Ranasi. A spirit-touched woman with her strength was a thing not seen in generations. The women's spirits were generous, it seemed, even as their counterparts whispered to the shamans of dire omens.

When Ilek'Inari had gathered his final materials, they departed the hillside in search of Ka'Ana'Tyat.

Ka'Ana'Tyat. The Birthplace of Visions. Arak'Jur had made the journey three times and never found it in the same place, though it was always on Sinari lands. Each tribe had at least one such sacred site, where the women would go to forge their connections to the spirits of the land, and the shamans first spoke with the spirits of things-to-come. He understood little of the details—it was not his place as guardian to know more than was required. Only that the women and shamans found their power along different paths than the guardians did. What the beast spirits held in common with the women's and shamans' spirits was a mystery reserved for wiser men than he.

They traveled for three days.

Passing through the highlands, they made their way down into the thickest parts of the forest, where it covered Sinari land like a fertile blanket. He hunted for their food and Corenna prepared it. Ilek'Inari performed a minor ritual each time they stopped, divining their destination from the whispers of the shamans' spirits. On they went, until the trees grew so thick they seemed to knot together, walls of wood and branch and vine.

This was the sign. It was always so, near Ka'Ana'Tyat. The land seemed to bend and warp itself into impossible scenes. If he came back this way on the next full moon, he would find it a forest like any other. But for now, they drew near a place of power.

A reverent glow settled on his charges' faces, Corenna with a practiced grace and Ilek'Inari with nervous excitement. They journeyed inward, past twisted branches and trees seeming to grow through one another, until they came upon a wide clearing at the heart of the wood. A canopy of branches parted to reveal a passageway sculpted from the shadows cast by the long arms of the trees.

Ka'Ana'Tyat.

They stepped forward, and a great roar echoed on the wind.

If the bear they'd slain before had roared, it was a drop of rainwater to the torrential storm they heard now. This was a peal of mighty thunder, a blast of raw power that could shear trees in half from the force of its bellow alone. This was a sound that few had ever heard, and survived.

An *una're.*

Somehow it had eluded the visions of Ka'Vos and Ka'Hinari both. The brown bear's elder brother, *una're* struck with a thunderous force that gave truth to the storms behind his roar. Arcing shocks blackened the ground where he ran, his claws dancing with streaks of lightning like fire from the skies. And now he came, crashing through the knotted wood, his keen senses alerted to intruders near this sacred place, a place he had claimed for his own. Few disputed *una're*'s claims when he made them.

Eyes pained, Arak'Jur turned toward his charges. Ilek'Inari was frozen in fear. Even Corenna had paled.

"Run," he said.

Arak'Jur leapt into the sky, coming down with the fury of the *ipek'a,* an ethereal blade forming around his hand like one of their scything claws. He scourged the *una're* along its side as he landed, ripping the Great Bear's flesh into a crevasse that soaked its legs in blood.

The beast roared as it reared up, its head twisting into a primal cry. Rage. Shock. This *una're* had likely never met a beast that could wound him, let alone stay toe to toe in a running fight. Now the creature dripped from the pricks of a dozen minor wounds. Not enough to fell him, but enough to keep him moving in the direction Arak'Jur needed him to go: away from Corenna and Ilek'Inari.

Arak'Jur's left hand was shattered and scored black, streaks of rotten flesh crawling up his arm where the bite of the *una're* had found purchase. No time to worry over that now. With time even the direst of his wounds would heal, unless he was slain outright; another gift of the guardian, the first granted after communing with the beast spirits. Proof against lasting injury, though the pain he endured in full.

He raced around the beast toward the entrance to Ka'Ana'Tyat, channeling the gift of *lakiri'in,* cousin to the water-beasts of the far south. The scaled reptiles were deadly quick when they went for a kill but tended toward sloth when not pressed to exert themselves; their gift was similar—a short burst of speed, fading as quickly as it came.

Another flurry of swipes from the *una're*'s claws raked the air overhead as he dove to the side. Shocking energy coursed into the ground, sending leaves and grass into the air with a smoldering hiss. Twisting toward the beast, Arak'Jur rolled with the driving attack, landing another sequence of empowered strikes along its flanks.

The blows he'd landed might be enough to slow it, if he could extend the chase long enough. The *una're* seemed to sense it, too, giving him a low growl. It snapped in his direction, forcing him to keep his distance as the *una're* recovered its footing. The two circled each other, the Great Bear showing him a measure of respect as each awaited the other's next move.

The wind began to blow cold.

"No," he called, his voice cracking from the pain. "No, Corenna!"

Too late. She stood with Ilek'Inari at her side, her face determined, eyes iced over with a wintry haze. The *una're* turned to consider her, and she sent a barrage of needlepoint icicles streaking through the air. The beast let out a bellowing roar as Corenna's ice took it across the shoulders, peppering its hide with bloody wounds. And then it charged.

Arak'Jur had already spent the gift of the *valak'ar,* his deadliest by far, and failed to land a blow. But he had saved the blessing of *mareh'et.*

He used it now, a nimbus of the Great Cat surrounding him, granting ethereal claws and a surge of strength and speed. The *una're* seemed to slow as he closed the gap, a shrill scream from Corenna echoing through the dense wood. He dove, and took the beast in the hind legs as it leapt.

Ilek'Inari's voice joined the chorus of war cries as the *una're* sailed through the air toward Corenna. A second volley of ice sprayed into the creature's roaring maw. Arak'Jur's strikes tore at its unprotected hindquarters, ripping the beast's tendons with the savage cuts of *mareh'et*.

But it was the simple cut of the bone knife in the hands of the apprentice shaman that scored the killing blow.

Corenna rolled away from the corpse of the *una're*. Beside her, Ilek'Inari had gone to his knees, eyes filmed over with white, in communion with the spirits.

It appeared Arak'Jur had found his apprentice.

13

SARINE

Fontcadeu Green
The Royal Palace, Rasailles

She let her pack fall, a soft rustle as it landed behind the garden wall, and she followed it a moment later, dropping to hide under the brush. It was always easier to slip into the royal gardens past nightfall; the meager stores of *Faith* that accrued where the nobles lived went much further when she could rely on a cloak of darkness in addition to her gifts. This late in the season the evening air had lost most of its sting, but she still wore a slim coat to go along with the usual linen shirt, calf boots, and trousers. And of course her pack, with extra charcoals and sheaves of paper. Ordinarily she wouldn't risk a return visit to the palace so soon—too dangerous, for the priests to find a pattern of errant bindings. But she'd spent the past days hovering close to the Sacre-Lin, fearful the man in the red coat might make good on his promise, that he could somehow track her down and expose her and her uncle to danger. She'd gotten nothing more than boredom for her concern. No invitation, no sign of the man who'd called himself Reyne d'Agarre. So, when rumors spread of a masquerade planned by the Duc-Governor, she'd resolved to quit her watch if nothing had come by the appointed date. Now the night had arrived, and so had she.

Staying low, she slid along the stone walls as she edged her way toward the green. It was slow going, weaving around the light cast by the ensconced lanterns along the wall. Worth every ounce of effort, though, if it meant prolonging the duration she could stay hidden. There was only so much *Faith* to be had in Rasailles, and she meant to bleed the wells dry before she left. Word was every seamstress, tailor, and papier-mâché mask maker in the city had been working long hours since the Duc announced his ball, each of them sworn to secrecy on behalf of their clientele.

Already some of the lowest-born made their entrances, callers announcing their names, ranks, and lineage to the accompaniment of long trumpets bearing the King's arms. The attendees entered through the main gate, following the winding walkway at a slow pace to show off their plumage before they gained the palace grounds proper. And plumage it was. It seemed the theme of the evening would be feathers, great displays of color festooning their masks and elaborate garb, men and women alike. There, an unlanded chevalier and his lady played the part of falconer and bird of prey, the rich greens and whites of their costumes springing to life whenever they passed beneath the torches lining the walkway. Behind them, a baroness and her escorts reenacted a Sardian harem, or at least a harem as one might imagine it taking place in a rookery.

Cloaked in shadows, even without the benefit of her bindings, she at times drew near enough to hear conversation the attendees must have thought private, as they walked in stately procession through the royal park.

"—oh, Percy, you must remember not to slouch tonight, my dear. We must impress the comte if we're to dispose him favorably to—"

"—a little bird told me the Vicomtesse d'Eilles would be 'ill' for tonight's festivities, owing to a black eye bestowed by the vicomte's own hand—"

"—I swear by the Exarch, if they serve those wretched little crevettes tonight, I've half a mind to belch on the serving dishes, you see if I don't—"

Zi had taken to strolling down the walkway himself, his eyes darting back and forth as he drank in the passersby. As ever, she was thankful she was the only one who could see him. His scales had taken on a pale green hue, ripening to a light yellow when he drew near some of the conversations.

After an eternity making her way through the outer garden she reached a bend in the path, level with the grand stone steps leading up to the palace receiving grounds. The grounds would be where the majority of the festivities would take place, but the stairs served her immediate purpose. The whole exercise of a promenade through the park was meant to be observed, after all. What better vantage point from which to sketch? She took a deep breath, closing her eyes as she drew in *Faith*. Fading from view, she crossed the walkway at a run and found herself an unobtrusive spot along the wide stone stairs. Moving under *Faith*'s shroud would deplete her stores ten times as fast, but so long as she stayed still she would have time to work.

The criers continued calling out the guest list as they arrived, offering a thorough primer on New Sarresant society. One at a time the coaches pulled up to the gate, unloaded their cargo, then drove off to the area designated for the drivers and teams. The nobles flowed out in a steady stream, careful to allow each party a comfortable distance before they began to walk. First came the seigneurs, the écuyers, the chevaliers—the lowest rungs on the social ladder, those who couldn't put on the airs of a fashionably late arrival. Some of these were not even noble, but who could deny New Sarresant's wealthiest citizens when they bankrolled most of the nobles' financial ventures? Too many favors owed to exclude them, and so they came, full of pride, knowing they pretended to a seat at better tables.

She sketched a few of these, confident most of her customers couldn't tell the difference between the costumes of the highest-born and those of the early arrivals. The gap between marquis and écuyer may well be an insurmountable chasm here at Rasailles, but in the Harbor district or the Riverways, any in attendance tonight were impossibly far above the wildest aspirations of the commonfolk. Did it work the same way in reverse? Were the city's merchants and financiers on a level with beggars and street thieves to the likes of the comtes and comtesses? A strange thought.

She continued to sketch as the titles rose progressively higher, chevaliers giving way to barons and vicomtes, interspersed with the odd comte and marquis. Zi lazed about the steps as she worked, draping himself across the stone tiers. His scales seemed pale, only a faint blue-green coloration reflecting the light cast by the lanterns behind them.

Her ears perked up as the caller announced the latest arrival.

"The Lance-Captain Donatien Revellion, graduating forthwith from the academy at New Sarresant, accompanied by the best wishes of his father the Marquis de Revellion, away serving the crown as diplomatic envoy to the Thellan colonies."

She set aside her half-finished sketch and began a new one. Lord Revellion's costume had a military theme, a blend of blue and gold feathers and silks to create an impression of the Sarresant officers' uniform. Working quickly, she had her sketch of his entrance complete by the time he circled the green and approached the stairs. As soon as the drawing was fixed and dried she slid it into her pack, rising to her feet.

Done so soon?

"Just joining the party," she whispered. "Come on."

A *Body* binding and a few handholds on the rough-cut walls of the inner keep gave her an excellent vantage over the area cordoned off for dancing. The courante-steps favored by the youths among the nobles were lively and up-tempo, requiring room to maneuver. They twirled and pranced to one now, percussionists beating out a three-quarter-time meter accompanied by rhythmic claps among the onlookers. Each costume's feathers came alive with the music, flares of color streaking past with every lift and turn of the steps.

The young Lady Cherrain, adorned in a wild costume meant to evoke the Oracle herself, seemed to be the star of the evening. Nothing less was expected from the daughter of the Duc-Governor, but she seemed to be shining particularly brightly, directing the courtiers as they moved from one dance to the next. Lord Revellion was a close second, his cavalry officer's costume giving him a serious air. All of them moved brilliantly, with a practiced grace bred from a lifetime of preparing for their places in society. She worked to capture their movement, pausing from time to time to allow herself the pleasure of taking it in. She doubted whether she could ever move like they did. She'd forget a step, tumble instead of spring, fall when she was meant to twist. And to think they all did it in unison, as if moved by a single mind. She tethered *Life* as she watched, empowering her senses to sharpen the colors, the movements, the magic of the evening.

She only once dropped a charcoal pen, but managed a lightning-quick

Shelter binding beneath it, a hazy blue barrier halting its fall just before it clattered onto the dance floor.

Zi's pallor had improved considerably. He was a rich, deep green punctuated by flashes of turquoises, reds, and yellows, and had managed to wrap himself around the pole mounting of a banner showing the King's arms, three flowers in gold-on-blue entwined at the stems, near the top of the wall. The King was not in residence, of course, nor were any of the princes or princesses of the blood; they were all across the sea in old Sarresant proper. The Duc-Governor presided over the festivities tonight, in a jet-black costume with a sinister look she supposed was meant to be the Nameless, the fallen enemy of the Gods. A bold choice, sure to spark rumors, which was likely the point.

The Duc rose to his feet as the music from the last dance died, then clapped his hands, a hush rippling through the receiving grounds as all turned their attention toward his seat in the center of the pavilion.

"Lords," the Duc-Governor announced. "Ladies. Your presence at this little fête is noted and appreciated by the crown." He inclined his head, acknowledging the light applause, before continuing.

"We gather tonight to honor the bravest among us." More applause. "The New Sarresant military academy has the reputation it does because it has never failed to produce the finest military officers this nation has ever known."

Still more applause, some of it genuine, though the Duc's sentiment didn't make much sense to her. Surely the school had at least once failed to produce the finest officers ever known. But he was playing to his audience, and his words seemed to have the desired effect.

"As you know, we are at war." Silence, thick and contemplative. "This is a time for heroism, a time for bravery, above all a time for sacrifice."

She bit back a laugh. This was their idea of sacrifice?

"Today our families send their best, our most noble and valiant, to lead our armies against the menace of the enemy. An enemy who thinks he can expand his borders, seize our ships, and not provoke us into action. These young men and women, graduates of the New Sarresant Academy, espouse the virtues of the Exarch: Courage. Vigilance. Duty. Our enemy has provoked us beyond tolerance or reason, and we will take the war to him, we will refuse his advances, we will never submit, we will be victorious!"

Thunderous applause.

When it died, the Duc spoke again, a shrewd look in his eye.

"But first, we will be entertained. Clear the green for the contest of archery!"

The crowd laughed, an easy release of tension. The nobles dispersed to ring the former dance floor in knots of animated conversation, while servants rushed to prepare the grounds for target shooting.

She rose to her feet, stretching, glad for a brief break in the action of the evening. Lucky for her they'd opted to repurpose the grounds she'd already positioned herself to sketch. Even so, she resolved to find a different vantage; it grew tiresome to sketch the same angles. She made a quick check of her stores and cursed softly under her breath. Running low on *Faith*, though the other energies were stocked well enough. She'd have enough for the next event or two, Gods willing. It took a short walk around the battlements of the keep to find another elevated angle from which to sketch the archery contest, an overlook close to the courtyard entrance. From here she could see the green, and the thick forest beyond, as well as the assembled mass of feathers and finery of the nobles. By the time she'd settled in, the servants had completed a hasty setup and the first contestants drew near the line.

The contest was simple; she'd seen it before during daylight on the green. Three targets, three arrows for each participant. A bull's-eye in each target was typically enough to win, but it could be trumped by three bull's-eyes hitting the same mark. "Hero's Gambit" the game was called, and few were bold enough to risk failure by trying for the second, superior brand of victory.

The criers were put to further use, calling out each challenger's name, rank, and number of stripes they'd earned during marksmanship evaluations at the academy. She doubted whether the army still taught archery or tested for ability with a bow, but traditions among the nobility died hard, when they died at all.

Pirouen de Boulange, scout-captain, three stripes, distinguished himself rather well for being the opening shot, though Gavrien Carailles, lance-lieutenant, no stripes, did not fare so well. Neither did Avrille de la Vessac, foot-captain, two stripes, or Eiron d'Orelle, lance-lieutenant, three stripes. A half-dozen more contestants tried their hand at the line without besting de Boulange's opening marks, until the crowd hushed with anticipation when the caller announced the next competitor.

"Darien de Sachant, scout-lieutenant, five stripes."

The first master marksman of the night stepped forward, and by the look of him he'd been invited to this fête only by virtue of his pending graduation from the academy. From the too-loud commentary among ladies near the wall, this was a soldier without a noble rank, here by recommendation of officers in the field rather than by the privilege of his birth. His costume, if you could call it that, was a simple affair of dyed linens with a half-domino mask, the likes of which you could buy from any number of vendors in the Market district. He stepped forward, slipping the mask off to unclutter his vision, then drew and loosed in a simple fluid motion. *Thunk.* Again. *Thunk.* Again. *Thunk.*

The crowd applauded politely as the servants dashed forward to retrieve the shafts from the circles at the center of each of the three targets. With a bowed apology, Darien de Sachant displaced Pirouen de Boulange in the winner's circle, awaiting the last remaining competitors to take their turn at the line.

Two more came and went without success before the caller announced, "Donatien Revellion, lance-captain, four stripes."

Lord Revellion strode forward to enthusiastic applause, following Darien de Sachant's example and tossing his mask down to the grass. He made a show of holding his bow aloft as he was handed his three arrows. With a quick flourish, he stuck an arrow by hand into the ground in front of him, in line with the center target. He stepped back, as if considering. When he drove a second arrow into the ground next to the first, in line with the same target, the crowd erupted with cheers. The third was a formality; Revellion would attempt the Hero's Gambit.

Sure you don't want to help him win?

She glared at Zi. "Don't you dare," she whispered.

Another flourish as he drew out the first arrow and took aim.

Thunk.

The crowd erupted again, and Revellion bowed to acknowledge it. When he stepped forward to pull up the second arrow, a wave of silence swept through the crowd, the sound of a hundred onlookers holding their breath, a silence so thick she could feel it press down around her.

Broken by a scream.

The assembled partygoers turned their heads with varying degrees of alarm. Guardsmen rushed from their posts toward the green. Trained soldiers among the nobles pushed forward, ushering the civilians back from whatever had caused the shrill cry.

Her heart surged, and she stuffed her drawing materials into her pack, an instinctive response to flee at the first sign of trouble. Always in the back of her head there was the fear that any commotion might mean she had been discovered.

Within moments, it was clear she was not the cause of this distress.

A massive beast, like a horse-sized house cat, padded its way up the stone stairs into view of the receiving grounds. Shrieks and screams echoed across the yard as the ranks of nobles broke in a panic. Only the soldiers and guardsmen held their ground, forming a semicircle around the creature. The beast was relaxed, seeming to enjoy the soldiers backing away wherever it stepped. It was covered in yellow-orange fur with a strange mix of stripes and spots, tightly muscled, taking its time with each stride. The thing radiated danger, as if it could pounce without warning, but was presently content to watch and evaluate its prey. And its eyes. She might have said they shone like fire, but she suspected they actually were fire. Dancing tongues of orange and yellow where other creatures would have had iris and pupil.

In a heartbeat she tethered *Body* and dropped from the top of the keep wall to the ground below. Zi appeared on her shoulder surging red and black; for once she was not the slightest bit perturbed at him for doubling her heart rate, with the attendant boost in energy and speed. Before she could decide how best to escape the grounds, the beast attacked.

It was laughable. Soldiers and guardsmen, swatted aside like mice. If not for her *Body* binding and Zi's gift of speed, she doubted she would have been able to see the creature move. It darted like a snake and struck with a terrible fury, its claws rending whatever it touched into bloody pulp. A half-dozen men were slain in an instant, a half-dozen more cast aside with grievous wounds. Undaunted, the remainder of the men charged forward in a second wave.

Without thinking, she dropped her *Faith* tether and found *Life* and *Body*, with a *Shelter* binding to put a barrier between the beast and the soldiers. It wouldn't hold for more than a few seconds, but it should be enough to deflect the creature's attention. A *Mind* binding sent out a handful of copies of herself in either direction, a further distraction as the copies closed in on the creature, and Zi lent his familiar red haze, speeding her movements and threatening to have her sicking up the contents of her stomach.

Her first unarmed strike took the beast in the left flank as it rebounded from her *Shelter* barrier, momentarily confused, darting a look between her and the various copies conjured by her *Mind* tether. The creature's hind leg cracked as she struck again, her fists empowered by *Body* and Zi's gifts, and the cat roared, whirling to face her before she could swing again. Lightning-quick, it snapped at her head, and she screamed.

A cocoon of white flared around her as the cat's jaws snapped shut, and she heard the sound of something shattering, a rush of hot energy blasting the creature backward. Somehow Zi had protected her. Her skin was still whole. Without pausing to think, she flew forward again. A wordless scream poured from her throat as she dove for its legs, feeling a sickening crunch as the already cracked bone shattered within.

The cat sank to the ground, jaws still working as it let out a piteous whine. With one more overhand blow she cracked its skull, and it fell silent.

The world went dark.

YOU KILLED HIM.

What was this? Where was she? What had happened?

Silence stretched on. Was she supposed to respond?

I killed it to save the people on the green, she thought.

HE WAS MAREH'ET. A FULL ADULT. IT WAS HIS RIGHT TO SLAY THE WEAK. YOU ARE BUT A PUP.

Mareh'what? she thought, confused.

HE WAS ONE OF MY CHILDREN. THE GREATEST OF ALL CATS. HOW DID YOU SLAY HIM?

I used my gifts, and Zi's.

A moment passed. A feeling pervaded her mind that whatever this voice was, it was considering her, weighing her. Had she angered it?

YOU BESTED HIM. A WOMAN. THIS IS NOT KNOWN TO US. ARE YOU CHOSEN? ARE YOU HER VOICE?

Whose voice? she asked. *Chosen by whom?*

THE GODDESS.

There are two Goddesses, she thought back to the voice. *Do you mean the Oracle, or the Veil?*

THERE IS ONLY ONE GODDESS, LITTLE PUP.

What? Well, her uncle and the rest of the Trithetic priesthood would have a bone to pick with that. What was this? Some kind of trick?

I don't know whether I'm chosen, she thought back finally.

VERY WELL. WOULD YOU HAVE A BOON OF ME?

I don't even know what you are, she thought back in anger. What was going on?

I AM THE SPIRIT OF MAREH'ET. I COULD GIVE YOU HIS GIFT. YOU WOULD BE A PUP NO LONGER.

What sort of gift?

TO KNOW WHAT IT IS TO BE GREAT. IT IS THE WAY OF THINGS, TO SHARE HIS SKIN.

Fine, but—

DONE.

Her body surged with light as she settled into a different form. She had four legs, powerful and lean, tipped with razor-sharp claws that could sunder meat and bone and steel with equal ease. She rushed through forests, across grasslands, hunting wherever she pleased. The thrill of the hunt rolled over her in a wave of pleasure, the satisfaction of toying with her prey after administering a mortal wound. She felt the moment of terror when her kills saw her flame-wreathed gaze, the moment they knew their death was certain, that the power of when and how it came rested solely in her choosing. She was the greatest of all cats, proud and strong.

It seemed to go on for a long time. But eventually the visions faded.

REMEMBER HIM.

The voice echoed through her head as she felt herself slide back into her body.

She blinked, her senses assaulted by the smell of stale air, damp stone, and raw sewage. Her nostrils curled, and she gagged, a taste on the air as foul as any storm drain beneath the Maw. Narrow slits of light poured through from above, painting lines of color on the dark stone floor.

Bars.

Not a sewer. A prison.

ELSEWHERE

INTERLUDE

VAS'KHAN'URO

Yanarat War Party
Nanerat Territory

The women would not fight.

He knew it even before he made the formal request. They were soft and weak, gifted magic they were too cowardly to wield. All agreed women were fit to raise children and cook meat. Some of his hunters—no, his *warriors*—preferred a woman's company when the nights grew long and the cold bit deep. But when the time came to act, to carry the mantle of the spirits against the tribe's enemies, women were good for little more than wasting time with prattle and deliberation.

When Arak'Uro became Vas'Khan'Uro, the men listened to his call.

He led the men out of the steam tent, cutting short the senseless debate that had droned until the sun disappeared from the sky. Two boys were missing and Ka'Erewun had seen the cause. Victims of the treacherous Nanerat, who would trade with his tribe and call them brothers, then slay their children in the night. Their erstwhile "friends" would learn what it meant to incur the fury of the Yanarat. The women would have him send an emissary to investigate. And so he would. But where the women's investigation ended with words, his ended with blood.

"Vas'Khan'Uro."

A solemn voice. Venari'Jatek, who had once been Ilek'Jatek, the apprentice guardian. His apprentice. Silently he closed his eyes and said a prayer to the spirits. Even before Venari'Jatek spoke, he knew.

"Vas'Khan'Uro. Honored warleader. They've found the boys."

He opened his eyes. "Show me."

They walked over the rocks and late-thawing ice of the northern tundra, the rest of the war party following in their wake. Whispers passed Venari'Jatek's news from man to man and then they were quiet. Four days' journey, each of them hoping Ka'Erewun's vision had been clouded, that the shaman had somehow made a mistake. They were ready to do what must be done for the defense of the tribe, but what man did not hope for peace when there was any chance for it, any chance at all?

The broken bodies dashed at the base of the rocks snuffed those hopes like so much sand on fire.

They were boys. Ice preserved their flesh where the carrion-eaters had not gnawed it away. Smooth skin beneath their cheekbones, mouths agape in surprise. His lip curled up in an involuntary snarl as he regarded the long spears still protruding from their bellies. This was no hunting accident, no misunderstanding. Those were spears of war, and they had been left here to remove all doubt of who placed them.

He fell to his knees and howled.

A chorus joined in behind him. It was right to rage for the dead. Beautiful boys, alight with the potential of youth. Kar'Duvek had been a gifted marksman, able to sight a bull moose at three hundred paces and bring it down with a single shot; he would have been *Valak*, of a surety. Kar'Urrin had a pretty face and a silver tongue. He might have been a *Ka*. Both would have been proud men of the Yanarat. Both had named him guardian. He had failed them. How many turns of the moon now had Ka'Erewun given his warnings, the whispers of the spirits' calls to war? He had failed to listen. He had let these beautiful boys run off, imagining they would be safe in the lands of the Nanerat, the tribe's allies. How often had he gone on such journeys in his youth, just he and a companion braving the wilds, full of life and possibility? The shaman would have seen it, were any great beasts nearby, and the guardian would have come to protect them from any creature beyond their ability to kill. He would have come, spirits be cursed; he would have saved them, preserved them, and kept them from this fate. But not even the shaman could foresee the treachery of men.

It fell to him now, as *Vas'Khan*, warleader, to avenge them. In a rage he called on the spirit of the *gun'dal*, mighty white bear of the North, and snapped both spears in two before the nimbus of the spirit's blessing faded from around him.

"I swear this now," he said, voice shaking, a pale mist revealing the heat of his breath. "Before the spirits. Before the tribe. I swear a blood curse on the Nanerat. I will bleed them. I will hunt them. The Yanarat make war, until the last ounce of Nanerat blood is spilled into the rivers and the sea."

He stood, slowly, looking down over the corpses of these two boys, freezing the image in his mind.

"This I swear, as *Vas'Khan*."

A quiet breeze full of winter's sting whipped around him and the rest of the warriors, the witnesses to his pledge.

The war party departed, according the boys the honor due fallen warriors: Their bodies lay undisturbed. An offering to the wilds, the last evidence of their courage.

The spirits favored them with fresh tracks three days later.

Hunters, from the look of their footfalls in the snow, but it could as easily be a war party like their own. Wide prints made by the shoes all hunters wore to traverse the ice, with shallow holes signaling they carried muskets or longbows, using them as staves to steady their footfalls on the snow. His warriors fanned out as they approached, making sure to keep the winds in a favorable direction. Men were not beasts, but the best among the hunters cultivated a keen sense that rivaled even the most wary prey.

His blood stirred as they drew near a copse of trees. He raised a hand, stifling a cry that boiled in his throat. When he passed by the first branches and caught sight of his enemy, he could contain it no longer, and he let slip a howl of rage as he charged.

The Nanerat hunters had taken a caribou and set to skinning their prize, unaware they too were being hunted. They started when Vas'Khan'Uro and his men poured from the trees, and the Yanarat warriors leveled their muskets, firing before the Nanerat could do more than cry out an alarm.

He rushed ahead of his men, calling on *gun'dal* as he crashed through the brush, crushing a man in the spectral grip of the Ghost Bear's claws, feeling blood and skin stretch and break as he tore his prey apart. Let the hunters use the weapons of the fair-skins. His was an old magic, and he would use it to show the Nanerat traitors the fury of their enemies. As *Arak* he might have obeyed the prohibitions on the use of magic to make war; as *Vas'Khan* he did what he must to lead his men to victory.

A gout of flame broke him out of his battle trance.

He felt it before he saw it, heat searing the air around him. By instinct he fell prone. Venari'Jatek had not been so quick. Beside him on the ground his former apprentice looked to him for help. The right side of Venari'Jatek's body was untouched, one eye opened wide in shock and fear. But the left side was black, charred and flaking, skin running down his body like slow trails of honey mixed with blood. He forced himself to swallow bile and rolled aside, springing to his feet.

"Arak'Uro!" a voice called, forceful but touched with surprise. He froze, then turned to meet it.

Asseena, spirit-touched of the Nanerat, flanked by Arak'Erai and a dozen of their hunters. She raised her voice again, her eyes gleaming bright red.

"I had not thought to find you among these betrayers. Among these murderers!"

"You dare?" he roared back. "You dare name the Yanarat betrayers?"

"What would you call it, *brother*?" Arak'Erai shouted at him, putting disdain into the last word.

He spat toward them, setting his feet to charge. He would die an honored warrior of the Yanarat.

"For Kar'Duvek, Kar'Urrin," he growled through gritted teeth.

"Don't," cautioned Asseena, her hands raised in a sign of warning. "Arak'Uro—"

Howling, he charged, drawing on the spirits of the *munat'ap*, and the *astahg*. He felt their blessings wash over him, their approval. He glowed with their sacred power, his by right when he'd slain them and earned the right to wear their skins. He smiled. He remembered.

Flame.

INTERLUDE

ALOUEN

Village of Oreste
Lorrine Province, Southern Sarresant Colonies

"You be the monster this time, okay?" Jeanette asked him.

He didn't feel like being the monster but he didn't feel like arguing, either. Easier to give her a turn so he could go back to playing the hero.

"All right," he said. "But I get to be a monster that flies."

She made a face. "Everyone knows monsters can't fly."

"This one can. I'm a big spider but with horns and bird wings."

He could imagine it in his head: a big gray spider, so big it could eat a cow in one bite. What sort of sound would a spider that big make? Maybe a buzzing noise. He tried it.

"Bzzzzzzzzz." He stretched his arms out like wings. "I'm coming for all the cows in the village. Better run and hide!"

"Alouen." Jeanette planted her hands on her waist like her mother did at suppertime. "This is serious; you can't fly."

He frowned. "Why not?"

She pointed westward. "Because, if any of them could fly the priests would have made it taller."

His shoulders slumped. She was right. The Great Barrier. It was tall, tall enough to see it even leagues away above the trees, but it wasn't as tall as birds flew. And it kept the monsters out. Everywhere, not just here in the village. If there were flying spider-birds they would have come over the wall and eaten their cows for real, not just make-believe.

"I don't want to be the monster anymore," he said.

"Oh come now, don't sulk."

"I'm not sulking. I just don't want to play monster."

She gave him a sigh, tossing her hair back over her shoulder. "Fine. You want to be the hero again then?"

"No. Let's play soldiers."

"Oh, Alouen, I'm not a good soldier. There aren't any soldiers in dresses."

No fair for her to remind him of that. He hadn't asked for his dresses to be taken away. His father had said it was time, though, on his fifth birthday. No more dresses, only breeches and shirts like a grown-up. It had made him feel big, before he remembered Jeanette wouldn't get new clothes when she turned five.

"Mother says there are girl soldiers. She says some of the best soldiers are girls."

She stuck out her tongue at him. "Fine, but I get to be from Sarresant."

He nodded along eagerly. It was rare for Jeanette to agree to play soldiers. He'd be from Gand and be the loser if it meant she would play.

"Halt!" he barked in his best impression of the thick accents of Gand. Not that he could remember having ever heard one of them talk, but the grown-ups often talked like they did when they told jokes or stories about the war. "We'll 'ave your lands, filthy Sarresant rats!"

Jeanette giggled, raising her arms up into the air. "Don't hurt me. I surrender."

"Hey, that's not how it—"

"Bang!" she called out. "Tricked you."

He grinned. "Aauuugh." He clutched at his belly. "But more of us are coming, filthy rat. You can't get us all with your tricks!"

"Yeah, but we're quicker than you," she said, turning to run.

This was always the fun part. No matter what game they played, the best parts were when he got to chase. Jeanette was fast even in her pretty dresses, and he loved to try and catch her, even if she almost always won in the end. But this time she got only a few paces away before he stopped with a frown.

She stuttered to a halt, turning back with a questioning look. "What is it, Alouen? What's wrong?"

"My mother is calling," he said.

She scrunched up her face, tilting her ear up to the wind. "Are you sure?"

He nodded. "Yeah, she says I'm to come in this instant, and you too if you're out here with me."

She made the pouting face she used when her parents wouldn't give her what she wanted, then brightened just as quick. "Well, she didn't say you couldn't race me there."

No warning, she just turned and ran. He followed, tracking through the first sprouts of the grain harvest coming up from the fields. The dirt was still wet from where it had rained a few days ago, enough that he was sure he'd track mud all over the house. He didn't care. It felt good to run, to chase after Jeanette even if she didn't try any of her zigging or zagging. That was probably why his mother liked her so much: Jeanette listened to the grown-ups and did what she thought they wanted, even if that meant coming straight home instead of playing for a few more minutes.

They crossed through the fields and ran up the wagon track that led onto the main road toward the rest of the village. She made a show of it, keeping just in front of him, but they both knew she would win. And she did, racing around the corner of the farmhouse and almost running into a tinker's wagon parked outside. Now that was a surprise. Jeanette turned back to him, wide-eyed and grinning with anticipation. A tinker visit before the harvest. No wonder his mother had called them in so early.

Together they scrambled up the front steps, expecting an early midwinter festival. Instead they tumbled through the door into a dour scene, as cold as the funeral for the Foubrens' baby that had died last winter. There was even a priest in his brown robe standing in the entryway. Mother's eyes were red as she hovered near the doorway to the kitchen, and father wore a worried look beside the hearth.

Right away he knew he didn't like the brown-robed man. But still the priest looked at him with a too-welcoming smile.

"So this is your boy," the priest said. "And the girl, Bernard and Therese's daughter?"

"That's right," mother said with frost in her voice. "His name is Alouen."

He'd never seen mother so distant. Her anger was hot when he'd seen it at all. More often she just told him and father what to do and got her way. He could tell she was mad now but for some reason she only stood there near the kitchen. Why couldn't she just make the man go away? Why couldn't she just give him and Jeanette whatever the tinker had brought?

"Alouen." The priest took the time to say his name slow. "Lovely name for a lovely boy." He turned back to mother and father. "You understand why I'm here?"

"We understand," father said.

He didn't understand. He wanted to ask but it seemed like the wrong thing. Jeanette looked at him, afraid, but he didn't know what to say.

"We thought..." mother said. "We thought no one would come. When his birthday came and went, when the new year passed. The law says—"

"The law says all children must be tested," the priest cut in.

"Before they are five years of age," said father.

"There is a magistrate in Lorrine if you have a grievance," the priest said, shedding some of the warmth he had pretended before. "But I assure you he will understand there has been a war going on. Villages along the Gand border are remote even in the best of times."

"Oh preposterous, we haven't seen a raid of any kind since the war began," mother said.

"Philippe and Marie d'Oreste, I am here to execute the laws of the crown. Will you stand in the way of that charge?"

Mother's face iced over, while father's shoulders slumped. Neither of them spoke.

The priest turned to Jeanette. She looked up at the brown-robed man with fear on her face, but she didn't move.

"Now. Since we have the boy and the girl here, we may as well handle them both."

Father frowned. "I should at least fetch Bernard and Therese."

"No need. This will be quick." He knelt down, looking Jeanette in the eye. "What was your name again, girl?"

Alouen stepped forward, full of distrust toward the brown-robed man. "Her name is Jeanette and you can't touch her."

"Alouen," father cautioned.

He didn't care. Jeanette was shaking, more afraid than he'd ever seen her. Jeanette wasn't afraid of anything.

"Jeanette," the priest repeated, looking between her and him. "And Alouen, you are a brave one. You could be a soldier if our test goes well. Would you like that, to be a soldier?"

Mother drew in a sharp breath. He would like to be a soldier, but he decided he didn't want to tell this man anything. "I would like for you to go away and leave us alone."

"He can't," Jeanette whispered. "He has to test us."

He frowned, looking back at Jeanette. What did she know? What hadn't she told him?

"That's right," the priest said. "Jeanette, did your parents tell you I would come?"

She nodded.

"Did they tell you how the test works?"

She nodded again, this time offering her hands outward, palms facing up as if she were going to play a game of slap-quick.

"Perfect. Now, this will be simple, just hold still a moment."

The priest rested his hands atop Jeanette's, wrapping around hers so he couldn't even see her fingers. The backs of the priest's hands were pink and scarred as if someone had driven a spike through the palms. It made Alouen shudder, except he'd barely had time to look before the priest closed his eyes, took a deep breath, and withdrew his hands.

"Well done, Jeanette," the priest said.

"That's it?" mother asked.

"That's it," the priest replied. "As I said, simple."

"Am I . . . ?" Jeanette whispered. "Can I . . . ?"

"You are healthy and whole, my dear. And you can tell your parents you passed the tests."

She let out the breath she'd been holding. He felt happy for her, seeing her relieved, the fear finally gone from her face.

"Your turn, my boy," the priest said.

He still didn't like the priest, but if it was this simple to be rid of him he could do it. He and Jeanette would be telling stories about this for the rest of summer. He strode forward, offering his hands palms-up the same as she had.

Mother held her breath. Father looked away. Jeanette looked at him with relief in her eyes, and he smiled at her. He could be as brave as she had been.

The priest knelt in front of him, taking his hands in a firm grip. He couldn't even feel the man's scars. He couldn't feel—

Terrible pain lanced through him. A ripping feeling like cords of white-hot wire burrowing into his skin. His vision shifted into black, and he saw a net of those cords beneath him, all crisscrossed lines beneath the house. Clouds of gray hung around each cord, with green dots hovering in the air around them. He liked the green dots. Even with the pain, even though he had never seen these lines before, a corner of his mind recognized them. They were why he could hear so good. Why he could see what others missed.

The world lurched back to normal.

"No," mother was sobbing. "No, no, no, no."

Father had risen to his feet. "No," he said.

Jeanette gaped down at his hands, horror on her face. He looked down in time to see a bloody ruin where his skin had been. His fingers were fine, but he had a gash the size of a walnut on the back of each hand. The priest wiped them both clean with a cloth before he could look for more than an instant. Strange. He didn't feel any pain now, only wonder over how his hands had been hurt.

"Alouen." The priest met his eyes. "You are a special boy. The King has need of you."

"No," father said again. "You can't have him. He was ours. You came too late."

"You know the law, Philippe d'Oreste. He is yours no longer. And you will be paid for your sacrifice."

What did the priest mean he wasn't father's?

"The Nameless can spit on your blood money," mother said, her anger finally boiling over.

The priest turned back to him. "Alouen, you are going to have to come with me. You have a gift that must be controlled. We will teach you to use it."

"I can't come with you," he said. "I have to stay here."

"You have to come with me. It will be hard, but this is the law. You know what the law is?"

He looked to mother, and to father. To Jeanette. What about Jeanette?

"What about Jeanette?" he asked.

"You must say your good-byes now."

Jeanette looked at him with tears in her eyes.

"Better if we make this quick." The priest rose to his feet.

Mother was sobbing, and father went to her.

Jeanette took his hands. She didn't even flinch away from the wounds.

"You get to be a hero now, Alouen," Jeanette said. "I'll tell stories about you."

He felt numb. He didn't want to be a hero anymore.

INTERLUDE

THE ORACLE

Meditation Chambers
Gods' Seat

From the corner of her eye Ad-Shi saw a lizard baking on a rock, storing its energy before the sun hid itself behind the storm bank. A speck in the shadow of her falcon eyes, but she knew it was there; every sense at her disposal screamed it to her. Tucking talons back against her compact body, she dove. This was nature, the power of tooth and claw and wing. She quivered, anticipating the feel of her beak slicing into its scaly flesh.

Paendurion had his war games. Axerian read his books and contemplated whatever riddles the mortals had produced in the time between their awakenings. Ad-Shi had the hunt.

She needed it. She needed a kill. Just as often, she chose to wear the skin of the lizard, or the elk. The wild surge of fear at being hunted could be a potent reminder of what it was to be alive. Today she needed to feel violence, the purity of murder without morality. There was no judgment in what the falcon did to its prey, any more than there could be judgment from mortals for the actions of one such as Ad-Shi. They did not understand. They could not understand.

This was the way. The Three bided their time, waiting for the anointed moment. Each cycle they awakened to find the world changed, but also unchanging. Always there were the lines of power: Order, tied to the leylines; Balance, tied to the serpents; and her magic, the Wild, derived from the spirits of land and beasts and things-to-come, separate but united in her grasp. Three lines, demanding three champions to face the ancient enemy. Three ascendants of every age, who left unchecked would rise to damn the world with their ignorance, if she and her fellows failed to stop them.

In a rush of wind and feathers she closed her talons around the fragile body of her prey. A moment ago the lizard had thought only of its next meal. Now it dangled helplessly as she rushed higher and higher into the sky. An electric shudder crackled up and down her spine as she opened her beak, announcing to the teeming mass of creatures below that a falcon hunted here, had made its kill.

DOES HE PLEASE YOU, SISTER?

He does, brother. I thank you for the allowance of his form.

HE IS A MIGHTY FALCON.

He is. He does you much honor. May I have him again, one day?

A brief pause. The spirits always took their time when asked for favors, no matter how slight.

YOU MAY.

Blessings, brother.

The voice faded as her reverie cleared. Ad-Shi sighed, her vision returning to the present.

"A good one today, hm?" Axerian looked up from his latest volume with his usual half smile.

She said nothing, only bowed her head, nodding once. When it was clear she would venture no further response, he laughed to himself and went back to his book.

The two of them sat on smooth stone benches opposite one another in the center of the cavernous chamber. She had long since grown accustomed to the feeling of this place that men had called the Gods' Seat in the tongue of the Amaros. Her people, the Vordu, had named it *Ujuru'i'alura*, which translated to much the same thing: "the place where Gods sleep." A more fitting description than her people could have imagined.

It was a place of stone, everywhere smooth stone as if carved by countless centuries of water through the bed of a river. Paendurion and Axerian felt at home here. To her, more and more often it felt like a cage.

Without the escape of her connections to the spirits she might have tasted madness long since. She calmed herself with a few deep breaths. Soon. The time was coming. She would do what she must, to prepare.

No sense delaying. With trained response cultivated by countless thousands of such exertions, she opened her mind into the realm of the spirits.

Spirit of things-to-come, hear my call.

The moments stretched on as her vision blurred once again. Stone gave way to emptiness, an overpowering sensation of void that had emptied her stomach when she learned this as an acolyte all those lifetimes ago. Nothingness. And then something.

CHILD. YOU SEEK ME. WHY?

I am no child, vision-spirit. I wield the gift of the Goddess of Life, and you will recognize the right of that power.

Energy surged within her, raw and untamed. A roiling blue mass that threatened to slither out of her grasp whenever she touched it, drew upon it, as she did now.

Long moments passed while she struggled to hold on. The silence broke in a wave of release.

VERY WELL. WHAT WOULD YOU HAVE OF ME?

To whom are you bound, vision-spirit?

More silence. The spirits of the beasts and of the land could be pliable, amicable even. Dealing with Vulture or Oak left her feeling refreshed and invigorated. The spirits of the great beasts and the sacred places were less giving, but in the end they knew their place, or she found it for them. Not so with the vision-spirits, accustomed as they were to less than equal relationships with those who sought them out.

Answer me. Now.

Another moment passed before its defiance broke.

I AM BOUND TO ONE CALLED *ILEK'RAHS*, OF THE OLESSI TRIBE.

Show me what you have revealed to him.

No words came, only a flood of images. Births. Beasts. An *anahret* drawing close to Olessi lands. Trade. Woodcarving. Successful hunts. Young men coming of age. A bonecarver. Paints. Dances. Great fires raging through the forests to the north. The sun shining. Stories. Pain. Food. Marriages and sickness. Remembrance ceremonies. Love.

When the spirit finished, she reached deep inside herself for the surging torrent of energy at her command. It kicked and twisted inside her, struggling to evade her grasp. She forced it, willed it into the vision-spirit as she thought to it once more.

You will add to what you have shown.

Another stream of images flowed, this time from her into the spirit. Death. War. Deception. Betrayal. Men girding themselves for war. Battles. Conflict. Expanding borders. Glory. A tribal leader setting aside the marks of a hunter for the mantle of a warleader. Guns and powder. Clouds of uncertainty around the tribal lands. Wounds. Cries of pain. Loss. Weeping mothers, broken husbands. Fire. Ruin.

Gasping, she released the vision and the power and collapsed to the ground, falling from the stone bench in a rush.

Axerian had already moved, lightning-quick, catching her before she landed.

He smoothed her hair back from her face, wiping away the tears that streaked her cheeks. She sobbed into his arms as he held her in a tight embrace.

"Shh," he whispered to her, a soothing sound. "We do only what we must."

She nodded, knowing it for truth. And deep within, a small part of her soul tore away.

She mourned its passing.

PART 2: SUMMER

SEASON OF THE EXARCH

14

ERRIS

1st Division Command Tent
Sarresant Territory, Near Villecours

The day's last orders were signed, the aides had been dismissed from her tent, and for a rare moment she had time alone. She spent it sitting atop her cot, knees cradled in her hands, remembering.

She went over her orders during what the colonial newspapers were already calling the Battle of Villecours, the troop movements and strategies, the moments of indecision between engagements, the areas where her commands had been weak. Fools passed up the opportunity to learn from their failures; greater fools ignored the lessons nested within success.

Villecours had been a rout. The enemy broke and gave up the field after her maneuver to strike down their commander and disrupt their reserve. Victory had followed almost too easily, but there were still weaknesses from which to learn. And blood on her hands.

One thousand six hundred and fifteen souls from Carailles's brigades. Dead. Because of her, and because of the strange golden light.

She hadn't been able to replicate it since the battle, nor make sense of it. Whatever happened to cause the golden light, she knew it had been her voice that ordered Vicomte-General Carailles's men to die. They had charged, and been butchered, and they'd done it on her word. In the harsh light of day, newly promoted Chevalier-General Erris d'Arrent spoke solemn praises for the late Vicomte-General Carailles and for the rest of the men who had fallen on the fields of Villecours. Here in her tent, away from the requirements of the service, she wept.

She doubled over, clutching at her belly to smother the pain of the images that danced across her vision. Fathers and mothers who would never come home; children who would grow up without them. Survivors who would live crippled and broken, a burden on those who loved them. Her body convulsed as she let herself feel the pain of it, and she covered her face with her hands, hair matted, eyes red, face slick with tears.

When morning came it found her stirring awake, disheveled and spent, but somehow having managed a few hours' sleep.

She ran her hands through the basin of water that had been brought for her. Warm water cleansed her skin, and she forced a brush through the tangles of her golden shoulder-length hair. More than once she'd considered shearing it to her scalp as many of the men did. It would offer some advantages in the field. But for one such as her, who relied on bindings and agility over brute strength in close combat, if an enemy combatant were quick enough to grasp her by the head she'd have problems beyond a few torn locks. In truth it was a vanity to keep it, but one she was loath to give up, and that was that.

She tied her hair back with a leather cord and donned her uniform. Pristine and pressed, with a single golden star on the collars and sleeves. She hadn't expected a promotion for years, if ever. But the 2nd Corps had a new commander, a nobleman come over from the Old World. She'd never met the man, nor served under him. But evidently Marquis-General Voren thought well enough of her, in spite of the no doubt scathing reports Vicomte-General Carailles had left behind, to approve her promotion.

So now she was Chevalier-General Erris d'Arrent.

The title was a formality, without attendant lands or incomes, but she was by rights a member of the peerage, and more important: She had the 1st Division. A full third of the 2nd Corps, two steps removed from Duc-General Cherrain himself. She had cavalry brigades, infantry, artillery, supply trains, and binders skilled with the military applications of *Life*, *Body*, *Shelter*, *Entropy*, *Death*, and *Mind*. Enough men to make a difference on every battlefield, and more than a little stake in choosing the ground on which those battles would be fought. All she needed was a season or two to train them up to an acceptable standard; all she had was a few weeks. She intended to make good use of the time.

Her preparations finished, she strode through the flaps of her tent into the light of the early morning sun.

"Good morning, sir," Sadrelle said with a salute as she emerged.

"Aide-Lieutenant," she said.

"The morning assemblies are being called," he said, and began reading aloud a few of the reports that had come in during the hours before dawn. The camp was quiet, with no contact reported with the enemy. And more important, no orders to prepare for a march.

"Very good, Lieutenant," she said, accepting a cup of hot tea from another aide as they walked. "Are the brigade commanders assembled for the morning briefing?"

"Almost, sir. I took the liberty of fetching maps of the area to the south. The wooded hills along the coast."

She raised an eyebrow. "And what makes you suppose I'd have an interest in conducting exercises there?"

"You had the Fourteenth stage mock engagements on similar ground, when you first took command, sir."

"Good, Aide-Lieutenant." She nodded approval. "I'll also need maps of the area farther south, where the woods break near the river. If we're to be here a while, I want to give my scouts room to dance."

He saluted, ducking away to carry out her order.

When she reached the planning area, those of her commanders who had arrived on time greeted her with pleasantries and proper respect. She'd make enough of a spectacle of the rest; they'd learn not to waste her time with tardiness or excuses. Whatever Carailles had allowed, the 1st Division under Erris d'Arrent would be a very different beast. Discipline for its own sake could be bent, with need and purpose. Discipline in service to the right orders—to her orders—was another thing entirely.

She went through the usual command routines at first, bluster mixed with stirring appeals to the rightness of their cause. She deviated a bit by recounting the army's moves over the last nine months, and those of the enemy. Having scouted a fair portion of those moves herself, she knew them well. And it set her up for the true purpose of the day: the beginnings of establishing her style of command. Where other generals blundered about, barely able to describe the trial and error that led to whatever successes they could claim, she intended to train her commanders to lead.

"Here," she said, pointing to one of the topographical maps, annotated with details from the 14th's reports. "Say we received word the enemy had taken this position in the night and begun fortifying. We are presently a morning's march away from deploying. His disposition threatens to harry our supply lines from the north. How would you respond?"

Her protégés among the assembled commanders, Lance-Captain d'Guile and Brigade-Colonel Vassail, each adopted wry smiles, knowing what she was about. D'Guile had temporary command of the 14th Light Cavalry, standing in for some marquis's son who recovered from injury in the capital. Brigade-Colonel Vassail had served under her command, two years past, when she was still a captain. Now Vassail commanded the remains of the 11th Light Cavalry, after the former commander and most of the horsemen had been killed at Villecours.

The rest of her commanders looked askance at one another, unsure who would speak first.

Finally Brigade-Colonel Chellac, who commanded the 16th Infantry, spoke up. "Sir, are we to assume we are in command of our own units? The First Division entire?"

She gave him a warm look. It was never easy to venture the first reply, and she meant to encourage boldness. "Say the First Division, and no more. The remainder of the Second Corps is deployed to the west."

Brigade-Colonel Savasse, recovered from the spotted fever and back in command of the 9th, rubbed his chin and replied, "Is there some threat to the west we ought to consider in this scenario?"

"Very good, Colonel. One must weigh the fullness of the situation before committing troops to one objective or another." She pointed to the western section of the map. "Let us say the remainder of the Second Corps is deployed here, and here, with the enemy arranged like so along this hillside to the south. You've been given a directive to deal with the element of the enemy army that has split to harry our supplies. What are your orders?"

Chellac spoke again, beginning to understand her meaning. "What size force has the enemy brought to the eastern encampment?"

Brigade-Colonel d'Ellain, also recovered from the fever and field-promoted to command the 12th Infantry in addition to his artillery crews, nodded, adding, "And do we trust our scouts' reports?"

Excellent. This lot would come along quickly. "The reports are good, firsthand accounts. The enemy has the full Third Corps of the First Gand Army entrenched in these hills, with the rest of the First Army deployed against our Second Corps here to the west."

Some grumbling then. Vicomte-Colonel de Tourvalle spoke, one of her infantry commanders. "You have us outnumbered three to one, on ground where our horse will be no better than infantry."

"Yes. What would you do?"

D'Guile and Vassail caught each other's eyes, having withheld participation as long as they could.

"I'd order the horsemen of the Eleventh and Fourteenth to harry the enemy position to the east, to ensure the Gand Third Corps could not join the main engagement," said d'Guile.

"And send the rest of the First Division around to the south to flank the enemy reserves," Vassail finished for him. "They'd be forced to abandon fortifications in plain view of the rest of our army."

Brigade-Colonel Royens, a young man but already a decorated veteran, laughed, deep and rich. "We'd earn ourselves a court-martial, ignoring orders." A few of the others nodded dubiously, though Royens continued, "I must say that open ground to the south is tempting, though, for cavalry maneuvers."

She said nothing, waiting.

Royens looked up and down the assembled commanders. "Yes, it's a bold plan. I rather think we'd stand a good chance of breaking their line."

"The enemy committed far too many men to harry supply lines, with the rest of their army engaged," Vassail said. "If the First Division is not deployed, the best thing we can do is continue to maneuver. Lance-Captain d'Guile's plan to pin down the enemy with an inferior force is the crème icing on the lemon cake."

Erris beamed.

"We'll start each day's briefing with a tactical exercise like this. In time we'll learn to trust each other's judgment. Under my command you will have tactical flexibility; I do not intend to give you rigid orders or positions to hold. Only goals to achieve, and even those are to be set aside when better opportunities present themselves.

"Oh, and one more thing. If you don't already make a habit of reading scouting reports thoroughly yourselves—not summarized by an aide—I insist you start. Information is the key to good judgment."

Her commanders murmured with varying degrees of enthusiasm. Well, she'd learn soon enough which ones took to her paradigm of command and which yearned for reassignment. Unlikely that she could grant it during wartime, but perhaps arrangements could be made. At worst she'd know who she could rely on and who needed more involved direction.

She continued. "Now, my aides tell me we're likely to be encamped here for some time while reinforcements and supplies are distributed throughout the army." Nods up and down the line. "I don't intend to waste the time. By midday I want us marching south by west into these hills. We'll stage mock maneuvers through the week. Vicomte-Colonel de Tourvalle, you'll have the Fifteenth, Third, and Sixteenth Infantry, along with the Fourteenth Light Cavalry and half of the Twelfth Artillery. Start deployment once you've crossed the mill, here." She pointed on the map.

"Brigade-Colonel Royens, you have the rest of the division. Swing to the south and begin your deployment here, around this bend in the river." She held up a hand to stop him before he could voice his objection. "Yes, I know the vicomte-colonel's men will reach their assigned position a half day ahead of yours. You decide how hard to push your soldiers' march to compensate."

Royens nodded, pursing his lips as he looked over the maps.

"I'll ride with my aides flying the division banners to judge your positions and the likely effectiveness of your engagements." She clapped her hands. "Dismissed. I suggest you move with all haste; no prizes for second."

They scrambled, all grins and bravado as the two sides clustered around their commanders, eager for first orders before they assembled to march.

A fine way to begin the season. She'd have this division in fighting shape soon enough, Gods willing.

15

ARAK'JUR

Deep Wilderness
Sinari Land

He stood frozen, still as a pond in the moments before dusk. The trunk of an oak gave him ample cover and the wind was favorable. He knew by instinct he was well hidden. He could observe and remain unseen.

Across the sparse grasses and trees his apprentice crept toward their quarry. Ilek'Inari had misjudged the angle; the wind would give him away before he closed to striking distance. Perhaps *una're*'s gifts would be enough to offset losing the advantage of surprise. Still, it was not well done. He'd have to upbraid his apprentice no matter the outcome.

The buck's ears pricked as it sipped from the stream, quick darting motions suggesting it had noticed something was amiss. No elk survived to produce a full rack without keen senses; this buck was not a grand specimen but he was an adult, if only recently matured. It was the season for such things, for comings of age. The forests and grasslands teemed with life on the cusp of maturity, but danger, too. Predators slept along with their prey when the days were cold, reemerging with the wet season showers. And in the long, hot season they hunted.

In the distance a pair of birds flew from a copse of bushes with a rush of feathers. A stroke of luck for his apprentice, if the buck mistook it for the source of his unease. It seemed he had. The animal's head lowered once more to lap at the smoothly flowing water. Ilek'Inari continued his approach, creeping across the grass in a low crouch, hiding behind trees where he could. The tribe's more gifted hunters would long since have taken the buck with bow or musket shot, but such was not the way of the guardians. Their work required honoring the beast spirits, and that meant they abstained from implements the beasts themselves did not employ.

The buck's head darted up. Ilek'Inari had used a boy's trick: a stone tossed to make a clatter from another direction. A master hunter would not risk the chance of alerting his prey, triggering flight instead of fear. Ilek'Inari found luck a second time. The buck froze, its head turned such that one eye could focus where the stone had sounded.

A pale hue of ethereal fur and claw surrounded Ilek'Inari as he called on *una're*. Too late the buck realized its mistake. It had time for a single jolting spring forward before it crashed to the ground, stricken out of the air by a mighty blow from his apprentice. Blue energy coursed across the buck's body as it slammed into the dirt, miniature lightning storms conjured by the power of the Great Bear. Its hide sparked and popped as the creature died, smoke hissing from its smoldering fur.

The air fell still with the familiar silence following a kill.

"Honored guardian," Ilek'Inari called. "How did I do?"

Grunting as he emerged from behind the tree, Arak'Jur jumped down the small ledge to the grass below. He raised a hand in a gesture of respect as he walked. "A fine kill, apprentice."

Arak'Jur knelt over the body of the buck when he reached its side, bowing his head in reverence for the creature's sacrifice. It was a sacred thing to kill using the gifts of the guardians. Ilek'Inari joined him on his knees, a moment of silence passing between them as they contemplated the hunt.

They used their bone knives to skin the beast before preparing its meat for the fire. Ilek'Inari took the rebuke over his failure to read the wind in good humor. The young man knew his limitations when it came to woodcraft. Ka'Vos had recognized the seeds of the shaman's gift early in Ilek'Inari's life, and it led to a childhood spent memorizing the tribe's stories and assisting in ritual preparations rather than joining the other boys at play with stick-spears and makeshift bows and arrows. At least it could be said Ilek'Inari had few bad habits, having few habits of any kind when it came to the hunt. And he listened, credit him for that.

"See here." Arak'Jur pointed as they stretched the buck's body in preparation for butchery. "You struck hard enough to crack its spine. A killing blow, yes. But a single hit here"—he pointed again, to the buck's torso—"even a glancing blow, and most beasts' hearts will stop when you strike with *una're*'s blessing."

"Is it truly like a storm?" Ilek'Inari asked. "The same energy?"

"It is. I have seen beasts struck during the tempests in the wet season. It is much the same. *Una're* carries the blessing of the fiercest storms, and he shares it with us."

Ilek'Inari nodded, pacing around the body of the elk in contemplation.

"I wonder. Why do we not converse with the spirits of elk, or other beasts when they are slain? Why only the great beasts?"

"You do wrong asking why. We are guardians, not shamans." He meant it as a subtle rebuke, though Ilek'Inari seemed to miss his intent.

"Yes, but you must have wondered. Do the elk and wolves not have a guardian spirit? I wonder what we might learn, conversing with the spirits of all creatures, and not only the most terrible."

Arak'Jur shrugged. "The lynx is quick, his claws are sharp. Is *mareh'et* so different? The *Ka* can see him, and when he is slain we speak to the spirit of his kind, and receive his blessings. That is the way of things." He said it with finality, intending it to be the end of the lesson.

"Your knowledge exceeds mine, of course." Ilek'Inari bowed his head. "Still, there have been more and more great beasts of late, have there not? New creatures, new bonds for the guardians—for us—to forge, new strength to defend our people."

"It is not our place to worry over matters of the spirits."

"Peace," Ilek'Inari said, raising a hand to concede the point. "I meant only that, as more creatures show themselves to us, perhaps the spirits of ordinary beasts will do the same, in time."

"It may be so. But *mareh'et* and his ilk are strong, and you would do better to concern yourself with facing him than worrying over his lesser kin."

Ilek'Inari paled.

"Ka'Vos didn't mention... *mareh'et*... nearby?"

Arak'Jur grinned. "No, my friend. But when the day comes, you will regret each moment spent worrying over the nature of the beasts, when you might have been preparing to face them."

This time the answer sufficed to end the conversation, returning their attention to skinning their kill. When it was ready they would carry the hide back to the village for tanning. Much of the meat would be left, but a buck's hide was too valuable to give to the carrion-eaters. A guardian and a guardian in training would have no shortage of kills to feed them on their journeys. They would not kill more than they required—such displays were vulgar in the extreme—but Ilek'Inari needed a great deal of practice. Many a buck, a wolf, or a bear would fall before he deemed his apprentice ready to face another great beast. Neither he nor Ilek'Inari had any illusions that the killing blow the younger man had landed on the *una're* was anything more than luck.

Such were their people's ways since they had come to these lands, though he struggled to make sense of Ilek'Inari's renewed apprenticeship. The only stories of men seeking to join a guardian's power with the shaman's magic were cautionary tales, of men possessed by lust for power, and disdain for the spirits' ways. A guardian's strength and a shaman's wisdom were separate paths, stemmed from spirits as different in kind as beasts were from men. Ilek'Inari was no full *Ka*, though the line was thin. And even apart from the threat of the forbidden, for the spirits to rob them of a new *Ka* precisely when his faith in Ka'Vos's abilities dwindled… it was as if fate played some cruel joke on him, and on his people.

And just as his guardianship had been unforeseen by the shamans, so now was his apprentice's.

Did it speak to a flaw in him, or only in their shaman? In other things Ka'Vos continued to see as he always had. Perhaps a curse, as Llanara had named it, though that was a bitter draught to swallow. Yet perhaps this was only the repayment he deserved: a cursed fate for failing to protect his family, failing the ones he loved most dear. The broken body of his wife in his hands as her skin flaked black from the bite of the *valak'ar*. His son, his brave son, who had fallen to the same. The vision of that day played again in his mind, and he let it come, bracing himself against the pain. *Rhealla. Kar'Elek.*

"Arak'Jur." His apprentice's voice was soft and full of sympathy. "Your heart is troubled."

He looked away. "These times are troubled."

"They are. I find myself lying awake deep into the night hours, asking why."

"Ilek'Inari." He turned back to regard his apprentice. "Our people have endured worse than this, and prospered. You will make a fine guardian, in time."

"But I would have made a better *Ka*."

He had no reply to that. Ilek'Inari had trained his entire life to become a shaman. The tribe watched him grow into a mediator, a conciliator, as he advanced in his training. There was more to being shaman than seeing and interpreting the whims of the spirits, and Ilek'Inari had gifts far beyond whatever skill he could claim at parting the veil of things-to-come.

"When the *una're* spoke to me, almost I thought I had become *Ka*."

He furrowed his brow. What did his apprentice mean?

Ilek'Inari went on. "We are trained as shamans to form a bond, a bond with a spirit of—"

He hissed. "Ilek'Inari, you know better than to speak of that which you know is forbidden. You must let go of such things."

"It is not so easy," the young man whispered, looking away. Arak'Jur was not certain he had been meant to hear.

So it was, with troubles of the heart. They passed easily from one man to another.

The remainder of their work was done in quiet contemplation. By nightfall they had finished taking what they could from the buck, and they slept beneath a canopy of oak and cedar trees.

"Now do you see?" he asked patiently.

Ilek'Inari searched once more, pacing around as he inspected the nearby brush. He shook his head and gave a flustered smile.

"I am sorry, Arak'Jur. It looks like brush to me."

"There, near the base of that elm."

Dropping to a knee, his apprentice inspected the tree more closely.

"These marks?" Ilek'Inari gestured, uncertain.

"Yes. Those. Tell me, what do we hunt today?"

"A wolf?"

Arak'Jur laughed. "A wolf that size would be a sight indeed. See the way the bark flakes off here, and here?" He waited for Ilek'Inari to nod. "A bear's claws made these marks, and freshly, too. We'll find him nearby, if we can keep to the trail."

His apprentice swallowed hard, but made no complaint. Good.

"You are ready. See there? The broken twigs, the leaves pushed aside? That is our path."

"Follow me, then," his apprentice said, pushing forward into the brush.

He stayed behind, keeping far enough back to allow Ilek'Inari to find the trail on his own. It was slow going, but Ilek'Inari did well. Twice he veered off the path but recognized his error and corrected it without prompting.

The third time his apprentice did not recover so quickly.

Sighing, Arak'Jur quickened his pace to intercept Ilek'Inari before they went too far astray. A disappointment. The thick foliage should have made it easier to follow the sign.

"Apprentice." He pushed past the thick brush, grown so tall it obscured sight. "Hold, we must turn back."

No response. He frowned, and called again, with only silence in reply. His pace quickened. Could Ka'Vos have missed another great beast, as he had the *una're* near Ka'Ana'Tyat? It was not unheard-of for a shaman to miss one from time to time. But two, not even a season apart? Coupled with his other concerns over the shaman's abilities, it would be grave indeed, perhaps too much to be borne. His heart raced as he prepared to draw upon the spirits' gifts.

He called out again as he crashed through brush at the base of a hill, emerging into a clearing. Ilek'Inari stood motionless ten paces ahead. He swept his vision across the area, seeking some sign of danger. Nothing. With a growl, he stormed toward his apprentice and grabbed hold of his shoulder, turning him to see his eyes glazed over, all white.

"Ilek'Inari!" he shouted, shaking his apprentice.

Blinking, Ilek'Inari came back into his senses.

"Explain yourself!" he demanded.

"I am sorry, honored guardian."

He said nothing in reply, merely glared.

"I felt an impression," Ilek'Inari continued. "Something terrible. Violence, coming from this direction, just ahead—"

"And so you spoke with the spirits of the *Ka*? This is forbidden. We hold the blessing of one kind of spirit, never two! You are a guardian's apprentice now. You cannot do this!"

"My training was not complete. I cannot speak with them, but I can listen—"

"You can do no such thing. The spirits will curse us, you fool!"

The younger man hung his head in shame. For a moment, silence hung between them. Then the meaning of his apprentice's words sank in. Violence?

A scream sounded through the trees ahead, then another, close behind. Instinct sparked his legs to move before he could consider any further.

Another scream etched it clearer in his mind. A woman's cry, or a child's.

Clear enough which, as they ran through the trees, and came upon its source. Two boys, splayed in the dirt of the forest floor, each with a spear through the belly. Long spears, marked in the old style, the sort the tribes had used for war before the fair-skins' arrival.

Ilek'Inari retched.

Arak'Jur drew upon the spirit of *lakiri'in*.

In a rush he tore through the trees, leaving his apprentice behind, fresh tracks leading the way. Heartbeats later he caught sight of his prey: a lone man fleeing through the grass. With *lakiri'in*'s speed he overtook the man easily, kicking his legs out and sending him sprawling into the dirt.

Arak'Jur stood over him, turning the man onto his back and pinning his shoulder to the ground.

He was greeted with eyes glazed as white as Ilek'Inari's had been. He knew this man. Ilek'Rahs, apprentice to the Olessi shaman, from the lands to the west.

16

SARINE

A Prison Cell
The Citadel, New Sarresant

Her world had dwindled to eight paces by eight paces, a bowl, and a bucket.

She sat on the far wall of her cell, as far from her bucket of excrement as she could manage. Once a day the brown-robed guards would come, making an opening in the *Shelter* around her cell to change out her bucket and fill her bowl with food. The rest of the day she sat, alone, against cold stone walls suffused with the smells of shit and piss and vomit.

Prison. She'd slain the beast and saved the attendees of the nobles' masquerade. She was a hero. A hero, and they rewarded her with a cell. She hadn't even been formally accused.

Tears sprang in her eyes, and she let them come.

Not for the injustice. She'd lived in the shadow of injustice every day of her life, writ in the hungry eyes of the denizens of the Maw while Rasailles's courtiers feasted and danced behind guarded gates. Not for the shit stink or the solitude—she had Zi for company, after all.

No, she cried for the ruin of pink flesh, the scars on the backs of her hands, as if a stake had been driven through either palm.

They'd finally caught her.

Since she was a little girl she'd been terrified of having her hands marked. She'd always run and hid when the brown robes came trawling through the streets, rounding up stray children to administer the tests. Zi had insisted she trust Father Thibeaux, and the man she came to call her uncle had never betrayed her, never tried to administer the test, even knowing what she could do. But now it was over. She'd been marked. Everywhere she went people would notice her, assuming she ever got out of this cell. She'd never be able to sit and sketch again without hiding behind shadows or *Faith.* And who would buy portraits from a freebinder anyway?

Off in the distance, muffled by uncounted layers of stone, a prisoner howled. Another voice joined the chorus, somewhat closer, and another. She thought about adding her own, but instead slumped against the stone walls, listening to the choir of rage and madness as she sank into despair.

Perhaps she could escape. This was a binder's prison; the *Shelter* around her cell made clear enough of that. But she could overpower the guards who came to bring mush and empty her bucket, and those guards would have keys. There was plenty of *Faith* here to keep her hidden, and *Death* if she needed to breach the shield around her cell. But after that, what? The priests would trace her leyline connections and find her, even if she used *Faith.* And she wasn't about to murder some poor prison guards just doing their job.

A thousand times she'd thought these thoughts, and a thousand times she'd failed to find a way that didn't require violence. In time she knew desperation might overcome her scruples. But it hadn't yet. And so she listened as the prisoners' chorus sang its screaming songs, a routine of pain and loneliness.

It took the sound of shuffling footsteps outside her door to jar her back to the moment.

She'd hardly heard them approach over the sound of the wailing cries, but even the slightest deviation from her routine was cause for heightened alert. She cast a quick glance over at her bucket to confirm it was still there, still empty. It stank horridly, but they'd emptied it that morning when they brought her meal. She had no window to see the sky, but surely it wasn't nighttime yet?

Gone.

What?

Then she felt it, too—the air suddenly sweeter, as if an enclosure had been removed. She'd never felt this when the priests came to change out her bucket or fill her bowl. Before she could reply to Zi, raps sounded on the iron door.

"Easy now, prisoner," a voice called through the door. A man's voice, but not ungentle. "The warden needs you cleaned up at once."

Her heart quickened and she sprang to her feet. "The warden. Why does he need…?" Her voice croaked, weary from howling, or lack of use; she wasn't sure which.

"No idea. Now if you please, prisoner, stand and face the back wall as we come in."

She complied with the instructions, and once again escape plans surfaced in her thoughts. She could overpower the priests, tether *Faith* to go invisible, and use whatever keys they had to escape this place. She could do it. She could—

The rusted creak of the door being opened scattered her courage. Two pairs of footsteps entered the room, rough hands affixing manacles around her wrists. They pivoted her around and she saw two guardsmen in leather tunics and a brown-robed priest of middle years, regarding her from across the room.

"Treat her gently," the priest said. "The warden asked she be brought to him in presentable condition." He smiled, a warm look that reminded her, against all expectations in this hellish place, of her uncle. "Apologies, child. The manacles are a necessity, but you don't have the look of our worst. I trust you understand you must behave meekly, and you will not be ill-treated."

She nodded, senses still numb.

"Very good then." He nodded to the two guardsmen who flanked her, each man gripping one of her arms. "Shall we?"

He turned and led the trio out of the cell. Recesses for doorways lined the outer edge of the hall into which they emerged, each one covered by a blue haze of *Shelter*. The walkways were smooth stone, sunlight trickling in from barred windows at either end of the hallway. The priest led them through the twists of the corridor, up one staircase and down another. From time to time she saw another brown-robed figure, but more often it was men garbed like her two escorts in leather tunics and breeches. Evidently the priests kept watch over a special area of the prison devoted to dangerous types like herself.

An amusing thought, that she would be considered among the most dangerous of the prisoners of the crown. Zi appeared just in front of the priest, trundling along as if he and not the jailor were leading the way. He was livelier than she'd seen him in days, his head perked up, scales alternating red and white. She supposed she was dangerous, between her leylines and Zi's gifts, and then there was the cat-spirit, the *mareh'et*...

The memory of it was fresh in her mind, the sensation of being the predator, of living and breathing and wielding the power of his form. A frightening magic, separate and different from anything she'd known before. The spirit seemed to beckon at the edge of her mind, a blessing waiting to be called upon whenever she had need. She'd been afraid to do it here.

The priest unlocked an iron grate, leading them into the chambers beyond. By the décor, she judged they'd left the prisoners' quarters. Paintings hung on the walls, carpets lay across the stone floors, and actual furniture could be seen through open doorways. They tracked up another flight of stairs before the priest motioned to her two escorts to wait behind. He led her into a chamber, where another brown-robed figure waited.

"Here she is." Her captor handed a set of keys to the second priest. "The one the warden wanted. Can you have her prepared promptly, Sister?"

"Of course." The woman spared a look for her as she took the keys. "I'll get her cleaned up."

"Sister Zoelle will take good care of you, child. We'll be waiting outside once she's finished."

She nodded. "Thank you."

The door closed, and the sister tsked as she looked her over. She must have looked a mess, skin covered in filth, clothes ragged, and hair more knots than otherwise.

"Now, child, whatever you did to find yourself here, I'll brook no nonsense, understood?"

She bowed her head as meekly as she could manage. The prospect of a warm bath—she saw the basin across the chamber—was enough to cull away any thoughts of ill behavior.

"I trust you're learning a lesson about the King's justice. What exactly was your crime, dear?" The sister arched an eyebrow at her in askance as she brandished a key and made to unlock the manacles around her wrists.

"Being somewhere I shouldn't. The wrong place, at the wrong time."

Tsking again, the sister asked, "Political, then?"

"You could say so."

The priestess sighed. "Too many, lately. Far too many."

Her manacles came off with a click as the latch turned, and the sister went about getting her cleaned up. True to her word, Sister Zoelle worked quickly. Sarine wanted nothing more than to soak in the hot water, letting the soap lather melt away the grime from her skin. The priestess would have none of it, scrubbing her clean with washcloths. This warden was a strange manner of jailor to insist on keeping prisoners in filth and then require them bathed before a summons. She supposed it was a means of distancing himself from the reality of his post. Regardless, she was thankful for his odd proclivities. She hadn't been well and truly bathed in far too long.

Once she'd been toweled dry and dressed in fresh clothes from the sister's armoire of simple linen shirts and long skirts, she found herself manacled once more and back in the company of the first priest and the two guardsmen, on her way to the warden's offices. After a short wait in a modestly appointed foyer, they were ushered inside.

The warden leaned forward, gesturing with his free hand for her to enter as his quill worked furiously at a piece of parchment. She was escorted into one of the chairs in front of his desk while the guards and the priest stood along the rear wall of the chamber. They made no motion to leave the room; evidently the warden wanted whatever protection their presence offered. She was a highly dangerous prisoner, after all.

Finishing whatever he'd been writing, the warden lifted the paper and blew to dry it, then set it aside and turned his attention to her.

"So," he said, voice clipped and stern. "This is the trespasser."

"Yes, my lord." No point trying to deny it; she'd been dragged here straight from the royal green.

"What were you doing on the palace grounds?"

What was this? It sounded like an approximation of a trial. Her heart beat faster as her mind went through all the arguments she'd practiced, all the things she intended to say before a magistrate should she ever get the chance. It appeared this was it, as close as she was like to get.

"My lord, I climbed the wall to sketch the nobles at masquerade. I thought I could sell the drawings to commonfolk in the markets to earn a few coins."

The warden paused a moment, considering her. When he spoke again, it was in another tongue, harsh and guttural. Zi's voice sounded in her head.

He asks whether you understand Gand speech.

She dissembled, or tried to. At once she understood where this was going. A strange girl, an unmarked binder, caught at a function of Sarresant nobles with a pack full of sketches. They were at war. It didn't take much to draw the conclusion that she might be a spy, or worse.

Mercifully, he seemed to accept her insistence that she couldn't understand.

He switched back to the Sarresant tongue. "That you risked yourself attacking the beast is the only reason your head is still attached to your shoulders, girl. I hope you know that."

She swallowed. "I saw it about to hurt them, I didn't stop to think—"

"Do you know what it was?"

She shook her head. "No, my lord."

"Do you know anything of the weakenings in the Great Barrier? They found holes to the north. Large ones. Large enough for the beast to have come through."

Again she shook her head. "No, my lord. I've never been to the Great Barrier."

He pursed his lips, considering her. "Very well. And yet you are a binder, a freebinder who had evaded the King's tests before you came into our keeping."

This was it; the moment she'd dreaded from the day she'd first realized her gift. Again, no point trying to deny it. "I am."

"A crime." He rose from behind his desk, motioning for the priest to step forward. "But there are worse ones. And it seems your actions earned you a patron among the nobles."

"My lord?" Footsteps approached her from behind, and a brown-robed figure leaned over her shoulder to unlock her manacles.

"You saved more than a few lives on the green, girl. One of them is thanking you to the tune of buying a royal marque, to pardon your binding. Provided I am satisfied you pose no further threat to the state or the peerage, you are free to go."

Her head swam. Had she heard him aright?

"Only one thing remains. Your name. I need your name, to affix to the letter of marque." He picked up his quill again, returning to the paper upon which he'd been writing when they entered.

"Sarine," she said numbly.

"Surname?"

"Thibeaux." Her uncle's name; she'd never known her parents to ask for another.

He wrote it down.

"Very good." He handed her the papers. "Take these to a marquist's shop bearing the King's seal. Remuneration is included with these orders."

She stared at the papers in her hand. A royal marque. The blue and gold tattoos, three flowers entwined, on the scarred hands of nobles or the priests and soldiers who had completed their years of service to the crown. It meant a sanction to use her bindings, and it cost more than her uncle's church.

"Your benefactor has sent a coach. He'd have come in person, but he suffered injury on the green when the beast attacked, and now recovers at his townhouse in the Gardens district. He wants to meet you, to thank you for what you did."

She looked up at him in a daze.

"His name is Lord Donatien Revellion, son of the marquis. You will take the coach, I expect?"

17

SARINE

The Coach, Approaching the Gardens
Southgate District, New Sarresant

The cushions helped mask the rough ride of wheels over cobblestone. In her brief trip from the Citadel to the Gardens, she arrived at the conclusion that one did not ride in such a conveyance for comfort. One did so for the view.

Only a few feet higher than walking, but it might as well have been a seat among the clouds. Ordinarily she'd have had to navigate the press, weaving through crowds, trying to avoid the busiest thoroughfares. In the Revellion coach they went where they pleased, the team trotting ahead while passersby on foot ducked to the side to avoid them. And the stares. Half-masked envy mixed with wonderment. Never in all her years at the Sacre-Lin had she seen such reverence, not for the Oracle, the Exarch, or the Veil. She could almost believe herself a Goddess, riding behind the gilded doors, behind transparent curtains of the thinnest lace. No wonder the nobles acted so far above the commonfolk. The evidence of their superiority was wrought plain, in the eyes of the tanner, the baker, the wretch, looking up at them mere feet away, but worlds apart.

They approached the gilded-iron gate in the ringwall surrounding the Gardens district and, with a shout from the driver, bypassed the line of couriers, merchants, and whoever else had waited on their pleasure.

The guards waved them through without so much as a glance inside the carriage. Past the gate, lush greens and lavish buildings welcomed them on either side, the cobblestones paved so smooth the wheels seemed to glide over the streets. Zi drank it in with the fervor of someone who hadn't eaten in days. She felt a similar hunger herself. She hadn't been more than a few weeks in the prison—a short stay, when rumor spoke of grandfathers grown old there—but it was enough. To go from daily sojourns through the heart of the city to a beast caged in a menagerie made her bones ache. She yearned to draw again, to watch, to observe. Through a sheet of fresh paper she could make sense of the world. Here, now, the prospect of what she was about to face seemed a load beyond what she could bear.

And yet all too soon the coach came to a stop.

The door swung open, and like a hand descended from the heavens, the coachman escorted her down the steps and onto the street.

The Revellion townhouse.

She'd seen it before, sketched it even. Fine construction that spoke of wealth without shouting it. A small garden and a waist-high black iron gate between the main door and the street. In the haze of a dream she acknowledged the curtsies and bows of the servants as they ushered her inside, up the stairs into a small receiving room. And there he sat, reclining on a long chaise with enough room for him to rest his feet comfortably; he did so, with one leg in finely cut trousers and a calf-high boot, the other wrapped in the bandages of a chirurgeon. One of the servants announced her by name, though she hadn't remembered giving it, and Lord Donatien Revellion's eyes widened as he gestured her into the room.

"You're here," he said. "Sarine." His voice was weak and strained, with only a hint of the rich tones she'd overheard in the Gardens. The way his chest constricted suggested more bandages hidden beneath his blue formal coat and linen shirt. Still, he adorned her name in gold when he said it, and whatever the frailness of his body, he was still Lord Revellion, all chiseled looks and pushed-back black hair.

"Yes," she replied, then hastened to add "my lord."

"They never told me your name. I suppose you couldn't have given it before. They said you passed out after the beast was slain."

She nodded, unsure what he wanted to hear.

He took a deep, steadying breath. "Unjust, what they did to you. You're a hero."

Ah, it felt good to hear him say it.

He went on. "I've passed most of the time since that night in a sleep, the *sommeil de la mort*, as the chirurgeons call it. I made arrangements for your release this morning, as soon as they'd told me you'd been taken. And now here you are." He smiled weakly and gestured to a chaise opposite where he reclined. "Please, sit, be welcome."

"Thank you, my lord," she said as she settled into a chair with more cushion than any bed upon which she'd ever slept. "The warden told me you wished to see me. That you'd arranged for my release, and..." She swallowed. "...and for a marque to pardon my binding. I owe you my thanks."

"I owe you my life, Sarine."

"I suppose, if—" Heat rose to her cheeks.

"As do half the city's peers," he continued. "How they could think to reward you with a cell is beyond me. I was in a rage over it. All for the crime of what, some drawings and an uninvited showing at our masquerade? You'd not have risked yourself fighting the beast if you'd been there to spy; any fool could've reasoned it." He coughed at the exertion, passion dissipating from his voice as he closed his eyes, lying back once more against the cushions. A moment later one eye snapped open. "You aren't a spy, are you?"

She laughed in spite of herself. "No, my lord, I'm not a spy. I'm an artist."

"I knew it." He closed his eyes again, smiling. "Far too much talent to waste on covertcy." He gestured absently toward the corner of the room.

"My pack!" The sight of it, dirt-covered and worn as it was, was a treasure beyond price after so long away from her sketching.

"You won't mind that I had a look? It must be said, you are a woman of many talents."

She felt another flush, but couldn't dim a smile as she retrieved the pack, thumbing through its contents. All there, to the last sketch.

"Thank you, my lord. Truly. Thank you."

He made a dismissive gesture. "Returning what is yours is the least I can do. I fear you esteem us too highly, though—the nobles, I mean. Your drawings are flattering, to be sure. Too flattering, for some."

"I draw what I see, my lord."

"Would that I had your gift—I could show you what I saw, when the beast attacked. You were a thing to behold. They say you slew it by yourself, quicker than a man could see."

Her smile faded, recalling long years of training herself to avoid even the barest mention of her gifts. And here they were, in the open, tugging at a knot forming in her stomach.

"It's nothing to be ashamed of," he said. "The shame is on us, the nobles. We take children who show talent and we train them to serve the crown. We fear what binders might do with freedom. I think your example shows we underestimate you, people like you, I mean."

"Few enough of the people on the streets are like me, my lord." She shuddered to imagine what the toughs and thugs would do if they had unfettered access to leylines; it was dangerous enough when the odd deserter from the army's binders made a go of becoming a gang boss.

"Well, and why not, when we expect so little of them? And all the while the nobles buy royal marques when our children fail the tests, to exempt them from service to the crown." He grimaced. "It is injustice, simple and plain."

The sentiment hung in the air as she contemplated a reply. Strange and unexpected to hear that sort of talk on the lips of a man who'd lived his life surrounded by gold and the privileges it bought. Still, she didn't dare affirm the idea; whatever her personal philosophies, he was still the son of a marquis.

A knock at the door of the study saved her from the need to demure. It swept open, revealing a thin, tall woman in House Revellion livery.

"You're s'posed to be resting, m'lord," the newcomer said in an ornery voice colored by country accents, sparing Sarine a derisive look that weighed her head to toe.

"Yes, yes, Agnes. Tell the docteur I feel fine, more than up for a little polite conversation."

She sniffed, gainsaying him by demeanor if not with words. "Very good, m'lord. Time to dress the wrappings, though, docteur's orders."

Revellion sighed and made an apologetic look in her direction. "No allaying her when Agnes gets like this." Another sniff from behind. He laughed, a weak sound accompanied by a pained wince. "Well enough.

I would see you again, my lady, if you'd receive me. This is hardly my best."

She looked down, remembering the times she had watched him on the green. No, not anywhere close to his best.

He took it as assent. "Can I send a message to you?"

"Yes, my lord. With Madame Guillon, at the Five Cats, in the Maw." Not the Sacre-Lin. She would not betray her uncle no matter how well-intentioned Lord Revellion seemed.

"The Maw! Sarine, let me find you lodgings elsewhere."

"My lord, I can take care of myself."

"I suppose you can at that." A soft laugh, and he met her eyes again. "Expect to hear from me soon, Sarine. And thank you again, for saving my life."

She bowed her head and, a short time later, found herself once more in the Revellion coach, this time bound for home.

Whatever the egalitarian notions espoused by Donatien Revellion, they were not shared by his father's coachman. Pulling up to the edge of the Maw, the man made clear she was to find the rest of the way herself. His lordship the marquis would not have it said that his carriage had visited the slums, not to mention the risk of showing wealth among the city's lowest born. Or something to that effect. In any case, the result was her, in a linen blouse and long skirts with her pack slung across her shoulder, watching as the last vestiges of the morning's dream drove away beneath the whip of a Revellion retainer.

Had it been real? She supposed she had the skirts for proof. And the royal writ, a slip of paper rolled up safely in her pack. Permission, bought and paid, to do what she'd kept hidden since she was a child. Here among the shuttered windows and ruined buildings of the Maw, the notion of royal permission for anything seemed out of place, a relic from another world. Her shield of paper would do little to keep her safe if the wrong sort took an interest as she walked. She made quick about it, heading toward the familiar spires of the Sacre-Lin.

On a lark, she tethered *Body.* Its red motes were always plentiful here in the Maw, almost as common as *Life,* the green haze that clung to leylines wherever men or beasts were near. She wasn't normally hesitant to use her gifts here in the Maw—few enough priests besides her uncle walked these streets, and far fewer soldiers trained with bindings to recognize her work. But even without the tattoos that would cover her hands after she presented her letter to the marquist, everything was different now. The strangeness of permission. That single slip of paper changed everything, and nothing. She might be spared arrest should a priest trace an errant leyline connection where none was expected, but she doubted the city watch would accept her *Faith*-powered sojourns any more readily now than they had before.

Lord Revellion, though. That was different.

He seemed pleasant, Zi thought to her as she walked.

She smiled. "Yes," she said, hushing her voice. "He did."

Zi seemed content to leave it at that, and so was she. How many times had she imagined it, sitting down with Revellion, face-to-face, the sole audience for his attention? And now she had been, and if his word held true, would be again.

She walked the rest of the way to the chapel on a cloud, the dreariness of the slums kept at bay by hope for things-to-come.

It wasn't until she reached the main stair she remembered her uncle hadn't seen her since the night of the masquerade. She rushed into the entryway, heart catching in her throat when she saw him sweeping the dais. She watched for a moment, frozen in place until he noticed her.

"My child," he said at last, accompanied by the muted echo of the empty hall. "You've come back."

Tears streaked down her cheeks as she ran to him, wrapping him in a fierce embrace. The shock of it must have given him pause, but an instant later he returned the gesture, just as strong.

"I thought you were lost," he said, compensating for a lump in his throat.

"I thought I was, too, uncle."

Together they shared tears and stories. He wept to hear of her treatment in the Citadel, and she to hear how he had thought her dead, or worse. But in time the conversation dwindled to more routine events, and by supper it had finally settled in that she was home.

Happily for her, her uncle had not been able to bear the thought of cleaning out her loft. All was as she'd left it, down to the disheveled blankets atop her makeshift mattress. The only exception was a pair of letters atop her small table, each bearing a wax seal marked with the letter *A*.

She held them up over the ledge of her loft. "Uncle," she called down. "What are these?"

His brows furrowed as he squinted up at the letters. "Oh. The first came the morning after you disappeared. The second was delivered a few days ago. I hadn't the heart to read them; I was afraid for their contents. But it appears I won't have to." He smiled up at her, his eyes deep, still touched with pain.

She returned his wistful look with warmth, then sat down, thumbed the seals of her letters, and began to read.

Both letters were much the same. Invitations. One to a fête held weeks ago, the other to a smaller gathering three days hence. Both signed *Reyne d'Agarre.*

A tingle shot down her spine. The man in the red coat. The man she'd seen in the Harbor, and met in the market.

How had he known where to find her?

18

ARAK'JUR

The Greatfire
Sinari Village

Low whispers ran through the assembly as every man and woman, every child, every dog and elder gathered on the grass. They'd begun piling wood for the fire after the midday meal, now built to a towering blaze roaring against the black of a moonless night. Some such fires burned to mark new names for the men: *Ka*s, *Arak*s, *Valak*s. The women called for gatherings to celebrate a safe return from one of their journeys, an especially difficult birth, or a death deserving of the tribe's collective mourning.

Tonight the fire burned for judgment.

Arak'Jur wore the full regalia of a guardian. The leather-and-hide breeches he wore daily had been set aside for a paneled skirt that revealed leg muscles and manhood when he moved, meant to signify through him the tribe's strength and virility. His chest was bare, decorated with red and black paint in a more intricate version of the hunter's *echtaka*. He wore a mantle of feathers culled from the greatest hunters among the birds of prey: eagle, hawk, falcon, and, at the center of a necklace, a single blood-red feather plucked from an *ipek'a*. Beads interspersed with golden discs hung around his wrists to complete the garb, highlighting the contributions of the tribe's craftswomen to his attire.

To his right Ka'Vos sat in the shaman's ritual garb, favoring concealment and mystery, all heavy hides behind ghost-white paint on his face. To his left Llanara wore the women's ceremonial dress, white from head to toe, but a line of red running from her forehead to her neckline where the women were traditionally painted blue. It had surprised him to learn Llanara had been selected by the women to sit in judgment tonight, in place of Ghella or another of the gray-haired mothers or grandmothers of the tribe, but he knew better than to question it. Women's business was none of his concern.

He stood, and a cloak of silence fell over the assembly before he reached his feet.

"Bring the accused before us." His voice was deep, reverberating in the open space of the gathering area. He spoke with the voice of the tribe tonight, and together with Ka'Vos and Llanara his word would stand as law.

Whispers passed through the crowd, seated cross-legged on the grass. Some few had the foresight to bring mats or woven blankets, expecting the proceedings to stretch deep into the evening hours. Only the Ranasi remained silent. Ka'Hinari himself had made the trip, in the company of Arak'Doren and a small host of their most accomplished hunters. Corenna had come as well, this time in formal dress rather than the ceremonial white, flanked by a pair of older Ranasi women at her side. The Olessi tribe sent only two hunters: Valak'Han and Valak'Buri, and one woman, unknown to him.

Two Sinari men emerged at the back of the crowd, holding between them the slumped figure of the accused: Ilek'Rahs, apprentice to the Olessi shaman, on the cusp of making his final journey to become a *Ka*.

His lip quivered as Ilek'Rahs was brought through the center walkway. Had he not apprehended the man with his own hand, he would scarce have believed it possible. The spirits of the *Ka* spoke to Ilek'Rahs. How any man could profane that sacred charge he could not fathom. The apprentice seemed resigned to his fate, his eyes lowered as he made a halfhearted attempt to walk while the Sinari hunters held his arms firmly between them.

"Ilek'Rahs," Arak'Jur's voice boomed. "You stand accused before the Sinari tribe, and the Ranasi. The Olessi tribe also bears witness." He made a gesture toward each, receiving a solemn nod in response.

"Before you speak in your own defense, I will make plain that of which you stand accused."

More whispers in the audience, in defiance of convention. Rumors had spread, as they always would, but he suspected few here knew the truth.

"Since I bore witness to your actions, I will speak for them. First, you are accused of entering Sinari lands uninvited." That much was clear enough and elicited no great reaction from the crowd. "Second, you are accused of murdering two boys of the Ranasi tribe: Kar'Larek, and Kar'Andu."

An angry hiss spread through the assembly as they exchanged heated murmurs.

He let it go on for a moment before he raised his fist.

"Third, you are accused of conspiring to sow discord between the Sinari and the Ranasi by killing the boys with long-spears marked in the Sinari style, on Sinari land."

Chaos, and shouted rage.

This time he made no move to silence the crowd, taking his seat beside Ka'Vos and Llanara on the oak bench opposite the greatfire. Ilek'Rahs bore a pained expression, wincing at each shrill cry, each shouted insult. The Sinari hunters who had escorted the accused to the center of the meeting place dropped Ilek'Rahs's arms, recoiling in disgust.

When it became clear the crowd would not settle themselves, Ka'Vos rose and motioned for quiet. Once the noise had dimmed the shaman spoke. "We would hear Ilek'Rahs's words."

A hush settled as Ka'Vos returned to his place on the bench. The tribes remained still enough to hear, though their eyes continued to burn.

Ilek'Rahs was cloaked in animal hide as befit his position as apprentice shaman, but he may as well have been naked.

"Speak!" called a voice in the crowd, then another.

Ilek'Rahs turned to regard the bench with a look of desperation, but remained silent.

Llanara tilted her head as if listening to some unseen voice, then nodded as she rose to her feet. She met Ilek'Rahs's eyes, and the tension within the apprentice melted away like a winter thaw.

"Do as they bid you, child of the Olessi," Llanara said.

The change in Ilek'Rahs was unnervingly quick, a transformation from cowering fear to a quiet confidence. The apprentice shaman turned to address the crowd.

"Thank you, honored matron," Ilek'Rahs said, pausing for a deep breath before he continued. "I hear the voices of the spirits of things-to-come."

"Cursed!" came a voice from the crowd, an easy cry for others to pick up. Ilek'Rahs roared back over the top of them, alight with energy.

"I hear them! I challenge any here to deny it!"

That seemed to satisfy, for the moment.

"I do not claim to understand the entirety of what they say. Can any here claim to understand them fully? Ka'Vos, will you claim it? Ka'Hinari?" He twisted wildly, regarding both men. The shamans stared back, faces stoic and unreadable.

"The Olessi do not make this claim. Yet we live by the surety of their protection, the same as the Ranasi, the same as the Sinari. By following the visions granted us, our peoples prosper. That is our way, has been our way since our peoples journeyed north—together—to claim these lands."

On another night, the words might have received nods of assent, expressions of support. Spoken by this man, on this night, they garnered only darker stares, the collective anger of the crowd turning cold to hear their precepts spoken by one so direly accused.

Ilek'Rahs noticed, and became frantic. "I only followed their voices, the visions granted by the spirits of things-to-come. I did nothing the spirits did not sanction."

Arak'Jur rose to his feet. "You admit it, then? You admit what you have done?"

Ilek'Rahs turned to him with pained eyes. The apprentice sagged his head, the fire of his passion gone, and nodded.

Anger boiled in Arak'Jur's belly, frosted over as the apprentice confirmed for the crowd what he already knew to be true. "I pronounce judgment," he said. "Death."

Ka'Vos rose. "I, too, pronounce death."

Llanara drew in a breath, considering. It came down to her: All voices must agree, for such a sentence to stand. All eyes were on her as she rose, her white garb giving her a subtle glow against the night sky.

"Death," she said, plain and clear.

Ilek'Rahs slumped to his knees.

Valak'Han of the Olessi stood from the front row and called out, "Elders of the Sinari, I beg the honor of carrying out this sentence. It is wise, and just. Let his own tribe condemn him now, that all may be washed clean of this."

Ka'Vos looked to him, as did Llanara.

He shook his head. No.

"Brother," he said. "You have the right, but you do not have the means."

The crowd stilled as he stepped forward.

"For blaspheming the spirits' will, for sowing discord between tribes, this man deserves to die by my hand. By the gift of the *valak'ar*."

Ilek'Rahs's eyes widened as he heard the words, and the apprentice cowered, raising a hand to ward away his fate.

Arak'Jur called upon the wraith-snake. A pale nimbus surrounded him, and he struck.

The blackened, rotting form of the Olessi apprentice slid to the ground, leaking a thick green ichor into the dirt and dust beside the fire. Crackling pops of the greatfire echoed across the meeting place as the moment hung in the air, a reverent silence shared by all.

The crowd dispersed.

His tribe returned to their tents, carrying the weight of what they had witnessed together, a testament to the madness of men and the power of the spirits. Only a few elders remained behind, as did the delegations from the neighboring tribes. Valak'Han of the Olessi came forward first, offering assurances that Ilek'Rahs had acted alone, promising the continued goodwill of his people. The Olessi woman was introduced as Ilek'Rahs's mother; she had faced the night's events stoically, having had the tale from Ka'Vos beforehand, both the accusations and the surety of her son's guilt. Still, Arak'Jur received her with all the dignity and the warmth he could muster. He knew the horror of losing a child.

Corenna had brought the victims' mothers from among the Ranasi. For him they showed a brave face, giving thanks for justice done. For Llanara and Corenna they broke down in tears, weeping for the loss of their boys. Once more he understood their pain. It would not pass easily, no matter the vengeance he'd exacted on their behalf. Arak'Doren met his eye with a look of firm approval, and Ka'Hinari as well. There were prescriptions older than the tribes themselves for dealing with men like Ilek'Rahs, men touched with madness that drove them to the unspeakable. Both Ranasi men affirmed he had done well. From such exchanges the tribes grew closer, a shared reminder of common views even in the face of tragedy. In the morning the Ranasi and Olessi would depart; none of the tribes would wish to linger on the cause of their coming together on this night. But they would come again, all the more tightly bound for what had transpired here.

After the delegations and the elders had departed, he and Llanara were left together by the smoking remains of the fire.

He held out an arm, and she took it.

"You did well tonight," he said.

She smiled, and squeezed his arm. "So did you."

They walked together.

"When you calmed Ilek'Rahs, before he spoke, that was…?" He could not finish the question.

"Yes."

He shivered. The new magic. Of all the youths the fair-skin Reyne d'Agarre had been given leave to train, only Llanara found the gift. The women had treated it as a sign that it belonged to them, and neither he nor Ka'Vos nor any of the other men had been able to pry its secrets free.

"Do you wonder," she said, "whether Ilek'Rahs might have been telling the truth?"

"You think it was the visions the other *Ka* have seen?"

"Who can tell what form they might take? Yes, I think it may be so."

A troubling thought. "Whatever the source, I am glad Ilek'Inari and I were there. It was a near thing."

"A near thing?" Her voice trailed off, then grew hushed, but full of certainty. "You think the Ranasi would have made war."

He nodded. "If they had been the ones to find the boys, who can say?"

"You speak wisdom."

He grunted, acknowledging the praise, and they walked the rest of the way in silence.

Later, after they had washed each other and removed their ceremonial dress, they lay together in his tent. He had not thought to find he had an appetite for pleasures after the events of the greatfire, but in this as in most things Llanara was persuasive. She stoked his passions with the fire of her own, and for a time they forgot themselves in violence and relief.

After he had spent himself she nestled against him, the richness of her black hair spilling across his chest.

"The women think me ready to journey to Ka'Ana'Tyat," she said, regarding him with a pleased smile.

He responded with a soft laugh. "That is women's business, Llanara. Am I supposed to know it?"

"No," she said, eyes alight.

He tightened his grip around her hair, tugging softly, and she bit her lip. He laughed once more, shaking his head. "Are you so determined to seek trouble?"

"Yes." This time she grinned, her hand trailing down his stomach.

He let go of her hair, reaching down to the nape of her neck, drawing her lips to his.

She drank it in, then lowered her head, biting at his skin. "Will it be you who escorts me, Arak'Jur?"

Her hand stirred him once more, and he groaned. "Llanara..."

She bit harder, working her way down his chest, and he expelled a breath.

"No," he said finally. "It is always the guardian of another tribe."

She nodded as if she had expected it all along, continuing lower.

"Be careful, Llanara," he said, wincing with pleasure.

She looked up at him. "I am always careful, Arak'Jur."

Thought fled from him.

After, they curled together and slept.

19

ERRIS

Lorrine River Crossing
Southern Sarresant Territory

She stood beside the banner of the 1st Division—her banner—watching the men of the 9th Infantry stream across the bridge. It was the 2nd Corps' third week at rest, and she'd taken the initiative to redeploy her men for continued training exercises near the sleepy agrarian city of Lorrine. It was a far cry from the bustling streets of New Sarresant or Villecours, but it was the largest settlement in the province that bore its name. Farther south there were only a handful of mining towns, farming hamlets, and the odd fishing village along the coast before civilization gave way to open wilderness. She'd already sought dispensation from the Vicomte de Lorrine to use his town as the focal point of this week's maneuvers. Her men had acquired a good sense of working together in the open; now she wished to drive home the importance of maneuver to defend, or assault, a key objective.

"Tell me, Brigade-Colonel," she said as they rode, "what did you think of how Colonel Chellac used the Ninth when he had command, in the exercises by the sea?"

Brigade-Colonel Savasse eyed her as he replied. "We were judged successful in holding the seaward approach, as you'll recall, sir."

"Yes. Would you have made the same assignment?"

"No. We'd have been better suited to the center lines, in the rocky bluffs overlooking the coast. Brigade-Colonel Chellac's assignment was lucky; Brigade-Colonel Royens attacked with infantry on the seaward side of the line. It could as easily have been cavalry, and we'd have been flanked."

"Did you have scouting reports? Perhaps it wasn't luck."

"We had reports, sir. No sense taking unnecessary risks by assuming the reports are accurate."

She nodded. "A fine point, Brigade-Colonel. Still, if Chellac had used the Ninth to cover the seaward approach, he couldn't have deployed the Sixteenth to protect the artillery on the bluffs."

She went on to explain Chellac's strategy: He'd maneuvered his counterpart, Brigade-Colonel Royens, into committing both units of his cavalry to the center flanks, then placed infantry to ring the artillery batteries in a critical position overlooking the approach to their main body. Savasse was, strictly speaking, correct: The ideal response from Royens would have been to ignore the central position, flanking with cavalry on the seaward approach, threatening to sweep around the hill from behind. But for that to work, Royens would have to have anticipated it and arrayed his forces thusly before he committed to the engagement. Dangerous to assume one could correctly guess the enemy's plan. Far too easy to give the enemy too little credit for brilliance, or too much.

"So, commander," she continued, "what are your thoughts on the upcoming exercise?"

"I've deployed three companies of the Fourteenth Cavalry to scout the plains to the east, where the trade roads converge into Lorrine."

"Only three companies?"

"Yes, sir. I have the fourth company of horse patrolling the river, and skirmishers from the Sixth Infantry setting up sweeps on the hilltops."

She nodded. It was neatly done. She'd expected Savasse to miss the river approach, which of course was the likeliest route of attack for Brigade-Colonel Vassail, though she doubted it would be the first one Vassail would try.

"What of the rest of your—" She stopped mid-sentence.

"Sir?" Savasse asked. She barely heard him.

Golden light.

She'd tried to find it again a dozen times since the battle, if only to prove to herself it had actually happened. Tried and failed. And yet here it was. Far off in the distance, a speck from the south. Pulsing like a star in the night sky, drawing her vision to the horizon. As if something needed her, called to her, pulled her awareness toward it.

Jiri came to a skidding halt, sensing her rider's sudden alert.

A sinking feeling gripped her. Last time she embraced the light, she'd caused the deaths of more than a thousand men. Victory, but death just the same.

"Sir?" Savasse repeated, reining in his own mount as the officers and aides in their column slowed alongside them. "Are you all right?"

"I'm fine, Brigade-Colonel," she replied. "Go on ahead with the rest of the command staff. I will catch up shortly."

"Sir?" he asked again.

"A binder's matter, Brigade-Colonel. Keep the column moving. That's an order."

He frowned, but saluted and spurred his mount forward. The rest of the aides followed at his heels, all save Aide-Lieutenant Sadrelle, who lingered behind.

"Respectfully, sir," Sadrelle said, "are you certain you're all right?"

The light pulled on her again, glimmering in the distance. No time to argue. Feeling it again she recognized it for what it must be: a new leyline energy, one she'd never encountered before. Born of *Need*, or perhaps *Hope*? Neither was a recognized type of binding, but the light seemed to radiate its nature to her, the same way she knew the energies familiar to her: *Body*, *Life*, and *Death*.

She closed her eyes, letting long training with the leylines take over. It was impossible to forge a connection more than a short distance away, yet for some reason she could sense this energy over an incredible distance. She reached out to form a tether, intending caution, surprised when the energy nearly tore itself from her grasp, fighting to snap into place.

Her vision shifted.

She was in a small town. Glancing down, she saw she wore the uniform of a Sarresant cavalry scout, though once again she was in a man's body. Strange. She was standing in a fountain square, surrounded by small buildings with thatched roofs and wood frames.

They were burning.

High-pitched screams came from behind her, and she pivoted to see a stream of barely clad women hurrying through the door into the square.

Whores were a common enough sight following any army, but these were a better breed, the sort to find more permanent employment in pleasure houses such as, she supposed, the one behind her.

She rushed toward one of them, grabbing hold of an arm, eliciting a shocked look and an even shriller cry. "Stop, madame!" she barked in a harsh baritone. "I would know what town this is. Where are we?"

It took a firm shake to get a response. "F-F-Fantain's Cross..." the whore managed before her eyes widened further and she screamed again.

She turned and saw the reason why. Gandsmen. Mounted cavalry in red coats rounding one of the thoroughfares into the main square, carrying torches alongside their sabers. She let the whore go as one of the Gand cavalrymen caught sight of her Sarresant uniform. She reached down to draw her sidearm, and found nothing there. Curse this soldier! He'd slipped away to go whoring in this village, this Fantain's Cross, and not thought to come armed? No matter. She closed her eyes, reaching out for *Body*. Once more, she found nothing. Panic rose in her throat. The Gandsmen had already started riding toward her.

She whirled around and ran.

Their horses ran faster.

She coughed and sputtered as her vision snapped back into focus, sitting atop Jiri in the dust beside the road as the Ninth Infantry marched beside her.

"Sir?" Aide-Lieutenant Sadrelle asked. "What's going on? Are you—?"

"Fantain's Cross," she said, then again. "Fantain's Cross! A village to the south. Muster the division entire. We move with all speed. Cancel the training exercise and send word to Marquis-General Voren that we may be engaged forthwith."

Sadrelle hesitated, uncertainty creasing his face.

"Move!" she bellowed, spurring Jiri into a full run.

They arrived two days later, and two days late.

Fantain's Cross was a blackened ruin, the beams of its wooden shops and houses left half-standing and ashen. Thatched roofs may as well have been tinder. Even the stone chapel had been scored black. The Gandsmen had been thorough; not a building in the small town had escaped the torch. A remarkable display by itself—it was a rare thing, to strike so brazenly at nonmilitary targets. The sort of thing a prudent commander avoided except at absolute necessity. One understood, on a campaign, that one was not always the aggressor. Orders to sack villages and towns would be repaid in force the next time one found themselves on the defending side. But those were the orders the enemy had given here.

It wasn't until they opened the chapel doors that they understood the extent of the barbarity.

The smell had been masked by the fumes and smoke billowing from the other buildings. When the great oak doors of the chapel gave way beneath the axes ordered to clear them, her first thought had been of some kind of twisted cookfire. Then she understood. Men did not smell so very differently from livestock when seared by flame. She'd retched and vomited at the sight and not been ashamed for it. She wasn't alone. The Gand commander had ordered the denizens of Fantain's Cross packed into the church while the fires raged through their homes. Then once all were inside the order had been given to set it ablaze. At first she'd harbored a vain hope that the dead had merely been stored there, some semblance of honor due the fallen. The scratch marks on the inside of the oak doors, on the walls themselves, put the truth to that lie.

"What do you make of it, sir?" asked Sadrelle, trailing behind her as she gave the orders to make this right. It was little enough comfort, dredging what remains they could from the ruin to give these villagers a proper burial. But the horror of it faded before hard labor spent undoing the damage. If her men had been sick at the sight of what lay within the church, they were all firm resolve now.

She looked down, taking a steadying breath before she replied. "Horrible. And meant to incite us, though to what I can't yet say. A dangerous turn for this war."

"You think high command will order response in kind?"

She nodded. "They will."

The gravity of that thought settled around them both, a somber cloak still hanging in the air when a scout from Vassail's 11th Light Cavalry approached on horseback, offering a salute as her mount came to a halt.

"Sir, Brigade-Colonel Vassail sends her compliments, and wishes to inform you she has found the trail of the Gandsmen, heading south-southeast toward the coastline."

"Very good, Horseman. Do we have any report on their composition?"

"We estimate some three mounted cavalry brigades, possibly more, taking the eastern trails."

Her eyes widened in surprise. "No infantry?"

"No, sir, no foot we've been able to discern, though the paths are thin. The brigade-colonel has the Eleventh arrayed in a broad search along the eastern flanks."

"Good. Return to the Eleventh and order them to maintain the search, but keep a clear forward patrol. Poor country for an ambush, but I want warning before any sign of an engagement."

"Yes, sir."

She dismissed the scout, who rode off at a gallop.

She turned to another aide and went on. "Send orders for Lance-Captain d'Guile. I want the Fourteenth Light Cavalry covering the western flank, fanned out for signs of movements there."

Another salute, another rider dispatched.

"You think they're looking to lead our cavalry on a chase?" Sadrelle asked.

"I know I'd have been tempted to give it, if I still commanded the Fourteenth."

He smiled ruefully. Sadrelle knew her temperament well enough. She'd have been off like a freshly scented bloodhound at the first sign of the butchers who had struck here. That it had been cavalry, all cavalry, was a piece clicking into place. The open country south of Lorrine might well be a poor site for an ambush, but if the enemy cavalry could rile them up and provoke a chase, they might be able to lure them into more dangerous ground south of the Gand border. Whatever the enemy's goal with this sickening display, it began with troops that needed to stay mobile, and that pointed toward a trap.

Credit to Vassail that she'd found these monsters' trail and not pursued straightaway. And just as well she hadn't, if the numbers the colonel reported proved to be accurate. Three full-strength brigades of horse? Possibly more? She doubted whether the entire Sarresant army could field eight thousand cavalry, and certainly not in one place, not without leaving the main body blind for having no scouts to patrol ahead, to watch its flanks. What could draw Gand into committing so many of its horse into a single maneuver?

And what kind of Gods-cursed wretches would carry out an order to do *this* to Fantain's Cross?

She shuddered.

She'd heard of atrocities being committed before; every soldier had. She'd seen the so-called exigencies of war firsthand, the product of a few isolated and overzealous men who blurred the line between innocents and enemy combatants. But she'd never seen nigh a division's strength worth of soldiers act in concert for anything approaching what had happened in this village. No survivors, her men reported. Not a single one. No children hiding in some armoire, no families closeted away in an attic. Every living soul, even the bodies of those who must surely have died during the sacking of the city, had been taken to the chapel and put to the torch.

Barbarians. Madmen. With any luck, she'd find them herself. A thought most unbecoming of a general, to be sure, but there it was. She wanted to find these animals and gut them like pigs, showing them their entrails one at a time on the edge of her saber. And the officers saved for last, given ample time to contemplate the orders they'd given as they waited for their turn to meet her blade.

Sadrelle walked with her, saying nothing, Gods bless the man. An appreciation of when to remain silent was a talent worth its weight in gold in aides-de-camp.

They reached the horse lines and she gave her final orders for the day: to see the remainder of the dead buried with dignity, then to form the division in an orderly march along the eastern routes, guided by Vassail's scouting reports. She herself would ride for the marquis-general's command tent to make a personal report and confer with high command. The 1st Division would give pursuit to these attackers, but she needed to place their maneuver within the broader scope of the army's strategy. The attack on Fantain's Cross was no simple raid. There was a more sinister purpose here. She felt the surety of it deep within her bones.

20

SARINE

Sacre-Lin Chapel
Maw District, New Sarresant

Three days had passed since Reyne d'Agarre's fête. She hadn't gone.

The thought of attending a salon, one of the private gatherings of the city's intellectuals and the elite, had an undeniable allure. But even aside his gold coin and the crates of pork and bread d'Agarre had given out to the citizens of the Maw, there was still the matter of how he came by the means for his charity. He was a thief, to say nothing of whatever else he could do with Zi's promptings of *Yellow* and *Green*.

Besides, her wardrobe was entirely unsuitable for the occasion. Imagining herself in coat and breeches beside the ladies in their fashions and finery had tipped the scales in favor of remaining at the Sacre-Lin. And so she hadn't gone, and that was that. It was unlikely a third invitation would be sent when the first two passed unremarked, and besides, she'd already exposed her gifts to the magistrates after the episode on the palace green. Whatever d'Agarre might have threatened her with had lost its teeth. She hadn't expected to see him again.

Which made it all the more surprising when he'd shown up to attend her uncle's sermon that morning.

He shone like a beacon in the fourth pew of the church, the buttons on his red coat reflecting the sun streaming through the chapel's stained-glass relief. She could scarce imagine a man less suited to his present company, sitting amid the wretches and wayward souls gathered to hear her uncle preach.

When d'Agarre arrived her uncle had spared only a glance before continuing on with the day's lesson. The congregation always enjoyed hearing this section of the holy books: the Grand Betrayal of the Nameless, who had once been the companion of the other Trithetic Gods before he betrayed their trust and became instead their immortal enemy. Today the focus was on the Exarch, foremost of the Gods, and his decision to allow the followers of the Nameless to rejoin his fold after their onetime master's treachery was revealed. It was a sweet story, amid the battles and the carnage of the Grand Betrayal; the violence drew in the crowd, but her uncle weaved in the true lesson—on the virtue of mercy—with a master's touch.

She watched from her loft, a knot growing in her stomach as d'Agarre took in the sermon, seemingly oblivious to her presence. Every word her uncle spoke brought them nearer to the moment when that façade would shatter. And finally, with a sweeping gesture and an admonishment to remember the virtues of which he had spoken, her uncle's service was done. The crowd seemed to pay d'Agarre no mind, shuffling out in their usual way, finding it within themselves to place the odd coin into the collection box as they passed through the chapel doors on their way to the street.

He is skilled, Zi thought to her.

She wrinkled her brow and gave Zi a look.

"You preach the Betrayal well, Father," Reyne d'Agarre said, still seated as the last member of the congregation left the chapel.

Her uncle bowed his head at the compliment. "To what does the Sacre-Lin owe the pleasure of your attendance, my lord?"

"I'm no lord, Father. Only a councilman." He stood to offer a bow. "The name is Reyne d'Agarre. I had a pair of letters delivered here and thought to inquire after their receipt."

"Passing odd, for you to come in person, Master d'Agarre. This district has no love for wealth."

D'Agarre laughed. "Nor I, Father, I assure you, though I know well the good that can come of prudence and effort well spent." Pausing, d'Agarre glanced up toward her loft, and their eyes met as she peered over the divide. "Sarine. Is there aught I can say to convince you to join me for the afternoon?"

"Sarine is needed—" her uncle began.

"Why?" she cut in, rising to her feet and looking down into the nave below. "Why me, Master d'Agarre? You've sent three invitations now, if I'm to assume you intend to deliver another today."

He nodded, withdrawing another folded letter from his coat and dangling it over the side of a pew.

"You saw what I did, in the Harbor, and the Maw," d'Agarre said. "And you must have heard news of my activities since."

"You're a thief," she said.

"I support a cause great enough to excuse petty thievery," he snapped back, his voice suddenly hot. "Come, walk with me, and you may understand the reason why."

"She'll have no part in it," her uncle interjected. "Best if you leave at once."

"No, uncle," she said. "I'll hear him out."

"Sarine—" her uncle said, looking up at her with a worried expression.

She understood his concern; Father Thibeaux had kept her safe from half a hundred perils that she knew, and surely another hundred she'd never seen: hunger, cold, priests, and press-gangs. It was poor repayment to court the attentions of a man who made a habit of confronting the city watch. But more than curiosity had burned in her since the Harbor. She'd sketched the beauty of the nobles' world scores of times, been drawn in by the possibilities of her meeting with Lord Revellion. In spite of their allure, she knew in her gut the injustice of it, of their lives of plenty when so many had so little. And until the Harbor, she'd never seen a man or woman dare to stand so boldly against what she knew was wrong.

"It's fine, uncle," she said, taking the ladder down from her loft. "If he meant ill, he wouldn't have come here alone."

D'Agarre bowed, extending a hand for hers when he arose. "My assurances, Father. I know well the dangers of this city. We will be safe."

Her uncle nodded warily, and d'Agarre gestured for her to lead the way through the chapel doors. She did. On their way out, d'Agarre paused a moment to take a pouch from inside his coat, setting it atop the collection box. Then they emerged together into the New Sarresant sun.

"Sarine." D'Agarre repeated her name with the same intensity he'd used before. "I hoped you might accept my invitations. I was disappointed by your absence."

She eyed him as they walked. He stepped lightly through the streets of the Maw, seeming unburdened, without concern at displaying wealth so openly in a district full of thieves. Evidently his charity had earned him a degree of familiarity among the city's worst sort. A dubious honor, though not without merit, given her uncle's efforts to do the same.

"I never mentioned the Sacre-Lin when we spoke in the market. Did you have me followed?"

He paused mid-stride, turning to give her a surprised look. "Gods no. What sort of man do you believe me to be?"

"The dangerous sort," she replied without thinking.

He feigned a wounded look before breaking into a grin. "The truth is you had half again as many drawings of the Sacre-Lin chapel as anything else on display in the market. A few inquiries among the priests as to the source of those stained-glass reliefs and I gambled it was likely the best place to find you."

"I see." Damn but that was obvious. She'd been a fool to display it so plainly. What if the city watch had made the same connection after prying into her drawings of the nobles?

"As to danger," d'Agarre continued, "from what I hear you are no small threat to public safety yourself."

Heat crept into her cheeks. He laughed.

"Nothing to be ashamed of. I had the truth of it from men who were there at Rasailles. They say you were something to behold."

She said nothing. It was still too close to a raw nerve. By instinct she hid her hands in the pockets of her coat, concealing the scarred flesh that marked her for what she was.

"No." D'Agarre stopped to lay a hand on her arm. "Don't hide it."

She looked away.

"Sarine, you have a gift far beyond their understanding. I had wondered if it was possible. In all the long years, in all the records we've kept, there has never been a single incidence of binding among our number. Binding is a rare talent, of course, but for us to have gone so long without one, it began to seem as if one gift precluded the other."

She frowned. What was he talking about? Binding was rare, yes, but even among the commonfolk there were enough freebinders, marked and unmarked, to hire if one had need of their services, and d'Agarre had proven he had no shortage of coin.

D'Agarre faced her before she could put words to the thought. "You are not alone in your gift."

"I know. My uncle taught me about bindings when I was—"

"No, Sarine. Your other gift."

On the grass beside the road a four-legged crystalline serpent appeared, scales flushed a deep green. It cocked its head at her, then bowed, folding itself in half at the neck as she had seen Zi do, countless times before.

She gasped.

"Mine is called Saruk. Have you learned the name of yours?"

"Zi," she whispered, trembling. "He never told me he could appear to others."

It was never needful.

D'Agarre nodded. "The *kaas* can be difficult, at times."

"The *kaas*?"

"Yes. Have you not read the book?"

She gave him a confused look.

"The Codex? Those of us with the gift can read its pages, and before long the *kaas* appear to forge their bond."

"I've never heard of a 'codex.' And who is 'we'? How many are there?"

D'Agarre frowned. "A handful here in New Sarresant. More elsewhere. Are you certain you've never read the book? It is the essence of the link between us and the *kaas*. Might you have lost it, as a child perhaps?"

"I was an orphan, on the streets of the Maw."

"That may explain it then. I shall have to have another copy made."

"How did you know? About Zi?"

"In the Maw, when we were attacked by the watch. You used *Red*."

So that's what Zi had meant with his cryptic colors. He'd never explained what he could do; it wasn't like her bindings, or the strange lure of the cat spirit. Zi just did what was needed, when it was needful.

She shivered, and her breath came quickly. D'Agarre noticed.

"It is all a bit overwhelming, I know."

She nodded, staring off into the distance, toward the district boundaries and the Riverways. Whatever she'd expected from a sojourn with Reyne d'Agarre, it had not been this.

"And you are a binder as well," he went on. "You are gifted beyond the dreams of the fools that call themselves noble. They play at power, but you have the truth of it. Real power, the chance to reshape the world according to your desires."

"Is that what you were doing in the Harbor, Master d'Agarre?"

She'd meant it as a flippant challenge, a distraction from the fever-dream come to life swimming inside her head. But he seemed to take it deadly serious.

"Yes, Sarine. That is precisely what I was doing in the Harbor."

She felt a chill.

"Come to my next salon. You will see. This city is rotten to its core."

"I—" she began.

"I know," he said. "I know you will have doubts. Let me persuade you. Let me—"

"I have nothing to wear," she said in a rush.

He blinked, then let out a laugh.

"An easily solvable problem," he said with a grin, tapping another coin purse on his belt.

21

ERRIS

2nd Corps Command Tents
Southern Sarresant Territory

The sun had set long before her entourage arrived at the command tents. Jiri and the rest of their mounts were seen to with expert care—she'd been impressed enough to compliment the marquis-general's handlers—and space had been found for her aides at the camp. They guided her to the general's tent straightaway.

Already a pleasant change from Vicomte-General Carailles. She'd met Marquis-General Voren only once, on the day she was promoted, and that had been all formal airs and solemn ceremony. Another officer in her shoes might have spent the idle weeks after Villecours licking their new commander's boots. Probably foolish on her part to have started field training right away, but she was who she was. If Voren thought ill of her for that, well, she had dealt with worse.

She stepped inside the tent and saluted.

Two men stood beside a long table strewn with maps. Vicomte-General Dulliers, commander of the 3rd Division, and Marquis-General Voren himself. Dulliers she'd met before, though she knew him better by reputation: a barely competent commander who had advanced more by looking the part than from any exceptional achievement. Voren was new to the colonies, having arrived on the *Queen Allisée* during the spring tides. He wore gold-wired spectacles, with gray hair at his temples, weathered skin, and a well-kept officer's uniform.

"Ah, there she is," Voren said, saluting in response. "The prodigal general comes before me at last. I was beginning to wonder when you'd make an appearance."

She stiffened, remaining at attention.

"At ease, Chevalier-General. I knew what I was getting when I asked for you to be given command of the First."

That was news. She hadn't been aware the marquis-general had been behind her promotion. "Sir. My men have been conducting training exercises along the coast these past weeks."

"Yes, I've read your reports. Thorough. And the last report. Fantain's Cross. The vicomte-general and I were just discussing what to make of it. Join us. We'd hear your account directly, if you will."

She gave it, omitting none of the grisly details. Voren listened intently, interrupting her only to ask for clarification on a handful of minor points. She managed to keep her emotions in check during the telling, though Vicomte-General Dulliers muttered a few curses to punctuate the worst of it. She concluded with her appraisal of the situation.

"So many enemy cavalry operating in the south suggests the main body of their army should be nearby, massing near the border, sir."

Voren nodded, massaging his chin as he studied the map. "Have your scouts reported contact with the enemy horse?"

"No, sir, only the trail, though I have my men deployed in a wide arc with orders not to pursue sightings of the enemy."

"A curious order," he said. "Explain your reasoning?"

"Sir, whenever the enemy moves so brazenly I suspect a trap. And I want discipline in the ranks. The men were riled up after Fantain's Cross. I'd as soon not have my scouts stumble into an ambush."

Voren gave her a considering look, then went back to studying the map. "What would you have ordered in that situation, Vicomte-General Dulliers?" he asked absently.

"Sir," the other man coughed. "I would have sent one brigade of light cavalry in pursuit of the enemy, with orders to follow the enemy horse back to their main body. And I would have kept one cavalry brigade near my division, to warn us if the enemy had moved around to flank us."

Stupid. The enemy wouldn't set off a beacon to grab their attention and then go riding home. Dulliers's tactic would succeed in little more than giving the enemy what he wanted: a unit of dead Sarresant cavalry.

The marquis-general pursed his lips as he stared at the map. "Very good, Vicomte-General. Do you have any further questions for Chevalier-General d'Arrent?" When the other man shook his head no, he continued. "Dismissed then. I would debrief her before I sleep."

"Yes, sir." The vicomte-general saluted once more as he departed, leaving her alone with their commander.

"He's a fool, isn't he?" the older man said with a sigh. Removing his spectacles, he placed them on the table with one hand and pressed the other to the bridge of his nose.

"Sir, Vicomte-General Dulliers has a reputation for steady, even-tempered command."

Voren tsked. "Not what I asked, Chevalier-General."

"Yes, sir, he's a fool."

Voren nodded as if the matter was settled, beckoning to her to approach the table. A series of ever-more-detailed maps lay atop it, showing the length of the border, from the coastline in the east to the Great Barrier in the west. The marquis-general had made fresh notes on one of the maps, a well-illustrated visual of the flatlands between Lorrine and the Gand border, where the bulk of her division was presently deployed.

"I wonder if you'd update me on your last-known positions, General d'Arrent," he said, gesturing.

She gave him the latest information she'd had before riding for the 2nd Corps' camp, and he went over the disposition of the remainder of his corps, and the rest of the army. They were en route to the south, casting a wide net over the trade roads as the soldiers marched.

"What troubles you, General?" Voren asked when he'd finished.

"I'm concerned we are spread out, in vulnerable positions here, and here." She pointed to the army's 1st Corps, strung out along the road from Villecours to Lorrine, then to the infantry and logistics wagons of the 2nd Corps' other two divisions, unprotected on the western flank. "We're at least three days' march from being able to deploy for battle, while the enemy is massed close enough to field his full complement of cavalry in a raid across our border."

He nodded, following her reasoning. "Your predecessor, the late Vicomte-General Carailles, left extensive notes on your command. He said you were insubordinate, with no respect for regulation, frequently attempting to assert authority above your station."

Just like so, a part of her guilt over Carailles's death dislodged and floated away like flotsam down a river. She said nothing in reply.

"Carailles was as blind as he was stupid," Voren said. "He failed to see your quality, or if he saw it he was afraid you'd shame him somehow. Small men are ever wary of excellence."

He let the sentiment linger in the air, and she felt a rush of pride. Flattering words, meant to evoke just such a reaction, and she knew it, but they were no less sweet to hear.

"I need to have your trust, General d'Arrent. Carailles was not deserving of it. I am. In time we will accomplish much, working together. For now, I ask for your faith."

She couldn't imagine the likes of Vicomte-General Carailles beseeching her trust so openly. In the army, one's superior simply *was*. A force of nature, like an early morning fog or a thunderstorm on watch duty, and often just as inconvenient. Could she trust the lives of her men to this man?

"Sir, I look forward to serving under your command."

He laughed softly. "Very well. I see your trust will be earned. So be it. Here, you can see the route I intend the rest of the corps to take southward, covering the west behind your division's advance scouts. I take it you assumed their raid on Fantain's Cross could be cover for a movement around our western flank?"

She nodded. "Yes, sir. I have my best, the Fourteenth Light Cavalry, scouting the approaches over the flatlands."

"Very good. The Fourteenth. That was your former command, yes?"

"Yes, sir."

"Then you know their quality. A word of caution, though: You mustn't fixate on a past command. The other brigade commanders will resent it, and you must be sure you are willing to risk them the same as any others."

Obviously. "Yes, sir."

"Be careful the pendulum does not swing too far in the other direction, too, General. It was a mistake I made in my youth, overusing an infantry regiment after I was promoted, to avoid showing favoritism. If I judge your leadership aright, your men would die for you. See to it they don't."

It was a struggle not to drop her jaw, hearing sense from a commanding officer.

"Yes, sir."

"Good. Let's see if we can't set a trap for these enemy cavalry. Never a more satisfying maneuver than when you can best an enemy commander at his own game."

She grinned. Together they pored over maps until the sun broke the horizon, and the rest of the camp stirred to begin the day.

She tethered *Body* to help invigorate her—and felt a pang of regret that Marquis-General Voren had no such respite from their all-night planning—as she strode forward into the training yard. A few whispers circulated among the onlookers, which she made a point of ignoring. She wasn't here for a morning warm-up, much as she might have enjoyed the exercise.

"Laurent!" she called, using her battle voice, the deep boom trained to carry over the din of fighting.

One of the two soldiers in the ring hesitated, dropping his guard for a fraction of a second. The wooden practice blade of the other soldier cracked as it struck Laurent's shoulder, causing his blade to fall and clatter into the dirt.

"Yield, yield!" Laurent stammered as he fell back, gripping his shoulder.

His opponent, who could only be Lance-Lieutenant Acherre, removed her face guard to confirm the same. Bowing with a flourish that extended her wooden blade toward the sky at an angle, Acherre's face lit up when she rose and saw her watching their duel.

"Thank you for the victory, Chevalier-General," Acherre said. "He was starting to get full of himself."

Erris laughed. "Is that so, Laurent? Well, for you Acherre has the restraint to keep from using *Mind* in practice bouts."

Wincing, the man regarded them both with a mock scowl. "I had her in another step."

She cocked an eyebrow at Acherre, who mimed "no" as she shook her head. They laughed again, together.

"Here to join in, sir?" Acherre asked as she stooped down to fetch Laurent's practice sword.

"I'm afraid not, Lance-Lieutenant." She gestured for Acherre to toss her Laurent's sword, which she did. "Still using the old broadsword-weighted blades, hm, Laurent? When are we going to get you a proper saber?"

"Bah," Laurent said. He snatched the sword from the air as she tossed it, whipping it around in a few practice swings. "You know I prefer the added weight. Some of us are strong enough to make use of it."

"We'll change his mind eventually, sir," Acherre said brightly.

"You didn't come all the way here to harangue me, did you, Chevalier-General? Begging your pardon, sir."

"Quite all right, Major. I'm not here to practice, but I *am* here for you, the pair of you. And Marquand. Where is the captain?"

"Sleeping it off again, sir, I'd expect," Laurent said.

She sighed. Of course. "You two finish your bout and stay at the training grounds. I'll be back to collect you after I've awoken Marquand."

"Yes, sir," they said in unison, turning back toward each other, raising face guards and falling into their fighting stances.

She left the training area, heading toward the tents of the 5th Infantry just as Acherre and Laurent began their dance. There was an unmistakable beauty when *Body* fullbinders crossed swords, even in practice. Rosline Acherre was ten years her junior, with a promising career ahead of her. Erris had offered what guidance she could, and the girl was a quick study. The same could be said of Laurent, or more properly Regiment-Major Remy Laurent. Laurent had great skill with *Body* and *Death*, enough to render him among the best swords in the army. Acherre had *Body* as well, and *Mind*, making her a terror unto herself when unleashed on enemy lines.

Foot-Captain Marquand, the third of the fullbinders assigned to the 3rd Division, had *Life, Death,* and the new *Entropy* bindings, placing him in the elite company of fullbinders, like Erris herself, who could handle three types of leyline energy. He also possessed an equally rare talent for drinking enough wine in a day to drown a regiment of cavalry, with enough to see to their horses after the men had had their fill.

She found him precisely where Regiment-Major Laurent said she might, a loud snore emanating from his tent while the rest of the camp flowed around him. The aides and soldiers of the 5th seemed to be making a point of averting their eyes from the sound, and she could guess why. Closing her eyes, her vision shifted and she found the inky clouds of *Death* pooled beneath a nearby medic's tent. She felt the familiar pang of nausea as she held a binding at the ready. It was always easier on the stomach to bind *Death* in the open, or better, near the enemy's camp, where there were fewer immediate reminders of what it represented. She kept her tether at the ready, reaching for a nearby bucket of water as she pushed aside the flaps of the foot-captain's tent.

"ORACLE'S TITS!" Marquand roared, leaping up from his now-drenched bedroll. In the space of a heartbeat, she bound *Death* through the *Entropy* binding she felt spring up around him, dissipating it into harmless wisps of vapor. Not a moment too soon. *Entropy*'s discovery had been hailed as a breakthrough by all save those who'd first found it; the binding was as unstable as the decay and chaos that caused it to accrue on the leylines. And when tethered, it caused whatever it touched to burst into flame.

"Good morning, Foot-Captain. I believe the expression you're looking for is 'Oracle's tits, *sir*.'"

Marquand sputtered and wiped his eyes, squinting under the glare of the light streaming through the tent flaps.

"Mmhh," he groaned. "Good to see you, Brigade-Colonel."

"It's 'Chevalier-General' now," she corrected, giving him a glare sharp enough to make him think twice about collapsing back onto his cot. That he'd thought about it once was beyond doubt. He eyed the still-dripping blankets longingly as he yawned, stretched, and settled on his feet.

"To what do I owe the pleasure, Chevalier-General d'Arrent?"

"Reassignment. Gather your things and head to the training yard on the double."

He muttered something that sounded like "Sir, yes, sir."

"On the double, Foot-Captain. The next bucket will be filled with leavings from the horses."

She let the tent flaps fall shut, stifling a private laugh. Few pleasures were reserved to those who abstained from drink while in the field, and this was the sweetest.

She'd almost made her way back to the yard when a commotion headed toward her, no mistaking its source. She sighed, turned, and saluted.

"Vicomte-General Dulliers, a pleasure to see you again so soon."

He returned her salute. "What is the meaning of this, d'Arrent?" He held aloft a crumpled piece of parchment.

"If you mislike the marquis-general's orders, I suggest you take it up with him."

"Gods damn you and Voren both for thieves and poachers. You'd cripple my division taking my fullbinders, and you know it damned well."

"Temporary reassignment, Vicomte-General. My men are already deployed along the front lines. Your brigades are days behind. Read the orders, I'm sure Marquis-General Voren has it all detailed for you."

"The Duc-General will hear of this absurdity."

"Yes, I'm sure he will."

He glared at her, then flung the parchment to the dirt as he wheeled around, making an exit worthy of a mummer on a stage. She watched him go, pitying the poor aide who would have to retrieve the orders from the mud.

Knowing firsthand the devastating effect a fullbinder could have on a battlefield, she could almost empathize with the vicomte-general's loss, however temporary. She'd have done worse than complain to the army's commander had she received such an order. The difference was she knew better than any of the other division commanders what to do with the likes of Laurent, Acherre, and Marquand. Gods bless Marquis-General Voren for seeing it. Together they'd devised a plan that would crush the enemy cavalry in one swift stroke, leaving the Gandsmen blind for the upcoming campaign. The Gandsmen had been fools, gathering so many horse for a single reckless maneuver. She still burned with hate remembering Fantain's Cross, but she could think of no better way to see justice done than breaking the enemy with the collected strength of every fullbinder in the 2nd Corps.

Smiling, she made her way back to the yard to collect her newest soldiers, already formulating joint tactics they'd put to good use in the weeks ahead.

22

ARAK'JUR

The Guardian's Tent
Sinari Village

The summons came by way of a young boy, just after daybreak. Once it would have been carried by Ilek'Inari, when the *Ilek* in his name was tied to the shaman's path rather than the guardian's. Arak'Jur had been planning to leave just after midday on another excursion into the wilds, making Ka'Vos's summons well timed, though he'd come to expect such things over a lifetime of dealing with the shamans. Whatever unease he'd felt over events of late, he knew well the power they held. If he mistrusted Ka'Vos's visions it was not because he doubted their power. It was because he feared it.

Hurriedly he dressed himself and left to answer the summons. Llanara had awoken along with the sun, regarding him in silence during his exchange with the shaman's messenger and his subsequent preparations. They exchanged fond looks before he departed, but he could not shake the feeling of late that she had some secret thought, some plan left unspoken. He supposed she would find the words in time. Llanara was wise enough; she would consult him when the time was right. Like as not it regarded her bold assertion that the women would find her ready for Ka'Ana'Tyat, a claim that had yet to bear fruit. Though it was possible that was the subject of today's summons.

He crossed the village quietly. Many tents had stirred awake before sunrise. There was much to do during the hot season: preparing food, harvesting grain and maize, curing hides, storing fish and meat. And mixed in with the oldest traditions, some would spend their days repairing iron cookware, cleaning firearms, sharpening steel, tending to horses, or doing something else that had been unknown to his people generations before. His own purpose had been a novelty, once—when the first guardian met with the first shaman to follow the guidance of the spirits of things-to-come. A reminder that change was not always to be feared, though it rang hollow as he walked, exchanging greetings with men and women along the path.

Ilek'Inari arrived at the shaman's tent moments after he did, the first time summons had been extended to both men at once.

A great beast then, of a surety.

Stepping together inside the tent confirmed it. Ka'Vos had stopped the ceiling of his tent while the fire burned within, filling it with ritual smoke. Ilek'Inari doubtless knew all of the secrets, the making of the powders and reagents that turned the smoke from one shifting color to the next, bringing life to wispy forms rendered above the fire. For Arak'Jur it was still magic, an old and potent form.

Ka'Vos wore his shaman's regalia, thick hides and ghost-white designs on his face and arms. No sooner had the entrance of the tent closed behind them than the shaman dusted a powder over the fire, evoking a resonant *boom* that brought both guardians to their knees in reverence.

"They come," Ka'Vos said, and let it linger while the smoke belched once, then again from the fire. First gray, then blue, the color of twilight.

"They come!" he said again, and pointed.

The form of a dog took shape in the smoke.

Ilek'Inari glanced between him and Ka'Vos's display. Arak'Jur shook his head. This was no form he recognized. Another new great beast, in a time when such revelations grew ever more common.

"Do you fear, guardians?" the shaman hissed, his voice channeling the countenance of whatever spirit spoke to them now. Ka'Vos reached within his garb and withdrew another handful of powder, tossing it into the fire. Red streams bloomed above the flames, and the dog's form twisted, writhed...

And split. Two dogs. Then four.

"You see what fear brings?" Ka'Vos's voice seemed to echo through the tent.

"Great spirits," Arak'Jur said, eyes still fixated on the dancing wisps making patterns in the air. "They feed on fear, like the *munat'ap*?"

"Fear is the least precious of their meals. See what violence brings!" Another powder, this time a deep black that seemed to contort the air around each figure.

The dog shapes split again. Eight. Sixteen. Again. Numbers beyond counting.

This time Ilek'Inari spoke. "If we cannot do them harm, great spirits, how can we protect our people?"

"Starve them, guardian."

A third powder, this time a chalky white. The dog shapes dissolved, one by one, until only a single shape remained.

Arak'Jur nodded, though Ilek'Inari still bore a look of confusion.

"What is its name, Great Spirit?" Arak'Jur asked.

Ka'Vos turned to him, his gaze still filmed over and milk-white. "They are *urus*."

The remainder of the ritual passed quickly once the name had been given, leaving them to sort out its meaning. Of the location they were certain, unexpected though it was. They would find the *urus* to the west, beyond the boundaries of Sinari land. It was not unheard-of for guardians to be called to the lands of their neighbors; some beasts required more strength than could be offered by a single tribe. Evidently this was one such.

Other shapes and faces had shown themselves during the visions, and on this point they were less certain. He saw Arak'Doren, signifying the Ranasi would respond, or at least that they would have received the same prompting through their shaman. The others he did not recognize through the haze, though they were many. He had never heard of a hunt requiring so many guardians—dozens at least if Ka'Vos's vision held true. Most of the forms were blurred as if etched in sand, fading away before any could solidify into faces he knew. In the end they resolved to trust the spirits' guidance. The Sinari endured as a people by responding to their call, safe in the knowledge that their protectors would guide them no matter the gravity of the threats on the horizon. If the *urus* were new and frightening, so be it. They had faced such before, and would again.

Preparations were made, and they set out before the sun reached its apex. It was the nature of the guardians to travel lightly. The tribe's hunters might live from the bounty of the land on a long hunt, and the women, too, gathering such fruits and herbs as could be found to sustain them. But none were truly at home in the wild, none save the guardians. Well, he was. Ilek'Inari would come to be, in time.

He took the opportunity to teach Ilek'Inari as they traveled, days spent learning the hills and forests of their land. Most men of the Sinari would have the skills of a hunter long since ingrained in their bones. To set a snare, to stalk and remain unseen, to survive exposed in the heat of the sun. In some ways, the hunter's craft mirrored the guardian's, and there he felt Ilek'Inari's shortcomings. But it was not so in all things, and surprisingly often he found his apprentice's naïveté refreshing.

Of Ilek'Inari's lingering bonds to the spirits of things-to-come, he was less pleased.

In his mind, Ilek'Inari had become a guardian when he killed the *una're*, and that should be the end of it. He misliked the nature of Ilek'Inari's renewed apprenticeship as surely as Ka'Vos did, and for that matter as surely as Ilek'Inari himself. It was not done, for a man to draw on the beast spirits as he listened to the spirits of things-to-come. A prohibition as old as the tribes themselves, which meant it had to have come from the spirits, in ancient days, when the first tribesmen ventured into the wild. The *why* of it had always been clear, to him, or clear enough to keep him from questioning further than he should. Men given power sought more of the same; it was the truth nested within the shamans' stories, enough to make him wary of it in any form.

Yet try as he might, Ilek'Inari claimed the bond of the *Ka* was not set aside so easily. Once formed, the bond with a single spirit would not dissipate, and if the compact had not been fully sealed, still it would not be broken. Arak'Jur might disapprove, and did, but even he could not set aside what was plain and clear: Ilek'Inari had been chosen as his apprentice and what would be, would be.

On the fifth day they arrived at the gathering place.

As was typical with tellings of the spirits, they knew they had come to the foreordained place the moment they arrived. Some echo of the smoke-shapes within Ka'Vos's tent had settled into their bones, and this place was imprinted in their minds. A field of wild grass between two hills with three boulders at its center. He had not come this way before, or if he had it had escaped his memory, but he would more readily believe the spirits had prepared it for the gathering to come. It was often so that the wilds would change at the spirits' whim. A guardian learned not to be troubled by unfamiliar ground.

They were the first to arrive, and so they waited. For who and how many, neither of them could say, though he assured his apprentice they would know when, and where to go, when the time was right.

Arak'Doren arrived next, and they exchanged stories of the latest goings-on of their tribes. Arak'Doren too had never encountered or heard tell of the *urus,* though Ka'Hinari and Ka'Vos were of a mind on how to handle the creatures. Arak'Var of the Olessi and his apprentice, Ilek'Uhrai, arrived next, followed by the guardians of the Vhurasi and the Ganherat from the south. All agreed their shamans had seen visions of many, many guardians together, more than they could recall in their lifetimes. And none of them had encountered *urus* before. They'd each been given the warning against fear—that such emotions were enticing to the beasts—but even so, a haze of dread threatened to settle around the camp as they waited. There would be dozens of guardians, the visions said. How long would it take for so many to make the journey from distant lands? And worse: What manner of beast required such strength arrayed against it?

On the morning of the third day it became clear. No more guardians would come, and they would wait no longer. *Urus* had arrived.

Arak'Doren spotted it first, giving the prearranged signal. A white dog padded into view at the edge of the field, coming to a stop and cocking its head as it regarded the stirrings of the camp. No tents to strike, nor much in the way of cookfires or supplies to pack; such things were not the way of the guardians. Only nine men roused from sleep, spread into a half circle surrounding the great beast as it watched.

Even from far away it was clear the creature's eyes were wrong. Not in the way of the *mareh'et,* where fires burned in empty sockets, or *anahret,* whose eyes spilled shadows like clouds of ash. *Urus*'s eyes were a pale blue one could find on any manner of wolf or dog, but its focused stare struck fear into one's bones. It swiveled its gaze between the assembled guardians, as if it watched, waiting for a sign to move.

When it was Arak'Jur's turn, he slowed his breathing and emptied his thoughts. No fear, or thought of violence. It seemed to work. The moment stretched thin, and almost he felt the creeping tendrils of fear at the edge of his vision. Almost. Then it was done, and the beast was on to the next man.

Seven were weighed before one was found wanting.

It was Ilek'Uhrai, the Olessi guardian's apprentice. Without warning, the beast's fur shifted from white to red, as if blood spilled onto its back, and where there had been a single dog, in the blink of an eye there were two.

"Still yourself," Arak'Var said in a calm, collected voice. Silence hung in the air and all could hear the master's instructions to his apprentice.

The pair of red *urus* started toward Ilek'Uhrai. The young man froze, darting rapid glances between the slavering forms of the great dogs and the stoic calm of his master. In an eyeblink, a third dog appeared next to the first two, and their fur grew darker, a richer shade of crimson.

"Apprentice, you must calm your fears," Arak'Var said again, managing to keep all tension from his voice.

Ilek'Uhrai closed his eyes, but his breath came quick, and the beasts crept onward.

A heartbeat later, the young man's eyes snapped open. "No!" Ilek'Uhrai cried, surging toward the encroaching *urus*, a pale nimbus of feather and claw surrounding him. The dogs' eyes seemed to brighten at the sight, and they rushed forward to meet him.

"Look away," Arak'Doren called to the rest of them in a steady voice. "Stay calm. And look away."

Arak'Jur closed his eyes and listened. A sickening crunch, a high-pitched war cry, and the sound of flesh ripping. Snaps of teeth and low growls. A *thump* as a body slammed into the dirt. Then another. More. A rush of wind, and a second war cry joined the first. He kept his eyes shut, his breath steady. More cries, and *thumps*. Then screams. And finally, silence.

A long moment passed before he opened his eyes.

No fewer than ten dogs, each black as jet, regarded him with their unblinking stare. He saw twice that number of dogs slain, bodies mangled and spewing blood into the long grass. The remaining *urus* affected not to notice their fallen, only pawed about turning their curious stares on the remaining men.

Mixed in with the bodies of the slain *urus* were the corpses of Ilek'Uhrai and Arak'Var. Master and apprentice, leaving the Olessi tribe without the protection of a guardian. An unspeakable tragedy for their shaman not to have foreseen it in time for another apprentice to be chosen and trained. A sign of the spirits' disfavor. A curse. No time to dwell on such matters now. Keeping his breath still, his mind empty, he moved from where he stood, a slow walk toward the *urus* pack. The initial contact had gone poorly, but that was no reason to deviate from the remainder of their plan.

"I approach without harm," he called, once he was certain the beasts would not attack. A wave of relief spread across the field, and the dogs' jet-black color seemed to wane, drained through the tips of their fur. Still the *urus* darted their eyes between the men, the weight of their gaze keeping check on any feelings of safety.

He pressed on, until he reached them.

Arak'Doren had tried to volunteer for this step in their plan, but the rest of the guardians would not allow it. The Ranasi had no apprentice guardian, and if this did not work, the man who tried it would be killed.

Arak'Jur walked through the pack. To his left and right the once-black dogs looked up at him with heads tilted. If they expected fear he made certain they didn't find it. When he emerged on the other side, toward the edge of the field, the dogs seemed to lose interest in him, turning their attention toward the rest of the men.

"Come," he said, and the rest of the guardians repeated what he had done, making their way through the tall grass, avoiding the corpses and any stray thoughts about how they came to be there.

All seven passed through without incident.

When the last guardian emerged on the far side of the pack, the dogs turned away and padded toward the far end of the field. Other men might have celebrated a victory to have escaped the beasts. But the *urus* treaded toward their tribes' lands. Not for the guardians the simple pleasures of survival. Arak'Jur gave the sign, and the rest of their number ran to the south and west. Only he remained behind, watching the *urus* make their way toward the wood at the edge of the grass.

He waited until the beasts had nearly disappeared from sight, and then he let fear take him.

He thought of the *urus*' slavering jaws, the unearthly way their fur reflected the emotions of men. He thought of the Olessi, how with their guardians slain they would stand defenseless against the wild. He thought of his first hunt as a boy, and the terror he'd felt when he faced a predator for the first time. He thought of Ka'Vos and his mysterious silence, the weight that settled over their people under the threat of the spirits' curse. He thought of Llanara. He thought of his slain wife, Rhealla, and their beautiful boy, Kar'Elek, the horrible sight of their bodies broken and twisted by the bite of the *valak'ar*.

As one, the *urus* halted their slow procession and turned to face him. Under their gaze his fear deepened, and he allowed it to bloom unchecked. The beasts' eyes grew wide, and their fur, which had faded to a soft gray, almost white, began to darken into a deep shade of red. They broke into a trot toward him, then a loping gait. Faster. Tongues lolled from their mouths as they swept across the field, betokening the hunger his fear had promised to sate.

He turned and ran. The *lakiri'in* gave him speed unknown to other beasts, and when it faded, *mareh'et* granted another surge of power. Still the *urus* came, relentless.

They were almost on him when he dropped to his knees and cleared his mind, calling on the spirit of *anahret* for a visage of perfect death. His fear vanished, and the *urus* came to a stuttering halt behind him. Once more their unnatural eyes searched, as if asking where the fear had gone. They paced about him where he lay, and the crimson color in their fur began to fade.

When they flushed red again, his heart surged, threatening to spark his emotion anew. He kept still. This was the plan. Once more the beasts fixed their gaze on the source of the fear, and they ran. In the distance, the Vhurasi guardian gave them fresh scent. They would follow.

So it went, onward to the south, to the west. Away from the tribes' lands. One after another, allowing fear to take hold, luring them forward, then shedding it at the last moment, in time for the next man to continue the chase. As they ran he came to understand the meaning of Ka'Vos's vision, and the others, who had seen guardians beyond counting fight to drive the beasts from their land: The *urus* would not be slain, but through the collective efforts of the guardians of every tribe, they could be diverted.

They ran for days, emboldened by the spirits, resting when they could and letting the beasts wander when they must. It was difficult work, far beyond the exertions required by most great beasts. Yet they endured. Ilek'Inari in particular seemed well suited to the task, with a deeper understanding of emotion than those who had not had a shaman's training. Arak'Jur swelled with pride to see it: a reminder that not all of a guardian's work was fighting and woodcraft. In the end, since they had not formulated a plan that led to slaying the beast, whatever gifts the *urus* spirit could bestow would remain hidden, the province of the spirits alone. It was enough to see the beast far away from their tribes' lands. It was enough to ensure their people were safe.

Many days later, exhausted and bone-weary, they made their way home.

23

SARINE

The Five Cats Tavern
Maw District, New Sarresant

"Come now, what's a lovely thing like you doing sitting alone?"

The young man who took the seat across from her gave her a rakish smile. He'd been eyeing her since she walked in, he and a small knot of fellows hovering together around one of the tables near the hearth. She knew the types: young men, loud and drunk and happy to proclaim it to anyone within earshot.

She smiled back. "Waiting for my meat pie, enjoying the music."

He made an exaggerated face, likely as much for the benefit of his fellows as for her. "That will never do. A pretty girl should be dancing."

On another night she might have accepted; the jongleur had two assistants beating a rhythm to accompany his eight-string mandolin, and more than a few men and women took to the common floor to try their hand at following the steps. But tonight her thoughts were on Madame Guillon, the proprietress of the Five Cats, and on the letter the tavernkeep was fetching from her workspace behind the kitchens. It had finally come.

In reply to her would-be suitor she removed the leather gloves she'd been wearing, placing her hands facedown on the table between them.

He gave her a curious look that melted into wide-eyed shock as he realized what he was seeing. A binder's scars alone might not have been enough to deter him—freebinders, those who had fled from ecclesiastical training or deserted the army, were common enough in the shadows of the city. But the spiraling tattoos that made the King's arms in blue and gold from wrist to knuckle were a sign of something else entirely. Not a marquist in the city would ink those patterns into her skin without a royal writ that cost more than an honest man made in a lifetime. Having them, and having them here in the Maw, could mean she was any number of things, not a one of which was suitable fare for a hardworking young man out for a drink with his fellows.

He paled, backing away from the table without another word. A bittersweet feeling. This was her, now. This was who she was. Nice enough to have a means to deter unwanted attentions, but not every attention was so undesirable. Before, she had blended into the city's underbelly like any other shadow. Now she shone like a beacon. Watching the young man scramble back to his friends with an ashen face and a story, watching them glance over at her with looks of shock and disbelief, she felt a piece of her old life torn away like roots pulled up by a winter storm.

A wax-sealed letter dropped to the table in front of her.

"Came this morning," Madame Guillon began. "From a courier right dressed up like—" She trailed off into silence. "Your hands."

She winced and reached for her gloves. "Madame Guillon, I—"

"I want no part of whatever you've mixed yourself in, girl. And I'll not have you involving my tavern neither. Take your letter and be on your way."

She bowed her head, fishing for a silver mark to leave on the table. Twice what a letter delivery was worth, but Madame Guillon only watched as she gathered her things. Whispers through the room clung to her like the stench of a sewer as she made her way out into the evening air, unexpected tears stinging the corners of her eyes.

She walked the streets of the Maw without care for appearances. Just as well none of the urchins or street toughs thought to take advantage. No telling what she might have done if they had.

Even her uncle knew better than to ask after her mood when she arrived at the chapel, leaving her to climb the ladder into her loft, break the wax *R* that sealed the letter, and begin to read.

Her uncle stared at her in the morning light cast by the stained glass of the main relief, his jaw firmly open beneath his gray mustaches.

"Is it too much?" she asked. "The clothier showed me what to do with the cosmetics. It's not too different from sketching, really, but I haven't had time to practice, or—"

"You look beautiful, child."

She smiled. She could feel the carmine on her lips, the powder dusting her cheeks, the kohl accenting her eyelashes. Was this how the noblewomen felt each day? As if they wore masks, but masks of their best selves. And the dress. Not a strict adherent to the haute couture of the court—she'd captured enough of the nobles' fashion in her sketches to know it—instead a simpler, sleeker cut that ran headlong against the extravagance of the season's trends. Where the noblewomen wore wide panniers and corsets painted bright with patterns of gold, the one she had chosen for today was a narrow-cut, close-bodied gown of paneled silk in a deep shade of crimson-accented blue. She felt a pang of guilt that she'd wear it first for Lord Revellion and not for Reyne d'Agarre, whose coin had paid the clothier's bill. Still, a gift was a gift. She was not some porcelain doll to be dressed up and paraded about at her owner's whim.

D'Agarre had instructed his clothier to spare no expense for her *accoutrements*, and she could only wonder at the small fortune the finished products must have cost. Six dresses cut, sewed, and delivered to the Sacre-Lin not two days after they'd visited the clothier's shop, with all the requisite cosmetics and accessories for each. D'Agarre had even made a gift of a box of pendants, rings, and all manner of precious stones. The better part of those she left in the box today, wearing only a simple silver chain and matching teardrops fitted to dangle from her ears. More than passing strange, for a man who professed support for *égalité* and the plight of the commonfolk to deal in such luxuries, but for the sake of Lord Revellion's summons, she felt a guilty satisfaction that he did. In all, it was her uncle's warm look that assured her she had not gone too far.

"You are a vision of the Veil herself," Father Thibeaux said with a smile. "And you will do fine with this Lord Revellion. Remember the nobles are flesh and blood beneath their finery, the same as you."

"Thank you, uncle," she said, giving him a kiss on the cheek.

She spared another look over her shoulder as she made her way to the chapel doors, finding him still smiling a rueful smile, as if he could scarce believe his eyes.

Tethering *Faith* as soon as she left the chapel, she made her way down the steps toward the ruined iron gate that marked the boundary to the Riverways. *Faith* was a necessity—she wasn't fool enough to imagine she could walk the streets of the Maw done up like this without attracting the wrong sort of attention—but her heart felt light in her chest as she walked, the same familiar sights of the slums taking on a new cast when viewed from behind the eyes of a well-dressed lady of means.

She found the coach waiting for her at the district boundary, just as Lord Revellion's letter had said. *Tomorrow morning, at the district gates if you won't permit my man to come to you directly.* With some dismay she noted the coachman was the same ornery fellow who had driven her the first time. Well, perhaps he would see her in a different light now.

She released *Faith*, shimmering into view standing just beside the painted door of the carriage.

"Aren't you going to help me up?" she asked in a sweet voice.

The coachman gave a start and a yelp, which was pleasing enough on its own, but nothing to the delight of seeing his jaw hang open when he finally turned to see. She coughed, and received a flurry of apologies as he jumped down to assist her up the steps.

This time, she hardly felt the rattling bounce of the wheels over cobblestone.

She drank in the sights as they rolled through the Riverways, resisting the urge to pinch herself awake from a dream. Zi luxuriated on the velvet cushions opposite her seat, his scales seeming to drink in the blue-green of the plush, and he looked up at her with an approving nod.

You look lovely, he thought to her.

To her unfeigned surprise, it made her blush.

"Thank you, Zi," she said quietly. She took a deep breath, meant to settle her nerves. Instead it drove home where she was, and where she was going. Before, it had been a dream to pass through the gate of the Revellion house, with all the haze of waking from a long sleep. Now, dressed as if she belonged there, it would be somehow more real. And looking the part was the easier trick by far. A gnawing worry tugged at her, split between riding in a coach that could be sold to see a hundred hungry families through the winter, and the creeping certainty she was about to show herself a fool.

They were halfway through Southgate before she realized they had not turned north and west toward the Gardens district.

She slid open the panel between the coach and the driver. "Where are we going?" she demanded, nerves adding more bite to her words than she'd intended. "This isn't the Gardens."

"Beg pardon, my lady," the coachman said. "My lord's instructions were to take you to meet him on the green at Rasailles."

"Thank you," she said in a numb voice, closing the panel. Rasailles. Last time she'd been to the palace they'd arrested her. What did he mean by it, inviting her to the green? He hadn't mentioned the palace in his letter. Was it a sign he disapproved of how she had been treated by his peers? A message to the nobles who'd deigned to have her imprisoned? Did he want to parade her about as a symbol of defiance, meant to spark some tension of which she couldn't possibly be aware? Or just to assure her it was safe now, that her status had been bought and paid for?

She rubbed her hands, feeling the scars and the fresh tattoos that covered her skin. It took effort not to fling the carriage door wide and make a break for the familiar. The costume of cosmetics and silk she had delighted in back at the chapel felt heavy on her skin as they rolled past the city gates, through the winding woods that separated the city from the palace grounds.

Her heart skipped again when they emerged from the trees onto the sculpted landscape of the palace, rolling to a slow stop before the stone walkway. Not too late to bind *Faith* and make a mad dash back into the forest. Not too late to wake from the dream.

"The commoner, Sarine Thibeaux of New Sarresant, at the behest of Lord Donatien Revellion, son of his lordship the Marquis Revellion."

The crier's voice might as well have been a trumpet blast, cutting across the garden like a knife through her belly. When the carriage door swung open it was as if the curtain had been pulled away at the public bath, revealing her naked skin to the warm summer air. She could feel eyes drawn toward her with predatory interest. A new name. A new face. Unspoken questions hovered around her as she emerged at the top of the coach's steps.

And there he was.

Standing this time, with a cane to support his injured leg, wearing a blue gold-embroidered coat cut in a style that evoked his military uniform. His black hair was pulled back and tied in a ribbon, his blue eyes looking up with, was it anticipation? Nerves? He stared as she emerged from the coach, his jaw hanging open where she had hoped for a welcoming smile.

"My lord?" she said as she stepped down. "Are you well?"

"Gods above. Sarine." He leaned forward to offer a hand while the other rested on his cane. "You're here. And you look..."

She lowered her eyes, relishing the effect of her work.

"...stunning," he finished. "How did—?"

"Thank you for the invitation to the palace green, Lord Revellion."

He closed his mouth at last. "Thank you for accepting it." He seemed to be making an effort not to stare, which threatened to make her blush again. Gods bless d'Agarre and his clothier. "You're full of surprises, I must say."

She took his arm and they began to walk. If the young lords and ladies in attendance had scented blood when the crier introduced her, they were in a frenzy now. A polite frenzy, of course, but she felt the weight of eyes and whispers with every step they took.

"You're looking well, my lord," she said, eyeing the cane.

He noticed, and gestured with it as he took her arm, leading her away from the carriage as it rolled away down the path. "The docteurs had me lying abed long enough. I thought it past time for some exercise. We paid for *Life* and *Body* bindings on the night of the attack, but it's been a slow recovery since."

She looked him up and down. They'd bound *him* with *Life* and *Body*?

"How does that work, my lord? You're not a binder yourself, are you?"

He gave her a surprised look. "Me? Gods no. My father paid a goodly sum to retain the services of a retired fullbinder here in the city." When she frowned, he added, "I take it you were never taught at an academy?"

"No. I was taught... well, I taught myself."

With a blink, she sensed a nearby strain of *Life* beneath the royal green. She'd never tried binding to anything other than herself, but perhaps if she pushed the energy just so, weaving the tether through his leg...

"You could hire a private tutor, it's not unheard-of among the noble families, though the priests charge—" His voice cut off as he took another step, suddenly relieved of the limp that had required the cane. He looked down at his leg, then back at her, wide-eyed. "Sarine! You can bind *Life*, too?"

She nodded, feeling a rush of uncertainty. Had she overstepped?

"Incredible. Best not let the lords-general catch wind of this, or you'll find yourself pressed into the service before you can blink." He laughed, as if he'd meant it for a joke.

She froze, left behind for a few steps before he turned back with a frown.

"Sarine...?"

A lifetime of hiding her gifts welled up in her belly, threatening to leave her retching on the side of the path.

At once concern shone on his face. "I misspoke," he said. "You are safe here—no one is going to force you into the army or anywhere else. Your talents are your own." He reached out a hand for hers, an earnest look in his eyes.

"Planning to introduce us to your secret companion, Lord Revellion?" an airy voice said from behind.

They turned together to find three women, each dressed in the mirror opposite of her simple fare: wide trains of silk in bright colors, golds and reds and blues. Young women all, each of them several years her junior, but with the countenance of noble-born ladies through and through. The two ladies flanking the one in the center she did not recognize, but their leader she knew the same way she had known Lord Revellion, through sketches from afar. Anne-Laure Cherrain, daughter of the Duc-Governor.

"Anne-Laure," Revellion said with an air of formality as he stepped back, offering a bow.

She realized a moment too late that a similar gesture would be expected of her, and made a curtsy that was met by a sniff from the Duc's daughter.

"A binder," one of the others whispered, loud enough for all to hear. "She's got binder's marques."

"So she does," Lady Cherrain said, lips pursed as she looked her over, up and down. Only then did she notice Lady Cherrain too bore the

King's sigil tattooed on the backs of her hands, the same blue-and-gold pattern of three flowers entwined that had been inked into her own skin.

"She is my guest, my lady," Revellion said, caution in his tone.

"She is *my* guest, Donatien. Or do I need remind you whose family resides in the palace?" Lady Cherrain walked a few paces around where Lord Revellion stood beside her on the path, weighing them both. "My father's seneschal passed word that your estate had withdrawn a considerable sum a fortnight past. Passing strange with your father away in the southern colonies, I thought."

Revellion frowned. "Records of the King's writ are—"

Lady Cherrain waved a tattooed hand dismissively. "Yes, yes. The priests did not betray your trust. But in these times a wise governor keeps an ear out for signs of the unusual. Never let it be said my father's daughter does not follow in his footsteps."

A cold look passed between them, the young noblewomen hanging at Lady Cherrain's side seeming to drip with excitement at the promise of somewhat more.

"Well," Lady Cherrain said, "let us be on our way, ladies. A pleasure to have met you, Madame Sarine."

She made another belated curtsy as the noblewomen strode away into the garden. Lord Revellion only stared after them with a stoic look that failed to hide the sparks kindling behind his eyes.

"She was lovely," Sarine offered after Lady Cherrain's retinue was well out of earshot, making her voice sweet as a sugared plum.

"Courtly intrigue," Revellion said. "Never mind that we're at war and half the city is starving or near enough to the brink." He gestured toward Lady Cherrain's back. "Oh no, it is of vital importance that we posture and pretend at knowing each other's secrets."

"As well ask a sailor not to curse or a baker not to sample his own wares," she said, watching the Duc's daughter sashay down the garden path.

He raised an eyebrow appreciatively. "You've read Morain?"

Who? "No. I meant only that—"

"A thing's essential nature," Revellion said. "Part of the *Ethics*. 'As well ask the sun not to set, the players not to dance upon the stage.' "

"I meant the opposite, actually. That she's learned to play a part, so that's what she does. I expect nobles will be hosting fêtes and playing parlor games while the city burns around them."

A moment passed before she realized how frankly she'd spoken. "Beg your pardon, my lord, of course."

"No," he said. "No, that's precisely it. You shouldn't have to apologize for speaking the truth. I find your company refreshing. All my life I've been raised to do just as you said: host fêtes and play parlor games. With you I can speak freely. Never ask my pardon for a thing."

"You surprise me, my lord. I never imagined I would hear these sorts of thoughts from the star courtier of Rasailles."

"Perhaps more of us will surprise you. Call it your first sight of the true face of Sarresant nobility."

She shook her head, ignoring the irony in his remark. "Not exactly my first," she said, rubbing her hands together, feeling the scars.

Revellion frowned. "Oh, Sarine, you must think me an ass."

"My lord?"

"I only now remembered your last visit to Rasailles ended with you clapped in irons. I should have thought it might upset you, that it might   "

"You're not an ass, my lord," she interrupted. "Only a nobleman."

He gave her a pained look.

She reached out and took his hand, offering him a warm smile, letting him lead onward along the pathway through the gardens.

24

ERRIS

1st Division Command Tent
Southern Sarresant Territory

Foot-Captain Marquand grimaced. Whether from the fruitlessness of their exertions or an afternoon of enforced sobriety, it was difficult to tell.

"Try again," he said, furrowing his brow in concentration.

She took a deep breath and closed her eyes, knowing it was wrong. This was never the way her visions had come. But she'd identified a new type of energy, a binding that felt like *Need*, or perhaps *Hope*, and she had to try something.

Beneath the camp she saw the familiar network of leylines, a crosshatch of energy pulsing with colors and forms. Three she recognized: the green pods of *Life*, the red motes of *Body*, and the inky clouds of *Death*. All the others were gray haze, indiscernible from one another and useless if she tried to bind them. There were six known leyline energies: *Body*, *Shelter*, *Life*, *Death*, *Mind*, and *Entropy*. The last two had been discovered in her lifetime, and if she was right, the golden light might be the latest in a chain of discoveries, extending back to the first days of empire, when their people and the peoples of the other great powers had expanded their claims, seeking new sources of power across the seas.

Marquand had reacted with skepticism when she confided to him her discovery of what appeared to be a new leyline energy. Rightly so.

Discovering new bindings was a thing done by scholars in academies, not soldiers in the field. Yet here they were, and besides herself Marquand was perhaps the most skilled binder in the army, for all he was equal parts scoundrel and drunkard. Straightaway they'd set to test her discovery, trying every exercise they could recall from their academy days. So far, nothing.

She shook her head, opening her eyes. "It isn't like the others. *Body, Life, Death.* I recognize them. I can find them and see the pattern. This is different."

Marquand grunted. "I'm '*hoping*' as hard as I can here. You're sure it seemed to center on the recipient of the effect, and not the leyline itself?"

"Yes. Both times so far it's been like I tethered the essence straight from the source, not through a leyline. There was no pooling of energy to tap into."

"Hm."

They remained quiet, each heavy in thought.

"What are you hoping for?" she asked. "Maybe the object of the emotion is significant."

"Um…"

"Marquand, if you are hoping for wine, I swear by the Exarch I will drown you in it when we're through."

He harrumphed. "Try again then."

"You are an incurable bastard, Foot-Captain," she said, repressing a laugh. "Try something I might care about. Both times it happened the need was something *significant*."

"All right, all right. Go," he said.

"What is it, then? What are you thinking of?"

"Try without my telling you first; maybe knowing clouds the waters."

She nodded, and closed her eyes once more. She knew it was here somewhere, the golden light she had embraced before stepping behind the eyes of the late Vicomte-General Carailles, and the unknown soldier of Fantain's Cross. It was all but unheard-of for a binder to learn a new type of leyline energy beyond the first few months of training. But evidently that was what had happened to her. Except they'd been at this for hours, with nothing—

Wait.

Beneath Marquand there was no new energy pooling, no swirling shapes she could suddenly decipher. That hadn't changed. But there *was* a single leyline that seemed to branch from the interconnected grid. Keeping focused, she traced the line upward, following its coils until she found a thin fleck of gold.

Heart racing, she tethered it. And her vision shifted.

Instead of watching Marquand's red face squinting in concentration, she saw herself standing in front of the table she used as a desk facing the tent's rear wall. Her stomach roiled and her head spun. It was as though she'd fallen through a mirror. She raised an arm, and Marquand's thickly muscled frame responded. She made a few sweeping gestures, then ran her fingers along the scruff of Marquand's unshaven stubble. Goodness, but it itched. And there *she* stood, seemingly in a daze, her eyes staring straight through Marquand. From the foot-captain's vantage, her own body seemed so small. She'd never been reckoned a tall woman, or even average height, but it was another thing to see it for herself.

As quickly as the shift had come, her vision snapped back as the reserve ran dry. Once more her senses returned to her body, and Marquand seemed to come to, his face pale, eyes wide.

"It worked. By the Gods, Marquand, it worked."

"Yes," he said, coughing. "Nameless take me if I ever let you do that to me again."

"That bad?"

"I could feel you rattling around in my head. Like a bloody bad dream, and I couldn't force myself awake."

"Tell me everything."

He went on at some length as they tried to piece it all together. There wasn't much more to it. He'd thought of victory over the Gandsmen and an end to the war, and between one eyeblink and the next she was looking through his eyes, waving his hands about of her accord. Just as quick he'd regained control. Whatever had passed between them, he hadn't harbored enough *Hope* to maintain the connection, or perhaps *Need* wasn't as strong as it had been when she'd used the light before.

When they'd exhausted his account, he requested leave to fetch a strong drink. She allowed it. Tethering bindings was draining under the best of conditions, and the fitful start and stop of her testing was far from that. She remained behind in the command tent, allowing her aides to deliver the reports they'd held while she and the foot-captain worked, all the less urgent communiqués that nonetheless required her attention. It was enough to make her envy the other binders in the army. Few enough binders were allowed to be promoted above the front lines, effective as they were in combat. Marquis-General Voren had judged her more dangerous to the enemy wielding a general's knot than a saber. She had every confidence he'd be proven right.

As to their testing with the *Need* binding, her mind raced with the thrill of success and the possibilities it implied. The effect was nothing short of incredible. The scouting possibilities alone, to say nothing of instantaneous transmission of communication…or commands. She could place herself in direct control of an engagement, guiding each unit of her division, seeing from multiple vantage points as a battle unfolded. It was an insurmountable advantage, provided she could arrange enough *Need* or *Hope* to power it. She still wasn't clear which force was responsible, but in time she would work it out. Say what Marquand would about refusing to repeat this afternoon's work, he'd do it. Without doubt he saw the potential in their discovery, and he mirrored her excitement, even if he chose to show it by getting fall-down drunk when he was supposed to be on duty.

A rap sounded on the post outside the entrance to her tent.

"Come," she called.

Aide-Lieutenant Sadrelle stepped through and saluted, wearing a grim expression in place of his usual knowing grin. "Sir. Word from the Fourteenth. They've picked up a fresh trail and are moving in pursuit of the enemy cavalry."

"Excellent news, Aide-Lieutenant." That was the opening ploy. The Gandsmen dangled the cheese of the entirety of their cavalry, hoping to lure her horsemen to follow them into the open ground past the southern border. But when they caught the 14th, especially with d'Guile in command of six fullbinders, the enemy would find they'd snared a bear instead of a mouse in their little trap.

Still, Sadrelle wouldn't be wearing such a dour expression if that were the whole of it. She waited for him to continue.

"More news, sir, from Brigade-Colonel Chellac and the Sixteenth. They reached the village of Oreste three days past, on the western flank."

Her stomach sank. She knew before he said it.

"Sir, it's another Fantain's Cross."

She breathed deep, keeping her voice steady, but cold as steel. "Pass word to Marquis-General Voren. The southern villages must be emptied. This will not happen again."

"Yes, sir."

"And have Jiri saddled. I mean to see this for myself."

Alone and unencumbered by the command staff of the 1st Division, she and Jiri made the trip in under a day. Under ordinary circumstances she'd never tolerate a commander riding anywhere alone, much less along the front in wartime. But for this, the Nameless could take the regulations. She'd given orders for the rest of the division to carry out her plan, to continue their march southward following on the heels of the 14th. No chance of her missing out on that engagement anyhow; on Jiri's back, with the aid of *Body* they could cover five times the ground of the next-swiftest cavalryman in the army. Call this little sojourn another privilege of general officership, or, more accurately, one of its heaviest burdens. To lose soldiers on a battlefield was painful enough. But innocents butchered by the enemy tore at the deepest pits of her stomach. How had this happened? Her men had been spread out to patrol the breadth of the border. The scouts should have seen it, should have given word. But there could be no anger toward her men; she was a general now, the responsibility fell to her. It may well have been that the enemy nurtured some newfound thirst for carnage—and make no mistake, she'd see to it the Gandsmen paid the price for what they'd done—but in her gut she knew the blood was on her hands.

She passed Brigade-Colonel Chellac on the southern road leading away from the ruins of the village, his men making a quick-time march to catch up with the rest of the division before they were engaged. He briefed her on what they'd found. Oreste was a small village, a collection of farms situated close enough to the woods to make it a stopover for fur traders on their way to Villecours, or headed south toward Gand in better times. Chellac had had a notion to supplement his brigade's stores in advance of what might be an extended campaign across the border. He'd ordered one of his regiments to divert from their westerly patrol and pay a visit to the village. But when they'd arrived they found smoke and ruin.

How long since it happened Chellac wasn't able to guess. His men reported the ashes cold, the buildings ruined, with none of the leisure or supplies for which they'd come. Oreste was far enough away, and isolated, that it may have been some time since the grisly attack, perhaps even before Fantain's Cross. They could tell her little else. After such a sobering encounter, Chellac was eager to make a report and move on to rejoin the remainder of the 1st Division. She could not fault them for that. But she had to know.

She let them continue on their march, and rode toward the ruins of the village.

It was much as Chellac's men reported. Timber frames charred and blackened where they hadn't collapsed into heaps of rubble. Streaks of soot crossed the dirt, blown by the wind, and no foliage of which to speak. All ash. Jiri carried her forward; together they drank in the grisly sight. Even her mount could sense the wrongness of this place, and Jiri's nerves were hard iron. Jiri would not flinch at being pushed to charge a fortified line of bayonets and sharpened stakes, and she'd done so more than once. But one could read the emotions of one's mount. They both knew this place stank of evil.

When they came to the small stone chapel, doors still sealed, a knot of dread formed in her throat. Had Chellac's men not known the details of Fantain's Cross? Or had they simply wanted to avoid seeing it firsthand? She afforded herself no such luxury. She hadn't brought an axe, though looking back on it perhaps she should have thought to. No matter. A fullbinder had other means of breaking through oak.

She tethered *Body*, as much as she could handle, enough to exhaust her in minutes. It would be enough. The oak doors were thick, heavy wood; they'd resisted the torch, but they did not resist her. Paying no mind to the damage it would cause to her saber's edge, she hacked through the wood in a rain of *Body*-enhanced blows. She could find time with a whetstone later. For now she had to see.

She kicked through the wooden paneling, releasing acrid smoke kept bottled up for days, enough to sting her eyes as she forced her way through the chapel doors. Yet where she expected bodies piled and seared as they had been in Fantain's Cross, she found only empty pews. A powerful relief washed over her, and tears came unbidden, streaking down her cheeks at being spared another horror. The sentiment lasted only a moment. There was no joy here, no reprieve from death and madness. If the Gandsmen hadn't burned these villagers in the sanctuary of their own chapel, they'd surely brought them to some other terrible end. This village had been torched weeks ago; Chellac's men were not wrong on that count. No chance any of the villagers had escaped this attack, or word would have reached her sooner.

She left the chapel and began her search for whatever signs the enemy had left. A mass grave or something equally vile. Of a surety, there would be some marker. This had been done to send a message, to sow fear among the people of Sarresant. The enemy would not leave his work hidden in shadows.

She found nothing.

She searched the ruins of buildings and houses, scoured the dirt that had once been the village green, even lowered a rope to test the water beneath the well in the central square. Nothing. It wasn't until she thought to shift her vision to check the residues of the ley-energy that she began to suspect she'd been wrong. *Body* in abundance, and little enough *Life*. But of *Death*, the ink-clouds she expected to find below every building, every street, she found no sign. Only small traces beneath the cemetery behind the chapel.

The people of Oreste had not been slain. They had been taken.

Knowing it, she seethed with rage. What designs could the enemy have that required a village worth of innocents? Was Gand practicing the slave trade once more, a relic the civilized nations of the world had long since left in the past? A weight settled onto her shoulders, a duty to uncover the fate of these villagers. She had to know. She needed to know.

Need.

Almost instinctively, she closed her eyes, letting need guide her.

There. Leagues away, far to the north. Golden light.

She embraced it. Her need, and the need of the people of Oreste.

Her vision shifted.

She was bound at the hands, rope bonds tied to a cord running through the column of villagers as they marched. Dozens of them, perhaps the entire population of Oreste. Perhaps more. They shambled forward at a slow pace by military standards. And there were military here, wearing the red coats of the Gandsmen, shepherding their prisoners along in a column two by two. The dust clouds and the thrumming of shambling steps ahead and behind confirmed it: This was an army on the march, not an escort of a few prisoners. These villagers were in the middle of the pack, far enough behind that the ground they covered had been tracked into a semblance of a trail. And no chance this was the end of the column. No commander with half a brain would march prisoners behind the main body, where they could slip away at the tail end of the line.

"Marie," a voice whispered beside her. "Marie, your eyes . . . ?"

She turned and saw a man of middling years, his clothing ragged and face unshaven.

"What's happened?" the man whispered. "You look like one of *them*." His voice dripped with venom.

"Where are we?" she asked in a coarse whisper.

"What? Marie, what's going on?"

"Where are we?" she repeated, adding a forceful emphasis long trained to give commands. "Tell me!"

The man seemed taken aback, but whispered back to her in a rush. "You know where we are. They've had us marching north for weeks." He gestured to the right of the column as if it were obvious. And it was.

The Great Barrier. The division between civilized land and the wild, where beasts native to the New World threatened to massacre any who ventured outside the safety of the wall. If the prisoners were marching north through colonial lands it should have been on their left.

They were on the wrong side.

25

ARAK'JUR

The Guardian's Tent
Sinari Village

Llanara's eyes glowed as she looked up at him, closing the book she'd had open on her lap. She was seated cross-legged on the floor of the tent they shared, a place he found her more and more often of late. He mistrusted the book, a gift from Reyne d'Agarre; he'd seen books before, curiosities traded from the fair-skins, claimed to be stores of wisdom, ink pressed into pulp as thin as grass. In his view such things were the province of the shamans if they had to be handled at all.

"My guardian," Llanara said, smiling. "Welcome home. I trust the hunt went well?"

"It did. The tribe is safe."

Her smile faded as he lowered himself to the pallet beside her. Weariness seeped through his muscles like water through a cloth. She must have seen some measure of it, folding her legs to the side as she edged toward him.

"You are troubled," she said.

"Two of our number fell, hunting the *urus*."

"Not Ilek'Inari . . . ?"

"No. He did well. Better than most. It was Arak'Var, and Ilek'Uhrai."

She paused, and he completed the thought for her.

"The Olessi guardian," he said. "Ilek'Uhrai was his apprentice."

It took another moment before the meaning of his words settled in.

"It's happening," she half-whispered, then spoke again, louder. "If both are dead, then the Olessi are without the guardians' magic."

"Yes." It was doom, simple and plain. No tribe could survive without guardians to ward away the great beasts. A sign of the spirits' disfavor, a sure mark of a curse. Guardians were slain often enough, and apprentices, too, but the shaman saw the coming of such things in time to be certain a new apprentice was found. For the Olessi shaman to have failed to see it meant their tribe was doubly cursed, abandoned by the spirits of things-to-come and the beast spirits both. Arak'Jur had lived with the fear of such a thing since becoming guardian; Ka'Vos hadn't foreseen his calling as Sinari guardian prior to Arak'Mul's death, but the spirits had provided for his people. The same *valak'ar* that killed the old guardian gave its blessing to make the new one, and so the Sinari endured. But the Olessi had lost both master and apprentice. Even if other tribes' guardians offered to protect them, no tribe could restore the favor they must have lost with the spirits, to face so dire a fate.

"There will be war," Llanara said.

He winced.

"How could it be otherwise?" she continued. "The Olessi will blame us for their guardians' deaths. Us, and the others who accompanied you on the hunt."

The same fears had played in his mind since facing the *urus*, and now she voiced them openly. "The Olessi have been friends and neighbors for generations," he said. "They were allies, against the Tanari."

"And now they are doomed. They will remember the men who were with their guardians when they fell. And they will remember the greatfire, where we condemned their shaman's apprentice, on your word, and Ilek'Inari's. After these events, they will see our justice in a different light."

He hadn't thought to connect Ilek'Rahs's madness to the guardians' deaths; the Olessi envoys had made every sign of humility and acceptance at the greatfire. But he could well imagine them taking another tone now, debating in their steam tents the wisdom of violence.

"If there was a danger of war, Ka'Vos would have seen it, and brought it before the elders."

"Would he?" Llanara said.

His argument rang hollow in his ears already; Llanara's doubt doused it in sand.

Llanara cast a glance toward the book she'd held before his arrival. "I know this is not easy. But I have seen the shape of these events, written in the book."

His back stiffened, and he regarded the leather-bound pages as he might have a venomous snake.

"It is time," Llanara continued. "Time for you to—"

"Llanara, do not toy with me. This thing, this gift of Reyne d'Agarre, if it speaks with the spirits of things-to-come, I cannot believe even the women would allow it."

"Peace. Calm yourself, Arak'Jur. The Codex merely allows me to better understand... certain things. Things of great import to us, to our people."

"I mislike the nature of this. Whatever our misgivings, it is neither your place nor mine to speak for the shamans. It was wisely done, to accept Reyne d'Agarre's offer, and I have said as much. But there are limits."

"That is where you are wrong," she said in a rush. "Reyne d'Agarre came to us because the time has come for this power, for this gift to reach our people. You spoke truth—the Olessi contemplate war against us, even now. But my gift will see where Ka'Vos has been blind, and we will face this, together. Our time is near, my love."

He frowned. "Your words frighten me."

"Why else?" she continued, her voice flush with passion. "Why else would this power come to us now, when Ka'Vos's gift falters? No, do not deny it—we both know it for truth. Ilek'Inari abandons their path, chosen to be guardian, and with my coming, the women of the Sinari will be the greatest of all the tribes. This is a time for change, and if that breeds fear, so be it. But you are *strong*, Arak'Jur. You will weather it, with me at your side."

When she finished, a cloud of stillness hung in the air.

"You must reconsider these thoughts, Llanara," he said. "You go too far."

"You do not go far enough!" she shouted back at him. "Always caution, always uncertainty. You claim to be the guardian of this people and yet you sit idly and watch as Ka'Vos's visions fail. You refuse the mantle of chief, of warleader, hoping these times will sort themselves without your intervention. I tell you plainly they will not. Your people need you to act, *honored guardian.*"

She made his title drip venom. He took it as a blow across the face.

Without another word, he rose and left the tent, leaving her shouts echoing behind him.

He walked into the trees, letting his feet carry him as his mind worked. His tent was on the edge of the village, on the cusp of the wild. He'd always chosen to live on the periphery, though his role as guardian kept him near the heart of the tribe's political life. Llanara would have preferred a tent closer to the village center. He knew it, but his place was between the two worlds, even if Llanara didn't understand.

He repeated her words in his mind as he walked. Her book—she called it a codex—was well beyond his understanding. If it held a vision of things-to-come, he could not believe it sanctioned by the spirits. Such a thing violated every taboo he held sacred. But the root of her argument rang true, even if he was loath to admit it. The Olessi would be enraged when the news reached them. For Ka'Vos to have seen nothing of it, given no premonition or warning, cast a dark shadow over his gift, at a time when Arak'Jur had misgivings enough without the need for further doubt.

And the rest of her argument. Was she right, that this was a time to act, to seize power in defiance of their councils, to claim the mantle of *Sa'Shem* or *Vas'Khan*? Few would oppose him, if he did. He was no coward, whatever Llanara wanted to think. But neither was he wise enough to lead by decree; in the councils, the collected wisdom of the tribe guided them all. Without the voices of men and women, old and young, the tribe could not be as strong. Yet for the councils to decide, they required true insight, and that meant the shaman, foremost above all. It came back to Ka'Vos. And much as he wished it were not so, and stung his pride to admit, where her argument touched the shaman Llanara had the right of it.

He walked through the night, weighing the words in his mind, considering all aspects of his resolve. It was not until the first strands of dawn appeared at the edge of the sky that he found himself walking back through the trees, returning to his tent.

He found Llanara where he'd left her, cross-legged on the floor of his tent, only this time the book was put away out of sight. She looked up at him as he entered, her face streaked with tears.

"Arak'Jur, I am sorry," she began, trailing off as he signaled her to let him speak.

"Llanara. I have given thought to your words."

"I pushed too hard. Please, you must understand..." Again her voice faded as he urged her to silence.

"I do understand," he said. "I cannot fault you for seeing more in me than I see in myself. And I know you wish only what is best for our people, as I do."

He sat opposite her and reached a hand to brush tears from her cheek. She leaned into his touch, nodding in agreement.

"You must understand," he continued. "I have known loss, and gained wisdom from it." She nodded again. She knew well the pain he felt at the deaths of his wife and child; she had helped him find what measure of peace he had made with their memories. "If I have shied away from a course that may lead us to war, it is only because I know too well the horrors that lie along that path."

She looked at him evenly, though he could see her guard beginning to rise. He raised a hand to ward away the argument he saw forming in her mind.

"Your new magic unnerves me," he said. "But I cannot deny wisdom, no matter the source. Our people would never have come to these lands if we did not listen, when the first shaman heard the voice of the spirits of things-to-come. And in this, you have the right of it. It is past time to confront Ka'Vos."

"When?" she asked, leaving the rest of it—the warmth and forgiveness, the pain of the words they'd exchanged—to linger in her eyes.

"Now. I see no reason to delay."

Fire rekindled, and they rose together, sharing a firm embrace before he left their tent.

"There will be war."

The words hung in the air with the weight of a stone. Llanara's words, delivered through his lips, as bitter as when she'd said them, and as true.

Ka'Vos stoked the coals of his fire, freshly kindled with the morning sun. An ordinary fire, orange and red, with none of the smoke of the ritual summons. It made the tent seem ordinary, somehow bereft of the supernatural, and Ka'Vos along with it. A dark omen, considering the nature of his visit.

"You must see the logic behind my fears," he continued. "The Vhurasi guardians offered to deliver the news of Arak'Var's death, and well they did. If it had been me, or Ilek'Inari, can you say of a certainty we would have been received as friends?"

Age seemed to hang from the shaman's bones, a weariness pervading his tent like the sting of sour milk.

"There may be truth in what you say," the shaman said at last. "Enough to bring it to the steam tent. At the next turning of the moon, we can speak of this, and contemplate how we might tame their aggression."

A predictable reply, and he could imagine how Llanara would respond to further discussion and delay. There was wisdom in it. But the time for such things had passed.

"Ka'Vos. I would know if the spirits have granted you the visions of war, the visions the other shamans claim have haunted them since the last turning of the seasons."

The shaman turned away. Pressing Ka'Vos on such a matter was taboo in the extreme, edging on blasphemy against the spirits themselves. A shaman's visions were his purview alone; it had been so for as long as there had been shamans at all. But it was past time to settle the matter. If Ka'Vos would not speak on it when faced with a neighbor all but certain to have seen the visions, and given cause to act on them...

"Yes." A single word, ringing like a sheet of shattered ice through his tent. "Yes, Arak'Jur. I have."

"The signs of war... you have seen them?"

The shaman nodded.

"You have seen them and said nothing? Kept them hidden? Hidden from the Sinari people, hidden from me?" His voice seethed with anger, growing hotter as he spoke.

"Yes."

"Why?" So much of his thought had been bent around this. He had contemplated dire omens, and worse possibilities: whether the shaman had lost his gift, or at least some part of it, whether their people had fallen out of favor with the spirits, or been cursed themselves. And now he had the start of it. Ka'Vos had spoken lies.

He asked again, with greater force. "Why, Ka'Vos? Why?"

The shaman's expression softened, regarding him with a calm look. "I do not trust what I have seen," he said.

Arak'Jur stared at him, saying nothing, demanding more.

"Imagine a companion carried by your side since you were a boy, a companion you know well, and, yes, whom you love. Now consider how you react when your companion begins to whisper madness in your ear. Where once you heard peace, and wisdom, there is hate, and evil."

"The spirits of things-to-come have always spoken truth," Arak'Jur said. "I fear these things as you do, but we cannot ignore truth for the sake of fear."

"No. When the spirits speak of horrors, the voice is changed. It is not always so. At times it is the same, familiar companion. But when the visions come, of war, of death... it is a different voice. A foul one."

"What could it be, if not the spirits themselves? You are the one speaking madness."

"Arak'Jur, the spirits would have us at war, every tribe seeking the blood of their neighbors. If the other tribes have thus far refrained, it is because their shamans have seen what I have seen and *chosen not to act*."

Ka'Vos's words struck him with the force of *una're*'s roar. Impossible. Unthinkable, for the shamans to hear the spirits' whispers and fail to give them heed. Far easier to believe Ka'Vos had gone mad than to accept a shared delusion among the wisest men of the tribes. Once again he heard Llanara's voice in his mind, urging him to anger. But this time he found caution.

"How can you be sure? All we have heard from Ka'Hinari, Ka'Airen, and the others is that there are signs, courses that may lead to war."

Ka'Vos barked a bitter laugh. "No, my friend. I have seen it behind Ka'Hinari's eyes. He sees what I see. The spirits have gone mad."

A chill went through the tent. The guardian's gift made his flesh proof against the harshest winds and snows, the hottest fires of the sun. It offered no protection now.

"I have been a coward," Ka'Vos said. "I have feared what the people would say, what you would say. But you were wise; you asked, and I have answered. And now we must act, together, against what comes."

"You would cast aside the spirits' guidance?"

"No," the shaman said with force, a sharp crack echoing through the tent. "No. We could not survive without them. But as I have said, it is not always madness." He paused, holding Arak'Jur's gaze. "We must reach out to the other shamans, and counsel them to do as I have done, to listen only when the spirits are pure. To discern when there is corruption and to lay it aside. We must do this together, or I fear what the future holds. It may be too late for the Olessi. But if we forge bonds, alliances against the aggression of tribes under sway of the mad spirits' visions, we will be strong enough to remain at peace."

The shaman's words went against everything he had been taught, everything on which he had come to rely. He was a guardian. It was his place to protect the people, to defend them from the terrors of the wild, to trust the shamans' wisdom. It was only by the grace of the spirits and the visions of the *Ka* that their people could prosper in these lands. But how could he trust Ka'Vos in this? In his heart he was unsure. He knew the pain of loss. If war came, fathers, wives, children . . . all would suffer, and few be spared. Even without the gift of the spirits of things-to-come, he could see it unfold. To go against the shaman's visions was to invite a curse. But if the spirits would lead them to war, was that not already a promise of ruin? How could a guardian do other than stand in the way of such things?

In the end it was the memories of Rhealla and Kar'Elek, the loss of his wife and son, that decided him. Ka'Vos had spoken lies; that much he could not change. But the shaman had done it to avoid death and pain spread among their people. For that cause, he could stand against the madness of war, no matter the source. Llanara would not approve, but he had acted, as she had urged. He had made his choice.

He raised his head, and nodded slowly.

"You speak wisdom, Ka'Vos. What must we do to guide our people toward peace?"

Relief washed over the shaman's face. "The Ranasi," he said. "Ka'Hinari will listen. And we need strength. It is past time Llanara be given the chance to visit Ka'Ana'Tyat."

26

SARINE

Sacre-Lin Chapel
Maw District, New Sarresant

"And so, my sons and daughters," her uncle said from the pulpit, "remember the example of the Oracle next time one of your fellows has slighted you. Remember the power to be had in the virtue of forgiveness. If in her wisdom the Oracle could find it in herself to let the Nameless flee from the blood on his hands, how can we fail to do the same when our neighbors do us wrong?

"Carry her example with you in the days to come. Be mindful of the strength she found there, how even the Exarch bent knee before her on that day. For there are times when the only path to virtue is to lay down the iron sword of justice, to right oneself by taking up the burdens of love and mercy."

His words hung in the air as the congregation stood and began their shuffle out the main doors of the chapel. A good turnout this morning. Sarine watched from above as the last few parishioners lingered in the pews, seeking some private word with their priest. She made guesses as to what they might be wanting. The thick-looking brute of a man had blood on his hands, some crime to which he wished to confess and be washed clean. The gray-haired old woman sought company and a few words of encouragement. The filthy urchin staring up at her wanted… She frowned. The boy *was* staring at her, a blank look as he met her eyes. Strange for a child such as that to attend a sermon, clad in mud, dust, and tattered rags. Had the boy come to try his hand at picking pockets or palming coins from the collection plate? She hadn't noticed him during the lesson, but he was there now, plain as day.

Before she could puzzle it out any further, the boy held up a hand toward her, clutching a rolled-up parchment sealed in wax.

She climbed down from her loft and found him still watching her, proffering his delivery in dirt-covered fingers with a blank look in his eyes. He made no move toward her as she approached, only maintained his empty stare.

"Is that for me?" she asked.

The boy gave a slow nod.

She reached for it, and he let go as soon as it touched her fingers.

"Do I owe—?" she started, but the boy spun around and ran, nearly trampling his way through the main door.

"Is everything all right?" her uncle called down to her, the commotion drawing the eyes of the other parishioners who'd lingered in the chapel.

"I'm fine," she replied, looking down at the rolled parchment the strange messenger had delivered. An ordinary letter by any account, save for the *A* impressed into the seal. Reyne d'Agarre. She wasted no time thumbing the wax.

S,

Sincerest apologies for the late notice. I'll be hosting friends tonight and hope to count you among them.

Number 6 on the Street of the Ironworks, Southgate.

—RdA

She'd known the letter's contents even before the seal had slipped loose, though she hadn't thought the invitation would be for tonight. Her mind raced. Could she actually attend his salon? And what a strange choice of courier. The urchins she'd known during her time on the street would have snatched away whatever coin d'Agarre had offered and then delivered his letter straight into the nearest pile of refuse.

"Another missive from your admirer?" her uncle asked, walking toward her as the last of the parishioners headed toward the exit.

"Uncle, he's hardly an admirer. He's, well..." Her mind worked trying to find a suitable description.

"He's in desperate need of a courier service," her uncle harrumphed.

"Yes," she said with a smile. "He is. Were all of his letters delivered like that?"

"Just so. If he means to avoid drawing attention, he's doing a poor job of it. Last time his boy handed me a parchment in the middle of a sermon."

She gave a soft laugh even as it occurred to her that avoiding notice was precisely the opposite of what d'Agarre was doing. Did he send urchins into Southgate? Or the Gardens? Here in the Maw it might be mistaken for an oddity; in the upper echelons of the city, such an invitation was tantamount to a disturbance of the peace. It was deliberate, she was sure. A symbol, but of what? Commitment to the poor, perhaps. Or mastery over them.

"He's the one responsible for my dresses," she said absently as she weighed the letter in her hands and its contents in her mind. "But not the marques; that was Lord Revellion."

"Sarine, you know you have powerful gifts," her uncle said. "The sort that attract powerful people. Just remember who you are. You aren't beholden to any interest other than your own."

She looked up at him. "Thank you, uncle."

"I worry for you, child, that's all."

"I know. I'll be—"

"M'lady?"

She turned to the main door and stifled a laugh. Revellion's coachman, the very man who'd refused to even set foot in the district before, now looking like a fish in a bucket as he stepped into the chapel. She'd finally relented and told Lord Revellion he could send missives to her here at the Sacre-Lin, and this sight was repayment aplenty for her trust.

"Can I help you, my son?" her uncle asked.

"A message for m'lady from his lordship, Father. The Lord Donatien Revellion, that is, son of the marquis."

Oh, a silver mark for his timing. She noted the coachman was somewhat more pliable since her trip to the palace. An effect of seeing her done up in d'Agarre's finery, perhaps? Or the tattoos on her hands?

She supposed an invitation from Lord Revellion settled the matter of whether she would attend d'Agarre's salon.

"Let me guess," she said. "Lord Revellion wishes the pleasure of my company this evening?"

He shook his head. "Beg pardon, m'lady, but his lordship wishes to see you as soon as you can. He instructed me to wait here until sundown if I had to, provided you were willing to see him."

She smiled. Time enough for both, then, and thank the Gods for that.

"Ah, Sarine, again you dazzle me," Lord Revellion said as she descended the coach.

He met her in the small yard between the iron gate and the door of his family's townhouse, offering an arm as she stepped down onto the grass. She'd chosen another simple dress, cut in a soft blue trimmed with white, with a gold chain set with moonstones and matching pearl earrings. Suitable for a midday rendezvous and an evening at a salon both, so she hoped.

"My lord," she said. "Thank you once again for your invitation."

He slid her arm through his. "I had thought to take a walk through the Gardens, though I daresay the ladies of the district would be set ablaze with envy if we did."

"It's a hot enough day, my lord. A few fires would not be amiss."

His eyes glimmered. "So be it."

They walked down a polished cobblestone street abuzz with midday foot traffic, horses and coaches both. One could hardly go half a league in the Gardens without crossing through a well-groomed stretch of park or greenbelt, and it was toward such a green they made way. More than one head turned to watch as the Revellion coach sped off, leaving the young lord and his mysterious companion out on promenade. She could all but hear their minds racing, hear the whispers planting the seeds of the latest scandal. But she was with Lord Revellion, and the Nameless could take their gossip for the wasted breath it was.

"Now," Revellion said, "you must tell me how you've come to possess not one but two dresses fit to start riots among the ladies of the court."

She felt a rising flush. "A... A patron, my lord."

He frowned, but nodded as they made way up the broad street. "I suppose that's only fair. You are a rare specimen. It stands to reason there would be others."

"Oh no," she said. "Nothing like that. Only someone interested in my gifts."

He looked relieved. "Well, you are exceptional there, too, my lady. Fullbinders sanctioned to practice freely by royal marque command their price, especially in wartime. I hope you're being paid commensurate with your worth."

Again she blushed.

"I see you've set aside the cane," she said.

"And not a moment too soon." He took her hand as they moved aside for a passing carriage. "The docteur assures me I'll be fit and ready to ride before the season's out."

"To ride?" she began, then remembered. "Ah yes, your deployment with the army."

"Yes," he said grimly. "I'm to take command of a cavalry brigade to the south. A prestigious assignment for a newly graduated officer. Father pulled more than a few strings."

The thought caught in her throat as they arrived at the smooth stone walkway leading onto the greenbelt. She'd barely grazed the surface of Lord Revellion's world, and suddenly her tenuous hold here seemed in jeopardy.

Still, by some miracle she kept her composure.

"He must be proud of you," she said.

"Oh yes. I have rarely done aught that would displease his grace the Marquis de Revellion. Would that I had your courage, Sarine."

"My courage? I'm an artist, my lord. You're the soldier."

"Give yourself due credit," he said as they walked beneath the shade of a copse of trees overlooking the grass. "You live where you please, free to pursue your dreams. You charge headlong into a mêlée with some wild native beast and save dozens of lives."

"You make me sound like a song come to life. I've never tried to do more than survive, and if I have gifts, shouldn't I use them to help others in need?"

"Yes, of course, but how many would do the same?" Lord Revellion's eyes were bright with passion, focused on her as if they had the walkway to themselves. "You gave no thought to the danger, or of the petty injustice my peers would visit on you for trespassing, or for wielding magic you were born to, as if you needed the permission of the crown. On the green you saw a need, and you acted. That's courage."

"What about you, my lord? You stood your ground when the beast attacked. If I am some brave heroine, you're at least as much a hero."

"You'd make a song of me, then?" he asked.

"Hah! I'm no singer."

"Naturally you'd include your own role, of course. Except I think I've heard this one before: the son of the marquis and the roguish heroine. I'm certain they still sing it in some playhouses somewhere in the city."

"You'll have to take me to hear it played, before you head off to the south."

The reminder soured the moment, and he came to a halt. "Sarine," he began.

"Donatien," she replied, cutting him short. "I understand."

He winced. "That's just it. Understanding. I thought I understood the arc of my life, too, before the night of the masquerade."

"And now? Have I so disrupted the course of your future, my lord?" For all the roil in her stomach wanted it to be true, she didn't dare embrace the possibility. Lords did not abdicate their titles for orphan girls from the Maw, no matter her idle fantasies.

"Now... now, you have given me a future. Without you I would be dead. Every breath I take is a gift from the Gods, and I won't waste it pursuing empty designs on my father's behalf."

"Don't I owe you the same, my lord?" she said. "Without you, I'd still be scratching the days on the walls of a cell."

He took her arm, and they walked farther down the spiraling pathway through the park. "Just as well we came into each other's lives then."

"Truly though," she pressed. "What would you do to change your future? I cannot imagine you running off to live in the Maw."

"I wouldn't last a day, is that it?"

She smiled, waiting for him to continue.

"All right, no, I couldn't run away so easily. But why did my family become nobility in the first place? Long ago, some ancestor of mine was chosen to lead, to better the lives of our people. And what have we done with that trust? Anymore our noble families struggle only to preserve their position. People are starving, Sarine, starving while we feast. It is shameful."

"Yes," she agreed.

"And the war," he continued, "there must be more to our people's lives than starving, dying for the ambitions of a few nobles. Word in the papers is there have been entire villages sacked, burned, and torched in the latest campaign, and thousands of refugees headed to the city, no matter we can hardly feed our citizens without them. So much suffering, for the pride of so few. Thousands die because we are too prideful to negotiate a peace."

"You think it could be brought to an end?"

"Yes, if the people were empowered to govern their own interests."

She eyed him askance, sweeping a look up and down the green to be certain none were close enough to hear. "That sounds like talk of *égalité*," she said quietly. "Men have been hanged for less."

He grit his teeth. "I cannot change what I was born to, but I can use my station to change the fate of others."

"Like me."

"Yes. Like you." He walked a few more paces before he spoke again in a quiet voice. "Sarine, you've shown me the need for moving beyond comforts to action. There are those within this city who feel the same. I've tried to make contact with them since I awoke after the night of the masquerade."

She maintained a tight grip on his arm as they walked. This was dangerous talk; she knew it as well as he did.

"Well, they've responded." He took a deep breath. "A letter this morning, from the hand of a street child covered in dirt and dust. Tell me, if I invited you to attend a salon with me, to hear them out, to hear what they would plan, would you come with me?"

"Reyne d'Agarre," she whispered.

Revellion's eyes widened in surprise. "You know him?"

"Well enough to have received an invitation myself." She swallowed the knot in her throat. "I met d'Agarre in the Market, and he came to the chapel. He's responsible for my dresses. He gifted them to me so I'd have something suitable to wear into society."

Revellion frowned. "I see," he said in a tone that suggested anything but.

"It's all right. As I said before, he's a patron at best. It's nothing like..."

She trailed off, heat going to her cheeks as she realized what she'd been about to say.

"Nothing like...?" Revellion asked, a trace of mirth creeping back into his eyes.

She looked down. "Your pardon, my lord. I meant only—"

He cut her short with a gentle arm around the small of her back, drawing her into a long kiss beneath the shade of the trees on either side of the path.

"Ah," she managed. "Yes. That."

He smiled. "Sarine, would you honor me with your company at d'Agarre's salon this evening?"

She must have nodded, judging from the look of relief and satisfaction on Donatien's face. In her mind she weighed whether she was ready to step across the divide between idle conversation and accepting an invitation that marked the beginning of somewhat more. But there was curiosity, too, and on the walk back through the green, Lord Revellion's proffered arm seemed to draw her closer than it had before.

27

ARAK'JUR

Wilderness
Near Ranasi Land

Arak'Doren had taken Llanara into his keeping early that morning. He'd had no opportunity to gauge with Arak'Doren the likely reception his plea for peace would get from Ka'Hinari and the rest of the Ranasi elders. It had been a gruff ceremony, a simple exchange and blessings wished on both sides before they journeyed their separate ways.

Llanara had accepted his decision to treat with the Ranasi as though she'd expected nothing else; a surprise, given the passion he'd stirred before confronting Ka'Vos, but less so in light of her strange book. Perhaps she was only encouraged by having received the call to Ka'Ana'Tyat. He was left with the memory of her stealing a look over her shoulder, her eyes filled with pride, flashing him a smile as she trailed behind Arak'Doren. She was a beauty, and intractable as a stone when she decided on her course. Well for him that she'd accepted a path to peace.

"A fine thing to see you in good spirits, Arak'Jur."

Ilek'Inari kept pace behind him as they walked through the wooded hills, approaching the lands of their neighbors. His apprentice would accompany him only to the edge of Ranasi territory. It still gave him pause to think of Ilek'Inari as the sole guardian of their people, however temporarily. He reassured himself that the spirits did not choose guardians lightly, though the nature of his message to the Ranasi—

questioning whether their people could continue to place their full trust in the spirits of things-to-come—put a hollowness to that sentiment he had never felt before.

"It is a fine day," he said. "And I am hopeful for what may come with the Ranasi."

"They will listen," his apprentice said. "Ka'Hinari has felt what we have felt. He will see this is the way."

"I hope you are right."

"Not all tribes will agree. But the Ranasi are wise, and they make a good beginning. Our word and theirs will sway others, and in the end there will be enough. Enough to ensure those few tribes who would make war would be deterred by our strength." Ilek'Inari gave him a reassuring smile. "This is a bold plan, but it is a good one."

He nodded. The reason was sound, and he had heard as much before. A thought entered his mind, and before he weighed its implications, he spoke. "Are the spirits truly mad?"

That halted them both. Arak'Jur had never before asked his apprentice to speak of the connection he still maintained with the shamans' spirits.

Ilek'Inari adopted a solemn expression, with warmth behind his eyes. His apprentice had a soft way with words, and when he spoke it seemed to touch something deep within.

"Yes," Ilek'Inari said. "They speak with two voices: one of wisdom, one of rage. The first is a joy. The second is dark, full of spite and hatred. What we do here is right. Be sure of it."

He nodded. "Almost I reconsider whether you would be the better emissary on behalf of our plan."

"Oh, of a surety." Ilek'Inari smiled. "If any would listen when I spoke. But if I carried this mantle, few would hear me out. You and Ka'Vos spoke wisdom: Your status commands respect I have not earned."

So like Ilek'Inari to be self-effacing, in a way no hunter of the tribe would bear. Not for the first time, he reflected Ilek'Inari would have made a good *Ka*.

The remainder of the morning passed quietly as they walked, and before the sun reached its apex they heard the rushing waters of the Nuwehrai, the river that marked the northern edge of Sinari territory.

"Spirits favor your journey, Arak'Jur," his apprentice said when they reached the embankment.

"And yours, my apprentice." Ilek'Inari had come a long way from the soft shaman in training, but still he harbored his doubts at the thought of leaving him to defend their people alone. One last time he repeated his instructions. "Pay heed to Ka'Vos, and do not hesitate to call upon Arak'Doren should a great beast emerge that the shaman deems beyond you. There is no shame in such—guardians have always worked together, and it will take time for you to be granted enough gifts to stand on your own."

Ilek'Inari bowed his head. "I will keep our people safe, my friend. Do you have a sense of how long you mean to be away?"

"A question for the spirits." He shrugged. "I only hope I will return soon, and with welcome news."

"Often the spirits give us echoes, premonitions of what will be. What you hope may well be so, and you can take heart in it."

With that they shared a firm embrace, forearm to forearm, and Ilek'Inari turned to go.

The Nuwehrai River ran fierce and strong near its source, far inland. Here it was a tranquil flow moving steadily toward the sea, a bountiful supply of food for Sinari and Ranasi both. He made quick work of the crossing, the cool water a welcome respite from the midday heat. And soon he found himself on Ranasi lands. A journey he had made often, but this time there was somewhat more, a heavier purpose adding weight to each step. Always before the nature of his travels had been certain. Rituals, greetings, the duties of a guardian. Now he ran through the words he planned to say, searching for gaps and pitfalls. What if Ka'Hinari dismissed him outright? What if the shaman agreed but the hunters could not be brought to reason? And the women, should they be consulted?

For all these, he thought of answers, possible courses that would see him through. He was no quick thinker, made to spar in the steam tents like Llanara. But in this he had the right of it, and the conviction gave him strength. Only one possibility haunted him: What if the mad spirits themselves, with foreknowledge of his speaking against them, had poisoned the Ranasi against his coming? Arak'Doren gave no sign of such, but this was as perfect an opening for treachery as they were like to get. Still, he could scarce believe it of their longtime neighbors and friends. No, he would not believe it. If their plan was to succeed, it would be born on the back of trust, and the Sinari would take the first step down that path. Suspicion and fear were easy, but peace was worth the price of risk.

When the sun had risen to its apex he called upon the blessing of the *ipek'a* and slew a pair of rabbits that rustled in a bush at his coming. A piece of the hunters' ancient wisdom declared that to chase two rabbits was to lose them both, but even the greatest hunters among the tribes did not know what it was to be *ipek'a*. He drew on *una're* to spark a pile of dry tinder with the blessing of the Great Bear's thunderous claws, and had a fire going in short order. With seasoning from a few herbs gathered near the riverbank, it would be a fine, fresh afternoon meal.

He'd scarce taken his second bite when he heard the crashing of grass and twigs trampled underfoot, coming toward him from the river. Springing to his feet, he whirled to face whatever approached. A frightened elk, perhaps, or a bear roused to anger...

His apprentice emerged from the brush, racing toward him, crying out as soon as he came into view.

"Arak'Jur!" Ilek'Inari called, breathless. "Arak'Jur, you must come."

"What? What has happened?"

"A vision," Ilek'Inari panted, still dripping from the swim across the river. "A vision of Ka'Ana'Tyat. I know I should not consult the *Ka* spirits, but I saw... I had to know..."

"What did you see?" he demanded. For once, he let the taboo of guardians speaking with spirits of things-to-come pass unremarked.

"Darkness," Ilek'Inari said, struggling to catch his breath. "Pain. It was shrouded in a haze. The pure voices, the old and wise spirits. They tried to speak. But before I came to understand their meaning, the tainted voices kept me from knowing the whole of it."

"You saw where to find Ka'Ana'Tyat?"

"Yes," his apprentice said. "Nearby. It would have been a short journey for Arak'Doren and Llanara."

Arak'Jur kicked dirt over his fire, smothering it into wisps of smoke, and the two guardians ran.

It took no small amount of self-control to let Ilek'Inari lead. He knew Ilek'Inari would find the way sooner than he could have hoped to do on his own, having seen Ka'Ana'Tyat in his vision. Yet every passing moment, he felt as if a predator stalked him at the edge of his sight. It had been his decision to leave Llanara in Arak'Doren's keeping. Had he been a fool? Would another woman he loved die for his shortcomings? Llanara wielded her strange new gift with confidence, but his heart sank, considering it. Little as he understood the nature of the power she'd gained under Reyne d'Agarre's tutelage, she was new to her gift, and Arak'Doren had a skill born of long practice. The image of Llanara, broken and torn as Rhealla had been, haunted him as he ran.

The nature of Ka'Ana'Tyat was to remain hidden. One day it might be found to the south of the village, on the very cusp of the fair-skins' Great Barrier. The next it would be found to the west, in the heart of the thick forest that marked the boundary between Sinari lands and those claimed by the Olessi. And always the land gave no sign Ka'Ana'Tyat was near, not until one drew near enough to feel the power of its magic. He knew these things, and in his mind he accepted what Ilek'Inari had seen, accepted that his apprentice knew the way. Yet each step was agony and doubt. Every tree that grew straight and tall, unwarped by Ka'Ana'Tyat's strange magic, every blade of grass that did not announce they drew near, all seemed to shout to him: *This is not the way.*

Until, at last, they arrived.

At the first sign of the trees stretching together, growing entwined in patterns that would block out the sky in a canopy of roots and branches, he expelled a breath in relief and ran. He had to find her. He called on the spirit of *lakiri'in* and surged ahead of Ilek'Inari in a blurred rush of speed. Inward he drove, into the heart of the wood, racing in the direction the branches grew thickest.

The sight of a three-clawed slash mark in the bark of one of the twisted trees hit him like a blow to the chest.

Those were the marks of *mareh'et*'s claws, and unless another great beast lay hidden here at Ka'Ana'Tyat it meant Arak'Doren had used that gift to strike. The Great Cat spirit's blessing cut as sure as the claws of the great beast itself. Fury bubbled in his throat. So, it was true. Treachery. One small solace: If Arak'Doren had channeled the gift of the *mareh'et* to turn on Llanara, the Ranasi guardian would not be able to call on it again when he arrived to exact the price of betrayal.

He saw more gashes carved in trees as he ran, signs Llanara may have evaded pursuit. He swelled with pride, imagining her fleeing the mad guardian's rage. Perhaps she had lasted long enough for *mareh'et*'s blessing to fade. Perhaps there was hope.

He ran.

The trees grew thick, branches blacking out the sky. They pressed inward, funneling him toward what awaited at their end: the great black opening marking the entrance to Ka'Ana'Tyat. He saw more claw marks, desperate gashes strewn about the path. Pulp, wood, dirt, and blood, crimson streaks and pools left behind where the claws, at last, found purchase. Still he pursued, following the sanguine trail until he crashed through the last thicket of twisted brush, onto the empty path leading toward the entrance to Ka'Ana'Tyat, and laid his eyes on its source.

Llanara knelt in the center of the clearing, cradling Arak'Doren's head in her arms, his broken body lying on the forest floor in a mockery of any angle bones were meant to shape. And beside them, the corpse of a full-grown *mareh'et*, the flames of its eyes extinguished in wisping trails of smoke.

"Llanara," he mouthed silently. Then once more, aloud, after his body had time to take in what his eyes had seen. "Llanara!"

"My guardian," she said, her face streaked with tears, the white paint of her ceremonial garb marked with blood and dirt. "Is it truly you?"

He rushed to her side. She sobbed again, holding the body of Arak'Doren as she leaned into his embrace.

"Llanara, what happened here? Ilek'Inari had a vision, a terrible vision."

"The beast gave no warning." She hung her head. "It struck from behind."

"Are you hurt?" He looked her over. She was covered in blood.

"No. Arak'Doren protected me well, even wounded as he was. Oh, Arak'Jur, he fought the beast until the very end!" She wailed the last, clutching the body of her protector.

"Shh, Llanara, you are safe. Arak'Doren slew the creature, he did his duty."

She responded with hot fire in her voice. "I slew the creature, after Arak'Doren fell."

He gave a start. "You slew the *mareh'et*?"

She nodded forcefully. "I did."

"And after . . . did you speak with a spirit . . . ?"

She looked up at him with puzzlement in her eyes. "Is that the way of it? No. I struck, and the fires of its eyes went out. I did not converse with any spirit."

He nodded, trying not to show the relief he felt. "Your gifts are strong, to slay a *mareh'et*. And you are safe."

"Why was it here, Arak'Jur? Ka'Vos made no mention of this beast. You say Ilek'Inari could see it, when he is no full *Ka*. Why has our shaman lost his power?"

He winced. "No *Ka* can see all comings."

"You excuse his weakness, and it cost Arak'Doren his life. Now the Ranasi are without a guardian, Arak'Jur!"

It was true. In the moment, he had been overwhelmed to find Llanara here, alive. Now the truth of the matter settled over him. Arak'Doren had no apprentice, and now the Ranasi, like the Olessi, were cursed by the loss of their guardians.

Before he could form a reply, the rustling brush heralded another arrival into the clearing: Ilek'Inari.

"By the spirits," his apprentice exclaimed, eyes wide as he looked back and forth between Llanara, Arak'Jur, and the bodies of Arak'Doren and the great beast. "What happened here?"

"Llanara has slain a *mareh'et*," he said solemnly, rising to his feet. "And the beast has claimed Arak'Doren's life."

Concern filled Ilek'Inari's eyes. "Honored sister," he said softly. "The spirits are cruel, to visit this upon you."

The tide of her anger seemed to break before Ilek'Inari's compassion, and she sobbed once more.

"See to it she has every comfort, while I am away," he said to Ilek'Inari. "An ordeal such as this would weigh heavy on any man or woman of the tribe."

"While you are away?" Llanara said. "You cannot mean to continue on to the Ranasi now!"

Ilek'Inari echoed the sentiment in his eyes, though he remained quiet.

"I must," Arak'Jur said. "The Ranasi will take Arak'Doren's death hard. Hard enough to shatter our hopes of peace, unless strong voices are there to quell their anger."

Llanara looked to Ilek'Inari as though she expected him to join her in protest. Instead the apprentice guardian stood, hovering over the *mareh'et*'s body and Arak'Doren's beside it. Whatever vision Ilek'Inari had seen to guide him and Arak'Jur here, it evidently hadn't prepared him for this.

"Spirits favor your journey, Arak'Jur," Ilek'Inari said. "The way to Ka'Ana'Tyat is barred to us, but there is always wisdom in peace."

Arak'Jur looked again at the Ranasi guardian's body, then met Llanara's eyes.

"Don't go," she said.

"Llanara, I must—"

"I know," she said. "But we need your strength. I need your strength. Without the blessings of Ka'Ana'Tyat, I am afraid for our people."

He frowned. The black opening stood across the clearing, a shadowed passage made from twisted branches. Twice, now, it had been guarded by great beasts, and though it was no mystery for him to understand, twice its would-be acolytes had been rebuffed.

"You are strong," he said. "You will endure without me, for whatever time it takes to plead our cause among our friends."

He expected heated words, arguments thrice crafted to anticipate his every objection. Instead she bowed her head, cradling Arak'Doren's body as she looked away.

From Llanara, it was as solid a concession as she was like to make. He took it as such, embracing Ilek'Inari and then Llanara in turn, after she rose to her feet. Her nails dug into his shoulder, and she held him for a long moment before they separated.

28

ERRIS

Prisoners' Camp
Outside the Great Barrier

Philippe," she whispered, careful to keep her eyes turned down beneath the hood they had procured for her. "Philippe, I'm back."

The sleeping figure beside her stirred awake, rolling onto his side and scanning across the camp for any sign of the guards.

"Marie," he whispered back, then caught himself. "Or, General, sir. We've stopped. Today. You told me to tell you, when it looked like, when we heard we'd reached the place."

Her heart surged. "You're certain? The Gand army has stopped marching?"

"Yes, ma'am, sir. One of the Cullier boys overheard it from the Gand officers. We're done moving north, they said."

"Very good, Philippe. You're certain the last river you crossed was the Anorelle? And the army has kept the same pace?"

"Yes, ma'am, sir." He swallowed. "The fourth river since they took us. Six days since we crossed it. At the same pace, or thereabouts, since we first went through the barrier down south."

"Excellent work, Philippe. Keep up your spirits. You'll hear from me again soon."

He nodded once more, and she saw hope mixed with fear in his eyes before she released the *Need* binding, slipping back into familiar skin, propped astride Jiri's saddle as the pair of them tracked along the northern road.

At last, the enemy army had stopped moving. Six days north of the Anorelle, and they'd been traveling at a slow pace through the rough terrain of the wildlands. Ten, perhaps twelve leagues a day, no more. That would put them within spitting distance of New Sarresant itself when they breached the barrier. The Nameless take the Gandsmen, and whichever of them had planned this march. A terrible risk, but it was genius, pure and simple. Once she might have believed it the last stroke of Major General Alrich of Haddingston, some contingency plan conceived before she felled him with her saber at the Battle of Villecours. She would have believed it quite impossible for the enemy to produce two brilliant commanders in succession.

Now she knew the truth.

Philippe had revealed it to her, on her second visit to the prisoners' camp, when he'd told her of the light that shone from behind his wife's eyes when she tethered *Need*. golden light, light of the very kind she had seen in the eyes of the peasant boy Alrich of Haddingston. That boy had been no tactical genius, no brilliant commander. He was merely a vessel. Just as Marie d'Oreste lent her senses to Erris through the conduit of her *Need*, so Alrich had lent his body to the true commander of the Gandsmen. And when she'd slain the peasant boy, the true commander stepped behind the eyes of another and hatched this plan to take their capital unawares. He'd ordered the Gand armies through the barrier to bypass their scouts, all the while leaving the bulk of his own cavalry to keep the Sarresant forces distracted with their atrocities, dancing through the foothills south of their border.

The sheer genius of it staggered her. Every detail, planned to perfection. And she had seen the worst of it with her own eyes: Either there were many *Need* binders at work in the Gand army or the enemy commander was no longer limited to a single vessel, if indeed he ever had been. No telling when she might run across an officer with the golden eyes when she wore Marie's skin; thus far she'd managed to avoid notice, but the reality of what she faced struck home like a knife to the gut. All of her ideas on how to use *Need* to command an army had been put in place here by her enemy. A tall enough order for the Sarresant army to stand against that, and with the march they'd stolen on her through the wildlands, it seemed unlikely there would even be another battle of consequence on this side of the ocean.

Still, she would not give up so easily. Even as hope faded, the spark of a plan kindled in the back of her mind. The priests. Everything depended on the priests. She heeled Jiri to a quickened pace, diverting from the northern trade roads to tack west into the shadow of the barrier.

The abbey at Arentaigne was asleep when she arrived, driving Jiri at a canter in the black of night. No alarm or cry went up as it might have done in a military camp, but Arentaigne was no outpost or hillside fort. Its abbey was one of a dozen such arrayed along the barrier, spread from New Sarresant to Lorrine, and the only one in riding distance between her and the enemy army.

A few scattered lamps were lit by the time she dismounted, casting a soft glow from the second-story rooms as she hitched Jiri to see to her water and feed.

"I need the head abbot at once," she shouted. Her words echoed across the stone walls of the outer courtyard, greeted with the beginnings of shuffling steps and muted voices in the distance. Not good enough. "Now, priests! Move!"

She withdrew a cloth to wipe Jiri's sweat. They'd ridden for two days without pause for sleep or rest, and only a thick sheen over the top of Jiri's coat gave any hint of the fatigue she knew her mount hid beneath the surface. *Body* could only go so far, but she would see it a few steps farther before they were done. She'd wasted no time, riding straight north from Oreste. There would be no time for the army to make the march. It was down to her. Her and these damned priests, if they could ever be roused from their sleep.

"What is the meaning of this?" a brown-robed figure asked from behind, shambling out into the open air holding an oil lamp. "Who are—?"

"Are you the head abbot?" she demanded, looking up from Jiri's water bag.

"No, I'm—"

"Get the shit out of your ears, priests!" she shouted again, loud as she could manage. "And get the head abbot here at once."

The first brown-robed figure stood dumbly, mouth agape as she shouted over the top of him. "Now you wait just one minute—"

"Say another word and I will kill you," she announced, plain as day. She would do no such thing, but she found a little barbarity went a long way when dealing with civilians. And she was in no mood to explain herself twice.

The priest's mouth worked soundlessly, eyes wide as his gaze fell to the pistol holstered on one side of her belt, and to the saber dangling from the other. Did the fool not even recognize a cavalry uniform?

Finally, after what seemed an eternity, another brown-robed figure stepped into view, casting a weighing look between the first priest and where she stood tending to Jiri. This one at least had the sense to notice the star insignia on her collar and sleeve.

"I am the head abbess here, General," the second priest began. "My name is Sister Elise. What is—?"

"*Shelter*," she interrupted. "How many do you have here who can bind *Shelter*?"

The abbess frowned. "Our services are ever at the disposal of the crown, but this is most—"

"Enough, Sister. There is an army of Gandsmen less than a day's march from New Sarresant and I need as many *Shelter* binders as you have under this roof to saddle and ride every horse in your stables to death to stop them. Do I make myself clear?"

The woman gave her a stunned look. "Yes, General. Yes."

"Now, how many *Shelter* binders do you have?"

"Eight, including myself. But none of us are trained for fighting. The charge of this abbey is to repair and maintain the bindings along the northwest border. We won't be of any use in a battle."

"That depends on the nature of the battle, Sister," she said, withdrawing the water bag from Jiri's muzzle. "This one is going to be fought in precisely your area of expertise."

By now a handful of priests had come clamoring into the courtyard. Sister Elise made a gesture for them to stay back and keep quiet.

"I don't take your meaning, General," Sister Elise said.

"I'll explain as we ride. Saddle every horse in your stable and rouse your *Shelter* binders. We move as soon as your people are ready."

She nearly had cause to regret her display at Arentaigne as they rode. A more diplomatic leader might have roused them in a more amicable fashion, but the requirements of the service ofttimes dictated speed over etiquette. In any case, being roused by rough words in the early hours of the morning would be the least of their concerns before this was over.

Eight priests and twelve horses. Only Jiri was able to keep pace without signs of flagging, though with two days' hard ride behind her even Jiri was strained. She'd explained the plan, and the stakes, as they rode. To her credit Sister Elise handled it well, and relayed the necessary information to her priests without troubling Erris to repeat any details. It left her to focus on keeping up the pace, ensuring none of them fell behind. Before long she took up the spare horses' lead lines to guide them, as it became clear none of the others were well suited to hard travel.

The first rays of morning sunlight saw them thirty leagues past the abbey, a day's march for a well-trained infantry brigade. Half what they needed to cover, if luck was on their side. She called the first halt to rest and change mounts as the sun cleared the eastern horizon. This near the coastline it made for a rich display of orange, purple, and gold, a fitting moment to break for some of the hard bread and cheese they'd packed from the abbey stores. She paced through the line, checking the horses for signs they might falter, selecting the weakest of the four to swap for their more rested counterparts. The least she could do short of diverting into a roadside village to procure fresh animals, little as she was like to find any decent horseflesh pulling a farm cart or tending to the harvest. Say what she would about Arentaigne, at least Sister Elise kept a good stable.

"Up," she called when she'd finished her inspection. "Time to move."

The priest who had woken first at the abbey gave her a sour face. "How much longer? Even by daylight our mounts aren't good for more than another hour or two at this pace."

"No," she replied. "No, I expect they're not."

The rest of them exchanged a look.

"You mean to have us walking?" The priest challenged her with a defiant glare.

"Brother Antonin—" Sister Elise said.

"I'd have you crawling through a pool of your own entrails if it meant a chance to save the city, you blind fool," she snapped back. "But no. No. If it comes to that, if your horses falter, then it means you run."

The priests said nothing more after she swung herself into Jiri's saddle and heeled her forward, though the exchange had soured whatever relief they'd had from food as they pressed on.

The first horse broke before they'd gone another five leagues, stuttering to a halt and refusing to budge no matter how the mare was coaxed. No amount of cursing proved effective, and so they left her behind, her rider transferred to one of the reserves. Sister Elise made as if to protest for a moment, cut off by a withering look before she could voice the complaint.

Two more horses went down before they left the road. One stuttered to a halt as the first had done, but the second went down in a heap, slowing enough not to injure its rider before it pitched itself into the dust. An effort Erris judged worthy of a quick end no matter the possibility of a battle to come. She'd drawn her pistol and fired before the priests could register her intent, a miniature thunderclap echoing across the sparse woodland. Sullen eyes regarded her after that, blessedly silent as they turned northwest, leaving the road behind as they fanned out toward the Great Barrier.

Whatever hope they'd harbored that she might reduce the pace was snuffed out as she nudged Jiri to a canter, weaving through the trees in the direction of the barrier. The last of the reserve mounts was used within the hour, a broken leg that earned another pistol shot to silence its shrill screams.

When the fifth horse went down she called another halt. They were close, so close. By her reckoning they should be within a handful of leagues from where the Gand army had stopped its march. Yet if they pressed on with riders doubling up, the rest would collapse before they made it another hour. She did another review of the horses, and split them without protest from the priests. The freshest, strongest mounts and riders would press on while those who needed a rest took it. Only Jiri had the strength to maintain her pace at the head of the column, and so it fell to her to ride with her vision shifted to the leylines, watching for connections. The rest would follow, keeping the towering blue haze of the barrier to their left until they came upon the place. Gods grant them the strength to catch up before it was too late.

Another hour passed, and exhaustion settled around her like a warm cloak in a winter storm. Shifting her vision to the leylines gave no sign of anything more than the erratic patches of *Life* and *Body* common in wild places, and of course the deep pool of gray haze she knew the priests would see as the white pearls of *Shelter*, the reserve that powered the Great Barrier itself.

Then finally, *Death*.

Her heart sank even as blood rushed through her veins. She'd found it, and she was not too late. A quarter league in the distance, but unmistakable: inky blackness pooling on the far side of the barrier. It was there, and it was growing. Her thoughts turned to Marie and Philippe, to the rest of the villagers of Oreste, and she offered a prayer to the Exarch on their behalf.

Sister Elise was the first to arrive.

"Is this it?" the sister asked, looking as bone-weary as her mount beneath her. "Is this the place?"

"This is it," she replied. "They are pooling *Death* now. The rest will begin soon."

Sister Elise nodded, allowing her mount to stutter to a halt as she lowered herself from its back.

"The rest of your priests," Erris said. "They're close?"

Again Sister Elise nodded. "We may not be soldiers, General, but we are far from weak."

She offered no reply to that, shifting her sight to find *Body*, tethering it through the sister.

The woman's eyes widened, then she bowed her head in thanks. "Thank you, General."

"The least I can do, Sister."

The most she could do in fact. Without being able to see or use *Shelter* she was as useless as a noble-born officer for this fight. She could ease the fatigue of the ride with *Body*, but not the deep exhaustion of working with the leylines themselves.

Three more priests arrived within a few minutes, paying truth to Sister Elise's claim. None looked less bone-weary than their abbess, and all were grateful for the *Body* Erris offered. *Death* continued to swell beneath the barrier, and in the few moments of respite she allowed herself to look for the golden shimmer that indicated her link to Marie d'Oreste. The connection was effortless to find after the initial bond was made; it had never taken more than a moment to find Marie, no matter the distance between them. Of course this time she expected to find nothing. She knew full well what the inky pool betokened for the Gandsmen's prisoners.

Yet there it was. Against all odds, she saw it there: *Need.* Marie was alive.

She expelled a sharp breath, turning the heads of the priests, more than one of them starting as if she had crept up on them from the shadows.

"What is it, General?" Sister Elise asked. "Have they started?"

"You'll know before I do, Sister. Watch the barrier. I have no gift for *Shelter.*"

The sister gave a grim nod. Erris could see the responsibility settle over the other woman. To her credit the abbess did not flinch.

Sister Elise took charge, speaking with the others and welcoming the fifth and sixth of their number when they arrived a few minutes later. Erris took the moment to rest, leaning against Jiri as her mount lay in the grass beside her. Fatigue washed over her. She had pushed herself and ridden these priests just as hard. Yet in their element she could almost dare to believe they were measured to the task. Sister Elise had a sharp way with command, a practiced sense of what her people could do. Just as well none of her binders could sense *Death,* though, or the enormity of their task might become a hurdle unto itself. Never mind that the strongest *Shelter* binders would have been forced into the army rather than the priesthood. Never mind that the enemy had almost certainly brought twice their number or more.

She grit her teeth, forcing those thoughts to die. No point in harboring doubts now. Everything hinged on the next few hours. *Shelter* crews like the priests of Arentaigne were used to repair the barrier when it weakened, drawing on the leylines to reinforce its towering wall. Using *Death* to disrupt the barrier, to create a breach willfully, was an abominable tactic, and all the more so for their using prisoners to do it rather than livestock. Men and women left greater pockets of inky *Death* when they were slain, but it was no less sickening to contemplate using it in battle.

She closed her eyes to ward away the thoughts, and once more found Marie. *Need* called to her, a shimmering light in the distance.

A risk to embrace it now, but the prisoners were marked for death regardless. If by chance there was some last information, some last words that could pass between them...

A glance at Sister Elise revealed the priests in good order. She could spare a few moments.

She reached out to *Need*, to Marie, and tethered herself to the golden light.

Her vision shifted.

Even before her eyes focused, she knew something was wrong. Where she'd expected the familiar rope tethers and ragged faces of the prisoners' camp, she was surrounded by luxury. Elaborately woven carpets strewn across the floors of a broad canvas tent, filled with actual furniture—a desk, tables, chairs, and a bed. Looking down, she saw Marie's familiar travel-worn dress. No mistake there. What was Marie doing in a tent like this?

"Ah, at last," came a voice from behind her. "I was hoping you'd make another appearance."

She spun, and found herself facing a tall man standing upright, wearing the red uniform of Gand. Dirt-colored hair specked with gray, a clean-shaven face just starting to show the lines of age, four stars on his collar. And a pulsing, golden light shining from behind his eyes.

He walked around the desk, towering over Marie.

"So pleasant to meet my enemies before I crush them," he said, his words touched with a foreign accent she couldn't place, stilted and severe. "An opportunity rarely afforded commanders who do not share our gifts, though I expect a fledgling like yourself does not truly understand."

"This is your doing," she said in a cold voice, not meaning it to be a question.

He laughed. "Yes. I've beaten you, with my little maneuver. The rest of this"—he made a dismissive gesture—"is a formality. We both know your city will fall."

She said nothing, fixing a look of hatred on her face. This man, or rather whoever was seeing from behind those golden eyes, was responsible for unconscionable brutality, murders, and worse. Fantain's Cross, Oreste, and how many others could be laid at his feet. Before he had taken control the Gandsmen had fought according to the precepts of war. Now they were monsters made flesh.

"Come now," he said, affecting a light tone as he sat in one of the cushioned chairs, motioning for her to do the same. "Don't sulk. I began the campaign with more matériel and a superior tactical position. It was only natural I should find victory here. Your city is situated foolishly close to the *Aegis* barrier; surely you must have expected a flanking maneuver backed with disruption bindings?"

She remained standing, eyes narrowing as she maintained her glare. "If you intend to kill Marie, do it and be done with it."

He arched an eyebrow. "Kill Marie? Your vessel, you mean? That is not the way these things are done. Your vessel will remain here, should the need arise to discuss terms. The right of the victor, as it were."

"You're no Gandsman." She knew it for a certainty. The accent was wrong, but intuition led the rest of the way. This man—this creature, in light of the horrors he'd commanded done—carried himself with a menace she'd never seen among the generals of any army.

He smiled. "No, I am not. But desperate men hungering for power will embrace whatever talent promises to get them there. The Gandsmen were halfway to empire when your king ordered his invasion, and it frightened my would-be puppeteers enough to hand the strings to me. It is enough, for now. I suppose you fight for Sarresant here in your colonies. One of their generals, perhaps?"

She knew better than to confirm it, and said nothing.

"No matter," he said. "It's obvious. You've little stake in the conflict across the sea, judging by the ineptitude of your forces there."

She'd heard enough. Turning away, she prepared to release the *Need* binding, feeling a pang of sorrow leaving Marie in the company of this creature.

The man leaned forward in his chair before she could release the binding, his tone growing cold. "I will find you, wherever you think to hide. I know you are here in the colonies. You will not ascend. I've beaten you today, and I will beat you again. Your city will burn, and your people be put to the sword until I find you."

She turned back to him slowly. He had reclined once more, wearing a smug look.

She struck him in the face, as hard as Marie could muster. Bless the woman for a life of hard work in the fields of Oreste, and a frame well built enough to deliver a solid blow. She knew from the way his head snapped back, eyes rolling up into his skull, that she'd produced the desired effect. Without waiting for further confirmation, she gathered her skirts and fled the tent.

The sounds of an army camp on the cusp of a march came to life around her when she emerged through the flaps. Couriers made their way between the tent lines even while the tents themselves were being struck by soldiers and camp followers alike. Thank the Gods for the chaos of it; on an ordinary day she'd never have escaped a general's tent unnoticed. As it was she fell into the familiar stance of urgent, deliberate movement, the old scout's trick of moving among enemies by hiding in plain sight. For Marie's sake, she would try to find someplace in the camp, somewhere she could hide and perhaps make an escape in the rush of what would come. There. A wagon ahead, at the edge of the camp, near the tree line, already loaded with tents and provisions, only awaiting a team to arrive to be hitched to drive it. She'd make for the wagon and slip among the cargo. If the Gandsmen succeeded in breaching the barrier, Marie could stow away and escape once they crossed into Sarresant territory. And if not, the wagon was near enough to the edge of the camp that she could make for the wilds. It was unlikely the enemy had sentries posted here—little need for that, considering.

A slim chance in either case, but preferable by far to another minute in the company of the monster in command of the Gand army. Ignoring the soldiers who moved through the camp paths around her, she affected not to notice the few stray curious looks she drew as she moved toward it. Gods be praised, none of the soldiers did more than look. She'd be at the wagon momentarily…

The *Need* binding withdrew, and her vision snapped back into her own skin.

"Chevalier-General!" one of the priests cried, shaking her arm.

"What is it?" she demanded, voice flush with anger as she shook loose the brown-robed man's grasp.

"Chevalier-General, it's begun."

Even without seeing the *Shelter* bindings, it was clear the priests had not been able to blunt the onslaught of *Death* from the Gand binders. That had been her plan: to rebuild the barrier as the Gandsmen tore it down, to trap the enemy army in the savage wildlands after they exhausted their reserve of *Death*. Yet now the swirling haze of the Great Barrier had paled to a thin white, almost pink hue. Where the color normally rushed with patterns like inks dripped down a page, it had slowed to a crawl, hardly moving. The priests focused as they stared up at the barrier, but the sweat dripping from their brows, the pained lines on each of their faces made clear the toll it had taken.

"Brother Antonin, Sister Jolene, the top-left quadrant," Sister Elise called. "Now!"

A ripping sound filled the air from high above as trails of blue haze vented out over their heads.

One of the priestesses shrieked, sinking to her knees before she slumped over onto the ground.

"No!" Sister Elise shouted. "Brother Marc, cover for her!"

Erris wasted no time, rushing to the side of the fallen priestess. She tethered thick strands of *Body*, purging the woman of every lingering bit of fatigue in her system, all save the exhaustion of working with the leylines, the deep exhaustion beyond her ability to heal.

Erris shook her head. "This one is out, Sister."

Sister Elise managed a few curses, the sort of which only a priest could know.

"It's going," called one of the men. "I can't—"

Another sound like a sheet torn in half, still far overhead. Nothing close to the ground, nothing low enough for troops to pass through, thank the Gods.

Sister Elise turned to her, a look of panic in her eyes.

"Sister Elise," Erris said to her, "the lives of every man and woman in New Sarresant depend on you. Is there any more that can be done?"

"I... there are so many. I need more strength. I need..." She trailed off, shame welling up in her eyes.

Erris nodded. She'd been preparing herself for this for the last hour, watching Sister Elise and her priests losing their struggle to repair the barrier. They couldn't stop the Gandsmen breaking through. No sense in dying here for the sake of pride, not when their horses might be able to speed them away with whatever measure of strength remained to them.

The order to withdraw formed on the tip of her tongue, and just as suddenly turned to ash.

Need.

A glimmer of light sparked and bloomed in Sister Elise, standing across from her. Perhaps if the other woman could not muster the strength required, Erris herself could step in and lead their effort.

She embraced the light, and felt her vision leap into the other woman's skin. She whirled about, ignoring the disorienting feeling of watching her body through another's eyes.

"Focus," she cried in Sister Elise's voice. "We must stop them!"

The rest of the priests started, but seemed to take heart from her unexpected words, knotting their faces in grim determination. Erris closed her eyes, shifting her vision to the leylines.

It was as if she saw another world.

In place of the familiar greens of *Life*, the red motes of *Body*, and the ink-clouds of *Death*, she saw only one, new pattern: white spheres like links of pearls, wrapping themselves around the leylines emanating from beneath the Great Barrier. *Shelter.* Breathing deep, she opened herself to the new energy, aiming to tether a full-strength binding, with all the power she could handle.

Nothing.

She tried again.

Nothing.

Her heart sank. Was this it, then? She could see the *Shelter* bindings through Sister Elise's eyes, but could no more tether them than if she had tried while wearing her own skin. Perhaps there was some technique, some trick to *Shelter* that differed from the leyline energies with which she had experience. Perhaps...

No.

If there were such a technique, she didn't have time to learn it now. She faced the cold reality of it like a blow to the gut. She let the *Need* binding fade.

"What was—?" Sister Elise sputtered, in control of her own body once more.

"I will explain later, Sister," she said. "For now, we must ride."

"It was as if I... such strength..."

"Move!"

The other woman blinked, then nodded. She turned to give instruction to the priests as Erris rushed to their makeshift horse line to retrieve their mounts. Jiri snorted in frustration, sensing her rider's mood. Erris shifted her vision to bind *Body* through Jiri to energize her for the ride ahead—and she froze. *Body* was there in abundance; it was always so in the wild, where beasts hunted beasts, and they were near an army camp besides. But there was more. Strands of pearls, white pearls along the lines where always before she had seen only hazy, formless strands of energy.

Shelter. The same energy she'd seen moments before, behind Sister Elise's eyes.

She tethered it, feeling it surge through her with all the force she could manage. The Great Barrier now rose before her in an entirely new light: Instead of formless energy coursing over swirls of ever-paler color, she could see the strands themselves, being ripped apart by the *Death* bindings of the Gandsmen. In anger, she tried desperately to rebuild the patterns as she saw them torn down. She could see similar efforts now, where the priests continued their struggle to maintain the barrier's strength.

"Sister Elise!" she called, even amid the distraction as she worked. "Do not stand down. I've found a means to aid you. We can stop them!"

If the priestess made any protest, she didn't hear. It was enough that the rest of the priests maintained their efforts. Erris lost herself in the struggle, pouring all her energy into rebuilding wherever the enemy tried to destroy. Where before the barrier had paled, its color seemed to stabilize. If they could hold on like this...

One of the priests cried out, drawing her attention back to the clearing in which they stood. A sickening feeling gripped her as she realized the cause: Another of their number had collapsed under the strain, the exhaustion taking a toll beyond his ability to maintain.

"No," she cried. "Hold on!"

They tried.

Another priest crumpled to the ground, and the white strands of *Shelter* began to slip once more.

Moving as fast as her senses allowed, she focused all of her will on the strands of the barrier. She tethered *Body* to speed her reflexes, and *Life* to sharpen her vision. And though she was untrained with *Shelter*, she was a fullbinder with more raw strength than any four half-trained priests. She sensed a crack forming in the wall and snuffed it out, pouring *Shelter* into the holes left by the enemy's use of *Death*.

She missed one. A fissure erupted above, a gash like torn cloth ripping in the wind.

She grit her teeth as she worked, pouring herself into each moment. The other priests worked around her, with Sister Elise barking commands in response to Erris's efforts. A crack welled up near the base of the wall, and she fought it down in a fury. But she missed another seam torn out above, cracking and breaking in a rush of wind. The barrier seemed to groan, as if the entirety of the wall bent in on itself.

And then it stopped.

In a moment, her efforts went to repairing and strengthening the barrier instead of staying one step ahead of the *Death* trying to rip the wall apart. It was as if the enemy had abruptly ceased his attack, and in mere moments the worst of the ripped seams knotted themselves together as if they had never been breached.

Only then did she realize the ink-clouds of *Death* were gone. Empty. The enemy had run out of prisoners to kill.

Her mood soured even in the moment of triumph.

"Is that it?" one of the priests asked.

"General?" Sister Elise looked to her.

She met their eyes, seeing a reflection of the exhaustion she felt caked into her bones. She nodded.

A whooping cry went up among the priests still standing.

"Rest now," she said. "And prepare ourselves for the enemy to try again."

Whatever celebration had been coming, it died with those words. She saw in their eyes a halfhearted protest, perhaps thinking their part was finished. Still, at that moment an order to rest was not like to be disobeyed. Most of the priests dropped to sit where they had stood, grateful for reprieve, however temporary.

That it would be temporary she had no doubt. Whoever that creature was, the strange, cold man who had spoken to her behind golden eyes in the Gand command tent, he'd ordered hundreds of innocents slain to fuel his plans. He would not balk at ordering his own soldiers slain for *Death* once his binders were rested enough for another attempt.

She slumped to the ground at Jiri's side. Her mount had already given in to sleep, too weary to remain standing. She felt the same exhaustion washing over her. She needed a week's rest, and she might have a few hours, if the Gods were good.

Golden light woke her, and she gasped, bolting upright quick enough to startle Jiri as she rose.

Too long. She'd slept too long. The sun's light dimmed in the west, above the Great Barrier. Panic flooded her before her vision focused on the barrier's swirling haze. It stood, thank the Gods. Somehow it stood.

"Up," she barked, rousing the priests arrayed among the trees. They'd slept as she had, exhausted from the ride to reach the barrier and their struggles to keep it whole. The fog she'd purged from her senses played again among the priests, but she paid it no mind. They'd proved their worth. They would be ready when the enemy tried again.

She shifted her sight to the leylines, and her stomach lurched.

Death.

Inky clouds of *Death* as wide as she had ever seen. Sour blackness clinging to the leylines, enough to drown a city, pooling on the far side of the barrier.

"It's coming!" she shouted. "They're trying again, now!"

Her words dispelled any vestiges of fatigue from the priests, and they locked eyes on the barrier, blinking to signify they'd shifted sight to the leylines, ready for whatever came.

The barrier stood. Unchanging, and undisturbed.

Death remained. Vast pools of blackness, a hundredfold larger than the enemy had used in their earlier assault. And golden light. It pulsed among the ink-clouds, bright enough she'd seen it even without shifting her sight to the leylines. She hadn't paid it attention, confronted by the shock of the barrier still standing, and of *Death*, but turned to it now. Marie.

She made the connection, and shifted her senses into a sea of blood.

Marie had tucked herself inside the wagon on the edge of the Gand camp, but the smell cut through the crates and canvas, thick enough for her to retch even through the bond of *Need*. Somehow the woman had stayed hidden from whatever had transpired outside the wagon. Prudence shouted at her to stay there, to stay cloistered away from whatever had produced the tide of *Death*. But even had it been her skin she risked, she needed to know. She dislodged herself from Marie's hiding place, rose from beneath the covered wagon, and stepped down into horror.

Dead soldiers in red coats, torn in pieces and strewn across grasses stained crimson from calf-deep pools of blood.

And dogs. Scores of dogs; hundreds. Corpses of dogs mixed in with the men and women, each one a copy of the others, their fur a twisted shade between red and black.

29

SARINE

The Revellion Coach
Southgate District, New Sarresant

No quarter of the city was truly foreign to her, but the twisting, narrow roads of Southgate came close. Perhaps it was merely the vantage offered by the Revellion coach, or the anticipation as they drew nearer to Reyne d'Agarre's manse. The district was a mix of work and wealth, a place where textile looms could be found alongside the estates of wealthy families, housing citizens who lacked only the requisite surname to have a place among the nobles of the Gardens, or at Rasailles. Always before the factory owners and other moneyed commonfolk residing in Southgate had seemed closer to the nobles than to the red-knuckled workers they employed. Now, riding beside the heir to the Marquis Revellion, the distance seemed greater in the opposite direction. Here where they had everything—lives of luxury, comfort, and the means to do what they would—the difference marked by blood could be seen for what it was: an insurmountable, inexorable divide.

She saw it on Donatien Revellion's face as the carriage rolled forward. For all his protestations of *égalité* and the principles of philosophers like Fantiere, it was clear even he could sense the height from which his family descended when they came to Southgate. Bless him for reacting as he did, with uncomfortable reserve rather than haughty disdain.

She put words to the thought. "Do you think the nobles could ever see them as equals?"

He turned to regard her as they rode, weighing the question. "The commonfolk, you mean?"

She nodded.

"That's part of our purpose tonight at Master d'Agarre's salon, no? To effect change, we must begin to bring down the barriers between us, between all men and women of all creeds and class. If they see me today as a nobleman, I hope they will soon regard me as no more than the sum of my talents."

"A noble sentiment, my lord," she said, eliciting a grin at the wordplay. "But I worry it will be easier by far for the commonfolk to see enemies, and not equals."

Despite her concerns, she appreciated the ideal. It was a fine vision: real equality, rule by merit and place by desert rather than the accident of birth. They'd passed the afternoon in just such conversation, after she'd agreed to attend Master d'Agarre's salon. Her agreement had melted away a tension in Lord Revellion she hadn't known was there. To her, the principles of *égalité* were a captivating intellectual exercise and little more. To Lord Revellion, they were barely short of treason, if they were short at all. He had more to lose by far, and when he showed that side of himself to her, he made himself vulnerable in a way she had not considered before. To find she embraced his ideals, and would accompany him as he began his journey to do more than think censured thoughts, to act on the strength of shared conviction, together—it had been a powerful exchange, on both sides.

Now they rode toward Master d'Agarre's salon. By itself such a thing was far from remarkable. The wealthy among New Sarresant's citizens hosted such affairs nightly, both nobles and moneyed commonfolk, and the circles mixed often enough to pass without comment. It was possible Donatien expected no more than talk—incendiary though it might be—but she'd seen enough from d'Agarre to know his organization ran deeper than idle sedition and rumormongering. He was behind the thefts that had racked the city for months. He'd fed the citizens of the Maw in the face of violence from the city watch. And he'd spoken to her of effecting change, real change. A chance to shape the world according to her will. She had no illusions of herself as some power-mad despot, but she'd seen firsthand what the *kaas* could do. Curiosity drove her to listen when d'Agarre spoke, as much for a chance to learn more about Zi's gifts as to help shape a better world for people like her, people who had grown up in the shadow of the powerful. It was a dream, but like her meeting with Lord Revellion, it was a dream that might yet prove true.

The d'Agarre manse was opulent, designed to make clear its residents lacked for little. Tall hedges ringed the boundary, with a canopy of evenly spaced trees providing privacy from the street and a line of blazing lanterns beckoning visitors toward the receiving grounds. Footmen in well-tailored livery received the coach as they pulled into the circle and halted the team. Lord Revellion made his exit first, then reached back to take her hand as she descended—no mean feat in the long blue skirts she'd chosen earlier in the day. They produced invitations for the benefit of the crier, and were ushered across the threshold into the manse with the appropriate acclaim.

Reyne d'Agarre stood at the foot of the grand staircase as they entered, crystal wineglass in hand, surrounded by a pack of well-dressed guests. His eyes lit up as the two of them were announced in sequence. The crier had been midway through the sequence of Revellion's introduction when d'Agarre excused himself from his company and moved to intercept them both before either had managed so much as to remove their coats.

"At last," d'Agarre said, accompanied by a deep bow. "Sarine, I am overjoyed to have your attendance at my humble gathering." He made another bow toward Lord Revellion. "And to have arrived on the arm of another of my guests—my lord, we are humbled by your presence."

She managed a more graceful curtsy than she might once have imagined herself capable. "Thank you, Master d'Agarre. Lord Revellion and I are both honored to attend."

"Indeed," Lord Revellion said. "Much has been said of your company, Master d'Agarre. I believe I speak for Sarine when I say we are eager to see what may come of this evening's diversions."

D'Agarre lowered his head in a gesture of humility. "I can only hope we meet your expectations. I've managed to arrange something of a surprise for this evening's entertainment." His eyes sparkled. "I believe the both of you will find it quite stimulating."

"He won't reveal the surprise, you know, no matter how you ask," another voice chimed in from behind. D'Agarre turned and smiled at the newcomer, a woman of middle years dressed in what was considered the height of the season's fashion: all embroidery, color, and volume.

"Allow me to present the Comtesse de Rillefort," d'Agarre said with a gesture. "Comtesse, the Lord Revellion and Madame Sarine."

Lord Revellion made a slight bow. "An unexpected pleasure to see you here, my lady."

Sarine made to echo the sentiment, but found the words dry on her tongue as the comtesse turned to regard her with a hawkish look.

"So you're Donatien's secret," she said, eyeing Sarine up and down. "You set the green ablaze with that dress you wore, you know, and I see you've topped it tonight. Sarine, was it? You're a vision, my dear; I hope you'll find time for me after Master d'Agarre has revealed his surprise."

D'Agarre feigned befuddlement, smiling back and forth between Sarine and the comtesse. "It seems the nobles among us are privy to goings-on I myself am not. What was this, about blazes and gardens?"

"Oh, I will tell you everything, my dear," the Comtesse de Rillefort said. "Let them settle in, while you and I gossip."

At that moment servants arrived to take their coats, and d'Agarre flashed another grin as he allowed the comtesse to lead him away. "Please, enjoy every comfort on offer," he said. "And we will speak later, be sure of it." He gave Sarine a meaningful look as he backed away.

Lord Revellion spoke softly to her as they walked together toward the sitting room, where most of the guests were congregating at the far side of the foyer. "It seems the company of radicals is not so very different from nobility after all. I wouldn't have thought the comtesse to number among this fold. She and her husband have always been steadfast supporters of Duc-Governor Cherrain."

"Perhaps d'Agarre's philosophy is not so open a secret, even in this company? This is a social affair, after all."

He frowned. "Perhaps."

As it happened, it was not the case. No sooner had they entered the sitting room than they stumbled onto an impassioned exchange over the rightful place of laborers in an egalitarian society. She eyed him with relief, which he returned tenfold. This was what he had come for, she knew well enough. Revellion's eyes seemed to glow as they found places among the cushioned chaises and drank in the debate. Not a minute had passed before he was contributing to the discussion, halting one of the men—who had the appearance of one of the moneyed factory owners from Southgate—on a subtle point of the philosophy of rights. His opponents in the debate fired back with heated rhetoric, and so it went for some time.

She followed the lines of logic easily enough on both sides, even if the terms and philosophers they quoted were often outside her frame of reference. More important to her was the feeling that here, for perhaps the first time, she was among people who thought as she did, but were also prepared to act. A frightening thought for a girl alone in the Maw, but here, in this company, an empowering one.

And Zi seemed to revel here, alive as she had rarely seen him.

His scales were alternatively a bright gold fit to adorn the queen and a burnished copper-red that reminded her of the sunrise over the harbor. He'd taken up a position on an empty cushion beside her, luxuriating as the ideas flew back and forth across the salon.

She nestled into the deep cushions and spoke softly to him, in a private whisper. "What do you think of him, Zi?"

Lord Revellion?

She nodded.

Good ideas. Ideas that lead to change, of the sort that accords with the lives to which your kind are best suited.

Almost she laughed in spite of herself. Since when had Zi become a philosopher? She felt a pang of frustration that, given the company, she couldn't bring herself to strike up a conversation and press Zi further. Even aside Reyne d'Agarre's revelation of his own... *kaas*... she could not so easily shake the habits of a lifetime of secrecy where Zi was concerned.

The conversation had progressed to more heated rhetoric when d'Agarre made his entry into the sitting room via a door at the back, the Comtesse de Rillefort on his arm. Their arrival was noticed by more than a few of the guests, but after d'Agarre seemed content to watch and listen, their attention drifted back to the debate. D'Agarre himself joined in after he'd heard enough to understand the basic structure of the arguments.

After a time, the comtesse moved to sit beside her, opposite the cushion Zi had made his own. She welcomed the other woman with a smile, which the comtesse returned in kind as she sipped wine from a crystal glass.

"His surprise is ready, you know," the comtesse said with a gleam in her eye, leaning forward to speak in quiet tones. "But he can't help himself from these sorts of exchanges."

"So he's revealed his secrets to you after all, then, my lady?"

"Some few of them," the comtesse replied. "Not least of which was your story. He says...well..." She gestured with her free hand to the cushion where Zi lay. And at once, a second *kaas* was there, beside Zi, with the same metallic scales and twisted coils of her longtime companion, only different somehow. She'd recognize Zi among a dozen of his kind, and just as surely she knew this new one was different from the one d'Agarre had showed her outside the Sacre-Lin.

She stifled a gasp, and the comtesse patted her arm in a soothing gesture. "It's all right," the other woman said. "Only we two can see him. They can be particular about revealing themselves. But Arix agreed with Master d'Agarre that you could be trusted with certain secrets."

"Arix? Your...?"

"Yes," the comtesse said. "My *kaas*. And yours is called?"

"Zi."

"Zi," the other woman confirmed, smiling as she cast a look about the room. "The *kaas* do love these debates, don't they?"

Sarine nodded. "Is this thing common among Master d'Agarre's guests? To have..." She swallowed. "A *kaas*?"

"Oh heavens no!" the comtesse exclaimed under her breath. "Only a bare few of us, which is no small part of his excitement to have met you. He says you came to yours without knowledge of the book—the Codex, I mean."

"Yes. He mentioned a book, when we spoke before. He made it sound of great import."

"And is it true you cannot recall having ever possessed such a thing, even as a child?"

She shook her head.

"Very interesting," the comtesse said behind a veiled smile. "Very interesting indeed. I wonder, do you suppose your Lord Revellion could spare your company for a time? Knowing Reyne, this philosophical dalliance is like to continue for another hour at least, surprises be damned. I'd as soon turn your attention toward somewhat more instructive, if you'd be favorably disposed."

Her heart fluttered. She'd lived with Zi for as long as she could remember, and still never come close to unlocking the mystery of her enigmatic companion. Lord Revellion sat beside her on the long chaise, presently intent on following a counterargument posed by one of the merchants in attendance. He met her glance briefly and beamed a smile toward her before returning his focus to the main debate.

"Donatien seems well enough occupied, my lady. I would learn more, if you would lead the way."

"Excellent," the comtesse said, setting her wineglass aside on a table situated between the couches. The other woman caught Reyne d'Agarre's eye, and an understanding seemed to pass between them.

The comtesse rose, gesturing for her to follow toward one of the doors along the back wall. Lord Revellion gave her an inquiring look, which she dismissed with a reassuring smile. It pleased her to see him so engaged, so in his element—not a thing she'd choose to disturb. Yet for her, the pleasures of the salon counted for little against the comtesse's promised foray into the unknown. It proved to be no short journey—the d'Agarre manse was expansive, to say the least—and they tracked through lavishly decorated hallways, down spiraled staircases of wrought iron until she was sure they must be belowground. The comtesse confirmed it was so when she asked, only demurring that some secrets were best kept well hidden from prying eyes. As if to drive the point home, when they came to a wood-paneled wall at the end of a long corridor, a sharp pull on one of the sconces clicked and swung a door open whose seams had been hidden only moments before. She sucked in a breath, feeling nerves that had built during their descent come in a sudden rush. The comtesse gave her a sympathetic look, then gestured for Sarine to follow her inside.

As she stepped through the once-hidden doorway, her breath caught again.

The chamber was massive, easily as large as the aboveground sitting room and foyer combined, and lined wall-to-wall with bookshelves tall enough to require stepladders distributed throughout the room. Wooden tables extended between the shelves, piled with books, loose parchment, maps, and writing materials of all sorts. She'd never imagined so many volumes gathered in one place; her uncle had told her of the royal libraries at Rasailles, and in the Old World, but she could scarce imagine any of them contained a more thorough collection than this. Yet somehow the splendor of so much accumulated knowledge paled beside the centerpiece of the room: In a circular space between the long rows of tables sat seven columns, waist-high, upon each of which rested an elevated display. Four of the displays were empty, but three of the columns hosted great tomes, books that even from across the chamber seemed to radiate an aura of allure, danger, and power.

"The Codex," her guide said simply. "Or the Codices, as it were."

Seven places. "So there are only seven others?" she asked, numbness lingering in her voice. "Others like me, I mean."

"Oh no. Only seven of us here in the colonies. There are more elsewhere, of course. Even one among the native tribes, since Reyne, brilliant man that he is, correctly interpreted the passage pertaining to the lands outside the Great Barrier."

She took a deep breath. "How did this come to be?"

"You mean the d'Agarre library, the Codex, the *kaas*...?" The comtesse's words trailed off. "You mean all of it, don't you?"

Sarine nodded weakly.

The comtesse took her arm with a gentle touch, guiding them both toward the heart of the chamber. "It begins with the book. Copies can be made at will, but its pages are no more than garbled nonsense to one without the gift. If a prospective acolyte can read it, it means there is a chance a *kaas* will manifest. If they do, then we have another member of our fold. The book itself is a guide, a tome of philosophy and mysteries we work to unravel. Not the least of which is where to find new acolytes. Though it is not always so. Arix has been the companion of my family, passed down mother to daughter since we received his Codex from the Gods themselves, when last they walked among the living."

Sarine's eyes drifted toward the tomes resting atop the white plinths at the center of the room. "The Gods?" she asked, doubt touching her voice.

The comtesse smiled. "Of course. Reyne mentioned you had been raised by a priest. Many of the priesthood speak of the Gods walking among us as allegories, stories meant to inspire us, myths contorted by the passage of time. I assure you it is not so. The Gods have visited our world, and they will come again."

She swallowed the dryness in her throat. "You understand that is... difficult to accept."

"Of course, my dear, but it is the truth nonetheless." The comtesse gestured to the great library around them. "Part of what we do here is keep the records, collecting the sources of our myths in an effort to prepare ourselves for the time of ascension—a chance for mortals to join the Gods' ranks, if we can solve the mysteries in time to follow where they lead. That is our dream. Not only to forge a better world for the men and women of Sarresant, but for all men, all women, everywhere. With the *kaas* and the Codex to guide us we have preserved much, and kept hidden from the eyes of those who might oppose us, whether from malice, or lack of understanding."

They came to a stop before one of the white columns, one of those where the display held a great tome, lying open there on the stand. So close, she could see the pages were covered in symbols like no lettering she had seen before.

"This one is mine," the comtesse said.

The words hung between them for a moment.

"May I?" Sarine asked.

The other woman gestured toward the book. "Yes, of course. They are meant to be studied. Reyne has already commissioned a new copy be made for you. Until then, one of ours will suffice."

She stepped forward to the base of the column and reached up to touch the open book. She expected some surge of energy, some shocking jolt when she made contact, but felt only paper and a thick binding behind, not so different from her uncle's best copies of the holy books back at the chapel. Now, turning the pages, she could see in detail the symbols covering each face, jagged edges mixed with soft curves amid circular patterns with a pleasing aesthetic but, at a glance, no apparent significance or meaning.

"Comtesse..." she began, ready to confess her lack of understanding.

"Listen to your *kaas*."

Zi appeared nestled atop the display, his tail flicking side to side as she turned the pages. She took a deep breath, expecting Zi to tell her what to do. Instead the moment lingered on, and he merely looked up at her, his eyes a dark shade of red as he met her gaze.

"Zi?" she whispered.

What?

"What does it say?"

This book?

"No, the letter I've been composing to the Sultan of Sardia. Of course this book!"

He tilted his head as he looked at her, silent.

Well, the comtesse had said the *kaas* could be difficult. Still, she wouldn't give up so easily. She glared at Zi, waiting for him to respond.

It's nonsense, he thought to her finally.

"What do you mean, nonsense?"

It's nonsense, he repeated. *Merely a conduit for Axerian to deliver his messages. He's corrupted the words.*

"Corrupted? And who is Axerian?"

The comtesse stepped forward with a gasp. "Where did you read that name?"

"I—I didn't read it, Zi said—"

"What page? What page were you looking at when he read it?"

She pointed. "This one. The one it was open to. Comtesse, what is the significance of—?"

"It's *his* name, Sarine. The Nameless. The enemy of the Gods."

A shock ran up her spine.

"It's one of our oldest secrets. Rarely spoken of even in the Codex. Can you read more? Anything at all?"

"Zi said it was corrupted, that—"

"Please try. Anything you can learn could be critical, especially so now."

She turned back to the book. Still the same strange symbols, carrying no more meaning than a sheaf of practice exercises with her charcoals.

"Well, Zi?"

It's nonsense. Corrupted nonsense.

She sighed, turning to the comtesse, prepared to ask her advice. Instead, before she could form the words, Zi thought to her again.

You could remove the corruption, if you want.

She turned back sharply. "What?"

See?

And at once, she could. All around the book, pale blue strands danced like sparks in the dead of night. Without knowing what they were, or why, she knew those strands were *wrong*. They did not belong here.

Reaching up to touch the pages once more, the lines bent themselves toward her, wrapping around her hand, and she recoiled.

"What is it?" the comtesse asked.

Take it in, Zi thought to her. *It belongs to you.*

"It's all right," Sarine said, her voice steady. "Zi is telling me how to read it." She reached for the book again, feeling the blue strands once more coalesce around her outstretched hand. "He says it is corrupted, that we can remove—"

She gasped as the blue energy snapped into her, all at once, leaving the book sitting as she had seen it at first, free of the strange sparking light. Deep within she felt a stirring sense of power, raw power that infused itself into her bones. A wild, coursing energy unlike any of Zi's gifts, or the leylines, or the strange blessing of the cat spirit from the gardens. It seemed to cry out in an echo of a long-forgotten song, a distant melody that warmed as it settled over her, leaving her with an abiding sense of finally, at last, coming home.

"Sarine, what have you done? Arix?"

"I don't know," she said. "Zi, what happened? I didn't mean…" Her words trailed off as the other woman fell silent, turning her head as if listening to another voice speak. Slowly the comtesse nodded, and tears began to form in her eyes.

"Oh, Sarine," the comtesse whispered. "Arix says you've freed him of a great burden. What did you do?"

"Zi called it 'removing the corruption.'" She gestured toward the book, still sitting atop the display. "I'm not certain exactly what it was, or how it was done."

"Arix spoke so plainly," the comtesse said reverently, her voice touched with awe. "Always before he spoke in riddles, and now he speaks as plainly as you speak to me now."

She flushed. "I'm not even certain what I did. Zi refused to read from the book before…whatever I did."

"Oh Gods, yes, the book! If Arix is speaking plainly now, imagine how easily we can translate its secrets."

She stepped aside, allowing the other woman to move forward and pore over the tome. At once the comtesse's laugh rang out through the room.

"Yes, yes," the comtesse said. "It's so simple. Reyne was right, this passage does pertain to the tribesfolk, but it says nothing of war as we thought, only that their ascendant will claim the gifts of the land as well as the spirits of the beasts. I wonder what that means? Still, I can read it so clearly. By the hand of the Exarch himself, this changes everything!"

"What changes everything, my dear?" A new voice came from behind.

They both turned to see Reyne d'Agarre in the entryway.

"Oh, Reyne," the comtesse exclaimed, surging across the floor of the library toward him in a rush. "Sarine has pierced the shroud around the Codex. She's revealed secrets and brought us forward in the translation by a hundred generations, she's—"

The words stopped dead, a length of steel suddenly protruding through the back of the comtesse's dress, accompanied by a pooling crimson stain. D'Agarre gave a shove and her body slumped to the carpeted floor, revealing a long knife in his hand, covered in blood. Sarine looked in horror as d'Agarre shuddered, tilting his head back as if he had tasted some exquisite delicacy, and forgotten she stood ten paces away watching. Her memory flashed to the Maw, to the sort of men who took joy in beating defenseless victims, long past the point of thieving or intimidation.

Before her shock faded he snapped his eyes level with hers. For an instant she saw a hunger there, a look of insatiable thirst. Then he ran at her.

Without thinking, she snapped her eyes shut and tethered *Faith*. D'Agarre barreled forward, vaulting the tables in a rush of speed. *Red,* Zi's voice echoed in her mind, as a red haze swirled at the edge of her vision and she felt Zi's gift course through her. A moment before he collided with her she dove aside, springing to her feet as he stabbed wildly at the air with his blade.

"Impossible," d'Agarre growled. "What power is this? Saruk, what is she using?"

Frantically d'Agarre swept his gaze around the room, until his face lit up with realization a moment before she saw it herself: The room had but one entrance. She rushed toward the door along the east wall, but he arrived first, barring it shut in a great crash.

"Now," he said in a lighter voice, "show yourself, Sarine. This is all a misunderstanding. Let me explain."

He said it facing the center of the room, a few paces ahead of her, his back turned as he brandished his long knife in a sweeping guard.

Swallowing hard, she crept forward as silently as she could. *Faith* kept her hidden, but it did nothing to protect her from d'Agarre's blade. Closer. Another step.

"The Codex gives us premonitions," d'Agarre was saying. "When we recognize a moment has arrived, our path demands we act without question. I only meant to protect you. The comtesse was—"

She tethered *Body*, leapt forward, and struck a blow to the side of his head. D'Agarre slumped down into a crumpled heap, strange white energy sputtering around him. Without pausing to check the extent of her victory, she threw the doors open and raced through the hallway, her heart thrumming in her ears even as she felt the *Faith* binding dissipate. No matter. She could feel her body's energy draining rapidly as she maintained the *Body* binding and Zi's gift. Would it be enough? No telling whether d'Agarre had alerted some household guard, or set some barricade to bar her exit.

As it happened, he had done neither. Instead, after some few false starts and wrong directions, she burst into the sitting room, to the great surprise of the guests still engaged in the evening's debate. Lord Revellion sprang to his feet at once, rushing to her side. She could scarce imagine the state she was in after her mad dash through the twisting corridors of the d'Agarre manse, but she could see it reflected in the looks she earned from the ladies and gentlemen of Reyne d'Agarre's salon. She managed a croaking whisper to Lord Revellion that they needed to leave, at once. Bless the man, he asked no questions, merely dispatched one of d'Agarre's servants to fetch their coats and ready the carriage. With every passing heartbeat she expected some alarm to be raised, a mantle of dread settling over every moment they lingered on the d'Agarre estate. Yet soon enough, they found themselves once more in the Revellion coach, the doors latching shut as the team began to move.

A wave of relief swept over her as they pulled out onto the cobblestone streets of Southgate, bound for the high walls of the Gardens. She saw in Lord Revellion's eyes a blend of questions and concern, and once again gave silent thanks for his having waited to question her until they were away.

"What is it, Sarine? What happened?"

A tide of fear broke through any façade of normalcy she'd managed before, and she wept.

"He killed her, Donatien. The Comtesse de Rillefort."

"What? Who killed her?"

"Reyne d'Agarre. I knocked him down and fled. Oh, Donatien, he meant to kill me as well. I fear we have all been deceived. He is no force for justice, or *égalité.* He is a madman, corrupted by some dark power, some terrible evil." She broke down once more, convulsing into sobs.

He reached for her, drawing her close beside him in a firm embrace. Ah, but it felt good, even amid the horrors of the evening.

ELSEWHERE

INTERLUDE

LOUIS-SALLET

Reception Hall
The Royal Palace, Sarresant

He arrived in the capital at midmorning, which placed him fourteenth in line for an audience with the King. Never mind the risks he'd taken running his ship through the Gand blockade around the port at Valais, never mind the treacherous landfall in a smuggler's cove farther down the coast, and never mind the horse he'd nearly ridden to death to bring the news he carried. Thirteen other petitioners had arrived before him that morning, and so thirteen others would be formally received before he entered the royal presence. How it galled. He watched tradesmen dressed in ragged echoes of last season's fashions ushered into the throne room, like as not planning to make complaint to His Royal Majesty about spice tariffs or lost goats or some such utterly trivial nonsense. And for him they brought out refreshments and bid him wait his turn. *His turn.* He had never waited nor wanted for anything in his life, and now he stood like some common fop slavering over his chance to diddle the prettiest whore in the pleasure house. Just so, the King would prostitute the realm with these pointless gestures. *Égalité*, they demanded, these hounds snapping at the table scraps of their betters, thinking themselves equals for the merest vestige of meat left clinging to a discarded bone.

He was Louis-Sallet de l'Arraignon, Prince of the Blood, third in line to the throne of Sarresant. And he did not have *equals*.

After the third of these walking insults had been called, he could suffer it no longer. Over the muted protest of one of the chamberlains, he pushed his way through the ironbound doors and shoved past the lowborn wretch who had been trundling down the hall on his way to petition the King. At least the fool had the sense to keep silent as his prince swept him aside. Louis-Sallet opened the door to the throne room with a glare, the attendant guardsmen properly cowed, recognizing him on sight. Striding through the opening, his lip curled in an amused smile as the crier made his announcement.

"Your Majesty," the shriveled old servant intoned, "I present the esteemed Master Davien Forelle, trade craftsman of the Cobblers' Guild, here to petition the crown on behalf of his fellow masters in the matter of a dispute with the Shipmasters' Guild over a damaged shipment of cured hides from the colonies in the New World."

The bureaucrat hadn't bothered to lift his wiry face from the parchment as he read, and so only at the end, after half the court was tittering at the absurdity of it, did the man give his prince a squinting look, perhaps recognizing that master cobblers did not wear velvet cloaks lined with ermine fur.

"That's right, father," Louis-Sallet said in a loud, clear voice aimed at the assembled courtiers as much as the throne. "I've taken up bootmaking. And I have a bone to pick with your shipmasters for their negligent stupidity."

Guffaws echoed through the chamber, the assembled peers unable to maintain the façade of dignity required when the King sat in judgment. Only the King himself, and the Dauphin standing beside the throne, maintained level expressions, each regarding him with flat, unreadable looks.

It was the Dauphin, Gau-Michel, Louis-Sallet's eldest half-brother and heir to the throne of Sarresant, who spoke.

"Last we'd heard, you and your band of... companions,"—his half-brother's voice dripped with scorn at the word—"were privateering off the Skovan coast. To what do we owe the pleasure of your swift return, brother?"

"I carry word from Thellan," he said, keeping his eyes locked on his father's. "They have entered the war."

A rash of whispers swept through the hall. Again the other two men remained stoic.

"If what you say is true, and the Thellan were prepared to accept our offer of alliance, would they not send one of their own to treat with us? We've had no word from any Thellan emissaries."

"That is because they have not accepted our offer. They are entering the war on the side of Gand."

Pandemonium.

"That was recklessly done, even for you," the Dauphin said. They'd adjourned to the council chambers after he'd delivered his news, and now his half-brother stood disapproving over one of the broad tables. "You had no cause to deliver this news before the court, or to be received in state."

He shrugged. "I thought it fitting to remind His Majesty that the trappings of nobility were once reserved for those of *proper* birth." It was intended as an insult; his half-brother's darkening scowl made clear it had been received as such.

"Peace, my sons." Their father, His Royal Majesty the King Gaurond, sat upright in the tall-backed chair at the head of the council table. He was an old man for all he took pains to give the appearance of strength. "Louis-Sallet, I would know how you came to possess this information. And whether you are certain as to its veracity."

"I am certain, Your Majesty. I sailed into the port at Al Adiz flying Thellan colors"—he made a point of ignoring his half-brother's snort—"and found two Gand ships of the line moored alongside the Thellan fleet."

"That's it? You put the court in an uproar because you saw two ships of our enemy, like as not prizes taken by Thellan sailors as spoils after a battle?"

"If the *Imperial* had been taken as a prize, we'd have had word, I think." He said it quietly, knowing even his half-brother had heard of the black-hulled ship captained by the Gand queen's son, a sight dreaded by sailors in every sea that touched civilized lands. Most ships of the line had a binder or two as part of their complement, with fullbinders stationed on the heaviest of the triple-decked behemoths. Rumors said the *Imperial* carried no fewer than six.

"Still," his father said in a measured tone, "the sight of the ships alone is not a surety. Were you able to confirm Prince Emerich's presence?"

"I saw the prince with my own eyes, in the company of an honor guard being escorted from the Al Adiz fortress. Alas, I was not able to charm my way into their private meeting rooms. But I came in all haste to deliver this news as soon as I had it."

"And yet you found time for theatrics in the throne room," his half-brother said.

"Even so," he said, holding a grin long enough to inflame the Dauphin, "you know as well as I, the heir himself would not come ashore and risk being taken hostage for less than talks of alliance."

The other two men eyed each other with sober looks.

"I suppose we must consult with the lords-general," the Dauphin said. "I hope it is not so, by the Gods I hope it."

"It is too much to ask you might have been mistaken in what you saw?" the King asked.

Louis-Sallet shook his head. "No, father. I have seen renditions aplenty of the Gand prince, and I would not mistake him, even from afar, nor the lines of his ship in the harbor. The Thellan treat with our enemies."

The room grew quiet.

"Father," he asked in a serious tone, "can we withstand the combined power of Thellan and Gand?"

The King frowned, then looked askance at his eldest son.

The Dauphin spoke. "If this news is true, there are few enough, perhaps none of the great powers that could stand against them. We are overtaxed protecting our colonies, and they pressure us there as well. A Thellan invasion from the south, while the Gandsmen press us across the straits..."

"It is not sure," the King said, resolute. "It is possible the Thellan will have rebuffed the overtures of the Gandsmen, or failed to agree on terms. Even if this comes to pass, we will have time. They must plan and marshal their forces. We can make overtures of our own."

"Overtures have been made already, father," the Dauphin said in a pained voice. "Perhaps the news of a combined Thellan and Gand alliance will sway the Skovan; perhaps we can bribe the Sardians with gold, marriages..."

Louis-Sallet suppressed the urge to spit. His brother proposed the same tired plots, when circumstances demanded boldness. He could have predicted this, and had done as much as he sailed and rode to deliver his news. Their survival required more, and so he had dared to consider the unthinkable. Time his half-brother be forced to do the same.

"We could give up the colonies in the New World," Louis-Sallet said.

"What?" his half-brother asked. "You cannot be serious."

"Consider it, brother. You said yourself we are overtaxed there. Gand and Thellan both hold lands across the sea; even if we can hold New Sarresant against them, will it come at the cost of our ancestral home? Even the jewel of the New World is not worth losing the old one."

"Madness," the Dauphin said, but already he could see his half-brother's mind working as he considered the idea. "We discovered *Entropy* only after the Thellan War, and *Mind* as a direct result of the founding of the colonies. Would we lose them, if we ceded the territory? We could not hope for victory without access to modern bindings. And what new terror might the Gandsmen discover, in sole possession of the New World? To say nothing of logistics. It is impossible. We would need to deploy our entire navy to ferry the troops across the sea. The crossing itself would take weeks, in either direction."

"We will have time," Louis-Sallet said. "Our father is quite right. They will not act at once; they will need time to prepare. Bugger the bindings; we can match them with numbers. Imagine our combined forces, the armies of New Sarresant and old, deployed together to threaten Gand across the straits. Imagine the bindings *we* might secure for ourselves, in sole possession of the Old World, rather than the New."

His half-brother swallowed hard. "It is unthinkable to give up our protection of the colonies. They are already close to the brink of an uprising. The trade revenue alone, should the ports fall into the hands of the Gandsmen, to say nothing of the implication that we cannot defend our citizens... We risk ruin to even consider this course of action."

"No more than we risk ruin if we do nothing."

The King rose to his feet, stilling their exchange.

"Sarresant will not fall," their father said. He let the words linger in the air, pausing to look them both in the eye.

"Of course, father—" the Dauphin began.

"Sarresant *will not fall*," the King repeated, silencing his heir. "Do you have a better plan, to achieve it?"

The Dauphin remained quiet.

"Very well. We will consider this course, bitter as it may be. Gau-Michel, you will meet with the admiralty and the lords-general to begin planning. Once our agents among the Thellan confirm the news we have heard today, our fleet will sail."

His half-brother bowed his head in assent.

"As for you, Louis-Sallet," the King continued, "you have brought us dire news today, but you will carry it further before this is through. The time has come for you to set aside the freedoms of youth. If the fleet sails to take on this heavy task, it will sail with you in command. You will carry my words across the sea, to call the sons and daughters of Sarresant back to defend their home."

His eyes gleamed. At last, a task worthy of the royal blood that flowed through his veins.

"I swear to you, your majesty, I will see it done."

INTERLUDE

KA'VOS

The Shaman's Tent
Sinari Village

WAR. YOU MUST LEAD THE SINARI PEOPLE TO WAR.

The words were accompanied by images of death, flickering faster than he could discern any individual scene. He was left only with the impression of mangled bodies lying twisted beneath a gray sky, blood mixing with new-fallen snow.

He sighed, and filled his lungs with a deep-drawn breath. It was meant to center him, to still his mind in preparation to better understand the spirits' gift. His training demanded he give the spirits' voice this measure of respect, to try to discern the nature of their sending. He could not do otherwise, even knowing already that he would disregard yet another vision of war, death, and blood.

He expelled the breath as he let go the feelings of hate and rage that stirred along with the images sent by the spirits of things-to-come. A little-known facet of the gift of the *Ka*, to feel oneself the emotions associated with each vision. The spirits were ill-adept at communicating with men. Where a man might speak his meaning plain, finding simple words to express a sentiment, the spirits sent sights, emotions, thoughts, words, even smells, tastes. A purifying experience each time the weight of a sending crashed into him. It left him humbled, but also wiser for having glimpsed beyond the limits of what it was to be a man. Even at their worst, the visions gave him that much.

He breathed evenly, calming himself until he was satisfied he had divined what he could from this latest onslaught. Precious little. Perhaps a warning against some dire shadow looming over the cold season. If it was a true sending, he would see it again. For now, it was enough to seal it away among the many such visions of its kind, unlikely to be corroborated, or even mentioned in future sendings. Such was the madness of the spirits. It seemed they grasped at any chance to stir him, to drive home whatever grotesque purpose was served by these images of violence and loss. If there was a pattern, or some deeper meaning, it eluded him.

DEATH COMES FOR YOU, KA'VOS. IT APPROACHES.

He sighed. Another torrent of images and feelings. Silently he thanked his mentor for the training that let him weather this madness with stoic grace. As a youth he might have gone mad himself to bear this. As a man, a trained *Ka* of the Sinari, he carried it with dignity and pride. Of the people of the Sinari, only perhaps Ilek'Inari had any glimmer of what he endured each day. A sending no less horrifying than this might come at any moment, and often did. He would remain strong. It was no small thing he asked of the *Ka* of other tribes, to live with these horrors and set them aside. But it could be done. The alternative was unthinkable.

A stirring at the entrance to his tent promised a welcome distraction. A kindness perhaps, sent from the untainted spirits even as some twisted few among them showed him their latest madness. He reached down and snuffed the incense burning in a bowl beside him, its smoky fragrance filling his tent. Such implements helped him focus when the visions came.

"Enter," he called, keeping his voice steady.

The canvas flap of his tent was pushed aside, and Llanara stepped through, her head lowered. Llanara, who wore red where tradition dictated blue. A powerful soul. The spirits had been silent regarding her new gift. He had expected guidance, and received nothing. Another mystery laid at their feet.

"Be welcome, daughter of the Sinari. To what do I owe the pleasure of your visit?"

She bowed her head further in a show of respect. "Good morning to you, shaman. May I sit?"

He gestured to an open mat across from his, opposite the fire crackling in the center of his tent. She lowered herself into a cross-legged position, closing her eyes as she inhaled the aroma of the incense mixing with the acrid smoke of the fire. He remained silent, regarding her with a patient expression. Long years of treating with both the spirits and the tribesfolk made plain when one of his people carried a burden. He would let her reveal its nature in due course.

"The air cools," she said. "It seems the hot season gives way faster than I can recall it having done before."

He smiled. "It is often so. Yet do not discount the fire spirits—we may think them deeply slumbering, and then be granted days of heat, to remind us of their power."

She nodded absently, then grew silent once more.

"Why have you come to see me this morning, Llanara?" At that moment another wave of grisly images flashed before his eyes, and he smelled blood near strong enough to make him retch. He offered another silent thanks to his onetime mentor, for the training that let him bear it without an outward sign. This daughter of the tribe needed his guidance, and he would give it no matter how the mad spirits tried to interfere.

"I grow worried," she said finally. "Worried for Arak'Jur. We have had no word yet from the Ranasi?"

He shook his head. "Not yet. The tidings he carried will be difficult for the Ranasi to bear, as you well know. His presence there will be a comfort, and he will stay as long as he is needed."

"His journey will lead him beyond Ranasi lands, will it not?"

He felt a surge of fear at that, though he outwardly dissembled, as he had with the spirits' visions. How much did she know of his and Arak'Jur's plan, to solicit allies among the other tribes? It was not a thing to speak of in the open, yet perhaps Arak'Jur had taken Llanara into his confidence before he left. She was his woman, after all. Still, his instincts urged caution, and he spoke with care.

"The spirits will guide Arak'Jur through the shamans' visions. Ka'Hinari carries their favor as surely as I do, and if it is needful for our guardian to journey farther than our neighbor's lands, such will be revealed to him."

"Of course, he will act as the visions guide him," she said. "But I am not alone in my worries. Others have raised their concerns to me, others among the women. The Olessi and the Ranasi have been stripped of their guardians. A dire time for our people, and now Arak'Jur journeys away from our village. If something were to happen to him..."

"I have seen nothing that would betoken danger to our elder guardian, and we still have Ilek'Inari."

"Yes, honored shaman, I trust it is as you say. But neither the Olessi nor the Ranasi *Ka* had foreknowledge of the loss of their guardians. And Ilek'Inari is still an apprentice."

He nodded grimly. "There is wisdom in your words, but this is the course set for Arak'Jur by the spirits."

"Is it?"

He felt ice grip his heart. She knew.

"What do you mean, Llanara?"

"Ka'Ana'Tyat is closed to us. When Ilek'Inari made his journey he found no opening, no break in the heart of the wood that revealed the entrance for which you bade him search. Only thick-entwined branches closing off every path that might have led farther. The women counseled me to seek the same opening, and I found none. Instead Ilek'Inari found *una're*, and I, *mareh'et*. Two great beasts, and you saw neither."

"No shaman sees the coming of every beast."

"This may be so, but these were no ordinary beasts wandering into our land. They guarded the way into Ka'Ana'Tyat, our most sacred place. I say again, Ka'Ana'Tyat is closed to us, Ka'Vos. And with it, I fear we have lost the power of the spirits' guidance."

"You speak madness, woman," he said, trying to put the emphasis of authority into his words, a tremble in his voice betraying his intent as he spoke.

"The spirits demand you lead us to war. Why do you hide it?"

"What?" He inhaled sharply. "How can you know this?" His mind raced. Llanara practiced her strange new magic, brought by the fair-skin Reyne d'Agarre—it was already taboo to mention it, claimed as it was by the women—but perhaps it let her speak with the spirits of things-to-come. A forbidden thing. His face darkened.

"Your new *gift*." He nearly spat the word, answering his own question.

"Yes. It is written in the Codex, and Vekis..." She trailed off, tilting her head as if she listened to some unseen spirit. "It appears Vekis will speak for himself."

A crystalline, four-legged serpent appeared on the floor of his tent, scaled coils looped beside the fire. Ka'Vos started, scrambling to his feet.

"What is—?"

You have led your people astray, shaman. The voice crashed into his head with a force that left him stunned, as much for its intensity as for speaking the words he had dreaded to hear.

"No," he pleaded in a whisper, sinking back to his knees. "I have only tried to protect this tribe."

Your spirits demand war, and if you will not give it, you must die.

His eyes widened. Before he could speak again, Llanara rose to her feet in a blurred motion, faster than should have been possible. Another plea formed on his lips, and died there as she struck.

The world went black.

INTERLUDE

THE EXARCH

Living Quarters
Gods' Seat

Paendurion roared, smashing a fist through the desk in the center of his chamber. In his anger he tethered the red motes of *Strength* without thinking. Splinters of mahogany scattered through the room, accompanied by a crunch as what remained of the desk crumbled into a pile of rubble at his feet.

His fist would bruise, but a simple binding of *Growth* would aid the healing, one of the principal advantages of Order magic over that of Balance and the Wild. As for the remains of his desk, the unseen servants who tended to the keeping of these chambers would have the mess sorted soon after he left the room. The least of the mysteries of this place that his people had called the Gods' Seat. Paendurion had resided here since he'd first ascended to become champion of Order, so many lifetimes ago. This was not the first piece of furniture he had destroyed.

How had she done it?

That his opponent was a woman he was reasonably confident; one could tell, in the nature of the *Vision* binding that manifests as golden light behind the eyes. Subtle differences when a woman controlled a woman or a man controlled a man, a certain familiarity in the movements of one's vessel. It was not a sure thing, but he'd had more practice with the leylines than any soul that had ever lived, or ever would, save perhaps only the Veil herself. And with the Goddess in stasis, in time he would eclipse even her skill. That was his right as first among the ascended, champion of Order, and leader of the Three.

And still, despite all his titles and past victories, he had been outmaneuvered by some fledgling come to her power in a single lifetime. She could not have known the *urus* was nearby when she sealed the barrier. Even Ad-Shi, who had been champion of the Wild for the same span of lifetimes as he had held his station, did not have sure knowledge of the movements of the great beasts, certainly less than would be required for the needs of strategic planning. Luck. That was all it was, and he was seasoned enough to know that in the end it counted for little. He calmed himself with the assurance that this setback would only make his ultimate triumph sweeter. This fledgling was good, but he was still Paendurion, called the Exarch in this age. He would find the would-be ascendant, and kill her, as he had done to all the others who'd sought to rise and take his place as champion.

Already his opponent had revealed too much. He knew she operated in the colonies of Sarresant, across the Endless Ocean, on the far side of the world. Such was the nature of peoples gifted with Order magic, to grow in strength as the network of leylines expanded, the network of territory loyal to a single throne. He suspected she had even been reckless enough to seal the barrier in person, judging from the strength of the counterbindings deployed against his efforts there. A bold gambit to take the field herself, but a tendency he could exploit in future campaigns.

Plans would be laid, and traps would be set. He would strike this fledgling hard, and snuff her out before even the barest hint of an ascension. When the moment arrived it would once again be he who stood to claim the mantle of Order. It would once again be he who matched wits with the ancient enemy, he who secured another cycle of peace.

"Another ruined desk, my friend? Or was it a table this time?"

Axerian stepped over the wood chips strewn across the room's fine carpets as he entered. Almost Paendurion chided the man for failing to knock, until he remembered he had smashed the door off its hinges on his own way into his living quarters. Well, he was past the point of pretending defeat did not sting. Let his companions among the Three see the product of his rage; it was of little consequence to him.

"A desk," he said, gesturing for Axerian to take up a seat on one of the couches. "And a worse setback in a single engagement than I've had since our first cycle."

His friend whistled as he sat, swinging his legs up to rest on a neighboring cushion. "Too much to hope you exaggerate?"

He moved to one of the couches himself, quelling for the moment the rage that stirred within. "No. She's cost me the bulk of my soldiers in the Vordu lands, across the seas."

Axerian winced for a moment, then straightened where he sat.

"She? Some common enemy general, or have you found—?"

"I have found her," he said, feeling a smug satisfaction he didn't bother to hide. "The Order ascendant for this cycle."

"Ah, Paendurion! First as ever. Ad-Shi will be delighted to hear the news; for all I know her search continues."

He gave a confident smile. It *was* something of a triumph, to have sure knowledge of his opponent. Knowledge worth the matériel he had sacrificed, though the humiliation of defeat stung no less for it.

Axerian continued. "Where have you found her? And I suppose I can assume you've already planned the next move?"

"She is across the sea. A general of Sarresant, among their colonies. And my next move is a strike. Twenty thousand men pulled from the Skovan front, carried on ships across the sea to assault New Sarresant, with support from levees in the Gand colonies. With her city besieged, this general will commit herself to the field, and when she does, she dies."

The words hung in the air as Axerian mulled it over. His friend had little enough grasp of military maneuvers, but it cost him little to humor the man with an explanation. Paendurion expected praise, but instead saw a frown creeping across the other man's expression.

"Axerian? You disapprove?"

"No," Axerian said quickly. "Only… Paendurion, have you ever lost control of a vessel, or a leyline, once you held it with the Veil's power?"

"Never." An odd question. "It is no easy thing to wield, but once I have established a connection? No, I have never lost control."

Axerian frowned, deep in thought.

"Why do you ask this?" he demanded in a sharp voice.

"Because I believe it has happened. A connection lost to me, and a *kaas*-mage with it. A contingency activated with mere moments to spare. In the city of New Sarresant."

Now Paendurion's expression grew dark, his mind turning to piece together the information at his disposal. Only one of the Gods' three champions, or the Gods themselves, could act in the manner Axerian described, and the Veil, their patron Goddess, was imprisoned here in the Seat. Improbable as it was, that left only one possibility.

"The Regnant. Or his champions."

Axerian nodded gravely. "The enemy has never managed to pierce the Divide between East and West before the ascensions were complete on our side, but I cannot foresee another cause. And if the Order ascendant is in New Sarresant as well..."

"You fear they work in concert," he said, a chill crawling up his spine. "Damn us all for fools, could it be true? How could we miss this possibility?"

"You are the strategist between us, my friend. I have a handful of agents remaining in New Sarresant, and I can ferry over more with your forces. And we can speak to Ad-Shi. Perhaps she has plans we might accelerate."

"Yes. Yes, by the Veil herself. Twenty thousand men will not be enough; I will divert all the strength I can spare to this assault. We will flush them out, these would-be ascendants and the Regnant's agents both, if we have to burn New Sarresant to the ground."

"Very well," Axerian said with a heavy voice. "I will leave you to make your preparations."

Paendurion nodded as his friend swept out of his chamber. He was already working golden threads of *Vision* bindings spliced with the roiling blue energy they siphoned from the Veil each time they awoke. Other men might have shied away from this burden, from the deeds necessary to seize the power it required. Lesser men. He had seen firsthand the horrors of what would come to pass if they failed. One more city destroyed was nothing beside the costs he had already paid, and would pay again. He had long ago made his peace with choosing the lesser evil, to serve the greater good.

PART 3: AUTUMN

SEASON OF THE NAMELESS

30

SARINE

The Revellion Townhouse
Gardens District, New Sarresant

She paced the length of the Revellion library, wearing a dark expression that matched the dawn light leaking through the windows. Sleep had come uneven when it came at all in the weeks since d'Agarre's salon, and she'd spent hours pondering the events of that night, searching for answers. She'd come up with precious little, beyond the surety that Reyne d'Agarre had murdered the Comtesse de Rillefort, and tried to do the same to her.

She'd begged her uncle to accept Lord Revellion's offer of protection, or at least to find shelter somewhere beyond d'Agarre's reach. It had been so certain to her, in the moments after the d'Agarre manse, that she and all who knew how to reach her were in danger. Yet for all her impassioned pleas, her uncle's assurance that none would dare defile a church had proven less naïve than she'd imagined. D'Agarre had been quiet. The city had been quiet. And still she was certain a shadow loomed across every quarter of New Sarresant, a shadow cast by Reyne d'Agarre.

"Tell me again, Zi," she said as she pivoted to begin another track around the library's outer wall. "You said the book was nonsense, but the comtesse seemed to see something of import, all the more so once you showed me how to remove the corruption."

An old script, he thought to her. *Very old.*

"Do you mean it was written in an ancient language?"

Yes.

Her eyes lit up. This was new. "How old?"

Her companion writhed on the reading table, lolling his head over the edge while she paced.

"Zi?" she asked, voice touched with impatience.

Sixteen cycles.

She sighed. More cryptic answers. "Sixteen cycles, what does that mean?"

He only stared at her.

"Gods' blessings, Zi, this is important," she insisted, turning mid-stride to focus him with a disapproving glare. Still he remained silent. "Well, what about 'Axerian'? The comtesse said it meant the Nameless."

Yes.

"And? You mean to tell me the enemy of the Gods himself is speaking to Reyne d'Agarre?"

Not speaking. The corruption interferes with my kind.

"Interferes?"

We do not share the same motivations.

Frustration seethed through her, and she sensed the same emotion in Zi. They'd tread over similar ground more than once since the salon, and neither seemed to be able to make clear their meaning to the other.

"Zi, I need to know what d'Agarre is planning. Did the passage you read give any hint of what he might do next?"

It was only stories.

She pressed her fingers to her temples. There must be some way to get a clear answer.

"Something troubling you this morning?"

Lord Revellion stood in the entryway, up and dressed for the day despite the early hour. He wore his military uniform, a blue just shy of black, with a double row of golden buttons left hanging open on his coat. A painful reminder that all of this was temporary; little enough chance their affair would continue after he rode south with the army. He held a letter, unsealed and opened in his hand.

"Zi is trying to help me make sense of the night of the salon," she said. "With little success." She swallowed, eyeing the letter. It had been a shock that Zi had been willing to show himself to Lord Revellion, and no less for him, she was sure. Zi had never given permission to reveal his existence to her uncle. The more she learned of her companion, the less she understood him.

Lord Revellion nodded absently as he read, striding forward to sit on one of the long benches.

"News from the army?" she asked. Word had come some weeks past of a great victory at the Great Barrier, soured by the flow of refugees into the city, men, women, and families displaced by battles in the south. Neither would absolve Donatien of his duty to serve. She'd been expecting a summons, and seeing him in full uniform suggested the time had finally come.

Instead he shook his head. "No. From my father."

Silence descended on the library as he read. Finally he laughed, crumpling the paper and tossing it onto the floor.

"My lord?" she asked.

"It's nonsense. Word has reached my father, word that I've been seen with you. He admonishes me to remember my place as a scion of a great house, to remember my duty to uphold the noble legacy of my blood."

She glanced down at the remains of the letter, feeling a stinging rebuke.

"Sarine, you need not concern yourself with what my father thinks. He's a fool, mired in tradition and more concerned with appearances than sense. There's no law against our seeing each other; how could there be, when half the noble families in the kingdom are marrying rich merchants to restock their coffers? No, if he's concerned about you, it's for your lack of a dowry, not your blood. And I don't give a damn about either."

She nodded, but couldn't escape the weight of Revellion's father's words. Whatever assurances he gave, Donatien Revellion was still the son of a marquis. It was one thing to shrug off the stares and whispers of gossip from afar, but this was closer, more immediate. She had no illusions of belonging in Lord Revellion's world any more than he would fit in on the streets of the Maw. Before d'Agarre's salon it seemed as though they were on the cusp of breaching that divide. Now he wore the midnight blue of the Sarresant army, their stolen weeks feeling more and more like a fleeting dream of summer.

And d'Agarre. A shiver ran up her spine remembering the sight of him exulting in the murder of the Comtesse de Rillefort. Whatever passed between her and the son of the Marquis Revellion, there was still a madman sowing dissent and violence at the heart of the city.

"Are you all right?" Revellion asked. "Truly, Sarine, my father is a thousand leagues away. You have no need to trouble yourself over his ridiculous notions of propriety. I meant it when I said—"

"I'm fine, Donatien," she said. "Only concerned. I trust your sense of how to deal with . . . all of this." She gestured to the décor and finery around them. "But d'Agarre is out there, planning. And whatever your father thinks, there's still the matter of your deployment."

She meant it kindly, but he took it with a wince. "My deployment. Yes, it will come soon. Today it's a ceremony at the academy, to honor my new commander for her role in the latest victory over the Gandsmen. But with the rest of the army being recalled to the city for resupply . . ."

"You'll make a fine commander," she said.

He sighed.

"Somehow I imagined all of this turning out differently," he said as he stood, walking to the large window overlooking the streets below. "Not us. I mean the city, the people. D'Agarre made it sound as if real change could be possible. I thought we'd drive for reform, make peace with Gand . . ."

"Donatien, I'm frightened of whatever he is planning. D'Agarre holds a seat on the Council-General, attends salons with the nobles and factory owners, and half the urchins in the city seem to be under his thumb. He has influence at every level of this city."

"You truly think he means to seize power?"

"I do."

Donatien turned his gaze through the clear glass window that dominated the library, looking out over the city as it stirred, the sun only just cresting the horizon.

"You know I agree with damn near every precept of his philosophy," he said. "And if the *kaas* give him the power to challenge the binders that support the regime . . . will there be another, better chance to effect change, real change?"

"I saw the madness behind his eyes." She shivered, remembering. "He murdered an ally to his cause, for no more reason than his book told him it was needful. What would stop him torching a village, or putting half a district to the guillotine, if it were written there for him to follow? Whatever his support for *égalité* or liberty, we do not want that man for a leader."

"You're right, of course," he said, with a lingering look out the window. "And now duty bids me take up arms to support the very state I would see reformed. I feel like a coward, swept along by fate when I would stand and fight."

She rose and stood beside him, looking out over the city. It wasn't easy to feel sympathy for him, in spite of their time together. He was a man of ideals, a product of the life of privilege he claimed to abhor. He'd spent his youth mastering courtly games and moonlighting with subversive texts while she and Zi dodged street gangs in the Maw. For her, equality of birth and rule by merit alone was a fact of life on the street: The strongest got their share, and the rest lined up to carve what they could from the scraps. In a way, the nobility only played out the same scene on a grander scale. At least if Lord Revellion was caught up in it, he had the sense to see the need for freedom from a life preoccupied with survival. That was no cowardice.

Reyne d'Agarre, though... he was a monster, a monster that claimed to hold the same beliefs, but she had seen the truth of it in the blood on the edge of his knife. Whatever madness drove him, he'd acted no different from the worst of the street toughs when it became clear she'd challenged his power, by cleansing the evil from the *kaas* of the Comtesse de Rillefort.

"We have to stop him," she said.

Her words brought Lord Revellion out of a reverie beside her. "Stop him?" He turned to look at her. "Ah, you mean d'Agarre."

She nodded. "You call it cowardice not to fight for what you believe. What does that make me, sitting idle here behind your walls? I've seen the evil that drives him, and I cannot stand by and watch his madness loosed on this city. We have to stop him."

"Sarine, you said yourself Reyne d'Agarre has influence throughout the city. And he attacked you at his manse. He may well want you killed."

"Well, and what of it? Why has he not sought me out since? I will tell you, Donatien: because I am *not* powerless."

"I know it." He gestured to the leg he still favored, even after months of recovery. "Remember how we met?"

She nodded, smiling. The beast at the masquerade.

He'd never asked after her gifts. It was strange to think she experienced the world from a different vantage than he did; but too, when they were together they refrained from speaking in depth about his upbringing as a noble, or the courtesies he'd learned among others of his standing. It felt as though acknowledging their differences shone a light on the unlikeliness of their pairing. Besides, it was simple enough, most of the time, to focus on the perspectives they shared.

Yet now, here it was.

"You can ask, Donatien," she said, keeping her voice calm. "I have nothing to hide from you."

"Very well. Understand, my knowledge of the leylines is limited, an academic study at best. And I know nothing of your Zi. Still, you revealed to me already you can bind *Body*, and *Life*."

She nodded.

"Well, is that the extent of your bindings? Can you sense another type of energy?"

"I can bind everything," she said. "My uncle claimed it was a rare thing, though he knew precious little beyond the most rudimentary training. He had only enough talent with *Life* to be taken and trained as a priest when he was a boy."

"Everything?" Revellion frowned. "Everything you can sense, yes? How many is that?"

"All of them. *Body*, *Shelter*, *Life*, *Death*, *Mind*, *Entropy*, and *Faith*."

A silence settled over the library.

She went on. "*Faith* I named myself—my uncle couldn't find mention of it in any of the holy books. It felt right, though. White clouds that gather where people have hope, hope in dark places."

"Sarine..."

"What?" she asked, feeling a creeping unease, the old worry of revealing what she had spent a lifetime keeping hidden. She'd sensed even as a child that it had been wrong for her uncle to train her. The one time she'd asked why, he'd demurred, promising to tell her when she was older. And now, even in the company of a man from whom she desired to keep no secrets, the sinking feeling returned.

Revellion swallowed and began again. "There are stories. Old stories of fullbinders, *true* fullbinders who could do what you are describing.

Now there are not more than a company's worth of binders in all of Sarresant, Old World and New, who can handle three types of leyline energies. And none in living memory who could handle more."

She flushed. "Well, I can."

"All six—seven!—types of energy. Do you know what this means? You're a true fullbinder, right out of the stories. Gods, but this is incredible. If the priests, or the..." He trailed off.

She said nothing, watching him.

He reached a hand around her shoulders, bringing her tight toward him. "Thank you," he said. "Thank you for sharing this with me."

Tears stung her eyes. Even now, after weeks in his company, it felt good to be accepted. It felt good to trust.

Telling of Zi's gifts was more difficult, owing to Revellion's lack of familiarity and her own limited knowledge of what Zi could do. She related what she knew: the bursts of speed and strength, the influencing of weakly held emotions and beliefs in others, the protective shield he conjured when she was at risk of physical harm. Almost she forgot the blessing she'd received from the Great Cat, but she related that as well, the strange encounter with the *marcb'et* spirit while her body had been comatose and moved to the Citadel the night of the masquerade.

When the telling was finished, she laughed weakly. "So you see, Reyne d'Agarre has good cause to fear *me*."

"I believe it," Revellion said with a grin, fading into seriousness as he continued. "Sarine, could you truly strike at him?"

The question sobered her as well. "I don't know. But I mean what I said: Whatever he claims for his motives, he must be stopped. Perhaps there is a way to gather evidence, something we could use to undermine him, or expose him to the Duc-Governor, or the Lords' Council."

"We know he holds subversive meetings among the moneyed classes from his manse, though I suspect neither of us will be receiving another invitation to one of those."

"No, likely not," she said with a wry smile. "We'll never produce proof of the comtesse's murder, and d'Agarre has too much wealth to receive more than a reprimand for seditious talk at his salons. But we know he treats with the commonfolk as well. I saw him in the Harbor, and the Maw. He's been behind the rash of thefts and riots in the city."

"Yes." Revellion nodded along with her reasoning. "That would get the Duc-Governor's attention. But how could we prove it? He's not like to exchange direct correspondence with street gangs and ruffians in the Maw."

"We'll find something. And unless I miss my guess, he'll have subverted high-ranking commanders within the army as well; he'd not risk instigating a coup d'état without some surety of military backing."

Revellion whistled. "I suspect you're right. By the Gods themselves, Sarine, you'd pit the two of us against a conspiracy that might extend halfway to the Old World."

"Start with your new posting? See what you can uncover, and I'll do the same among the city's rougher quarters."

"All right. Though for the life of me, even after hearing the sum of your gifts, I still mislike the thought of you going into danger alone." He held up his hands to ward off her objections. "I know, I know, you've lived in the Maw since you were a child. Still, you've survived by avoiding the worst elements there, not by courting them."

"I know how to remain hidden, Donatien. In fact..."

She slid her eyes shut for a moment. There: a thin strand of *Faith* in this very room. A sign from the Gods if ever there was one. She tethered it, and allowed herself a smile at the startled gasp from Lord Revellion when she faded from view.

"You see?" she said as she released the binding. "I will be safe."

He barked a laugh after he'd settled himself. "Oh, Sarine. Reyne d'Agarre chose poorly when he made you his enemy."

"Yes," she said. "Yes, he did."

31

ERRIS

Academy Grounds
Gardens District, New Sarresant

The reflection in the standing mirror bore only token resemblance to Erris d'Arrent. At Duc-General Cherrain's insistence she'd allowed a pair of groomers free rein over her appearance this morning. If they'd tried it with anything less than a direct order from the Duc, she'd have tossed them both into the nearest sewage canal. As it was, she bore it with as much grace as a child raised first by a trapper and then by the army could muster.

She took a step back, regarding the groomers' work. Her shoulder-length hair had been pulled into a knot at the nape of her neck, tight enough to make her scalp itch. A layer of cosmetics covering her face made her look more like a porcelain doll than an actual woman, let alone a soldier. They'd even replaced her dress uniform with a freshly tailored version cut to her exact measurements, fixing a pair of gold epaulets to her shoulders, the dangling tassels making her feel more than a touch ridiculous. The twin knots of rank, one on either collar and the forearm of each sleeve, completed the picture.

Her lead groomer nodded with satisfaction, pronouncing her attire complete. She pitied the man, poor fool that he was. What an utterly pointless vocation.

The officers' arrival in the northern colonies was the purpose for the day's affair, of course. Let them claim it was to celebrate her victory over the Gandsmen, to recognize her courage or whatever other horseshit justified the occasion in their minds. She'd been around nobles and gentlemen since she first made brigade-colonel five years ago, after the Thellan campaigns. She knew how they thought. A medal ceremony was an easy excuse to throw one of their lavish parties, but without her they would have found another reason, sure as sunrise.

"This way if you please, General d'Arrent." A servant in the Duc's livery beckoned. "The ceremony is due to begin."

Praise the Exarch for that; best to get it over with as quick as she could. She said nothing, following the man through a hallway and into a large chamber where the procession was already forming up. A faux military march, styled like the commencement ceremonies here at the academy. She'd graduated here, ten lifetimes ago. Even then she'd felt like a wolf given a seat at the dinner table, having to work twice as hard as her blue-blooded fellows for half the accolades. Trappers' daughters, especially trappers' daughters bearing binder's scars that marked them property of the King, did not graduate first in their class from any school, let alone the New Sarresant Academy. That she hadn't actually been granted the honor had mattered not at all. She knew she'd had the best marks in her year, and she'd made damn sure every pig-tit-suckling nobleman in her class knew it, too.

"The Exarch's blessings on you, Chevalier-General." Sister Elise bowed from behind her, near the head of the line.

"Sister. You'll have to tell me how you managed to escape the Duc's groomers."

"Privileges of the faith." The sister smiled.

She returned the gesture, but couldn't manage much in the way of warmth. A day like today only reminded her that knighthood had come along with her promotion to command of the 1st Division. Ceremonies like this would be the rule now, where before they'd been avoidable more often than not.

"General," another woman beside her said in a quiet voice, inclining her head.

"Marie," she said, this time with genuine affection. "Has the city treated you well?"

"I will land on my feet, General, thank you."

Erris nodded, turning her attention back to the academy steward as he gave instructions to the entire procession. The horrors Marie d'Oreste had endured these past months were beyond imagining, even for a soldier and a veteran of two wars. It had been at Erris's urging—no, at her insistence—that Marie be given a place of honor equal to her own today. The woman had earned it. It had been through Marie's eyes she witnessed the devastation wrought on the Gandsmen, when she forced the woman against every ounce of good sense to go back to their camp. The massive pools of *Death* that had swollen nigh to bursting had had her whipping the priests into a frenzy, steeling them for an attack that never came. Instead the inky clouds congealed into sickly pits of tar clinging to the leylines, as deep and thick as she had ever seen. And then Marie had given her the truth of it: a slaughter, men torn limb from limb, with pools of gore so deep the grass flooded beneath the trees, and only the bodies of dogs mixed in with men to give the cause. Beasts of some sort, the very creatures against which the Great Barrier had been built so long ago, that had threatened the colonies upon their founding here in the New World.

She shuddered, remembering the sight.

Standing beside them she could almost sense the golden thread of *Need* that bound her to these women, to Marie d'Oreste and to Sister Elise of Arentaigne. Their victory had bought time. Her orders had been to stand down here in the city while the nobles made a show of brokering an end to hostilities—with the Gand army destroyed, it put Sarresant on favorable negotiating terms, at least here in the colonies. Yet this time it was different. Sarresant had invaded as a preemptive measure, a check on Gand expansion, but she knew that no terms of trade or territorial concessions would end this war. Her spine chilled, recalling her conversation with the enemy's golden-eyed commander. So long as that creature was in command, there would be no peace.

The steward gave the order to march, and their column swept onto the grass with a military band playing fanfare to accompany their steps. Muted, polite applause greeted them as they were ushered into place below the stage, upon which the army's commanders sat on one side and the civilian leaders, noncommissioned members of the Lords' Council or the elected commoners of the Council-General, sat on the other. Duc-General Cherrain stood welcoming Erris and her companions on the dais at the center of the platform. A cousin of the King, High Commander of the army, and governor of the colonies. He was an imposing figure in his uniform, looking every bit the part of the dashing, cunning leader. One could hardly rise to his station without looking the part.

The Duc gestured for quiet after the last of their column was settled into place.

"We gather today for valor's sake," the Duc began. "To honor sons and daughters of Sarresant, whose bravery exemplifies the highest ideals of our people, our faith, our nation."

The rest of her companions' eyes were fixed on the stage as the Duc spoke, though her attention began to wander almost immediately. She'd heard speeches of this nature too often and found they rarely deviated from the script: praise the heroes, denounce the enemy, generalize to a greater message of shared struggle leading to inevitable triumph. In her view, the army would function a sight better if generals learned that soldiers, not speeches, led to victory.

It came as a shock when she realized after a few minutes that the crowd had gone quiet, every eye turning to stare at her.

"Chevalier-General d'Arrent?" the Duc repeated, looking down at her with a raised eyebrow and a beckoning hand.

She cleared her throat. "Sir?" she asked, feeling a flush at her collar. Those damned groomers had cut the uniform too tight, a sensation not helped by the crowd tittering with the polite laughter of the nobility, spurred by the Duc's amused grin.

"I asked if you would share a few thoughts on our enemy, and the events leading up to your victory. A view from the front lines, as it were."

She blinked, feeling herself rise from where she sat on one of the wooden benches that had been dragged onto the grass in front of the stage. What sort of game was this, to invite her to speak unprepared, without forewarning? Had the Duc invited her here to honor her or to make her look a fool? Applause sounded once again as she strode up the steps to the center of the platform, echoing in her ears as if it came from far away. The Duc took his seat behind her, and she turned to see half a thousand eyes fixed on her. Powerful eyes. Judging eyes.

And there in the front row, the priests of Arentaigne, and Marie d'Oreste. She took a deep breath. If they could do what she had asked of them at the barrier, a speech before the peers of the realm was a challenge she could meet, unflinching.

"Our enemy," she said in a quiet voice, then repeated it louder, more firm. "Our enemy. I have fought the enemies of the crown for nigh on eleven years. I have matched wits with enemy generals, I have slain enemy soldiers by my own hand. I tell you this true: I have faced no enemy I have feared so much as the commander of these Gandsmen."

That stilled whatever mirth had settled over the crowd from her unexpected invitation to the stage. Good. If the Duc-General wanted a view from the front lines, she would give one.

"Well spoken, d'Arrent," Marquis-General Voren said, tipping his crystal wineglass in her direction as he approached. "I suspect not quite the display the Duc-General had in mind when he planned his little ambush."

She suppressed the instinct to salute, opting for a subtle bow more appropriate to their surroundings. Already she felt out of place at the Duc's reception here at the Rasailles palace; the last thing she needed was to remind them all that Erris d'Arrent was a common-born soldier first, come to nobility by virtue of a field promotion. Not that they were like to forget it.

"Thank you, sir," she replied. "I tried to keep my descriptions authentic."

He nodded with an amused look. "Oh, you achieved it, Chevalier-General. Half the ladies to whom I've spoken are skipping the hors d'oeuvres, and the men are wondering aloud what madman supported you for promotion to the peerage." He sipped his wine. "Then they remember that madman was me."

She felt her cheeks redden. "Sir, if I've embarrassed you—"

He waved her off. "Not at all. If the sensibilities of polite society are easily offended, it's only to keep the gossip flowing freely. All of this will be forgotten when the next scandal breaks. Besides, that token becomes you. You more than earned it."

Her fingers went to the medallion she wore on a ribbon around her collar. The Legion of Valor. The highest military decoration given by the crown of Sarresant, the sort most often given to the dead. She'd never put much stock in medals or ceremony, but even she had to admit it felt damned good when the Duc-General placed it around her neck. Even if he had been somewhat red at the ears after her gruesome description of the events of the summer campaign. Well, he'd asked for it.

"Thank you again, sir," she said. "I assume I have the reports you made to high command to thank for the honor."

"How not? By the Gods, d'Arrent, when you're the only soldier present at a battle, there isn't much room to quibble over whom to pin medals on after the fact. Besides," he continued, eyes sparkling, "I suspect the lack of noble-born honorees was precisely the cause for Cherrain's little ambush. Our peers are little accustomed to being shut away from glory."

She raised an eyebrow. Would the Duc-General of the army and the governor of the colonies be so petty? She supposed she knew the answer without asking. "Again, sir, I regret if I caused you embarrassment today."

"Think no more on it, d'Arrent. Try to enjoy our time in the city. We get so few opportunities between campaigns to immerse ourselves in the privilege of our ranks." His tone suggested he was at least half-serious.

"Sir, with your arrival I'd expected to make my report to you in person on the events at the barrier. There have been troubling developments."

"More troubling than the account you just gave to the nobility?"

"Yes, sir. Details I withheld from the official reports. You'll need to see it in person, sir." She'd tried to describe the golden light of *Need* and the threat posed by the enemy commander's use of it in her written accounts. In the end she'd resolved to recount the information in person. Without seeing it firsthand, she'd not have believed it possible; she could expect the army's commanders to require the same proof.

This time he regarded her with genuine interest. "Very well, Chevalier-General, I'll have an aide deliver you a summons for a debrief. In the meantime, do try to enjoy the Duc's hospitality. I expect your brigade commanders will still enjoy the pleasure of your company, even if the rest of society may keep their distance." He said it without malice, although she still felt another creeping flush at her collar. She hadn't meant to do more than give them an honest account of the soldiering life. Perhaps she'd gone a bit too far with her descriptions of Fantain's Cross.

"Ah, speaking of which." Voren gestured toward another pack of nobles making their entrance into the foyer. "I don't believe you've yet had the pleasure of meeting your newest brigade-colonel."

That piqued her attention. She turned to see a young man approaching at the marquis-general's behest, looking fresh-faced enough to confirm the rumor that the new commander of the 14th Light Cavalry was among this year's graduates from the New Sarresant Academy.

"His father is an old acquaintance of mine," the marquis-general continued. "But the instructors here at the academy say he shows promise. I wanted him posted under my best division commander. Chevalier-General Erris d'Arrent, I present Brigade-Colonel Donatien Revellion."

The newcomer gave a crisp salute, the precise sort she'd managed to avoid giving before.

"Chevalier-General, sir," he said, remaining at attention. "An honor to serve under your command."

"At ease, Brigade-Colonel," she said. "We're at a salon, not on a scouting patrol."

Voren laughed, clapping them both on the shoulder. "Don't be too hard on him, Chevalier-General." With a wink, the general took his leave, making his way across the foyer to another waiting group of guests.

The young colonel made a visible effort to relax, a calculated attempt that fell somewhat short of natural. She stifled a laugh in spite of herself, retaining a cool expression as she looked him over, head to toe.

"Donatien Revellion," she said. "The new commander of the Fourteenth Light Cavalry."

"Yes, sir."

"Your first command?" she asked, masking the irony behind the question. Of course it was his first command. This boy was greener than the first sapling of spring.

"Yes, sir. And may I say, it is an honor to follow in your footsteps. I studied your exploits with the Fourteenth at the academy."

"You know the unit's history."

"Yes, sir," he said, eyes shining. "Every battle, every engagement during the Gand campaign, and many of the battles during the Thellan War as well."

"Tell me then, Donatien Revellion. Why should the veterans of the Fourteenth follow the orders of a freshly graduated nobleman's son granted their command by virtue of who his father knows?"

She expected him to react the way noble brats typically did, as if she'd struck him across the face. One of the few pleasures of having to deal with their lot, and an essential step if she was to break down a lifetime of easy comforts and begin to build a real commander out of him.

Instead he nodded, wearing a solemn expression. "I understand, sir. I haven't earned this post, but I will do my duty. If the men follow me out of obligation at first, I hope in due time I will earn their respect."

She kept her expression cool, revealing none of the surprise she felt at his words. Perhaps there was hope for him, though just as likely he had merely given more than a token thought as to how best to kiss her ass.

"Just remember you know less than horse piss and you have everything to learn, Colonel."

He nodded gravely. "Yes, sir."

"You've reported to the Fourteenth's camp outside the city walls?"

"Not yet, sir."

"Good. You can accompany me tomorrow morning when I ride to the command tents."

The boy made another attempt to salute, which she dismissed with an eyebrow. Gods but this was the last thing she needed. To have to train a fresh commander, and like as not one who thought too highly of himself to shut up and do what d'Guile and Pourrain told him to.

At least having a subordinate here gave her some measure of protection from the nobles' glowering eyes.

She thought of a question about his training, a comparison between her days at the academy and whatever they were teaching now. Only she never got to ask it. A crash at the foyer entrance drew her eyes, and those of every guest assembled in the room. She turned to see what looked like one of the Duc's servants, a portly man clad in velvet livery, making a mad dash through the chamber, rushing down the gallery toward the Duc's private audience room.

Without thinking, she bound *Body* and ran.

In the space of a heartbeat she cut the servant off mid-stride, interposing herself between the man and the gilded doors behind which the Duc entertained a select coterie of guests.

"Out of my way, madame!" the servant barked, fighting to free himself from the leyline-enhanced grip she'd fastened around his forearm.

"Explain yourself at once," she snapped back, halting him where he stood.

"He's here," the servant gasped, out of breath. "Here at the palace. He's come straight from the harbor!"

"What? Who is here?"

"The Crown-Prince. The Duc must be alerted. The Nameless take you, woman, let go!"

She released her grip, turning with a confused expression toward the foyer entrance. The latest arrival to the Duc's reception stood there, silhouetted against gilded doors swung wide to accommodate him: a tall, hawk-nosed man with an ermine-lined cloak of royal blue and all the haughtiness of youth mixed with power. A pair of guardsmen in purple uniforms flanked him on either side. Fullbinders, wearing the sigil of the royal bodyguards, the Aegis of the King.

The newcomer's eyes settled on the servant's backside, and the long chamber echoed with the lordling's laughter.

"That's right, run and tell him, little man," the man called, seeming to relish every pair of eyes he drew among the noble guests. "Tell him Louis-Sallet has arrived."

32

ARAK'JUR

Ka'Hinari's Tent
Ranasi Village

The Ranasi will accept the offer of alliance."

Relief washed over him as Ka'Hinari uttered the words. It was not a binding promise—that would come later, after the final deliberations in the steam tent. But the shaman's backing went far with his people. If Ka'Hinari believed they had consensus, then it would be so.

If he surprised Ka'Hinari by wrapping him in a bear hug, the shaman didn't show it. Laughter rang through the tent, and Arak'Jur's gesture was returned with a fierce strength belied by the other man's aged frame. Corenna's steady visage slipped as well, and she joined him in a tight embrace after he and Ka'Hinari separated.

It had taken four formal audiences like this one, presenting his cause before the Ranasi shaman and—much as it surprised him to learn it—before Corenna, who stood as foremost among their women, for him to reach this end. And now he had it. The Sinari would not face the other tribes alone.

"Honored brother," Corenna said, speaking as if their pact had already been sealed. "Thank you. For you to approach us took great courage and strength of will. I cannot say we would have made the same overture." She eyed Ka'Hinari with purpose. "But I am pleased that you did."

"Thank you, honored sister," he said, at last allowing himself to relax in spite of the formality of their meeting. "Neither Ka'Vos nor I could countenance the thought of what the spirits seek. War, between the Sinari and Ranasi? Unthinkable."

"Unthinkable," Ka'Hinari agreed. "It will not happen, so long as I am *Ka*. But you have gone further. To take the step of making a pledge of alliance in the open, before the people of our tribes... it is a bold plan, but I say again it is a wise one."

"Will we speak of my request then, to approach others, other tribes who might take up the mantle of peace?"

Ka'Hinari and Corenna exchanged a look.

"Yes," she said. Ka'Hinari's expression changed as if he was about to speak, but Corenna silenced him with a hand laid across his forearm. "Yes. Father, we have discussed this. The Sinari have taken this bold step, risking their guardian's life coming to us with their plan, and we can do no less."

"You would go yourself," the older man said in an accusing tone.

"And what of it? Am I more valuable to the Ranasi than Arak'Jur is to his people? We speak blasphemy before the spirits, it is only fitting we send an envoy worthy of the import of our cause. The other tribes would not consider words carried by any of lesser standing."

Arak'Jur remained silent, letting the moment pass between them. He made no pretense of understanding the relationship between Corenna and her father, nor did he claim to understand the strange role she seemed to play in the workings of the Ranasi tribe. Certainly Ka'Vos did not keep council with the women for considerations such as this, nor did he and Ilek'Inari consult women in their responsibilities as guardians.

Ka'Hinari gave a grudging nod, and Corenna turned toward him.

"The Nanerat," she said. "They will hear our plea."

"Corenna—" her father began.

"I know, father. Their lands are far from here, across the peaks that do not shed ice even in the hot seasons. Yet the Nanerat will listen, and I cannot say the same for our neighbors."

Arak'Jur rubbed his chin, considering. "I know their guardian, Arak'Erai. We hunted *lakiri'in* together in the lands of the Vhurasi to the south. A good man. Even-tempered."

"A common trait among the Nanerat," Corenna said carefully, drawing a warning glance from her father.

He raised an eyebrow. What did the traits of the Nanerat betoken that would draw censure from the Ranasi shaman?

Corenna sighed. "Must we tread so cautiously around the forbidden?"

And now he understood, wincing at the same moment as Ka'Hinari. Women's secrets. A lifetime of adherence to the ways of the spirits sent chills down his spine at the thought of letting her continue. Just as the magic of their people had been divided between men and women, so the tribes had followed the spirits' example, keeping men's rituals and women's ways separate. It had been so since the first tribes had listened to the spirits' call, on pain of a curse, the risk of straying from the spirits' ways. An uncomfortable reminder that their purpose put them on such a course now.

"It is no more comfortable for me to hear the ways of men," Corenna said. "But we have chosen to walk this path together, and if it will avoid war..." Her shoulders dropped into a submissive posture. "Tell me what to do, father."

The shaman looked toward Arak'Jur, as if asking his permission. He gave it with a slow nod. Corenna spoke wisdom, much as it pained him to admit it.

"Very well, Corenna," Ka'Hinari said. "Tell him."

"The places of power," she began. "From which the women draw their magic, where the bonds are forged with the *Ka*. Each tribe has at least one, and each bestows its power on the women who are chosen to journey there."

He nodded; he knew as much from his role as escort on many such journeys, to Ka'Ana'Tyat, and as a proxy for other tribes' guardians when their women or apprentice shamans visited their own sites.

She continued. "The sources we have claimed are bound to the land, but to the people as well. From Hanet'Li'Tyat here in Ranasi land, I draw the power to harness Wind. From Moru'Ona'Tyat on Yanarat land, Ice."

Now his skin crawled. This was forbidden knowledge. He forced himself to listen as she went on.

"The source and the spirits from which we draw it give us power, but ask that we give up somewhat in return. By dwelling on their land we agree to the compact. We let the spirits influence us, our temperaments, the very way we think and feel. We are more than we were without them, and they grow stronger for their bond with us. Always they speak of a Goddess, who will need our strength in times to come."

He nodded slowly. "It is the same with the beast spirits. They have grown stronger, and more numerous, of late. And they speak of a Goddess who will need our strength in turn."

"I believed my father's visions the first steps toward this time of need, but you have shown us otherwise. If dark voices corrupt the spirits' visions, perhaps the time is already upon us. Our enemy stirs the passions of our people toward war; we must look north, to the spirits' most peaceful children, to find the strength to resist its call."

"The spirits' most peaceful...?" he said, finding the words dry in his throat.

"Yes," Corenna said. "As I said, we take from the spirits' gifts, in more than just our magic. The Ranasi people are renowned for our strength, but also our willingness to bend with the tides of fate, just as the wind does. The Yanarat are cold, brittle, and deadly sharp when their veneer of serenity is cracked—this is the influence of the ice spirits."

"And the Nancrat?"

"Their sacred site is called Nanck'Hai'Tyat, and it is said its gift is peace. The serenity of the mountain spring, a centering found in the thin air atop the great peaks. If there is a tribe that can weather this onslaught of madness from the spirits, it is the Nancrat."

He swallowed hard. "It is a long journey."

"It is," she said. "By the grace of the spirits, it is."

"And a hard one," he continued. "But we will soon find the passes through the peaks blocked with sleet and ice, is it not so?"

Corenna nodded. "If we are to make this journey, it cannot wait. I can be prepared to travel when the sun rises tomorrow, after our alliance has been sealed. If the portents are favorable for us to be so long away from our lands..." She looked to Ka'Hinari.

The shaman nodded. "I will spend the night in contemplation."

The deliberations in the steam tent were contentious, but it was clear from the start that Ka'Hinari knew his people well. He, Corenna, and Arak'Jur had crafted the delivery with attention paid to every detail. They agreed the shaman should speak first, revealing the nature of the spirits' madness. Whether to speak of the spirits at all had been a point of disagreement; even he and Ka'Vos had not yet laid the truth before the elders of the Sinari. Ka'Hinari had been firm in his resolve, insisting the Ranasi could weather such tidings and emerge stronger for knowing the truth. He was proven correct. Ka'Hinari's words were met with a torrent of anger and suspicion that nonetheless stilled itself into a calm before the shaman's unwavering certainty. The revelation by Corenna of the link between her people and the spirits of the wind echoed in his mind during the proceedings. He could see in the Ranasi all the fury of a late season windstorm, great strength that still relented against a steadfast cliffside. A strange thing, women's secrets.

When Ka'Hinari finished, the tribe had all but convinced itself of the wisdom of his words. Yet turning their backs on the spirits, or at least the voices calling for madness and war, left even the most radical among them feeling isolated, alone. Even with Ka'Hinari's assurance that the madness did not taint the spirits in all things, a cloud of unease settled over the tent, thick as the steam vapor billowing from the heated rocks at its center.

And so, when Arak'Jur stepped forward to give the ancient plea for alliance, it came as a balm for fresh wounds. Many among the Ranasi elders had known him before he came to their village, and all had heard the news of their guardian's death at Ka'Ana'Tyat from his account. When he knelt before them, his chest bare, and produced the stone knife he had brought into the tent, many wept, hoping for the very words he then delivered.

"Our blood for your blood," he said, drawing the blade across his forearm. "The Sinari would stand with the Ranasi, in the eyes of our people, and the spirits."

Agreement came swiftly.

After, he approached Corenna, waiting as she spoke with the last group of women to depart the tent. She'd offered soothing words to many such, answering sentiments better addressed intimately, after the group had made its decision. He'd given no few words of encouragement himself, affirming the strength of his people's commitment to this course. When she finished, dismissing the women to whom she had spoken with a comforting gesture and a smile, she turned her attention to him.

"It is done then," he said.

"Yes. You did well. My father was wise to trust your words, no matter that your arrival carried ill tidings."

A moment of quiet hung around them in memory and homage to Arak'Doren. They began to walk the path down through the center of the village, toward the shaman's tent.

"We travel north, then," she said after a time. "If the visions are favorable."

"Your father has already begun his meditation?"

"He left as soon as the pact was sealed. We will hear from him after the sun rises tomorrow, but do not worry yourself. The signs will be favorable."

He eyed her with a weighing look. Was this another of her secrets?

"Not a vision," she said, addressing his unspoken concern. "Just confidence. The spirits continue to guide us, even if some few of them have gone mad. Whatever happens does so of a purpose. Our steps would not so clearly point toward the Nanerat if we were not meant to take them."

He relaxed. "I hope it is so," he said. "Though the way ahead vexes me still. It will not be an easy path."

"Spoken like a Sinari," she said with a smile.

This time when he eyed her, she returned it with a sympathy that confirmed his fear. Now she was most assuredly speaking of the women's secrets.

"You did not say what manner of spirits the women find at Ka'Ana'Tyat," he said. "And I am not certain I wish to know."

"I could not reveal it for certain, anyhow. The path was barred to me when we ventured there. I have not been to Ka'Ana'Tyat, nor conversed with the powers that dwell there. Yet it is no secret your people are preoccupied with things-to-come. They call your sacred place the Birthplace of Visions. Perhaps it is no coincidence."

He shook his head in awe, considering the possibility.

"You have journeyed to Nanerat lands before?" he asked, changing the topic.

"I have, though I have not entered Nanek'Hai'Tyat. As with the Sinari sacred place, the way was closed, guarded by a great beast the Nanerat *Ka* had not foreseen."

Now he reacted with surprise. "This is a thing common to other tribes?" His thoughts went to the *una're* they had encountered together, with Ilek'Inari, and to the *mareh'et* that had slain Arak'Doren.

"I believe it is a common thing, yes," she said. "For the last turn of seasons at least. Tied to the madness my father hears from the spirits, perhaps? We don't know for sure."

He exhaled in a rush. "I'd thought it a sign of a curse."

"We feared the same," she said. "When Ilek'Luren was slain visiting Hanet'Li'Tyat..." She trailed off. "We feared to speak of it, even to you, even having shared what we saw with Ilek'Inari at Ka'Ana'Tyat."

"It is well we share blood-bond now, through the pacts of alliance. If the spirits curse us, let us suffer their wrath together."

She smiled, and took his arm in a gesture of acceptance. "Thank you. Those are comforting words in times such as these."

"Do you believe all tribes' sacred sites are sealed in this manner?" he asked, his mind still weighing the implications of this new revelation.

"None among them will speak of it, to me or my father. Even the Nanerat were less than pleased when I reported the way was sealed."

"Perhaps you were right, and the time of need is upon us. Perhaps this is the punishment meted out by the mad spirits, for refusing their call to war."

"An unpleasant thought," she said.

"Even so."

They walked the last few steps with that sentiment hanging in the air, a dark cast over the day's events. When they arrived, they saw thick tufts of smoke winding their way through the openings at the top of the shaman's tent. Even past dusk, it was clear these were not confined to the ordinary whites and grays: Instead they were colored darker shades, deep hues that spoke to the work of the shaman conducted within.

"Well," Corenna said as they came to a stop, giving him a warm look as she let go of his arm. "We will have much to discuss on our travels."

"Rest well, Corenna."

"And you, Arak'Jur," she replied, lowering her head in a sign of respect before she entered the tent.

In the morning, the omens were pronounced favorable. With Ka'Hinari's blessing, they left the village bound for Nanerat lands, far to the north.

33

ERRIS

Waterfront
Harbor District, New Sarresant

The New Sarresant harbor resembled nothing so much as a densely wooded forest. Everywhere she looked across the waters of the bay, ships' masts reached into the sky, with more arriving by the hour. Mooring lines snaked in a tangle she could not begin to decipher, and a fleet of smaller boats swarmed in the channels between the hulls of the warships, carrying men, orders, and supplies to and from the shore. Louis-Sallet de l'Arraignon had brought chaos in his wake, and as yet, his purpose had not been revealed outside whatever meetings he'd held with the Lords' Council and the army high command. A strange turn, to redeploy so much of the royal navy into the waters of the New World. Perhaps a blockade in force, or a ferrying operation for an amphibious strike far to the south? All would become clear in time; no sense attempting to divine the whims of lords. Until then, the denizens of the Harbor district made what accommodations they could for this influx of sailors and soldiers from across the sea.

The Harbor-folk scurried in every direction this afternoon, most with jobs to do for the harbormasters, and the rest looking to hawk whatever wares they could scrounge for sale. Whether it was a hot meat pie or the attentions of a whore, men who'd spent weeks aboard a ship denied any semblance of comfort were not known for their discerning tastes.

Almost she pitied the city's rat population, being cooked up and passed as pork or beef. As for the whores, well. In the coming days, even the least among them would be wooed with fervor ordinarily reserved for blushing highborn virgins.

She made her way through the streets toward the 2nd Corps headquarters, and thank the Gods she was not pressed for time. Marquis-General Voren had shown either uncanny foresight or exceptionally ill luck, opting to establish his command here by the seaside during their tenure in the city. The day the army arrived in the city he'd made arrangements to host the officers of the 2nd Corps in apartments along the docks. Good for an old man's constitution to be near the sea, he'd said. And that very night, Louis-Sallet's flagship had arrived, with the rest of the fleet close on his heels. So now she and the other banner generals under Voren's command occupied the most coveted space this side of Rasailles. It made delivering orders a damned frustrating exercise, to say nothing of trying to keep appointments anywhere close to their allotted hours. Left up to her, she'd have the officers sleeping in tents with the rest of the soldiers outside the city walls. But she supposed it also had the effect of making Voren's command the envy of every admiral and ship's captain who came ashore for lodging. A political game, and if she herself would not have chosen to play, that did not keep her from admiring her commander's moves.

After an interminable walk through the press, she arrived at the Tank & Twine, the three-storied inn Voren had commandeered for 2nd Corps business. As soon as she stepped across the threshold into the common room she was assaulted by the smell of spiced meats and fresh-baked bread, rich enough to remind her stomach she hadn't yet eaten today. She kicked the mud from her boots and called an order to a passing kitchen maid, asking it be served directly to Voren's private chamber. If her commander issued summons at midday to a common room, he couldn't object to her taking a meal while they spoke. Like as not he made a point of arranging his conferences at such hours precisely to show his peers how well stocked they kept the Tank & Twine's larder.

She scanned the common room, finding no sign of Marquand. He was late, or perhaps already gone upstairs to begin their meeting with the marquis-general. Knowing the foot-captain, she knew where she would place her coin. No sense waiting for him. With a sigh she climbed the wooden stairs, letting the general's aide know she had arrived.

"Chevalier-General d'Arrent," Voren said as she entered. He waved her forward without looking up from the report over which he stood, leaning against his desk. "Apologies for the delay in scheduling your debrief. Things have been hectic since the Crown-Prince's arrival."

"Of course, sir," she said, taking a seat in one of his cushioned chairs, the quality of which suggested he'd had them brought in rather than found them here at the inn. She made herself comfortable as she waited for the general to finish reading his report.

The click of his spectacles being folded and placed on the desk signaled he'd reached the end. "All right, d'Arrent," he said. "Let's have an account of these details you omitted from the official report."

"Yes, sir. I'd hoped to show you in person, but it begins with the scout's reports I mentioned in the official account."

"I thought as much. The cavalry deployments mentioned in your report would never have caught the enemy movements through the Great Barrier. I assume it was an agent sent to infiltrate their ranks? Hence the need for secrecy?"

"No, sir. Not exactly."

He said nothing, waiting for her to continue.

She took a deep breath. "Sir, I believe I have discovered a new leyline binding. One that allows for communication, and observation over great distances. My personal redeployment north to the barrier, and the involvement of the priests of Arentaigne, were both a result of this observation. I was near the Gand border when I saw the vision from Marie d'Oreste's eyes. Or, sir, that is how it is done: through a vessel, with sufficient need in both myself and the subject."

Her commander sat back in the leather-upholstered chair behind his desk. "Start at the beginning, d'Arrent. Explain the details of how this works, and remember I have not had your education where the leylines are concerned."

She gave him a full accounting, explaining the golden light, *Need*, the shift in control of the vessel whose eyes she stepped behind. In spite of his professed ignorance, he grasped the concepts of *Need* bindings quick enough. By the time she'd finished, the unasked question hung in the air like a dark cloud, always the first concern when a new form of warfare was discovered.

"Does the enemy have it?" Voren asked. "Can enemy generals issue orders over great distances, take command personally?"

"Yes, sir. I recognized it for what it was only after the events at the barrier. We'd seen the telltale golden light before, at Villecours, behind the eyes of a man called Alrich of Haddingston. The enemy has at least one *Need* binder."

The marquis-general frowned, rapping his spectacles against the wood of his desk in one hand with the other pressed to the side of his head.

"And sir, I believe the *Need* binder is the High Commander of their armies."

Silence stretched between them as Voren contemplated, filled only by the tapping of the general's spectacles on his desk.

Finally he let them drop in a clatter. "They've had this for what, perhaps six months? And at what scale? Can it be used to command divisions? Brigades? Gods be good, d'Arrent, no wonder their *Need* binder is in command. Can you imagine what you could do with a network of communication like that?"

"I'd considered it, sir," she said wryly. "However, I haven't been able to use it with more than a single vessel concurrently, so command would be limited to large-scale operations. But with the right placement of *Need* vessels in tactically significant positions within a battle plan..."

Voren cursed. "Well, this explains the presence of our Crown-Prince."

"Sir?"

"He's brought the bulk of the royal navy here to redeploy us, Chevalier-General. He's taking the army back across the sea to defend Sarresant proper. They've been losing the war on the ground there"—he gave a soft, bitter laugh—"for the past six months."

"Sir," she began, heat creeping into her voice, "if they redeploy us back to the Old World, how can the colonies stand against the Gandsmen? They are doubtless mustering fresh levies even as we speak."

"Perhaps the Duc-Governor can broker a peace. If not..." His voice lingered. "Then the colonies will fall."

She slumped into the cushions of her chair, stunned. Could it be true? It was clear the navy was here for a grand purpose, but to evacuate the army from the colonies? This was her home. This was her men's home. Nominally they owed allegiance to the crown, but she'd never seen a scion of the de l'Arraignon line before Louis-Sallet made his trip across the sea. If their armies boarded his ships and sailed away, thousands would die. Tens of thousands. New Sarresant would be sacked. Villecours would burn. She'd seen the barbarity of the enemy commander firsthand, at Fantain's Cross, and Oreste. Could they abandon their people, their homes to the mercy of such a man?

The door to the general's private room banged open before she could reply. Foot-Captain Marquand stumbled in unannounced, wielding a freshly cooked chicken leg in one hand and a tray she could only assume had been meant for her in the other. Thankfully, Voren looked amused. The general's aide rushed to the doorway a moment later, stuttering an apology. Marquand affected not to hear, offering a gesture that might have been a salute before he crashed down into one of the long couches at the far side of the room.

Voren leaned back in his chair, eyebrow raised. "One of yours, d'Arrent?"

"Yes, sir," she said, with a glare for Marquand. "One of our fullbinders, in need of a reminder that his talents do not confer the sort of privilege he seems to think they do."

"Very well. Why have you invited him here? Can he be trusted with strategic confidence?" The look he gave Marquand suggested what he thought of that.

"Yes, sir, he can be trusted. He's a drunken fool, but he's loyal to... to the army." She'd been about to say he was loyal to Sarresant, but the words soured in her mouth in light of the revelation of Louis-Sallet's intent.

Marquand coughed. "He's sitting right here, sir."

She ignored him, returning her attention to her commander. "Sir, I've called him here to demonstrate firsthand the power of *Need*."

"Now hold on a minute," Marquand said, setting down the grease-soaked remains of her lunch on the upholstery beside him. "You never said anything about—"

She slid her eyes shut, and found the golden thread of *Need* within Marquand, ignoring his sputtering protests. It proved far easier to repeat with a subject with whom she was familiar, snapping into place as easily as she might have tethered any other binding. The reserve of *Need* was small but, driven by her own requirement to show her commander, proved sufficient.

Once again the feeling of seeing herself, her eyes rolled back as if stunned or in a trance, sitting in the cushioned chair opposite Marquand's place on the couch, made her stomach turn. Voren's eyes went wide, and he rose to his feet.

"This is it?" her commander asked, craning his head to regard Marquand in a wholly different light. "This is the *Need* binding?"

"Yes, sir," she said with Marquand's voice, straining to control the slurring effects of whatever wine he'd drowned himself in this morning. "I see through his eyes, and control his movements."

"Fascinating," Voren said, rubbing his chin.

The reserve of *Need* ran dry, and her vision slid back behind familiar eyes.

"Fuck you, d'Arrent!" Marquand roared, springing to his feet. Or at least, he might have done, if his knees hadn't buckled beneath him halfway up. Sputtering a few more choice curses, he scrambled to pick himself up off the ground.

She turned to look down at him, shaking her head. "Find a trough to soak your head, Marquand. That's a direct order."

He knew better than to try her. For other men, the presence of two senior generals might have been enough to corral their behavior toward some semblance of normalcy, no matter how much they'd had to drink. For Marquand, she knew it was only the memory of a few sound thrashings in the dueling grounds that kept him restrained. He stormed out of the meeting room, still hurling curses. She pitied whoever came between the foot-captain and the nearest flagon of wine.

"Well," Voren said after he'd gone, wearing another amused look. "I suppose I can infer the binding has unpleasant aftereffects?"

"Perhaps, sir. I have not as yet had time to give it a proper study."

"Find the time. Requisition whatever resources you require; I will see it approved. We cannot fight another campaign without the full use of this ability."

"Yes, sir," she said, feeling a renewed pang of concern. "Will it be in the Old World then? The next campaign?"

Voren sighed, rubbing the bridge of his nose. "See to your new leyline binding, d'Arrent."

"Sir, I cannot believe the crown would give this order." She knew she overstepped in pressing her commander after he'd given her a cue to leave. She didn't care. "Are you certain the Crown-Prince means for us to leave the colonies undefended?"

"He'd have given the order already if he had given proper forethought to the consequences."

"Sir?" she asked.

"What would you choose, d'Arrent, between right and duty? Could you board that ship, knowing you consigned the people of New Sarresant to death and torment at the hands of our enemies?"

She made no reply.

"Louis-Sallet de l'Arraignon is a boy," Voren said finally. "Untested, young. He's hatched a brilliant plan and sailed across the sea to see it done. Now he faces the reality of his dreams, and he blinks."

She sat in silence, regarding her commander. Voren was an old man, but no ancient graybeard for all that. Yet he seemed taxed, brought low beneath the weight of the orders he would soon be asked to give.

"We are soldiers," he said abruptly. "We are soldiers, and we do not blink."

"Yes, sir," she said, hearing the hollowness of her own words. It was almost beyond thinking, questioning an order. Years of training ingrained obedience in her bones. The pointless regulations she could set aside easily enough, but a direct order from the crown? It was not her place to question. It was not Marquis-General Voren's place to question. Yet here they stood, contemplating the bedlam Louis-Sallet would unleash on this city when he gave the order for its protectors, for natives of the colonies to board ships and sail off across the sea. Her men would be asked to turn their weapons on their own people before the end. There would be riots, and worse.

"See to your new binding, Chevalier-General," Voren repeated in a weary voice. "I expect a full report within a few days' time."

"Yes, sir," she said again, rising to salute. Her commander gave the counter-salute and she made her exit, down through the common room and once more onto the bustling streets of the Harbor. Whatever else was coming, she had work to do.

34

SARINE

An Unmarked Street
Maw District, New Sarresant

She kept to the shadows whenever she could. *Faith* was abundant in the Maw, but her body had limits when it came to maintaining leyline tethers. Fatigue was a hindrance she could do without; no telling how much longer the evening's pursuit would continue.

She'd followed these two since sundown, when they left from a back entrance of Reyne d'Agarre's estate. Right away it had been clear these were no ordinary guests, nor were they the servants and gardeners who frequented the grounds. One was a wiry man of middling height, lean, with a hip-scabbard dangling from his belt. The other man towered over his companion, a brute who went without a cloak despite the chill creeping into the autumn breeze. Together they made a beeline through Southgate, crossing through the Market district at the center of the city, traveling along the Riverways just far enough to cross the river and make their entrance into the Maw.

These two were the first she'd followed who did more than routine comings and goings, errands to the butcher shop or the candlemaker or any of the dozens of other artisans and merchants required to keep an estate like d'Agarre's running in good order. She'd hoped they would lead her into the Gardens, the Harbor, or the military camps outside the city. Still, she might learn somewhat about d'Agarre's operations, even here in the slums. And neither of these men had a look suggesting they kept permanent residence in the Maw; with luck, she might follow them after they'd conducted whatever business they were about, and make a connection elsewhere. For now, vigilant pursuit.

Her breath caught as they came to a halt, and the larger of the two men craned his neck to look up and down the street. By reflex she tethered *Faith* and faded from view, slivers of a second before he saw her. The Nameless take her luck; she'd been caught between hiding spots as she tailed them. She'd kept a good distance behind, but the bigger man had already cast a suspicious eye once back in the Market, a sign he thought they might be followed. He hadn't seen her, thank the Gods, but if she kindled further suspicion they might abandon the night's errand. Seconds passed, and it seemed she'd been quick enough this time, or at least the man gave no outward sign that anything was amiss. He turned his attention back to the building in front of which they'd stopped. A warehouse. Storage space was cheap in the Maw, provided you didn't mind the constant threat of local toughs breaking in and stealing your goods. There were a few less reputable merchants who did business in the district, and it seemed one was working here in spite of the late hour. The upper floors of the warehouse streamed light back out onto the street, and even from two blocks away she could hear the sounds of activity coming from the building. The shorter, wiry man gestured to someone on the other side of the main door, and she could hear raised voices.

No telling whether the men she followed or the men inside the warehouse might be binders, able to detect her leyline tethers. But she was here for information, and a few risks had to be taken to get it.

She tethered *Mind*, fixing the binding to a point beside the men rather than into herself. Had she done the latter, it would have sent out copies of her, exact mimics made of light and energy. Instead, as soon as the tether snapped in place her senses seemed to leap forward; she saw and heard as if she stood just beside the men.

"...drops from the lily petals," the wiry man finished, just as her senses shifted.

Some kind of pass-phrase? She cursed under her breath for having missed the entirety of it.

A pair of eyes through an opened slat in the door replied, even as they looked him up and down. "And the fish will swim upstream with the morning tide. Thank the Gods you've arrived."

"Everything's in order then?" the big man said in a gruff voice.

"Yes, everything's ready. Come around the back to make your entrance. Tell 'em 'Margot waters the lemon trees' and they'll let you in."

The slat slid shut and the two men walked the alley between the lighted warehouse and the dark one beside it, leaving her view. She released the *Mind* binding, feeling her senses snap back where they belonged. A grueling binding to maintain, not least for the dizziness that followed when she let it go. She paused, safely hidden in the shadows, to let the effects fade. Whatever was going on inside that warehouse pertained to d'Agarre's plans, of a certainty. And she had the password to the back door if not the front. She could always tether *Faith* and wait to squeeze inside if they opened for someone else, but no telling whether any more arrivals were expected.

"What do you think, Zi?" she whispered. "Worth trying to sneak inside?"

Her companion materialized on her shoulder, his scales as bright a red as she had ever seen them.

Yes, he thought to her, then faded once more from view.

Well, that settled that.

She lingered in the shadows long enough to be certain the two men had made their entrance, then took a deep breath and let her *Faith* dissipate. She strode toward the rear entrance of the lighted warehouse with a show of outward confidence. As she drew near she heard once more the dull buzz of activity within. This was more than a few secret conspirators. No telling precisely what she might find inside, but it sounded like a crowd. As usual for the Maw, she had enough *Faith* and *Body* to get away unseen, in haste, if she had to. She'd gotten into places she wasn't meant to be scores of times for the benefit of her sketches. She could do this. One more deep breath for good measure, and she approached the door.

The slat was shut when she arrived. She rapped the door twice, firm and clear. A long moment passed, time enough for her nerve to threaten to fade, before the slat whipped open without so much as a warning. A pair of suspicious eyes regarded her from the other side. Young eyes, absent crow's-feet or any other adornment of age.

"What do you want?" came the voice from beyond the door. Her first thought had been to use charm, but in the moment she decided confidence was the better approach. The street rats of the Maw had little enough use for pretty girls or flattery, but they respected strength, and they were used to being too unimportant to be noticed.

She affected an air of detachment, only deigning to look the young man in the eyes for a moment before glancing back toward the street as if her mind were occupied by other matters.

"Margot waters the lemon trees," she said nonchalantly. "Here with a follow-on delivery from the estate."

The eyes on the other side of the slat narrowed, suggesting a frown.

"Is there a problem with your hearing, boy?" she demanded, letting a touch of irritation into her voice.

"No, m'lady, only, they've started and—"

"Gods damn it, you mean to tell me I'm late? Open the bloody door then."

She kept the satisfaction from her face when she heard the sound of locks being unlatched. The door swung inward, revealing a lanky youth.

"Thank you, boy," she said, striding by him with a sense of purpose. She nodded ahead, toward the hallway that forked left and right. "Which way to the meeting?"

"Either way," he mumbled. "Just in the center of the warehouse there." He pointed down the hallway.

She turned her back on him, walking down the right fork without sparing a glance back over her shoulder. With any luck he'd see nothing more than someone more important than he was, on business he didn't need to understand.

Now that she'd made it inside, her suspicion of a crowd gathering here was confirmed in spades. She tethered *Faith* as soon as she was clear of the youth and the door, fading from view. A long corridor wound its way around the outer edge of the building, the windows lining the inner wall giving her a view into the warehouse proper. Inside she could see the makings of a grand reception, with dozens of men and women—perhaps half a hundred or more—assembled beneath a series of crates piled along the west wall in a kind of makeshift stage. Most of the attendees had the look typical of Maw denizens: ragged clothes, gaunt faces, eyes that alternated between desperation, fear, and rage. Some few street toughs in leathers, but most were the types that hid from thugs when they came calling. A strange mix. She emerged at the back of the room, still shrouded in *Faith* for the time being, just as the smaller of the men she'd followed here, the wiry one with the dueling sword, climbed atop the crates and turned to address the room.

"Thank you," the man said in a clear voice that carried through the hall, stilling the murmurs and chattering of the crowd. "Thank you for coming to hear my words tonight."

He waited for silence to fall before he continued. "I know you have all heard promises before, promises of protection, perhaps. Of food. Empty words from men who would place themselves above you. Rich men, clawing for a seat on the Council-General. Bosses looking to legitimize their gangs. Nobles. Priests."

"What makes you any different?" a voice called from the crowd.

"Because," the man shouted back, his voice coming alive with a chilling intensity. "Because I can deliver on the promise of my words. Others promise bread; I promise blood."

At this, the larger of the two men approached the stage, carrying a wide crate. With a grunt and the focused attention of everyone in the room, he hefted it up to the speaker, who wasted no time prying the top open. He reached inside and withdrew a long-barreled musket, obviously meant for the army camps outside the city, and a hush fell over the crowd.

"You see? The time for action approaches. I do not ask you, the least of the citizens of this city, to bide your time with the comfort of promises. I propose instead to give you the power to forge your own way. Strength is the answer, brothers and sisters. *Égalité* will never come from the deliberations of men with everything to lose. Only the desperate can change the world."

Murmurs spread through the room, hot with anger, affirmations of what had been said.

Yellow, Zi thought to her. What? Almost she asked after it, then remembered Zi had said the same when Reyne d'Agarre had stolen the crates at the Harbor, and again before the violence in the Maw. Was this man using the same gift? Did this man have a *kaas* as well?

"You fear to act," the man said, a challenge to the crowd. "You fear to act because the priests and the soldiers have magic they claim comes from the Gods, and they wield it like reins fastened about your necks. But I tell you now: Our cause is not without a power of our own."

In a blink, he moved from one end of the stage to the other, too fast to be seen without the benefit of a *Life* binding to sharpen her senses. A gasp rose from the crowd and he moved again, drawing the dueling blade at his side in a threatening stance, then moved once more, seeming to fade in and out across the stage.

Red, Zi thought, as the crowd took up a cheer.

That confirmed it. This man had a *kaas.* That was what Zi's promptings meant. The red haze around her vision when Zi granted his gift—the wiry man was using it now. She shifted her sight to the leylines to be sure, and found nothing, none of the telltale connections that would reveal a *Body* tether.

"With this power we need not fear to oppose our so-called masters. With us to lead you, with weapons in your hands and fire in your hearts, you need not bow to men who suppose themselves your betters. Change is coming, and you will bring it. You, the hungry, the poor. You will set fire to their great council halls, their lavish manses, their chapels and cathedrals."

Now the crowd roared. Hands reached for the weapons, and the larger man gave them out, throwing rifles one at a time into the assembly. The speaker observed the exchange for a time, then turned to a pair of boys lingering near the stage, giving some order that had them scurrying toward the warehouse's main entrance.

"Even here," the speaker called out. "Even here in the Maw, they dare build obscenities in the name of their Gods, the Gods of oppression and misery for the common man. I say: enough. We send them a message tonight. Take up your arms, and march with me. March to purge with fire the excess of their overreach. Tonight it begins." He pivoted toward the wide doors behind him, still firmly shut, and raised his sword. "Tonight we burn the Sacre-Lin chapel to ash."

His words rang in her ears. They couldn't. Her uncle had serviced the denizens of the Maw district for years, fed the poor and taken in the sick. She'd seen the lavishness of the priesthood firsthand, from the Exarch's Basilica in the Gardens to a dozen other chapels and cathedrals scattered throughout the city. But no residents of the Maw could confuse her uncle's charity for pompous grandeur. Yet the speaker's cry had been taken up among the crowd, anger burning in their eyes as they called for fire and blood.

It had to be the *kaas*'s influence. Which meant Zi could stop it.

A yellow haze flared at the edge of her vision before she could form the thought into a request, and she felt a tableau of emotion from the crowd: passion, anxiety, hope, righteous anger. Without saying how, she massaged them all toward shame for contemplating the man's words. Shame, and fear.

As one the crowd turned their heads in a growing panic, as if she'd sounded a thunderclap over their heads. At the same moment the wiry man closed his eyes, drawing in a breath and wearing an expression of raptured bliss. "Sarine," he said in a voice barely above a whisper.

She let her *Faith* dissipate. Zi appeared at her feet, his neck arched up in a menacing pose, body flushed a radiant yellow like the glint of the sun on the surface of still water. The crowd wavered, pressing themselves to the sides of the room, even the toughest-looking among them seeming to cower in newfound fear.

"Your *kaas* is strong," the man called out into the now-quiet chamber. "D'Agarre warned me as much."

The doors to the warehouse rattled open behind him, wooden planks rolling to the side revealing the street beyond. The speaker laughed softly to himself, jumping down from the crates to the floor of the warehouse, drawing his thin dueling sword and holding it point downward at his side.

The crowd broke in terror, throwing muskets to the ground as they dispersed in a chaotic rush through the warehouse doors. Not quite the raging mob the man had tried to conjure with his little speech. Even his companion, the larger man, fled with the others into the night of the Maw. The speaker affected not to notice, only paced toward her, keeping his sword at a low guard.

"So," the man said as the last few of the crowd trickled out through the main doors. "Shall we?"

She held her ground as he approached. "Why?" she asked. "Why the Sacre-Lin? Why now?"

"Did you think you could skulk around d'Agarre's estate unobserved? As to why, let us say some of us are less patient than others. One way or another, I knew I'd have your attention tonight."

He came to a stop ten paces away, fixing an empty smile on her.

"Now. Let's see if Reyne d'Agarre's fear of you is justified."

Unprompted, Zi's scales flushed from gold to red. She felt herself speed up, her heart racing through her chest. Without the surge of energy from Zi and the *Life* binding she had already tethered, she might not have seen the bunching of muscles in the man's left leg, the shift in his balance. As it was, when he sprang forward, sweeping his sword around in a whirling cut, she sidestepped with room to spare.

He spun with a flourish, shifting to a high guard as he came about.

"Oh yes," the man said. "This will be most satisfying."

She crouched low, stepping back to create distance between herself and the long reach of his blade. She'd never even carried a dagger before, but found herself wanting one now. Even with her gifts his steel was deadly, and he had *Red* as well. It would be a risk to try to get in close, but she had no choice; *Entropy* might send the whole warehouse up in flames.

Once more the man charged forward in a lunge, darting strikes slicing the air. This time she added *Body* to her leyline bindings, giving her enough speed to dance out of the way. Dashing behind him as he rushed toward where she had stood, she delivered a *Body*- and *Red*-assisted kick to the man's leg. With her combined gifts it would have been enough to shatter bone had it not impacted on a glowing barrier that sprung up between them at the last possible instant.

White, came the thought from Zi, echoing in her mind.

So, a power from the *kaas.* Memory sparked, seeing it; Zi had protected her the same way, from the giant cat at Rasailles, though whatever the nature of the shield, the force of her blow had still sent the man crashing to the ground. He recovered almost at once, springing to his feet and bringing his sword up between them. Now a touch of fear kindled behind his eyes. Reaching up to his collar, he unclasped his cloak, letting it tumble to the floor of the warehouse. Then he leaned back in a defensive stance, waiting.

Her turn to attack. With another surge of energy from Zi she charged in an uncoordinated flurry. It was clear her opponent had the edge of a lifetime's training over her, but she had the advantages of speed and strength. Even so, she found herself hurtling toward him off balance, her strikes pushed aside by his steel as he swept around in an attempt to anticipate the angle of her attack.

He struck her, an impaling cut that would have run her through the belly if not for her own shield of *White*. But she struck as well, and this time he had no such protection. Her attack caught him in the chest, sending him sprawling to the ground gasping for air even as she rebounded off the edge of his blade.

"Yield," she demanded in a rasp, still struggling for air. "Yield and foreswear your service to Reyne d'Agarre."

He spat a cruel laugh as he scrambled to his feet. "I do not serve d'Agarre. It is the Codex that demands your death, abomination."

She shook her head. "Your Codex is tainted by evil. And you must see you cannot win this fight."

"I see you are an untrained girl with the magic of the priests. And your *kaas* has already used its *White*."

He stepped back and took up a defensive posture, waiting.

Anger welled within her. Was that how it worked? Could Zi only shield her once, or at least once in a span of time? The lack of knowledge made attacking a foolish risk. Whatever advantage she had in raw speed was tempered by her enemy's trained reflexes; if she tried another charge, it might well go against her. But this man intended to murder her uncle. She could not just leave him here, but nor could she strike with only *Red* and *Body*, without the benefit of Zi's protection.

Then she remembered *mareh'et*.

She took a step back, and her enemy smirked, opening his mouth as if he intended to speak. Whatever he'd meant to say died on the vine as she surrounded herself with the nimbus of the Great Cat.

His eyes went wide, though his blade never wavered from his guard. It stayed suspended in air as she flew toward him, bolstered by Zi, by the leylines, and by the spirit of the Great Cat. In an instant she stepped inside his reach, shearing through tunic, flesh, and bone with one swipe of the spirit's ethereal claws. A fountain of blood and entrails spilled out through his belly as his sword clattered to the ground, shock wrought on his face. An echo of a memory danced behind her eyes: the hunter victorious, the predator sated with the blood of a kill.

For a moment a golden rush took her, a cascade of honey trickling down her spine. Pleasure. Quivering, unfiltered pleasure, enough to consume her senses and leave her hungering for more.

Then it faded, and the horror of what she had done struck her with all the force of the man's discarded steel.

35

ARAK'JUR

Wilderness
Jintani Land

He turned to the gift of the *ipek'a* to procure the evening meal. Soaring through the air, propelled on hind legs capable of crushing a man in the blink of an eye, he remembered what it was to inspire fear in his prey. The moment of pride when a kill showed through in his feathers, painting him the color of fresh blood. A warning to all who beheld his glory: Here was a predator without peer, victorious and triumphant.

Today he bestowed death on a fine specimen of bird, the largest male in a flock of turkey he'd caught rooting around a running stream. The bird was larger than he and Corenna could eat in one meal, but the pride of the *ipek'a* spirit demanded he choose the largest and strongest of the flock. *Ipek'a* was no scavenger to pick off the weak and sickly, and the female he'd slain to earn the spirit's blessing was an exemplar of her kind. Such was how he honored her memory, by hunting as she would have done, providing food for those under his protection.

The stream proved a fine stopping place for the day's travel. Corenna had built a fire, hobbling their horses and refilling their waterskins by the time he returned.

"Do you suppose we have crossed into Jintani lands?" Corenna asked as she stoked the fire.

He grunted, half in response to her question and half for a stubborn patch of feathers pulled from the hide of the turkey. "It may be so," he said. "We are far from the lands I know well. I do not have a feeling for the sacred places of the northerly tribes."

"I came along the coast when I traveled north," she said, casting a fond glance to the east. "I do not know the Jintani well."

"They cannot be less hospitable than the Uktani."

"Yes," she said with an apologetic tone.

The Uktani were the northern neighbors of Corenna's people. Corenna had assured him she knew Ka'Ureh, their shaman, and they could expect a warm reception in the Uktani village. She'd been hopeful they might plant the seeds of peace, if the signs were favorable. Instead their approach had been rebuffed by a patrol of armed warriors, wielding long muskets traded for from the fair-skins. It had not come to violence, but it had been a near thing.

"You've traveled with the Jintani guardian?" she asked.

He nodded. "I have. Arak'Atan was a young man, barely more than an apprentice when he came south. I mourned the passing of his master. They say a *valak'ar* visited the Jintani, soon after I met him."

"I recall hearing of it when I was a girl. Arak'Doren frightened me half to death with stories of the wraith-snake."

"A well-placed fear." *Rhealla. Kar'Elek.* He stripped the last of the feathers from the bird, trying to suppress the memories.

"Arak'Doren was always envious of you. That you'd slain a *valak'ar*, earned the gift of their spirit."

He regarded her with a sharp look, from which she did not flinch.

He sighed. "I suppose you and I are past the point of speaking of that which should be forbidden."

"Yes," she said simply.

"Did Arak'Doren truly speak openly of our gifts to you, Corenna? Even before your father's decision to set aside the madness among the spirits?"

"He did. Honored guardian, I know all of this unsettles you, but the signs of change have been coming for some time now. The Ranasi are swift to adapt; it is part of who we are."

"It gives me much to consider," he said, rising to his feet. A brief search revealed a suitable branch nearby. Taking care to avoid piercing the breast, he spit the turkey and handed it to Corenna to place over the fire.

"Is there anything you wish to know about my gifts?" she asked.

He flinched.

"We are blood-allies now. One and the same people, before the spirits. If we are to stand before what comes, we must know each other's secrets."

It was not done, for men to speak of women's magic, or the reverse. The spirits themselves had provided the pattern for the first tribes, and his people had honored their ways since: Men hunted beasts to become *Arak*s, or conversed with spirits to become *Ka*s. Women found their own sources of power, and strong as they were, they were not for him to understand. Of the little he knew, he felt a proper sense of shame. Yet there was wisdom in Corenna's words, in the secrets she had already revealed. Even now he could feel the weight of a shadow on his shoulders, a threat stirring beyond the horizon of what was to come. He was no shaman, but he could sense it all the same, in the betrayal of the spirits, the madness of their incessant calls to war.

"You have sought the gifts of many tribes," he began, speaking slowly.

"I have."

"Why?"

She gave him a pensive look. "How many great beasts' gifts do you wield?"

"I thought we were speaking of your magic," he said.

She held up a hand. "Please, if you will."

"Seven, then."

"This is reckoned to be many, among the guardians, is it not?"

"More than most, fewer than some."

"I hold five connections to the spirits of the land. Neither I nor any matron of the Ranasi knows of a woman in living memory who held more."

He held her gaze, waiting for her to continue.

"Why do you suppose that is?" she asked. "Why are the women of our people discouraged from seeking out the powers of other tribes?"

He frowned, thinking on the journeys among the women of the Sinari. A painful thing, to consider what had always been taboo. And it was true enough that few such journeys were undertaken, though he had never been privy to the reasons why. "I know little of women's secrets," he managed at last.

"And yet you ask after my journeys as if they are a thing worthy of rebuke. No." She forestalled his objection. "No, I know you asked without malice. Even so, you are not the first to do so. I too can sense these are troubled times, and it is my judgment and the judgment of my father that we need every gift, every power we can bring to bear on what lies before us."

"A wise course," he said. It was. With Arak'Doren slain, the strength of the Ranasi rested on Corenna's shoulders. Taboo or not, he could see the wisdom in her words.

"Apologies, honored guardian. This is a topic about which I am easily incited to passion. I do not know the source of our people's enmity toward women's power, but it is a true thing, and I have borne the weight of it since I was a child."

"I understand. Yet it is not always so. Has word reached you of Llanara?"

"Your woman, yes?" Corenna asked. "What of her?"

"She bears a gift of which even I am loath to speak. A new magic, brought to us by the fair-skins."

Corenna hissed, recoiling from his words as a hand from flame. He stopped, eyeing her with a weighted look.

"I'm sorry," she said. "Here I speak of casting aside taboos to prepare for the future, then condemn you for the same. But even so, the fair-skins? Can they be trusted?"

"The Sinari elders debated it long hours in the steam tent, but we decided it was the wisest course, for the same reason you pursue so many connections to the land. Now is a time to gather our strength. And Llanara has claimed the magic for her own. Not all among us fear the strength of women."

She lowered her eyes. "I didn't mean to imply you thought less of me for my gifts."

"The new magic does frighten me," he continued. "But no more than any other course before us. It is good we can share these burdens, without judgment."

"It is," she agreed. "Do you know the nature of her gift? The one Llanara has claimed?"

"It is tied to a spirit-made-flesh, a four-legged serpent that rarely shows its form. It is as if Llanara has a great beast for a companion, calling on its blessing at her whim."

"Could you liken it to a beast of our lands?"

He shook his head. "As the *mareh'et* inspires awe, so does the serpent-spirit. But that is the least of it, I think, though she has not spoken of it with me."

"You believe her gift stronger than yours?"

He laughed at that.

"What?" she asked. "Is it not a fair consideration?"

"Only a vulgar one. By the spirits, Corenna, at least among the guardians we do not compare our strength so openly. Our gifts are meant to protect our people."

"Even so," she said. "If the fair-skins have this power, I would know how we compare."

"I cannot say. Without knowing the extent of what the serpent-spirit can do, I can say only that his gifts would need be mighty indeed to stand against *mareh'et*, *una're*, *valak'ar*, and the rest of the blessings I hold."

She pursed her lips, considering. "Do you suppose your magic could best mine?"

"Corenna!" He barked another laugh at the audacity of the question.

"I know," she said. "Vulgar. But again, it is a fair consideration. Who can say in the madness to come that women and guardians will not join the ranks of the warriors, tribe against tribe?"

A sobering thought.

"It may even be wise for us to practice, together," she said, eyeing him with a look that gauged his reaction with careful precision.

He returned it, steady and calm. "You have been thinking on this for some time, haven't you?"

She nodded. "Yes."

"If I caused you harm—"

Her back stiffened where she sat by the fire. "We heal quickly, the same as the guardians do."

"One does not heal from the bite of a *valak'ar*."

"Well and just the same, for a sheet of ice through the heart," she said, her voice dripping with a sudden fire. "Arak'Jur, I am frightened of what is to come. Whatever we can do to prepare ourselves, to prepare each other, we must do it. Your gifts have been tested in ways mine have not. I would learn from you." She lowered her eyes again. "Please."

He eyed her for a long moment.

"Very well," he said. "For now, we eat, and sleep. In the morning, we will see."

He awoke to find Corenna had a fire going, with the remnants of their turkey cooked and apportioned for his morning meal. Doing a poor job of hiding her anticipation, Corenna watched him eat.

"You did sleep, I hope?" he asked between bites.

She returned his smile, a slight flush in her cheeks. "Is my eagerness so plain?"

"It is," he said.

She stood, stretching with her arms above her head, offering him a demure smile as she backed away to let him eat while she attended to the horses, leading them on a rope line well away from the clearing where they'd slept. He watched her go. Corenna was a small woman, as things went. Half a head shorter than Llanara, and slender where Llanara was toned and lithe. Even so, Corenna was strong, and had held her own during their travels, even at a guardian's pace.

He'd nearly finished by the time she returned. Wise, to lead the horses away; the creatures would not take well to the sort of display he knew Corenna had in mind. Yet she said nothing as she returned, only lingered nearby until he tossed the last bone to the ground.

"All right," he said. "Time for practice?"

She nearly leapt forward. "Yes." Then a moment later. "How shall we do this?"

"Did you and Arak'Doren never . . . ?"

"No. He thought it vulgar, when I made the request."

"And yet you persuade me," he said, amused.

"Circumstances have changed, as we said—"

"I know, Corenna. No sense making a decision twice."

She gave a satisfied nod. "Then, how shall we proceed?"

"I know little of your limits. With my gifts, the spirit grants a blessing for a short time, thereafter withholding their power until suitable time has passed."

"The same with mine. How long must you wait between blessings? The women's magic varies, and I cannot say why. I suspect it has to do with pleasing the spirits."

He nodded. "Just so with the guardian's magic. When their gifts are put to vulgar use, the spirits can withhold their blessing for some time."

"Then perhaps we will see for ourselves what the spirits think of our exercise."

"A wise point."

"Shall we begin, then?" she asked.

"You wish me to attack you?"

She grinned. "If you can."

One moment she stood, smiling at him with her deep brown eyes. The next, her pupils frosted over, and a lance of ice sprang from her fingertips. Without thinking he drew on *lakiri'in*, throwing himself to the ground with all of the great reptile's speed. A near thing. He could feel a searing pain down his lower back where the tip had sliced his skin.

He let instinct take over, rolling to the side as another salvo came roaring through the air, peppering the dirt with hunks of ice. He sprang to his feet, racing forward in a blur, bolstered by the gift of *lakiri'in*. Corenna seemed to move as if submerged in water, pivoting toward him. Too slow. His unarmed strike took her across the chest, even as he swept her legs from beneath her with a swift kick to the back of her calves.

The explosion of earth beneath his feet as she fell took him by surprise, sending him sailing backward through the air. His lungs expelled air in a crunch as he landed, skidding in the dirt on the other side of the camp. Calling on *ipek'a*, he crouched low and launched himself into the air, trusting his instinct to vector him down on top of where Corenna stood. Instead he crashed into a barrier of stone, conjured from nothing just above her head. Once more he fell, bracing his arms behind his neck as the stone came down with him, encasing him in a prison of earth and rock.

Growling, he called for *una're*, using the thunder-bear's claws to carve him free of Corenna's trap. A single swipe, even with his arms restrained, and the stone shattered in an explosive burst, showering the clearing with fragments of granite. In the cover of dust that followed, he rolled to the side and drew upon *juna'ren*, feeling his skin take on a camouflage of the patterns and hues of the scene around him. Time to set a trap.

The dust settled enough to see Corenna edging forward, craning her neck to catch sight of him, her eyes glazed over in a slate gray. A few steps and she would be close enough for *mareh'et* to catch her. He stilled his breath, waiting.

She frowned, opening her mouth as if to speak, then closed it abruptly, wearing instead a look of renewed determination. Her eyes went black, and he saw twisted shadows emerge from her fingertips, sweeping across the camp in an unsettling display, like vines of darkness growing through the morning sunlight. So much for his ploy; he knew better than to let one of those touch him. Perhaps she was close enough after all. He waited until she looked away, then drew on *mareh'et* and sprang toward her with a great leap.

Almost. He'd nearly reached her with *mareh'et*'s spectral claws when he crashed through a solid wall of air that sent him spinning as if he'd dived through a screaming gale. He twisted in midair, violent torrents of wind threatening to tear him to pieces as he fell. He struck the ground with a wet sound, splayed on his belly, facedown in the dirt.

"Arak'Jur!" Corenna called, rushing toward him. "I am sorry, I reacted without thinking. Please forgive me..."

She knelt at his side, probing him for sign of injury, feeling his skin grown cold. "No," she whispered. "Please, no. Spirits, please."

Still he lay there, giving off every sign of death. She grabbed him by the shoulder, tears beginning to fall on his skin.

He waited until she turned him on his back to speak.

"You would be dead, honored sister, if I called now upon the *valak'ar*."

She recoiled from him, then struck him lightly across the chest. "Arak'Jur, you are cruel!" She struck again, and he began to laugh. "How did you do this? I saw you dead. I would have sworn it to the spirits themselves."

"The gift of the *anahret*," he said with a weak smile.

She choked a laugh through the remains of her tears, wiping at her eyes. "A cruel trick."

He nodded as he closed his eyes, resting his head back against the dirt. "May as well keep that fire going, and retrieve the horses. I expect we've lost a day or two to our practice."

He felt her at his side once more. "You are hurt."

"We heal quickly," he said. "Thank you, Corenna. Vulgar it may have been, but a refreshing exercise, nonetheless."

"Spirits send we need not use what we have practiced."

He opened one eye to see her looking down at him, her eyes still full of concern.

He managed a slow nod in spite of the pain. "Spirits send it may be so."

36

ERRIS

Marquand's Tent
1st Division Camp, Outside New Sarresant

"No. Bloody no. Not if the Exarch himself came down and licked my boots for the privilege."

She sighed. Whatever else he was, Foot-Captain Marquand was an incurable bastard.

"You really don't have a choice, you know," she said.

He scowled at her.

"Is it so awful? Marie seemed unfazed by the experience, and Sister Elise described it as 'enlightening,' once she passed the shock of it."

"You can enlighten the piss from my cock, and the same goes for the priestess."

"Is that what you're afraid of, soldier? That I'll step behind your eyes, reach down, and find you're packing somewhat less than you've boasted?"

"Fuck you, d'Arrent."

"I'd put a knife in your belly if you tried."

Another dark look. Well, this was going nowhere. She slid her eyes shut and shifted her vision to the leyline grid beneath them. Still orderly lines for the most part, this close to the city. It could be difficult to trace the patterns when one strayed too far from civilization. Here it was simple. *Body*, always abundant near the army. *Life*, abundant virtually everywhere. Of *Death* she saw only a few small clouds, bless the Gods—never a comfortable leyline energy to encounter, knowing its source. And *Shelter*. *Shelter*. It seemed a waking dream that she could still see it, white strands like pearls along the leylines where there had only ever been formless haze. Since the barrier, when she stepped behind Sister Elise's eyes and grasped *Shelter* for the first time, the ability had not faded. A miracle, a legend from a story. She had four bindings now, and with *Need*... who could say how many more she could gain by stepping behind her vessels' eyes? Perhaps all of them.

And it was time to see if she could do it again.

She found *Need* within the foot-captain. A much larger reserve than usual. Strange. She found it difficult to believe Marquand was suddenly overcome by a need for her to bind her senses to his. Another key to understanding how *Need* worked, perhaps? Perhaps the vessel's need sparked the initial connection, and thereafter it was driven by hers. It would be a marked departure from the rest of the leyline energies, if so.

"You sodding cunt," Marquand began when he saw her eyes close. "You tyrannical, shit-stained, whore-loving—"

Ah, much better.

Not that it was pleasant stepping behind Marquand's eyes. She could feel the wine sloshing through his senses, as if she had donned a veil of fog. A wonder the man was able to function at all.

His reluctance to allow the binding was another puzzling question. She seemed to be able to take control at will, no matter his objections. If that was so, what was to prevent the enemy commander from seizing the golden light beneath key officers of the Sarresant army at the height of a battle? Perhaps Marquand's acquiescence was required the first time they established a connection, then not again. It did seem much simpler to tether *Need* through a vessel on subsequent attempts, after the first link was made. But even so, that first link could be established through subterfuge, and she had not required consent from Marie, Sister Elise, Vicomte-General Carailles, or the unnamed soldier from Fantain's Cross. There was a mystery here, and she would damned well see it unraveled.

But first, *Entropy*.

Taking a slow breath to steady the dizzying sensation brought by the wine in the foot-captain's belly, she slid Marquand's eyes shut and let herself see the leylines as he did.

Life and *Death* remained. But where she typically saw the red motes of *Body* and the white pearls of *Shelter*, Marquand saw only gray haze, and so it was when she regarded the leylines through his eyes. No *Body* or *Shelter*. Instead she saw purple cubes, snaking at right angles in a grid that seemed to suggest a pattern without ever actually confirming one.

Entropy. The newest binding—well, the newest apart from *Need*. Discovered during her lifetime, in the midst of the Thellan War, after Sarresant seized half the territory Thellan had claimed in the New World. An energy built from decay, chaos, things in order being unmade.

Reading descriptions of the various ley patterns couldn't hope to do it justice. She knew from her studies long ago, after she had first been taken away from her father and told she would become a soldier, when they had forced her to learn every pattern in hopes she might recognize somewhat more than she had first been able. A vain joke. Seeing a ley-energy for the first time was unmistakable. The gray haze of patterns one could not tether and bind paled before the colors and patterns of a known energy like midnight before sunrise.

She reached for the *Entropy* energy, still wearing Marquand's skin, and found nothing. Just as it had been with Sister Elise at the barrier, she could not touch the leylines through her vessel's eyes. She made another attempt to be sure, then gave a satisfied nod when she failed again.

She released the *Need* binding, spurring another stream of invective from Marquand. She didn't bother listening. Instead she closed her eyes, shifting her vision while her heart raced.

Entropy.

Red motes, black ink-clouds, green pods, white pearls, and purple cubes. *Body*, *Death*, *Life*, *Shelter*, *Entropy*. Just like that, Erris d'Arrent became the first binder in recorded history to command five leyline bindings, and well on her way to have all six. She laughed in spite of herself. It had worked.

Marquand scowled deeper. "You think this kind of mind-fucking is funny, d'Arrent? This is no better than forcing yourself on some kitchen maid no matter that she's screaming 'no.' "

"You're right, Marquand. I apologize."

"This is beyond the boundaries of duty, this is—Wait, you what?"

"I apologize. You're right: It is an invasion of your person."

"Well, damn right," he said, still eyeing her with suspicion.

"Even so, Foot-Captain. Care to see the fruits of today's efforts?"

He glowered at her.

She bound *Entropy* through the tips of her leather glove, the thinnest sliver she could manage. A hiss of steam rose from the doeskin leather; she snuffed it out before it could do more.

Marquand scrambled to his feet, eyes wide.

"Oracle's tits, that's impossible. That's *Entropy*."

"Yes it is, Captain. And I'm going to need your help to see just how far this can go."

Discretion proved the greatest challenge in selecting candidates for *Need* bindings. Revealing her ability to see through others' eyes to Marquis-General Voren had itself been a risk, if not to her life then at least to her station as a battle commander in the army. She wasn't fool enough to imagine new and vast sources of power going unnoticed by the ruling class. That she learn its use was a necessity born of circumstance; they couldn't hope to triumph against an enemy with *Need* if they didn't make use of it themselves. But she noted Voren had kept her ability quiet pending further investigation, and that was certainly no accident. Easy to imagine herself the target of innumerable intrigues once word spread of the new binding. Now, adding the ability to bind five—or more, if the binding worked as it had with *Mind*—types of leyline energies was a threat to any chance of her ever earning out her royal marque, of ever attaining the hand tattoos that marked her a free woman. Not that she would know what to do with herself outside the army. But she had no desire to live bound in some academy while priests and scholars demanded to know exactly how she did it.

She could trust Marquand. For all his bluster and love of drink, he was a loyal man not without subtlety. He understood at once the need for tact when approaching binders to further experiment with *Need*, and had offered to round up candidates himself to buffer Erris from prying commanders and uncomfortable questions. Too, it had been Marquand's suggestion that they limit their initial investigations to binders, men and women already known to him, and to her. She'd agreed at once with his reasoning that the strange golden light—until now only the subject of rumors regarding some dark force employed by the enemy—would be better received as one of the mysteries of the leylines if the vessels were binders themselves. And there was an opportunity to identify new *Need* binders. That would be a coup. They'd decided to start first by screening the binders of the 1st Division for the ability, hoping to learn what they could before reaching out to other commanders. And if she was able to complete her arsenal of leyline bindings during the testing, so much the better.

"Lance-Lieutenant Acherre here for you, sir," Sadrelle called from the entrance to her tent.

"Very good. Send her in."

Acherre ducked under the tent flap and made her salute. The young woman was all vibrant energy, the restless need for action of a cavalry officer without orders. Erris recognized it all too well. Acherre had taken to wearing her blond hair pulled back in the same fashion as Erris herself. That combined with the lieutenant's insignia at her collar and the scabbarded saber dangling from her belt made Erris feel as if she were on the wrong side of a looking glass, seeing the image of herself ten years before.

"At ease, Lance-Lieutenant," she said, giving the counter-salute and gesturing to one of her chairs. "Make yourself comfortable, if you wish."

"Thank you, sir," Acherre said as she sat. "I was disappointed when your aide led me here rather than toward the city. They say the corps commander secured us every well-appointed waterfront townhouse in the Harbor."

"They exaggerate," she said with a wry smile that suggested they did not exaggerate much. "And I prefer to work here when I can. Too many soft cushions and I'll feel it next time I'm in Jiri's saddle. How is training going with your mount? Oboros, was it?"

"Yes, sir. The training is slower with me than it is with him. *Body* comes naturally enough to us both, but *Mind* is a challenge."

"How so?"

"I have trouble making the images appear convincing enough when I'm mimicking Oboros, rather than just myself. I'll keep working at it, sir. We won't disappoint you."

It was a challenge, of a certainty. Learning a horse's tendencies—its senses, the limits of its own awareness—was an undertaking measured in years, to reach the mount's full potential.

"You have my every confidence, Lance-Lieutenant," she said. "Trained cavalry fullbinders and their mounts are the heart of any army."

They shared a laugh at that. Pride in one's branch of service was a time-honored tradition, not lightly given up even by generals who were supposed to be above such concerns.

"The truth is, Acherre," she continued, "I've summoned you here as a binder today, not a cavalry officer."

"Sir?" Acherre asked.

"I need to trust your discretion, Lance-Lieutenant. At our corps commander's orders, I am pursuing a weapon we believe the enemy has at his disposal. What we discuss here is strictly confidential, on pain of treason. Do you understand?"

"Yes, sir, I understand," Acherre said. "Is this related to the golden light used by the enemy commanders?"

She tried to mask her surprise. "What do you know of it?"

"All of the binders have been talking about it, sir, since the scouting reports from Villecours. They say the Gand army has dozens of them, and we haven't been able to find a combination of bindings to produce the effect."

She sighed. Leave it to soldiers to gossip like highborn ladies at a masquerade. No sense hiding it.

"It's called a *Need* binding, and I need to see if you can handle one."

"Sir? Do you believe it involves *Body*, or *Mind*?"

She shook her head. "No. It's a new energy."

Acherre's eyes went wide. "A new energy? Sir, I haven't seen any new forms around the leylines since I was a girl."

"Neither had I, Lance-Lieutenant."

It took a moment for the meaning of those words to settle in. When it did, Acherre looked at her with awe. "Sir, you can use this new form?"

She nodded. "Yes, and I need to see if you can handle one side, or the other. There are two parts in a *Need* binding. I warn you, Foot-Captain Marquand finds it a less than pleasant experience."

"Anything, sir. Just tell me what to do." Her eyes shone with hunger. Once again Erris recognized herself in this young woman.

"Let's start by seeing if you can be on the receiving end. Focus on a feeling of need—something you hope for, something powerful. The binding works differently than most. It requires the subject, the vessel, to share a strong feeling of need with the binder. You allow yourself to feel a strong need, say for victory over the Gandsmen. I'll do the rest."

"Yes, sir." Acherre nodded, settling into her chair and taking a deep breath.

She closed her eyes, shifting her vision to the leylines, and saw at once the telltale colors and patterns of the ley-energies with which she was now familiar: *Body*, *Life*, *Shelter*, *Entropy*, and a few ink-clouds of *Death*. *Need* was so similar to the others for how she observed it, tethered it to produce an effect, but in other respects it was maddeningly different. Where every other energy pooled around the grid of lines, waiting to be used by any binder who could establish a connection, *Need* seemed to be a private reserve, tied to an individual and dependent on a connection between the binder and the source.

The moments drew on as she searched for Acherre's *Need*. She traced the grid of leylines in her mind, searching for some sign of the golden light. The other patterns seemed to swarm around her, clouding her vision. An irritating distraction. For a moment she wondered if learning to recognize more types of leyline energies would be a detriment to establishing new *Need* connections.

Then she saw it.

It was small. A single thread from the broader grid of the leyline patterns, branching up until it seemed to merge with the young woman in front of her. Not her physical form—she had heard it said that the leylines existed in the space between what was real and what was not. Yet nonetheless this single thread traced itself into a pattern that she knew instinctively was tied to Lance-Lieutenant Acherre. She focused on the golden light pooling at the source of the thread. *Need*. How had she missed it before? Now, having seen Acherre's thread, the pulsing light beckoned to her, inviting her to establish a tether like a garden flower opening itself to the sun. None of her previous vessels had been so warm, or welcoming. It piqued her sense of caution, and when she reached out to establish a binding, it was with the same tender care one might apply to testing the currents of an unfamiliar stream.

She willed the binding into place, and her senses shifted. One moment she had been Erris d'Arrent; the next she became Rosline Acherre.

Always before there was a rigidity to the sharing of senses, a hard delineation between her sense of self and the vessel over whom she assumed control. Behind Acherre's eyes, she felt as if she could run a footrace. Energy surged within, a wellspring of youthful vigor. In other respects the binding seemed to function as it always had, but there was a comfort here. A familiarity like returning to camp after a successful sortie, like the warmth of a hot meal after days spent sleeping in the mud.

She closed Acherre's eyes at once, shifting her vision to the leylines. *Body*, of course, but also a new form, spiraling blue coils entwining themselves around the leylines as they raced about almost too fast to see. She felt a certain pride that the blue coils seemed more common beneath her tent, for all they were scarce throughout the camp. Some truth after all in the old joke about military intelligence.

Mind.

An amusing thought, that binders like Acherre could see telltale sign of the exercise of intellect. Perhaps she ought to perform more arithmetic exercises, or bouts of philosophy or other such nonsense before *Mind* binders came calling.

Reaching out, she tested once more whether she could form a tether while bound to a *Need* vessel. And once more she found nothing, as good as binding empty air. Good. At least she seemed to be learning some of the rules for how this binding worked.

Before she released the connection, she spoke for Acherre's benefit, using the other woman's voice. "So you see, Lance-Lieutenant," she said, "through a *Need* binding, one could deliver orders, see a battle unfold firsthand. A multitude of possibilities."

She let her binding fade, her senses slipping back into her body. She spared a moment to flicker her vision to the leylines to confirm *Mind* was now among the energies she could see, and it was, thank the Gods. Time enough later to experiment with its use; she trusted Acherre more than most officers under her command, but this was a matter best kept to those who needed to know.

Acherre's arm trembled as she lifted it, regarding her own limb as if it were a foreign entity.

"Are you all right, Lance-Lieutenant?" Erris asked.

"Yes, sir," Acherre said, near breathless. "That was... that was an incredible experience, sir."

"My apologies if I frightened you. Had you suspected the nature of the *Need* connection from your scouting reports?"

Acherre swallowed. "No, sir. But if the golden light means someone else is seeing through the enemy officers' eyes, directing their maneuvers—"

She finished the thought. "Yes, Lance-Lieutenant. One commander, able to control the entirety of the enemy army. There may be more *Need* binders elsewhere, of course, but I have reason to suspect it is a single binder deciding strategy for the Gandsmen here in the New World, and quite possibly the Old World as well."

A moment of silence lingered as Acherre contemplated the implications of the news. Finally, the younger woman looked up at her. "Is he good, sir?"

"Good?" She gave a soft laugh. "You mean a competent strategist? Yes, Acherre. He's bloody good."

"Well, you have it, too, sir. *Need*." She said it with all the confidence of youth, as if the mere observation that Erris had the same power neutralized the enemy's advantage.

"Yes," she replied, projecting a confidence she could not claim was real. "Yes, Lance-Lieutenant, I do. And we must see whether you can handle *Need* from the other side."

"Yes, sir. Just tell me what to do." Acherre closed her eyes in preparation.

"No, Lance-Lieutenant," she said. "My first experience with the golden light came unbidden, without shifting my sight."

Acherre frowned. "I've never tethered bindings without seeing the leylines."

"Nor had I, but it came instinctively in the moment. I doubt we'll be able to replicate it here, on demand." She felt a pang of guilt over that, but she had no intention of offering herself as a test subject. Marquand was right; it was a violation of the sort that made her skin crawl, and if she maintained a double standard concerning the use of the binding on others, well, she wasn't entirely sure what to think about her hypocrisy. One problem at a time.

"How will I recognize it, sir?" Acherre asked.

"I first saw it as a shining light," she said, remembering the field at Villecours. "It seemed to melt away from my vision, as if it shone from a great distance."

Acherre frowned. "A pulse of golden light, like a glimmer at the corner of my eye?"

"Yes, Lance-Lieutenant, precisely. Look for a sign of that nature, and you will—"

"Sir, I've seen a pulse of light in the distance since you broke the tether. I assumed it was an aftereffect of the binding."

"What?" she exclaimed. "Where?"

Acherre pointed. "Behind you, sir."

She swiveled about in her seat, seeing nothing. "You're certain, Acherre?"

"Yes, sir, it hasn't dimmed at all, though it is difficult to keep in focus."

"Try to bind it, just as you would *Body* or *Mind*," she said, rising to her feet. "Once you can sense the golden light it functions identically to the other leyline energies."

A look of determination creased Acherre's face.

"Focus, Lance-Lieutenant."

"I am, sir. I just can't. It won't come. It's as if I am trying to bind a stone."

"Gods damn it, try harder!" she barked. "If you can see *Need* it means someone is in danger, something to which you have a connection, something..." She trailed off.

The light had appeared for her.

She tethered it at once, and felt her vision snap behind the eyes of a man half a world away. She couldn't say how she knew how far the binding had carried her senses. A thinness perhaps, a strain on the binding. In any case, the black sky above confirmed it for her; in New Sarresant the sun was a few hours shy of twilight. Wherever this man was, it was on the far side of the world.

Salt in the air suggested she was near the sea, and a glance at the horizon confirmed it. Water, yes, but also wood. If she had thought the harbor of New Sarresant resembled a forest, it was a thin copse of saplings compared to the sight in front of her. Dozens of ships. Hundreds. And a massive gangway down the center, extending for a league or more into the sea. Torches lined the way, illuminating the teeming mass of soldiers in clean ranks as they marched up onto the ramps attached to the closest ships.

Gand uniforms. Gand soldiers.

Her mind struggled to process what she was seeing. Soldiers marched in ranks all the way out onto the dike through the center of the harbor, winding back through the city in neat blocks that would have satisfied any parade sergeant. Fifty thousand if she had to guess, maybe more. Two armies' worth at least, loaded onto tall ships worthy of making the crossing to the New World. Her stomach sank. These ships were bound for New Sarresant; she knew it in her bones.

"Ho there, what are you about then?"

The voice startled her, and it took a moment to understand the words. Her command of the Gand tongue was far from perfect, but it was enough.

The man whose skin she wore had wedged himself between a stack of crates and the side of a tall building, likely a storeroom. An excellent hiding place, all but invisible to passersby, with a solid view of the harbor. The sort of place she might have chosen herself had she been the one to take on this scouting mission, a hidden vantage that required hours of quiet waiting. He'd likely been there since the night before, patiently observing the goings-on by the waterfront. Whatever else her vessel was, he was a master scout. Yet he'd been found. The voice that had called out belonged to a newcomer wearing a Gand sergeant's uniform, peering into the crack. Quite the attentive soldier to take note of this particular spot.

"By the Gods," the sergeant exclaimed in the Gand tongue. "One of the light-blessed."

Gods damn it. The bloody golden light behind the eyes. That was what had given away her vessel's hiding place. The poor scout had infiltrated whatever Gand town this was, managed to skulk his way into an impeccable observation point, and she'd ruined it all. Reaching down, she thumbed the hilt of the dagger she felt hanging from the scout's belt. Nothing for it now but to gamble.

"Come here," she called in the Gand tongue. Clearly the man whom she'd made her vessel had a far better command of their language than she herself did; the words seemed to roll from his tongue with a natural ease.

The Gand sergeant obeyed at once, leaning in toward the crack behind which she was hidden. Whatever these "light-blessed" were to the Gandsmen, clearly they knew the phenomenon well enough not to question. Gods but she was lifetimes behind the enemy commander for implementation of *Need*.

She edged forward, right to the street. Then she drew the dagger and rammed it through the bottom of the sergeant's chin in a fluid motion. With *Body* it would have been a sure, silent kill. As it was, the man cried out in a gurgling scream as he collapsed onto the street. Frantic, she scrambled out from behind the crates, looking up and down the waterfront. Oh yes, they had heard. Soldiers were coming.

"Forgive me, my friend," she said aloud, not to the dying Gand sergeant, but for the benefit of the scout whose skin she wore through the power of *Need*. "You have done your duty by Sarresant. Your work today will save thousands of lives."

She closed her eyes, as much to hide the telltale glow from the oncoming soldiers as to steel herself for what she had to do next.

"But you must understand," she continued, "I cannot allow you to be captured."

With as firm a grip as she could manage, she plunged the dagger into her own belly. A searing pain tore through her, vomit and blood mixing at the back of her throat.

Ten paces across the street. Ten paces to the waterfront.

She cracked her eyes a fraction to see the way clear, then sprinted, feeling adrenaline course through the scout's veins. The enemy soldiers understood now, and came rushing on. Too late. She vaulted the stone wall at the water's edge, and the scout hurdled over the side, crashing into the deathly cold of the sea.

She released the binding.

Acherre was still seated, her face streaked with tears. Seeing Erris regain control of herself, the lance-lieutenant stiffened, wiping her cheeks.

"Sir," Acherre began, "I apologize. I will try harder, I will—"

"Enough!" she cried. "Gods damn it, we have bigger problems. Run and saddle Jiri, Lance-Lieutenant, now! We ride for the city, for high command."

"Sir?"

"Go, soldier!"

Acherre ran.

Erris watched her leave the tent, then sagged against the side of the table, tears threatening to overwhelm her. Gods, the pain. It had to be done. It had to be. Time enough to gather herself, and be strong, on the ride into the city. For now she let herself feel the pain of it, offering up a silent prayer for the scout she'd left bleeding in the water on the far side of the world.

37

SARINE

The Revellion Townhouse
Gardens District, New Sarresant

"She's incredible, Sarine," Donatien said. "I've learned more in a week under her instruction than all last year at the academy."

An inward sigh. She could feign enough interest to escape notice when he started up this line of conversation, but it was becoming harder by the day.

"What did she have you practicing today?" she asked.

"Mock maneuvers near the coast, outside the city. She had us drilling with flotsam in the shallows, 'simulating an amphibious landing,' she called it. Half of the division attacking, half defending. Chaotic, of course, but she insisted we learn precision even in unpredictable circumstances."

He went on to recount some brilliant maneuver he'd performed, sufficient to earn the accolades of Chevalier-General Erris d'Arrent herself. In her head she spoke Donatien's commander's name with mock reverence, a deification worthy of the Exarch, if not for the sarcastic bite nested within. She'd hoped this would be different, when they'd committed to the cause of standing in the way of Reyne d'Agarre. It seemed Donatien had forgotten, and left her prowling the streets on her own. An unfair assessment, and she knew it in her head, but that didn't erase the feeling.

"Why do you think she has you planning for an invasion by sea?" she asked after he finished. "Does it have anything to do with the Crown-Prince's arrival?"

The question surprised him, though he made an effort to hide it. "Just an exercise," he began, then adopted a contemplative look. "Though I suppose it is possible she expects an attack. I've heard no reports to confirm it, either way."

"Half the royal navy is here in New Sarresant," Sarine said. "More, perhaps. Word has been on every tongue in the city, speculating why. And still we hear nothing."

She knew it sounded as though she was accusing him. He seemed to take it in stride.

"The consensus among the First Division's officers is we may be planning an assault in the south. Perhaps that's why the general has us working by the sea: to simulate an offensive maneuver. I wonder if she'll have us running joint exercises with the navy next."

She nodded absently, looking out through the glass of the Revellion library. The city seemed hushed in the twilight hours, torches being lit along the streets as the sun faded away behind them.

"D'Agarre has been quiet since the ships arrived," she said, changing the subject.

Revellion started, as if he'd already been lost in thought, planning for his next maneuver. He made a quick recovery. "Nothing since the night in the warehouse?"

She shook her head. "Not even any gatherings at the d'Agarre manse. He leaves to call on a few houses during the daylight hours, but without a pattern I can tell. Nothing to indicate what he's planning."

"The man you fought, he intimated they knew you were watching."

"Yes. But that's not it. D'Agarre wouldn't cease his plans on my account."

"Well," Donatien said, scratching his chin. "Perhaps it's the presence of the Crown-Prince, and the army. So many soldiers stationed here in the city would make it difficult to act."

"Perhaps. Or perhaps he's biding his time. If he has allies in the army, they are well poised to strike, now better than ever."

He frowned. "I'm trying to learn what I can, Sarine. I'm only a brigade commander, and new to my post. It will take time."

"I know," she said, holding up a hand to forestall his protest. She couldn't blame his efforts, even if she hungered for better results. She sighed, sitting on a cushioned bench beside the window. "I only wish we had more. He means to seize power, but that could be a strike at Rasailles, the Gardens, the council halls...we need to know what he intends if we're going to stop him."

"I'll press the chevalier-general. I have a private meeting with her tomorrow."

She nodded, snuffing the flare of jealousy that caught in her throat.

"Has your uncle reconsidered your request to leave the Sacre-Lin?"

"No," she said. She'd begged her uncle again before she left this morning, and gotten the same reception she'd had for the past week. "He knows they're targeting it, targeting him to get to me. He doesn't take the threat seriously, only reassures me the Gods will watch out for him."

"I'm sorry, Sarine. Would you like me to accompany you next time? We must be able to get him to see reason."

"Yes, if you would," she said. Damn her uncle and his stubbornness. "Anything to get him to listen."

"Tomorrow afternoon?"

She nodded. "Thank you."

He moved to sit beside her, wrapping an arm around her shoulders, joining her in looking through the window. Whatever her frustrations, it still felt good to sit beside him, to feel the warmth of him, the steadiness of his touch. She would deal with her petty jealousy in her own way. Of course the division commander had no designs on Lord Revellion. And if it turned out she was mistaken, she had plenty of tools at her disposal to deal with that. Even if they did say Erris d'Arrent was a fullbinder.

Down below, a lone merchant's wagon trundled up the thoroughfare, flanked by a pair of guardsmen in their long blue cloaks. Otherwise the streets were empty. A quiet presaging the evening's traffic. Inevitably, when the sun went down, the nobles of the Gardens district set to their fêtes and gatherings, no matter the rationing elsewhere in the city, no matter the army encamped mere leagues away. The man in the warehouse had spoken the same sort of words she'd heard from Reyne d'Agarre, and she remembered the appeal they held, even now. The people of this city hungered. For food, yes, but also for blood, for the prizes bloodshed might purchase. Why did it have to be d'Agarre? The corruption, the strange blue energy she'd siphoned away from their strange book, it had been tied to the madness she saw behind d'Agarre's eyes, and the eyes of the man she'd fought in the Maw. The man she'd killed. Sickness roiled in her stomach at the memory, a nausea she made no effort to quell. His face still haunted her, though she'd never learned his name. Another feeling, just as sick and twice as sure: He would not be the last man she killed, before all this was through.

"Will you teach me to fight?" she asked abruptly.

It earned her a questioning look, though Donatien still held her as they sat together beside the window.

"Teach you?" he asked. "I expect you'd give me a sound thrashing if we sparred."

"I mean without my gifts, or with fewer at least."

"What's bringing this on? The warehouse?"

"The man there knew how to use a sword. Even with my advantages, I've never been trained. If I knew how to fight, even the basics, perhaps it would help."

"Of course. I'll see if I can secure some practice blades from the quartermasters."

She nodded, leaning back into his arms. The sun had set, streetlamps casting circles of light on the cobblestone below. A luxury of the Gardens. When the sun set in the Maw, the streets became living shadows, lit by the occasional bonfire dared by the stronger groups of toughs. So it went, subtleties that escaped the notice of the privileged. It was as if they didn't see the tinder they piled atop the commonfolk, more and more each day. Soon, that first spark would catch.

"What do you suppose he's doing now?" Donatien asked, bringing her back to the moment.

She knew without asking who "he" was. "Sitting in his manse," she said. "D'Agarre hasn't left after sundown since the Crown-Prince arrived."

"You'd have taken to sleeping on the street in Southgate by now otherwise?"

"Probably." She smiled. She'd spent the bulk of her days there as it was, tailing anyone suspicious when they left the manse, without any successes since the night of the warehouse. She still wasn't sure what she was hoping to uncover, or what she would do if she did find something.

But already her efforts had prevented a riot in the Maw, and saved her uncle's life. If nothing else, she'd learned the pattern of d'Agarre's days, and his household. Soon she might risk venturing inside. To what precise end, she couldn't say, only that each passing day she felt more and more certain the answer lay beneath the d'Agarre estate, in the hidden chamber where the Comtesse de Rillefort had begun to reveal their secrets.

"Sorry to disturb you, m'lord," a woman's voice intoned with a sniff from the entrance to the library. Agnes, one of the servants, who had made no secret that she disapproved of her, and of her relationship with the young lord.

Donatien craned his neck around from where they sat. "What is it, Agnes?"

"A visitor for you, m'lord. Uninvited." Another sniff. "Waiting in the sitting room downstairs, if it please your lordship."

"Does this visitor have a name, Agnes?"

"Umm," Agnes began. "I can't . . . well, that's strange. I can't recall, m'lord. He seemed important, so I let him in."

Sarine leaned forward, rising to her feet as she caught Donatien's eye.

"Thank you, Agnes," he said, dismissing the maidservant and turning his attention back to her.

"You don't think—?" she began.

Donatien stood, offering her a hand. "Either way, I trust you won't mind accompanying me downstairs?"

Sure enough, when they walked together arm in arm into the receiving room, they found Reyne d'Agarre reclining on one of the long couches. He rose when they entered, sweeping a formal bow in his waist-length red coat.

"What are you doing here?" she demanded.

He feigned a wounded look in Donatien's direction. "Is that how they greet guests in the Revellion household?"

"What are you doing here?" Donatien repeated, just as firm.

D'Agarre gave an exaggerated sigh, sitting once more. "A pleasure to see you both again."

Neither she nor Donatien budged from the entryway, each fixing cold stares in d'Agarre's direction.

"I assumed you'd been hoping for an audience with me, Sarine, given how often my men report your presence in Southgate." He looked her over, giving every appearance of relaxed comfort. "Quite a trick you have, disappearing from sight. Unknown in even the most arcane circles of binders. I expect they'd be quite interested to learn of its use."

Once, it might have been enough to lodge panic in her throat. Coming from d'Agarre it fanned already kindling sparks of anger. "If you're here to threaten me, I can show you a few more things they don't know."

"Please," he said. "Once I counted both of you friends, or at least fellow conspirators." He grinned. "Hear me out. I bear you no ill will."

Her glare turned hot. "You tried to incite a riot to burn down the Sacre-Lin, and claim you bear me no ill will?"

"The very reason I am here," he said, his tone all penitence and sincerity. "Your provocateur acted without my blessing, against my orders in fact. I swear it by the strong arm of the Exarch. But for that isolated incident, the city has been quiet of late, has it not? If I meant you harm, could you believe it would be so?"

She and Donatien exchanged a look.

"Please, both of you, afford me the chance to speak. I ask nothing more."

A long moment passed before she nodded reluctantly. Together, she and Donatien entered the room and sat opposite d'Agarre.

He gave a satisfied nod. "Thank you."

"Say what you will, then," Donatien said.

D'Agarre seemed to ignore the chill reception, continuing as if he'd been welcomed with open arms. "Well, then. Let us start with the actions of my fellow. Sarine, I imagine you had already supposed de Merrain had a *kaas*. I will confirm it for you: He was one of us."

De Merrain. The man she'd killed. Having a name to attach to the face did little to settle her conscience, but it was something. She said nothing in reply.

"You must understand," d'Agarre continued. "The nature of the *kaas* is different for each of us, and the nature of the Codex. A lamentable thing that you have yet to study it."

Once more her anger flared. "Your book is corrupted, and corrupting you," she said. "As you well know, seeing as that is the reason you murdered the Comtesse de Rillefort."

"You might say otherwise if you would only study its words, Sarine. It is nothing short of a handbook for greatness, of a sort few men, or women, could imagine."

"I'll have nothing to do with it, or with you."

He held her gaze, then bowed his head. "Be that as it may, the point stands. De Merrain acted as he did at the urging of his *kaas*, and not in furtherance of any design of mine."

"Why should she believe that?" Revellion said. "And what is to prevent another of your fellows deciding they too have interpreted your Codex as calling for her head?"

"If I meant either of you harm, I assure you I could have effected it. My organization is formidable, as you both may have an inkling by now. The point I'm making with respect to the *kaas* is that, whatever grudge you have, it need not be with me. Just as one binder cannot be held responsible for the actions of another binder, so it is with me. Wielding the same power does not qualify me to suffer for their misdeeds. It is not just."

"And what of the death of the Comtesse de Rillefort, d'Agarre?" she repeated. "Or your attempt on my life immediately thereafter? Am I to forget these things?"

"The comtesse had betrayed my organization, a matter that need not concern you. Afterward, what passed between you and I was a misunderstanding I have come here in part to correct. I greatly lament the loss of both of you as fellows in furtherance of our cause."

"You mean to foment revolution against the nobility," she said.

"I do," he said. "I make no secret of it. Have you both not heard the arguments against the corruption of the old regime? Have you not made such arguments yourselves?"

She glared at him. "No argument I've made induces me to support the leadership of a madman."

He frowned, casting a look toward Revellion as if for help. Donatien sat in silence, regarding him with a cool expression.

"If you feel that way, then I can only implore you to stay out of my way. You cannot support the Crown-Prince's plans, can you? I'd believed the two of you to be persons of conscience."

"What plans?" Revellion demanded. "What do you speak of, d'Agarre?"

"You mean word has not reached you?" d'Agarre said with a glimmer in his eye.

"Say what you mean to say," Sarine said.

"Louis-Sallet means to take the army back across the sea, and leave the colonies to burn. I, and others, have lobbied to change his mind, but he will give the order within a fortnight."

A stunned silence descended on the room.

"Inquire with the navy, or the logistics divisions if you don't believe," d'Agarre said. "I swear, it's the truth."

"Did we not win a great victory against the Gandsmen, not two months past?" Donatien asked. "Why would the crown take such drastic action?"

"I cannot speak to their reasons, except to say that word from across the sea is the war goes badly there. All I know of a surety is that I will not allow New Sarresant to fall, not for the glory of a king who has never set foot on our shores."

D'Agarre rose to his feet.

"I'll leave you to consider my words. Whatever our disagreements, I believe we share a common goal. If you decide to change your minds, you know where to find me."

He made another formal bow and exited the room. Silence hung in the air until they heard the servants close the front door behind him.

"By the Gods themselves." Donatien slumped back in his chair. "Can it be true? Could the Crown-Prince really... Sarine, where are you going?"

She'd already risen to her feet, striding toward the door.

"He's out and about in the city. What better cover could he ask for than giving me news like this to consider? I mean to follow him."

"Sarine—" Revellion began. She didn't wait for him to finish. No time for deliberation. A quick scan of the streets found her mark: d'Agarre in his red coat, already making his way toward the district boundary.

38

SARINE

Street of the Crown Bridge
Riverways District, New Sarresant

Ducking from shadow to shadow through the lamplit streets had proved Reyne d'Agarre had no intention of going directly back to his manse. The first turn he'd taken out of the Gardens gate, leading east toward the Harbor, had been a sweet vindication. Whatever else he was, d'Agarre was crafty enough to do exactly as she'd thought, and screen his activity behind the cover of his revelations to her and Lord Revellion.

She stayed some distance behind as he walked, trusting to *Life* bindings to sharpen her sight. She'd expected him to take a carriage or some other means of conveyance, but d'Agarre seemed content to stay afoot, with no sign of stopping to converse, conspire, or plot. Now he was entering the Riverways district across one of the old stone bridges that spanned the Verrain River as it wound through the center of the city. The bridge was a marvel of construction, a monument to the engineering prowess of New Sarresant's first settlers, some three hundred years past. But it also lacked for foot traffic on this particular evening, and so she waited for d'Agarre to have nearly made the crossing before she dared it herself.

Lamplight from either shore of the river painted half circles on the flowing waters, with gaps of darkness stretched between. No boats, and no foot traffic in sight. Since the Crown-Prince's arrival, the city had bustled as if it were the height of summer, with soldiers, sailors, and officers scurrying this way and that, giving even the city's most venerable quarters the feel of a glorified army camp. And yet tonight there was a lull. Strange. Once she was satisfied d'Agarre was far enough ahead, she ducked her head low and followed, taking the sloping cobblestone at a quick pace, feeling the winds blow cold on her cheeks as she emerged from behind the cover of the Riverways' shops and storefronts.

Unbidden, the memory of the scene in Donatien's parlor played in her mind. Could d'Agarre's revelation be true, that the Crown-Prince meant to give the order to withdraw the army from the colonies? It would be an unmitigated disaster. The commonfolk had little to lose as it was, without the promise of their city being sacked. The spirit of *égalité* already stirred rage and bloodthirst dangerously close to a boiling point, and a proclamation of withdrawal at the behest of the crown would be enough to tip the cauldron into the streets. There would be blood, and the peaceful revolution Lord Revellion imagined would be revealed for the childish fantasy she'd always feared it was. She knew the people of this city. She'd lived among them, captured their likenesses in sketches and portraits of every walk of life, from the lowest urchin to the haughtiest courtier. If Prince Louis-Sallet de l'Arraignon gave the order to withdraw, the only question remaining would be how many binders remained loyal to the crown, and if there weren't enough, how many pikes and guillotines could be found for the heads of whichever nobles were close at hand.

Perhaps the prince could change his mind, or perhaps d'Agarre had lied.

To her and Donatien's knowledge, no order had yet been given. It was not beyond possibility the Crown-Prince had come intending one course and decided differently after seeing the state of the city, of the colonies. Surely he could see the desperation, the hunger in his people's eyes. Surely he would not order the soldiers of the colonies to abandon their families to the ravages of their enemy. Hollow sentiments, even as she thought them. She knew the nobles were capable of such callousness. No one raised in the Maw could trust very far in the wisdom of the wealthy. Better if d'Agarre had lied; easier by far to find hope there, however slight.

As she crested the arch of the bridge, a knot of panic flared as her reverie broke, returning her to the moment. She'd lost him. The street ran straight on into the Riverways before it forked, not nearly far enough for d'Agarre to have disappeared from view if he'd continued at the same pace. Had he noticed her? If he'd broken into a run before she'd started along the bridge he might have slipped away. Gods damn it. She shifted her vision, hoping to find a source of *Mind*, unlikely as that was in the middle of a bridge on the river. To her surprise it was there, just on the far bank, beneath what appeared to be waterfront houses and empty streets. She tethered it, shifting her senses forward at the extreme edge of her ability. In an instant she could see from a point at the intersection of two streets, up ahead on the far side of the bridge. Swiveling in both directions, she saw no sign of d'Agarre's red coat. Nothing for her but to sit and wait, if he'd gone inside one of the buildings, though without the promise of at least having seen him enter that seemed a fool's gambit. Perhaps he had doubled back beneath the bridge, making his way down to the waterfront? There was some hope there, if she was quick. She released the first binding as she ran across the bridge, preparing another tether of *Mind*, this time positioned along the water's edge. She completed the binding and instantly her senses shifted, as if she were standing along the embankment.

"... falls before the summer moon," came a voice just beside her, beneath the arch of the bridge. D'Agarre's voice. As ever, the disorientation brought on by a projected *Mind* binding took a moment to fade. When it did, she saw him standing before a reinforced iron grate on the sloping dirt walkway that ran alongside the shore of the river. Another man stood on the opposite side of the grate. The sewers?

"Good to see you've made it, sir," the other man replied as he moved to unlock a section of the grate she hadn't noticed before that was cut into a makeshift door.

"I wouldn't miss it, my friend," d'Agarre said, clapping the man on the shoulder as he entered, then disappeared into the tunnel behind.

She let the binding fade. The Nameless brand her for a fool. All this time, she'd been watching the d'Agarre estate, hoping for some sign of a gathering, some notion of who might be conspiring with him. And instead he'd been delving into the city sewers, like as not from an entrance on the grounds of his bloody manse. Kiss the tip of the Exarch's longblade for all the sense she had.

She pressed on, gritting her teeth. She had half the password, assuming that was what she'd heard Reyne give, and it wasn't like to do her much good. Overpowering the gate guard would reveal her presence in time, though that was an option. *Faith* might work, provided more conspirators came to give the man cause to open the gate, though a brief check of the leyline stores nearby cast doubt on how long she'd be able to remain hidden once she was inside.

Use those men, Zi thought to her.

No sooner had he finished the thought than a group of what looked like sailors rounded the corner up ahead from the Riverways. Heading toward her on otherwise empty streets.

"How?" she whispered to Zi. Already they'd noticed her.

They are nervous. Be what they expect.

How that was supposed to help she hadn't the faintest idea. But Zi had gotten her out of worse situations before. She put on a brave face, as if she belonged nowhere else in the world but at the foot of the Crown Bridge, above the entrance to a secret meeting in the sewers.

The sailors eyed her with uncertainty, as if their roles had been reversed, and she were the burly group of sailors, while they were the lone girl out for a walk at night. Gods but Zi was right; they were nervous.

No sooner had they come within earshot of her than one of them blurted out, "The springtime rain falls—"

"—falls before the summer moon," she completed in a rush. "Yes, I know. I'm here for it, too."

The relief across the sailors' faces was palpable. Bless you, Zi.

"After you, gentlemen," she said, motioning down the incline toward the waterfront.

They took her cue, shambling together like a pack of foreigners at the market. She took the lead at the grate, giving the password with confidence on behalf of the group. The man standing guard swung the makeshift door open without fanfare, welcoming them inside with a beckoning gesture and an easy smile.

"It's my first meeting," she said, lingering behind the sailors as they pressed on into the sewer tunnels. "Any words of advice?"

"Plenty of fresh faces tonight. Wouldn't worry about it. Which district are you from?"

"The Maw."

She could as easily have claimed the Market, or the Harbor, or even Southgate if she'd had a mind to. But in the moment, she felt compelled to give an honest answer. The Maw was home, and if he pressed her for details to verify her answer, she'd rather not have to think. The slums were a part of her, as sure as Zi or any other of her gifts. She could wear them with pride.

He whistled, looking her up and down appreciatively. "Never known the Maw gangs to pick a woman to speak for 'em. You must be something."

She made an exaggerated curtsy, eliciting a laugh from the man. "I can hold my own," she said.

"You'll do all right. Just head on down." He pointed down the sewer shaft, where she could see flickering torchlight around a sharp bend up ahead. "The sub-bosses'll sort you by district and give orders for you to relay to your boys back in the Maw. You might even catch a glimpse of the man himself tonight. He came down not a moment before you did, swear by the Oracle herself."

"Now that would be something," she said, letting the amusement show through in her expression. With luck he'd take it for a rogue's swagger, the kind she'd seen so many times before among the toughs of the Maw. "Thank you for your help."

He knuckled his brow, turning back to keep watch through the grate as she strode forward into the tunnel. It was well lit, with torches placed in sconces along the stone walls every twenty paces. She could hear the ribald joking of the sailors up ahead—a sign they'd recovered their nerve, at least in part—but she opted to hang back, taking in the twists and turns of the sewers for herself. More than once she crossed an intersection or a chamber that led off in another direction, pitch-black without the benefit of torches to light the way, and a good thing, too. With only a single lit passageway, one could hardly get lost. The network of passages and drainage chambers seemed to extend in every direction, like a honeycomb of tightly packed routes beneath the streets. How had she never thought of the sewers? It seemed so obvious in hindsight, a hidden place to distribute information, weapons, and loyal revolutionaries throughout the city. Even the smell was not half so bad as she imagined it would be; every child raised in the Maw was accustomed to stale piss and excrement.

It made a damn near perfect refuge for conspiracy. The guard had even said she *might* get a glimpse of d'Agarre himself, as if there would be too many of them here to guarantee it. How many attendees were expected at this meeting?

The noise drifting through the tunnels as they pressed on offered half an answer. A dull roar, the kind she heard on a slow day at the market, when the stalls two streets over had somehow attracted a bustle of traffic despite the relative quiet around her. And the gate guard had said she would be given orders here to relay back to her men in the Maw. Every man or woman she saw down here tonight represented a cell of would-be revolutionaries back in their home districts. By the Gods, just how deep did these sentiments run? She feared she had an inkling. And she'd have wished them well, if not for what she had seen that evening beneath the d'Agarre manse. Whatever his intentions, Reyne d'Agarre was mad. Evil. She shivered, remembering.

"Hold there, missy," a man said from the doorway ahead. A portly graybeard, wearing a red sash draped across his left shoulder and clutching a sheaf of papers. Not an invite list, surely? She'd already given the password once...

"The springtime rain falls before the summer moon," she said. No harm giving it again.

The man arched a bushel of an eyebrow at her. "I'm sure it does," he said. "Now which district are you from?"

"The Maw."

He glanced down at the papers in his hand, thumbing through them until he produced whatever it was he'd sought.

"Name?"

"Arianne," she lied. She steeled herself, preparing to be found wanting. She had no desire to harm this old man, but Gods be damned if she was about to give up now, this close to seeing the inner workings of d'Agarre's revolution. And there were plenty of dark tunnels nearby, plenty of places to hide an unconscious doorman if it came to that.

"All right, Arianne of the Maw," he said in a perfunctory tone, glancing down at the sheaf of paper in his hand. "You're going to want to take four rights, then a left. Sub-Boss Guyard has your instructions tonight. That's four rights, then a left. Repeat it back to me if you please."

"Four rights, then a left."

"Just so. Off with you then."

She suppressed the desire to exhale in relief. Pushing past the old man, she emerged into a cavernous chamber that must have served as the main sluiceway for the Riverways district above. Half a dozen passageways led off in as many directions, this time each one lit by torches along the walls. Four rights, he had said. Did that mean she was to take the rightmost passage, or—?

"Yes, you'll want the rightmost passage," the old man's voice called to her over his shoulder. A common question, apparently.

The sound of activity came from all around, down each of the six passageways. Once more she crossed dark tunnels leading away, supposing she was to ignore the unlit routes. She came to a torchlit passage leading right, and she took it, then again. A large chamber revealed her first gathering of people, a dozen or so rough-looking men, including the sailors with whom she had entered at the grate. They were arranged in a half circle with one man at the center, who spoke with passion, draped in a red sash like the one the graybeard had worn. Her arrival was noted by a few turned heads, but she kept her head down and pressed on to take her third right turn, then her fourth. No small temptation to tether *Faith* and have a look around, but there would be time enough for that later. For now, she'd maintain the ruse of being here as one of them, and see where it led.

One last left turn, and she'd reached her destination. Ten toughs eyed each other with a hostility fit to pale even the most seasoned tavernkeep. She'd seen her share of conflicts between the toughs and street gangs, and had the good sense to run for the nearest shadows when two rival groups came into proximity of each other. To bring ten at once into a single chamber in the sewers was asking for fireworks. And, as yet, no man-in-a-red-sash to keep the peace. Either their sub-boss had not yet arrived or these toughs had polished him off as an appetizer and tossed his body down one of the darker passages to rot.

Her arrival drew the immediate attention of every man in the room.

"What's this then?" a tall, thickly muscled man with a long mustache demanded. "They sent us a snack to pass the time?"

"Looks right delicious," another man added, this one bare-chested despite the cold outside, sporting a makeshift patch over his left eye.

She edged back toward the entrance. *Faith* was looking more attractive by the minute.

Do you want to fight them? Zi thought.

"No," she hissed under her breath.

"What's that, girly?" the first man asked with a leer.

She took a deep breath.

"Look," she said. "We're all here of a purpose. Let's wait and see what this sub-boss has to say."

The men looked back and forth at each other, then erupted into laughter.

At that moment, Zi chose to appear on the floor of the chamber. She couldn't say how, but she knew he had chosen to be visible to these men, the same way d'Agarre's *kaas* had shown himself to her back in the Maw. Zi's scales flared gold, a glinting sheen like the midday sun, bright enough to fill the chamber with radiant warmth.

As one, the men cowered away from Zi, pressing their backs to the walls.

"What I mean to say is," she said in a quiet voice, "we were chosen for this meeting because we each have our strengths. Let's leave it at that, shall we?"

Zi vanished, but the effect of his display was no less pronounced for his absence. As one, the men dully nodded their heads, mumbling incoherent protestations and wards against the influence of the Nameless.

"What under the Veil's skirts is going on here?"

A man in a red sash had emerged from one of the unlit passageways at the back of the chamber. So, d'Agarre's lieutenants knew the sewers even without the benefit of the torches. Good to know.

"Just straightening out a misunderstanding," she said lightly, with a glance around the room. Had the bare-chested man's pants been wet before Zi's display? She didn't think so.

The newcomer's eyes narrowed. "I thought it had been made clear to the lot of you that our cause transcends your petty squabbles."

More murmured sounds from around the room, evidently penitent enough to satisfy.

"Very well," he began again. "I am Sub-Boss Guyard, and you lot speak for the denizens of the Maw. We're going to need your sort, in the days to come, when the moment arrives."

"And when is that?" she asked. May as well cut straight to the heart of it.

"You're here to learn what to do after you get the signal. You should know already it will come when it comes. Your task is to be ready when it does."

She affected a bored look that clashed with the terror she saw behind the eyes of every other man in the room. They struggled to hide it, but knowing its source she could see behind their respective façades. What Sub-Boss Guyard thought of it was anyone's guess.

"Right," Guyard continued. "When the time comes, we'll have weapons prepared for you and your men, stored here in the sewers beneath the Riverways, and the Harbor."

"Why not the sewers beneath the Maw?" she said.

Was that the wrong question? Right away she saw the men around the room cringe, redoubling whatever signs of fear they'd given off a moment before.

"Are you daft, woman? Is your gang so fresh-faced that you haven't tried the sewers on the north side of the river?"

"And what if we haven't?"

More murmurs from around the room. A few derisive snorts.

"It seems your fellows know better than to go down there. One of you care to enlighten our companion?"

The mustached fellow piped up in a hushed voice. "The beast."

"That's right," Guyard said. "The beast. Any true Maw gang can speak to it firsthand. This summer past, anyone with a presence in the tunnels beneath the north side had it cleaned out, right quick."

She shrugged, putting on airs of the bravado any street tough would try to show in the face of such a charge. Inwardly she wondered. What did d'Agarre have going on in the sewers north of the river?

"As I was saying, we will have muskets, balls, and powder stored for your people here, in these tunnels. When you get the signal, you come down here and retrieve them, first thing. And don't even think of looking for them early; we'll know if you do, and I think the lot of you have an understanding by now of just how deep our organization goes."

More murmurs, this time with a hint of defiance from around the room. A sign the impact of Zi's little display was wearing off. Perhaps her cue to start thinking about making an exit.

"Don't think about starting a brawl down here, either," Guyard warned, pointing a finger around the room. "Or settling old scores. You'll only be wasting better opportunities for riches aboveground. You see, I've secured something of a plum assignment for the gangs of the Maw. If you're quick, you boys will be among the first to sack the Gardens."

That got appreciative noises, even a whistle or two. She felt her stomach sink. In a salon, disguised by rhetoric and philosophy, revolution for the sake of *égalité* sounded lofty, even noble. Here in the sewers she could see it for what it was, or at least the bloody shadow behind the thing. This was the true beast d'Agarre would unleash on her city: the fury kindling behind the eyes of these brutes, and the men for whom they stood.

"Now," Guyard went on, "if you can wait here without killing each other, I'll fetch the big boss himself. I know he'll want to say a thing or two to the best and brightest of the Maw."

With that, the sub-boss turned back toward the dark tunnel from which he'd entered, leaving the ring of toughs behind, already licking their chops over the promised spoils. Time for her to go.

Tethering *Faith*, she faded from view, enjoying the exclamations of shock she drew once more from the men who had been eyeing her and plotting some simple form of revenge. She knew they'd talk. Guyard at least would mention the strange girl if the gang toughs didn't. If Reyne d'Agarre himself was coming to speak to this lot, he'd leave knowing she had been here.

Let him. Let him know she knew his secrets. She'd bring all this crashing down around him soon enough.

39

ARAK'JUR

Ruins of the Jintani Village
Jintani Land

Fire.

It had raged here, the sort of cleansing blaze that transformed the thickest forest into charred, twisted ruin. A gift his people had used since before they received the spirits' magic, purifying flame to clear the forest so it could be born again. In the wake of fire's terrible path, a man could not help but feel submission, awe, reverence for the power of the wild.

But one did not expect to see it strike a village.

The Jintani tents had been reduced to tattered scraps where they stood at all, blackened pillars slumping toward the ground, broken and charred, trailing smoke that promised heat still waiting in the embers. He bore the sight as stoically as could be managed, leading both their horses on rope lines as they walked around the edge of the ruin.

Corenna rose from where she'd doubled over beside him, wiping bile from her mouth. He offered a steadying hand, which she accepted without shame.

"How?" she managed, her voice as weak as her skin was pale.

"I don't know," he said. "Perhaps some ill fate befell the Jintani shaman. Perhaps they had no forewarning."

Corenna tried a calming breath that caught in her throat. She turned again, retching. Taking a step forward, he saw the likely cause: blackened bones lying across the ground where one of the tents had stood, just ahead. Child-sized bones. He closed his eyes, drawing a deep breath. Where sickness took Corenna, he felt instead a shuddering rage.

This did not happen to their people. The shamans had a sacred trust, to see the coming of threats in time for the guardians to protect them. Great beasts, yes, but also the disasters of the wild. Famines, droughts, quakes, fires. When a tribe faced the coming of such, they were granted visions in time to find safety. And yet here that trust had failed. An entire village caught without warning, reduced to ash. Unthinkable. A sign of the worst disfavor, the direst curse, as though the Jintani had somehow provoked the spirits and lost the guidance of their shaman.

And whatever the Jintani had done, the thought rose in his mind: Could it be worse than his and Ka'Vos's plan, to ignore the whispers of the spirits? Standing now before their awesome power, he felt a fool. His people courted the same fate, while Arak'Jur, their guardian, was far to the north seeking allies to support their blasphemy.

He howled, letting loose the torrent of anger that boiled in his belly. Let Corenna grieve with tears and sickness, the way of a woman. He would grieve with the roar of a man.

When the first shock of it passed they resolved to enter the ruined village, stopping to tie their horses to a tree and stow their supplies. The dirt was still warm, mixed with ash and soot, but enough time had passed to safely traverse the grounds and see what they could find. Like as not some of the Jintani had fled into the woods to escape the onrush of the flames. If there was hope to be found it lay there. Yet from the first tents they passed, it was clear few of their number had been given warning before the fire struck. Charred bones lay curled within the scorch marks that outlined where each tent had stood.

"Nighttime," Corenna said, her voice touched with hollow grief. "The fire must have come while they slept."

He could see it was true. For so many to have been within their tents it would have had to be so.

"Could it have spread so quickly?" he asked. "It seems as though the men and women in these tents had no forewarning, even as the flames struck behind us."

"Perhaps up ahead, it will be different."

They pressed on, bearing hope like a mantle of heavy stone. But it was the same in tent after tent, even the communal steam tents, and the ritual grounds. Bones. The village had been a shelter for the Jintani people, a ward against the wilds, a place of happiness and life. And now their village had become their dying ground. It was the highest sign of honor, to leave the fallen where they died. A cruel twist of irony that the spirits had afforded such an honor to the Jintani, leaving them to rest in the open. Anger flared once more, almost enough to spur a desire to bury these bones within the earth, if only to spite the spirits' gift. There was no honor here, only death.

When they reached the edge of the wood, he turned back to survey the village from the other side, still feeling a surging anger, tempered by an ever-growing knot of worry. He had ventured too far from his people. If he returned to find the same fate visited on the Sinari—

"Arak'Jur," Corenna called to him, her voice unsteady.

"What is it? Have you found a trail?"

"No," she said. "Only, why have we seen no sign of the fire around the village?"

He blinked, turning to see where she stood. It was true. There was no trace of the devastation in the trees and brush surrounding the village. "We've walked a path from east to west," he began, speaking slowly. "The village is broad, surrounded by brush and trees on all sides. The fire must have come from the north, or the south."

She nodded, though she wore a look of dread. "Can we walk around the village? I would know where this began."

He gave her a long look, seeing the uncertainty behind her eyes. They had traveled together long enough for him to sense when she had more to say. "What is it, Corenna?"

"Arak'Jur, I . . ." She swallowed and began again. "I fear this fire was no natural blaze. I fear this was the women's gift."

Even standing among the heat of the ashes and smoke, the thought struck him like the breath of a winter storm.

He did not let himself believe until they crested the last hill, circled the last bend of wilderness surrounding the remains of the village. Everywhere they walked it was the same: brush, grass, trees all untouched by the inferno that had raged mere paces away. Wherever there had been village, now was smoking ash. The wilds remained untouched.

"Who?" he asked. "Which tribe's women could do this?" The voice within decrying the question as forbidden was muted to a distant echo.

"I do not know for certain," Corenna said. "There are whispers of peoples far to the west, living among mountains of fire. Perhaps some among their number, or a woman who has made that journey."

"You are certain it is the women's gift?"

She shook her head. "No. I am no *Ka*, to see and speak with surety. But to control a flame, to direct it like this—I have seen no other power that would serve to explain it."

A silence settled between them as they each regarded the ruin, alone with their thoughts.

"Could it be the new magic?" Corenna asked at once. "The fair-skins' gift?"

A comforting thought, to lay such barbarity at the feet of the fair-skins instead of their own people. Still, he found it unlikely they would strike at the Jintani, so far to the north. He shook his head. "No. I have seen no sign they wield such power. And I believe if they were to attack us, it would come to the Sinari first, or one of the other tribes living along their barrier."

Corenna nodded, accepting his reasoning.

"Did you find any sign of tracks leading away from the village?" she asked. "Of survivors?"

"None."

The wind changed direction, turning the smoke toward where they stood. They ducked low to avoid it, though they could not escape the smell. Charred wood, burnt hide, and the sickly sweet aroma of meat on a cookfire. Enough to unsettle even him, and it sent Corenna doubled over once more, retching into the dirt, her stomach long since empty. He went to her, taking her by the arm when she finished.

"Time for us to go," he said.

She offered no protest.

They retrieved their mounts, walking and riding in silence for the better part of the day, once again making their way north, toward the base of the great mountains that marked the edge of Nanerat land. Their worry went unspoken, though he knew it dominated Corenna's thoughts as well as his own. War. What else could bring the ruin of the Jintani? And what would they find among the Nanerat, a people Corenna had described as peaceful, meditative in nature? He tried to shut out the images his mind tried to paint for him, re-creations of the grisly scene they had left behind.

What little he had known of war and its horrors came from stories, cautionary tales passed down by the elders to temper the ardor of young men. There had been no war in living memory, and even then, what little violence was spoken of in the stories was confined to the men of the tribes. Hunters took up the war-names, and with them the long-hafted spears of battle, and the muskets of the fair-skins since their coming. It was vulgar for a guardian to use his gifts to fight men, though the worst stories told of such: raging man-beasts channeling the gifts of the spirits into a twisted mockery of their intended use.

Not even the most vulgar, violent stories spoke of women following the men into battle.

He found it hard to countenance the thought, yet he could not dismiss it. Bearing gifts like Corenna's, before the threat of a rival tribe bent on their extinction, how could the women refuse to fight? The question gnawed at what little reservation remained to him, after a journey spent shattering taboos at Corenna's side. Finally, he asked it, turning back to her mid-stride as they pressed through the foothills.

"Corenna, do the women tell stories of war?"

She winced, revealing a lingering sense of the forbidden, even for her. "I trust you don't mean the leaders' tales, of young men's tempers."

"No," he said, waiting.

She looked him in the eye, her gaze steady. "There are wars fought for aggression, for tempers flared hot, for wounds that can be quenched only by blood. In these, women do not involve themselves."

Still he waited.

"And there are other kinds," Corenna continued. "Wars that burn cold, conflicts that can be settled only by the extinction of a people, one side or the other. The women pass down these rituals. When such a war is pronounced, the spirit-touched among the women take up arms, under the guidance of the most favored among them."

He looked at her, straining to keep the horror he felt from showing in his eyes. Women fighting alongside the hunters, the warriors... unthinkable.

She looked down as they walked. "Have you never wondered why women possess the gifts we do? Guardians protect us from the great beasts; shamans see their coming, and ensure we prosper from the land. Women protect us from our enemies, and from each other."

Stunned silence fell between them.

"It will be my calling," she said before he could form a reply, in a voice barely above a whisper. "I can feel it in my bones. I've felt it since I was a girl."

"You believe our course leads to war," he said.

"Yes. If not today, then soon. It will be my charge, before I die, to lead the women of the Ranasi against our enemies."

They walked for a few paces in silence before he spoke again.

"If it is so, then much depends on this journey. We must secure allies. If war comes, we will face it together."

Once more she looked up at him, this time with tears welling in her eyes. "Thank you, Arak'Jur."

He stopped, reaching for her to draw her close into a comforting embrace. The horrors they had witnessed washed over them both as she stood in his arms, holding her as she clung to his chest.

When they reached the first slopes, they turned their horses loose, the uneven ground proving too difficult for the beasts to traverse. Corenna withdrew what supplies they needed from the animals' packs, not least of which was a coat of thick furs she had brought along, knowing they journeyed into the northlands on the cusp of the seasons of biting cold. He made do with the blessing of the guardians for warmth, bare-chested even as the air grew thin. Hardiness was part of the spirits' gift, and it served him well here.

On the fourth day since they left the ruin of the Jintani village behind, they reached the pass.

Neither had known of a route through the mountains, and both had been prepared to scale the heights to reach the Nanerat lands beyond, if it came to that. As it was, the sloping valley winding its way between two of the larger peaks was a clear sign from the spirits, well tracked by herds of bison and elk grazing their way west before the cold set in. They slew one such, an elk that had fallen behind its brothers and sisters, and made a feast of it to celebrate. Over the fire they exchanged plans for how to deal with the Nanerat, and speculation over the state of affairs here in the North. Neither the Ranasi nor the Sinari had dealt with the Jintani, the Nanerat, or their other northerly neighbors in some time, not since Corenna's journey into Yanarat lands.

"It could not be the Yanarat," Corenna said. "Their gift is frost, fitting for their frozen shores and wary temperament. I could believe they had gone to war—they are an unfriendly, suspicious people—but the Jintani village was no doing of theirs."

"Perhaps one of the tribes to the west?" he asked.

"It would have to be, though I know little of them. The Eranat along the northern coast, and the Hurusi inland. Farther west, I have heard only tales of great rolling plains, lakes as deep as the sea. I do not know their people."

He rubbed his chin. "I have met the guardian of the Hurusi, Arak'Dal. He had an easy nature, and a great many gifts of the spirits, as such things are reckoned."

"Could you believe his people capable of…?" She let the question taper off, though he took her meaning.

"I could hardly believe any of the tribes capable of committing such an act." He sighed. "Though I did not know Arak'Dal well enough to say it was not possible."

The fire crackled to fill the silence between them, each contemplating the course ahead, and the horrors behind.

His instincts gave only a moment's warning.

Enough time for *lakiri'in* to grant his blessing, a blinding rush of speed hurling him away, rolling into the dirt. A heartbeat later, a great gout of flame seared the ground where he had been, accompanied by a deafening roar as the air itself caught fire. He sprang to his feet, whirling toward the shadows from whence the fire had been thrown, still surging with *lakiri'in*'s blessing. Corenna shot to her feet, her eyes misted over a pale blue.

"Show yourself!" Corenna cried out, even as his sharpened senses made out a trio of figures standing in the darkness twenty paces ahead.

The one in the center raised an arm, and the figures at her side lowered muskets they had leveled in a firing position.

"Stay where you are," the one at the center commanded. A woman's voice.

"Who are you?" Arak'Jur shouted back, staying low, ready to spring away at the first sign of her flame. "How dare you attack us, when we have done you no wrong!"

"I am Asseena, daughter of the Nanerat," the figure in the center said. "Our shaman warned us we would find a guardian here, but said nothing of a woman in your company."

The wind shifted, and his senses revealed a dozen more warriors, approaching from all sides.

"I am Corenna, daughter of the Ranasi," Corenna said. "I am known to Ka'Ruwan, who gave me his blessing, some seasons past. We come as envoys of peace."

The first three shapes leaned toward each other, conferring.

"Speak," the woman, Asseena, said. "Convince us you mean no harm to our people, or we leave your bodies here, as an offering to the spirits."

Mareh'et beckoned at the edge of his vision, but Corenna stepped forward before he could call on its gift.

"We will speak," Corenna said. "If you will listen. We have traveled far, and we are only two, though we carry the spirits' blessings, and the strength of our tribes."

The implied threat hung in the air in spite of Corenna's offer of peace. Asseena stood her ground, and her men held their guns in place.

"We will listen, honored sister," Asseena said. "But we make no promises for what follows, should we mislike what you have come to say."

40

ERRIS

Private Receiving Room
The Royal Palace, Rasailles

For a series of chambers that saw use at best once in a decade, the crown apartments were opulent beyond anything she might have imagined. Wasteful in the extreme, for Duc Cherrain to keep a staff on retainer to clean and service an entire wing of the palace that had no inhabitants save when the royals made the trek across the sea. Clearly the men and women who served here took pride in their work—not a mite of dust or a frayed seam anywhere in sight. How like those in charge to misuse talent. At least the fruits of the servants' efforts saw use now with Louis-Sallet in residence. It had taken longer than it should have by far for Marquis-General Voren to secure them this audience with the prince, but at last the summons had come. And now she, Lance-Lieutenant Acherre, and Voren himself sat in these luxuriously appointed chambers, waiting on the pleasure of His Royal Majesty.

She was not one to be overawed by titles, but in this place even the most jaded skeptic could not help but feel a touch of humility. That was the intended effect, of course. Portraits of the scions of the de l'Arraignon line hung on every wall of the royal wing, extending back for seven generations of kings and queens. In this particular chamber—the private receiving room fit for small audiences, away from the main throne room—they were watched over by a portrait of Louis-Toulard. Politics had never been her strong suit, but she knew her military history as well as any academy instructor. It had been Louis-Toulard who led Sarresant in its first great war against Thellan in the modern age, to secure the Ventane Reach, repelling the final claim the Thellan lords had on the ancestral lands of the people of Sarresant. They said he had been a *Body* binder himself, unafraid to lead the armies on the front lines as they clashed with their enemy. Would that they had such a man on the throne to lead them now. From all she'd heard of Louis-Sallet and his father, Gaurond, her expectations had been set low indeed. Even so, surely they would convince him here and now to give up the folly of ordering the colonies' armies to return with him across the sea. In light of her last vision, there could be no other decision.

"His Royal Highness, the Crown-Prince Louis-Sallet de l'Arraignon."

The crier's words brought their party to attention, snapping into salutes, fist to chest. Civilians might be expected to bend the knee, genuflecting before the divine right of the royal line. Soldiers were accorded more respect, even junior officers like Acherre. And so they stood rigid for some time; evidently the crier had been somewhat overzealous in announcing the arrival of His Highness. That, or Louis-Sallet had taken his time traversing the length of the mirror gallery leading to the receiving room.

It appeared to be the latter, as the prince entered at last, staggering a few steps at a time until he collapsed with a grin into the luxuriously appointed chair at the head of the room. He was piss-drunk; she could smell the stink halfway across the chamber. By the Gods themselves. She had chosen Acherre for this meeting precisely because she wouldn't trust Marquand within five leagues of the royal palace. And now this. At least Marquand wouldn't have noticed the smell.

The prince's guards flanked Louis-Sallet as if nothing were amiss, two men in purple tabards bearing the royal insignia. The Aegis of the King, the elite handpicked bodyguards of the de l'Arraignon line. Fullbinders all, and a narrow thing she had escaped being chosen for such service herself. Only her prowess at the academy and in the field had spared her, she was sure. Even so, if it were known that she had command of six bindings now—seven, if she included *Need*—nothing would stop the crown from settling a purple tabard around her neck like a collar and chain. Imagining herself shackled to their drunken sot of a prince made her feel a pang of pity on behalf of his present handlers. Perhaps the crown's greatest waste, keeping so many fullbinders out of the army. Flowerguards, they were called by most, never mind their proper name.

"Voren!" the Crown-Prince bellowed, slurring his words together in a slow cascade. "How wonderful to see you again. I expect my brother's hide is still stinging from the tongue-lashing you gave him."

"Your Majesty," Voren acknowledged, still standing at attention.

"Oh come to," the prince said. "At ease and all that. Be seated. What have you brought me? The stewards say you insisted it be kept secret."

A wise choice, one she had counseled when she had presented her vision to the marquis-general. Only a handful of soldiers knew the truth of the impending Gand invasion; a precaution, until they knew for certain the prince's foolish order to withdraw would not be given. She suspected the sharpest of her brigade commanders had already guessed at her purpose from the training exercises she'd been running along the coast, but she would not confirm it without the assurance of this meeting.

"Yes, Majesty," Voren replied as he sat, while she and Acherre remained at attention. "First, a demonstration of a new weapon."

That got the prince's attention, never mind the drink. He leaned forward. "A binding?"

"Yes, Your Majesty. Chevalier-General d'Arrent, if you would, please?"

"Sir," she replied with a fresh salute, turning to the Crown-Prince. "Your Majesty. The binding is *Need*, a new type of leyline energy." That got even the flowerguards to perk up from their lazy poise behind the prince's seat. A new binding was exceedingly rare; for centuries there had been only *Body*, *Life*, and *Shelter*, until the great powers' expansion revealed new powers, in turn driving them to more and greater conquests. Even so, discoveries came once in a generation at best. *Need* would be the third in three decades, a coup for Sarresant, never mind that Gand seemed to have had it first.

She continued. "The energy allows a *Need* binder to establish a link with a willing vessel, whereby the binder assumes control over their actions, seeing through their eyes similar to a projected *Mind* binding, but with full control."

"And you are a binder of this new energy, Chevalier-General?"

"Yes, Your Majesty. Lance-Lieutenant Acherre"—she inclined her head toward the other woman—"can see the energy but cannot bind it—we don't yet understand why."

The prince cast a glance over his shoulder at the flowerguardsmen behind him, before turning back to her. "Continue with your demonstration."

She nodded. "Lance-Lieutenant, if you would please excuse yourself."

That earned a reproachful eyebrow from the prince.

"Part of the demonstration, Your Majesty," she said. "Your pardon, please, if you would excuse the lance-lieutenant."

He lifted a finger in approval, and Acherre saluted once more before seeing herself out of the reception chamber.

"Now, Your Majesty, if you would provide me a phrase, one the lance-lieutenant has not heard."

Louis-Sallet chuckled. "A parlor game, Chevalier-General? Very well. Your phrase is 'you wouldn't know sense if it bit you in the ass.' I believe that was your parting line to my brother, was it not, Voren?"

She nodded, ignoring the repartee between the prince and her commander. She had what she needed. Shifting her vision, she saw the *Need* energy pooling beneath Lance-Lieutenant Acherre on the other side of the door. As ever, finding Acherre's *Need* was a trivial thing, like donning a well-worn glove. Perhaps that was the benefit of Acherre being able to see the *Need* energy, even if the lieutenant had thus far failed to bind it; compared to Marquand, or any of her other vessels, Acherre seemed to *fit*.

She tethered the binding and made the link. Her senses slid behind Acherre's, with none of the lurching disorientation she felt with the others. One moment she was standing in the receiving room; the next she was on the far side of the door in the long hallway beyond.

Pushing her way back into the receiving room, she was met with startled looks from the prince and his flowerguard.

"The golden eyes are the sign of the connection," she said with Acherre's voice. "And the phrase is, 'you wouldn't know sense if it bit you in the ass.'" Ah, but it felt good to say that to a prince, never mind the circumstances.

She let the binding go.

"Well," the prince said, his senses seeming to sharpen by the moment. "Now that was something."

"You see, Your Majesty," Voren said, "there is truth to the rumors of the golden light behind the enemies' eyes. And this is what it betokens: command from afar, by a binder of *Need*."

"I know damned well what it betokens, Voren!" the prince spat. He leaned forward as if to continue the tirade and found himself sliding out of the chair. If not for the timely intervention of one of his flowerguard, the prince might have graced the floor with his royal face. She knew to hide her disgust, but it was no easy thing. This man held the fate of the colonies, of the army in his hands?

"Of course, Your Majesty," Voren said, continuing as if the prince had kept his composure and his seat. "And you can doubtless see the advantages this binding offers for command."

"Are there others?" one of the flowerguard piped up, the one not presently occupied with helping the prince recover his seat. A young man, likely only recently graduated from one of the academies of the Old World. "Can it be taught?"

She met his eyes, seeing in him a hunger for new power. She remembered well the feeling from her youth. This flowerguard had likely only just emerged from adolescence, thinking the door forever closed on developing new abilities. To hear a binder a dozen years his senior had come into a new binding—to say nothing of the other new energies she kept hidden for now—would kindle similar hopes and aspirations in every binder with a shred of ambition anywhere in Sarresant.

"As I've said, Lance-Lieutenant Acherre can see *Need*, but so far I am the only one who can bind it, apart from however many the enemy has."

"How long have you had it?" the prince asked in a soft voice.

She tensed at the question. There was an accusatory tone there, no mistaking.

"Chevalier-General d'Arrent came into this ability at the conclusion of the summer campaign, Majesty," Voren said. "We worked together to understand it. Duc-General Cherrain awarded her the Legion of Valor for its use in defending the city."

"'The city' refers to Sarresant itself, Voren, not this up-jumped newborn of a settlement. Never forget this is *New* Sarresant."

"Of course, Your Majesty." Once again Voren dissembled expertly, a sign of long practice dealing with the nobility. Not a skill she ever hoped to cultivate.

"And the Legion of Valor," Louis-Sallet mused, his words running together. "There's an honor that once meant something. Not a thing meant for commonfolk."

Voren turned and gave her a look, wilting the retort on the tip of her tongue. She drew a breath instead, urging herself to calm.

"Majesty, there is more," Voren continued. "Chevalier-General d'Arrent has established a *Need* connection with one of our spies, working from within Gand itself."

"How exactly is a 'connection' established?" the prince interrupted. "What's to prevent this binding from taking control of someone important at a critical moment, someone like me?"

"It doesn't work that way," she asserted. "The *Need* link has to be voluntary, at least for the first binding, which is also the most difficult to establish. It depends on a shared need, or a hope, between the binder and the vessel. An enemy *Need* binder couldn't link with you unless you were already a traitor."

Louis-Sallet's face grew dark.

"... Your Majesty," she added belatedly.

"Forgiveness, Your Majesty," Voren interjected. "As we've said, we are still learning the limits of this ability. Its functioning can be explained later." He gave her a pointed look. "What matters now is the news Chevalier-General d'Arrent brings from the spy across the sea."

"They mean to invade the colonies, Your Majesty," she said. "Fifty, perhaps sixty thousand men, at least ten dozen ships, likely more. I saw them firsthand."

Silence descended between them. The prince mouthed her words once more to himself, chewing on the thought like a dog worrying at a bone.

"How do you know they intend to sail across the sea?" the prince demanded. "Perhaps they merely intend a strike along our shores. Or perhaps they mean to invade Skovan lands, or surprise Thellan across the western channels."

"I saw only their provisions, Majesty—the ships were being loaded for a long journey. And beyond that, I have come to understand the enemy commander. He has displayed a pattern of bold, unpredictable moves. I believe he intends to strike here." She left unspoken her belief that the mysterious enemy commander intended to attack the colonies precisely because she was here. He had promised as much, back in their exchange in the Gand camp, when she had seen through the eyes of Marie d'Oreste.

"Why would they . . . ?" The prince snorted. "No, never mind that." He waved a hand in a dismissive gesture. "Voren, you bring me a great new weapon; for that I give thanks. But this news, this changes nothing."

He rose to his feet, stumbling into the arms of one of his flowerguard.

The rest of the room rose to stand as well, snapping to attention and watching as Louis-Sallet batted away the aid offered him, struggling to stand on his own.

"We will speak on this new binding again," the prince said, turning to make his way out of the room. The youth among the prince's bodyguards met her eyes on his way out, but Louis-Sallet managed to make his exit without another word.

The mood in the room was sullen, and quiet, as a royal steward led the three of them back to Voren's carriage. Hardly a fitting conveyance for a pair of cavalry officers, but Voren had insisted, back in the Harbor. Now she doubly regretted her acquiescence, wanting nothing more than to saddle herself onto Jiri's back and fly. She had dealt with her share of incompetent fools in her career, but never a man so doggedly stupid as the Crown-Prince Louis-Sallet de l'Arraignon.

Acherre seemed stunned as they were seated in the carriage and Voren gave word to the driver to see them off. The poor lance-lieutenant had been brought up, nigh indoctrinated on tales of the divine right of the House de l'Arraignon since she was a girl, the same as every binder when they were taken for their training and service to the crown. And now she'd seen the face behind the mask. An ugly sight.

"We do the best we can," she said to Acherre.

"Yes, sir," Acherre said, sounding hollow.

"We do at that," Voren said. "Though that went poorly. I had hoped even the chance of an invasion might temper him." He removed his spectacles, rubbing the bridge of his nose.

"Marquis-General, sir," she said, "I am certain the enemy means to invade. I feared to say as much to the prince, but I spoke with the enemy commander, through our vessels. He intends to find me, and see me dead."

Voren regarded her for a moment, the jostling carriage casting a shifting light across the lines of his face.

"I do not believe it will matter," he said at last. "Louis-Sallet has made up his mind. He intends to give his order."

"Sir?" Acherre asked. "He cannot mean for us to abandon the colonies, can he? The people will be left defenseless."

Voren laughed, a mirthless, empty sound. "Oh he can, Lance-Lieutenant. And he means to. The only question that remains is whether we will let him."

A storm cloud settled over the carriage with those words. Treason. Voren knew it, as did she.

Settling his spectacles back into place, Voren looked her in the eye.

"There is an organization," he began. "One that—"

Thundering hooves approaching the carriage cut him off. One of the riders barked an order to the driver, and their team slowed.

"What in the Exarch's name is this?" Voren demanded, pulling back the window drapes.

Two riders in purple drew close, peering inside the carriage. The flowerguards, the Aegis of the King. Once again the young man with the hungry look met her eyes.

"Chevalier-General Erris d'Arrent," the young flowerguard began with a nod. "Lance-Lieutenant Rosline Acherre. Both of you are under arrest, by the order of Prince Louis-Sallet de l'Arraignon."

41

ARAK'JUR

Meeting Grounds
Nanerat Village

The smell of cooked fish seasoned with unfamiliar spices greeted him as he sat beside the cookfires. A welcome respite from a long journey, though his and Corenna's passage through the mountains had ended in a fashion neither had foreseen. The trek to the village had been cold, with promises they would speak on affairs between the northern tribes when they arrived.

Arak'Jur had taken his first bites of the evening meal before he understood the reason for the Nanerat's aggression. Empty places near every fire, and far too few men for the number of tents.

He paused between bites, turning to regard Asseena, seated to his right.

"Asseena," he began.

"Yes, Arak'Jur," she replied before he could begin his thought. "War has come to the Nanerat. The greater number of our men are dead."

He set the remains of his fish on the mat in front of him. "Your shaman?" he asked quietly.

"Ka'Ruwan was murdered by Arak'Atan of the Jintani. Ilek'Hannat survives him." She nodded to a man in white hides, seated beside her. "He speaks with the spirits of things-to-come on behalf of our tribe."

"And your guardian?"

"Arak'Erai fell to Arak'Atan as well." She paused, meeting his eyes with a look of understanding mixed with sorrow. "You see why we feared a vision of a guardian drawing near our village."

The rest of the tribe continued eating in a muted din as her words repeated in his mind. This was no celebratory feast. This was a people clinging to an echo of life as they waited to die.

"Oh, Asseena," Corenna said. "Honored sister, I am sorry. The Ranasi mourn your losses."

"As do the Sinari," he added automatically, even as he contemplated the bleakness of what had been revealed. They were a cursed people, of a certainty.

"And what is that worth?" the apprentice shaman demanded from the place beside Asseena. "The mourning of tribes two moons or more away?"

"Peace, Ilek'Hannat," Asseena said.

Still the sentiment hung in the air. Arak'Jur knew well enough his people could do little to help the Nanerat.

"Did Arak'Erai have an apprentice?" Arak'Jur asked.

"No," Ilek'Hannat replied. "We have lost the guardians' magic."

Arak'Jur suppressed a wince, only just managing to keep his features smooth. Unthinkable.

"What of the neighboring tribes?" Corenna asked. "I have traveled among the Yanarat; have you reached out to them for aid?"

Asseena and Ilek'Hannat shared a look.

"They were the first to attack us, honored sister," Asseena said. "Two seasons past. Arak'Uro led a war party onto our lands, armed with the guardians' magic and the fair-skins' muskets. I suppose he died as Vas'Khan'Uro." Her voice resonated with sadness, though she kept her back straight, her eyes level.

Corenna met her gaze. "Will you tell us what has transpired here, from the beginning?"

"There is little more to tell," Asseena said. "The Yanarat struck, and then the Hurusi. The Jintani approached us with offers of alliance against the madness of our neighbors, then murdered us the very night we sealed the blood-oath."

"The spirits have forsaken us," Ilek'Hannat spat. "They have decided they have no need for their most peaceful children."

"Then you have heard the madness of the shamans' spirits," Arak'Jur said. "You have heard their calls for war."

A dawning recognition passed between Ilek'Hannat and Asseena, and they turned to him as one.

"This is why we've come," Corenna said. "Our peoples have heard it, too, and sealed our own blood-oath of alliance against that madness. We will not go to war."

"We have heard this before, from the Jintani," Ilek'Hannat said. "What is to prevent you from killing us where we stand, for being fool enough to listen to your talk of peace?"

"What indeed?" Arak'Jur demanded, his blood suddenly hot. "You have no guardian. If I wished this tribe dead, it would be so. I will not be spoken to as if I am a spirit-cursed dog."

"You will not find us so defenseless, guardian of the Sinari," Ilek'Hannat said in a rush, met by Asseena's upraised hand.

"Peace," Asseena urged. "He speaks wisdom, Ilek'Hannat. We cannot mistrust every tribe for the folly of one misguided neighbor."

"You welcome the viper twice into your tent, woman," the apprentice shaman barked, rising to his feet. "Be it on your head, but do not risk the life of the tribe for your foolishness."

Corenna laid a hand on Arak'Jur's forearm, forestalling whatever reply he might have made. Instead, the three of them watched Ilek'Hannat storm away, a scene that drew eyes around the other fires as the rest of the tribe ate.

Asseena sighed.

"He hears their voices," she said. "The spirits' madness of which you speak. It is hard on him."

"Ilek'Hannat would have had you go to war?" Arak'Jur asked.

Asseena nodded. "He urged that course, 'to preempt attacks from our neighbors,' he said, long ago. How wise he seems now."

"Fear of madness is poor reason to take up the mantle of madness yourselves," Corenna said. "I name it wisdom, to have sought the path of peace, whatever the consequences."

"I recall Ka'Ruwan made the same argument," Asseena said with a bleak smile. "Yet wisdom is a poor companion, when the nights grow long, and the winds blow cold."

"Not all among the tribes have heeded the spirits' calls for war," Arak'Jur replied. "The Nanerat are not alone."

Asseena nodded. "You speak of peace, and we would hear your words," she said. "But first I would know: Will you help us hunt Arak'Atan?"

He recoiled from the question.

Asseena continued before he could reply. "He hunts us, Arak'Jur. When Nanerat women gather the last seeds and herbs before the cold spirits claim dominion over the seasons, they do so knowing Arak'Atan may strike at them from the shadows. When our hunters and fishers sleep in their tents, they do so in fear they may never wake. Ilek'Hannat is no full *Ka*, he sees only glimpses of what may come, but he says Arak'Atan is shrouded in a haze that clouds the vision of the spirits. He cannot reveal where Arak'Atan hides. He cannot give enough warning to keep us safe. Arak'Atan strikes, and we die."

"Arak'Atan is alone?" he asked.

"He is the last of the Jintani."

"Asseena," Corenna asked, "were you behind the burning of the Jintani village?"

Asseena eyed him, appearing to search for some sign of discomfort at speaking of the women's magic. When he gave none, she nodded and made her reply.

"Yes," she said. "After they betrayed our blood-oath. One of their women swore to me the Jintani would see my people dead to the last child. In the face of such madness, the path to peace is soaked in blood."

"It is said among the women that the magic of the Nanerat is peace," Corenna said carefully.

Once more Asseena looked to him. "Is this a thing of which you speak to men, in the South?"

"It is," Arak'Jur replied with firmness. "In these times, it is. If knowledge of our gifts will help us stand against the enemies of peace, it is a small blasphemy beside turning our backs on the madness of the spirits."

Asseena nodded slowly. "Perhaps there is wisdom in this. Yes, then. Our gift is peace. But peace without strength is only weakness. Our women wield the magic of fire, the blood of the mountains upon which we dwell, to keep our people safe."

"And you used it to burn their village," Corenna said, turning her eyes away, toward the greatfire.

The sight of the Jintani village had been a horror to them both. But seeing it again in his memory, with the backdrop of the Nanerat on the cusp of death themselves, he understood. To protect his people, to stop an enemy committed to the course of madness—he could use the gifts of the spirits to strike at his enemies, and could not condemn the Nanerat for doing the same.

"She did what had to be done," he said.

Asseena eyed him with surprise. "Yes," she said.

Corenna said nothing. He knew her well enough to see the current of doubt below the surface. So be it. Reasoned wisdom was a luxury of innocence. He understood the pain of loss.

In the moment, he made his decision.

"Honored sister," he said. "Yes. I will help you kill Arak'Atan."

"I mislike this course," Corenna said, pacing across their tent. It was large, a conical design fit to shelter a family from the harshest winds of the foothills. How it had come to be empty he had known without asking. They could have had their pick of such even without their status as honored guests of the Nanerat.

"Share your misgivings, Corenna."

"We traveled north to find peace," she said. "To seek allies against the madness of war. I cannot forget the Jintani village. To think Asseena capable of such slaughter—"

"They faced an enemy bent on their destruction," he said.

"She murdered children!"

"Was any less done to them? To hear it from the men, Arak'Atan was not alone in his brutality, only his effectiveness. The guardian's gift was never meant to be used this way. It is an abomination."

"I feel no differently about the women's gift being used to fire a village."

He sighed, rising from where he sat on the mats lining the floor of the tent. Fetching one of their freshly refilled waterskins, he took a long drink, offering the same to Corenna. Pure, cool water direct from the springs of the peaks. A welcome refreshment after weeks in the wild.

"It is unwise to judge from afar," he said finally. "Could you speak truly, that you would have done otherwise in her place? If it were Ka'Hinari and the Ranasi people being murdered by an implacable enemy, an enemy convinced your people's destruction was the will of the spirits?"

"I fear it," Corenna said, the righteous anger behind her eyes melting away. "I fear what we will find ourselves capable of, all of us, before the end."

"Will you travel with me, to hunt the Jintani guardian?"

She looked away.

"I need your aid, Corenna. Arak'Atan bore many gifts when I knew him as a youth, and he has surely gained in strength since. Even if the spirits bless me with their favor, the hunt is far from sure."

"This is a terrible thing you ask, Arak'Jur. It has ever been the place of the guardians to mete out justice. It is different, for a woman."

He said no more, letting silence fill the tent. She was not wrong; under ordinary circumstances, he would never have asked her aid. The elders of every tribe handled mundane matters of punishment, but the guardians alone bore the mantle of death. Some crimes demanded no less. Yet in this, even the oldest stories offered no wisdom. The spirits did not idly grant their gifts; for a guardian to transgress so deeply was a sign of sickness among the spirits themselves. Another such sign, in a time where evidence of corruption was all too common.

Corenna turned once more, and he saw fear in her eyes. Fear, and resolve.

"I will aid you. I have not come so far to abandon our course now, though this deed will weigh heavy on my shoulders."

"You have a strong back, Corenna of the Ranasi."

That elicited a soft laugh. "You had best hope for the spirits' sake I do."

He smiled at her, seeing once again the image of the young woman she was, contrasted with the power she wielded, so far beyond her small stature. *Rhealla,* he remembered, thinking how his onetime wife had moved with the same surety, the same confidence. Neither his dead wife nor Corenna standing before him had Llanara's brash intelligence, or her fiery wit. Theirs was a deeper wisdom, the poise of a path well traveled, and remembered.

"So, how is this done?" she asked. "Sinari men don *echtaka* paint before a hunt, do they not?"

His turn to laugh. "You would wear the guise of a hunter?"

She bowed her head. "I follow your guidance, Arak'Jur."

"First we seek the blessing of the shaman. Ilek'Hannat is only an apprentice, but if he can beseech the spirits for a glimpse of Arak'Atan, it will serve us well."

Corenna drew a breath, drawing herself up to her full height. "Lead on, then."

"You would begin the hunt tonight?"

"Do we have cause to wait?"

He had no proper reply to that. Lifting the flap of the tent, he followed behind as she ducked beneath it into the frigid air of the Nanerat village.

Ilek'Hannat was already burning incense when they arrived.

Odd, that the prescience of the shamans could still surprise him, after a lifetime of trusting to their visions. Even a half-trained apprentice spoke with the voice of things-to-come, enough to bring Arak'Jur to his knees in reverence for the spirits' guidance. Such was proper, in their presence. Corenna followed his lead, flanking him as though she were an apprentice guardian herself. It may well be they lived in a time for change, for the disruptive and new. Nigh unthinkable for a woman to attend such a ceremony, but Ilek'Hannat bore it without comment. A time for change, yes, but this ritual was the means behind their peoples' protection from the ravages of the wild, since the first tribes had gone in search for the richness of these lands. So it was, that the old and new bled together, like the wisps of colored smoke tracing through the air of the shaman's tent.

"He hides," the apprentice said, speaking in the ethereal tones of the spirits. "He shrouds himself unseen, the predator you seek."

A puff of blue smoke belched from the flame at the center of the tent. Corenna gasped as it shifted into the form of a man above them.

"Arak'Atan," Arak'Jur said.

"His form twists, and he evades us!" Ilek'Hannat's mouth curled into a snarl. "We cannot see him."

"He is called Arak'Atan," Arak'Jur repeated. "And we would have whatever knowledge you can offer."

The apprentice convulsed where he stood, falling to his knees. Droplets of blood ran from his nose, falling to paint the dirt before the fire.

"He is hidden," the apprentice whispered.

"Find him," he commanded. "And tell us what you see."

A thundercrack sounded from the fire, and a black cloud began to spill forth from the depth of the cinders.

"The *valak'ar*. He carries its gift! Flee from death!"

Arak'Jur rose to his feet, raising a fist to the fire. "I carry the gift of the wraith-snake as well. I do not fear its bite. Reveal what you have seen."

"The *astahg*."

Orange smoke coiled in a thick cloud, then vanished, only to reappear a handspan away.

"Speak of its gift!" he demanded.

"The great stag, mirrored in the shadows, a hunter where there should be prey."

He considered the smoke, turning the words over in his mind.

"And *mareh'et*." Ilek'Hannat spoke again. "*Juna'ren. Ipek'a*."

"These I know," he said. "Are there others?"

Ilek'Hannat turned to look him in the eye, carrying a far-off look he recognized from years spent receiving visions from Ka'Vos. But there was more. A shroud of mist, as if the apprentice's sight was soiled by some strange corruption. Still he held Ilek'Hannat's gaze, even as a blood-red cloud of smoke erupted from the center of the fire, surging upward in a violent torrent. The smoke poured out of the fire like blood seeping from a wound, and Ilek'Hannat began to laugh. A wild sound, echoing through the tent, sounding more akin to a scream than any expression of mirth. Blood flew as Ilek'Hannat's body shook, droplets dissolving into the smoke wherever the two collided.

"Enough!" Arak'Jur demanded. "Release him."

"Death!" the apprentice cried, still howling with laughter. "He has touched that which is forbidden. The time of change comes! An Ascendant of the Wild!"

Arak'Jur strode forward into the smoke and struck Ilek'Hannat across the face, hard enough to put him in the dirt.

The fire dissipated into embers, smoke vanishing in a rush. The tent fell silent, save for the slow crackling of the fire, and the heated, shallow breathing from Corenna behind him.

"Is he . . . ?" she began.

"The spirits can be cruel masters," he said, kneeling beside Ilek'Hannat's finally dormant form. "But he lives."

She rose to her feet. "Is it proper for us to tend to him?"

He shook his head, joining her on his feet. "The spirits will see to his recovery. What passes between the shamans and their spirits is not for us to know."

She nodded, her face pale. He had never before seen such a display. Was it merely an *Ilek* channeling spirits beyond his ability, or a sign of worse portents, the incipient madness he had feared since Ka'Vos's revelation, so many lifetimes ago? His heart raced, though he kept his outward composure. Once more he lifted the tent flap, following behind Corenna.

Asseena stood alone, waiting outside the shaman's tent to receive them.

"Ilek'Hannat told me he would prepare the ritual tonight," Asseena began, stifling tears.

"He lives, honored sister," he said.

Asseena let loose a rush of breath. "Thank the spirits," she said. "It sounded as if death itself walked inside that tent."

Corenna moved to her side, offering a steadying arm. "Your apprentice shaman has a powerful gift, sister."

"And Arak'Atan?" Asseena asked. "Was Ilek'Hannat able to reveal his location?"

Corenna gave her a look of sympathy, then shook her head. "No. Ilek'Hannat saw as much and more as we might have hoped, but he could not see where the Jintani guardian hides."

True enough, that the spirits channeled by Ilek'Hannat had failed to pierce the shroud around their quarry. But at times, failure to see was sight enough.

"I know where he is," Arak'Jur said.

That drew looks from both women.

"Since this madness began, no shaman has seen the coming of great beasts at our sacred places. Yet they have been there, each time. If Arak'Atan is hidden from the spirits of things-to-come, he hides where they are already blind."

Corenna's eyes went wide.

"Would he dare?" Asseena asked, her skin pale even by the light of the moon. "To enter another tribe's sacred place without their blessing—"

"Arak'Atan is there," he said. "Ilek'Hannat's gift is powerful. If it were otherwise, the apprentice shaman would have seen it."

"Then go," Asseena said. "I give you the blessing of the Nanerat. You may enter Nanek'Hai'Tyat."

42

SARINE

The Revellion Townhouse
Gardens District, New Sarresant

Is m'lady going to lie abed all morning?"

She squinted. It had been a rough night; she could have wished for any of a hundred sights more pleasant to awaken her than the maid's all-too-familiar look of disdain.

"Good morning, Agnes," she croaked, turning to stretch into the untouched portion of the bed. It wasn't the first night she'd spent at the townhouse, but it was the first without waking to Donatien beside her. Last night's exchange had been heated. A painful reminder, to wake alone.

She rose to sit against the pillows. "Is Lord Revellion at breakfast already?"

"His lordship is out. On an errand, m'lady." Agnes sniffed. "I'd have them linens if you please. Some of us have work to do."

Sarine rubbed her eyes, allowing Agnes to collect the bedsheets as she rose to her feet.

Unpleasant creature, Zi thought to her.

She bit back a bitter laugh, drawing another look from the maid as Agnes swept out of the room, bundle of would-be washings in hand.

"I've known worse," she said after Agnes had gone. She opened the window shutters to pour in sunlight and the quiet hum of activity in the

Gardens below. Zi appeared on the edge beside the opening, his scales a soft blue, mirroring the cloudless autumn sky.

You plan to hunt today?

She selected a pair of sturdy trousers and a tight-fitting coat from the armoire Donatien had made available for her use. "Over the objections of one Lord Donatien Revellion. Yes, I do."

Zi seemed content with that, resting his head on his coils and looking down on the streets below as she settled into the day's attire. She and Donatien had argued well into the early hours, like as not part of the reason Agnes had decided to wake her. Spiteful woman, but no point in dwelling on it. She rather liked the way Zi put it: She had a hunt ahead of her today.

"What do you suppose d'Agarre might have hidden down there, in the sewers?"

You were there.

"No, Zi, not those tunnels. The north-side ones. His men called it a 'beast.' They might describe one of your kind that way. If the Maw gangs have seen a *kaas* there, it means d'Agarre or one of his lieutenants has been there, hiding something. Or guarding it. Either way I mean to find out what it is."

He closed his eyes in reply, lolling his head to the side as if scratching an itch against the awning.

Well, she hadn't expected him to be of any help. She'd been speculating on d'Agarre's plans since the night at his salon. Today she'd get another piece to the puzzle. She'd already begun to understand the extent of his organization: their stockpiles of weapons in the sewers, their secret paths and pass-phrases, their coordinated efforts to mobilize the people of the city. It was what to do next that vexed her.

Finished dressing, she joined Zi along the window's edge.

She was afraid.

As an untutored girl, and later with the limited understanding and guidance of her uncle, she'd been naïve enough to think her gifts special, but within the bounds of normalcy. So much had changed in recent months. The truth was she'd learned to enjoy the comforts of the Gardens, of Revellion's affections no matter their recent discord, and to come forward, to report Reyne d'Agarre's activities to the Lords' Council, was to risk it all on the hope they would hear her out, and act.

Why did it have to be her? Surely the signs could be seen in the anger on the streets, passed from ear to ear among the commonfolk of every district. Surely the mighty lords of Sarresant did not need word carried from Sarine of the Maw to see the threat taking root at the heart of their city. Better for her to lie low, to escape notice. To let others see Reyne d'Agarre for what he was.

Even as she thought it, she knew it for an empty daydream. Yes, there were binders and fullbinders aplenty in the ranks of the city's priests, and the army. But she had seen firsthand the power exerted by the *kaas. Yellow,* Zi had named it. A mob, roused to murderous rage, then scattered by fear. She had never paused to fully consider her companion or the nature of his strange gift, but she began to see it now. The terror he'd inspired among the men in the sewers, and all the times throughout her memory she had survived the wrath of evil men, when by rights she should have died on the streets of the Maw long ago. Even the kindness of her uncle, his willingness to train her, keep her talents hidden from the crown. The more she reflected on it, the more it became clear. Zi could affect the emotions, even perhaps the thoughts of others. And whatever Zi could do, so could the *kaas* of Reyne d'Agarre. She'd seen him use it, scattering soldiers in the Harbor... and inducing the city watch to fire into the crowd, at the farmers' market in the Maw. The realization clicked in her mind like the hammer of a pistol. Another evil to lay at his feet; another atrocity no doubt prescribed by his corrupted book.

With that magic at his side, there was no greater power in all of New Sarresant. None save her. Gods damn her soul if she would abandon New Sarresant to the whims of the evil she'd seen behind d'Agarre's eyes, not when she had the power to stand in its way. The book, their *Codex*; that was the root of it. D'Agarre had been willing to murder a woman he counted a friend moments before, because the scene had been written in his book, or he'd interpreted it as such. What if the next premonition pointed to burning half the city, or guillotining every child who refused to perform some other unspeakable horror? Whatever her sympathy to d'Agarre's cause, he was mad for his devotion to that book, and every other *kaas*-mage along with him. Hadn't they proved it, targeting the Sacre-Lin, a place of peace and refuge for the poor, because the man called de Merrain interpreted a passage to mean he ought to burn the chapel as a means of getting her attention?

Damn Donatien Revellion and his dream of peaceful revolution, and damn Reyne d'Agarre and every one of his fellows for the evil they would unleash upon her city. How could she fail to act? D'Agarre could use his *kaas* to incite revolution, well and good; she could do the same to sway the lords.

Today the sewer, tomorrow the council? Zi asked. His scales had taken on a faint hue of gold, mixed with the blue they had been before.

She took a deep breath. "Yes. Yes, I think so."

Relief washed over her, the simple act of deciding. Zi nodded, returning his head to rest.

"Sarine."

She started, turning to find Lord Revellion standing in the doorway. He appeared shaken, his skin pale, eyes red.

"Donatien. I didn't hear you come in."

"About last night. I'm sorry. I spoke rashly."

She suppressed a surge of emotion. "We both did."

"Sarine, they've arrested her," he said abruptly.

"Who?"

"My commander, Chevalier-General d'Arrent."

"What?" She rose to her feet. "Why?"

"For reporting on the enemy's plans to the Crown-Prince. I had it from the corps commander himself, from Marquis-General Voren. The Gandsmen are planning to invade the colonies. A fleet sails across the sea even now to sack New Sarresant."

"*What*? An invasion? And they arrested her for reporting it, why? Why would…" Her voice trailed off. "Because the Crown-Prince really is going to order the army back to the Old World."

"Yes. By the Gods, yes." He entered the room, sitting on the edge of their bed, running both hands through his hair. "Voren confirmed it for us, for all of the division and brigade commanders, this morning."

Her heart sank. "The prince gave the order?"

"No. Voren asked whether we could command our men to refuse it."

A moment passed before the weight of his words sank in.

"Treason," she said.

"Revolution," Donatien said, lowering his hands as he looked up at her. "It's happening, Sarine. The Lords' Council convenes tomorrow, to receive the Crown-Prince. And when he gives the order—"

"Gods above, you mean to seize power."

"Not us. Not Voren."

"Who then? Voren's commander? The Duc-General?"

"Sarine. Voren has been approached by Reyne d'Agarre."

Her eyes widened.

"No," she said.

"You must see reason. I know how you feel about d'Agarre, but you cannot consign us to follow the Crown-Prince's order, not with a Gand invasion already crossing the sea. Whatever your misgivings, you must see this is the wisest course, the only course left to us."

His words washed over her in a distant hum.

"Sarine? Where are you going?"

"I mean to oppose him," she said. "With or without your help."

She strode past him before he could reply, then descended the stairs and pushed out the door of the Revellion townhouse, into the biting chill of the autumn air.

She gagged, making a pointed effort to ignore the pliable textures beneath her feet as she walked along the stone beside the main channels of waste. Such filth. No wonder the gangs had abandoned these tunnels. Like as not they'd simply grown disgusted, and invented the tale of some deadly beast living down here to salvage their pride. That or they all fell ill from exposure to the refuse.

In the east-side tunnels beneath the Riverways and the Harbor the smell had been rank, the aged pungency of stale piss. Here beneath the Maw the slop was fresh, delivered by bucket from the streets above. No river channels to vent away the leavings, not here. Digging out complex waterways must have been judged an expense too far, for the benefit of the Maw. If she'd ever wondered why the streets reeked during rainstorms, well. Now she knew.

Another squish beneath her boot threatened to have her retching into the stream. She shivered, trying to block it out of her mind.

Mm, Zi thought to her. *This place is strong.*

She coughed when her mouth opened to form a reply, feeling the acrid tang of the smell on her tongue even with her nostrils plugged. "Strong?" she managed, followed by another cough. "Yes, this place is certainly that."

Strong emotions.

She raised an eyebrow. True enough, if disgust qualified. "What do you mean, Zi?"

Long ago. Not now.

"How long?" She coughed once more.

No reply, only a dim sensation, like the last flickers of a candle before it burned out.

She shook her head, spitting to get the taste out of her mouth. No doubt murders and worse had happened down here. And if d'Agarre had something hidden, that could account for strong emotions as well. All she had to do was find it.

She took a left turn at a three-way junction on a whim, then another left down a side channel ahead. She'd procured a hooded lantern for the journey, though she tried to keep from shining light to illuminate the filth beneath her feet more than absolutely necessary. She knew from living on the streets above that the Maw did not have extensive sewer tunneling, only drain grates along the most populated avenues. Even so it seemed she walked for leagues, making left turns and rights, searching for some sign of d'Agarre's presence. Nothing. And no patterns, no familiar turns or corridors, though she must have retraced her steps at least once or twice.

Finally she came to a halt in frustration. "Do none of these tunnels connect to each other?"

Strong emotions.

"Not helpful, Zi."

She shone light back the way she'd come, toward a large room that had four connecting passages. She could have sworn it was only three connections when she'd come through moments before. Was the smell playing tricks on her other senses? She trudged back, sweeping her lantern to be sure she hadn't confused a shadow for a tunnel. Sure enough, there was a fourth way. Strange. But wasn't that why she was down here? After what felt like an hour or more trekking through filth, anything strange was a welcome sight. She took the new corridor instead.

Three more turns revealed nothing new, and nothing familiar. Gods take this place, and its rotting stench. Once more she cast light the way she'd come, with a vain hope of another mysterious passage. No such luck, only the same stone walkway covered in filth beside a channel nigh overflowing with more of the same.

Still, whatever was down here, she meant to find it. With a sigh, she turned back, resolved to continue on.

She'd almost started walking again when a shadow bent at the edge of her vision. Something had moved.

She whipped back around.

"Who's there?" she called out, shining her lantern back down the passage.

Zi flared in her mind before she even saw it.

MOVE.

A brilliant white glow snapped into place around her, only the barest sliver of a moment before the creature's jaws closed around her leg. She caught a glimpse before the thing released its hold, jolting back into the sludge of the channel. Scales. Not metallic, like Zi's. A reptile's scales, and a long snout filled with teeth that might have been enjoying her leg for a snack if Zi hadn't reacted on her behalf.

And *fast.* By the Gods, even with *Body*, Zi's gift, and the *mareh'et*'s blessing together she wasn't sure she could move like that.

Only one way to find out.

A nimbus of the Great Cat surrounded her, Zi pushed her heart to beat faster in her chest, and she laced the threads of *Body* into a binding with all of her strength. Time seemed to slow to a crawl, the droplets of moisture collecting on the ceiling falling toward the floor as if suspended in glass.

There, again in the channel.

This time she saw it swimming through the waste, so fast a cloud of steam rose around it, solid waste turning to vapor before it could touch the creature's scales. She dove to the stone floor as it lunged, ignoring the filth that caked her as she hit the ground and the rattling clank of her lantern rolling across stone. The beast sailed through where she had stood, seeming to hang in the air as its massive jaws snapped closed around what would have been her torso.

Gods, the thing was *fast.* Time was running out. She had enough *Body*, and Zi's gifts usually held for some time, but *mareh'et* would not grant his blessing forever, and she needed all three at once to begin to match this thing for speed. Rolling onto her back, she slid her eyes shut, searching for *Entropy.* Any moment now…

It came again, skittering its stumpy legs on the stone walkway beside the channel. The creature looked as if it would have been at home lazing by the side of a river somewhere, basking in sunlight. It had no cause to move like this; nothing about it suggested such unbridled speed. Even so, it came. And this time she was ready.

A hairbreadth before it connected with her leg, she tethered a thick binding of *Entropy* into the body of the beast, as thick as she could manage.

It exploded.

And the world dimmed.

YOU KILLED HER.

She recognized it at once, this formless void. The place where she had met the spirit of the Great Cat. Even without vision she knew, and she could sense the presence of another entity, one that spoke directly into her mind.

She was bloody fast.

YES. SHE WAS *LAKIRI'IN.* IT IS HER GIFT.

What was she doing in the sewers?

Silence stretched on for a moment, and she sensed… anger?

COMPELLED, it thought to her at last. FORCED HERE, BY THE POWER OF THE GODDESS.

The title sparked her memory. The cat spirit had spoken to her of a goddess as well. What did it mean? Some goddess of these spirits? Either way, the compulsion of some wild beast in these sewers pointed exactly toward her purpose here: Reyne d'Agarre's secret. Could the *kaas* control these beasts?

You were forced here, she thought. *For what purpose? Was it to serve Reyne d'Agarre?*

LAKIRI'IN SERVES NONE SAVE THE GODDESS. SHE WAS CALLED HERE TO PROTECT TANIR'RAS'TYAT.

Tanir'Ra…? The words sounded foreign in her mind. Somewhere deep within, another voice sounded. *The Birthplace of Storms.* Zi's voice?

ARE YOU CHOSEN?

I don't know, she responded truthfully. The spirit had asked this before as well. *What does it mean to be chosen?*

YOU ARE A WOMAN WHO WIELDS THE POWER OF THE GUARDIAN. THIS IS NOT KNOWN TO US. A CHANGE.

And that means I am chosen?

YOU ARE STRONG. BUT YOU WOULD KNOW, IF YOU WERE MEANT TO STAND FOR THE WILD.

Another silence. Should she claim it, without knowing? Whatever customs to which this spirit adhered, they were foreign to her.

No, she finally thought back. *If I would know already, then I am not chosen.*

VERY WELL. WOULD YOU HAVE THE BOON OF THE *LAKIRI'IN*?

Yes.

Light surged within her, and she felt her senses mold themselves into a scaled form, one that walked on four legs. Her stumpy limbs seemed barely able to support her weight, and it took a great effort to move. She had a long snout, lined with razor-sharp teeth, and a tail that curled around half again the length of her body, ribbed with spines and knobbled ridges. Water. She needed liquid. And the sun. Without them, her body was languorous and slow. Better to rest, to conserve energy. To wait. In time prey would approach. She was no hunter, to stalk and chase down her kills. Such was beneath her. She felt the pleasure of watching, waiting for the moment when it pleased her to strike. She felt her muscles surge with the life of fire stored from the sun, all outward sign of sloth dispelled in a glorious instant of unleashed fury. A single snap of her jaws and the mightiest beast fell dead before it saw her stir from the water. A fine meal. And then back to rest. She was *lakiri'in*, the swiftest of all predators, and her speed condemned any creature fool enough to draw too near to death.

REMEMBER HER.

The voice echoed through her head, and she slid back into her body.

She coughed and sputtered, gagging on the fumes of the sludge that caked the side of her face. By reflex, she raised a hand to wipe herself clean, only belatedly realizing her hands were every bit as filthy. That was all her stomach could handle, and she rolled onto her side, heaving yesterday's meals into the channel.

You're back, Zi thought to her.

"Yes," she managed, this time having sense enough to wipe away the flecks of bile with a clean sleeve of her jacket. "And with some idea of what d'Agarre concealed here. Tana'Rastir... or was it..."

Tanir'Ras'Tyat, Zi spoke into her mind, even as she simultaneously heard his voice speaking different words, in her own tongue: *The Birthplace of Storms.*

"So that *was* you, translating what the spirit said. Could you hear it, while it spoke to me?"

No response. Ah, but Zi could be frustrating. She rose to sit against the far wall of the corridor, recovering her breath and letting her stomach settle. How long had she been down here? By some miracle her lantern still burned, but beyond that there was no way to tell from the slop and the darkness, and come to think of it she hadn't seen a vent to the surface in half a dozen turns or more. Was it better to turn back now, or press on? Clearly whatever set the *lakiri'in* to guard this place did so to protect something of value. And even if she could find it once more, nothing prevented another one of these creatures coming back, diving at her again from the sludge. Zi had been quick with his shield this time, but there was no guarantee he could do it again.

She rose to her feet. Time enough to rest after she'd uncovered the secrets of this place.

She retrieved her lantern, lighting the path forward as she began to walk. Only this time the tunnel seemed to extend onward in the direction she'd been walking, her light revealing only more blackness stretching on up ahead. No offshoots, no intersections, no chambers. Her heart beat faster as she made her way down the passage. This was it. Whatever she'd come here for, surely it lay at the end of this tunnel.

She walked another fifty paces before her light shone on a wall of solid stone, right in the center of the path. A dead end.

And yet...

Something about the stone spoke to her. The wall should not be there. It was *wrong.* She knew without knowing how, a premonition as sure as the knowledge of who she was, the gifts she held, the very essence of her being.

Corruption, Zi whispered inside her mind.

She walked forward.

Take it in, Zi thought to her. *It belongs to you.*

At once she saw the pale blue strands, the same energy she had seen in the depths of d'Agarre's manse, around the Codex of the Comtesse de Rillefort. They hovered here around the stone that barred this path. She raised a hand, and the strands arced away from the wall, drawn to her as if they longed for release, longed to return home. With a sucking snap, the last of them danced along her arm, coming to rest deep within her, and the wall vanished like a shadow cast before a torch.

Blackness loomed beyond, a void that seemed to beckon, like a mother's embrace. Fear melted away, and Zi pulsed a sense of rightness in her mind.

She took a step forward, across the threshold, and once more her body melted away.

SARINE.

The voice spoke to her, at once similar to the spirits of cat and reptile, but different. Older. Deeper, anchored to the land in a way that suggested it had seen and weathered trials beyond counting.

BE WELCOME IN TANIR'RAS'TYAT, DAUGHTER OF SARRESANT. BE WELCOME IN THE BIRTHPLACE OF STORMS.

43

ERRIS

A Prison Cell
The Citadel, New Sarresant

The arrest played itself over and over in her mind.

Almost she wished she had tethered *Body*, drawn her saber, and rushed the flowerguards. An uneven fight, with the pair of them mounted and her on foot, but she liked her chances better than she liked being caged behind *Shelter* in the bowels of the Citadel. Those fresh-faced boys had never been blooded. Killing men, feeling the sickening crunch as your saber parted flesh to strike the bone beneath, it changed you. It took a warrior to see it, and neither of the flowerguards had the look. She could have killed them both. But what would follow if she had? Flight into the countryside? Defection? Unthinkable. None of those roads led to command, and if there was one thing she was born for it was leading men into battle. She couldn't give that up for the satisfaction of resisting arrest.

Besides, with *Need* she might as well have been free.

Her reserve was strong today; it seemed knowledge of the Gand invasion force had redoubled her capacity, though Marquand was as stubborn as ever. She'd weighed his objections, and her promise not to bind him again without his consent, and found both wanting in light of circumstance. He would do his duty. She tethered the binding, and found herself once more in the Tank & Twine.

"Thank the Gods, d'Arrent," Voren said. "I thought the foot-captain would never cease his whining."

Voren settled his spectacles into place and stood, walking around his desk toward the smaller table, strewn with maps, on the far side of his makeshift office.

"Sir," she said with Marquand's voice, "any word on arranging my release?"

"No. I'd hoped a sober Louis-Sallet might recant his foolishness in the light of day, but he seems committed to his idiocy, not least in the matter of your arrest."

The heat behind his words caught her by surprise. She'd done her share of bad-mouthing her superiors, of course, but this was the Crown-Prince.

"D'Arrent, our time is short, is it not?" Voren asked.

"Yes, sir, I can maintain this *Need* binding for a quarter hour perhaps, before exhausting my supply."

He tsked. "Not nearly enough. We have planning to do."

She glanced down at the maps, spread across Voren's table. "Sir, I can formulate tactics in the cell. Have Marquand stay with you, or somewhere supplied with accurate maps, so I can bind to him when my *Need* supplies regenerate, if I must review details. We're working up counter-strategies to the Gand invasion?"

Voren raised a hand, forestalling her review of current deployments. "In time, d'Arrent."

"Sir?"

"Chevalier-General, events are being set in motion. Under better circumstances, I'd have given you more time to acclimate yourself to this idea, but we are running out of time."

Her memory returned to the coach, when he had spoken of refusing to obey the Crown-Prince.

"Sir—" she began, but once again he cut her off.

"There is an organization in the city that plots revolution, violent revolution against the crown. I mean to support this organization, with as many of my soldiers as will follow my orders."

Voren allowed her time to consider his words, reclining to watch her reactions, writ on the face of Foot-Captain Marquand.

"*Violent* revolution, sir?" she managed at last.

"Part of what we need to plan. I mean to seize power with minimal casualties, but with Reyne d'Agarre's organization we can mollify the commonfolk and moneyed classes together. An arduous task without his foundation to build from. He imagines the Council-General can be invested with real power after the Lords' Council is dissolved, and I mean to oblige him, for now."

Her head spun, and for once she wished Marquand had been filled with his usual amount of drink. The games of kings and princes were so far beyond her imagining as to be folktales, stories from the priests of the Gods' travels. She was a soldier. She needed an objective, an army, a battlefield. Leave it to men with elaborate surnames and noble titles to worry over who would rule.

"What part do I play in this, sir?"

"I need your support, d'Arrent. You are my best commander, and if what you've seen of the Gand invasion is true, without your newfound *Need* bindings we are lost. Can you refuse the Crown-Prince's order to accompany him across the sea? To do so is to support this revolution. There is no other way. And, if you'll pardon my speaking frankly, your arrest and imprisonment should make this an easy decision. But it is yours to make."

The oaths of service she'd taken on graduating from the academy flashed through her memory. To uphold the realm. To defend Sarresant from all its enemies, without and within. To obey her officers, and the King. Her memory cast her further back, to the day she'd been taken. She'd been eleven, six full years past the mandated age of testing. Perhaps her father had sensed something different about his daughter, enough to keep her hidden as they ranged through the countryside. Blissful years, in her memory. Her father had raised her like a son, teaching her to ride, to hunt and fight and skin their kills for pelts. And then one day he had been slow to rouse from the inn, too deep in his cups the night before. A brown-robed man had laid a hand on her, scarring her with binder's marks and tearing her life away from her forever. She'd gone to the binders' camp years behind the other children, and pushed herself relentlessly to catch up, driving until she met and exceeded her teachers' standards of perfection. While the other children learned obedience, had the lesson of humility instilled into their bones, Erris d'Arrent learned only excellence. It had been enough for them, then.

And so now, when Louis-Sallet de l'Arraignon demanded obedience, demanded loyalty enough to allow her homeland to burn, the Crown-Prince would reap what her teachers had sown years before: only excellence, nothing more.

"Sir," she said, "you have my support."

"You are sure, Chevalier-General? This will be no easy path to tread. It means blood on all of our hands, before the end."

"Sir, my time is drawing short. If we have planning to do, we best get started."

Her commander nodded. "Thank you, d'Arrent." He leaned forward, shuffling through the maps until he produced the one he sought. "Our first priorities must be the palace and the harbor. If we can seize the Crown-Prince and the Duc-Governor it will go easier, convincing any would-be loyalists to stand down. And I worry the navy will flee the city if we do not secure the ships. Either way, we'll need a pretext to begin deploying men inside the city."

"Training exercises," she said. "I've been conducting them with my men since we arrived. How much time do we have?"

"The Prince intends to give his order before the council tomorrow evening."

"Tomorrow…? Gods damn us all," she cursed, the words flowing from Marquand's mouth with familiar ease. "Your pardon, sir."

Voren waved away her apology. "I believe the men will follow us in this, d'Arrent. Do you agree?"

Nigh every soldier in the army had been born in the colonies. They would take the order hard—Sarresant soldiers were men and women of honor—but there was always a higher duty to home. If there would be difficulties they would come from the binders, trained almost from birth to believe themselves property of the crown. But she herself would serve as an example there; there would be conflict, but with swift, decisive action it could be settled to their advantage.

"Sir, I agree. There may be some small trouble, but most will follow. I am more concerned for the binders, and the priests. The crown's training is thorough. Not all of them will bend easily."

He nodded. "We have assurances from the prelates, and I've spoken with our senior binders in the Second Corps, but you are no doubt correct. As I said, this will be no easy path, for any of us."

"What of the men who won't follow you, sir? Or the captains and sailors of the navy who crossed the sea with Louis-Sallet?"

Voren gave her a grim look. "Blood on our hands, d'Arrent."

Her stomach turned. One thing to decide in the abstract, another to order her men to kill their fellow soldiers and sailors for the crime of loyalty, for upholding oaths they'd sworn themselves.

"You will give them the opportunity to support us, at least?"

"Of course."

She turned back to the maps. Time was short. Best get to work.

"Sir," Acherre whispered, "are you back?"

She sat forward, propping herself up on her elbows from where she'd lain on the dusty floor of the cell. Disorienting. She hadn't been lying down when she made the *Need* connection with Marquand.

"Yes, Lance-Lieutenant," she replied. "You moved me?"

"Yes, sir. The guards came with the midday meal." Acherre nodded toward the door, where a pair of bowls rested on the ground. "I told them you were asleep."

"Quick thinking, Lance-Lieutenant." Troubling that Acherre could move her body while her senses were suppressed by the *Need* binding. Would that lack of awareness persist in the face of real danger, if she suffered pain, or wounds? Yet another area for which she lacked understanding, another set of unknowns she'd need to test. Too damned many of those lately.

"Were you able to make contact, sir?" Acherre asked. "With the general?"

"Yes. Troubling news. You were born here in New Sarresant, right, Acherre?"

"Yes, sir. My father was a wine seller in the Market district, before they took me away for training."

"Have you seen him since?"

"No, sir."

Credit the binders' training for that. Connecting with family again after the academy was not explicitly prohibited, only frowned on to the point of taboo. They were soldiers, not citizens. Regulars could retire from the army after a completed tour, go home to wives, husbands, children. Binders, and especially fullbinders, served until they made their marque. Twenty years on an officer's pay, if somewhat fewer on a general's.

"Could you obey the Crown-Prince's command, if he gave it?" she asked.

"To leave the colonies, sir, to defend the Old World?"

She nodded.

Acherre went quiet.

"Could *you*, sir?" Acherre finally asked, a searching look behind her eyes.

"No," she said with finality. "And I don't mean to. Voren intends to join the Second Corps to the cause of revolution if Louis-Sallet goes ahead with his folly."

Acherre sat back against the stone walls of the cell, looking up at the ceiling as she let out a breath.

"Then I would follow you, sir."

"Very good, Lance-Lieutenant." She made an effort not to show her relief. It was no sure thing. Voren was right: This would be a hard road, before the end. "Voren expects Louis-Sallet to give his order at the Lords' Council, tomorrow night."

"Sir? Will there be enough time to deploy our men into the city?"

"Not if we overreach. Too many objectives and we'll never hold them all."

"The marquis-general has you planning this, doesn't he?"

"That's right, Lance-Lieutenant. *Need* is a powerful tool."

They exchanged a look, and Acherre returned her smile.

"Now, as to our objectives," she said. "Voren has placed a high priority on securing the harbor, and I agree. We must protect the ships if we are to have any hope of standing against the Gand invasion force. Bless Louis-Sallet for doing one thing right and bringing the navy with him. If we can secure those ships, prevent the admirals from fleeing the city, we may well have a fighting chance against what's coming."

"Sir," Acherre said, "is it wise to assume the remainder of the army will not oppose us?"

"We have to roll the dice, Lance-Lieutenant. Our composition is the same as theirs, levees from the colonies. They won't like the prince's order any more than we do. I don't have the men to fight a pitched battle against our own soldiers. The priority must be the ships."

Acherre leaned forward, listening intently as she laid out the rest of her plans. It helped to have a foil for planning, and Acherre asked more than a few pertinent questions. The most pressing issue was redeploying the men into the city, starting at first light, and doing it without attracting undue attention from the prince, or the rest of the army. They might manage a handful of brigades moving into the city before the fighting started. The rest of the corps would have to be mobilized and ready to move when they gave the order.

Timing would be tight, which meant detailed and specific logistics, down to the smallest fighting company of the barest regiment. And all of this planned and delivered in a day, while she was imprisoned, with access to maps only as fast as her *Need* reserves replenished. She was mad to even attempt it.

She grinned as she checked her *Need* stores. Mad, yes. But she'd done worse.

To her surprise she'd already recovered a small portion of *Need*; it seemed to regenerate more quickly when she focused herself on tasks and ideas for which she felt a sense of urgency. Not a large quantity available, but it would be enough for a brief review of the Harbor maps.

She closed her eyes, tethering the binding, and reached out for Foot-Captain Marquand.

Her senses snapped into place, and she stuttered to a halt mid-stride. A jolting sensation. She'd expected to find him seated behind Voren's maps. Instead he was out in the city, sauntering down the street alone.

She squinted into the unexpected sunlight. The Riverways. Marquand was wandering the Riverways, probably looking for some hole to crawl into before he drank himself into tomorrow.

"You listen to me, Foot-Captain," she hissed in Marquand's voice, for his benefit. "I need those maps. Get your wine-soaked ass back to the Harbor and do your duty or I'll flay your fucking hide for my personal battle standard."

She let the binding fade. Much as she wanted to lay into Marquand further, or perhaps take him to a rooftop and jump off just to teach him a lesson in obedience, *Need* was far too precious today to waste on mere discipline. He'd received the order. Drunkard he may be, but she'd never known him to fail in his duty, not when it mattered. More likely his little jaunt was a momentary lapse in judgment. Perhaps he'd failed to grasp the urgency of the situation. The alternative—that he'd grasped it perfectly well, and chose this moment to break—no, she could hardly bring herself to countenance that possibility. He could not mean to shirk his duty now.

Or worse, he could have decided his duty lay in working against them.

She could scarce believe it. Not of Marquand. Yet it was treason for which they asked. Who could say what steel lay at the core of any man or woman, without peeling back the skin to reveal it? She'd seen Marquand so piss-drunk he couldn't remember his name, but she'd also seen him lead a charge of fifty men against a regiment of five hundred without batting an eye. If he decided to warn the Crown-Prince…

No. Time enough to settle that if it came to it. It would take him an hour at least to reach Rasailles. She'd check in on him then, and if he had indeed made his way to the palace, she'd bury his own dagger in his belly. For now she had planning to do, damn Marquand for a bloody fool.

Her other vessels were unlikely to be anywhere useful. But she had to try.

She reached for Marie d'Oreste, and slid her senses into place. At once she was assaulted by the smell of blood, and rot. A soldier lay on a table in front of her, writhing out of her grip, howling in pain. The chirurgeon whipped his bone saw away with a curse when the patient slipped loose, invective trailing off when he noticed what could only have been the golden light behind Marie's eyes.

A field hospital. Gods damn it, Marie was in the camps outside the city. A fine bloody time to be nursing the wounded. Bless the woman for her charity, but there was no time.

"Marie," she said, "I need you to find Marquis-General Voren of the Second Corps. He's at the Tank and Twine in the Harbor district. Move on the double."

"What's going on here?" the chirurgeon demanded.

She let the binding fade.

"Sir?" Acherre asked as her senses returned to their cell. "Is somewhat amiss?"

No time.

She reached for Sister Elise, feeling her reserves of *Need* dwindling.

This time she sat astride a horse, on a slow walk amid a caravan of the same making their way along a road. Brown robes all around her, riding, walking, driving wagons. Nowhere near the city; they were returning to their abbey at Arentaigne.

No point sending a message. Too far. She let the binding fade.

"Sir?" Acherre again.

"No time, Lance-Lieutenant."

She needed a new connection. Now. She closed her eyes, letting the feeling of need overwhelm her. She imagined the Crown-Prince subduing their attempt at a coup, ordering the remains of the army back across the sea. She let herself feel the horror of the enemy invasion force making an uncontested landing within the New Sarresant harbor, commencing the butchery the enemy commander had promised, back in his command tent when she'd worn Marie d'Oreste's skin.

The golden light flickered at the edge of her vision. For a moment it seemed as if it would spring up, welcoming her embrace like the rays of an autumn sunrise.

And then, nothing. Her stores were exhausted.

She tethered *Body* and slammed a fist into the wall of her cell. Stone cracked and chipped, shards knifing through the air in a cloud of dust before it broke, and her fist connected with the *Shelter* binding beneath the wall. With a snapping sound, the force repelled her strike, sending her backward across the cell, throwing her into the far wall and knocking the breath from her lungs.

She gave a choking laugh, once she'd sucked in enough air for it. She'd been a fool. Expending all her *Need* to study the maps had been foolish in the extreme. Without it she was isolated, at the mercy of her body taking the time to generate more leyline energy. She took another deep, steadying breath.

"Sir?" Acherre asked once more, lowering the arm she'd used to shield herself from the shards of stone. "Is there anything I might do to help?"

Before she could reply, a hard rapping came on the door.

"Enough of that, prisoners!" shouted a stern voice. A woman, some priest who had been tapped to maintain the *Shelter* bindings today. Erris didn't envy her that posting: A binder of any real strength could overpower the guards at a moment's notice whenever they dropped the *Shelter* shield for meals, fresh linens, waste collection, or anything else besides. It was only the threat of the remainder of the Citadel's guard, and the binders among them, that might give a prisoner pause. Little enough surety in that, for the woman assigned to hold the barrier.

"We'll behave ourselves, sister," she called back. No reason to put fear into an innocent woman.

She turned back to Acherre. "And no, Lance-Lieutenant. Nothing to be done now. Not until my *Need* stores replenish."

Acherre frowned, but made no complaint.

"For now, we continue our work."

"Yes, sir."

It was slower going than she might have hoped without reference to Voren's maps of the city. General strategy only, directives for each unit with plans for how to deliver messages without drawing the notice of the city guard, or the other corps of the army. Still, they made progress, and before long she was satisfied with their framework for deploying the brigades toward the Harbor. Time to turn attention to the remainder of their men, stationed in the camps. They'd need to make a quick-time march through the woods between the city and Rasailles without drawing overmuch attention, in hopes of securing the Duc's family and the Crown-Prince before any loyalist opposition could take the field.

A thundercrack from below broke her concentration.

Acherre rose to her feet at once, with Erris not far behind. Dust fell from the ceiling as the walls shook.

"An attack?" the lance-lieutenant asked.

"Well ahead of schedule if so. Voren couldn't have moved the corps into the city so quickly."

Another boom, this time closer.

"That's coming from inside the Citadel," Acherre said.

Muffled shouting came from the hallway beyond the door, followed by another peal of thunder and rattling of the walls.

"Prepare yourself, Lance-Lieutenant," she said. "The *Shelter* barrier should protect us as well as it imprisons. But if the priestess falls, the barrier won't sustain itself."

More shouting from outside the door. Closer.

"Here!" a voice cried. The same priestess who had rebuked them before. "They're in here!"

"Open it then," a voice called. A gruff voice. A familiar voice.

By the Gods themselves. He couldn't. Even he wasn't that stupid.

The ironbound door swung open to reveal Foot-Captain Marquand, holding the brown-robed priestess by the arm.

"Good afternoon, Chevalier-General," Marquand said, grinning.

"You wine-sodden fool. What do you think you're doing?"

"The way I see it, what's a little prison break when we're already committed to treason? This way, you can leave me the bloody fuck out of your work."

Acherre stepped forward. "You murdered the Citadel guards?"

Marquand raised his free hand in a warding gesture. "Just a few *Entropy* bindings. No one hurt, so long as they cooperate." He said the last while tightening his grip on the priestess's arm, eliciting a whimper.

"Oh let her go, Marquand," she said, shaking her head. "You truly are an incurable bastard."

"Yes, sir," he replied, eyes gleaming.

She sighed, stepping forward.

"Let's go, Acherre. We have work to do."

44

ARAK'JUR

Approaching Nanek'Hai'Tyat
Nanerat Land

Bones. He lifted a blackened femur with a delicate touch. He'd feared the worst when they'd glimpsed the charred remains of some creature here among the permanent snowfall atop the Nanerat peaks. No fear needed now: He knew it for a certainty. These were bones from a man.

"Asseena's work?" he asked.

"It may be so," Corenna replied. "Perhaps they tracked the last of Arak'Atan's warriors here, into the peaks."

He frowned, setting the bone back down amid the scorched earth. A dignified end, if it were true; whatever scavengers lived here, so high up the mountainside, had been at the corpse. Some Jintani warrior, feeding the circle of Nanerat life, left to stand where he died.

That, or a lightning storm. It was not beyond possibility, and had been his first thought when they saw the blackened earth that had melted away the snow. Only the bones made him think twice. But if there had been pursuit here, on the very peak leading to their sacred place, would Asseena not have revealed it when he asked after Arak'Atan? Searching here had been his notion. A troubling thought, if there was more to her tribe's conflict with the Jintani than she had let on. Perhaps it was only a storm after all.

The peaks of the Nanerat towered above the foothills. On an overcast day, the summits pierced the heart of the sky, extending past the cover of the clouds. According to the Nanerat tribesmen, those were places for the spirits, certain death to any who attempted to scale their heights. Some few of the others could be scaled, and this was one such. One of the sacred mountains, set aside for the Nanerat by the spirits themselves. Having made the ascent he could well believe it. The twisting paths and switchbacks that covered the peak seemed to have been crafted to allow for the frailties of men. Treacherous, yes, and demanding of respect, but always under the protective gaze of the spirits. One could not help but feel their presence in this place. He and Corenna climbed higher, watched the world below dwindle, and he found himself overcome with its beauty. This was a place of peace and meditation, a place to let oneself be awed by the land, humbled before the power of the natural world. Even as a hunter, here to shed blood, the majesty of the peaks had a magic unto itself, older and deeper than any gift of the spirits.

Trees grew thin as they climbed, until they were replaced by sparse brush, clawing for survival through a layer of permanent snow. Even the air seemed thinner, a sensation he had not expected. The guardian's gift made him strong, but he felt the need to breathe deep and often, and Corenna fared somewhat worse. From the beginning she'd requested they take stops to allow her to rest, to conserve her strength for the climb. He trusted to her knowledge—she had made the climb before—and did so without complaint. She'd wrapped herself in a Nanerat design of thick hides and furs she insisted left her surprisingly nimble, though he remained skeptical of the protection it offered from the cold. For himself, simple leggings, bare skin, and the blessings of the spirits sufficed, and if he would never claim Corenna was weak, still it could be said the strength of her gifts lay elsewhere. The winds were cruel and sharp here, and he was sure she felt every tooth of their bite.

Four days. And every one, he rebuked himself for allowing Corenna to join this hunt. She'd never hear it, if he gave voice to his concerns, and he kept silent. Yet for all the power she brought to bear through the women's gifts, she risked her life making this ascent. The spirits of the Nanerat had been cruel indeed to force such trials on their women, keeping their sacred place high atop these peaks. Yet Asseena and her ilk had made this journey in reverence, knowing wisdom and power awaited them at the summit. Corenna expected only blood, and still pushed on.

"Arak'Jur," she called, pointing up ahead.

"Another path?" he asked. Then he saw it.

A boulder, near the size of a man, lay ahead. Only instead of resting along the steep mountainside, threatening to cascade down to cause an avalanche or worse, it hovered a handspan or more above the snow, suspended in air. He looked again to confirm it, and it was so: No part of the stone touched the ground.

A moment of silence passed between them.

"Nanek'Hai'Tyat," Corenna whispered.

"Yes," he said. "We draw near."

They exchanged a look, and he saw grim determination in Corenna's eyes. No more needed be said. Whatever fatigue might have settled in as they made the day's climb was gone in an instant.

They pressed on, winding their way around the slopes on paths just wide enough, as if they'd been cut to allow their passage. And everywhere they saw the signs. Stones and clumps of earth floated around them, gliding through the air as if it were water. Always the land was altered near a place of the spirits, but he had never seen such a display as this. As they curved around the face of the mountain, more earth and snow seemed to be suspended in the air than lay beneath their feet. No sign of such had been visible from below, yet here it was. They spiraled around the path, moving upward until, at last, they crested the final rise.

At the far side of a field of floating stone and snow, one last spire rose to the sky, with a black cave opening etched into its side. The entrance to Nanek'Hai'Tyat.

They'd arrived.

And they'd found their quarry.

Arak'Atan stood, waiting, in the middle of the field, flanked by a pair of full-grown *ipek'a*. Arak'Jur stepped forward, placing himself between Corenna and the deadly beasts.

"Be welcome, friends from the South," Arak'Atan called. "The spirits have whispered to me of your coming, and so long as you mean to join yourself to their cause, you have nothing to fear here."

He eyed the man warily, darting glances back and forth between the Jintani guardian and the *ipek'a* at his sides. The sight exposed a raw nerve. Great beasts could not be tamed; they lived to kill, the manifestation of the raw destructive power of the wild. And yet here they stood, long necks twisted to focus their hawkish eyes on the newcomers, seemingly content to be still and observe. Their feathers were white, which meant neither had made a kill in some time. By rights they should have slain Arak'Atan on the spot and trumpeted the news of their victory as a warning to any creatures lurking nearby. Arak'Jur knew the ways of *ipek'a*; he had worn that skin himself, by the grace of the spirits. Yet neither beast moved, only watched and waited.

"How have you done this, Arak'Atan?" he called, still warding Corenna behind him. "*Ipek'a* is no companion to men."

"Much has changed for our people, and our gifts. The *ipek'a* and I serve the same cause. If you serve it as well, you will find us welcome allies."

The unspoken threat hung in the air, bolstered by the reserved posture of the Jintani guardian.

"You make war on the Nanerat," Corenna called back to him, managing to keep her voice neutral.

"I do."

Even from a distance, he could feel Arak'Atan's gaze studying them, weighing them against some hidden expectation. The *ipek'a* seemed to do the same, mimicking the guardian's posture. *Ipek'a* was a fierce predator, but they were little more than that. When he had worn its skin, the *ipek'a* spirit had never revealed the curious, burning intelligence he saw now, lurking behind these creatures' eyes. Was this in their nature? Had some part of it been kept from him? He couldn't believe it. Something else was at work here.

He looked again, and whatever was behind those eyes dawned with understanding at the same moment he saw it for what it was. Evil. Madness.

The *ipek'a* trumpeted a warning blast that echoed across the mountaintop, scattering floating motes of snow and earth before the sheer force of its call.

Arak'Atan made an exaggerated sigh.

"It seems you do not share our cause, brother. I take it our honored sister stands with you as well."

"We stand against war and madness, Arak'Atan," Corenna called back. The Jintani guardian nodded as if he had expected no less.

Without warning, one of the *ipek'a* launched itself into the air, crashing through the floating stones as if they were no more than nettling thistle. Arak'Jur sprang away from where it would land, keeping watch on Arak'Atan and the first *ipek'a*, still gnashing its jaws after letting loose its thundering cry. Corenna remained where she was. In the moment his heart surged with a desire to call upon *lakiri'in*, to race back and defend her. Just as quick he reminded himself she was more than capable of seeing to her own protection. His calling was as guardian, but to be overmindful of Corenna was to hamstring them both. He knew it, and cordoned off the portion of his mind that worried for her safety. Time now to look to his own gifts, and trust that she could handle her part.

The *ipek'a* landed, crashing full force into a barrier of stone Corenna conjured above her head at the last instant. A sickening screech as it swiped its scything claw across the stone, then a crunch as the rest of its massive body collided into her shield. Yes, Corenna could manage.

He shifted his focus back to Arak'Atan. The other guardian made a wordless snarl as the first of his beast companions rolled to the ground, dazed. A nimbus of cat surrounded the Jintani guardian. *Mareh'et*. A powerful gift, one that Arak'Jur preferred to save until need was dire. It seemed Arak'Atan had no such predilections. Even so, it could be countered with speed.

The Jintani guardian, joined by the other great beast, lowered his head and charged at Corenna. Arak'Jur called upon *lakiri'in*, and his limbs surged with energy. He raced across the field, taking Arak'Atan with a shoulder charge at full speed.

The two men collided, rolling together into a puff of snow floating at chest height. No time to consider what the other *ipek'a* was doing; Corenna would see it coming, and be on guard. He slammed a fist into Arak'Atan's jaw before the other man could react, his limbs still surging with speed. Before they hit the ground he rained a succession of blows on Arak'Atan, with time enough to set himself for the counterattack he knew would come. And come it did. What *mareh'et* lacked in pure speed he made up for in the gift of his ethereal claws. Arak'Atan landed one savage cut across his left torso, with a second strike missing his head only for their crashing together into the dirt.

A lance of pain tore through him as blood sprayed into the snow, and another arcing cut went for his shoulder as they tangled together on the ground. He twisted inside the other man's guard, landing another rain of blows to deflect the striking arm. Arak'Atan returned a backhanded slash, enough to send him sailing into the air with another rip across the chest. He sprang to his feet the moment he landed, still surging with *lakiri'in*'s gift, and raced forward before Arak'Atan had risen to his knees.

An instant before he crashed into the Jintani guardian, he called upon *una're*, the Great Bear. This time there was no rain of blows, only a single, savage strike connecting with Arak'Atan's left eye socket.

Hissing and popping accompanied the blow as electricity surged into Arak'Atan. Pockmarks scored the side of his face, and his eye split into pulp around Arak'Jur's fist. A full-strength hit carrying *una're*'s blessing would end a fight with any lesser man, but Arak'Atan carried the guardian's gift. No sooner had the first sparks crackled over his skin than the Jintani guardian blinked out of existence, like a fire snuffed by sand. One moment he was there, on the receiving end of Arak'Jur's strike, and the next he had vanished. Arak'Jur struck again for surety, to verify the man had not employed the gift of *juna'ren* to camouflage himself in plain sight, and met only air and snow.

"*Astahg!*" he cried out, for Corenna's benefit. "The gift of *astahg* is to vanish and reappear. Stay on your guard."

He sprang to his feet, turning to survey the rest of the fight. Corenna had held off the charge of the second *ipek'a* with another shield of stone, and switched now to her gift of ice to go on the attack. The great birdlike creatures howled as she peppered them with massive shards of deadly ice, enough to forestall any instinct they might have had to spring toward her.

Scanning the field, he saw no sign of Arak'Atan. He needed to get close to Corenna, to guard her back against an unseen strike. Maintaining *una're*'s gift meant he would be too slow to cover the distance. With *lakiri'in* spent, that meant *mareh'et*.

He raced toward her, channeling the cat spirit. A gamble, if Arak'Atan could wait out *mareh'et*'s blessing, but one he had to take.

He closed the distance, still without sign of Arak'Atan. Just as well. If the other man thought to recover himself it meant Arak'Jur could field his gifts against the *ipek'a*. He took one of them from behind, tearing through its feathery hide even as Corenna provided distracting shots of ice to hold the beast's attention. It went down into the snow, a desperate bleating cry stilling in the creature's throat as it died.

"Down!" he shouted. Too late.

Arak'Atan had reappeared behind Corenna and caught her with a swift kick that took her legs out from beneath her, sending her into the snow. Shoving one of the floating stones out of his way, Arak'Jur sped toward them, forcing the other man to back away before he could land a killing strike. He watched as Arak'Atan's form shifted colors, blending into the haze of white and red, snow and blood. *Juna'ren*'s blessing. He would have to stay near Corenna until she recovered her footing; a second unseen strike could well be fatal, especially while she was down.

By now the second *ipek'a* realized the shards of ice had ceased, and recovered enough to make another trumpet blast, this time less steady, less sure without the backing of its fallen pack mate. Arak'Jur called upon the *juna'ren*'s gift as well, feeling his form blend into the landscape behind him. Two could play at hiding.

The remaining *ipek'a* bobbed its head around the floating motes of snow, peering toward where he stood at Corenna's side. But the great beast would see only the fallen form of the woman who had just pelted it with a dozen icy spears. She'd risen to her knees, propping herself up in the heartbeats it took for him to close the gap. Enough time for the *ipek'a* to push off with its powerful hind legs, propelling itself upward, aiming to fall atop her with deadly precision.

He moved aside, on full alert for Arak'Atan. With only *juna'ren*'s blessing he couldn't withstand the force of an *ipek'a*'s leap.

Corenna seemed to sense the danger, rolling onto her side and filming her eyes over with pale blue. A concentrated gale of wind whipped into the *ipek'a* even as it crashed toward her, and he saw its innards torn open, entrails spilling down onto Corenna where she lay, pinning her to the ground. As opportune a moment as Arak'Atan was like to get. Sure enough, the Jintani guardian appeared in midair sailing toward her, having called upon the blessing of *ipek'a* himself.

Without thinking, Arak'Jur did the same, invoking *ipek'a*'s gift and launching himself into the sky.

The two men collided at full force, grappling each other as they plummeted to the ground. They struck the snow and bounced apart, each man rolling to his feet. Arak'Jur leaned back on his legs, trusting the blessing of *ipek'a* to hold for another flying leap. He pushed off, sailing toward Arak'Atan, expecting the other man to do the same.

Instead, the Jintani guardian held his ground, locking his remaining good eye on Arak'Jur. His pupil went red, bright red. The color of fire.

Women's magic. Impossible.

A spear of flame seared the air around him, and he felt his skin crack and burn as he crashed into the ground, skidding helplessly to land at Arak'Atan's feet. Pain enveloped him, a desperate stabbing pain coming from every inch of his body, salved only by the gentle cooling of the snow.

Arak'Atan stepped toward him, his left eye a mash of bloody flesh, his right eye filmed over with a red glow. Hatred twisted Arak'Atan's gaze, and the Jintani guardian raised a hand, invoking another torrent of fire to scour the ground before him. When the flames cleared, Arak'Jur had fallen still.

Arak'Atan exhaled sharply, dropping to a knee beside his body.

A long moment passed, and Arak'Jur did not stir.

"You see, honored guardian," Arak'Atan said, "much has changed, by the will of the spirits."

Arak'Jur released the gift of *anahret*, setting aside their perfect semblance of death, and took up the gift of the *valak'ar*. His joints screamed pain as the serpent granted its blessing, his skin flaking and cracked from the fire. But he found strength enough to reach upward, striking through the Jintani guardian's skin to inject the wraith-snake's deadly poison into his heart.

He saw Arak'Atan's one working eye widen, the red glow replaced by an empty, far-off look. And then his own vision blurred, the world seeming to fall away as he slipped back into the snow.

He awoke to the sweet smell of cooked meat, and a haze of burning pain.

A mumble died in his throat, formless words choked off by a searing fire. The slightest tremble ignited sparks hidden beneath his skin, and he fell still, followed by the dull echo of the pain. His eyes wouldn't open.

"Arak'Jur?" Corenna's voice. Even the vibrations of her words were spear points in his side, though there was warmth there as well. The succor of his mother, and of Rhealla, his onetime wife. Comfort.

He heard Corenna's voice again, a muted wind that rolled over him in a wave of pain.

Once more the world faded away. At the edge of consciousness, he heard another voice, barely above a whisper.

It is time, guardian of the Sinari.

Come to us.

His eyes slid open, and he felt himself choke and sputter.

Corenna withdrew a cloth from his mouth with a gasp, leaning over where he lay.

"Arak'Jur," she said. "Are you awake?"

This time the pain was a distant companion, though his senses felt snared down by mud.

He managed a nod, and a murmur of assent, feeling the taste of meat and broth in his throat.

Corenna replaced her cloth by the side of the fire, atop the small clay bowl she had used to cook meals on their journey. Distantly he wondered where she had managed to scrounge enough brush to light the fire, here atop the Nanerat sacred mountain. No mistaking where they were; she did not have the strength to have carried him elsewhere, and the floating motes of earth and snow made it clear enough by themselves.

"I've done what I can for your wounds," she said in a soft voice, kneeling once more at his side. "Don't exert yourself."

He drew in a deep breath, letting the pain ripple through him, testing its limits. Bearable.

"The guardians heal quickly," he said, forcing himself to lift his head, and look down.

"Don't—" she began, trailing off as she watched his reaction.

She'd kept his body exposed to the cold. Certain death for another man, but a salve against the stinging burns for him. Thank the spirits she'd had the sense not to waste her furs on him; she wouldn't have survived without them. She knew his body could handle the elements.

As for his skin, well.

It was a ruin. Hairless, cracked, and crossed with seams as if he'd been stitched together by needles. Still swollen red where the cuts ran deepest, and a tender, flushed shade of bronze even at its best.

He managed a weak laugh. "It seems I've seen better days."

"Arak'Jur—"

"Thank you, Corenna. Without your aid I would be dead."

She turned away, trying to hide a stifled sob.

He sat up, and she snapped back to face him. "No, you must rest."

"I will recover," he said, feeling his muscles cry out in protest. Even so, they obeyed. "How long have I slept?"

"Two days."

He nodded. A good length of time, where the guardians' healing gift was concerned.

"Arak'Jur, I was afraid you would not wake, that you had fallen, that I had failed you."

"You fought well, Corenna. You did honor to your tribe."

This time she didn't hide her tears. He reached for her, drawing her close. She stiffened, like as not worried she would do him some injury. He held her tighter, and she softened, sobbing against his chest.

"Thank you," she said when they separated. "I haven't hurt you, have I?"

"I'll survive," he said.

She smiled, and he straightened where he sat, stretching his back. Spirits, but it burned, even now.

"Do you mean to stand?" she asked.

In reply, he curled his legs beneath him, ignoring the pain, and rose to his knees. She rose, offering him an arm. He took it, rising to his feet.

"Ah, but that feels good." It did. The icy rush of pain washed out by the vigor of blood coursing through his body.

She let go his hand, making a show of inspecting him from all angles. "A surprising thing, the guardian's gift," she said. "You'll be descending the mountain before nightfall."

He gave a weak smile as he drew another deep breath, like drinking from a spring of pure water laced with flame, and swept a look across the field. An otherworldly place. By now clumps of blood mixed with snow and earth had joined the other motes floating above the ground, giving a crimson cast to the sunlight piercing down from the cloudless sky. And there, at the far edge of the mountaintop, the last spire, and the cave entrance to the sacred place of the Nanerat.

"Did you . . . ?" he asked, glancing between her, the cave entrance, and the fire burning beside them.

She gave him a questioning look. "Did I what?"

"Did you enter Nanek'Hai'Tyat? Did you receive its blessing? Is that how you came to make the cookfire?"

She frowned. "No. I gathered brush for half a day to make the fire. And I see no means of entering Nanek'Hai'Tyat. It must be as the Ranasi, and Sinari sacred places: sealed shut by the spirits."

"Sealed?" he asked, furrowing his brow. "You attempted to enter the cave, and were rebuked?"

"What cave, Arak'Jur?"

He looked once more, checking to make certain his eyes had not deceived him. It was there, a black opening in the side of the crag rising up at the far edge of the field.

"There," he said, pointing. "You cannot see it?"

"No. Are you certain?"

"I see it now," he said. And at once, his memory sparked. "At Ka'Ana'Tyat, you said it was sealed as well. Could you see an opening there, when we made the journey with Ilek'Inari?"

She shook her head slowly. "No. Our sacred places have been sealed shut since the spirits began their whispering madness."

"Corenna, no. Arak'Atan bore the gift of this place, the fire he used to scourge my skin. And I can see a cave there, leading into the heart of the mountain."

Her mouth fell open. "By the spirits," she whispered.

They shared a long look.

"Go," she said.

Come, a voice echoed, at the far edge of his hearing, like a whisper on the wind.

"Corenna—"

"Go," she repeated, more firm.

"This is women's magic, or a shaman's. It is not my place to—"

"Would you turn your back on such a gift, Arak'Jur? Would you ignore its promise, the power to defend our peoples? If the spirits will you to receive their blessing, I would sooner it pass to you than to men like Arak'Atan."

"It is forbidden."

"The spirits will speak for themselves of what is forbidden. Go, Arak'Jur."

He held her eyes.

"Go, spirits curse you." She wore a smile, laced with bitterness. "Before you see me overcome with envy that they chose you and not me."

"Corenna..."

"Go."

He went.

ARAK'JUR.

The voice thundered through him, though he felt no pain. His body was distant, a memory of a memory. Had he been hurt? Here, he was whole. Here, he was aware.

BE WELCOME IN NANEK'HAI'TYAT, SON OF THE SINARI. BE WELCOME IN THE BIRTHPLACE OF PEACE.

It was the same sensation as with the great beasts, yet different as well. Softer. Older. Wiser.

My thanks for your welcome, spirits of peace.

IT IS AN OLD THING, FOR A GUARDIAN TO COME TO US. ONE WE HAD ALMOST FORGOTTEN. BUT THE TIME IS SOON UPON US. THE GODDESS WILL SOON HAVE NEED OF YOUR STRENGTH. ARE YOU CHOSEN?

Always they asked this, when he slew the great beasts. Almost he replied as he always had. Yet this time, it was not the same.

You chose me to enter here, though it is no place for a guardian.

YES. A GUARDIAN WHO WIELDS THE MAGIC OF WAR. A CHAMPION OF THE WILD.

A light washed over him, bathing him in blue radiance. He could see a face, silhouetted by the light. A woman, but none he knew.

WALK HER PATH. BECOME HER CHAMPION. SEEK ASCENSION TO THE SEAT OF THE GODS.

She is not known to me, he thought. *Nor is the calling or place of which you speak.*

A silence echoed between them, and then he had a sensation of twisting, shifting, as if the ground he stood on bent beneath his feet. Mist gathered around him, and he had a vision.

Death. Corrosion and decay, plague and fire. All the lands of the world crushed by the weight of torment and suffering.

THIS IS HIS WAY. THE ENEMY.

He saw his son broken, pierced by the fangs of the *valak'ar*. His wife, who had cast herself before the creature with a wail of agony.

Stop this, he pleaded in his mind.

THIS IS THE HOMAGE HE REQUIRES. THE REGNANT. THE ANCIENT ENEMY.

Please.

WALK HER PATH. STAND AGAINST HIS CHAMPIONS.

I stand against evil, and madness. Why do you show me these things?

Another silence, and still the images played on. Death. Suffering.

You are spirits of peace. Stop.

Torment. Anguish.

Why would you grant your gift to one such as Arak'Atan?

A reckless demand, bordering on insult to the spirits themselves. As soon as he made it, the mist faded away, leaving behind only emptiness, a vast void surrounding him on all sides.

Fear crept in. Had he overstepped?

EVEN THE POWER OF THE GODDESS CANNOT STOP AN ASCENSION. WE HAD ALMOST FORGOTTEN OUR WAYS. BUT WE FOUND YOU, FOUND YOUR PEOPLE. WE CALLED TO YOU, SUMMONED YOU TO LIVE AMONG US, TO HELP US REMEMBER. YOU CAME. AND NOW THE TIME DRAWS NEAR.

A relief to hear them speak again. Even so, the meaning behind the spirits' words eluded him. He thought as much to them. *Spirits, I do not understand.*

ALL WILL BECOME CLEAR. WE WILL REMEMBER, TOGETHER. WALK HER PATH.

I will stand against evil, no matter its source.

IT WILL SERVE.

Once more the blue light shone around him, a face masked in shadow looking down on him from afar. He heard a faint sound, a melody carried on the whisper of a breath, hidden behind the light. A songbird's greeting, in the morning after a storm. A requiem, sung for the fallen after a great hunt.

It held for a long moment before fading away. A dim whisper echoed in his mind as the song fell silent, but he could not make out the words.

WOULD YOU HAVE OUR BOON, SON OF THE SINARI?

Great spirits, I would.

Energy pulsed through him, and he felt the weight of roots sunk deep within the earth. He was the great mountain, stoic and ageless. He felt the stirring wind, beginning as the clouds themselves broke against his peak, rushing down his slopes in a gale of biting cold. Spring water bubbled beneath his surface, and the rains poured down on him, the cleansing draught of life flowing down to the creatures below. He stood against the turning of the sun, lifetimes upon lifetimes coming and going in his shade. He felt what it was for the mountains to be born, the slow crushing of one land into another, jutting great spires of rock up into the dome of the sky. He felt the liquid secret at the mountain's heart, the price paid for tranquil serenity. Flame given form, simmering deep within. A promise, delivered in vengeful fury. He felt himself torn apart under the weight of violence, billowing smoke and ash that blackened the sky. He was the mountain, the earth given form, and his blood was fire.

The vision faded.

REMEMBER US.

The voice echoed through his head, and he expected the blackness to fade, returning him to the mountaintop. Instead he lingered, on the precipice of nothing.

Was this part of the women's secrets? Had he missed some part of their sending?

Another whisper formed at the edge of his mind, then again. Too faint to understand, but growing in strength, as if each repetition added voices to its chorus.

At last, he understood their words.

"Let us speak."

Again.

"Let him see."

Now he heard a mix of voices. "He is ours." "He belongs to us." "He must see."

Let them speak, he thought into the void.

At once the voice of the mountain, the voice of the spirits of Nanek'Hai'Tyat, returned. YOU WOULD HEAR THEM?

Who are they?

THE SPIRITS OF KA'ANA'TYAT. THE SPIRITS OF YOUR PEOPLE.

Yes, he thought at once. *Let them speak!*

The whispers coalesced as one.

"Arak'Jur," they whispered. "We are dying. Save us."

What? he thought. *What has happened?*

"War," the voices whispered together. "War has come to the Sinari."

45

SARINE

Lords' Council
Southgate District, New Sarresant

"The hall will come to order."

The command echoed through the ornate chambers, accompanied by a crash of steel as guardsmen snapped to attention. The lords and ladies reacted slowly, as if they accepted the inevitability of the words but were in no hurry to be the first to comply.

From the gallery above, Sarine looked down on a parade of plumage as the last conversations lingered on, banter tossed back and forth as the nobles found their seats. Only the steel-clad soldiers ringing the chamber upheld the gravity of what was supposed to be the principal governing body of the colonies. For the rest, a show of the latest fashions in the city: golds, crimsons, purples, and blues, with jeweled necklaces, studded scabbards, elaborate hairpieces, and slim-cut dresses. The last brought an unbidden smile. Whatever his failings, Reyne d'Agarre had employed a visionary clothier on her behalf; it seemed her little garden jaunts at Lord Revellion's side had set something of a trend.

Idly she wondered just how much of the politics decided in this chamber came about by virtue of these displays of fashion and wealth. Clear enough from the start that the Lords' Council deliberated few matters of actual import. She'd nestled herself into place hours ago, alongside the other petitioners, and heard every name, every title called by the crier as they entered. She'd expected marquis, comtes, and comtesses, or at least their heirs, and heard instead too many second sons and daughters for the families represented here to be conducting their true business. Even so, it was an impressive display, enough to overawe the commoners who flanked her, dressed in their best finery and still a pale glimmer beside the bonfire of the nobility.

She'd tensed when the crier had called "his lordship Donatien Revellion." It had taken no small amount of argument to convince Donatien to sponsor her petition tonight—without his patronage, she'd never have been admitted to speak before the Lords' Council—and he'd given it only on the firm condition she limit herself to presenting the activities of Reyne d'Agarre, leaving out the planned military coup to which Revellion himself was now complicit. He'd even insisted on giving some other pretext for her making the petition, thinking to insulate himself from the wrath of those loyal to d'Agarre. She hadn't been able to convince him he was being a fool. As if men inclined to bloody revolution would be forgiving of disloyalty in any form, no matter if he claimed he had not known her purpose. That was not the way of the world. She knew little enough of high courts and politics, but she knew the coming days would be anything but the bloodless affair of which she knew Donatien still dreamed. And she had no intention of leaving out the treachery of the military.

She cast another long look down below, where Donatien had taken his seat. Would he forgive her betrayal, understanding she did it only to try to stem the tide of violence? She was not naïve enough to believe it, no matter her hopes. Tonight in all probability marked the end of her affair with the son of a lord. All for the best, though the cut stung no less for being self-inflicted.

"Order now, order, I say."

A clatter of steel sounded as the soldiers ringing the chamber snapped to attention, giving the lie to the illusion that they were decorative statues, dressed in the full-plate relics of a bygone age. The room fell silent at last.

"Very good then. The Lords' Council of New Sarresant is hereby convened and in session, his royal stewardship the Right Honorable Julien Duroux presiding, standing in for his grace the Royal Governor the Duc-General Cherrain, here to receive petitions from the assembled lords and ladies, or of designates with grievances appropriate to this council as so judged by the assembled peers."

"Your Right Honorable Stewardship, I have a grievance." One of the young lords rose from his seat, a tall man with a pointed jaw and a solemn air.

The steward, seated behind an imposing oak rostrum atop a dais at the center of the room, leaned forward to eye the speaker. "Lord Lemais, your name was not submitted to the docket for consideration."

"Nevertheless, your honor, I would speak, if it please the council."

The steward frowned, glancing down to shuffle a sheaf of paper sitting before him on the lectern. "Very well, Lord Lemais. Yours is the only matter brought before us by a peer tonight, and as such you may speak first."

The young lord nodded as if he had expected nothing less, and turned his back on the steward, addressing the nobles directly.

"My lords, I have a grievance of the direst nature, testimony of deeds most heinous and foul."

His words brought a cloud of reverent silence among the petitioners waiting in the gallery, though the nobles seated on the floor below seemed somewhat less enchanted, stirring and exchanging glances back and forth across the hall.

"Let it be known," the lord continued, "that one of our very own peers stands accused tonight." He pointed. "Yes, let it be known that the Lady Cherie Salliere has knowingly, and with malice aforethought, thrown such a gala for her seasonal debut that none of us shall be able to top it."

The floor filled with raucous laughter as a dozen more young lords and ladies called out to second the motion. Muted laughter passed through the gallery overlooking the floor, the bubble of their rapt attention popped by the unanticipated mirth.

"Order, order in the hall."

The steel-clad soldiers snapped to attention, a small thunderclap that silenced the room.

"You will excuse me, Lord Lemais, if I table the motion without putting it to the floor."

The young lord bowed with a flourish, accepting his defeat, and retook his seat, met with a round of backslapping from nearby fellows.

"Perhaps we can resume with council business?" The steward coughed as he arranged the papers on the lectern, raising a hand in the direction of the gallery with a beckoning gesture. "Our next petitioner is the Honorable Master Kellon, here at the behest of her ladyship Racine l'Euillard, daughter of the esteemed Marquise l'Euillard of the colony that bears her name, absent from this council to attend to private matters. Bailiff, if you would kindly escort Master Kellon to the floor."

A man rose from his place seated behind her in the gallery, drawing the eyes of the other petitioners as one of the soldiers escorted him down through a rear exit. A lull on the floor provided opportunity for more private exchanges between the nobles, whispers and gossip passing between them, unchallenged by another call to order. It seemed the wiry man at the head of the chamber opted to pick his battles. She wondered what the steward must have been like as a youth. Not so very different from Donatien, she suspected: all progressive philosophy and love for the law. And now he was a shepherd for the indolent children of the nobility. He'd have made a good candidate for a sketch, if she'd had her pack. One of the sort she saved for herself, even while other sketches showing the opulence of this chamber would sell quick as apple cakes on a summer afternoon.

"Now," the steward began, "Master Kellon, you've come before the Lords' Council on a matter of redress for the exigencies of war along the southern border, is that correct?"

The petitioner stepped forward, sparing a nervous look around the chamber before he replied. "Yes, my lord." That drew a snigger or two from the nobles, as the steward halted the man before he could continue.

"I am a steward, Master Kellon, in service at the pleasure of the Duc. Not a lord. Resume your account, if you please."

"Yes, my . . . steward." A few more choked-back laughs at that, though the man carried on. "I was chosen to speak for the farmers of the village of Alès, to plead for hardship. We had stocked our stores for the coming winter, but with the quartering of the army over the past season, we have little left for the cold months. I had hoped to—"

"You plead hardship on account of being asked to feed our own soldiers?" one of the lords called, from the far side of the chamber. The speaker rose to his feet, drawing eyes away from Master Kellon.

"The chair recognizes Lord Courtenay."

The lord made a half nod toward the steward, then turned back to address the room. "What are we to make of this? I'd expected a grievance to at least include some tales of border raids, an atrocity or two for spice. Instead we hear the lament of a farmhand fretting that he might be asked to do his share during a time of war." Murmurs of assent passed through the room. "At least entertain us, if you mean to ask for our largesse, good master. And besides, this sounds a matter for the Council-General, to me."

Master Kellon's eyes went wide. "My lord, I… I mean only to—"

The steward spoke, cutting short the man's protest. "The chair concurs with Lord Courtenay's sentiment that this matter seems best heard by the Council-General. Might we hear from the petitioner's sponsor for extenuating circumstance? Lady l'Euillard, if you please?"

A girl stood, seated only a few paces away from the rostrum. She could not be more than ten or eleven years old, yet bedecked all the same in fashions and jewels that could fetch gold enough to feed the poor man's village for a season by themselves.

"My lords and ladies." The child's voice quavered. "Forgive me if I have erred in judgment. Master Kellon lives on my family's land, and so he came to us. My household chamberlain was moved by his plea, and asked me the favor of endorsing the request. I fear I have made a mistake, and I beg the council's forgiveness."

Another young lord stood at once. "I cannot bear to see a child so moved, especially one as lovely as the Lady l'Euillard. I move to support this claim, trusting to the virtue of innocence to decide the merit of our charity."

A lady's voice called out a second, and the room soon shared murmurs of assent.

"Very well," said the steward in a tired voice. "We have a motion, and a second. Lord Courtenay, will you maintain your opposition?"

The first young man stood once more. "My lords, my ladies, I could not in good conscience stand against such worthy sentiment. House Courtenay stands with the motion."

"Will any other houses champion an opposition?"

When none came forward, the steward nodded. "Then the motion carries. Look to the clerks for remuneration of your claims, Master Kellon."

The man stammered a bewildered protest that he hadn't named an amount before evidently thinking better of it and accepting the bailiff's escort from the chamber.

"Our next petitioner is the Honorable Master Stevren, at the behest of Lord Petreuil Forbin, son of the Lord Admiral the Comte de Forbin, away from this council serving honorably in the crown's navy."

So it went, for another petitioner, then another. There seemed little rhyme or reason to the order they were called; one might ask for the council's blessing for a mining venture into the southern hills, the next for sanction against a neighbor's encroachment of the property boundaries of their townhouse. A sure enough bet that none of them had a matter half so urgent as news of a violent group seeding weapons caches in the sewers, intent on bloody revolution. It took no small measure of self-control to restrain herself from taking to the floor and demanding their attention. She'd almost reached the end of her reserve, and never mind the consequences, when the steward finally shuffled a paper and intoned the words for which she'd been waiting.

"Our next petitioner is Madame Sarine Thibeaux of New Sarresant, at the behest of Lord Donatien Revellion, son of his lordship the Marquis Revellion, away from this council serving the crown as diplomatic envoy to the Thellan colonies in the south."

No sooner had she risen from her seat than Zi's voice sounded in her head.

Yellow.

Good. Someone else might have cared about persuading the council by the force of their argument alone. For her, it was enough that they listen, and if that took Zi's gift, so be it.

She walked through the back of the gallery, descending the steps with one of the steel-clad soldiers at her side, and presented herself on the floor of the council, every eye crawling over her, weighing her, whispering to their neighbor without diverting their gaze. An unsettling feeling.

It took the laughter of the chamber to snap her back to the moment. A harsh sound, cruel and mocking.

The steward coughed. "Madame Sarine? Must I repeat myself? I *said* the nature of the matter you wish to bring before the council is a garment maker's subsidy, is that correct?"

"No," she said.

"No?" The steward wrinkled his nose as he looked down at his sheaf of papers. "Am I mistaken somehow—?"

"No, honorable master, you are not mistaken. I deceived the Lord

Revellion as to the nature of the matter I wished to bring before this council. I bring information too sensitive, too dire to share with any but the collected nobles of this city." The room stirred at that, with most of the looks directed toward where Donatien sat, near the entryway.

"Irregular," the steward said. "Most irregular. Realize you risk imprisonment for insulting this council. I would hear from Lord Revellion as to whether he wishes to press—"

She cut in. "I bear news of a plot to seize power in the city, to foment revolution of the commonfolk against the crown."

A mantle of silence thick as a springtime fog settled over the chamber, the quips of the young nobles dying on their lips, unspoken.

"You offer proof of this allegation?" the steward asked.

"Search the sewers," she said. "The east-side tunnels beneath the Riverways. They've stockpiled weapons and supplies there, with men prepared to act on their orders in all quarters of the city. They are led by a man called Reyne d'Agarre, a member of the Council-General."

Murmurs around the room at that, heated whispers and glares that seemed... angry?

"Why should we listen to this nonsense?" one of the young lords demanded, rising from his seat. "She comes before us under false pretense, dishonoring one of our own with every word she speaks, and slanders an elected member of the commoners' council."

"I concur with the sentiment," came another voice. "Her very presence offends this chamber."

More nobles made to rise, a tide of anger surging through the room. It hit her like a wave, an affirmation of the voice inside her that cautioned against boldness.

"Order," the steward called, evoking another steel crash as the soldiers came to attention.

The steward continued, looking down on her with a neutral expression. "You understand the severity of this claim, Madame Sarine. Master d'Agarre is a respected member of the Council-General."

She took a steadying breath. She hadn't come so far to wilt beneath a few withering glares.

"Honored Steward, there is more. The conspiracy extends further, all the way to the highest ranks of the army, to—"

A trumpet blast smothered her words in brass, and at once the nobles throughout the room rose to their feet. She turned, cut off mid-sentence, to see the crier march through the entryway of the chamber.

"Presenting His Royal Highness, the Crown-Prince Louis-Sallet de l'Arraignon, third in line to the throne of Sarresant, Prince of the Blood and trueborn son of the King Gaurond, may his reign last a hundred years."

Even before the crier had finished, a pair of guards in slick leather and purple tabards entered the chamber, casting looks in every direction. The way they flicked their eyes shut confirmed for her they were binders, looking for errant connections. Just as well she hadn't panicked herself into a *Life* binding, or some other ill-advised comfort.

Evidently satisfied, the purple-tabarded guardsmen nodded toward the crier as he finished his announcement, and the Crown-Prince made his entry.

He was tall, an imposing figure, all the more so for the lavish cloak of blue velvet trailing behind him. The nobles of the council bent the knee together, casting their eyes to the ground as Louis-Sallet de l'Arraignon strode toward the dais. In a rush, the steward vacated his seat, doubling over with papers falling loose to the ground around him. The Prince affected not to notice, taking the high seat in a single smooth gesture.

"So," the prince said, "this is what passes for a Lords' Council, on this side of the sea."

The nobles retook their seats, with nervous glances for one another and a tenuous silence otherwise.

"Your M-M-Majesty," the steward began, his eyes still downcast beside the rostrum. "We had heard testimony of a r-r-rather shocking nature, before—"

"Who is this wretch who dares speak to his prince unbidden? I will hear no more of your bleating."

"B-b-but your M-M-Majesty—"

"Aegis-Guard Fiorain, if this man speaks again in my presence, kill him."

One of the purple-garbed guardsmen stepped forward, interposing himself between the steward and the prince, even as the steward threatened to choke on his own tongue. "Yes, Your Majesty."

The Prince raised his eyes to sweep across the chamber, passing over her as if she were not standing at the petitioner's mark. "I am not here to listen to your nonsense, nobles of New Sarresant." He put venom into the last words. "I am here to command. I am here because once, long ago, your ancestors did service to the glory of Sarresant, glory you seem to have forgotten."

His speech continued, but she didn't listen. Inwardly she despaired. Perhaps coming to this council was folly. Even without the damned fool of a prince choosing this moment to extoll the nobility on the virtues of their birthrights, she wouldn't have convinced them to do more than arrest her, at best. And she knew better than to tempt Louis-Sallet de l'Arraignon. That would earn her no better than a death sentence, and a fight to escape his binder guards when she refused to lie down and accept fate meted out by the hands of her betters. A bitter thought. Wasn't that at the heart of this struggle, in the end? But no. Reyne d'Agarre had murder in his heart. And time was running short, if she was to stop him from the violence for which she knew he yearned.

In a heartbeat, her instincts snapped her out of her reverie.

Movement. She'd seen movement, a blur at the edge of her vision.

The chamber slowed as Zi bestowed his gift, and a *Body* tether slid into place. She cast a searching look about the chamber. There. One of the soldiers, clad head to toe in polished steel plate, was moving toward the prince from behind. Too fast to be unaided. Either he was a *Body* fullbinder or he had some other gift at his disposal.

Two more of the soldiers began to move, the ones to the left and right of the first, all three stationed along the far wall of the chamber behind the rostrum where the prince made his speech.

Red, came the thought from Zi as she began her sprint toward them.

Moments flickered past. She'd covered half the distance before anyone in the chamber reacted, but react they did. Drawn-out screams or cries of alarm from most, slowed down but still audible, with fingers raised to point where she'd been moments before. Only the two purple-garbed guardsmen moved toward her, each one speeding up to double the speed of a normal man the moment they noticed her approach. Still half what she could bring to bear. It wouldn't be enough. Her movement had drawn the room's attention away from the three steel-clad soldiers surging toward the prince from behind. They were mere steps away from Louis-Sallet's unarmored back.

She needed more. In mid-stride she called upon *lakiri'in*, a gift too new to be triggered by reflex. She hadn't used it yet, and certainly not in conjunction with *Body* and Zi's *Red.* With the boon of all three at once, she *flew.* Leaping up to the rail surrounding the front of the rostrum, she sprang into the air, sailing over the purple guards, who now seemed to be moving as if mired in a deep bog. She landed on her feet between the prince and his first assailant, lashing out with a *Body*-enhanced kick that sent the soldier sprawling back. No time to watch him fall. She spun and went after the soldier to her left, delivering an equally powerful blow that dented the steel of his breastplate, pushing the man off balance. Good enough. Another pivot to the last man.

Draining, came the thought from Zi. *Black. He's taking it.*

The world sped up as one of her boons left her in a sudden shock. Zi's *Red* was gone.

Even so, she crashed into the final soldier, pushing him away with a two-handed shove. But not before the long knife he carried had been buried in the Crown-Prince's back.

She stared, eyes wide with horror, as the screams from the room hit her in a crash. The remainder of the steel-clad guardsmen who had ringed the chamber began to move. And blood spilled to the floor as the prince fell sideways from his high seat.

The third soldier, now lying on his back a few paces away from the prince, reached up to raise the visor of his full-helm, a twisted look of pleasure on his face. A look she'd seen before. Reyne d'Agarre. He met her eyes, and smiled.

She screamed in a fury and flew toward him.

Only, she crashed into a swirling ghostly barrier that had sprung up around her on all sides. *Shelter.* One of the purple guards came into her view, hands raised as he worked the shield.

D'Agarre scrambled to his feet and called out, "Assassin! Seize her!"

"Zi, I need you!" she cried.

A black haze stirred at the edge of her vision, and the *Shelter* barrier around her shimmered, growing thin as Zi worked.

Then the purple guardsman's barrier snapped back to strength. *Black,* came the thought from Zi again. Concentration writ on d'Agarre's face suggested the cause. How? Had he managed some way to subvert Zi's gift, to drain away his energy? She felt a rising surge of panic.

Snapping her eyes shut, she found the tiny cloud of *Death* beneath the prince. It had to be enough. She tethered it into the *Shelter* barrier, even as Zi's power wavered. The inky blackness enveloped the shield and tore a small opening. She dove for it, scraping the edge of the barrier as it closed behind her, throwing her to the ground with thunderous force. Springing to her feet, she rounded on the purple guards. Without Zi's gift, she'd not get another chance if they managed to enclose her again.

She drew on *Mind* and a half-dozen copies of herself sprang into place, each one moving of its own accord. Let them roll the dice and guess which one was right.

Before she could strike, the world sped up again. *Body* had run out. How? Was d'Agarre behind this, too? It had not been a deep supply, and the purple guards had tapped it as well, but it should have held longer than this. Still, she had *lakiri'in*. And the purple guards had nothing now.

All seven Sarines ran toward the purple guard who had held the shield around her, and another shield sprang into place around one of them. He guessed wrong. A split second later she landed a full-force punch in the middle of his nose, bone-searing pain spreading through her hand. Without *Body* she was just a slender girl without training for fisticuffs. But bolstered by the momentum of her speed, it was enough to lay him out flat, his tabard ripping as he crashed backward into the railing.

One problem solved. She whirled about and felt her heart sink. D'Agarre and the other two soldiers who had assaulted the prince were making their way toward the exit. Almost she sprang to pursue, and then she saw what was happening in the rest of the chamber.

Screams, and not on her account. The remainder of the steel-clad soldiers had moved from where they stood on the wall, but not to apprehend her, as she'd assumed. Instead they were laying into the nobles with their long halberds, cutting down their fashionable dress like wheat at a harvest. D'Agarre had not just infiltrated and turned some few of the council soldiers—he had subverted them all to his cause. The other purple guard had already abandoned his fight with her, running into the main hall to defend the nobles. And d'Agarre was fleeing the chamber.

Another day, Zi thought to her.

Frustration wrenched her gut. Gods damn it. She had to defend them. Spoiled, overindulgent, entitled sots they might be, but they were dying, and Donatien was among them. Without her they had no chance against men in full plate.

Gritting her teeth, she channeled *mareh'et*'s gift.

Justice for d'Agarre would have to wait.

ELSEWHERE

INTERLUDE

JIAOSHEN

Great and Noble House of the Crane
Shinsuke Province, the Jun Empire

He took his afternoon tea on the grass beneath the cherry blossoms. It had been an affectation in his youth, one that had grown on him as his skin pruned with age. The young Jiaoshen had taken great pains to maintain appearances. The Great and Noble House of the Crane expected no less from her favorite son. Once, it had been a house to fear, not so long ago. Once, these halls were alive with children's laughter, sweet and pure.

Now an old man sipped tea beneath a canopy of late-blooming sakura trees.

The servants kept to the daily rituals, which they performed with the excellence of long practice. When the sun had passed its zenith just so, they approached from the appointed door at the southwest of the courtyard. Thin slippers barely rustled the ground as they carried the trays, swift footsteps carrying them in imitation of the *aryu*, an homage to the wind spirits. It was to wind and water the Great and Noble House of the Crane owed its first allegiance. The tea ceremony was perhaps the purest expression of that loyalty, a fact of which he reminded himself often. The blade-dance was an ugly thing in comparison. But such was his gift; he had no aptitude for tea service.

Beside him on the grass lay his implement, a manacle in the shape of a blade, never farther than arm's length since the day he'd taken it up. Folded steel, honed to an edge that was his duty to maintain. It was the masterwork of another man, the fulfillment of another calling. It fell to the Great and Noble House of the Crab to smith the weapons, for their allegiance was to earth and stone. His blade had cost his house dearly, a price paid in more than gold and gemstones. But he had not been the one who sacrificed for the sake of trade. It fell to lower souls to trade their gifts away for glories. Unthinkable, for a blade-dancer to traffic in such fare.

No, the price he paid was in a calling left unfulfilled. Smiths could create masterwork blades. Tea service could be sipped and enjoyed. Those gifted at masonry or carpentry could relax beneath the fruits of their labors, solid roofs and sturdy walls around them. Gifted mathematicians could see truths, and philosophers, too, in their way. All around him, men and women grew ripe with age, their talents put to good use. They created; they built; they left a legacy of finished works adored by all.

Jiaoshen waited.

He waited for a challenge, for an enemy. He waited for someone foolish enough to test the mettle of the Crane in open combat. In his youth, he thought it the honor of all honors to be adopted into this bloodline. It could be said well and truly that no house in all of the Everlasting Empire boasted a finer tradition of swordsmen than the Great and Noble House of the Crane. Now, seasoned with age, he had come to see that ruin came in many forms, not always borne on the edge of a sword. Tragedy could strike, an earthquake, or the great tsunami that showed the disfavor of the *koryu*, the water spirits. An ill-advised trade, a caravan taken by bandits as it lumbered across the steppes. Seeds could fail to take root; crops could wither. Blight. Plague.

And pride.

Pride above all. Pride in the glory of the honored tradition of his house. Pride that turned away generations of hopefuls, come to him to learn at his hand. Pride that scoffed to teach the unworthy, that shunned the thought of adopting fresh blood into a legacy that traced its line unbroken to the last God-Emperor himself. Pride that grew old, content with a reputation that made clear: Seeking a place with the Cranes was naught but wasted effort. Pride that convinced itself the waning reputation of the Cranes was a woeful mistake, that one day a worthy student would come and shine bright the glories of his house once more.

The smiths had their steel. The carpenters had their woodwork. The traders had their fortunes. And Jiaoshen had his pride.

The servants finished the tea ceremony, and he sat contemplating. He remained there under the cherry blossoms until evening fell. As the sun hid beyond the horizon, more servants rushed to light the paper lanterns that decorated the courtyard. Still he sat, cross-legged on the grass beside his sword.

The servants had relit the lanterns twice by the time the stranger entered and sat across from him.

The stranger was dressed all in white to signify he was *hanarun*, unclaimed by a bloodline. His head was covered by a hood and a mask, like one of the *jinata*, though it would have been a queer tactic for one of their assassins to approach him so boldly, and in white instead of their traditional black. The man wore white gloves, and laid a sheathed blade in a white scabbard beside him on the grass before he sat.

Jiaoshen met his eyes. Young eyes, ringed by smooth skin visible above his mask.

"Honored master," the voice said in accented tones, though the newcomer spoke the Jun tongue. "I have come seeking your skill with the blade."

Almost Jiaoshen flew into a rage and dismissed this upstart from his presence. He dared to beseech the Great and Noble House of the Crane without bothering to learn the proper forms for the *hanarun*'s request? A long, indrawn breath kept him centered. Let this young fool speak what he will. Jiaoshen would respond in proper form.

"Bloodless," he intoned, voice rasped from the hours he had spent in silence. "Crane has need. Would you make an offering?"

The newcomer bowed his head. A gesture of refusal?

"No, honored master. I do not stand before you as *hanarun*."

"You wear white," Jiaoshen said, breaking the ritual exchange.

"Once, this was worn to signify a man's intent to take up the God-Emperor's path."

He nearly laughed. Perhaps the claim was true; Jiaoshen was no philosopher, to remember ancient writings and whispered memories. Instead, he asked, "This is your intent then? You seek to become a God?"

The man nodded gravely. Was he serious?

He did laugh at that. "Well then, young man, you must tell me. How can the Great and Noble House of the Crane assist you on your divine path?"

"As I said, I have come seeking your skill with the blade."

It took a moment for Jiaoshen to realize his meaning. Blasphemy.

He snatched his scabbard and rose to his feet in a smooth motion, teeth grinding in a snarl.

The young man looked up at him, still cross-legged on the grass.

"You are an old man," the newcomer observed in even tones. "You could surrender willingly."

"Make your challenge," he spat, voice dripping with cold venom.

The stranger sighed, reaching for his scabbard as he stood.

"Very well." The stranger drew steel, and Jiaoshen copied the motion fluidly, like water from a cloud. "Jiaoshen of the Great and Noble House of the Crane, I challenge you to the *surakai*, my gifts wagered against yours."

Jiaoshen had never heard of the *surakai* but he took the boy's meaning clearly enough. This was forbidden. He knew deep in his bones. This was wrong.

"I accept."

Nodding as if it were a foregone conclusion, the stranger paused to remove the white glove from his left hand. Jiaoshen stifled a gasp as the stranger revealed a hand twisted and black, covered in sores, with protruding veins of blue and purple.

"What vileness is this?" he demanded, a touch of fear creeping into his voice.

"Not all gifts are won easily, honored master," the stranger said softly.

Locking eyes, he felt fear settle in, deep into his old bones. What had he done?

"Begin," the stranger said, setting his guard. By the ancient rites of the duel, first attack went to the man who had been challenged.

Swallowing hard, Jiaoshen let his long years of practice take over. He snapped into the One Thousand Fans, a two-handed form that rained high cuts from the left and the right.

His opponent adopted the Steps of the Wind, considered the perfect complement. Together, the blade-dancers executed the opening stanza in unison, the prearranged steps playing out precisely as they should. Neither man flinched or made a mistake, and so the steel rang out its song, a rhythm of cuts and parries that Jiaoshen had practiced ten thousand times before. The blade-dance was art refined to science. The slightest misstep would result in a killing blow, on either side. Every move and countermove had been prescribed, practiced, and tested. The end result a beautiful harmony that filled the courtyard now, blade against blade, steel against steel.

The passage ended, and Jiaoshen bowed in spite of himself. He felt tears streak down his face at the beauty of the dance.

"You would have been a worthy apprentice," he said softly.

"You would have been a worthy teacher, honored master."

The stranger's turn to begin the next stanza. The man in white raised his blade in his right hand, and brought the twisted mockery of his left up level with the hilt. This was no form he recognized.

The left hand pulsed then, a sickly purple glow.

Jiaoshen felt his lungs constrict, and recognized sorcery for what it was before he died.

INTERLUDE

LLANARA

Among the Tents
Ranasi Village

Thundercracks sounded through the tents, smoke from the warriors' muskets billowing toward her in a mimicry of an early morning fog. The ash and powder stung her skin, burned when she inhaled it into her lungs. A delicate pain, like the screams carried on the wind, from across the village. She smiled, listening to the sounds of her men charging forward. Her warriors.

Her fingers shook from the memory of her kills, and she slowed her pace, walking between the tents, savoring the sights and smells of the victory around her.

A red haze flared at the edge of her vision.

Unbidden, her senses quickened into a semblance of a viper. Another victim, hiding among the tents. Vekis coiled around her forearm, though she hardly needed to glance at him to know his scales would be flushed reds and pinks, the soft shades of fear rather than the deeper crimson of anger and hate. So, one of the Ranasi had thought to hide, perhaps to slip away after she and the rest of her tribe were distracted by celebration of their victory. A foolish idea, born of cowardice.

She tried the entrance of each tent along her path, looking inside to find the straggler. Empty, each one, until she pulled a flap back to be greeted by incense smoke, and an old man seated cross-legged beside his fire.

"You are the vessel for the madness of the spirits," the old man said as she entered. He was dressed in the full regalia of a shaman, covered head to toe in paint and furs. Had he been donning the ritual garb since their attack started? What a fool.

He bowed his head. "Kill me, and be done with it."

Her eyes narrowed, though she said nothing. Always the men needed to believe themselves in control. As if he had the power to give her permission. As if she required his acquiescence.

After he was dead, she left his tent, quivering from the kill. Her legs shook, the raw pain of exertion in the name of pleasure. Her *kaas* drank the red, pooled deep until it shifted to black, sharing it with her as their victim died. A mind-shattering sensation, no duller for having spent the morning invoking it again and again.

"Llanara," a man spoke from behind. "The village is clear."

She welcomed Venari'Anor with a gesture. A warrior now, where before he had been Valak'Anor, among the foremost hunters and traders of the tribe. He had not dared style himself *Vas'Khan*. That title—warleader—belonged to her, even if tribal custom did not allow her to take it in the open. When Arak'Jur returned she would offer it to him, and no one else. Only the guardian had gifts deserving of a place at her side.

Vekis's scales flared green, and Venari'Anor's eyes closed as he drew in a sharp breath, letting it out slow. She felt a tinge of jealousy as her *kaas* shared the pleasure of their kill. The feeling faded as quick as it had come, replaced by arousal, seeing him touched by her power.

"You see, honored brother," she said, laying a hand on his forearm, "obedience to the will of the spirits is its own reward."

He reached for her, and she allowed it. Arak'Jur may have first rights to her, but he was far away, and fighting kindled fire in her blood. A pale echo of the sensation bestowed by Vekis's gift, but her body hungered for it all the same.

He took her there in the open, on the paths between the tents.

When he finished, she rose to stand, adjusting her skirts into place.

"Has there been sign of Ilek'Inari?" she asked.

"No, spirit-blessed," Venari'Anor said, still kneeling in the dirt, his long rifle dropped beside them. "He was with us when we crossed the river, but none of the warriors have seen him since the attack began."

She frowned. "He could not have fallen. The Ranasi guardian is dead, and Arak'Doren had no apprentice. No common warrior could kill a guardian, even an *Ilek* training to become one."

Venari'Anor nodded, but said nothing.

She waved him away. "See to the rest of our people. If you have word of Ilek'Inari, send it to me at once."

He rose to his feet and went.

Troubling. The Sinari would take it amiss if a guardian had fallen, even if Ilek'Inari was merely an apprentice. Could Arak'Doren have trained another guardian in secret, before his death? Perhaps the Ranasi shaman had seen her intent and given warning? But no, if that were so, their attack on the Ranasi could not have gone so well.

It had happened exactly as it was written in her Codex. Vekis had whispered its meaning to her, every step, from Ka'Ana'Tyat to their glorious entrance into the Ranasi village. He had promised her the Ranasi would greet them as friends, and be unprepared for their attack. He had promised her the Sinari people would accept her leadership once Ka'Vos was gone. He had even promised that the *mareh'et* would aid her in killing Arak'Doren, then lie down and let her kill it when the deed was done. It was enough to believe what her people said: She was truly spirit-blessed. What was Vekis but a spirit given form, known only to her and the chosen few to whom she allowed him to appear? Her companion had knowledge of things-to-come, more sure and steady than any shaman. And armed with that knowledge, her people would rise.

"Can you see what has become of Ilek'Inari?" she asked her companion. "Has he fallen?"

I cannot see one man, unless he is of great import. Ilek'Inari is irrelevant.

"Without a guardian, my people will grow concerned."

Irrelevant.

She nodded, trusting Vekis's wisdom. If it came to it, she would weigh her gifts against any guardian's. Her people were safe. If they worried over not having a guardian to protect them from the wilds, perhaps it was only a vestige of the past, one more thing to be cast aside as they tread a new path.

Mmm.

Another flush of deep red, and black. More kills nearby. Odd. Venari'Anor had reported the village clear.

Shouts, then the cracks of musket fire. The sounds of fighting, not merely cleaning up some last few Ranasi villagers. She rushed toward it. A pack of hunters returning to the village, perhaps. Yet another sign of the spirits' favor, if her people had come upon the Ranasi without their full complement of men.

She rounded a pair of large tents at the edge of the tribal meeting ground and had barely a moment's warning before throwing herself into the dirt. The poles and canvas of an entire tent sailed overhead, a pair of warriors flying with it to crash in a heap in the field behind her. She choked on dust, recovering her breath, then looked up and saw the source. Not hunters returning to the village. Women. Baskets of fruits and seeds had been discarded beside them as the rest of their number cowered behind one, standing in the center of the space. An old matron, eyes misted gray, facing down a dozen Sinari warriors approaching her from all sides.

"Cowards!" the woman cried, waving her hands as a torrent of wind whipped toward one of the Sinari warriors, cutting him down where he stood. "Spirit-cursed! You dare to strike us after offering blood-oath!"

The rest of the warriors edged back, hiding behind Ranasi tents, ramming powder and musket balls to reload their weapons.

"Red," she whispered to Vekis as she crawled to her knees. "Now."

No need.

"What?" she hissed.

We have enough Black to drain her.

She watched as Vekis's scales darkened, and the matron rounded on the warriors, her hands raised again.

"Vekis—?"

It is done.

This time, no rush of wind blasted through the tents. The look of horror on the old woman's face was proof enough of whatever Vekis had done. And her warriors took its meaning as motivation to strike, stepping out from behind their cover, muskets leveled to fire.

Her eyes rolled back as Vekis shared the pleasure of each kill, the women's screams punctuating each thundercrack of the guns. The men, too, shared in it, as Vekis's scales flushed green. Confirmation that this was the will of the spirits. This was the path the Sinari were meant to tread.

She lay in the dirt after it had finished, basking in the afterglow.

"What was that?" she whispered to her companion. "What did you do to stop her?"

Black.

"Black," she murmured to herself. A new gift. "It takes away the magic of others?"

Silence.

"Vekis, I would know more. You harvest it from killing our enemies?"

More silence. A maddening trait. It meant she was close, so close to understanding.

She had come to know the *kaas* were secretive creatures, but she had become adept at divining their mysteries. Already she'd learned more than Reyne d'Agarre had ever known of their nature. Not Reyne d'Agarre's fault, merely a limitation of his kind. He was a fair-skin, where she had the wisdom of the spirits to aid her in understanding, the inborn gift of every Sinari woman. Intuition. Without it, Reyne d'Agarre could grasp only the smallest measure of the spirits' grand plan. He had been a fool to give her this gift, but it had been inevitable. It was the spirits' will that she take up this charge.

In the moment, she had a vision, extending beyond their war on the Ranasi. She would lead, not only the Sinari, but all the tribes who would follow the call of the spirits and take up arms for war. A grand chieftain, the likes of which there had never been, not in the most ancient stories.

"Vekis, with the Ranasi destroyed, we will reach out to the other tribes, those who would not turn their back on the spirits' call."

Yes. The Olessi, and the Vhurasi. And more. Allies will be provided, in furtherance of your cause.

"Allies?" This was new.

A great army, come for bloodshed, an aid to greatness on ascension's path.

She weighed Vekis's words in her mind. He spoke in riddles, but she could tease them apart, piece together the whole from the fragments of each part.

"The fair-skins," she said. "They sprout from the earth like weeds behind their barrier. Our path leads there. The spirits mean for us to attack the fair-skins' city."

Silence.

She smiled.

INTERLUDE

THE NAMELESS

Library
Gods' Seat

A stack of dusted tomes gave off a rank odor beside him as he worked. The powers that maintained this place took care to ensure he had the small comforts—the musty rot of old leather, the frayed edges of vellum and papyri, the ribbed spines of the same editions he had studied as a boy, in the great libraries of his people, long dead these many centuries. Try as he might to clean the dust or care for the scrolls as he unwound them, always he found this chamber and its tomes precisely as they had been when he first ascended, when he first claimed the mantle of the champion of Balance. Only a new awakening brought change, and the rare new tomes produced while they waited for the moment of ascension; these were the sweetest delicacy offered by this life of almost-Godhood. The best and brightest minds of each age, compiled for his pleasure, adjoined to the classics in this, the greatest library the world had ever known.

Today he perused the work of a modern essayist, a pamphleteer working in the native tongue of the people of Sarresant. *Treatise on the Virtues*, by one Jaquin Fantiere. Delightful reasoning, an echo of some of the Jukari masters, who during his boyhood had made their arguments against the tyranny of the Amaros Empire. Did it reveal some deeper truth, when philosophers of disparate era and circumstance came to identical conclusions? Was there some essential human ideal in cleaving to freedom of thought, freedom of opportunity, and all the rest of Fantiere's creed?

He smiled, relishing a particularly succulent argument on a point of epistemology, calling into question the knowability of truth when facts corresponded with beliefs by accidental means. Fantiere intended it as satire: His readers were never meant to take it at face value when he pointed out that the nobles were best suited to rule despite basing the foundations of their lordship on faulty assumptions of inherent superiority. But there was sound logic underlying the philosopher's mocking tone, and Axerian appreciated it even as he turned the irony on its head.

The people of this cycle named him their enemy. The Nameless. Amusing to see how close they could come to the truth and still fall so very short of understanding. He was no more the enemy of the Gods than he was a God himself. Sixteen cycles ago he'd been an ordinary man, the same as his protégés among the *kaas*-mages tied to him through the book they called their Codex. Sixteen times now he'd watched and nurtured would-be champions as they drew near ascension, the very path he'd followed as a Jukari philosopher, uncounted years before. But where his path had ended with triumph—the cleansing of the Regnant's vile influence, the forging of a world of sunlight, joy, and knowledge—the ascendants of this age would end their path on the edge of his curved *shenai* blades, as their fellows had done in the sixteen ages prior to this one. Such was the way of things now. A better way, for all it stung to pay the price of wisdom. The soul of the world could not be left in the hands of the unproven.

He set the *Treatise* down beside a stack of holy books, thumbing open his copy of the Codex to a passage he had written that morning. Clearer perhaps if he borrowed from Fantiere. A better idiom, more likely to be interpreted correctly by his intended audience. He dipped his quill in the inkpot, mulling over the words as he reached within for the coursing blue energy that was the source of the Codex's link with its brothers and sisters, the relics he had handed down the last time the Three had walked the earth.

Mmm, Xeraxet sounded in his mind. *More violence?*

"It seems appropriate, considering," he said, licking the edge of the quill even as the coils of blue energy fought to escape his grasp. A desperate struggle to control the Goddess's power, but a familiar one. No need for outward sign when the conclusion was inevitable.

Xeraxet appeared on the edge of the table, his scales a flickering shade of purple and black. Onyx eyes stared their disapproval, and he laughed. "Soon, my friend. These will be the last missives for some time. A great many threads to stitch together, before the end."

His *kaas* said nothing further, only laid its head back down and watched him write. The words came out in a flowing sequence, verse punctuated by the power of the Veil, sealing his every line into the pages to see them mirrored and reread by the *kaas* of every would-be ascendant of Balance in the world.

Satisfied, he blew the ink dry and sat back, rereading his work.

It was done.

Nerves blossomed in his stomach. He'd put this off long enough. The Codex would keep, and if centuries of life were enough to let him recognize when he dallied to avoid an unpleasant task, well, he had not found the secret to eliminating such delays altogether.

Is it time?

His eyes went back to the book, lying open on the desk. Perhaps another line...

"No," he said, as much to Xeraxet as to himself. "No," he repeated, standing. "I would see her first."

Xeraxet glowered, frustration seething through his coal-black scales.

As you wish.

He stared up at the Goddess, frozen in her crystal prison.

For a moment he pictured the chamber as it had been at the moment of his ascension. Empty, save for a surging mass of energy at its heart. She had been there, watching, beckoning him forward to complete the seal, to bind himself as her champion of Balance. It had been his idea, the betrayal, when he and Paendurion and Ad-Shi turned their gifts on her at the moment of their victory. No sooner had the last of the Regnant's champions fallen than he had tapped into the raw energy of the Seat of the Gods, using it to bind the Goddess while his companions took their first taste of her power.

It had worked. He'd half-expected it not to. But they'd frozen her in her prison, siphoning away the Goddess's power to keep them alive between awakenings. The Gods' Seat had never been more than a temporary refuge, a place where her champions would rest between their ascensions and the moment of conflict with the ancient enemy. Now it was home for him, Paendurion, and Ad-Shi. Who better to stand against the Regnant, to ensure the world never again fell under his shadow? The Three had proved themselves once. With the Veil's power to sustain them, to aid them in snuffing out their challengers among the would-be ascendants of every age, they could ensure the world they'd built would endure, free of the Regnant's corruption. For sixteen cycles now his plan had worked. And the Veil herself was the price.

He gazed up at her, encased in crystal, a vision of perfection. The flowing ribbons around her made it seem as though she moved, the light casting twisting shadows as it streamed through the edges of her prison. How much more did she know? How much more did they need from her, even now after sixteen cycles of victory? Especially now.

"What would you tell us, if you could?" he asked. "What secrets have we missed?"

Only silence in response. That serene look, eyes closed as the ribbons seemed to swirl around her.

Why do you speak to her still?

He smiled. "Perhaps one day she will answer."

Not likely.

"One should never presume the past is a predictor of the possible."

Quoting your own verse?

"Who will remember it otherwise?"

More silence. He smiled again.

Silence suited his mood, else he'd not have come here. A sad thought, that his library full of wisdom went unheeded in this age. The fools of this age had no idea the true nature of the enemy. And now, if he'd interpreted events aright, the Regnant's champions had managed to pierce the Divide, had come to the Vordu lands, where the would-be ascendants of Order, Balance, and Wild drew nearer the moment of reckoning. The Regnant's ascendants had never managed to pass through before, but he could think of no better explanation. A greater threat than any they had faced in sixteen cycles of Godhood. Enough to send a trickle of fear through his veins as he stared, looking up at the Goddess in her prison.

Again he studied her, tracing the smooth curve of her skin. She had fought the enemy for countless lifetimes, long before he, Paendurion, and Ad-Shi tasted the first breath of their mortal lives. She had fought, and lost. The world during the time of the Amaros, the Jukari, and the Vordu had been a shadow of the lush beauty it held now, even with the ravages of destruction visited upon it by the Three.

Yet always, despite it all, she was venerated.

The Veil. It was as if some part of her rested in the deepest thoughts of every man and woman. Always they found a place for her in their myths and legends. Always they remembered the Goddess.

If he failed, would the world remember him?

He thought not. For a cycle or two perhaps, if the conflicts over the Gods' Seat were contained. If by some measure Ad-Shi and Paendurion could find victory without him. If they failed altogether and the Regnant was allowed to reclaim the Seat, there was little enough hope for any of their memories. Perhaps even the Veil would fade then, in time.

"You mean to go through with this, don't you?"

Ad-Shi's voice rang through the chamber despite her small stature, and the softness of her words.

He turned to the entryway, meeting her eyes. Deep pools of brown, eyes that could measure a man in a moment. He didn't bother to smile; she would see through it. They understood each other, Ad-Shi and he.

"I do, sister," he said. "Our enemy grows bold. We must be equally bold to match him."

She raised a hand, forestalling his words as she swept into the chamber. "I have heard these words. Know that I disapprove."

"And Paendurion? Is our champion of Order still smashing his furniture?"

It might have earned him a smile under better circumstances. Instead she held her expression, cool and even. "You have ever walked close to the edge, but this course is folly, even for you."

"Nevertheless, I am decided."

She came to a stop a few paces away, ignoring the crystal at the center of the chamber. "Axerian, do you mean to fail?"

"No, Ad-Shi, I do not mean to fail."

"What am I to do, if you fall short?"

His heart softened. Few could understand the burden they carried. More than once Ad-Shi had turned to him for comfort, and he to her.

"There is still a chance. Before an ascendant completes the seal, before the path is closed to—"

"I know this already. You ask me to dance along the edge of a knife."

He bowed his head. "Yes. It is a narrow thing."

A moment of silence stretched between them. Ad-Shi focused on him, avoiding looking toward the crystal humming at the center of the room.

"Please," she said, pain showing in her eyes.

"Ad-Shi, I must do this."

She held his gaze, then spun and walked away.

"Ad-Shi," he called after her. "Ad-Shi, please."

He took a step toward her, but she made no move to stop.

He let her go.

Tears welled as he turned back to the crystal.

Now is it time?

He took a deep breath, keeping his eyes fixed on the Goddess's face as he spoke. "Yes, my friend. It is time."

You understand once I exhaust my reserves, you must ascend once more to return here.

"Yes. I understand."

Very well.

He gave a last look, sadness touching him as he traced the lines of the ribbons flowing around the Goddess's frozen form. She remained still, exactly as she'd been when he bound her so many years before.

"Forgive me," he whispered to her as his *kaas* began.

A thousand colors flashed before his eyes. His body pulsed with energy, and time distorted, sped to a crawl. Hours passed. Minutes. He heard a scream, dwindling to nothing on a distant horizon, and felt the walls around him twist away. A shroud of darkness enveloped him, choking away his senses in a violent spasm. He was a wisp of wind, a drop in the ocean, a sheath of skin pierced by a needle under the raking claws of a desert sun. He was a God, and then no longer. A gift rescinded. A destiny refused.

He was a man, like any other, standing on the streets of the Market district.

He released his breath.

Flakes of snow settled atop his arms and shoulders, a gentle caress welcoming him home.

PART 4: WINTER

SEASON OF THE VEIL

46

ERRIS

Foudroyant, *Main Deck*
Harbor District, New Sarresant

A wall of *Shelter* sprang up below the crow's nest, five spans above her head. Puffs of mist leaked out as a volley of pistol and carbine shot struck against the shield, dissipated into harmless vapor. Gods damn it. It'd been too much to hope *Life* was the extent of this bastard's talents.

"Cowards!" he cried from above. "Traitors!"

Raising her pistol, Erris braced herself against the mizzenmast. This piece of cowshit had killed four of her men before they sighted him, hiding like a coward amid the *Foudroyant*'s rigging. He was a bloody good shot, though, she'd give him that much.

"The Nameless will have you all," the man cried. "Woe to those who walk the traitors' path. Woe to those who abandon faith."

Any moment now. She could have torn his shield apart with *Death*, but she had no desire to climb up there and settle it hand-to-hand. She kept her pistol arm steady.

"Curse the lot of you for fools. Curse you with the wrath of the holy Veil, for hers is vengeance. Vengeance for the betrayed."

In an eyeblink the *Shelter* vanished, and the long barrel of a sighted rifle cleared the edge of the crow's nest. He was quick; he'd need only a moment to fire before he raised the shield again.

She was faster.

Three shots rang out, sparks lighting against the sails as they whipped in the wind. His rifle clattered over the edge of his perch, falling to the deck below. A man-shaped silhouette slumped over, and no *Shelter* sprang up again. Cheers went up from the dock, and she stood to acknowledge them, then vaulted the wood railing around the ship's masts and made her way back to the gangplank to disembark the ship.

"Fine shooting, sir," Aide-Lieutenant Sadrelle said as she stepped back into place among the officers of the 1st Division.

"Same to you men," she said with a nod to acknowledge the rest of her command staff. The *Shelter*-binder-turned-sniper had been patient in the extreme, hiding in the rigging, waiting until he saw the stripes and stars of officers' insignia before he started shooting. "How is Lance-Captain Pourrain? Is he—?"

Sadrelle met her eyes with a grim look and shook his head.

"Bloody coward," she said.

Nods of assent among her aides as a courier approached from the northern Harbor, where sounds of fighting still rang in the distance.

"Word from Brigade-Colonel Savasse, sir," the courier said. "The crew of Rear-Admiral Dubois's fleet is subdued and surrendering. He asks whether he should devote his strength to keeping them under guard, or to bolster Brigade-Colonel Vassail's lines in the northern Harbor."

"Neither," she said. "Have Savasse make for Brigade-Colonel Chellac's position with the Sixteenth, at the boundary of the Harbor district. Deliver the prisoners into Chellac's keeping, then move the rest of his brigade to reinforce Vassail from the west."

"Yes, sir," the courier said.

"Hold here," she said to the rest of her officers. Damn but this would be easier if she had brought Jiri into the city to carry her forward while she worked.

She tethered *Need*, reaching out for Lance-Lieutenant Acherre.

"—break them, damn it. We can push—" Brigade-Colonel Vassail cut herself off, turning toward Acherre. "Chevalier-General, sir. What orders?"

"Savasse's Ninth Brigade will be coming to reinforce your line within the quarter hour. Plan accordingly, Colonel."

"Sir, yes, sir. These sailors are hardly organized. We'll break them, sir."

"Aim to take prisoners, Vassail. These are men loyal to Sarresant."

"Yes, sir," Vassail said, offering a salute. She returned it, then dropped the *Need* binding, her senses shifting back to familiar skin.

"Any surprises, sir?" one of her captains asked.

"Nothing new," she said as a line of captured sailors walked past, hands folded atop their heads. "Vassail expects the battle decided soon."

Gods send it was true, with as few casualties as they could manage. To think of Sarresant sailors as the enemy—it roiled her gut. At least her brigades had taken to the *Need* bindings like trout to a stream. Marquand's philosophical objections notwithstanding, the remainder of her vessels had seen the power offered by *Need* and accepted it as another duty owed the army. So now their movements were coordinated as if she'd planned out every countermaneuver, every possible contingency. She could imagine the few admirals who still held out resistance despairing at the sight of it, seeing her reserves flow and surge with every shift of the line. A beautiful dance, and this was only the start. The rest of the army would follow suit as soon as she could put *Need* vessels in place. Gods grant her enough time to get them ready before the Gand invasion arrived, and perhaps a few winter squalls to delay the Gandsmen at sea while they were at it.

"Hold again," she said, reaching for *Need*, and her connection to Marie d'Oreste.

"Ah, Chevalier-General," Voren said, seated across from her around the wide table at the center of the room. "Just in time."

A man standing at the other end of the room unbuttoned his bright red coat, a long knife coated with blood resting on the table in front of him. He looked up and met Marie's eyes as his fellows found their seats to his left and right.

"So, Voren, this is your secret," the man said, nodding toward Marie.

"No secret, Master d'Agarre," Voren replied. "Call it a weapon now. One of the most effective in service to our cause."

The man Voren had called d'Agarre smiled, taking his seat and gesturing toward his knife. "Can it compare to the blade that took the life of our Crown-Prince?"

Voren kept his eyes steady, focused on d'Agarre. "You did the deed yourself then?"

"It's done, General. The Lords' Council is broken, and my people are taking the streets. The city will be ours in a matter of days."

Voren nodded, wearing a grim look. "As bloodless as we can manage."

"What word from the army?" d'Agarre asked.

"The chevalier-general was about to make a report I expect. General, have you met with the High Admiral?"

"Not yet, sir. On my way to the tavern where he's being held now." She eyed the far end of the table. Strange to be making reports to civilians. "The rest of my division has secured the Harbor. Some last fighting with the sailors in the north of the district, near the border with the Riverways. I expect the matter to be decided within the hour."

"So easily?" D'Agarre laughed. "You break the strength of the Sarresant Navy in an evening?"

"Best hope they are not broken, Master d'Agarre," she said. "We'll need those ships when the Gandsmen arrive."

"Peace, Chevalier-General," Voren said. "Keep checking in with us on the hour if you please. Thank the Gods for your *Need* bindings. Yours is the only quadrant of the city with clear reports thus far."

She raised an eyebrow. "Sir, is the rest of the city—?"

"Chaotic, d'Arrent. To be expected, considering. From the sound of it Vicomte-General Dulliers is encountering opposition from the Duc's loyalists at Rasailles, but we have little more than that for now."

"Yes, sir," she said, sparing a long look toward the end of the table, where d'Agarre sat behind his bloodstained blade. What sort of man was this, to whom Voren had tied their fortunes? Not a thing she'd considered before; politics was the concern of men and women with titles and lands, not trappers' daughters. Credit her binder's training, perhaps, for instilling in her a sense that this sphere—the forum for deciding *why* and not *how*—was no province of hers. Yet here she was.

She released *Need.*

The streets had bloomed with activity around her, soldiers, prisoners, quartermasters, couriers, men, and horses tracking up and down the waterfront, as if it were a high summer afternoon and not a night that carried the beginnings of the first winter storm.

"Welcome back, sir," Sadrelle said as her eyes regained focus. He'd done well these past months. Perhaps it was time to consider a promotion.

"The Crown-Prince is dead," she said.

Her words hung in the air, muting the din of activity around them. The rest of her aides and officers trailed a half step behind as the weight of her news settled around their shoulders. Credit their discipline that they made no comment as they made way toward the lights of the Tank & Twine.

Already the tavern hummed with activity. The onetime headquarters of the 2nd Corps, though Voren's flag had been moved in light of tonight's affairs. Yet having secured the southern Harbor, the logistics officers were already moving back in, resuming operations as if violent revolution were no more a setback than a snapped wagon axle, a hailstorm, or a bog. There was comfort in that, in a job well done trusted to men and women of competence. Not for the first time she wondered whether *Need* wouldn't have been better employed in service to the quartermasters.

The smells coming from the kitchen offered comforts of a different sort, warming the air with the scent of spices and simmering meats. Her people stepped behind her through the door, kicking snow from their boots and eyeing her for permission to place an order with the cooks. She gave it. This business was not like to be easy, or brief. Not bothering to remove her long coat, she asked after the prisoner and, receiving confirmation he was being held in Voren's former chambers, made her way upstairs.

"He's inside?" she asked the sentries posted to either side of the door.

"Yes, sir, General," the senior of the two men replied, sergeant's stripes on his sleeve.

"You boys are with Vassail's cavalry, yes?"

"Yes, sir," they replied together.

"How was the prisoner taken? Were either of you present?"

"I was there, sir," the sergeant said. "It was a binder, one of ours I mean. She broke through their line and captured the admiral with a blade to his throat, out from the middle of a company of his sailors. Damnedest thing I ever saw, beg your pardon, sir."

Bloody fool of a girl. Acherre had been ordered to keep herself out of the fighting. What if Erris had made a *Need* connection in the middle of Acherre's heroics? The girl thought with her saber instead of her head. Still, if she'd captured the High Admiral by herself, perhaps Acherre had earned herself a medal along with a tongue-lashing when this was over.

"How is our prisoner's disposition?" she asked. "I trust he's taken to our hospitality with the grace typical of the nobility?"

"Ah, yes, sir," the sergeant said. "I would say the typical amount of grace."

She clapped him on the shoulder. "Rest easy, men. And fine work today."

"Thank you, sir." They saluted and she returned the gesture, then rapped twice on the door for politeness' sake before pushing it open and making her entrance.

"Enter, by all means," the prisoner said, beckoning her inside. "It is almost time for tea after all."

"High Admiral Tuyard," she said, offering a slight bow.

The High Admiral was seated on one of Voren's cushioned chaises, reclining into the velvet with his feet resting on one of the armrests, looking more like a bored socialite at a salon than a captured flag officer of the Sarresant Navy. He was younger than she expected, not a day over fifty and likely somewhat less, with a full head of hair and a well-tailored uniform she expected saw more use at the aforementioned salons than it did on the decks of any warship.

"And whom do I have the honor of addressing?" the admiral said, eyeing the single star on her sleeves and collar. "Knowing how the governor hands out peerages, I expect you are the chevalier of the privy detail? Perhaps the marquis of a lumberyard?"

"I would think," she said quietly, closing the thick oak doors behind her, "that a defeated military commander would have better sense than to insult his victorious opponent."

"Quite right, of course, General," High Admiral Tuyard said. "You are to be commended on your noble victory. Tell me, what was the most difficult part? Was it the skulking in shadows beforehand or the actual moment when you knifed your fellow countrymen in the back?"

"No countryman of mine would have attempted to order this army to abandon its home soil," she shot back, her voice suddenly heated.

His eyes widened, then he laughed. "Louis-Sallet actually gave the order? Bloody fool of a prince."

She said nothing, merely stood, watching.

"Please, General, sit," the admiral said, gesturing to one of the couches. "I told him this would happen. I bloody told him. Well, perhaps not *this*." He gestured again, sweeping to encompass the whole of the Harbor. "But none of the docile compliance for which our Prince of the Blood was hoping."

She frowned. "I am here as a courtesy, High Admiral."

"You are here to persuade me to back your little coup. Or to begin the process of bribery in any case, whether you know it or no. Tell me, whose hand is pulling your strings, General? Is it the Duc-Governor? Has Cherrain turned his coat for good and all?"

"I am here at the behest of Marquis-General Voren, the—"

The admiral laughed again. "Voren? Oh, this should be rich. No pardon for the wordplay—I expect to be lavished like a Sardian haremite before this is through."

She gave him a cold look. Gods but she detested this sort of officer. No doubt he'd made his lieutenant's stripe before he'd even set foot on a ship, captain by the time he could shave. If High Admiral Tuyard knew enough about naval maneuver to avoid sailing his fleet into a forest she would eat boot leather for a month.

"Do you have a message for me to carry to Marquis-General Voren on your behalf, High Admiral?"

"Oh, I'll do better than that, General," he said, swinging his feet down to rest on the carpet. "I'll accompany you to let Voren make his offer in person."

"Admiral, that is hardly—"

"Chevalier-General, you have need of my men and ships, do you not? We may as well dispense with formalities. I have no desire to rot in a prison waiting for my shrew of a wife to pay an exorbitant ransom. You can tell Voren I'm open to being bought, or you can bring me to him and expedite this little charade."

Her thoughts went to the Gand fleet. They were coming, and if High Admiral Tuyard could bring the loyalty of some number of his officers, they might stand a fighting chance of harrying the Gandsmen away from a favorable landing. Too much to hope they could field enough ships to defeat the Gand Navy on the open waters, but if they had sea power to back the army, if they could force the fight onto ground of their choosing, it might be enough to tilt the engagement in their favor.

The admiral smiled, watching her weigh his words. "What will it be, General?"

"Best fetch your coat, Admiral."

47

SARINE

Sacre-Lin Chapel
Maw District, New Sarresant

She rolled to the left, trusting her instinct to dance away from danger.

Wrong.

She knew it, even as her body committed itself to the maneuver. He was ready for it, already pivoted into a lunge that would catch her through the heart. Hesitation only ensured the inevitable. Her guard was down, and she felt the point of the saber take her hard in the chest.

Coughing, she stepped back.

"Sarine, are you hurt?"

Donatien lowered his blunted practice sword, worry creasing his face. A few of the nobles who had been sitting nearby shared a collective wince on her behalf, only adding to the shame. They looked to her as a protector, and she made a mess of simple footwork?

She waved away Donatien's concern, gritting her teeth and settling once more into an offensive posture. Rapier extended forward. Elbow bent, just slightly. Feet a pace and a half apart, facing her opponent at a quarter turn. Off-hand dagger held point-skyward at her side. Breathing even. Shoulders relaxed.

Are you sure you don't want Red?

"Gods damn it!" she exclaimed, as Donatien's first attack found its mark.

He stepped back, lowering his sword. The nobles winced again.

"Is everything—?"

"I'm fine," she spat. "*He* distracted me. Go again."

"Perhaps we should—"

"Please. Donatien. I'm fine."

"We've been at this for some time now. I could use a rest."

Her first impulse was to argue. A chorus of aching muscles supported Donatien's notion, though, enough to give her pause. *Body* and *Life* bindings could spell them both, but perhaps he was right. She lowered her weapons, reaching instead for a flask of water on a stool beside their makeshift dueling ground.

All around them the nobles seemed caught by surprise, making hurried attempts to appear occupied by other means now that their practice bouts had paused. A hundred pairs of eyes, looking more like they belonged in the Maw with every passing day, dirt and dust soiling the finery they had worn to the Lords' Council. She'd saved the majority of their number in the madness that followed d'Agarre's attack, and earned herself a different sort of prison sentence for it, shackled to the chapel to protect her charges. She'd been a damned fool, bringing this lot to the Sacre-Lin. They would have died if she'd turned them loose; in the moment, it was all that had mattered. But now d'Agarre was out there, and she was here, trapped by the vise of her own charity.

"You're improving, my lady," Regiment-Major Laurent said, watching from the atrium wall. "One of these days you'll have to let me show you some of the finer points of incorporating *Body* into your swordplay."

"Better to learn the basics, in my view," Donatien said, stepping forward to lay his practice sword against the wall of the chapel.

"Those *are* the basics for her, my lord," Laurent said. "If she's to learn to take full advantage—"

"Please, both of you," she said, lowering her water flask. She'd just as soon avoid another of these sorts of exchanges. Laurent commanded a troop of loyalists, soldiers and priests who'd been swept up along with the remnants of the Lords' Council during d'Agarre's attack and now found themselves here, under her protection at the Sacre-Lin. She was grateful for the extra hands, and Laurent was a *Body* binder to boot, but from the tone of these exchanges, he felt the sting of confinement as sure as she did.

"Major Laurent," she said, "how are things outside?"

"Quiet," Laurent said. "It seems the revolution has drawn the inhabitants of the Maw elsewhere in the city. Spoils to be had in richer quarters, I expect." His lip curled as he said the last, not hiding his contempt.

"Perhaps if the crown spent less coin on masquerades and warmongering," Donatien said, "and more on stockpiling food for—"

"Enough!" she demanded.

Both men fell silent, Donatien bowing his head while Laurent held a knowing smirk. She sighed. Whatever she'd imagined when she led the nobles here to the chapel, it hadn't been this. They'd been shut in for days, eating through her uncle's larder. If the close quarters wore tempers thin from time to time, well, that was to be expected. And if she needed some space to breathe, who could speak against that?

"Sarine?" Donatien said. "Where are you going?"

His words grated on her skin, and she pushed through the atrium doors into the central nave, leaving both of them behind without another word.

All around her the nobles stirred, some offering greetings and warmth as she passed, with the rest giving her no more than dull stares. Fine silks and lace held dirt and dust as sure as common linen, and a few days' sleeping on chapel benches had the nobles looking like a mummer's parody of the council they had been. Yet in spite of it all, their demeanor hadn't descended into the spoiled whining she'd feared would greet her the morning after the prince's death, when she'd lain awake in her loft wondering what in the Nameless's twisted mind had possessed her to bring them here. No, the children of the noble houses of New Sarresant bore their ordeal with grace and poise. Perhaps it was only shock, left over in abundance from that terrible night. Whatever the cause, she said a silent prayer to the Oracle in thanks. She had enough on her shoulders. The small kindness of the nobles' best behavior was a sure sign the Gods were good.

The smell of stew simmering over a fire pervaded the chapel, and she walked through the priest's entrance to find her uncle leaning over a deep iron cookpot, testing the broth with a wooden spoon. His face brightened when she entered the room, and he beckoned to her, holding the spoon up for her benefit.

"Try a sip," he said. "Tell me if it's ready."

She did, a hot mix of spices and chicken warming her throat and belly. "It tastes lovely, uncle," she said, earning a nod of satisfaction. "But it also tastes as though you're aiming to burn through our stores in a week."

"Bah. How can I conscience stockpiling foodstuffs with so many hungry mouths to feed? 'Charity reveals the best self, even as—' "

" '—even as it raises us to new heights,' " she said. "Second virtue of the Veil, fourth parable."

He smiled. "Give me a hand with the pot? More space if we serve it in the chapel main."

"Of course," she said, flicking her eyes closed to tether a strand of *Body* into them both as she leaned down to grip the pot by its iron handles. His eyes went wide as they hefted the pot, finding it no more a burden than her pack of sketching materials on a light day.

After a moment he realized what she'd done and gave her an easy laugh. "You are an exceptional girl, my child."

"And you are still going to need to conserve our supplies, uncle. Those are winter storms outside, and this city has gone mad."

He nodded as they walked the pot out into the central nave. "You're right, of course. Still, I trust in the Gods."

"Uncle, the Gods aren't going to be able to scrounge cheap cabbage, let alone chicken and spices."

"Peace," he said as they settled the pot beneath the dais. "Let us enjoy what we have, today."

She sighed as the nobles began to form a line around the side of the wide chamber. "I'll fetch the bowls," she said, walking back to the kitchen. Just as well her uncle made a habit of serving soup to the poor wretches of the Maw in the cold months. Between the few donations they received from their parishioners and the coin she earned selling her sketches, they'd been able to stock the larder well above what the Sacre-Lin's stipend from the Basilica could provide. But the smoke rising from the Gardens made clear there wouldn't be any more wagons from the Church, and she'd been hard-pressed to venture more than a few streets from the chapel for fear of d'Agarre's people seizing the moment to strike.

"Do you need a hand there?" Donatien asked after she'd deposited the first stack of bowls, making her way back into the kitchens.

"If you don't mind," she said. "Grab the spoons, there beside the basin."

He hefted the wood crate, walking beside her. "I'm sorry for that, back there," he said. "I didn't mean to—"

"It's fine, Donatien."

They carted the rest of the utensils in silence, watching as the nobles lined up to receive their soup, looking for all the world like the usual urchins if you could see past the silks and jewelry. Her uncle shooed both her and Donatien away, insisting he could handle the service, and that they each receive full bowls, "for the benefit of our protectors," as if he himself wouldn't skim the dregs of the broth after everyone else had eaten.

She carried hers back to the atrium, as far as she could from the crowd of nobles. Donatien followed, sitting cross-legged beside her.

"Has there been any word from the city?" he asked after they'd eaten a few spoonfuls.

"Not much," she said. "Most honest folk are staying indoors, as cut off as we are."

"And the fires in the Gardens?"

"You know as much as I do," she said.

He nodded, taking another sip of his broth, looking down in silence.

It was obvious what he was thinking. "Look," she said. "I've already told you, I can't go tracking halfway across the city. If I leave and the chapel is attacked—"

"I know," he said. "You're right. It's only that I can't stand sitting here while—"

"If you want to participate so much, go rejoin your army and lay siege to the Gardens your bloody self."

He winced as if she'd struck him.

Eyes from across the chamber turned toward them.

"Sarine, please—"

"I need time to think," she said, dropping her spoon into her bowl and rising to her feet.

"At least take a coat," he said as she paced toward the main door. She made no sign she'd heard him, only unlatched the door and let herself out into the flurry. The swirling snow suited her mood, stinging against her skin as the wind cut through the Maw, leaving a layer of untracked powder. For some reason the cold didn't trouble her, despite her loose linen shirt leaving her neck and forearms exposed.

The beast spirits, Zi thought to her. *It's part of their gift.*

Shock pushed away the anger that had simmered beneath her skin. Zi never spoke so openly. "What is? Not feeling the cold?"

Yes.

She stared out into the storm, feeling the wind as if for the first time. "What else are you not telling me, Zi?"

Silence. She sighed, settling in on the chapel steps. Gods but she hoped Donatien didn't get it into his head to follow her, to bring her a coat or whatever other noble excuse he'd drum up to work his way under her skin. Not fair, she knew. His intentions were good. He only felt his own version of the pressure that threatened to smother her here at the chapel.

The city was boiling over, and she was hiding like a rat.

D'Agarre was out there; the army was out there. For all she knew the fires in the Gardens were pyres, built to sacrifice the nobles en masse on the altar of *égalité*, or whatever other excuse d'Agarre could find to fuel the madness she had seen behind his eyes. People were dying. Her people, the people of the city. And the Gandsmen, Donatien had told her they were coming. She felt caught in the eye of a storm, shackled to the lives of the nobles she had saved. And Donatien. Gods, but she felt trapped. She'd betrayed his trust at the council, when she started to reveal the treachery of the army after promising to leave it out of her account. He'd said nothing of it in the days since, nor of his duty to the army he had deserted. He only remained there by her side as the city burned.

He shouldn't be here.

She frowned. "I know Donatien supports the ideals of these revolutionaries, but—"

No. Him.

She looked into the snowfall, tethering *Life* by reflex as she struggled to find something unexpected in the haze of the storm. She saw nothing, only white streets lined with white rooftops beneath a pale gray sky. Frowning, she began to ask what Zi meant. Then she saw.

A lone silhouette, dressed all in black, making his way toward the chapel.

Fear spiked in her veins. "Who is he, Zi?"

Too soon. Too soon for him to have left the Seat.

She rose to her feet. One man was little cause for alarm by himself—she had *Body* binders in the chapel, and a squad of trained soldiers to boot. But it could mean d'Agarre had finally realized she'd survived the council. It could be a warning against what was coming next, though she couldn't imagine d'Agarre would be fool enough to come himself.

The man in black continued his approach, now visible even without the aid of *Life*. She had to assume he was either a binder or a *kaas*-mage to be so brazen. It could not be an accident that he was bound for the Sacre-Lin. She stepped forward into the street, the chapel at her back. The man came to a stop twenty paces away, facing her through the snow on the wind. He drew the blades from his belt, a pair of short swords no more than half an arm in length with a sloped, curved design she had never seen in use by any soldier or gentleman of Sarresant.

"Sarine," the man called. "The one they say guards this chapel."

"Who approaches?" she called back.

"An arrogant move. To come here, to hide in plain sight. Did you imagine the Three would not respond?"

"What is he talking about, Zi?" As if in answer, Zi materialized on the snow in front of her, his tiny frame puffed up to his full height, interposed between the newcomer and where she stood before the chapel.

Red, came the thought from Zi.

So, the man was a *kaas*-mage after all.

She tethered *Body* and felt Zi's *Red* pulse at the edge of her vision, steeling herself for a fight.

The man lowered his swords, abandoning a fighting stance as he stepped forward into the wind.

"Impossible," he said in a voice barely above a whisper, caught by her *Life* binding.

She kept her guard, expecting a trick.

It is not impossible, Zi thought. Without knowing how, she knew Zi had made himself heard by the man.

"You are bound," the man in black said. "You cannot be here."

"Zi, what is he talking about?" she said.

Now she was close enough to see his face, a tall man with a hooknose. His eyes had gone wide, his face pale.

You know less than you imagine.

"She doesn't know, does she?" he asked.

"What is this?" she asked, heat touching her voice. "What's going on, Zi?"

Why have you come here? Zi asked.

"You thought you could cleanse away our efforts and not draw a response?" the man said, sheathing his blades. "What were we to believe? We thought it was the Regnant's work. I risked everything to come down, and now I find this."

"Enough," she said. "Who is this man, Zi? Explain yourself."

He is Axerian.

Axerian. The name stirred her memory, taking her back to d'Agarre's manse. To the revelations of the Comtesse de Rillefort, before she'd been slain on the edge of d'Agarre's long knife.

In this age, he is called the Nameless.

Zi's words tore through her, confirming her memory. The Nameless. The Enemy of the Gods.

"Yes, my lady, I have that dubious honor this cycle," Axerian said, affecting a slight nod. "No more truth there than in any other myth, I assure you."

"You..." Her jaw worked, trying to make sense of what she was hearing. "You are the one responsible for Reyne d'Agarre, for the corruption there, with his Codex."

He seemed surprised. "That's right," he said. "I am, and in a way I've come here to rectify that mistake."

Axerian, Zi thought, in a manner that made clear it was meant as a warning.

"Let him speak," she said. Her head swam, looking him up and down. The Nameless. A God, or near enough for the difference not to matter. Here, on the steps of her uncle's chapel. Madness.

"I mean to stop d'Agarre's ascension, of course," Axerian said. "Him and the others of his kind, those with the *kaas*."

That is not your place.

"How?" she asked. "How would you stop d'Agarre?"

"Restoring peace to the city, if I can," he said. "And if not..."

"What?"

He met her eyes. She found his gaze strangely normal, an ordinary shade of brown, but touched with a reserve of fear all the more out of place in the eyes of a God.

"If not," he said, "then I must hunt the *kaas*-mages down and extinguish them, every one."

Their madness is your doing, Axerian.

"You mean for her to ascend in my place?"

No. That is not possible.

"Stop," she said, looking between Zi and Axerian beside him. "What are you talking about? I don't understand. What is 'ascension'?"

"Passage to the throne of the Gods, my lady, to secure a place as a champion of—"

Axerian, no. She is not ready.

Fury boiled in her stomach. "Zi?"

I am sorry, Sarine.

Axerian bowed his head, taking a step back.

"How dare you?" she said. "What do you know, Zi? Tell me now, this instant!"

It is not my place to decide. Forgive me.

"What?" she shouted. "Why is it anyone's place to decide what I should be told?"

Silence. She glared at Zi, rage building beneath her skin.

"Be this as it may," Axerian said, "I accept that the fault for the *kaas*-mages' madness is mine. But surely both of you can agree they cannot be allowed to…" He trailed off, looking down at Zi. "…fulfill their goals. Are my aims at odds with yours, my lady? Would it be remiss to ask for your help?"

Her vision still simmered with heat. "What sort of help?" she said.

"Peace may be beyond reach, unless I can contact…" He paused, and shook his head. "No. I mean to kill them, my lady. That is the sort of help I need."

"Well, Zi?" she asked, anger dripping from her voice. "Am I allowed to work against d'Agarre?"

Zi looked up at her, silent and staring as the snow fell around him.

"I can't help you," she said, breaking off her stare, looking down at the base of the chapel steps. "I'm needed here, to defend these people."

Axerian frowned. "Why not set a warding? Few enough could break one, save perhaps a *kaas* on the cusp of ascension."

No. She is not ready.

Anger flared again. Zi's refusal was a bitter draught of betrayal. And now to be pointedly told she was powerless to stop d'Agarre, powerless to do more than sit in the chapel while he sent the city into madness…

"Apologies, my old friend," Axerian said. "But I am going to need your lady's assistance if I am to have any hope of success."

Axerian closed his eyes, and an arc of blue lightning coursed around his arm. A coil of energy she'd seen before, beneath the d'Agarre manse surrounding the Codex of the Comtesse de Rillefort, and again at the strange place called Tanir'Ras'Tyat in the sewers beneath the Maw. It seemed to call to her even as he shaped it, sculpting it into a lattice of brilliant color. Then it vanished.

"It should work with any of your gifts, of course," Axerian said. "I only know the use of it with the *kaas*'s powers."

"What did you do? What was that?"

"A warding, as I said. Do you need me to show you again?"

Don't use it, Zi thought to her. *You aren't ready.*

Muting Zi's voice to a buzz in her head, she thought through what she had seen Axerian do. The use of the power was simple enough, but from where had he drawn it? The same energy, the blue sparks, but it came from within him as if he had tapped some internal reservoir. Perhaps she'd absorbed some of it, before. If she could only find it…

There. A song at the edge of her mind, a sorrowful voice that wrapped itself around her as she let it come forward. She reached for it by instinct, feeling it course through her. For an instant her vision flashed to another place, a wide, empty stone chamber behind a thick pane of…glass? It blurred and disappeared, leaving behind a coil of pure energy in her hands.

"You've got it," Axerian said. "Now fold it around one of your gifts, and you'll make a warding. Once it's set, you can channel a power of the *kaas* —or one of the leylines or spirits—as if you were there in person, and stronger, with less fatigue in the wielding."

His words floated through her mind, but she understood without further instruction. She blinked to see the leylines, finding *Faith,* her oldest, most trusted gift. Twisting the binding through the blue energy from the distant song, she tethered it into the chapel, and watched as the Sacre-Lin chapel faded from view.

"Hah, now that's a sight I haven't seen in a long time," Axerian said, grinning. "Though if I may suggest, you'll want *Yellow* instead, or *Shelter.* Vanishing chapels tend to draw more attention than they hide."

She released her tether of *Faith* and the chapel reappeared. Only this time she could sense the latticework of blue energy she had created, waiting for her to tether another binding into it.

"I think I've got it," she said, awe touching her voice. "Thank you."

"Your gift, not mine," he said, bowing his head. "And perhaps now you can lend me your help in return."

Zi glared at her, as angry—or whatever passed for that, for a *kaas*—as she'd ever seen him.

"You'll have it," she said. "To bring down d'Agarre, and those loyal to him? Yes. I will."

48

ERRIS

Council Street
Southgate District, New Sarresant

Jiri slowed to a walk as they turned down the wide street that ran between the council buildings. The first winter storms had abated, but their leavings stuck to the ground like a blanket of ice and sleet. Long icicles hung from rooftops, ominous spears threatening to impale passersby when the ice cracked and dropped. A good sign that there were people on the streets at all, never mind the weather. And there were a great many today, enough bodies to pack the gallery and make her late for Councilman d'Agarre's meeting. Ostensibly a meeting of some body called the "Transitional Reform Council," but neither she nor Voren had any illusions which puppeteer pulled those strings.

"What do you make of it, sir?" Sadrelle asked, riding beside her.

She frowned, looking up ahead. A swarming crowd, out of place both for the cold and the city's politics, but she hadn't taken any especial note of it. Such gatherings were common in better times.

"Nothing of great import, Aide-Lieutenant," she said. "A sign of the city's recovering health."

"Sir?" Sadrelle asked, in a tone that suggested she had just ordered a bath drawn and filled with calf's blood.

Only then did she notice the commotion in the center of the swarm, where it appeared a man had decided to go out naked into the cold, drawing a crowd to watch the spectacle of it. A heartbeat later she noticed a rather fine-looking coat being held aloft in a mocking fashion by one of the onlookers.

"Oh, Gods damn it," she said, spurring Jiri into the press. She fell into her battle voice, calling for the crowd to move aside. Jiri was large enough to draw attention by herself, and trampling through the square got them to make way at once.

"What goes on here?" she called out, reining Jiri to a halt. "Who is this man?"

The naked man cowered on hands and knees, looking up toward her with dullness in his eyes. She saw bruises on his legs and back, with flushed skin on his chest that would bloom to purple soon enough.

Rage shone in the eyes of the crowd, with a pair of large men—one of whom held the coat she'd seen from afar—standing at the front rank on either side. "No concern of yours, Captain," one of them said. "Just a tribunal on behalf of the people of New Sarresant."

"She's a general, you bloody fool," Sadrelle called as his mount reined to a halt behind her.

"She's fixing to be next if she doesn't mind her business," the man shouted back.

That made the crowd nervous; credit them with sense enough not to assault soldiers in broad daylight. Even so, the man's words hung in the air, adding their own sort of chill to the biting cold.

She said nothing in reply, merely held a hand high enough for the crowd to see as she peeled off her glove, letting it drop to the ground at Jiri's side. Gasps came from all around as their eyes settled on the broken skin on the back of her hand. By the time her second glove fell to the ground, the crowd had edged itself back a few paces, the men at the head sharing uncertain looks.

"He's one of them," one of the men offered, with an exaggerated spitting gesture even as he backed away. "One of the nobles. It's no more than they deserve."

"Go back to your homes," she said in the voice she used for battlefield speeches. "And give this man back his clothes."

The crowd broke, and coat, breeches, hose, and shirt were tossed forward from among the onlookers. "It's justice," the first man yelled back. "We'll have them all before we're through."

She ignored it, dropping from Jiri's saddle and tethering *Body* and *Life* as she knelt at the naked man's side. He sucked in a wheezing breath, a sickly gurgle suggesting a pierced lung.

"Don't speak," she said. "We need to get you inside."

Sadrelle brought the man's coat to drape it over him as she tethered a strand of *Body* for herself. "Carefully, Aide-Lieutenant, get his feet. We have to move him."

The man groaned as they hoisted him together, her *Body*-enhanced muscles enough to keep him steady as she made her way toward the council building. A warm fire and her bindings might be enough, but it would be a near thing.

"You missed quite a show, d'Arrent," Voren said, leaning forward over his desk. "Councilman d'Agarre was apoplectic. Says the army are 'a glorified pack of half-trained barbarians,' I believe his words were."

"My apologies, sir," she said, taking a seat across from him in the temporary chambers he'd claimed for himself here at the Council General.

"How is Vicomte Ouvrille?"

"He died, sir."

Voren grimaced. "I'm sorry to hear that. I didn't know him, not well at any rate. I'll see to it his family is notified."

"Sir, is this what the revolution means, to d'Agarre?" she asked. "To his followers?"

"There is no shortage of hate toward the nobility, d'Arrent."

"Much of it well deserved, sir, all due respect. But that isn't what I asked. What are Councilman d'Agarre's intentions?"

"Peace, Chevalier-General," Voren said. "Reyne d'Agarre is a young man, and an idealist. But he has no illusions that he can hold power without our backing, and that means he tolerates the nobility, or at least the vestiges of it within the army. And control of this city ultimately falls to us."

"The men speak of worse than the Vicomte Ouvrille got, sir. Angry mobs calling themselves tribunals, seizing the watch's guillotines to put on public displays of bloodletting."

"Well, and what of it, d'Arrent? It's no order I gave, but still better than the city would have had if Louis-Sallet had gotten his way. There are realities to this sort of business; surely you can understand that."

A long moment passed.

"Yes, sir," she said finally.

Voren sat back in his chair. He was right, of course; she never imagined their refusal to obey the Crown-Prince would result in bloodless resistance. But it was one thing to countenance a degree of lawlessness, quite another to make it an end unto itself.

"You did well with the vicomte," Voren continued. "Good to show the citizens our strength. No need for the city to devolve into chaos."

"Yes, sir," she said.

"D'Agarre unleashed his invective on us for want of just such control," Voren went on. "He claimed two of his lieutenants were killed here in the city. Assassinated, to hear him tell it. What would you make of that, General?"

"Two men murdered, sir? I'd call it a slow night, since d'Agarre's people started barricading the streets."

Voren barked a short laugh. "Truly though. D'Agarre claims they were men of influence within his ranks, men he claims were skilled enough fighters that anything short of a fullbinder shouldn't have stood against them."

She snorted.

"Yes, General, I know," Voren said. "Humor him. What do we know of the fullbinders that have gone missing from our ranks? Are there any among the priests who might have access to *Body*, *Entropy*, *Death*?"

"Few enough," she said. "And those would have been trained to healing or stewardship, not for combat."

"Our fullbinders, then."

"Laurent is the most skilled to have gone missing. Perhaps four or five more. And Louis-Sallet's flowerguards, if they survived the council. I can get a full report from the Second Corps by tomorrow."

He nodded. "Do it, if you please, General. But do it for the full army, not only the Second."

"Sir?"

A spark showed in Voren's eyes as he rose from behind his desk.

"It's time, General d'Arrent. My attentions are going to be on securing the governance of the city, and the Gandsmen are coming. Your *Need* bindings will have to be implemented in more than just the Second Corps." He opened a drawer, withdrawing a small wooden box and placing it on the desk, pushing it toward her. "It's time we begin planning our defenses in earnest."

She kept emotion from showing even as her heart raced.

He opened the wooden box, tilting the lid back and revealing a pair of gold pins. Five stars in a circle. "Congratulations, General. Or shall I say 'High Commander.' The armies of New Sarresant are yours, Erris d'Arrent."

He broke into a wide grin. "Yours if you want them, that is," he said.

Her head spun. Sixty thousand souls under her command. The fate of the colonies in her hands.

"Sir, I was a brigade commander not six months ago..."

"And the finest mind in the army," he finished for her. "Take the posting, d'Arrent. Not a soul in the colonies would do it better; we both know it for truth."

Her jaw worked, and she found herself nodding.

"Yes, sir," she said. "Thank you, sir."

He beamed, coming out from behind the desk as she rose, belatedly, to attention.

"We'll have to get you a new coat tailored for your rank, but for now these will do." He leaned down and withdrew the gold pins, fixing them into place as she stood before him.

When he was done he stepped back, offering her a salute. She returned it, feeling a rush of pride even as the weight of it settled onto her shoulders.

The remainder of her pleasantries with Voren passed in a blur, her head spinning as she considered the implications for command. No time for training exercises to mold the existing unit commanders toward her preferred way of thinking, but then again a decentralized style might be unnecessary in an army equipped with *Need*. One vessel for each brigade commander should be sufficient, with two or three assigned to each cavalry unit for redundancy's sake to ensure the accuracy of her field reports. And the navy. She'd have to speak with High Admiral Tuyard at once for full manpower reports and preliminary planning for the invasion.

Fifty thousand infantry, the lion's share veterans of the spring and summer campaigns, with eight thousand horse. Two hundred wheeled cannons and their firing teams. Crew enough for perhaps eighty ships, with at least sixteen men-o'-war. More details after she spoke with the admiral, gun counts and the status of each ship's complement. Three hundred binders with varying degrees of combat-relevant talents and training, and forty-odd fullbinders. All told they would be outnumbered by the Gandsmen four-to-three or perhaps three-to-two, with the enemy's command structure already leveraging *Need* to the hilt. But she had the choosing of the ground, and her men would be fighting on their home soil.

Two weeks until the enemy arrived, perhaps more. Her connection with the scout on the far side of the world had revealed only the enemy's preparations; it could have been days, perhaps a week or more before the last ship was ready to sail. Her men were rested in spite of the chaos in the city. The enemy soldiers would be coming off a hard voyage through winter storms. The first step would be to find them. A patrol sweep, ships spread along the coastline to catch sight of enemy sails on the horizon. Scouts posted along the barrier as well; she wouldn't be caught by a flanking maneuver again, in case the enemy had levees marching north from their colonies. Then deployment in the field, once she knew where they would invade.

These things and more ran through her head. Ammunition stores. Snowfall. The ground upon which they would fight—always that, above other considerations. If Tuyard could harry the Gandsmen to make landfall in the south, they might prepare an ambush in the narrows where the southern rivers fed into the sea.

"Sir, is everything well with the marquis-general?" Sadrelle asked, falling into step beside her as she made her exit from Voren's offices into the council halls.

"Sadrelle," she said, "I've been promoted to High Commander of the army. We need to rouse the division commands and begin vetting our supplies and disposition in the—" She cut herself off, turning to look sharply at her aide who had fallen a step behind, wearing a look of surprise. "You support our victory, do you not, Aide-Lieutenant?"

"Sir, I... Congratulations," Sadrelle stammered, quickening his steps to catch up. "Yes, of course I support our efforts and hope for victory. Why would—?"

His words washed over her as she shifted her vision to the leylines, searching for the threads of gold. In another time she might have worried over the implications of forging *Need* connections without the informed consent of her vessels; now, with mere weeks to plan a full defense of her homeland, such concerns paled before the immediate needs of the army. She found *Need*, snapping a connection into place between her and Sadrelle. Her vision shifted into his skin for an instant before she released the binding. Good enough. She could find him again.

Her aide sucked in a breath, his eyes wide with shock as she resumed her brisk pace toward the council stable yard.

"Move, Aide-Lieutenant," she called over her shoulder. "Gather the division commanders of every corps, tell them to report to high command on the double."

She took a few more long strides, then stopped. "And have them bring an aide. Someone known to be loyal to our cause."

Flicking her eyes shut, she made a check of her stores. *Need* in abundance, springing from her like a fountain of gold.

Voren had spoken truly: It was time, past time, to begin laying the groundwork for victory.

49

ARAK'JUR

Approaching the Ranasi Village
Ranasi Land

Their journey had been swift, on new horses borrowed from Nanerat tribesmen at the base of the snowy pass. Each day began before sunrise, and ended long after the sun had set. Short days in the cold season, made longer by hard travel, with an uncertain end.

The spirits who had spoken to him at Nanek'Hai'Tyat had confirmed his worst fear. War. Whether the Sinari men had taken up weapons and battle names, or merely fallen victim to aggression Ka'Vos had not been able to see, he could not say. The question gnawed at him like a wolf at a haunch of a fallen elk. Would he return home to find his people at arms defending their land, or slain by the hand of an enemy? Every day he drew closer to an answer, and his dread built with every step.

Corenna shared his fears as they traveled, but there was warmth there, too. In the late hours, when they waited for sleep to come, they risked whispers of possible futures, daring to imagine a world where their peoples stood together. Perhaps war was inevitable, but if the blood-oaths had been honored, the pacts sealed between Ka'Vos and Ka'Hinari, they could be returning to find their tribes united in victory over the aggression of their enemies.

As they drew near the northern boundary of Ranasi lands, Corenna's mood lightened. The flowing waters of the Anakhrai River marked the edge of her home, and together they dared to hope for a reception there, of Ranasi and envoys from the Sinari standing together to welcome their return.

Instead they found the riverbank empty. By itself no great cause for concern; even the best shamans could not foresee every coming and going. They crossed the waters in nervous silence, anticipation building with every step as they tracked their way through forested hills toward the Ranasi village. Whatever their hopes, each of them knew well enough the darker side of what was possible. Until they had confirmation of what had transpired in their absence, hope would flicker like a flame under a rough wind.

Wisps of smoke above the trees in the distance—signs of a greatfire in the Ranasi village—confirmed their arrival, at last.

Unable to hold herself to even the quick pace they had kept for days, Corenna nudged her mount forward through the tree line as he followed behind. Together they emerged into a village frozen in place, the paths deserted, tent flaps hanging loose in the wind. Panic stirred in his belly as they tethered their mounts, and Corenna rushed from tent to tent, seeking signs of life. He left her to it, heading straight for the village meeting ground. A fire burned there, no mistaking the smoke trailing into the sky above it.

Thank the spirits he arrived first. Enough time to turn back, to meet Corenna on the path and stop her before she could reach its source.

"Don't," he said, holding her as she struggled against him.

"What is it, Arak'Jur?" Her voice quavered, threatening to break.

"Don't," he repeated, keeping himself interposed between her and the pathway to the meeting grounds. "You do not want to see."

"Let me go."

"Corenna—"

He meant to reason with her, to spare her the pain. He hadn't allowed himself to feel the shock of it, concerned only with sheltering her from the horror ahead.

Instead a blast of earth beneath his feet sent him soaring away from her, crashing to the ground beside one of the empty tents in a cascade of dirt and stone. He snapped to his feet, but not before a howl sounded from the grounds ahead. A desperate plea, and then a scream. No, she cried out in denial. Let it be false. Let it be anything other than what it was.

When he emerged behind her, Corenna was on her knees, weeping into the dirt.

He approached with caution, staying silent. Enough to let her feel his presence, to let her know that whatever else had happened here in her village, at this moment she was not alone.

"I left them," she whispered, curled beside the fire.

He had carried her from the ruins of her village, away from the terrible pyre as she clung to him in tears. Now they camped to the south, at the base of a hill dusted with snowfall, fleeing from the memory of what they had witnessed.

"Corenna, you strove for peace—"

"I left them! My father, the brothers and sisters of my tribe, my people. Our guardian was slain and I left them without a protector. Their blood is on my hands."

He fell silent. His assurances were hollow. In her place he would blame himself; spirits forbid it came to that when they reached Sinari lands. A possibility they had not yet escaped, and he knew it well. If he could not assuage her pain, he could remind her he felt some measure of the same.

"Ka'Vos honored the blood-oath," he said quietly. "I saw Sinari men among the dead."

Her anger cracked, her expression softening once more into tears. "Oh, Arak'Jur, what have we done?"

The fire hissed and popped, casting shadows into the night. Stillness surrounded them, settling over the snow-covered hills of the Ranasi as if the spirits themselves mourned what had befallen their children. Perhaps some few had survived; he didn't have the stomach to sort through the wreckage of that terrible pyre to make an accounting of the dead. But the truth was clear: The Ranasi tribe was no more. And some among the Sinari had stood with their blood brothers and sisters. What fate might that betoken for his people? The question festered inside him.

But even as he felt it threaten to take hold, he knew despair was not the way. They had chosen the right path, and he could not doubt it now when faced with the price.

He met Corenna's eyes, and saw strength within her. Quivering for the cold, and for the uncertainty of convictions tested by horror. A fire burned there—dimmed by wind and snow, but no less for it.

"We have done only what was right," he said. "Against this madness, our people could not stand alone."

"And what do we do now?" she asked, voice shaken. "We travel to Sinari lands; what then?"

"We make war."

The answer stoked the fire behind her eyes, but she tempered it with reserve, a steadying breath that misted into the night air.

"Is it wisdom," she said slowly, "to trade peace for vengeance?"

He considered her words. Even in the grasp of anguish, she was right to urge caution. Anger boiled beneath his skin. He would have given much to have the ones responsible for the Ranasi village before him now, to cut them down like weeds and break them with the power of his gifts. The spirits would understand and forgive the vulgar use of their blessings; *una're* or *ipek'a* protected their young with savage ferocity. And men were not as simple as the predators of the wild. Even the greatest predators limited their killing to food, territory, or the perception of a threat. Only men could be corrupted by madness.

"There cannot be peace in the face of such evil," he said. "No tribe can be safe, so long as those who would commit such acts walk upon our lands."

She nodded, a solemn gesture, full of poise. And then she broke, turning away.

He moved to lie beside her, offering his warmth against the biting winds. No more words passed between them, only quiet tears of pain and grief.

Sleep found them both, and they awoke long past first light.

A haze settled around them as they made preparations for travel; he saw it in the distant look behind Corenna's eyes. For himself, he felt once more the creeping dread of the unknown, made worse by the atrocity they left behind. He expected no comforts from Corenna, though he offered what little he could as they crossed the land of her people. Corenna kept a hard pace, but said little. He understood.

When they reached the waters of the Nuwehrai, they turned inland in search of narrows where they could fell a tree for a crossing. Too late in the season to make the swim; floes of ice slid along the slow current as a warning, if the snowfall and chill in the air were not caution enough. Little concern for him—the gift of the guardian was strong—but he would not ask it of Corenna, and she did not offer.

Rounding a long bend in the arm of the river, he saw a pair of tall oaks had already been put to the task, bridging the water where the banks drew close. Freshly done, at least since he'd been away. They'd nearly reached them when a man rose from where he sat at the base of the wide trunks, on the Ranasi side of the river.

"Arak'Jur?" the man called, his voice caked by disbelief.

He raised a hand in reply. Drawing nearer, a tenuous relief spread through him.

Ilek'Inari.

"My apprentice," he called back as they closed the gap. He expected some manner of warmth from Ilek'Inari—it was his apprentice's nature, even in the worst of times. Yet instead he saw a pale cast to the younger man's face, a trembling, unsteady look in his eyes. And when his apprentice looked past him to settle on Corenna, Ilek'Inari's expression twisted into a grimace, as if he recoiled from the source of a fresh wound.

His stomach sank.

"What news?" he asked, fearing his apprentice's next words as he had feared little else in his life.

"You've seen it," Ilek'Inari said. "The Ranasi village."

"What do you know of my people?" Corenna said.

Once more Ilek'Inari turned to look at her, then winced and looked away.

"Ilek'Inari," Arak'Jur said, "tell us what has passed here."

"Madness," his apprentice said, eyes downcast. "She corrupted them. The new magic. I should have seen it. I should have—"

"Slow down," he said. "What has happened? What news of our people?"

"The Sinari have gone mad, Arak'Jur. Llanara's power has twisted our people into vile shells of what they were. The atrocity of the Ranasi village, it was done by our hand. The Sinari fell on the Ranasi with the fair-skins' muskets, beguiled and goaded by her magic."

Ilek'Inari's words faded into a dull hum, the void following a thunderclap.

Corenna's eyes widened to pale moons, her jaw working as if she meant to speak.

"No," he said. "It cannot be so."

"It is," Ilek'Inari said. "Spirits curse us all, it is the truth."

"What was your part in this, apprentice guardian of the Sinari?" The ice in Corenna's words took him aback, and he saw a pale film cover her eyes in mist.

"Corenna," he said. "No. Ilek'Inari cannot have known—"

"I will have the words from his mouth, Arak'Jur!"

Ilek'Inari met her eyes with pain in his own. "I fled, honored sister. I knew their intent, and I fled. Spirits curse me for a coward; I could not stand against her."

Corenna quivered on the edge of fury, checked by the barest shred of restraint.

"Corenna—" he said.

"Arak'Jur!" she shouted at him, stepping back. "How am I not to believe this part of your plan from the start? Arak'Doren fell on your lands, and then you came to us speaking of peace, you drew me away, you left us open to be murdered like defenseless children."

The shock of her words struck him like a blow, and he watched the rage boil behind her eyes, searching him as she spoke.

He fell to his knees.

"Kill me, if you believe it," he said. "If the spirits of your people whisper to you of my part in this, then exact your revenge. The Sinari guardian as first payment for our betrayal."

She held steady, her gaze fixed to his. Then he saw the film of her magic fade from her eyes, replaced by tears and pain. He rose and moved to her side, cradling her in a firm embrace as he looked back to his apprentice.

"Tell us all, Ilek'Inari. Tell us what evil has taken our people."

His apprentice nodded, still watching Corenna with a lingering concern as he began to speak. He told of Ka'Vos's death, how Llanara had proclaimed it the will of the spirits. How he had opposed her in the steam tent, stunned to find himself dismissed before a rising tide of passion and a growing thirst for blood. Llanara's new magic had hold over them, he claimed, and before Ilek'Inari could understand the depth of her power, she had assumed a position of leadership and guidance over the tribe.

As he listened, a knot of anger took root in his stomach. He had been a fool to ignore her strange new gift. That Llanara had her share of ambition he knew well—no secret to him she had sought his companionship in some part due to his status as a guardian of the tribe. But he had never imagined such madness in her. The more he listened, the darker his spirit grew.

Corenna had recovered herself as best she could, sitting cross-legged in the snow beside him.

"Her gift," Corenna said. "It came to her through the hands of a fair-skin, did it not?"

"Yes," Arak'Jur said. "From a man called Reyne d'Agarre. He visited the village a number of times, instructing Llanara."

"I do not understand; the fair-skins have not stirred from behind their barrier in ten generations. If the fair-skins wished us destroyed, could they not have made war? Why plant such a pernicious seed among our people?"

"Llanara claimed her gift was related to the spirits' visions," Ilek'Inari said. "That she spoke on their behalf. The elders swore she could make a spirit appear to them, to confirm her words."

Arak'Jur nodded. "I saw such a thing, the day Reyne d'Agarre first came to our village. Llanara may well have spoken true—yet if her gifts are of the spirits, they are tainted by the evil against which we have struggled for so long."

"And her power corrupts the mind," Corenna said. "Inspiring madness. Yet it does not appear to have taken hold in you, Ilek'Inari?"

"No, honored sister," his apprentice said. "I watched my people succumb to heated emotion as Llanara spoke, and felt none of the passion that stirred within them. They marched to war, to the unspeakable. And I was powerless to dissuade them."

If what Ilek'Inari had said was true, his people may already be lost. None among the Sinari would countenance such atrocities—his people loved peace, had shown wisdom enough to walk its path even as others gave in to the urgings of the spirits. Perhaps if he could reach Llanara, confront her...

"Where is she now?" he asked. "What does she intend?"

"I fled from the tribe, hiding in the wilds when I came to understand their purpose. I had a vision of your return, and came here. I have not heard tell of her plans since."

He and Corenna shared a look.

"We must seek her out," he said. "And put an end to this corruption."

Corenna nodded. "Then we travel to the Sinari village." She rose to her feet, dusting snow from her furs.

"Wait," he said. "Can you forgive my people, Corenna?"

Her back stiffened.

"I must know you can lay blame for this at its source," he said. "The madness of the spirits, of Llanara's vile gift, and not the men and women corrupted by its power."

She took a long moment, looking between him and Ilek'Inari.

Finally she spoke. "I can judge what I see. No more, no less. If all is as Ilek'Inari has said, then I will content myself with finding Llanara. Finding her, and seeing her dead."

He held her gaze, searching the pained look in her eyes.

She spoke again, voice wavering. "Do not ask me for less than this."

He saw anger in her, the grief of loss. Fury, but also hope. She could find forgiveness, when the moment had passed, but now she wore the pain of the horrors she had borne like an open wound.

He rose to his feet, taking her hand in a steady grasp.

"If what has been done to my people can be undone, it must be so. After, it is the place of a guardian to mete out justice."

Her eyes closed as she nodded, fresh tears streaking down her face.

"I swear to you, Corenna of the Ranasi, by the spirits of our lands—I will see justice done, for the blood of your people."

50

SARINE

Public Tribunal
Market District, New Sarresant

Sarine, please. Listen.

The buzz of the crowd made ignoring Zi that much easier. Anger seethed beneath her skin at his words, fitting with the mood of the men and women around her. She had often sold her sketches here in the central market, what felt like an age ago. Now the only wares on offer were flavors of violence, death disguised as justice. And rage. The hunger for food she had seen so often in the eyes of her fellow citizens had been replaced by a hunger for blood. They clamored together, congregating at the base of a hastily erected platform in the middle of the fountain square, watching as d'Agarre's men prepared the stage for the afternoon's work.

A cold sky looked down on their gathering, empty and blue with the promise of ice lingering now the storms had gone. A few of the crowd called out, impatient to see the accused, or just to profess their support for the causes of freedom and *égalité*. Most were content to wait, breath misting in the biting cold.

Sarine, Zi tried again. *Please.*

She cleared her mind, focusing on watching the stage for signs of another *kaas*.

The wound of Zi's betrayal was too raw, too near the surface to listen to him speak. Her relationship with Zi had never been easily understood, but it was one thing to know her companion had a strange, often cryptic manner and another entirely to have him intervene to keep her from knowing the truth of her place and purpose. When she'd been a girl her gifts had been mysteries, mysteries she was content to leave alone. She'd had no cause to believe herself more than an orphan girl upon whom Father Thibeaux had taken pity, enough to keep her from being taken and trained as he had been, as all children were when they showed the signs.

Now she saw Zi's touch in it, in what she had once believed to be her uncle's charity and good heart. It made her anger flare again. How far did her companion's reach extend? Had every step of her life been some machination toward a deeper purpose, a hidden path she walked unknowing to satisfy Zi's design? She had counted him more than a friend. Zi was part of her, had saved her from the horrors of the streets. Without Zi she would have been dead a hundred times over. She had never truly questioned him before, but now she began to see the childish mistake of that blind trust. Hadn't d'Agarre been led to his madness by the same force, his *kaas*? Could she assume Zi was not guiding her toward a similar end?

I have not been corrupted, Zi thought to her. *I do not compel you, only protect you from that for which you are not prepared to face.*

"Shut up, Zi," she whispered, tears stinging the corners of her eyes.

He complied for the moment, thank the Gods, falling silent in the recesses of her mind. Just as well that one of d'Agarre's men chose that moment to unveil the instrument of the afternoon's justice: a guillotine, on loan or stolen from the city watch. The man climbed the side of the elevated stage, drawing eyes and excited whispers as he pulled back the linen sheet that had been draped over it for just such a dramatic effect. He pulled the cord and the steel blade rose up, glinting in the afternoon sun, with all the promise of swift death the next time it fell. Excited whispers became hushed anticipation as he tied the cord, stepping back with a twisted grin.

"Citizens of New Sarresant," another man proclaimed as he strode up the steps, raising his arms to draw their attention. "Citizens, we gather here today to see justice done, before a tribunal of the peers of the accused.

"I speak, of course, of you, the citizens of our city. For as we know in our hearts, we are all one peerage, never mind what our onetime King might have had us believe. A lie, I call it!" He paused for effect, his words having already stilled the crowd to silence. "A lie, to claim nobility, to claim the exaltation we owe to the Gods. Do these so-called nobles not eat, the same as we do? Do they not sleep and shit and fuck?"

He stepped back, gesturing toward the guillotine, where the steel blade had been raised taut and fastened beside him. "Tell me, my brothers and sisters. Do the nobles not bleed red and true, the same as any man?"

Cries shattered the silence of the crowd as the man put on a broad smile. He let the moment linger before turning behind his stage and calling out, "Bring forth the accused!"

She scanned the crowd as d'Agarre's men hauled their captive up the steps, drawing jeers and cries of hate. No sign of manipulation from d'Agarre's *kaas*-mages; this crowd was a fire that needed little in the way of kindling. It seemed their captive was an army officer today, though the uniform seemed strange to her eyes, looping tethers in place of buttons on the coat, with a cut unlike any she had seen in the days since the army had moved into the city. The accused bore the mockery of the crowd with stoic grace, eyes upraised to the horizon as if the assembled citizens were beneath his notice. If the prisoner had calculated it as an act of defiance it had the desired effect, spurring the onlookers to hurl insults with ever-increasing fury even as the plain-looking man at the center of the stage raised his hands to beg for calm.

"Citizens," the man called, then again. "Citizens, please." The crowd paid him little mind, stirred to a frenzy by the officer's haughty disdain. If not for Zi's warnings she might have thought the display a product of the *kaas*'s influence—*Yellow*, to irritate the emotions. That Zi had not abated in using his gifts on her behalf stirred mixed feelings; she'd grown accustomed to his magics and his warnings, even as she resented their source. Enough that Zi would reveal one of d'Agarre's *kaas*-mages here today, if they were foolish enough to show themselves. Across the square she met Axerian's eyes, the hook-nosed God standing as she was, waiting hidden in the crowd for sign of a *kaas*'s powers in use. He gave a subtle shake of his head, indicating he had detected nothing so far, and she returned the same gesture.

The Nameless. Working with her to hunt Reyne d'Agarre's lieutenants, and d'Agarre along with them if he dared to show himself. Her head spun as she reflected on their strange alliance, a God walking the streets of the market, breaking bread with her at suppertime. An oddity beyond belief, but there it was all the same.

"State your name for the tribunal, prisoner," the speaker demanded, having wrested a measure of control over the crowd. The officer-turned-prisoner looked back at him for a long moment, the crowd's energy as taut as the cord that upheld the guillotine's blade. And then he spat at the speaker's feet, a subtle gesture without exaggeration.

Once more a tide of insults broke against the officer's iron exterior, redoubled in force when the first man—the one who had tied the cord—donned a black hood in plain view of the crowd. Always before at the executions she'd attended the headsman wore his mask from start to end, a messenger of death, faceless, unknowable, inhuman. This man had gone from grinning bystander to executioner in a moment, a perversion of the typical ceremony that only added to the gruesome spectacle.

She'd seen enough. If there was a *kaas*-mage here they would not reveal themselves; no outside power would be needed to stir this crowd. One last chance to draw them out.

Yellow flared at the edge of her vision. She hadn't asked for it, but it was there at the moment she willed it. A sign of Zi's attentiveness, and another spark to fuel the anger in the back of her mind. She felt his power weave through the crowd, reading their emotions: rage, hatred, envy, satisfaction. Zi replaced them all with shame and fear.

The crowd broke.

Even the headsman tore off his hood, flinging down his axe and leaving the guillotine cord taut and uncut as he fled into the snow. Across the square Axerian stood, watching for signs as the crowd surged around him. The officer looked bewildered watching from the stage, as even the speaker dove from the platform in a flying leap, running away on a hobbled ankle.

Only one woman stood her ground, her eyes wide as saucers as she darted uncomprehending looks at her fellows, who moments before had been raging and screaming for blood.

She and Axerian closed on the woman from opposite sides of the square, stalking toward her like alley cats sighting a wounded pigeon.

"What is—?" the woman started, pivoting between them. "I don't—"

Understanding dawned in the woman's eyes and she flung herself at their feet. "Mercy, please. Please!" the woman cried. "I never meant to touch the lines, I swear it. I'll never do it again, I swear on the Exarch himself, please."

The tension melted away, she and Axerian exchanging a look on hearing the woman's pleading cries. Axerian reached her first, kneeling and peeling away one of her woolen gloves. Binder's marks.

"Please!" the woman cried, twisting beneath his grasp. "Please, I swear!"

He let go of her arm, standing in a swift motion. "You're free to go, my dear," he said. "So long as you honor the Gods."

Her eyes remained wide, looking between them before she scrambled to her knees. "Oh thank you, my lord, my lady, thank you. I swear it, I do. I promise."

She watched the woman run, trailing after the other members of the crowd, long since vanished down snow-covered streets.

"A freebinder," she said.

"*Yellow* is a fickle thing," Axerian said. "Xeraxet detected nothing here, only an ordinary slice of mob justice."

She looked up to the stage where the officer stared at them, as if unsure whether he should flee along with his captors.

"You're free, my lord," she called to him. "Do you have a safe haven here in the city? Or with the army outside the walls?"

The officer steadied himself, giving a slight shake of his head as he considered them both. "My thanks," he managed at last. "Who are you, madam? And what was…?" He left the question unfinished, glancing around the square.

"'And he came forth from shadow, and his eyes were the twinned pearls of a viper, shining the light of judgment upon the souls of the unworthy,'" Axerian said. She recognized the passage, from an old translation of the holy books.

"We're enemies of Reyne d'Agarre," she said firmly. "I can escort you back to the camps if you like. Bold of them, to risk abducting an officer. I hadn't seen it before today."

The man knelt, stepping down from the front of the stage. "I'm no officer of this army, madam," he said. "My name is Vaudreuil, a captain in His Majesty's navy. Master and commander of the *Redoubtable*. My crew and I have been imprisoned here in your city since we refused the High Admiral's dictum to support the rebels."

"Ah," Axerian said. "I take it you'd as soon we not return you to your cell."

The captain frowned.

"There is a safe place here in the city, Captain," she said. "A haven for the nobles and others we've managed to rescue from d'Agarre's mobs. I can take you there if you prefer."

"What did you do here, madam?" the captain asked. "How did you scatter these people? A new binding?"

"Of a sorts. And my name is Sarine. This is Axerian."

"Thank you both, again," the captain said with a slight bow. "And yes, failing a way to use that binding to return me to my crew and my ship, a haven from the madness of this city would be welcome."

She nodded, and a spark of an idea took hold in her mind.

"Follow me then, Captain."

"I'm telling you, I think I could do it," she said, keeping her voice low. "I don't know why I didn't think of it before. With Zi's power, and my gifts, I could get all of them to the Harbor."

"A ship," Donatien said, scratching his chin where stubble had blossomed into the makings of a full beard in the absence of enough razors to go round at the chapel. "It would be a risk, and this city is still—"

"This city is still mad. They are killing nobles in the streets, Donatien. We can't stay here forever."

He winced, reclining up against the wooden paneling that separated her loft from the chapel nave below. "There is bound to be chaos," he said. "Until order can be established, until elections, real elections can be held."

"You don't understand," she whispered back in a rush. "Whatever d'Agarre might have claimed to believe, whatever philosophy was debated at the salons, this all has a mind of its own now. If order is going to be restored, it's going to be done on the back of noble corpses."

He frowned.

"Ask Captain Vaudreuil," she said. "Ask him how close he came to being executed for the crime of *probably* being noble."

Donatien went quiet, turning around and rising to his knees to observe the goings-on in the chapel below. She let him have his look, remaining seated beside him. After a moment he spoke. "So, you'd secure us a ship and have us sail away," he said. "Bound for where? Villecours? The Old World?"

A fair question. She hadn't considered it.

"This madness isn't going to stay confined to the city," she offered.

"The Old World, then," he said. She gave a tenuous nod, and he continued. "You know most of us have never made the crossing. We're all ostensibly peers to the King and the families of his court, but the Revellion family here in the colonies has no significant ties to the Revellions of the old country. Much the same for the rest of us. We'd be putting ourselves at the mercy of the King's charity."

"Better than anyone would get from d'Agarre."

He slumped beside her.

"None of this is what I wanted," he said. "I imagined reform, yes, and perhaps even some measure of violence, if only in furtherance of the cause. Not this."

"I know. You're a good man, Donatien Revellion."

He reached an arm around her, sharing a moment of mutual contemplation.

He gestured to one of her sketches, a portrait of her uncle displayed above the small chest that held her wardrobe, half street clothes and half tailored by way of the generosity of Reyne d'Agarre. "You hardly draw anymore," he said.

"I've had more on my mind of late," she said, smiling as she remembered the struggle it had been to get her uncle to sit still long enough for that particular sketch. Such was her uncle's nature, always active, always working. And never a word of complaint, even when she brought a hundred noble refugees to his door.

Allowing herself a moment of reverie, she had missed Donatien tensing beside her. "And where is your Axerian tonight?" he asked.

"Donatien. He's not *my* Axerian. He comes to the chapel when he has information. I've told you—"

"I know," Donatien said. "He's helping you with d'Agarre. But I don't like him, Sarine. Something about him makes me uneasy."

He is dangerous. He cannot be trusted.

Anger burned hot as Zi's thoughts rang through her mind. But before she could reply to Zi, Donatien pulled away.

"Fine," he said. "I understand. I'll stay out of your way."

"No. It's only—"

"You don't have to explain," he said, rising to his feet.

"Donatien," she said quietly. "Sit, please."

He gave her a long look, then settled back onto the floor of her loft.

"It's Zi," she said. "He's keeping secrets from me. It's put me on edge. I'm sorry."

"Secrets," he said slowly.

"Yes. More than that I can't say, only that he knows something of my nature, of the bond with the *kaas*. Something he isn't telling me."

"Well. If he knows somewhat of your nature, perhaps he'd tell me. I'm still trying to figure it out."

A laugh came unbidden, and Donatien gave a wry grin.

"Truly though, Sarine," he continued, "I'm only worried for you. And I think your idea with the ship has some merit. You're right that we can't stay here forever, not with the city like this."

"And the Gandsmen," she said. "They're still coming."

"Just so. Perhaps leaving the city is our best option." They shared a look, and she could almost hear the unasked question simmering behind his eyes: Would she be on the ship, if they managed to secure it?

"I'll talk to Captain Vaudreuil," she said before he could speak. "He said his crew had been imprisoned. I'll need to find out where, and arrange to find supplies as well."

Donatien rose to his feet. "I can start getting the nobles organized to move. The last of the wounded should be recovered within a few days. We'll cover ground much faster than we did before."

"Thank you, Donatien," she said, rising along with him, accepting an arm as he helped her descend the ladder from her loft.

In the back of her mind she acknowledged for herself the answer to Donatien's unasked question: She wouldn't be on that ship. Not unless Reyne d'Agarre was a corpse, dead and buried by her hand, and the rest of his *kaas*-mages along with him, before it sailed. She laid the innocent lives lost in the city at their feet, from the Crown-Prince to the lowliest urchin caught up and trampled by the chaos. And she would see them pay the price for their corruption before this was through. By the Exarch and the Oracle and all that was good, it was time she use her gifts to do more than survive. It was time she shoulder the responsibilities of who and what she was.

You must not continue on this path, Zi thought to her. *You are not ready to bear this burden.*

She ignored him, feeling the weight of the nobles' expectations as she made her way through the crowd.

51

ARAK'JUR

Outlying Tents
Sinari Village

Once, he'd imagined his return to the Sinari village would be accompanied by exultant celebration. An occasion for a feast to mark the alliances they'd sealed. A jubilant welcome for their guardian come home. Food, warmth, and the comforts of the familiar.

Instead he tread on ground that stank of death. Not the bitter flame he and Corenna had witnessed on Jintani lands, nor the wrenching sorrow visited upon the Ranasi. The Sinari village clung to an aura of rot like a wound festering in the heat of the sun.

He saw it in his people's eyes, turning away as he strode through familiar pathways. No warm reception, only shame and guilt enough to overpower the relief his homecoming should have brought. Arak'Jur returned, and his people hid away cloistered in their tents, shielding themselves from a biting wind that had nothing to do with the cold spirits breathing their frost across the land.

What Corenna or Ilek'Inari might have thought, he could not say. He spared no looks over his shoulder as the three of them made their way through the village. One destination weighed on his mind. One purpose. The guardians were the keepers of justice for the tribe, and he meant to fulfill that calling today.

He reached his tent, where Llanara would have remained in residence.

Empty.

Corenna showed him a mask of forced serenity, while Ilek'Inari looked to him with sympathy and concern. Neither mattered. He pushed past them, reaving his way back into the village. He tore the flaps open at the first tent he reached along the path, again greeted by an empty space. Another, met by the same.

Finally he found a tent with a cowering set of eyes, watching his furious entrance behind the shelter of a blanket. Ghella, onetime leader of the Sinari women, huddled away from the light as much as the cold, with a wince as recognition dawned in her eyes.

"Where is she?" he demanded, ice in his voice.

"You've come back," Ghella whispered, loud enough to carry across her tent.

"Where is she?" he repeated.

"I…I…"

He stormed into the tent, tearing away the old woman's blanket and lifting her to her feet in a fluid motion.

"Answer me now! I would see her pay for what she has done!"

"Arak'Jur." Ilek'Inari's voice came from behind.

He released his hold on Ghella with a pang of disgust as she crumpled to her knees, sobbing.

"Justice, Ilek'Inari," he said. "I will have it, if I have to flay it out of every complicit elder of this tribe. How, Ghella? Honored sister, how? How could you allow this?"

"Calm," Ilek'Inari said gently. "Remember Llanara's magic. Ghella may know little of what transpired."

He turned back to the sobbing form, doubled over on the woven rugs of her tent.

"I would have it from her," he said. "Speak. Now."

Corenna entered the tent, watching with a quiet expression that bespoke a boiling anger beneath the surface. He knew Corenna well enough by now to see it, and he knew its cause. Ghella looked up as she entered, and recognition dawned with spreading horror on the old woman's face.

"Oh, sister," Ghella said in a ragged voice. "I'm sorry."

"Answers, woman," he demanded, evoking another pained look from the elder as she turned back to him, tears welling in her eyes.

Ilek'Inari dropped to a knee beside her.

"Please," Ilek'Inari said. "Tell us what has happened."

"She claimed to speak with the voice of the spirits," Ghella managed, her eyes downcast with shame and grief.

The moment stretched, and anger simmered in his belly, reflected in the stillness of Corenna's gaze.

Ilek'Inari spoke again. "Go on, sister. Tell us."

"W-w-when she spoke," Ghella said. "When she spoke it was as if, as if the spirits themselves embraced us, whispered the truth of her words. As if their will was made real. As if I could touch it. Every thought that agreed with Llanara's words was met by rapture; any thought against her was cold and empty. It swept us all along, until…"

She glanced at Corenna once more, her expression wrenched into pain. Ilek'Inari looked up at them with her, as if to absolve her of her involvement.

"Why can you see the madness of it now?" Arak'Jur demanded. "Why now, and not before?"

"She is gone," Ghella said. "She took our warriors south, and when she left us the spirits' blessing went with her. We were left with the knowledge of what we did."

"All of you?" Corenna asked, her voice quavering. "All of the tribe went with her to betray my people?"

Ghella looked on her once again, eyes red and raw as she nodded. "Yes. Spirits curse us, yes."

Corenna turned to him, shaking as she struggled to maintain her composure. "I… I cannot be here, Arak'Jur, I…"

"Corenna—"

"No, I have to go."

He saw the glimmer of mist creeping into her eyes, the sign of her gift made manifest. Without another word, Corenna whirled and ran from the tent.

"Corenna!" he called, stepping to the entrance in her wake.

She gave no sign of turning back, fleeing toward the wilderness outside the village.

He let her go. The pain of his people's betrayal stung deep for him; for her, it would be a grief no affection could bridge. If she needed time and space to grieve, he would give it to her.

Ghella had once again begun to sob, witnessing the fruits of her madness firsthand.

"We must assemble the elders that remain in the village," he said to Ilek'Inari. "I will address them all. And if Llanara gave any sign of her intent, of where I might find her, I would have it from their mouths."

His apprentice nodded. "A wise course."

"Gather them, Ilek'Inari. Tell them I will receive them in the steam tent."

He took the time to adorn himself with *echtaka* paint, thick bars beneath either eye devolving into swirling patterns covering the rest of the skin he could reach. The full decorum of a guardian's markings required a woman's or an apprentice's assistance to apply, but this would serve. In a way, the partial covering of *echtaka* paint he wore stood as a symbol of his distance from the tribe—patches of russet skin showing through the unmarked gaps on his shoulders and lower back a declaration that the Sinari were unworthy of providing their guardian proper support. Otherwise he was covered head to toe, even his manhood bearing the marks of deference to the spirits.

Hours passed before he was finished. Ilek'Inari would have long since gathered the elders, but they would not leave the steam tent before he arrived. The burden of their shame would weigh them down, keep them pinioned where they sat, however long he took to prepare. He had intended only the token marks he wore for tribal ceremonies, not a full marking. Yet there was a salve in it as he worked, in decorating his body with the patterns of his calling and his people. He even found new designs, or perhaps ancient patterns lost to the passage of time. Glyphs of sorrow and regret; lines to evoke the pain and suffering of his people, of Corenna's. Of the Jintani, and the Nanerat. Of the spirits themselves, as their children bled against the awakening madness of the world.

When he was done, he emerged into the ice of the midday air, naked as he walked the pathways of the village. Shadowed eyes watched him pass, cowering behind tent flaps as if meeting his gaze would invite condemnation. He held his head high, bearing the mantle of Sinari pride. If none among them could bear the shame of it, he could. He who was second only to Llanara for the depth of his failure. From her, he would have justice. But for the rest, he could carry his people through this despair, painted outside and in with the guilt of their shortcomings.

He could meet the weighing eyes of the world and declare: Yes, we have failed. But we are Sinari. We endure.

The steam tent was half-full, with the most aged of elders, those who could not carry a weapon, or otherwise fight alongside Llanara's whispered madness. As one, they cringed away from his coming, as if the tent vented away hope alongside the gush of steam when he raised the flap to enter.

With purpose, he strode to the center, where Ilek'Inari sat tending to the heated rocks suspended over the fire.

"Elders," he said, sweeping a challenging look across the tent. "You imagine I am here to pronounce judgment. And I am."

He paused, letting his words settle, drawing hesitant looks as the silence stretched on.

"I am," he repeated. "But no more upon you than on myself. First, the woman Llanara. I pronounce death, and declare her anathema to the Sinari. In lieu of judgment from the shamans or the highest of the women, I ask the support of the elders of this tribe."

Only the hiss of water on rocks met his words.

"Do you imagine you are unworthy to condemn her?" he said. "That your compliance in her madness deprives you of standing to denounce it? I say no. You are elders of the Sinari. Speak, now. Speak for our people."

"We are shamed," replied Valak'Ser, a pruned elder who had led the hunters in his day. "Shamed, or cursed."

"Both," came more than a few voices, with accompanying murmurs of assent.

"Llanara compelled you with magic, a gift of the fair-skins—"

"We are cursed, then," said Valak'Ser. "If the spirits of things-to-come allowed it to come to pass, if they gave no warning through our shaman, then they have turned their backs on us, and we deserve death."

"No," he said. "I reject the spirits of things-to-come."

Gasps echoed through the tent.

"I have rejected their guidance since Ka'Vos refused to accede to their whispers for war. Ilek'Inari has heard them as well. The shamans' spirits have gone mad. Some malign force has corrupted them, and if it is within my power I would root it out. Failing that, I will not let their cancerous whispers destroy our people. I reject them, even knowing some among their number are pure and true. The spirits guide us, but no more can they bind us. We listen, but cannot be compelled to follow. This must become our way, if we are to survive."

"Madness," one of the elders whispered.

"Madness is the war the spirits have demanded," he said. "It is the blood on the hands of our people. I cannot walk that path. I judge Llanara must die, that her pernicious gift is cleansed away from this tribe. As to the rest, if I can bring back our hunters—our warriors—I will."

Ilek'Inari rose to his feet. "Arak'Jur speaks the truth. I have heard the corruption, and we have erred in keeping it from you. Forgive us."

Steam poured from the rocks at the center of the tent, a low hiss that drowned out whatever other sound was made within its walls as the elders contemplated Ilek'Inari's words, and his own.

Valak'Ser spoke again. "Arak'Jur. Almost I hoped you returned to us as a scourge, to exact blood for blood. Instead you speak of another kind of madness, no less vile to my ears." He paused a moment. "But I cannot see another way."

Murmurs among the elders were cut short as Valak'Ser turned to face them. "If Llanara spoke with the voice of the spirits, as she claimed, could you countenance another drive to war?"

"I cannot believe she spoke on their behalf," Ilek'Inari said. "But the message was the same. The spirits of things-to-come call for blood."

More murmurs, and looks exchanged, but none rose to speak.

"Can you give your blessing to my judgment, elders?" he asked. "I say Llanara must die, that what can be saved of our people, may be saved."

"Yes," Valak'Ser replied slowly. "I will carry the stain of our betrayal until my last breath, but I will carry on until that day. Our tribe must endure."

"Yes," came another voice.

Then the tide burst, and the tent descended into tearful unity.

He broke the moment with an upraised hand.

"I would know her plans," he said. "Where can I find her?"

"South," Valak'Ser said. "The lands of our neighbors. She sought allies. And enemies."

"Which tribes were meant as friends?" Ilek'Inari asked. "And which for . . ." He trailed off, a sickly pale on his face.

Valak'Ser shook his head. "She kept her own counsel." The rest of the elders nodded their assent.

“She told none of you?” Arak’Jur asked.

“No, honored guardian.”

His stomach twisted. To think so many of his tribe carried on under the burden of her terrible gift, compelled to hideous acts in the name of her madness. He couldn’t delay. Even a day spent without surety meant unspeakable horrors on the conscience of his people.

“Then I must make a request,” he said. “I would go to Ka’Ana’Tyat.”

Even Ilek’Inari gave him a twisted look, full of confusion. “Honored guardian, you are no shaman,” his apprentice said.

“I do not seek to become one. But the gift of our people is vision. And I would have knowledge of where to find Llanara, of how to see her dead.”

The men among the elders furrowed their brows, but a dawning clarity showed in the women’s eyes.

“You are a man,” came the reply, on the lips of more than one woman. Ghella’s voice emerged the strongest, now full of renewed confidence since he had found her in her tent.

“You are a man,” Ghella said again. “You cannot know the secrets of our magic, nor can you speak to the spirits of Ka’Ana’Tyat in this fashion.”

“I can,” he said. “And I would do it with your blessing.”

Before she could make further protest, he drew upon the spirit of the Mountain, feeling his eyes flood red, the color of flame.

The tent gasped.

“I carry the gift of the Nanerat,” he said. “The women’s magic. The war magic. As the chosen of the spirits.”

Voices stirred among the women, swelling with the beginnings of anger.

“No,” Ghella said, turning to address the other women. “No. He could not have this power without the spirits’ blessing. Do any among you deny the spirits of Visions would aid him in finding Llanara, in redeeming our tribe?”

The challenge hung in the air, but none rose to claim it.

“Very well,” she said. “You have our blessing, Arak’Jur. Visit Ka’Ana’Tyat, and find her.”

Her voice caught, and he saw in her eyes a kindling hope behind a veil of grief.

“Find her,” she repeated. “And bring our people home.”

52

ERRIS

Glorieux, *Quarter Deck*
The Endless Ocean

The rigging of the mainsail creaked as the ship rolled in the morning chop, thick waves pushing against her hull with force belying their small size. Pushing her west, back toward the coast of New Sarresant. The *Glorieux* was a small frigate—thirty-two guns on a single deck—but she deserved her name. By all accounts she was the fastest ship in the fleet. The admirals had suggested her to lead the farthest patrol sweeps, part of a net cast far and wide across the western reach of the Endless Ocean. Her captain boasted his ship could cover twice the distance of any other with a strong wind and an open sea.

"No sign of the Gand ships, High Commander," the captain reported after they exchanged salutes. "We encountered a flotilla of Thellan merchant galleons with a pair of frigates for an escort last night, running south-southwest on a course toward the Thellan colonies. Another ship tailed behind their wake, just off the horizon. No flags, with movements on deck disorderly and un-navylike. Pirates, sir. We tacked clear and continued our sweep to the north."

She nodded. "How long before this fog clears?"

"Likely by midday, sir."

"Very good, Captain," she said. "I will return then for further report."

"Yes, sir," he said, offering another salute.

She returned it.

Need faded and she returned to the chambers she had claimed for high command. Her requirements there had been surprisingly easy to meet. Expansive space, with close access to the burgeoning center of government here in Southgate. Multiple entryways to allow for messengers coming and going without disrupting operations. Private offices for the generals and admirals and their support staff, more senior commanders in one place than had ever been achieved during wartime.

The Lords' Council chambers had proved perfect for her needs.

Voren had laughed at the symbolism of it, seeing to it the new assembly passed a resolution funding whatever she needed to transform the grounds. And transform them she had. In place of the rows of chairs and elevated dais, she'd had massive oak tables brought in and dedicated to each potential theater of battle. Cartographers were paid lordly sums to paint them with exactly accurate detail, while engineers built detachable surfaces, allowing her to customize the chamber for any operations, at any scale. And miniatures, miniatures by the hundreds: ships, horse, men, binders, wagons, supplies. At a glance any of her commanders could see a battle as she did in her mind's eye, as a bird might see it flying overhead. With *Need* to provide accurate reports from vessels placed with each unit, they could confer and decide grand strategy at the smallest tactical levels, the movements of each regiment contributing toward the greater victory of the army. A greater upheaval to command than any in a hundred years, but the men had taken to it at once, seeing the benefits in coordination, information, and mobility. Gods send it was enough. Gods send they were ready.

"*Glorieux* reports no sign of the Gand ships," she announced for the benefit of the table in front of her, painted a deep blue and strewn with miniatures representing the sweep of her ships in the western reaches of the ocean. "Continuing on in the fog bank, heading north, same course."

Aides scrambled to update the display with the latest information, while the officers around the table shared weighing looks.

"That completes the morning sweep, yes, High Commander?" one of the captains asked.

"Yes," she said. "When I recover enough *Need* I will return to the ships stuck in that fog bank. Expect a midday update."

The table affirmed her words, returning to studying the plans they'd laid for the naval engagement, refining every detail in light of the fleet's current position, the quadrants of the sea already swept, and the remaining angles of approach the Gand fleet might take.

She moved on, toward the table indicating the movements of the army as they marched south.

"Where do you need reports, gentlemen?" she asked.

The table saluted her approach, giving her the key troop positions and supplies for which they needed information. Efficient and orderly; thank the Gods the majority of the actual generals and admirals had deemed themselves too important to participate in her newly designed central command. Instead she'd interviewed their staff and found the aides, seconds, and subcommanders who'd kept the high officers afloat, consolidating as many of them here at the Lords' Council as she could spare from the front lines.

She chose the five most pressing updates, cycling through them one by one, careful to conserve her *Need*. When she'd finished, she saluted the officers and aides who ringed the table, then excused herself to her private quarters, adjoining the hall. Sadrelle remained behind, posted at her door to wake her in time for midday.

They'd found no more *Need* binders.

Only a small handful who could—like Acherre—see the golden light. But none who could tether it. None who might spell her from the fatigue of coordinating the army, the navy, the supply trains, the scouts, even the priests she had posted along the Great Barrier, just in case.

A great disappointment. Fifteen years ago she might have preened at the thought that she was unique, that her talents were rare and unprecedented. Now she felt only exhaustion. All of this effort on her behalf and it would fall to her to be the lynchpin of the entire command. Conserving her energy was of the utmost importance, and so she slept between bindings in an effort to ward off the crippling fatigue lingering at the edge of her consciousness. No time to be exhausted. The enemy was coming. She knew it, felt the surety of it at her very core.

Where were they? What had she missed?

She slept.

"Sir, you asked for me to wake you at midday."

Sadrelle's voice. By some miracle she had fallen asleep straightaway, an eyeblink between lying down—still in full dress uniform—and being roused for another round of reports.

She rubbed the sleep from her eyes, her field training coming to the fore as her senses forced her body out of its fog. Rising to her feet, she thanked the lieutenant, rinsing her face with a splash of cold water and looking over her appearance in the stand mirror. This chamber had been a sitting room, a private office of some lord or another. Now it was hers. High Commander Erris d'Arrent. The face looking back from the mirror had already aged a few years since the last time she'd bothered examining herself.

Her eyes went to the backs of her hands, scarred as ever. No marques there—not for her, not until she'd completed the service she owed the King. Only now there was no debt. They said the citizens' assembly had declared the abduction of children an abomination, that instead there was to be publicly funded education for those who passed the binder's test, enough to prevent them harming themselves or others with their gift. Voren had seen to it there was still compulsory military service for fullbinders and those especially skilled with *Body*, *Mind*, and *Entropy*. So it was that the arc of her life, the path of service to earn a royal marque upon retirement, was only a memory now. She was a free woman, as free to bind the leylines as any noble-born who bought themselves a dispensation. Somehow she felt no differently for her freedom.

She made her way back to the main hall, checking in with the navy officers arrayed around the table showing the current maps of the Endless Ocean. All agreed it was likely the fog had burned off by now.

She found her vessels by instinct, as easy as telling one finger from another, no matter that she had hundreds of them now.

Lieutenant Gavrien, aboard the *Solitaire*. Seaman Colliers, of the *Concorde*. Seaman Baumont, of the *Frelon*. More.

All quiet, on open seas.

Finally the last vessel called to her, the midshipman aboard the *Glorieux*. She stepped into his skin, feeling the rush of the salt spray on the air, hearing the sails snap into the wind.

"Sir." The captain saluted beside her, the golden eyes giving him sign she had come even before her senses had settled.

"Report, Captain," she said. "Tell me you've sighted them."

"No, sir." He shook his head. "Nothing to report."

She closed her eyes, suppressing a sigh of frustration. Without another word she let go the binding, returning to the council chambers.

"Anything, sir?" one of her officers asked.

She shook her head.

"Could we have missed a span of the sea?" she asked. "Could they be out there, sailing past our lines?"

The captains and aides exchanged a look. "It's possible, sir," one of them spoke. "The ocean is vast. But we have been as thorough as we can with our numbers."

"Unless they had foreknowledge of our disposition—" another began.

"With so many Gand ships, they would—"

"Enough." She raised a hand, signaling them to quiet. "Recheck the coverage of our patrols. If there has been a window the Gandsmen could have slipped through, we must know where, and when they could make a landing."

"Yes, sir," the table replied.

Crossing the chamber, she went to a long table depicting the lands around the city itself. The forests that ran to the north, the cleared farmland to the south, crisscrossed by trade roads running into the southern colonies. And the Great Barrier. Fifty leagues north of the city, the lands of the colonies ended and the wilds began, the true wildlands behind the barrier itself. Lone figures represented her scouts along the barrier, spaced leagues apart, the brown-robed priests watching for signs of *Death*.

Had she been foolish to post so few? Could the enemy have made his crossing in the far north, threatening to breach the barrier in a repeat of his summer gambit?

A suicidal move even without the threat of the great beasts. New Sarresant would stand in the way of whatever southern progress they could hope to make, forcing a fight to take it that would bleed the Gand numbers and entangle their supply train. The wiser course by far was to threaten New Sarresant to force her deployment, then to sail south and make landfall in a safe port or natural harbor. An army loosed behind her borders meant the Gandsmen could maneuver in the open to find themselves a fight on favorable ground. Pinning themselves into the walls of New Sarresant meant a bloodbath.

Only, hadn't the enemy commander promised her as much?

She shivered.

Checking her stores of *Need*, she found a good amount remaining. The priests along the barrier weren't due for a report for another day at least, but her senses itched to find whatever piece of this puzzle had gone missing.

She reached for Sister Elise, reunited with the priests of Arentaigne on duty in the north.

At once the towering haze of blue film came into view, dwarfing the trees at its base. Even now the barrier inspired awe, forcing the eyes higher, ever higher, to try to catch a glimpse of its end. Here alongside it one felt small indeed.

"Sister, what is...?" a voice beside her asked. "Your eyes...?" A pause before recognition dawned. "Oh. Oh, yes. Commander."

Another brown-robed priest stood next to Sister Elise, a young woman she didn't recognize from their prior efforts to seal the barrier.

"Any report, Sister?"

"No, Commander," the priestess said. "See for yourself, it's as quiet as ever. Not even any weakening or stretches in need of repair."

She sighed in full, not bothering to hide her disappointment.

"You can bind *Shelter*?" she asked.

"Oh no, I'm a *Death* binder, Commander," the priestess replied. "The abbess thought it wise to pair us with her *Shelter* binders to help them spot, ah, enemy activities."

She nodded. A wise decision.

She closed her eyes, shifting her vision to the leylines. As she'd expected, the only energies she could see while wearing Sister Elise's skin were the white pearls of *Shelter*—the only energy with which the abbess was skilled. The rest was gray haze, for all that she would have been able to make out the fine details if she saw it with her own eyes.

The Great Barrier itself was a construct of pure *Shelter*, sustaining itself from the stores it generated, the swelling pools of white at its base. All around it the leylines curved in disorderly fashion, as they often did in the wilder, untamed places of the world. Gray haze clung to them, fed by the activity of the surrounding forest. There would be *Life* in abundance, and *Body*, and *Death*. It was the latter they had cause to fear; a few pools of inky *Death* were to be expected in the wild, but a swelling indicated the Gandsmen could be preparing to attempt another breach.

She scanned the barrier up and down with her vision shifted. No flaws in the *Shelter* that she could see. But there, on the far side, a thick haze did settle around the twisting lines, thicker than she would have expected from just the activity of the wild.

"That there," she said to the priestess. "That haze. It isn't . . . ?"

"Oh no, Commander," the priestess said. "I've been watching that. No *Death* at all. It's probably *Life*, a herd of animals perhaps. We've seen a few of those, moving up the barrier."

"Could it be soldiers?"

The question seemed to take the priestess by surprise. "I suppose it could be. But, sir, wouldn't we have warning from *Death* if they were trying to . . . ?" She swallowed.

"Yes, Sister. But even so, any large concentration of *Life* might mean—" The words died on her tongue.

One moment the barrier stood, a hundred spans high and more. The next it vanished, an enormous bore the size of the council hall cut away from the swirling haze. And behind it stood a woman in white, a native tribeswoman, her face painted with lines of red, grinning as she leveled a look at the two of them, standing there.

Beside the woman was a cat, a cat the size of a horse with eyes of flame, flanked by a host of painted tribesmen, hefting muskets and cheering.

And red coats, the red coats of Gand. Long ranks of them beside the natives, muskets shouldered as they began to march.

53

ARAK'JUR

Ka'Ana'Tyat
Sinari Land

I see no opening," Corenna said, the pain of it touching her voice. Hope had kindled when they reunited outside the Sinari village, sharing a purpose as they made for the Birthplace of Visions. A *juna'ren* lying in wait had been the first sign; since the madness of the spirits began, there was always a great beast warding the sacred places. Expecting it made its ambush far less deadly, and Corenna had dispatched the creature with a spear of ice through its throat.

And now, the entrance.

Arak'Jur saw it, plain as he saw her face. Twisted branches came together to form a passage into darkness.

"I'm sorry, Corenna," he said.

"Why?" she said. "Am I so unworthy?"

She turned to address the trees. "Have the Ranasi so offended you, great spirits, that we must be purged root and stem, only for you to spit in our eyes when we plead for help?"

He understood. For a guardian it would be as if the spirits denied their gift at the moment of the kill. An unthinkable loss; such ritual was at the heart of who and what he was. Corenna lived that horror now, barred entry to the sacred places and starved of the connections to the land that fueled the essence of her magic. Especially for one such as she, who had striven more than any woman in his memory to prepare herself for war, the spirits' prohibition would wound her to the core.

"You're not alone in this," he said, pacing around where she stood in the narrow clearing. "Ilek'Inari could not complete his final rites when we—"

"Could you see the way inside then?" she demanded. "When you first brought us here?"

He grew quiet. The memory was clear. He had seen the entrance then, just as he saw it now.

"You could," she said, with a nod to punctuate the accusation. "Why? Why did the spirits choose you?"

"I don't understand any better than you."

She turned away.

"I'm sorry, Arak'Jur," she said. "It's wrong to turn my anger on you. Forgive me."

She drew a slow breath as he watched her, and yearned for some way to make her whole.

"Go then," she said. "Enter and find what we seek."

He turned toward the entrance, where looming shadows pooled into darkness. Then he stopped and turned back toward her.

"Try to enter," he said. "Walk the path. You say you cannot see the way. I can. It is there. This is a thing of the spirits' corruption, no more."

"Arak'Jur, even if the spirits are maddened by corruption, it would invite a curse if I—"

"We are past such concerns," he said.

She held his eyes, then nodded.

She approached, striding forward toward the twisting knots of branches. A confident step carried her almost to the cusp, but when she came to the edge of the opening her fists struck upon what looked to him like the shadows themselves.

She turned back, a look of despair on her face.

"With me, then," he said, extending a hand.

She took it, and together they stepped forward.

He heard her breath catch before the world faded away to blackness, dissolving his consciousness into the presence of the spirits.

The spirits, and Corenna at his side.

ARAK'JUR.

He felt the words thunder through him even as another voice sounded: CORENNA.

BE WELCOME IN KA'ANA'TYAT, SON OF THE SINARI, DAUGHTER OF THE RANASI. BE WELCOME IN THE BIRTHPLACE OF VISIONS.

The way was barred, he thought.

YES.

A great silence lingered, though he felt the warmth of Corenna's presence beside him. If she spoke, he could not hear it, though he felt her there, huddled close as if they sheltered together by a fire.

Why? he asked at last.

WHAT THE POWER OF THE GODDESS DEMANDS, WE MUST GIVE.

Can you be made free of this burden?

Another long silence.

YOU ARE CHOSEN.

Again the spirits declared him "chosen," as if he was meant to understand. Ilek'Inari had not known its meaning. Not even the oldest stories in their people's memory spoke of such a thing, though perhaps Ka'Vos had taken the secret with him into death. He knew only that the spirits asked after it, finding the supplicants of each tribe wanting. And now had the spirits confirmed it was his mantle to bear.

What does it mean to be chosen?

IT IS THE OLD WAY. WE DID NOT REMEMBER, BEFORE. WE WERE WRONG TO TURN ASIDE THE GUARDIANS. NOW WE UNDERSTAND. YOU MUST SEEK OUT OUR POWER. ASCEND, AS CHAMPION OF THE WILD. MARK YOUR PLACE AT THE SEAT OF THE GODS.

A vulgar thought. Guardians did not seek out the gifts of the spirits, only followed the shamans' visions to ward against the great beasts that threatened the tribe.

NO.

He had given no voice to the thought, but the spirits responded all the same.

NO. GATHER OUR GIFTS. THE TIME APPROACHES. THE GOD STIRS. THE GODDESS HAS NEED OF HER CHAMPIONS.

The words washed over him with the force of thunder. If there was corruption here—and he had not ruled it out—he could not feel it.

Great spirits, he thought. *I will try.*

IT WILL SERVE. WOULD YOU HAVE OUR BOON?

Yes, he thought, bracing himself to receive their gift.

Nothing came, only silence.

Spirits? he asked.

OURS IS THE BOON OF VISIONS. ONE FOR THINGS PASSED, AND ONE FOR THINGS-TO-COME.

A sensation pervaded his thoughts, of himself asking the spirits for answers.

You wish me to ask for visions?

YES. ONE REQUEST FOR THE PAST. ONE FOR THINGS-TO-COME.

Doubt flooded his mind.

Had Corenna known this would be the boon of Ka'Ana'Tyat? Had she come prepared? For his part, his mind ran dry even as he weighed a dozen and more possibilities.

In the distance he felt a muted sensation, as if Corenna spoke to him through water, then he heard the same dull rumbling as the spirit spoke in return. Strain as he might, he could make out none of the words.

CORENNA OF THE RANASI'S ANSWERS BELONG TO HER ALONE. ASK, IF YOU WOULD HAVE YOURS.

Two questions? he asked.

YES. ASK.

The past. He could have the truth of Ka'Vos's death, surety of Corenna's devotion, or the steps that had led to Llanara's betrayal. What paths he might have walked instead, had he never taken up the mantle of the guardian. He could ask after the corruption of the spirits themselves, delving into the mysteries of their madness.

But in the end, all of these were stones cast into the river of time. He would continue on his present course—to protect his people from the ravages of war—no matter the spirits' revelations pertaining to Llanara, Ka'Vos, or even their own corruption.

Instead he sought a balm of knowledge, to salve a wound that would not heal alone.

Spirits, he began, *I would know whether I could have saved my wife, Rhealla, and my son, Kar'Elek. Whether I could have taken some action, some other course. Whether I might have returned to the village sooner, or spoken to the shaman in time to receive warning. Whether—*

YOU BEAR NO FAULT FOR THEIR DEATHS, ARAK'JUR.

The voice interrupted his thought, a peal of thunder crashing through him, mixing agony and relief.

BE FREE OF THIS BURDEN.

He felt it drain away. Grief bled through him, replaced with the sure knowledge of the spirits' words. In an instant he saw the vivid truth of that terrible day, when he had returned to the village and found the *valak'ar* slaughtering the bravest among his people, those who had stood against it, buying time for the rest to flee. He saw his wife among the first to rush forward, leading the beast away from the tents. He saw her stand firm as it coiled toward her, heard her cry out as her last thoughts echoed in his mind: thoughts of loss and sadness, but also pride. Thoughts of him and of their son. Of love. A deep and abiding love that the wraith-snake's venom could not wash away.

He watched in agony as his son picked up a spear fallen from the hand of a master hunter. He watched as his beautiful boy strode forward, confident he did only as his father would have done in his place. Once more he heard the final thoughts: Did I do it right, father? Was I a worthy son?

He saw himself. Rushing into the village, armed with no more than a hunting spear, daring to expose his flesh to the *valak'ar*'s deadly bite. He watched as it killed Arak'Mul, and he struck it down, rending the creature into bloody ruin, its corpse steaming like the ashes of a dying flame.

There was nothing more. He had done what could be done. Tides of grief and pain threatened to drown him, but through the spirits' eyes he could see the truth. He would mourn their loss, but he need not carry the burden of guilt any longer.

Pain seared through him as the visions faded.

REMEMBER THEM.

Thank you, great spirits, he thought.

ONE MORE. FOR THINGS-TO-COME. ASK.

This one was simpler.

Llanara, he thought.

The visions came at once.

54

SARINE

A Wide Street
Riverways District, New Sarresant

The street shook, windows rattling in their frames.

She felt it more than heard it, a deep boom reverberating through her *Life*-empowered senses. It sounded like a thunderclap, for all that it was midday and the sky was clear and blue. Behind her the column of nobles trailed in tight clusters, credit to Donatien for drilling them in soldiers' marching formations. She paused, looking over her shoulder to the northwest, the direction from which they had come.

Another boom, this time enough to rattle her teeth.

Regiment-Major Laurent turned to look, the same as she had. "What under the Nameless—?" he managed, before yet another boom cut him short.

"Cannon fire," Captain Vaudreuil said, flanking her at the head of the column. "Someone is setting off artillery."

"Keep moving," she said, raising her voice. "Let's go, everyone keep up." More than a few heads had turned, startled back into line by the sound of her voice. She looked up and down the line, seeing no sign of any attacks nearby; the booms were far enough away, and in the direction from which they had come, not the way they traveled now.

Still, her uncle.

He'd insisted she leave him behind, and nothing short of clubbing him over the head and tying him to a pack horse would have been enough to change his mind. She'd almost done that very thing, his choices be damned. Her stomach wrenched at the thought that he'd stayed behind, doubly so now if Vaudreuil was right. Artillery, northwest of the city. Almost enough to see her turn back to the Maw just to be certain he was safe. Instead she checked her leyline tethers through the strange power Axerian had called a warding, the blue sparks that even days later had not diminished. *Shelter* would hold if *Faith* did not, with the chapel itself an ample supply of both.

Vaudreuil trotted at her side, in full dress uniform of a navy captain, as the booms sounded again.

"What do you make of it, Captain?" she asked. Laurent loped along beside her, listening in as they spoke.

"I can't begin to guess," Vaudreuil said. "I had little information about the goings-on in this wretched city—ah, begging your pardon."

"Perhaps a training exercise," Laurent said. "I know the new High Commander personally. D'Arrent was ever fond of her war games." That had been one of the few learnings they'd been able to glean from excursions into the city—Erris d'Arrent had high command of the army. Donatien had been silent on it, and she hadn't pressed.

"Cannons though, so near the city?" she said.

Laurent's brow furrowed as he took another look over his shoulder. "She might," he said dubiously.

Nodding, and hoping it proved to be no more than that, she kept them moving down the wide streets of the Riverways, angling toward the Harbor district. The booms echoing in the distance added uncertainty to their slow advance, though they already took a great risk moving through the city in daylight. Vaudreuil had insisted their best chance was to sail on the evening tide, and that meant taking the time to secure supplies and free his crew beforehand. And now this. Gods send that nothing else went awry before she saw these people to safety.

As if to mock her pleas, a small company of men strode into view at an intersection ahead, carrying muskets but out of uniform. Almost she reached for *Yellow* before they continued on course, heading west on a different street. Off-duty soldiers, perhaps, but far more likely to be d'Agarre's people, armed citizens. And they were marching in the direction of the cannons. She shared looks with Laurent, Vaudreuil, and the nobles around her, feeling the uncertainty she was sure was common up and down the line.

They tacked east, staying north of the river as they made way toward the Harbor district. Two leagues perhaps to cross through the rest of the city. They had somehow managed to avoid one patrol already, and made good time as they followed the streets winding along the banks of the river. Perhaps whatever trouble was brewing in the northwest corner of the city would leave them behind as they gained the ship.

"They'll be in one of the warehouses along the harbor," Vaudreuil had said when she'd asked after his crew. He'd proceeded to give her every detail he could remember, and offered to go with her to help spur the men to obedience. It would be a delicate thing to use *Yellow* to scatter whatever guards had been set without affecting the sailors, but Zi could do it. Whatever else his failings, she retained full confidence in his gifts.

She thought she knew the warehouse Vaudreuil had described, and went over the plans in her head as they moved. A side approach would be best, using one of the back alleys both in and out. Even now there was plenty of traffic in the harbor. She'd as soon keep the attention she drew to a minimum.

Thoughts of planning died as they rounded a left turn toward the district boundary. Gods damn it. Another company of militia, this one fifty strong or more and all carrying muskets, rushing up the very street down which they meant to march.

So much for luck.

"Stay back," she called to the nobles behind her.

The militiamen showed no signs of stopping. Flares of *Yellow* sprang up at the edges of her vision. The militia were close enough for her to feel their emotions, using the power of Zi's gift: dread, determination, worry, anticipation. She reached out to them, intending to amplify the fear already nestled there.

Instead Zi whispered into her mind. *Green.*

A moment of confusion, backed by a rising fury. Had he worked against her? Had he used the power of *Green*—to manipulate positive emotions—to offset her *Yellow*?

No, Zi thought to her. *Not me.*

Then she saw the man at the head of the militia company, a man carrying no musket, shouting commands, looking toward her column with rage in his eyes. She didn't recognize the man, but he seemed to know her, staring into her eyes as he barked out orders to fire.

She had a bare moment before the militiamen dropped to their knees, leveling their muskets to shoot.

Shelter sprang up as the whipcracks of musket shot went off, wisps of smoke rising where they dissolved into harmless vapor. A battle cry rose up from behind the barrier she had constructed. *Red,* came the warning from Zi.

"I can't break them!" she cried. "They have a *kaas*-mage. Laurent!"

Major Laurent seemed to blur as he tethered *Body,* drawing his sword with grim determination, huddled behind her barrier.

Yellow, thought Zi.

No. She willed *Green* into place, countering her enemy's attempt to scatter her line in the same manner she had seen him do moments before.

"What should we do?" Laurent called to her.

They had moments, mere moments only before the militia covered the ground between them. And what if this enemy *kaas*-mage had access to *Black,* the power d'Agarre had used to drain away her bindings? What if he pierced through her *Shelter* and left them exposed?

"I didn't want to have to kill them," she said. "I—"

"No time, we have to attack!" Laurent shouted back.

Careful, Zi thought.

She dropped her *Shelter* binding and called on the power she'd found hidden in the sewers, granted by the strange voices at once similar to the *mareh'et* and *lakiri'in,* and yet also different. War-spirits, they had named themselves. Spirits of the storm.

Air ripped as she discharged their gift, streaks of lightning arcing from her hands into the onrushing militiamen. She was right; they'd almost been upon her barrier, a mere twenty paces shy of racing around her *Shelter* and crashing into the nobles. Their eyes narrowed with hate as her barrier vanished, replaced with shock and terror as her power struck home, streaking from man to man as it snaked through their line.

Screams, terrible screams as a crushing boom followed her gift.

White, Zi thought to her, and it was so: The man at the head of the column stood untouched, surrounded by a pulsing white shield.

But she heard nothing, saw nothing. The world seemed to blur.

A feeling bloomed in her mind, a swelling tide from the tips of her fingers down the back of her spine.

Pleasure.

She teetered on the edge, an abyss of golden warmth beckoning her for what seemed an eternity. Her mind drew in the feeling, shuddering as the sensation of needles pricked all across her skin. Joy, and a thirst for more. A thirst for blood. Pure bliss that stretched every moment into an hour, every heartbeat into a void of thoughtless rapture.

Fight it, Zi thought to her. *Come back.*

She blinked. It called to her, stirring a yearning from deep inside her. A picture shrouded in mist, struggling to be made real.

Screams. High-pitched screams.

The world came back into focus.

She saw Laurent, his face twisted in surprise as his head lay skewed apart from his torso, a sure sign his neck had been snapped. And Vaudreuil, twisted in an echo of the same, his fine naval uniform ditched into crimson snow. She saw bodies around her, bodies dressed in sullied clothes that had once been fine. Bodies of the nobles, torn and bloody.

Red flared at the edge of her vision, and she tethered *Body*, whirling to face the source. The *kaas*-mage had been loosed in her company, and they had broken before his attack, scattering into the street in a panic. The man laughed, a look of madness in his eyes as he ran after them.

She moved.

A raging flurry, drawing upon *mareh'et* to complement the rest of her gifts. She closed the distance between them in a heartbeat, striking the man in the back with one of the Great Cat's ethereal claws. His *White* already exhausted, the man folded like paper into the slush remaining on the street.

As he died she felt the faintest stirring of the sensation that had crippled her before, a droplet of pleasure washing over her mind.

And then grief.

"Sarine," Donatien said.

She affected not to hear him, lost in a sea of gray. It was her fault. It had been her responsibility to protect these people, and she had failed.

The remainder of their journey passed in a daze, long streets made for wagonloads of goods hauled from the ships, reaching out from the harbor like the fingers of a corpse. She walked their paths inward, knowing she had blood on her hands. Never mind the men she had cut down like chaff with the gifts of the storm spirits; she had lost a dozen or more of her charges before coming to her senses. Zi had tried to warn her, tried to stay her from this course. She was a fool.

"Sarine," Donatien said again. "Isn't that . . . ?"

She looked up.

Axerian stood in a relaxed posture, hands at his waist, short curved blades dangling from his belt. Waiting for them at the end of the last street, where their path ended at the entrance to the harbor.

"It wasn't your fault," Donatien said quietly as they moved toward where Axerian stood.

The nobles behind them moved in a ragged procession, as if they carried some glimmer of the burden on her shoulders. She looked back and saw their haunted eyes reflecting her guilt, wincing as she turned away. It *was* her fault.

"Sarine, I—" Donatien said.

"Donatien," she said. "Let it be. Please."

He said nothing more and she didn't look back.

Axerian grinned at her approach, the first she'd seen him since the day they'd rescued the captain. If he noticed the hollowness she felt behind her eyes he made no comment on it. This had been his way since he'd first come to the chapel: showing up when he had word of d'Agarre's activities, then vanishing for days at a time, only to reappear wearing a half smile as if his arrival were a matter of course.

"Trouble crossing the city?" Axerian said, casting a glance up and down her column as he fell into step beside her.

She nodded. No need to bear repeating the details.

"We ran into d'Agarre's militia," Donatien said. "Isn't that what you are supposed to be out stopping?"

The upbraiding sounded foolish to her ears. Not that Donatien had cause to know he was speaking to a God.

Axerian seemed similarly amused. "How under the heavens did you manage without me, my noble lordling?"

"There was a *kaas*-mage with them," she said.

Axerian's eyes shone as his smile faded into a look of concern. "Ah," was all he said.

"Sarine cut the man down," Donatien said as he walked a step behind. "She saved us all."

"You'd hardly be standing here if she hadn't, my lord," Axerian said, his smile returning.

"Why are you here?" she asked Axerian, coming to a halt at the mouth of the harbor. The streets beyond were quiet for all that it was still midafternoon. She glanced down the docks, craning her neck to try to tell one ship from another. They all looked the same to her, knots of rigging and white sails packed and bound to masts as tall as buildings. Some empty, some swarming with sailors preparing to sail. If Captain Vaudreuil had been here he could have shown the way to the *Redoubtable*, but he was dead. Because of her.

"As it happens, I have need of your assistance," Axerian said. "The city has need of your assistance. There have been certain developments over the last two days."

His words flowed through her like water through a sieve. She cast another blank look up and down the harbor. "After," she said. "First I have to save the nobles, to get them to the ship."

He grinned more broadly. "I'd guessed you might do that."

"What do you mean?" she said.

"My dear," he said, a spark showing in his eyes, "I took the liberty of releasing the *Redoubtable*'s crew and seeing to it they were provisioned for a lengthy voyage. I trust I guessed aright?"

"What? You sent them away?"

He laughed, forestalling the beginnings of her anger. "No, no. I know you too well. As soon as the captain gave his name I knew you'd come. I have the crew set and waiting for your charges, here at the northern docks."

She gave him a long look.

"Shall we?" he asked, offering an arm.

With a wordless nod, she disdained his gesture as she strode past him. He laughed again, walking beside her as the column of nobles trailed in their wake. A glance behind revealed Donatien simmering but silent, meeting her eyes with a look that nonetheless bespoke compassion.

They made the short walk to the north end of the harbor in relative silence, passing sailors eyeing them with dubious looks. She was past caring. So long as they made it to the ship.

Yellow, came the thought from Zi.

Panic flooded her veins, whirling around to find the source.

Axerian held out a hand as a calming gesture. "It's only me," he said. "A warding, to ensure the ship could remain here safely. There, see?"

The sensation faded from her mind, though her pulse did not slow. She nodded.

And there it was. A cheer went up from the nobles when they read the name etched on its hull.

The *Redoubtable.*

She found a stack of crates, and seated herself atop one, watching as the nobles made their way onto the ship. The crew had made quick work of preparations, unfurling rope lines and barking orders across the deck. Vaudreuil's first officer—the captain now—had assured her they'd be under way within the hour. She'd stolen away to have a few moments to herself. Here on the dock, before she had to say her goodbyes.

The thought came again: She was a fool.

"What was it, Zi?" she whispered. "What happened to me?"

Black, he thought to her.

"Killing?"

Yes.

She brought her knees up to her chin, wrapping her arms around them as she rocked in silence.

It is one of the ways Axerian corrupts his ascendants, Zi thought. *He uses the Veil's power to compel my kind not to intercede.*

Her thoughts went back to the night of the salon, to the look of madness in Reyne d'Agarre's eyes when he killed the Comtesse de Rillefort. Had she worn the same look as her charges died around her?

"There are plenty of murderers in the world. Why me? Why does it affect me? Because of our bond?"

Yes. It is the price of our gift. You feel some margin of what I collect.

"This all sounds like things for which I am not prepared," she said, allowing some measure of bitterness to creep into her voice.

It is my nature to protect you.

"I know, Zi," she said, tears sliding from her eyes. "I'm sorry."

The moment lingered, sailors shouting as they worked, relief showing on the nobles' faces as they walked up the gangplanks. How she wished for a moment she could be like them, not for their finery and poise even in the face of adversity, but for the small kindness of being able to board a ship and sail away from everything. The freedom of it beckoned to her, the adventure of the unknown.

"Do you know anything of what Axerian spoke? The danger to the city?"

No. I know only what I see, the same as you do.

She nodded.

But it may be d'Agarre. He will be close to ascension.

"Zi, will you explain what ascension is, please?"

A long silence stretched, and she felt a measure of anger come creeping back, never mind the softness she had felt before.

The Seat of the Gods, he thought to her. *Three champions, one for each line, at each awakening. Three to decide the fate of creation for each cycle. Three for Life, Three for Death.*

She turned his words over in her mind, repeating them to herself.

"I don't understand," she said.

The champions decide the image of the world, vying for balance between the Goddess and the God. Life and Death.

"The image of the world...? And what is a champion?"

Pain lanced through her mind, though it was no sensation of hers.

Please, he thought. *You are not ready.*

Understanding dawned. "Zi, does it hurt you to tell me these things?"

Only if you are not ready to hear them. It is part of the bond. Like the union of the spirits and the aspects of gold along the ley-threads; there is an appointed time. I am sorry.

"It's all right," she said quietly. "I'm sorry, too, Zi. I'm a fool."

So are we all, when we are young.

She laughed at that, rich and true in spite of her grief. Imagining Zi as a young version of himself was more than she could manage. He was just Zi. As far as she was concerned he had always been exactly as he was.

"Feeling better?" Donatien asked, approaching from the base of the gangplanks leading onto the deck of the ship.

She looked up at him, feeling some of her mirth drain away. "Donatien, I—"

"You're not coming aboard the ship," he finished for her.

Tears welled up, and she shook her head, reaching a hand up to wipe them away as Donatien came to sit beside her.

"Sarine, it's all right," he said. "I understand. I knew this was coming, even if I didn't want to admit it to myself."

"Thank you," she said, stifling another wave of emotion.

Donatien offered his arm, and she leaned against him, a roil of conflicting feelings coursing through her. He held her as they listened to the sailors work, making final preparations before the ship cast off.

"You will stop him," Donatien said after a time. "D'Agarre I mean."

She nodded.

"Did Axerian disappear again?" he asked.

She nodded again. "I told him I needed a moment. He said to meet him at the chapel."

"Did he know what was happening in the city? The cannons?"

"I don't know. He didn't say anything more."

"Be careful with him," Donatien said. "If he can help you, let him, but—"

"You're right," she said. "And I will."

They sat together for a long moment, until one of the sailors called out. Final boarding.

Donatien rose to his feet, turning to look at her.

"You are an amazing woman, Sarine," he said. "I've been privileged to have loved you."

"Thank you, Donatien," she said, rising into his arms one last time. "Thank you for everything."

They held together as long as they could before breaking away, and she watched as he rounded the dock, looking back at her as he boarded the ship.

Emotions swelled within her as the mooring lines were cut. Relief for the ones she had saved, regret for the ones she had lost. Sadness for Donatien, but sweetness, too; the same for Zi.

And determination. A rising swell of determination from deep within her bones. It was past time to see this decided, one way or another.

55

ERRIS

High Command
Southgate District, New Sarresant

She leaned over a hastily painted table showing the winding streets of the Gardens, watching as the aides adjusted the placement of red, green, and blue figures.

"Gods damn it," she cursed, drawing solemn nods from around the table.

They'd been too slow. Another half day and they might have staged a battle in the northern plains, between New Sarresant and the barrier. Instead three full brigades of Gand infantry had begun their march into the city, with batteries of artillery in place to shell the Gardens, screening their movements. Those were the red figures. The green figures—hastily painted when it became clear there would be another player on this stage—were the nightmares made flesh set loose on the streets of the city. Tribesmen, natives of the New World. And the terrible beast, the horse-cat that by all accounts was fighting at the tribesmen's side. She might not have believed it but for seeing it with her own eyes, through the power of *Need*: a horse-sized cat with eyes of flame.

All of them marching together. All of them attacking the city.

Madness.

There was no other explanation. If the Gandsmen had wanted to take New Sarresant, the civilized thing was to maneuver in the open field until they defeated her army, then obtain a formal surrender. That was how wars were waged. Indiscriminately firing artillery into a city was barbarism of the highest order, to say nothing of marching soldiers through its gates, inviting a pitched battle street-to-street. Even in the best-executed versions of her battle plans, thousands would die, on both sides. Tens of thousands. And still the enemy came, willing to bleed his own ranks if it meant the same in hers.

"How many of them are there?" Reyne d'Agarre asked. The man stuck out as if he'd worn white to a funeral, dressed in a red coat amid a sea of blue uniforms. If he noticed the insult of wearing the enemy's colors into her command hall he didn't seem to care, staring blithely at the figures.

"Sixty thousand soldiers that we've confirmed, Assemblyman," one of her aides replied. "With perhaps another corps' worth as yet undeployed."

"Making the final count...?" d'Agarre asked.

"Eighty thousand," she finished for him. "Give or take."

"Sir, the Eighty-Third will be engaged presently," another of the aides said, pointing, as if she hadn't been watching that section of the map for the past half hour. News of the Gandsmen's arrival north of the city had spread like an arc of lightning through the ranks of her soldiers deployed along the colonial trade roads, but they were still hours away from reaching New Sarresant in force. Shorthanded as she was, she'd drawn a line of battle across the southwest sections of the city, putting her forces in place to flank any attempts to seize the bridges across the Verrain River—the natural choke points of the city. The 83rd was the first unit to take up a place along the waterfront. More would be coming to reinforce with every passing hour, but a good many of her soldiers were too damn far behind.

"And how many of the green figures?" d'Agarre was asking. "The tribesmen?"

"We don't know," an aide replied. "Perhaps twenty thousand, perhaps fewer. Scouts have had difficulties assessing accurate reports."

"Difficulties?" d'Agarre said.

"They're being killed, Assemblyman," Erris said absently, looking over the long train of figures representing her troops on their march into the city. She'd managed some semblance of order by virtue of her *Need* bindings, but less than she might have liked. Everything hinged on holding the line until her full strength arrived. It meant the Gardens was a lost cause, and that Southgate would fall if the enemy so much as breathed heavily in the wrong direction, but if she could hold, her men could pin the enemy troops in the Riverways if they maneuvered east to try to cross the bridges. And that meant she would protect the harbor, the gateway to the city.

"Sir, we could use an update here, from the Forty-Second," an aide said, leaning over the table. "Brigade-Colonel Iman should have deployed along the west flank by now, and the tribesmen are moving fast."

She nodded. "Very well. I'll check in on the Eighty-Third and Forty-Second. Anything else?"

The table shook their heads, as d'Agarre asked, "How many soldiers do we have again?"

Gods but he was an annoyance. Here to represent the interests of the people, or whatever nonsense to which Voren had agreed without consulting her.

"Sixty thousand," she snapped. "Plus however many of your citizens you can convince to pick up a musket."

He nodded as she turned her attention back to the maps, burning the disposition of the battle lines into her memory. She'd had light blue figures painted as well, to represent d'Agarre's militia, but in her mind the count was sixty thousand, no matter what outlandish numbers of armed civilians the man claimed he could put in the field. A good amount of her own soldiers had languished under commanders worth less than shit stuck to her boot; so much the worse for untrained militiamen. They'd be lucky to avoid discharging their muskets while trying to reload. Perhaps if it came to it—if the circumstances were truly dire—she could find a use for them, but that would be paying the butcher in his own coin.

She drew a deep breath, and reached for *Need.*

"Line of battle, boys," a voice bellowed in her ear. "Let's give these dogs hot lead to chew on."

The roar of friendly soldiers accompanied the command as blue uniforms rushed in front of her, a double-quick march to man a hastily erected barricade of furniture in the middle of the street. Artillery boomed overhead as the Gandsmen continued spitting fire into her city, with Gods only knew what targets in mind. Enough to keep her from attempting a maneuver to seize the northern walls, which was likely the point. Still, a brutal tactic, to shell civilians.

"Colonel," she yelled over the din. "Regiment-Colonel, report!"

"High Commander. Good of you to join us." He removed his hat, a wide-brimmed sort better suited to the hot months, waving it overhead. "Here, boys, they're coming. Dig in and show them what it costs! Show them the price they pay for treading on New Sarresant soil!"

She turned to see the first line of red coats appear at the far end of the street, then just as quickly vanish behind a billowing cloud of smoke as the front ranks fired.

"We're engaged, Commander," the colonel roared. "That's my report. The Eighty-Third is engaged, under heavy fire at the boundary of the Riverways." His eyes shone, a man thoroughly in his element. There was a reason she'd placed the 83rd at the head of the line. "Reload, boys, reload. Back line forward, give them another volley!"

She released *Need*.

"The Eighty-Third reports contact with the enemy," she said. "Two blocks north of King Louis-Fachard Square."

Aides scrambled to push the figures into place.

She reached for another golden thread, this one tied to a foot-lieutenant whose name she couldn't remember. Even so she knew by instinct it was the right woman, the second to Brigade-Colonel Iman with the 42nd, on the far west flank, approaching the Gardens.

Bloodcurdling shrieks pierced her ears as soon as the tether snapped into place.

Howls of pain, and ululating cries like nothing she had heard before. Her vision came into focus just in time for her reflexes to take over, hefting the musket she carried to parry the thrust of a bayonet. A hulking man filled her vision, his skin the color of bronze painted with bright colors, garbed in the furs of some kind of animal she didn't recognize.

"*Uluv'a cha'be!*" he shouted, diving at her.

She pivoted, reaching for *Body* by instinct only to find nothing there. Gods damn it but she wished she had access to her ley bindings while she used *Need*. She managed to get out of his way, dancing backward toward the line of friendly soldiers.

Only there was no such line. A panicked look over her shoulder revealed blue coats fleeing before an onslaught of tribesmen dressed and painted like the man in front of her. She was alone, and surrounded.

Gritting her teeth, she wheeled her musket around, swinging it like a club. Her soldiers hadn't even managed to fix bayonets. What had happened here?

Her musket connected with the tribesman's head, putting him off balance and sending him crashing into the cobblestone. That drew the attention of two of his fellows, nodding in her direction as they leveled their guns. Behind them she heard laughter, high and rich. A woman stood watching them, her face painted white with a red stripe down the center. The same woman she had seen at the barrier? Erris stepped back, squaring her feet, and felt musket shot pierce her gut.

Pain.

Need faded, and she sucked in air.

"Sir?" the aides exclaimed, one of them managing to catch her before she fell forward.

"What is it?" d'Agarre said from the opposite end of the table. "Is there some kind of—?"

"The Forty-Second is broken," she managed, coughing as her senses came to accept the fact that the shots had not actually pierced her own flesh. "We need to reinforce the west flank. Binders, I need binders. What do we have close to the Gardens?"

Her aides scrambled to find the information, poring over deployment reports and scanning the figures on the table.

"The tribesmen, right, Commander?" d'Agarre asked, looking thoughtful as he considered the scene-in-miniature.

"Assemblyman, due respect but I have a battle to fight," she snapped, turning her attention back to her aides as they worked.

"Was there a woman among them?" he asked in an even tone. "Their leader perhaps?"

Shock ripped the words from her throat. "What—?" she managed, then swallowed to recover her breath. "How could you know that?"

He smiled, nodding as if she had given him news of a victory. "Leave the tribes to me, Commander," he said. "My people can stand against their magic."

"Are you mad?" she said, even the aides turning to regard him with a measure of disbelief. "I just told you they broke a full regiment of my soldiers."

"Save your binders, Commander," d'Agarre said, his eyes shining as he wheeled about to make for the exit. "The left flank is mine."

He was a madman. Did he want to die? She'd seen it before among soldiers in hopeless situations, suicidal charges to bring death at a time of their choosing rather than wait for the inevitable. He boasted great numbers in his militia. She couldn't countenance him sending innocent men and women to die for a vain dream of glory.

"No," she said. "D'Agarre, that's an order. Stop at once."

He did, turning to face her with a cold stare in his eyes.

"You do not command me, Erris d'Arrent. Unless you mean to fight a battle here and now, I suggest you turn your attention to the conflict you know. Deal with the Gandsmen. Leave the rest to me."

The entire chamber fell silent by the time he was through. One did not hear—or countenance—that sort of talk to *anyone* in the military, let alone the High Commander of the army.

"Sergeant-at-arms," she said, loud enough for the room to hear. "Clap that man in irons."

D'Agarre laughed. No one in the room moved.

She cast a glare at the sergeant, finding him standing stock-still and frozen, looking back at her as his body trembled. If she didn't know better she would say the man was overcome with terror, the sort that raw recruits got when they were forced into a line of battle for the first time. What under the Gods?

"Don't waste your efforts, Commander," d'Agarre said. "And don't presume to believe you know all of the mysteries in this world."

He left the chamber.

The air seemed to rush back into the room, her aides and officers sharing looks of bewilderment and anger.

"Is anyone hurt?" she said.

"No, sir," mumbled the voices standing nearby, as the rest of the room shook their heads.

They looked as if they couldn't believe what they had just seen, and she couldn't blame a one of them. What in the Nameless's twisted mind had she just witnessed? D'Agarre was an assemblyman, and a member of the Council-General before his coup d'état. Not the sort of man known for martial prowess, and he had just spoken to a fullbinder as if she were a child, inspired a room full of soldiers to a state just shy of full-blown panic, then walked away. Was he a binder after all? Is that what the tribesmen were doing, some version of whatever she had just seen from d'Agarre?

"Sir," one of her aides piped up, "you wanted reports on binders near the west flank...?"

"Yes," she said, feeling her mind refocus on the details of the battle, never mind d'Agarre's madness. "Yes, what do we have?"

"A contingent of *Shelter* binders with the Sixth Division, sir, currently with the Twenty-Second Infantry two leagues from the Gardens, and another company of *Body* binders with the Eleventh Light Cavalry to the east."

"Vassail's brigade?" she asked.

"Yes, sir, that's right."

"Foot-Captain Marquand is with her," she said.

The aide frowned, looking down at the reports he'd been reading. "Sir, are you certain?" he asked. "I have no mention here of any of our *Entropy* binders with—"

"He'll be with her, Lieutenant."

"Yes, sir," said the aide. "Will you order them to the west to cover for the Forty-Second?"

She glanced down at the table, taking in the details of their deployment. She'd given Vassail a company of binders, knowing the brigade-colonel could make full use of them even without her direct guidance. The west flank was a weak point—if the enemy swept around it, the Gandsmen could pincer her line from north and south, cutting off her ability to reinforce with the reserve now pouring into the city. She didn't have the strength to hold the bridges directly, but so long as her men held in Southgate and the Gardens, the enemy had to deal with her before he moved. For all a collapse in the west would expose her, she had to concentrate strength to be in position to respond if he tried the attack anyway. And with d'Agarre about to unleash some sort of madcap chaos on the left wing...

"No." She made a snap decision. "No. We give d'Agarre what he wants. A distraction on the west flank serves our strategy. We'll pull the line eastward after we give up the Gardens."

"Very good, sir," the men and women around the table murmured.

Only one thing remained.

She reached for Marie d'Oreste, one of the few vessels she had not committed to the fighting.

Her vision slid into place in an open square, surrounded by men and women in thick coats, carrying muskets held aloft as they listened to a man shouting from the base of a statue at their center.

"—come to our city, and invade us?" the man shouted. "No! We will fight them all, show them we are willing to bleed for our ideals. Who is with me?"

The crowd roared around her as she felt a musket in her own hands, Marie's hands.

The woman had joined d'Agarre's militia.

"Marie," she said softly, knowing the woman would remember her words even if no one in the crowd could hear, "I need you to find Reyne d'Agarre to the west of the city, and stay close to him, or at least stay with his people. I need to see what happens there. If it gets bad, I will send reinforcements."

It would be enough. She let *Need* go, returning to the high command, studying the map to plan for a sequence of ambushes as the battle lines pushed back through the Gardens. She could do this. The enemy commander had *Need*, with the advantage of numbers and twenty thousand screaming tribesmen besides, but this was her city. She would see to it the Gandsmen paid in blood for every block of every street they took.

56

SARINE

District Boundary
Maw District, New Sarresant

She'd passed four more militia companies massing in the streets as she made her way west through the city, each one crying out for *égalité*, hoisting homemade banners sporting various sigils and designs as they tromped through the remains of the snow. A trivial thing to avoid them, now that she'd seen her charges safely aboard the *Redoubtable*. But still, the militia's presence on the streets was alarming. D'Agarre's people had already driven the nobles into hiding, if not outright spilled their blood in the mock tribunals. What was the purpose of a second revolution?

Was he moving against the army now?

A bitter thought, made worse by the raw pit in her stomach. Bitter and sweet, her exchanges with both Donatien and Zi. And all of it punctuated by a stream of thunderclaps and smoke coming from the northwest.

Her pace quickened, moving toward the chapel, hearing the booms grow ever louder, ever closer. Little chance it was a training exercise, going on for so long, and with d'Agarre's people massing in the streets. The smoke was rising over the Gardens again, and for all the Maw was separated from the chaos by the bridges of the Riverways, still a knot of worry grew on her uncle's behalf. Her *Shelter* held through the warding—remarkable how little effort it required to sustain it, with the blue sparks—and so did *Faith*. But still, having reached the rusted iron gates that marked the district boundary, her heartbeat quickened to match her steps as she raced toward the Sacre-Lin.

Faith snapped into place by reflex as another company of d'Agarre's militia came roaring into view. She heard them before she saw them, shouting and whooping as if they embarked on some grand adventure. They held their muskets high as they ran in a disorderly pack, more akin to feral dogs feeding from the leavings at the butcher's shop than to men.

She let them pass undisturbed. More important to be certain her uncle was safe.

She arrived at the chapel, dropping her bindings for long enough to race up the steps and throw open the main door.

"Uncle," she called, stepping into the atrium court. "Is everything all right?"

Her heart spiked as no reply came. She crossed the atrium and called out once more as she made way into the central nave.

"Ah, my child, you're back," her uncle said, smiling as he rose from one of the pews. "And you never told me your friend was a Trithetic scholar."

Axerian stood beside him, a glimmer in his eye.

"I trust all went well with the nobles?" her uncle said.

"Yes. They're safe." She cast a look up and down the chapel, detecting no sign of distress in her uncle or the stone- and glass-work of the Sacre-Lin. "Everything is all right here? D'Agarre's people are everywhere outside, I was worried for—"

"I'm fine, child," her uncle said. "Your protection has worked wonders these past days."

Axerian offered a bow to her uncle. "If you'll excuse me, Father, we'll have to settle the matter of the essential virtues of the Veil on another occasion, if it pleases."

"Of course," her uncle said. "Yes, of course. I'll need to catalog the larder with our guests gone, take stock of what we'll need to make it through till spring." He shuffled toward the back rooms, turning back to regard her with a fond look. "You take care, child, and bring this one around more often. Most stimulating conversation, most stimulating indeed."

"I will, uncle," she said. "I'm glad to see you safe."

"Everything settled at the docks?" Axerian asked after her uncle had closed the door behind him.

"Yes," she said. "And thank you for your help."

"It was no inconvenience at all," he said, eyes shining.

"How did you get into the chapel? My bindings held. You shouldn't have been able to see it, let alone enter."

"I have my ways. And I'm not so sure your Zi would approve of my sharing the details."

He used Black, Zi thought to her.

"Zi says you used *Black*."

Axerian gave a short laugh, walking out from behind the benches and gesturing for her to follow. "Let's get moving," he said. "We have some rather important business to which we must attend."

"Wait." He stopped, turning to her with a questioning look. "You know I had to kill the militiamen. When the *kaas*-mage attacked us in the Riverways."

"Yes, and my thanks for dispatching another of their number. We're close, now. So close to ensuring we avert disaster."

He said it reverently, with a passion she couldn't summon for herself. Always before there had been fire in her belly at the thought of striking back at d'Agarre, but now she was left with her failure in the Riverways, a weight that settled behind her eyes, raw and laced with guilt.

"I felt something, when they died. It distracted me." Memories came back, of blood and broken bodies, and she closed her eyes to ward them away before she spoke again. "Zi said it's part of our bond."

Axerian's manner shifted, from carefree passion to heartfelt concern. "Yes," he said. "*Black*. It can be intense."

"Zi also said that is the manner you corrupted d'Agarre, and the others."

Axerian winced, affecting an exaggerated look of pain. "True. I won't hide from it. A regrettable thing, and one for which I am here in part to make amends." He eyed her as if making sure she'd heard his words before he continued. "Zi was right about your bond. You must take care not to expose yourself to too much of any of the emotions he collects. There is no danger so long as you proceed with caution, and temperance. It's why my path was named Balance, years ago."

She nodded slowly.

"As to the rest," he continued, "there will be time enough after to explain, in as much detail as Zi will allow." He smiled, offering a slight bow as if he could see Zi there to offer deference. "For now, you should know there is real danger here in the city."

"Danger? D'Agarre's people? The cannons?"

"Only the first part of it. It seems my onetime fellows—yes, your Exarch and Oracle—have accelerated their plans here on the Vordu continent, that is to say, your New World."

"What do you mean?"

"I mean their influence has been cast here, and in force. Paendurion's troops are attacking the city even as we speak. Your Gandsmen, I believe. And Ad-Shi has brought—"

"What?" she started. "You mean the smoke, the soldiers... Oh, Gods." She turned toward the main door. "We have to get out there, I have to defend the city, I—"

"Wait, Sarine, remember Zi's warning. You cannot throw yourself into the fighting."

"Uncle, we're leaving," she called, rounding on the door, then pivoting back. "Wait, no, he has to go, he can't stay here."

"Sarine, please," Axerian said. "Hear me out."

"What?" she demanded, a rising panic in her belly.

"This is what d'Agarre wants, him and the other *kaas*-mages. Ascension is..." He trailed off, eyeing her with a pointed look.

"What? What is it?"

"Zi?" he asked, making her companion's name a question, clearly a request for permission to speak. Despite it all, anger simmered again. He had no right, no more than Zi did, to withhold information from her. No right to—

Tell her, Zi thought to them both.

Axerian's eyes lingered for a moment before he nodded. "Ascension is the product of amassing power enough to trigger passage to the Gods' Seat. For the *kaas*, the true path is a depth of experience, an abiding knowledge of the various facets of life—but there are shortcuts."

She said nothing, waiting for him to speak.

"Killing," he said. "Ordinarily a *kaas* would find such a path abhorrent. But in light of certain... influences"—he bowed his head, gesturing toward himself—"d'Agarre and the others will not balk. They will be sparks to powder in the heat of a battle, whether they know it or not."

"So what would you have me do? You say I can't fight. Am I to just watch the city burn while I hunt down Reyne d'Agarre?"

"More than just a city will burn if any of them ascends, Sarine," he said, his eyes filled with pain. "Please."

"I need to see my uncle to safety," she said numbly.

"Nowhere in this city is as safe as this chapel, protected by your gifts through a warding."

Her objections crumbled as another wave of cannon fire rattled gravel in the chapel windowsills. *Shelter* would keep her uncle safe. Damn him for not being on board the *Redoubtable*. Damn her for not putting him there herself.

"All right," she said finally. "How do we find the *kaas*-mages in the middle of a battle?"

Axerian's eyes shone once more. "Listen to Zi—he'll warn you if any *kaas* powers are used nearby. We'll each go our own way to cover more ground. But take care if d'Agarre or his fellows are close to ascension. They will emit fields of *Yellow* and *Green* like nothing you've seen, swelling to drive half the city mad, before the end. If you encounter such a thing, even the beginnings of it, do not attempt to confront them alone. Come find me, and we face them together. Otherwise"—he gave a grim smile—"take them down."

"Everything all right?" her uncle asked, peeking his head out from around the priest's door at the back of the hall.

She looked back over Axerian's shoulder, meeting her uncle's eyes. "Stay here in the chapel, uncle. Please. Stay inside until this is over. Keep yourself safe."

He looked taken aback for a moment, then gave her a warm smile.

"I will, child," he said. "But look to yourself as well, for my sake. And may the Gods watch over you both."

57

ERRIS

High Command
Southgate District, New Sarresant

"Sir, the enemy column should be moving down Canopy Street." One of her aides pointed over the table to a line of red figures representing the enemy soldiers.

As he was speaking another aide pushed a different figure, a miniature field cannon, atop the Basilica in the Gardens, and two more moved red figures into place behind them to mark that they had entered the city walls. Scouts' reports delivered by hand flew through the chamber, a complement to the battlefield updates provided by her *Need*. The new way was faster, more accurate, but try as she might she couldn't be everywhere at once. So far her line had repelled the Gandsmen's advances into the city, setting traps in narrow alleys to suggest their objective was attrition, and a strong line from the Gardens to the Riverways, rather than a focused defense of the bridges on the eastern flank. Every hour bought her fresh reserves, and the enemy seemed to be prodding her, moving slowly, giving her the precious time she needed. A minor swing in her favor, but the battle was far from decided yet.

"I'm giving orders to the Nineteenth to execute the ambush on Canopy Street now," she said. "We'll need binders to hold the enemy's advance in the meantime. Bring the Third Division's company forward, here," she said, pointing. "Send a courier on foot."

Crisp replies in the affirmative, and her attention was already back to the table in front of her. If the 19th's ambush worked they could flank around and threaten the Gand artillery placements, a distraction easily worth an hour or more by itself. And an awful risk. The 19th had the right flank—she gambled on the enemy believing that position too critical to abandon for the sake of an ambush. Mentally she made a note for backup plans in either case: If the attack was successful, the 11th would deploy behind them, bolstered by the binders from 3rd Division, with more than enough firepower to screen the brunt of the Gand vanguard while Royens's soldiers seized the heights. If they failed, the 11th would be there to pincer any attempt by the enemy to make for the river to the east.

Good enough.

She tethered *Need*, connecting with the foot-lieutenant second to Regiment-Major Amarond's 19th Infantry.

"High Commander, sir," a hard voice whispered beside her. "Bloody fine to see you."

Her vision came into focus, surrounded by wood paneling and heavy linen curtains, velvet furniture and portraits hung on the walls. Blue uniforms packed into the back side of the room, two dozen men shying away from the windowpane, their number spiraling out into the stairwell behind. Every one of them as silent as the grave.

They were inside a residence, overlooking Canopy Street mere minutes before the enemy marched down its length, if her earlier reports and orders were any indicator.

"Damn fine work, Major," she said in a soft voice. "The whole regiment is hidden like this?"

"Yes, sir. In townhouses up and down the street. Those bastards won't know what hit them."

"How did you manage it? You were deployed along the river not half an hour ago."

"Ah, yes, sir," the major said. "I expected you'd order us to position for an ambush, so I took the initiative, sir."

She suppressed a laugh even as frustration bloomed in the back of her mind. This was the legacy of a long chain of idiot commanders. Major Amarond had been right this time, but he'd also magnified her risk. With the right flank exposed for this amount of time...

No. No time to worry over it now.

"Very good, Major. Your men are in position to attack as soon as you see the Gand column reach the end of the street. We have reports they have overextended here, and you can expect few enemy reinforcements if you hit them hard and fast."

"Yes, sir," Amarond said with a grim smile.

"Gods be with you and your men," she said, and released *Need*.

She looked down at the table, to the right flank along the Verrain River. Only the Old Bridge stood in the north, with the ruined slums of the Maw past its far bank. If Amarond had been moving his people into place for the last half hour that meant the bridge had been damn near vacant and her right flank along with it. In fact, looking at it now with fresh eyes, the bridge looked to be the far likelier target for her to have set up an ambush: a plum position left undefended for a considerable length of time. Quite possible the sheer obviousness of such a trap was the reason the enemy had taken the risk of overextending into the southern Gardens, believing her to have committed her forces elsewhere. A stroke of luck. Gods knew she would need a few of those today.

"I need eyes here," she said, pointing to the Old Bridge. "Do we have any fresh reports?"

"Yes, sir," an aide replied. "Fifteen minutes past; the placements on the map reflect that report, sir."

Very good. She looked it over again. Very good indeed. The enemy was nowhere close to the northern approach, a half league away with soldiers intended to reinforce the units they'd marched down into the southern Gardens. The very units Amarond would be carving to pieces shortly.

She made her way across the room, weaving through the couriers, officers, and aides as they rushed through the chamber, offering hasty salutes she had no time to return. The cartographers had produced paper maps detailing the western flank of the Gardens in lieu of having time to properly paint one of her tables. A sea of light blue and green figures, representing d'Agarre's ragtag militia and the nightmarish fighters of the tribesmen. Gods be praised that they seemed content to hold the Gardens, or perhaps that d'Agarre was good for his word before he'd stormed out of high command. If those reports were accurate, the tribesmen seemed to be held down by d'Agarre and his militia, confined in place for the last hour or more.

"How accurate are these troop counts and placements?" she said, looking over the positions of each figure.

"Our best guesses, sir," one of them replied. "The scouts still can't get near it."

Impossible to fight a battle blind. Without accurate reports her hands might as well be tied to her boots. If d'Agarre couldn't deliver on his promise, if the tribesmen broke loose and rounded on her flanks, there would be havoc from Southgate to the front lines.

At least she had Marie. She'd have some warning if the lines began to break.

Time to check in on it now, while Major Amarond executed his ambush. She found *Need*, reaching out for Marie, and stepped into chaos.

Shouts, and stinging smoke. A rough hand shoved her, and she staggered into the path of another man, charging through her as if she weren't there. Her feet tangled together, and she fell, scraping Marie's forearms on cobbled stone. Roiling fear churned in Marie's belly, though the *Need* connection seemed to insulate her from the worst of it.

She coughed, and blinked until the scene cleared. Militiamen, fleeing with no semblance of order or discipline. Street clothes and cloaks, running from the city, climbing the outer wall, though entire sections were knocked down not ten paces from where they scrambled over the stone.

She was in the Gardens, but not where her aides had placed the light blue figurines, along the border with Southgate. This was the northern part of the district, near the outer wall. Whatever company Marie had joined herself to must have broken, taken by a panic fierce enough to scatter them halfway across the city.

The same fear spread in her mind. Not for the militia's sake, or Marie's; if these men and women had broken, there might well be nothing left on her west flank. She'd been a fool to trust d'Agarre. With luck she could redeploy. If the Gods smiled on her, there might be time, before—

"*Am'i nar il cha.*" A man's voice cut through the smoke. "*Corenna s'an chak. Ti ok'rai.*"

She rose, pushing up from the ground. The speaker stood at an opening in the wall. No militiaman, nor even a citizen of the colonies. A tall man, bare-chested and bronze-skinned, though she could no more than half-discern it through the layers of black and red paint in swirling designs from beneath his eyes to his forearms, chest, and back.

A moment later she saw the woman at his side, a bronze-skinned, thin-set figure in a brown wrap of furs and sewn hide.

Tribesfolk. The source of the breaches in the barrier.

"*Ki na, luki a'il cha,*" the woman said, pointing at her, at Marie. "*Sa ni'cor, na iral ok'rai.*"

Hatred surged, and she burned their faces in her mind, preparing to release the *Need* binding. Marie would have to run, and she wouldn't wager a husk of week-old bread for her chances. But if her vessel died, it would be for New Sarresant. It fell to Erris to see she died for victory.

"Your eyes," the man said in a half-broken version of the Sarresant tongue, gesturing to help her understand. "Spirits sent you. A sign, for we to follow."

What was this? She reached her feet, and neither the tribesman nor the woman made a move to attack. Instead they strode forward, the man with his arms wide, in a slight bow, a posture of peace.

"I am Erris d'Arrent," she said. "High Commander of the Army of New Sarresant."

"Erys de Aru," the man replied, then gestured to himself. "*Arak'Jur, dhakai dan Sinari o'na chai.*" He said it slowly, then pointed to the woman. "*Corenna, ana'i bat dan Ranasi o'na chai.*"

"Why have you entered New Sarresant?" she asked.

"Madness," the man replied. "My people, driven here, by a woman, *Llanara a'il cha kapan.* We find her. Kill. Then our people leave in peace. You show us. Show us where."

She frowned. They had to mean the strange woman she'd seen at the barrier, and again on the western flank. The woman in white with her face painted red. Could it be so simple, to kill her and have done with it? She had no notion of what the tribesfolk's magic could do. Perhaps the strange woman was the source, and clear enough neither this tribesman nor the woman at his side feared the madness roiling on the western flank.

"You kill her—the woman in red—and the madness ends?" she asked.

The man nodded, fervor in his eyes. A terrifying sight, made all the worse by children's stories of the wild men and women native to the New World. But all the better for her if they were terrible. She wasn't fool enough to leave a loaded musket lying on the ground, whatever its source.

"You'll find her to the south," Erris said. "Near the district boundary, though I can't be sure the precise—"

Resolve flared in Marie's belly, strong enough to feel it through her *Need*.

She stopped mid-sentence.

"You know where the woman is?" she asked, and the feeling flared again. The man gave a questioning look. Certainty glowed like an ember in Marie's belly, alongside a hunger for vengeance.

"This woman will guide you," she said, taking care to speak slowly for their benefit as much as Marie's. "Follow her, and Gods send you do what you came to do."

58

SARINE

Old Bridge
Riverways District, New Sarresant

She'd made it halfway across the bridge when she saw the soldiers. Blue coats running through the streets of the Riverways toward the riverbank.

Her first reaction was pride. Strange.

Seeing troops on the streets of her city, she might have expected anger, fear, worry. Instead she found pride, pride on behalf of the fighting men and women of Sarresant. There was a connection there, a debt paid in the courage of soldiers willing to stand up and fight against their common enemies. No Gandsmen in sight, and she expected to feel a swelling of hate for those, for the invaders who had come to threaten her home. The thundercracks of cannon fire prevailed in the distance, promising the Gandsmen were close at hand. She was near enough now to smell the smoke that had risen like a storm cloud to hover above the Gardens.

Watching the blue coats approach in the distance made her step lighter, against all odds. She had stood alone, or near enough, against the specter of d'Agarre's madness for so long that the sight of dozens, hundreds perhaps, of brothers and sisters in arms eased a burden from her shoulders, a burden she hadn't known was there.

It took another moment before she realized the soldiers were breaking, fleeing toward the bridge. Scattered by fear, just as the militiamen had been, and the nobles, and the sailors in the Harbor a lifetime ago.

Her instincts took over, and she raced forward. "Zi," she cried out, "I need *Green*."

He gave it, color flaring at the corners of her vision. She felt a tableau of emotion—terror, uncertainty, shame, disbelief—and smothered the fear, urging as many as she could reach toward calm.

She flew toward them in a rush, covering ground with the aid of a *Body* tether she had slid into place by reflex. "Zi, where is the *kaas*-mage? If these men were scattered by *Yellow*—"

This wasn't Yellow.

The first ranks of soldiers flowed around her, shock written on their faces. They darted glances at each other, at her, over their shoulders at whatever had broken their line. A few slowed their pace as they moved past her, giving her questioning looks as if they couldn't quite understand why they had stopped running.

"What's going on ahead?" she asked a handful of them. "How many enemy soldiers?"

A crashing boom filled the air before any of them could reply, and she saw flames spout above a building not two blocks west.

"A monster," one of the soldiers said, looking back with wide eyes even though he had come to a halt. "Don't go that way if you value your life."

Another gout of fire shattered the glass of nearby buildings, the air sucking westward in a sickening rush.

She grit her teeth and ran toward it.

One block flew by, and a dozen more pops and crackles sounded up ahead.

"Bring your worst, you chicken-fucking up-jumped rat-mongrel," a deep voice shouted, loud enough to echo across the walls of nearby buildings. Another bang sent fire rushing around the corner. Still she pressed on, another heartbeat before she rounded the intersection and came face-to-face with the source of the soldiers' panicked flight.

Mareh'et.

A blast of flame struck in front of the creature's feet when it tried to step forward, sending it skittering to the side. Standing in the middle of the street, surrounded by pockmarked cobblestone and the blasted-out remnants of nearby buildings, was a man in a captain's uniform, his eyes burning with fury as he roared obscenities at the Great Cat.

"Come on, you reeking pigshit," he shouted. "Try me again if you have the nerve."

She saw the cat had already landed a savage cut on the captain's leg, his uniform torn and shredded, caked with blood. The beast seemed content to probe forward, provoking blasts of fire when it came too close. *Entropy*, for the fire, and *Life* to keep him standing; evidently this captain was a fullbinder. Just as well she hadn't rushed in. With him tossing fireballs she'd as soon keep her distance.

She tethered strands of *Entropy* herself, loosing a torrent of caustic air that exploded behind the beast. The creature moved too fast to hit it directly, but it took notice of her, spinning back into a crouch.

The captain's eyes went wide for a moment before he saw her.

Cornered, the beast sprang forward, evoking another stream of curses as the captain exploded the ground in front of him, sending cobblestone into the air. Except this time she was there, too, setting her own *Entropy* bindings to cut off its retreat, anticipating *mareh'et*'s propensity for games of cat-and-mouse. A sizzling burst of cat flesh erupted into fire, eliciting a yowling whine from the creature, a growl befitting its massive size. It darted another look between them before springing back, then turned and loped northward in a blinding flash.

"That's right," the captain called out, sagging down against his wounded leg. "That's bloody right."

She rushed to his side, tethering *Body* into him as she cradled him toward the ruined cobblestone at his feet. He blinked, fixing his eyes on her. His breath reeked of drink almost as much as his coat, and he winced as he tried to laugh.

"*Body*, too?" the captain asked. "Where the fuck did you come from, girl?"

"Shh," she said. "Don't speak, you're hurt."

His eyes went to the tattoos on her hands, the royal marque permitting her bindings by the grace of the King. He scowled.

"Bloody fucking nobles," he said before his eyes rolled into his head and he passed out in the middle of the street.

The stench of blood and alcohol mixed with sweat proved worse than actually carrying him, restless as he was, hoisted like a newborn babe in her arms. She'd made the mistake of tethering *Life* along with *Body* when she'd first hefted him up, nearly dropping him when the acrid smell made its way onto her tongue through amplified senses, thick enough to taste bile and twice as strong as whatever drink the captain had been favoring that morning.

He'd started to come to three blocks to the south, murmuring something about lambskin and fresh grapes. She'd figured it wise to avoid the routed troops to the east and the sounds of cannon fire to the west. That left south for the likeliest place to find friendly soldiers, fool as she was for trying to save the captain's life. It had certainly been a damned sight easier to carry him before he decided to start moaning and turning in her arms.

She turned down Canopy Street, the long avenue leading toward Southgate and the Market, and nearly choked again at the sight of whatever battle had been fought here. Bodies piled up in the entryways of the shops and townhouses lining the street, far too many blue coats for every red, as if the Sarresant soldiers had been shut up inside the buildings and butchered when they tried to come out. The street reeked with the smell of powder, guttering flames still burning in storefront windows and shattered glass strewn across the cobblestone. So many dead, with the quiet of a graveyard hanging in the air despite the sounds of fighting nearby.

Tears stung her eyes as she walked past the bodies of the fallen, the shock of it coming home to rest. Gods be good, perhaps the price of *Black* was worth paying, if it meant she could stand against this sort of slaughter. And no telling where the city's inhabitants had gone, fleeing before the advancing armies on both sides. How many innocents would die today? How many more in the weeks to come? Carrying the body of one wounded man in a vain attempt to reunite him with his fellows only underscored the futility of her efforts. What was one life worth? What was she doing?

We do what we must, with the burdens we are allotted to carry.

Zi's voice echoed softly in her mind. It sounded like something her uncle might say, though she knew it was no scripture of any of the Gods.

She said nothing in reply, only held tight to the captain's body as she walked.

After an eternity a line of soldiers came into view, holed up behind a makeshift barricade. Blue coats. Thank the Gods.

"It's Foot-Captain Marquand," one of the soldiers whispered in an awed voice when she reached the line, making her way through their roadblock as the others pitched in to shift the debris. "Get the brigade-colonel," another shouted.

A half-dozen voices weighed in with varying degrees of alarm before one of the soldiers, a young woman with a stripe on her collar, bothered to help her lower the captain to the ground.

"Thank the Gods," the woman said. "We had reports the companies sent north had been routed. Are there enemy soldiers behind you?"

"No," she said. "None that I saw. It was a *mareh—*" She stopped herself. "A giant cat."

When the other woman's eyes widened with a knowing nod, she continued.

"The captain and I managed to drive it off," she said. "I may have wounded it."

The soldier's eyes flicked toward her hands, which she had left bare despite the cold, and registered with a nod the inks etched into her broken skin. "You're a *Body* binder?" the soldier asked. "Noble-born?"

"Yes. A *Body* binder, I mean. My marques were a gift." She stopped herself as the soldier gave her a questioning look. A story for another time; irrelevant now. "I tethered what I could into the captain. I couldn't leave him. I figured if I could bring him to soldiers, he would be safe."

The soldier pulled off her gloves, laying hands on the captain's chest. Scarred hands, though without any inks to speak of. "You're in luck. We have a good number of the army's remaining fullbinders here, for as long as we can hold this position."

She exhaled, letting out a breath she hadn't known she'd been keeping in.

"My name is Acherre," the woman said. "Lance-Lieutenant Acherre, assigned to the Eleventh Light Cavalry."

"Sarine," she offered in reply. It felt odd to give her name, but concern over her identity seemed trivial compared against the horrors around them. Men and women were dying here, and hundreds more lay dead on streets nearby, the cost of a failed ambush or some other maneuver down the boundary between the Gardens and the Riverways. Lying about her name felt frivolous, a concern for a different time and circumstance.

"What's this I hear about Marquand managing to drag himself back here?" a sharp voice called out from behind. She turned to see another woman, flanked by a pair of men who rushed to Marquand's side as Acherre stood, facing the newcomer with a military salute.

"Sir," Acherre said, "this woman rescued Foot-Captain Marquand from the horse-cat, Brigade-Colonel Vassail, sir."

The brigade-colonel eyed Marquand with careful concern, for all her demeanor belied her expression. "Serves him bloody well right for disobeying orders," the colonel said. "Do you have a name?" she asked, turning toward Sarine, adding a belated "my lady" after catching sight of the marques on the backs of her hands.

"Sarine," she offered, finding it an easier fit the second time around.

"She's a *Body* binder, sir," Acherre said.

"Is that right?" Vassail said. "Have you ever considered military service? I assure you, the pay is top-notch." The brigade-colonel laughed bitterly, turning toward an aide approaching at her side. "Gods know we can use all the binders we can get today."

At once the colonel's demeanor changed from relaxed confidence to a crisp salute. It took a second look at the aide to hazard a guess at why: Instead of pupil-and-iris, the aide's eyes shone with a pure, golden light. The sight of it struck her in the gut, a hammer blow, though she couldn't have explained why.

Acherre laid a hand on her arm in a calming gesture as the brigade-colonel spoke: "High Commander, sir, what orders?"

"Redeployment, Colonel," the aide said. "The west flank is collapsed, or will be soon enough. I need the Eleventh to execute a forced march into the Gardens."

"Sir, scouts' reports say—"

"I know bloody well what the reports say. I need you to get in place on the double, and hold the line."

"I'm at less than a third strength," Vassail said, wearing a grim expression. "We've been driven back. I've lost half my binders already. I can't—"

"Gods damn it, Vassail, I need you," the aide said in a harsh voice. "Tell me you can do it."

Vassail drew a deep breath. "Yes, sir," she said. "We move at once."

The golden light faded as quickly as it had come. Breath came hard, and Sarine shifted her vision in time to see the last vestiges of the light pull away into the distance. It was like no binding she had seen before. High Commander, the brigade-colonel had said. Somehow that tether had connected the colonel's aide to Donatien's old commander.

"Going to need you, Acherre," the brigade-colonel said. "Gods damn it, we could have used Marquand, too." With that she strode away in a flurry, shouting orders as the soldiers around them began to swarm like hornets.

Acherre turned toward her, a sympathetic look mixed with determination on her face. "We really could use you, even if only for *Body* to help the wounded until the *Life* binders can get to them."

"What was that?" she asked. "The golden light?"

"Our latest weapon, my lady. High Commander d'Arrent directs the battle, and we follow her commands."

She nodded absently, looking up and down the line as the blue coats formed up facing west. Something in that light had called to her, an echo of a long-forgotten memory. Gone now, though the sight of it lingered in her eyes.

She cast a long glance toward the soldiers, feeling strangeness settle on her skin. What was she doing? She was no soldier. Reyne d'Agarre was out there, and the other *kaas*-mages. Axerian was counting on her, and he'd insisted the stakes were far greater than the lives of one company of soldiers, greater even than the city itself. And if she let herself go too far, if *Black* took hold of her mind...

No. None of that mattered. She couldn't let these men and women die.

"I can fight," she said. "Just show me where to stand."

59

ARAK'JUR

Street of the Cobblers
Gardens District, New Sarresant

"*Elle est à proximité*," the strange woman said, the one who'd first called herself Erys—or something akin to it—and then Marie. "*Le feu est trois rues au sud*."

The fair-skins' tongue seemed to flow together, a flow of words and nasal sounds he'd never been able to master. But he understood enough. The woman was near, and the fire. An echo of the vision he'd been granted at Ka'Ana'Tyat, as sure as their strange fair-skinned guide had been. He walked through their city in the haze of a dream, as though he had passed through the fire and chaos already, and so he had. Every line, every path of stone and smoke cloud rising into the sky; he'd seen it before, by the grace of the spirits. And it led to Llanara.

Corenna kept pace at his side, a distant look in her eyes. She'd seen the vision, too. He knew without asking. How they would enter the fair-skins' city, and be greeted by a woman with eyes of gold, who knew the way into madness. As it was when he followed the shamans' visions, so it was here in the city: Every step was a confirmation they followed the will of the spirits, though the sights around them wrenched his gut, more akin to terrors than a dream.

Dead men and boys, and women, too. Cold bodies broken on paths of stone, tribesfolk mixed with fair-skins. Olessi, Vhurasi, Ganherat,

Sinari. Thunder sounded in the distance, and the lesser booms of musket shot, but the way was quiet, peopled only by the dead.

"*Par ici,*" the woman, Marie, said. This way.

He and Corenna followed, turning a corner around a building of wood and stone. He'd heard stories of the fair-skins' city, passed down by traders who had glimpsed the sights beyond their barrier, but he had scarce believed the truth could match the tales. Foolishness, as he saw it. So many people in one place, trusting to a single barrier to protect them from the wild. If a tribe multiplied as the fair-skins had done, they would attract doom from a dozen great beasts, come to feast on their flesh as much as their pride. And when their blood ran hot, and one tribe's disagreement with another spilled over into fighting, the deaths would number into the thousands, to say nothing of the costs of outright war. He saw the truth of it littering the streets as they walked, bodies echoing the stain of Llanara's madness.

A scream was his only warning before a young man charged their guide.

A Ganherat warrior, from the feathers braided into his hair, leaping out from one of the buildings, with three more behind him. They poured into the street in a rush, ululating war cries as if they attacked a pack of enemies, instead of an unarmed woman in the company of a guardian and a woman of the tribes.

Arak'Jur sprang forward, putting a forearm in the way of the first warrior's attack, sweeping a kick to tangle his legs, putting him into the snow. Two of his fellows rushed to take the first one's place, snarling as though they were beasts, and not men.

Unarmed strikes rained as they lunged for Marie, leaping toward her, ignoring Arak'Jur and Corenna both. He grabbed hold of one of the men by the torso, hurling him into his fellows and pressing all four when they lost their footing.

"Enough!" he shouted. "What madness is this?"

They ignored him, scrambling to their hands and knees.

"Arak'Jur!" Corenna shouted from behind. He glanced to see her restraining Marie, who in the span of a heartbeat had gone from determined resolve to panicked flight.

Then, as quick as it had come, their madness passed.

The warriors stared up at him, stunned, and Marie relaxed in Corenna's grip.

"The Sinari guardian," one of the tribesmen said. "How—?"

"She foretold it," another warrior said, in hushed tones of awe. "His return, at the moment of our triumph."

"What goes on here?" Arak'Jur demanded, standing over the men as they slowly rose to their feet.

"*La folie,*" Marie said, her voice hoarse. "*Dans des vagues de peur et de panique.*"

He met her eyes, and she gestured on the way they'd been going. "*La femme, et Reyne d'Agarre.*"

He hadn't understood the first part of her words, but he grasped the second. *The woman*, and the name: Reyne d'Agarre. Her teacher. The first source of Llanara's madness.

"You must go to her," a Ganherat warrior said, a look of reverence on his face, as if he hadn't been screaming for blood moments before.

He met Corenna's eyes, and they shared a nod. The vision confirmed it, though neither had remembered the crazed warriors until the path became clear.

The four young men led the way, with Marie and Corenna at his side. Unease settled in his gut as they walked. Was this the form Llanara's magic took? The terror that had driven his people to murder the Ranasi, and who could say how many more in the days since. The Ganherat warriors seemed at ease, keeping a steady pace as they tracked down the fair-skins' paths of stone. More warriors stood idle on the streets, first offering greetings when their company approached, then falling into step behind when they laid eyes on him, with murmured whispers of his title, that the Sinari guardian had returned. If the madness came again, he might well have to strike them down. He felt the surety of Corenna at his side, and the spirits' gifts, calling to him at the edge of his vision. Blood soaked the snow, and the hides and wraps of the tribesmen, but they pressed on, with no sign of whatever had stirred them to frenzy.

Smoke in the distance grew as they approached, more and more warriors falling into step, or parting to clear the way. A greatfire burned at the center of a square, where a web of paths converged, leading all directions into the city. Steps rose toward where the fire had been built, and a figure in white stood atop them, revealed as the crowd stepped aside, leaving the way clear to approach the rise.

Llanara.

Her face beamed, radiant even from afar, in a twisted imitation of the fond looks they had once shared. The crowd mirrored her warmth, buzzing appreciation for every step their procession took toward the center.

When they'd covered half the distance, Llanara raised a hand, invoking silence across the square.

"The spirits have heard us, honored brothers and sisters," she said, her voice ringing clear. "Our warleader has returned."

The warriors erupted with cheers. She met his eyes amid the roar of the crowd, giving him the subtle smile she used when an opponent hadn't yet realized she'd won an argument.

"Warriors," she cried over the din, "I tell you now—he is warleader, but he will not take the mantle of *Vas'Khan*."

That grabbed hold of their attention, and their cheers died down as Llanara continued to speak.

"No, he will not be Vas'Khan'Jur. The spirits demand more for him, for our guardian and first among the men of our people."

She took long, strutting steps around the center of the clearing, seeming to relish the anticipation as the crowd hung on her every word. He only stared, an empty hate chilling him to the core.

"If *Vas'Khan* is the warleader of a tribe, then it is fitting that Arak'Jur take a new name, one that has never before been spoken among our people. A name whispered to me by the spirits. He will be Arak'Khan'Jur. Chosen by the spirits, a warleader for all tribes."

The name passed through the throng in whispers, met with nods of approval. They cried it out, tested it on their tongues. Arak'Khan'Jur.

"Come forward, Arak'Khan'Jur. Take your place at the head of your warriors."

She smiled again as the crowd broke into a roar, giving him a sweet look full of warmth. As if she expected humility or thanks; as if she had never considered he might react with anything other than acceptance.

She beamed amid the thunder of the crowd, fixed on him as he approached. As he drew near he saw the familiar lines of her face, the passion in her eyes. He could see the memory of the woman she had been, the relief she had offered to salve the loss of his wife and son.

"Welcome home, my guardian," she said.

He called upon the *valak'ar* and struck, surrounded by a deadly nimbus of the wraith-snake.

A flare of white surrounded her before he connected, repelling him with enough force to throw him to the ground.

Shock showed on Llanara's face, and it rippled outward through the crowd, the cheers near the center replaced by gasps of disbelief.

"No," Llanara said, looking down on him with pain in her eyes. "No, Arak'Jur. Why?"

He felt the shock of it hit him. The vision had ended here.

His mouth went dry, and he saw her tilt her head as if listening to an unspoken voice.

A dark look crept into her eyes.

60

ERRIS

High Command
Southgate District, New Sarresant

The lines hadn't moved. All her preparation, shifting reserves into place to be able to threaten an eastward assault, when it came. Superior numbers meant the enemy had the initiative, but instead of attacking, he probed, testing her without committing to an engagement.

She'd been near certain the Gandsmen would drive east toward the river, securing the crossings to threaten the harbor. If they took and held the docks, they could bring up ships to bombard attempts to attack their position, striking at the rest of the city at their leisure. Yet the enemy seemed content to wait, deploying to force her to extend from the Riverways to Southgate. She'd tried a series of ambushes designed to goad him into an attack, and been rebuffed, with no counter.

It made no sense. Which meant it had to be a trap.

"Sir, do you have any vessels near the Basilica?" one of her captains asked. "Our scouts haven't reported in. If the enemy attacks down Rouard Street we'll be caught blind."

She shook her head, wincing as an aide removed one of the blue figures from the map. Sauvignon Street, where she'd tried another ambush. The bulk of those men were dead now. The enemy had responded instantly, as if he had known it was coming.

Their commander was too bloody good. Maybe that was his plan:

bleed her dry, staring across the dying ground between their lines, waiting for her to be the first to commit, when every ounce of her experience said he should have the choosing of the ground.

She flicked her eyes closed, finding *Need.*

"Pull back to the heights at Courtesan's Hill," she barked, not waiting for her vision to clear. "Withdraw, and tighten the line."

The roar of musket fire was the only response, and she felt a stabbing pain take her in the stomach, knocking her to the ground.

"Sir!" another voice called out as she fell. "What were your orders, sir?" A foot-captain loomed over her as her vision clouded red, two bars on his collar. Where was the brigade-colonel?

"Retreat," she croaked. "Hold the hill."

Need fell away from her, and she sagged against the table.

"Gods damn it!" she yelled, pounding a fist as she caught herself.

The aides around her started, scrambling to ensure the red and blue figures had not been dislodged from their intended positions.

"My vessel has been lost, with the Thirty-Eighth," she said bitterly. "Issue the order by courier. We have to pull the line eastward to cut the enemy off from reaching the Jardins-Pêche Bridge."

"Sir, can we risk weakening the center?" a captain asked. "Fresh scouts' reports suggest the Gandsmen are holding steady at the district line, exchanging fire with—"

"Gods damn it, of course they are. But their reserves are coming up, the same as ours. We stretch the line eastward, or we risk the bridges when they deploy."

"Sir, yes, sir," the aide said, as another looked up from the map. "We can move the Nineteenth into position to support, and the rest of de Tourvalle's division. It will expose us on the west flank, though, sir, and the center."

"Vassail's Eleventh is already moving to reinforce the western line," she said. "She can keep the tribesfolk pinned down." She looked down at the maps, trying to plan a step ahead. "As for the center, a strike there would only allow us to fall back to the river, closing off our line. He'd never gain the bridges if he committed to that attack."

"Perhaps he doesn't mean to take the bridges," a voice said from behind.

The aides rose to attention from the table, saluting the new arrival.

"Marquis-General Voren," she said, not bothering to keep the fatigue from her voice. "Thank the Gods you're here."

"D'Arrent," Voren said with a half nod, stepping forward to lean against the table by her side. "Apologies for my delayed arrival. It turns out the logistics corps can be put to good use evacuating our citizens to safety, so long as we don't allow the assembly to administer the details." He smiled. "Now, have you considered whether the enemy may be after another target?"

She looked over the map again. Southgate was the industrial center of the city, but apart from Courtesan's Hill it was flat, with no especially defensible ground. It controlled the southern road via its eponymous gate but had no direct access to the sea, with wide fields of grass and parks cutting the district in half. Holding them offered no great advantage. The Riverways to the east were the key to the city, and the Jardins-Pêche Bridge was the southernmost crossing point. Ignoring it meant the Gandsmen intended to push south, where the only notable objective was...

"The council chamber?" she offered. "You think he'd strike us here?"

Voren pursed his lips, studying the arrangement of the figures on the map. "Are you prepared for it?"

"It would be nothing more than a symbolic gesture. There are strategic objectives to take, objectives far more important to securing the city."

Even as she said it, her memory went back to the exchanges she'd had with the strange commander of the enemy army. He'd promised to bleed her city, yes, but he'd also promised to kill *her*. Perhaps it had been more than a hyperbolic threat after all.

"The command is yours, of course," Voren said, offering her a slight bow.

"No," she said. "No, you may be right, General." She pointed to the map. "We'll draw in the eastern line, and bring the reserve up on the council monument grounds. A touch slower to reinforce the flank, but a nasty surprise if he strikes the center."

"And the west flank? Held by the militia, yes?"

She nodded. "For the time being. I have reports they've broken, but the tribesfolk have yet to advance. I've sent Vassail's brigade to reinforce. They'll be in position to threaten a counterattack, if the enemy is massing toward the center."

Voren nodded. "A wise precaution. Good to see the battle is not over yet."

"I'm glad you're here, General," she said, turning back to the chamber at large. "Sadrelle," she called. "I need you to ride, Aide-Lieutenant."

"Sir." Sadrelle saluted. "What orders?"

"I need eyes in the north, along the border of the Riverways and the Maw. Stay well clear of the enemy, but get me eyes on his reserve as they deploy from the Gardens. If they're heading east, we need enough warning to pull back to the bridges. If they move toward the center, we respond in kind. Either way, I need to see it firsthand, when it happens."

"Yes, sir," he said, saluting.

"Keep yourself safe, Lieutenant."

Sadrelle pivoted toward the exit leading to the stables. With any luck he'd be in place by the time she had Vassail and the reserve redeployed to check a movement toward the center. Whatever the reason behind the enemy's caution, he'd given her an opening to seize the initiative for herself. Voren was right. This battle wasn't over yet.

"It's a graveyard, Commander," Vassail said in haunted tones. "I've never seen anything like it."

Erris swallowed bile, through the throat of the aide-sergeant she'd placed with the 11th. A sea of dead men and women, where her aides had placed the light blue and green markers to signify the western front. Pools of blood stained the snow, frozen black, paying no heed to whether a corpse was pale-skinned or bronze. If there had been battle lines they had long since disintegrated; fur-clad tribesmen mixed with wool-coated militia in pockets of dead lining the streets and greenbelts as far as she could see.

"It's d'Agarre," a hushed voice said beside the colonel.

She turned to see a civilian, a brown-haired young woman wearing only a linen shirt in spite of the cold, bearing royal marques on the backs of her hands.

"Report," Erris said. "Who is this woman, and how is Councilman d'Agarre—"

A torrent of fear rose in her vessel's gut, the same overpowering emotion she'd felt in Marie d'Oreste, and Vassail's brigade broke in terror.

In a heartbeat, orderly lines of dismounted cavalry shattered in a rout.

Soldiers she would trust to hold against three divisions charging them over open fields suddenly flung their weapons to the ground, abandoning their posts in panicked flight.

Lance-Lieutenant Acherre gaped, along with a handful of other binders; every man or woman with scars on their hands seemed unaffected, while the rest broke like raw recruits at the vanguard of a charge.

"No!" the young woman in civilian clothes screamed. "Zi, *Green*. Now!"

As quick as it had come, the terror vanished.

"What under the Nameless is going on here?" Erris said, turning toward the young woman as the rest of Vassail's brigade stared at each other in stunned silence, returning to their posts.

"D'Agarre is out there," the young woman replied. "And another *kaas*-mage; at least one more. I can hold it for now. It isn't as strong when they use it over such a great distance, but—"

"Sir!" a sergeant shouted, pointing. "Contact with the enemy!"

Erris pivoted, with Vassail at her side. Across the greenbelts, rows of red-coated Gand infantry marched forward, thick lines coming to a halt at the extreme edge of the Gardens. At least a division's full strength, and not a man among them set foot on the dying ground between their line and Vassail's.

"They're marshaling for an attack," Erris said. "Waiting for their reserve. Gods above, how long have they been massing here?"

"Sir," Vassail said, "do you think they aim to flank us? The western line is as good as broken. They could sweep around, cut off our supply lines, and—"

"No," she said. "Nothing was stopping them from that maneuver prior to your arrival. If they had a means to counteract whatever madness is going on here, they would've used it already."

"It would take another *kaas*-mage," the young woman, the civilian, said.

"What is your name, girl?" Erris said. A sight beyond the strange, seeing a civilian moving with the ranks of military binders, but this girl seemed to have knowledge of the situation, and she'd done something to forestall the madness that had infected the Gardens.

"Sarine," the girl replied. "And Zi can use *Green* to stop their *Yellow*, so long as his stores—"

"Sarine," she echoed back, cutting the girl short. "There's no time for details. You said you can hold off whatever it is affecting this part of the city. I need to know it for sure. Are you certain—beyond certain—you can keep Vassail's brigade in place?"

The girl—Sarine—seemed taken aback, the usual surprise when a civilian was confronted with military discipline. But a moment later she nodded, a look of iron in her eyes.

Good enough. Victory went to the commander who could adjust to the reality of a battle, whether they understood it or no.

"Move north," she said to Vassail. "Take your brigade just outside of firing distance of their line, and wait for further orders."

"Sir?" the colonel said. "Do you mean for us to goad them into an attack?"

"I mean for you to check their reserve, until we can reinforce the center. This is his first mistake, Vassail. He's tipped his hand. The chaos here has given him cover, but now we know where he means to attack. I mean to be ready for it, with your men positioned to threaten his flanks when he does."

Vassail's eyes shone. "Yes, sir."

"*Every* reserve, High Commander?" Voren asked her privately, a few steps away from the table. "Are you certain?"

"He's mustering an attack on the council hall," she replied. "He's been massing soldiers at the center. As soon as he brings up his reserve, they'll strike."

"It's an awful risk, Commander. You yourself pointed out the bridges were the more strategic targets."

"And you pointed out he might value the symbolism more highly," she said, turning back to the map and pointing to the southeast quadrant. "We have four brigades as yet undeployed, two of them fresh from the Second Corps. If we can hit him as he's crossing the monument grounds here, we can cut his line in half."

Voren nodded slowly. "You have scouts in place to check the approaches to the east, to be sure?"

"I sent Sadrelle out a quarter hour ago; he should be in position by now."

The chamber scrambled around them, seeing that her orders were delivered. *Need* was in thin enough supply she couldn't spare it for routine repositioning, especially for reserves. Gods but she wished they'd been able to find more binders capable of handling *Need*. More mysteries for which she simply didn't have time.

"Very well, Commander," Voren said. "Gods' blessings on you, and on the army."

She nodded, delivering the last of her orders to aides standing around the table. Still no updates carried by hand from any of her scouts operating in the southern Gardens. Sadrelle would ride quickly, but there was the option to use *Need* as well—it was why she'd sent him. Every instinct told her she was right, that the enemy was coming here, and not to the east. Still, she had to be sure.

She reached out for Sadrelle, tethering a strand of her precious remaining quantity of *Need*.

Pain.

It overwhelmed her, sucking the wind from her lungs, lancing through Sadrelle's body with every movement.

Pain, but no cold. She was indoors.

"Ah, excellent, that didn't take long at all."

She quivered as she turned, looking up to see a tall man in the uniform of a Gand captain looming over her where she lay on the floor of the room, a golden light shining from behind his eyes. And behind him, the looming form of a cat the size of Jiri, smoke rising from its eye sockets as flame licked the tips of its fur.

"It seems your luck has run out, General," the Gand captain said. "You made a fine show of it, but even here within a city, on ground that favors the defender, you are no match for me."

The cat paced across the long chamber, its hackles brushing against the tips of a chandelier hung between a grand staircase forking off in either direction. Her eyes shifted into focus well enough to see that the room around them was a ruin. A theater perhaps, or one of the great manses of the city.

She looked down and saw a red stain on Sadrelle's shirt. Pistol shot. Through a lung, if the fire in her throat was any indicator. She coughed blood, an involuntary spasm from Sadrelle's body she could not help but obey, even under the control of *Need*. "Monster," she spat.

The man smiled. "Shame about the injury to your vessel. It does dampen things. Such an uncivilized age, to refuse a standing pair."

"You . . . attack the city . . ." she managed through the pain.

"Ah yes, why did I attack the city when I could have simply outmaneuvered you in the field?" He made a mockery of a grave nod. "It's true, casualties will be higher this way. But a protracted siege when the enemy's champions are active in the West seems a foolish gambit to me, wouldn't you agree?"

She closed her eyes. Pain shuttered thought, but this man was a blustering fool for all his genius. She could goad him.

"Hidden . . ." she said. "You won't . . . find . . ."

"Oh, I've already found you, whelpling. My forces are surrounding you as we speak. An obvious ploy to keep your *kaas*-mage close at hand. You'll have to explain how you managed to turn one of them to your cause."

His words began to fade in her ears, but she had the confirmation she needed: He was coming for her. The attack would come at the council hall. Sadrelle's sacrifice would not be in vain.

The cat whipped its massive head toward the entryway, its flame-eyes focused on the double oaken doors, though her vision blurred from the pain.

The Gand captain raised his head from where he stood over her. "What is it?" he asked.

A man in black burst through the doorway, and the captain's eyes narrowed. "You," he said darkly. "I was wondering how long it would take—"

"Time to scold me later, my friend," the newcomer said. "We have a problem. The cleansing of the Veil's power—I've found its source. It isn't the Regnant at all."

The Gand captain gave him a long look, then turned back toward her.

"Forgive me," he said, dropping to a knee. "But there are limits to civility, even among the civilized."

With that he drew a dagger and rammed it beneath her ribs.

61

ARAK'JUR

The Greatfire
Gardens District, New Sarresant

Llanara held his eyes, creeping rage replacing the love that had been there moments before.

"You've betrayed me," Llanara said.

Fear bloomed beneath his skin, fear of a sort he had not known since the day the *valak'ar* attacked the village. Llanara's eyes remained fixed on him, pools of brown falling away into depths that had not been there when she had shared his bed. An abyss. Madness, in the core of her soul.

A ripple passed through the crowd. Gasps, shuffling steps, as though Llanara had done something to keep them all at bay, and now they wavered as she did, staring at him with hate.

A cracking sound came from behind. Spears of ice flew toward her, shattering on a shield of white that sprang up at the last moment, scattering fragments around the steps.

The crowd roared.

Llanara moved, faster than should have been possible, equal to the blinding speed of *lakiri'in*, and he drew on the reptile's gift to match her, springing to his feet to interpose himself between her and Corenna. Men and women screamed as he struck, kicking at her, and met the white shield again. The impact blew them both apart, Llanara staggering back as he was sent to the ground.

"You've betrayed me, Arak'Jur," she cried out again, raw pain in her voice. "We could have had more than any pair in the history of our tribe. We could have been—"

Another salvo of ice flew at her, a blast of cold wind rushing through the square as Corenna advanced.

"Madwoman!" Corenna screamed, her ice impacting on webs of white springing up around Llanara's body.

The crowd surged away, widening a gap around the steps at the center of the square. Some broke and ran; others stared, and some few descended into fighting among each other, the same frothing madness they had seen before, when the Ganherat warriors attacked Marie.

"Is she your woman now?" Llanara asked.

Arak'Jur sprang to his feet, still bolstered by *lakiri'in.* But he froze as an aura of black enveloped Llanara, and in a heartbeat her eyes frosted over, the same misty blue Corenna showed when she channeled the gift of ice.

Impossible. Llanara had never made the journey north.

"Corenna!" he cried. Too late. Llanara loosed a spear of ice, streaking toward Corenna in a flash, taking her in the hip and sending her crumpling to the ground in a howl of pain.

The film of frost dissipated from Llanara's eyes as she turned back to him. "You see, my love? You see what you have given up?"

He roared, calling upon *mareh'et.*

White flared around Llanara again as he struck, the spirit-claws of the Great Cat slicing against her shield, a force great enough to shear through bone, to heave her across the square. Instead she held her ground without flinching from his attacks, looking up at him with pity in her eyes.

She reached a hand to grasp his throat. Fast. Faster than *lakiri'in*, and stronger than *una're.* She forced him to his knees.

"Did you not love me, Arak'Jur? Did you forget me on your travels?"

He gasped for air, and the crowd around them broke as she stared, rage burning in her eyes. Her anger seemed to bleed through the square, howls and shouts descending into pockets of violence. White flared around her as he struck her forearms, channeling *una're*'s gift to send shocks through her as he tried to pry loose her grip.

"Please..." he managed. "Llanara...our people..."

"Our people are on the cusp of greatness!" she shouted at him. "How could you?" Tears streaked from her eyes, a sudden rush of hate in her voice. "How could you do this to me?"

A torrent of wind whipped against them both, and Llanara's shield of white flickered for an instant, dashing them to the ground. The crowd screamed but kept their distance, as though some force repelled them from the center of the square.

He called upon *ipek'a* to give himself the strength to stand, watching Llanara rise as Corenna pressed forward, hobbled with blood streaking down her leg.

"Monster!" Corenna yelled, a raging whirlwind pouring out from her hands, breaking against the renewed strength of Llanara's shield. "Spirit-cursed madwoman."

Llanara's eyes narrowed, and once more a black aura surrounded her.

This time he was ready. He drew upon the gift of the Mountain, the fire held deep within its heart.

Fire bellowed from his hands as Corenna maintained her onslaught of wind, and Llanara howled, turning toward the pillars of flame he channeled into where she stood. No sooner had her gaze settled on him than he felt Llanara's cloud of blackness closing in, ethereal claws seeming to reach inside him, tearing the Mountain's gift from his grasp. His flame sputtered out as Llanara's white shield flickered again, letting Corenna knock her to the ground.

With a wordless snarl, Llanara's eyes went red and she turned the gift of fire toward Corenna, meeting a barrier of earth conjured from nothing as Corenna's eyes hardened to wield the power of stone. Llanara maintained her attack, a stream of fire threatening to break through Corenna's defense as it melted stone into liquid, licking around the edges in a roar of primal energy.

Corenna fell back a step as Llanara crawled to her knees. Hatred creased Llanara's face as she rose, surrounded by the gift of his stolen fire. He saw another flicker, a guttering light as the white shield around her diminished.

He leapt.

He remembered the triumphant roar, the pride of the *ipek'a* female trumpeting her kill to all who could hear, the thrill of the hunt, the terror inspired by every blood-red feather. And he remembered the fury of the protector enraged, fearless before the enemies of her pack.

He crashed through the earthen shield, through the billowing flame, feeling his skin crack and blister as it scorched his body. The pain seared conscious thought from his mind, leaving only instinct. Hunger. Rage.

He came down with the full force of *ipek'a*'s scything claws, shearing through the remnants of Llanara's shield as he snapped her spine in a sickening crunch.

They tumbled onto the ground before the greatfire, entwined together in a mockery of everything they once had shared.

The madness across the square guttered out in an instant.

Llanara met his eyes with a look of fear, lying beside him on the cold stone. Ragged breath escaped her lungs.

"No . . ." she whispered. "Vekis . . . said . . . ascension."

Hatred simmered, just beneath a boil. She'd done this to his people. Dead men and women lay broken in the snow, victims of each other's hand as much as the fair-skins', brought on by her madness. The woman he once had loved.

"Now . . . nothing to stop him," Llanara said. "Our people . . ."

Light seemed to go out of her eyes. She died, and in an instant, all the fury that had passed through the crowd returned in a surging mass of hate and screams.

62

SARINE

A Greenbelt
Gardens District, New Sarresant

"Stay outside their range," the brigade-colonel's aide ordered. Or, more properly, with the golden light, an order given by High Commander Erris d'Arrent. Strange to consider she'd never met the woman in person; in her eyes, it was hard to think of the High Commander as anything but a gruff, balding veteran in a sergeant's uniform.

The aide continued. "Stay back, but let them see you fortify. Make sure they know you'll be a thorn in their side when they attack."

"Sir, are you certain?" Brigade-Colonel Vassail said. "It's difficult to see what's going on out there, but I think they're on the move. My scouts report artillery being brought up from the Basilica."

"They're redeploying into Southgate, preparing for an assault across the monument grounds. Just stay in position to threaten the approach and get scouts posted to watch their reserve."

"Sir, yes, sir."

The golden light faded, leaving the sergeant sputtering and shaking his head. Vassail had already moved on to deliver orders farther down the line.

Sarine held her place next to a company of musketmen, interleaved with the dismounted cavalry she'd come to understand was the original composition of Vassail's brigade. They'd picked up the remains of other units broken or otherwise without direction in the fighting. Out of uniform she felt alone in a sea of blue coats, made worse by the stares and whispers she drew from the men and women when she passed by.

Without her *Green* to stop it, the men would long since have fallen to the *Yellow* emanating in waves from the north, and west. Somehow the soldiers seemed to know she held their emotions in her hands: fear, pride, resolve, faith in their commanders. The *kaas* she felt pulling in the distance were stoking the flames of fear, and she pushed against them, keeping Vassail's soldiers in place, for now.

She needed to go, to find Axerian, to face d'Agarre with him. But abandoning these soldiers meant consigning them to the madness, the same bloodlust that had turned the beauty of the Gardens into a dying ground.

"How is it you go without a winter coat, without gloves?" Acherre asked, a few paces away at the point between one company and the next.

She looked toward the lieutenant, finding warmth behind the question. "I must have forgotten them before I went out," she said, drawing a laugh from Acherre and uneasy looks from the men around her.

"If it's a binder's trick, I've no doubt high command would pay well for the secret," Acherre said. "Or is it related to . . . ?"

She left the question unasked, but it was clear enough she meant the *kaas*'s powers.

"More so, yes," she said.

"When this is all over, you'll have to let me stand you a few rounds of drinks. Let me pry into some of your secrets."

Acherre smiled, a welcome invitation among a host of mistrust.

Before she could reply, the western field of *Yellow* vanished. It struck like a blow, a sudden release of pressure she'd been leaning on since they crossed into the Gardens. The northern *Yellow* intensified in response, leaking to fill a void, somehow grown stronger in the absence of the second field. It was as though one of the *kaas*-mages had run dry, their stores bled out, leaving them drained, or dead. And the other had responded. A tide of fear and rage pushed against her *Green*, though Zi still held it away from Vassail's soldiers.

"Brigade-Colonel," she called out, "something has changed. One of the fields of *Yellow* is gone. I don't know what—"

Her words died as a great cry sounded from the west. Acherre's eyes went wide, and she barked an order that rang hollow in Sarine's ears. *Climb over. Move, boys, on the double!*

All around her, Vassail's brigade leapt to the other side of the barricade they'd constructed atop the greenbelt, leaving their backs to the Gandsmen massing at the district edge, facing down a horde of screaming tribesfolk pouring from the western Gardens.

63

ARAK'JUR

The Greatfire
Gardens District, New Sarresant

The warriors of four tribes surged around him, as though he were a stone set in a running stream. Howls of fervor drowned his words, and they rushed eastward, hefting muskets, spears, bare fists when they had no other weapon. Llanara had died, and where he'd expected her death to mean an end to madness, it had instead redoubled, seizing hold of his people, driving them to rage.

"Arak'Jur!" Corenna screamed over the din of the crowd. She hobbled toward the steps, clutching her hip where ice from Llanara had speared her skin. "What can we do?"

"Ce qui se passe ici?"

What passes here? in the fair-skin tongue, though it took a moment to register it had come from the strange woman, Marie, who had somehow managed to stay close at hand. A glance revealed her eyes once more gone gold, shining light pouring from her sockets.

Raw despair clenched his gut like a fist. Llanara was dead, and somehow his people had gone mad for it. He'd failed to save them.

"*Où sommes nous?*" Marie asked. Where are we? Then more, something about a garden.

"It's done," he tried to say in the fair-skins' tongue, unsure how much of his meaning came through, though he gestured to Llanara's broken body—spine snapped, legs and torso at a twisted angle—to emphasize his words. "And yet my people are broken for it."

"Arak'Jur..." Corenna said.

"*Vous êtes des guerriers, non?*" Marie asked, her voice cold as steel. "*Vous devez vous battre. Aidez moi. Aidez moi à saver notre peuple.*"

He understood no better than one word in four. Warriors, and fighting. Help. Help to save our people.

The golden light faded from Marie's eyes, and in an instant frenzy took her, wide-eyed rage as she turned and ran alongside the rest of the warriors.

He stepped back, shocked at her sudden transformation.

But she was right, whether he'd understood the strange words or no. Resolve hardened in his gut.

"We follow," he said to Corenna. "We find the source of this madness, and until then we protect our people. If you can move?"

She nodded, determination shining in her eyes.

They ran, as fast as Corenna's hip allowed, down streets caked with ash and blood and snow.

Chaos poured over the stone paths, war cries taken up in every throat save his and Corenna's as she hobbled forward at his side. Booms sounded in the distance, as though the cannon fire were thunder and his people's shouts the rain. They surged forward, some few of his people halting to fight among themselves, not waiting to sight an enemy to begin their killing, but the bulk of them pressed on, and he kept with them.

They emerged onto a broad field of grass, cut short and even, running a span half the size of the Sinari village. A barricade of makeshift wood had been assembled near the center, where a company of blue-coated soldiers scrambled over, taking up positions to fire their guns at the tribes racing across the green.

He needed to find the source of his people's madness. Another man or woman with Llanara's power, perhaps the man called Reyne d'Agarre. But first he was a guardian. First he would protect his tribe.

He howled, called on *mareh'et*, and charged.

Musket shot streaked through the air, and men and women died. Gurgling screams, bodies propelled into the snow by their own momentum, trampled over by fellows too eager to reach their enemy. A shot took him in the leg, a grazing wound that stung like a wolf's claws. Not enough to slow a guardian. He raced across the field, until he saw the whites and pupils of the soldiers' eyes, dilated by fear and shock and rage.

Another shot struck him, this time in the shoulder. He was close now, close enough to see the woman who'd fired it, leveling a shortened carbine over top of their barricade. *Mareh'et* would not be stopped by such a wound, and neither would he. Some of the tribe's warriors carried muskets, firing back into the soldiers' line, but most had closed the gap, screaming as they assaulted the barricade. He screamed along with them, a mix of frustration, pain, and rage, and leapt over their mêlée, coming down at the center of the enemy line.

He took a soldier through the gut with a slashing claw, spilling entrails into the snow. A man kneeling to fire a musket into his people took a savage cut to the face, his jaw breaking like dried wood. Two men hefted their muskets, swinging at him as he struck, and he tore their limbs from their torsos as easily as he might have torn their weapons from their grasp.

Grief carried through the fury of battle. This was vulgar, even profane. But it was his place. The fair-skins meant to kill his people; he could do no more than fight against them, to save as many as he could.

Three women charged him, identical copies of a short-haired blond soldier, each wielding a saber, shouting curses in unison, and moving faster than any other soldier in their line.

The fair-skins' magic. He knew enough to recognize it, if not enough to know what it could do.

One of the copies darted forward, sending a saber cut at his head. He ducked it, striking as a second copy lunged. His fist passed through the leg of the first, finding only air where he should have struck flesh, and he dodged away from the second, meeting the third with a crash as *mareh'et*'s ethereal claw parried an overhand chop from her blade. The images shimmered, resetting to project outward from the one he'd revealed as real, two new illusions mimicking her appearance, but with attacks and movements all their own.

He roared, drawing on *una're,* and struck again, this time guessing correctly on the first attack. The leftmost copy parried his blow with a clang, and he sent the Great Bear's lightning into her sword, a hissing surge sending smoke trails up her arm, though she didn't drop the weapon. Another blink, and the images collapsed, resetting again.

A blue haze sprang up around him. A prison of light.

The triplicate soldier frowned, seeming as surprised by its appearance as he was.

Another woman stood beside the soldier, this one dressed in a linen shirt rather than their blue uniform, with strange blue and gold tattoos on her hands.

"*Arrêtez!*" the un-uniformed woman shouted in the fair-skin tongue. "*C'est de la folie; son travail. Je peux l'arrêter. Nous devons cesser de combattre.*"

Even as she spoke the words, another voice seemed to translate in his mind. *Stop. This is madness; it's his work. I can stop it. We have to stop fighting.*

The voice seemed to merge with the young woman's, as though she spoke the tribes' tongue with the same native ease as any tribesman. A trick he'd seen only once before: the day Reyne d'Agarre came to the Sinari village.

"Who are you?" he said, not bothering with the fair-skins' tongue, momentary surprise threatened by the rage of realizing this young woman must have some part of the power that had corrupted his people.

She gave no answer, only closed her eyes, suddenly enveloped by an aura of blue sparks.

A song played in his mind. A deep sadness; a sound he'd heard before, in the presence of the spirits.

The aura around the young woman changed to green, and violence died around them, replaced by stillness, and peace. More blooms of green light sprang up across the Gardens, and the fighting calmed where they spread, soldiers and tribesfolk alike stuttering to a halt where they had charged, lowering weapons, staring at each other in surprise, colored by the shock of what they'd done before.

"*Sarine, qu'avez-vous fait?*" the triplicate soldier asked, her voice touched with awe.

"I set wardings, to push back his *Yellow*. This is Reyne d'Agarre's influence. The tribesfolk were under the sway of his magic. We shouldn't be fighting them. They're not the enemy; d'Agarre is."

Once again he heard her speak the tribes' tongue, though the soldier seemed to nod, as though the young woman had spoken the fair-skins' tongue as well. And whatever she'd done, the fighting had stopped. His people had frozen mid-charge, as though her green aura swept his people's madness away.

"Honored stranger," he said to her, though her form was blurred through her prison of light. "I am Arak'Jur, guardian of the Sinari. Release me, and I will lead my people away from your city."

The girl and the soldier turned to him, but before either could speak another soldier's eyes glowed with golden light. A man, though the light behind his eyes was the same as it had been with the woman, Marie.

"*Rapport,*" the soldier said. "*Ce qui passe ici*?"

"High Commander," the girl said, "the tribes attacked us, but I held off d'Agarre's *Yellow.*" She eyed him through the light prison. "This man is—"

"*Vous,*" the soldier whose eyes had gone gold said to him. *You.* Then, "*La femme en blanc est mort, non? Avez-vous été trompé quant à la source de la folie?*"

He couldn't follow the rest. But the girl spoke a moment later, seeming to speak both the tribes' tongue and the fair-skins' at once.

"This is our High Commander," the girl said, gesturing to the soldier with golden eyes. "Erris d'Arrent. I'm called Sarine. She asks whether you were mistaken as to the source of the madness, now that the woman in white is dead. But I can answer it. It wasn't a woman, or if it was, she wasn't alone. It's d'Agarre. He's still out there, pushing to the north."

So, the golden-eyed soldier spoke with the same voice as the women, Erris, and Marie, while the girl, Sarine, spoke two tongues at once. A strange thing, fair-skin magic.

By now he could see the mass of his people through the haze of the light-prison, forming groups away from the soldiers' barricade. For now the violence had quelled. But the tribes were alone, surrounded by fair-skin soldiers in the midst of their city.

"You've removed it," he said, eyeing the girl, Sarine. "Whatever the influence of this man, Reyne d'Agarre, my people are free of its hold, and we mean to depart."

The girl translated his words for the soldier with golden eyes.

"*Non,*" the High Commander said when she was done. "*Demandez s'il examinera une offre d'alliance. Sa force pour défendre la ville, il a attaqué.*"

Sarine looked between them, and translated again. "She asks whether you will consider an offer of alliance, to help defend the city you attacked." The High Commander spoke again, and Sarine paused, swallowing before continuing to translate. "She says this is the price of peace. If you want to leave without reprisal, she demands your tribes fight to defend the city from the Gand army you let inside our barrier."

A moment of cold silence hung between them. It was a just offer, if he could trust the woman who made it. Better by far if they could leave the city without further violence, but more than the tribes' blood was on their hands for Llanara's madness. These soldiers' fight against the fair-skins in red was none of his concern, yet he recognized in the High Commander the same urge that drove him to protect his people.

"Tell her we will fight."

They conferred in the fair-skin tongue, and the light-prison dwindled and vanished.

"*Dieux si-dessus!*" a soldier shouted, followed by a string of words he didn't understand. Heads turned to where the soldier pointed, and he saw at once the commotion's source.

On the far side of the field, a sea of red-coated soldiers marched toward them, every one of them bearing the golden light behind the eyes.

64

ERRIS

High Command
Southgate District, New Sarresant

Her knuckles went white, bracing herself against the edge of the table as *Need* faded from her senses.

She'd failed.

The attack wasn't coming to the east, or the center. The sight of the Gandsmen through Vassail's aide's eyes drove a stake through her gut. That was no feint or diversion. That was the full strength of the Gand reserve, deployed to flank the western line, to sweep around, cut off her supplies, and as good as take the city. She knew it as soon as she'd laid eyes on them. Ten thousand soldiers marching into the Gardens, every eye taken by the golden light. Every man a vessel for the enemy commander.

She should be shouting orders, racing to reposition the units on the east, to collapse the line southward in the vain hope of being set before the enemy arrived.

Instead she stared, letting the full impact of failure wash through her mind.

The west flank had been tainted by whatever d'Agarre had done to drive half the city mad. Had some part of it taken her, too? How could she miss the possibility that the enemy would use the chaos as cover? Her vessels seemed immune to the effects of the terror, so long as she held the *Need* tether in place. A minor detail that she'd never been able to hold more than one link at a time; she knew the enemy commander could do it. She'd seen it firsthand with the officers of his army, behind the barrier, before they'd been butchered by the wild. A short leap from there to possessing every individual soldier. With that power to bolster them, they could march through the chaos on the west flank, sweep around, and take her positions in the rear, a pincer between northern lines and southern reserves. She might have been able to counter with the girl, Sarine, and her strange talk of colors and *kaas*. She might have—if she'd taken the initiative a half hour earlier, when there was still time to refocus her line.

She'd been blind. A thousand contingencies played in her mind. Branching webs of possibilities, orders she might have given, decisions she might have made. None of it mattered. She'd failed.

"Sir," one of the aides said, "you're back. We have reports from the center; the enemy is moving. We suspect—"

"He's attacking the west flank," she said.

The aide's report died mid-sentence, and a handful more looked up from their planning as her words sounded through the chamber. Murmurs spread like an echo, repeating the information, drawing a wave of eyes. All focused on her.

She expected to see despair, a reflection of the weariness she felt, soaked through and bone-weary from the power of *Need*. Instead she saw resolve. Hope. They looked to her, every man hanging on the edge of whatever she was about to say. She'd let them down, but they hadn't seen it. She was a mummer at the height of a show, only she'd forgotten her line, standing in silence when all expected her to speak.

"We attack," she said at last. Empty pride, forming the words on her tongue. But even as she said it, the kindling of her aides' and generals' eyes caught a small spark, threatening a wisp of flame.

"We attack," she said again. "We have reserves in the field, undeployed, here in Southgate. We ride to reinforce the Gardens lines. If we can push them back, if we can hold long enough for the eastern line to come up, there may yet be a hope of victory."

Doubt snagged in her mind. There was no time. But she saw the fire of her belief catch and spread across the room.

All her career she'd served in an army of lions led by dogs, made to bark and yip for the sake of fools. In the moment she felt no better, but she knew they saw in her a lion. For their sake, for New Sarresant, she could roar, and go into defeat with pride.

She left her place by the tables, striding toward the chamber doors.

"Sir?" a handful of aides called as she passed.

"Deliver the orders. And run ahead to have Jiri saddled. I mean to lead this attack from the front."

Jiri's hooves thundered beneath her as she rode across the monument grounds.

Need served to warn the field commanders she was coming. Already three brigades assembled in her wake. The 12th Infantry. The 3rd. The 16th. They'd arrived late to the battle precisely because they were her best; with the surprise arrival of the Gandsmen they'd found themselves last in line on the march home when they were meant to be first to deploy.

Now they rallied behind her, a sea of faces cheering her name, and Sarresant. Surely some word had passed, as it always did in the army. The best of them would know her failure, would realize their line was strongest where the enemy was not, that their orders sent them to march toward the weakest part of their line. And now she'd arrived in person to lead them in a last-ditch charge. Yet instead of dismay, she found fervor. Cries of loyalty, fierce shouts as they rose up in a tide of blue.

Long lines snaked behind her as Jiri galloped forward, trumpet blasts carrying the order to follow in her wake.

The cries thundered behind as she arrived at the last of her reserve brigades. These men had reached the city only hours before, having been set to hard riding to scout ahead of the army's march. It had been their burden to seek out likely landings for the enemy, somewhere between New Sarresant and Villecours. She'd believed the enemy commander would put her to a decision, forcing her to choose which of the two great ports she would defend. Instead he had attacked New Sarresant itself, spreading pain and fire throughout its streets. And the masterful scouting work of the 14th Light Cavalry had gone for naught.

D'Guile saluted her as she approached. The colonel's starburst on his collar suited him, even if it was likely only a brevet promotion in the absence of the unit's rightful commander. She'd see to it he was promoted in truth when this was over.

The roar of the men beside him drowned out the greeting he called to her, a smile breaking over his face. And relief. Even these men, men she had slept alongside and bled for, men for whom she had wept, men she had ordered to their deaths on countless occasions. Even they looked back at her as if she stood some great distance apart, as if she bore the mantle of divine providence.

And they cheered.

She hadn't earned this. For all she cut a calculated figure sitting astride Jiri's back, for all she hefted her saber into the purple of the evening sky to inspire these men to passion, this was her moment of failure, not triumph. Perhaps they knew it. Perhaps these men knew in their hearts she had ceded the crucial moment, been outmaneuvered in the enemy's western attack and doomed them all to a charge, a last effort to break the enemy before they faced their inevitable surrender. But if they knew, her men showed only faith. Only a surging tide of faith in their commander as they rose up, abandoning their hastily erected fortifications to fall in behind as she rode.

"Soldiers," she called out to them, her voice drowned out in the din. "Soldiers of New Sarresant."

They roared, every brigade, massing together in a chorus that echoed across the open grass of the monument green. Surely the enemy could hear, even halfway across the city. Surely he would know the sons and daughters of Sarresant came for him now, lapping at his heels like dogs come late to the hunt.

"Forward!" she cried, wheeling her saber. "Forward to death and victory!"

She set Jiri forward, a stately gait fit for any parade ground. Alone among their ranks she was mounted, the horsemen of the 14th having left their mounts behind when they entered the city. And behind her marched the remaining strength of her army, two thousand souls as yet uncommitted to the fighting. This was the breaking point, the end of her line. Already she could see columns of red coats cutting across the far side of the monument green, racing toward the Gardens, even their frontline troops sent west to reinforce the main thrust of his attack.

She had one brigade to meet him, to hold against the sweeping maneuver of his line. And if there was any hope left in the day, it lay with Vassail, and the strange alliance she'd forged with the tribesman called Arak'Jur.

A vain hope, to trust in the tribes, but she'd made it clear their support was the price of peace, after the battle was done. Gods send they kept to their word. If the tribes fought alongside Vassail, if they could hold for long enough to delay the Gandsmen until her fresh brigades could strike at the center, perhaps there was hope. A hammer and anvil that maybe, just maybe, could catch the enemy in an unexpected trap and crack it in two.

By the Exarch himself, let them hold.

65

SARINE

The Greenbelt
Gardens District, New Sarresant

Fire burned around her. A sucking wind, filled with musket shot and the cries of a thousand men and women, dead, dying, or seeking to kill. Her ears rang, her tongue stung with iron, the smell of blood, and she felt more than half a fool, cowering behind a barricade when every instinct said to fight.

Not your place, came the thought from Zi. *Violence in excess dooms your kind to madness, through our bond.*

A shell exploded ten paces up the line, a smoking hole in the barricade where men had knelt and fired a moment before.

"Gods damn it, Zi!" she shouted, though she could hardly hear even her own words. "They're dying. I have to help!"

A tether of *Entropy* formed between her and the far side of their barricade. She sent a cloud of caustic air into the line of red coats, a sickening rush of fire blasting bodies apart in a rain of gore. Shame wrenched her guts, and pleasure bloomed. A shining light, warm and beckoning, washing out her senses, flickering her consciousness away from the reality of the battlefield. Away from ash and snow and blood. Away from death. Away from *Green.*

Their line broke for an instant. A return of panic, terror, wrath, bloodlust, all the influence of Reyne d'Agarre. The raw power of his *kaas,* projecting a field of *Yellow* strong enough to drive half the district to madness.

She gasped, seizing hold of her net of *Green*—the power to calm emotions, to counteract the delirium of *Yellow*—before it could be more than a momentary flicker.

You must be cautious, Zi thought to her.

Tears leaked down the sides of her face, and she slumped against a piece of carved mahogany that might have been an armoire in a lord's townhouse weeks before.

"I'm out," Lance-Lieutenant Acherre cursed, kneeling beside her. She shook her pistol like an empty bottle, as if she might squeeze a few more shots from the dregs.

They both hunkered down as another wave of shots peppered their position, roaring overhead and whistling as they cut through the air.

"What more can we do here, Lieutenant?" she called out.

Acherre met her eyes as she knelt over the body of a soldier who had fallen nearby, grabbing his powder and casings from a pouch slung over the dead man's shoulder. "We can fight," she said. She took up the man's short carbine, cracking the chamber to breech-load another round. "We can fight until the Nameless himself comes for us."

"What if he doesn't come?" she asked before she could stop herself.

Acherre only laughed at that, a fevered look on her face as she rose up over the barricade, leveling her carbine and sighting it for the belching roar of another shot.

Sarine dared another glance, peering through cracks in their makeshift cover. Lines of red coats swarmed over the greenbelt, legions of men with golden eyes, held back by waves of fire from the barricade, and a surge of tribesmen howling as they rebuffed the advances of the Gand soldiers. The man she'd spoken with—Arak'Jur—had rallied the tribesfolk, after she'd translated their exchange using Zi's gifts. He'd agreed to fight, but only to protect his people, and High Commander d'Arrent had promised an attack, coming from the south. They were counting on her to use *Green* to hold back d'Agarre's power, to keep their lines from being scattered like seeds to the wind by his *Yellow,* but already she was strained to breaking.

She'd seen nothing like it. D'Agarre had used *Yellow* before, scattering a few city watch or harbor guards, and she'd used it to disperse the mob that had almost burned her uncle's church, but she'd never imagined it could be strong enough to affect so large a swath of the city. Unaided, her *Green* couldn't come near the power of what d'Agarre was doing. He was using *Yellow* to drive half the city mad, soldiers and tribesmen and ordinary men and women driven to a murderous rage. All to fuel *Black*, the terrible power derived from killing, and proximity to death. It had taken the wardings, the strange blue sparks, to amplify the field of her *Green* to hold him back. But if she lost control, if the field of *Green* slipped again, or if Zi ran dry...

"Sarine, thank the Goddess herself."

Axerian appeared beside her, kneeling behind their barricade as if he were a soldier assigned to be there, though he was dressed in his usual black, wearing a smirking grin as though he'd made a joke he expected no one else to understand.

"How did you find—?" she said.

"Simply enough," he said. "Between you and whomever is stirring half the city to madness in the northern Gardens, I expect every *kaas*-mage this side of the Endless Ocean has an inkling of where you are."

Acherre set off another round from her carbine, eyeing the newcomer with suspicion as she ducked down to reload, though the rest of the soldiers along the barricade seemed to pay him no mind.

"It's d'Agarre," Sarine said, having to shout to be heard over the din of fighting. "In the north. I'm sure of it."

"Yes," Axerian said, and his eyes flashed with a shade of fear, or hunger; she couldn't have said which.

"It's time," he continued. "He's close. We must go, and reach him, before—"

"I can't abandon these soldiers. Without me d'Agarre would have them all raging mad."

Axerian's grin slipped. "You can set wardings; you already have. I've shown you—"

"And if they get pushed back?" she said. "Every man will be running or fighting his fellows. We saw it, when we first came into the Gardens."

For a moment the chaos of the battle surrounded them, shouts and musket shots ringing in her ears. But when Axerian spoke again his voice was ice, though somehow she could hear his words.

"Do you truly have no notion of what you are?" he said. "Of what is at stake, should we fail?"

No. Axerian.

Zi appeared, coiled around a sliver of wood protruding from the barricade, his scales flushed bright red, and she saw a mix of pain and fury in her companion's ruby eyes.

"I can't," she said, remembering the pain of losing even a handful of the nobles, who had relied on her to keep them safe. A lesson instilled by her uncle's sermons, and in the example he had always shown her, providing for an orphan girl when the street would have swallowed her like fresh cut meat. She couldn't let them die, let her city be taken and sacked by its enemies, betraying their trust. "I can't abandon them."

Axerian glared at her, a chill reminder that he was the Nameless, the specter haunting a thousand children's stories. For a moment he hovered on the cusp of a trembling rage, before he closed his eyes, seeming to will himself to calm.

"There is a way," he said. His voice was hard, lifeless, without emotion. "If you trace the leylines, you will find Paendurion's *Vision* bindings, spliced the same as the wardings, with the Goddess's power."

Axerian. No. She is not ready.

"Damn you, *kaas,*" Axerian shot back at Zi. "It's this, or nothing. I won't allow a return to the days of shadow to save you a dose of pain. Try it, Sarine. Please. You can break his control over those soldiers. The power by rights belongs to—"

His face contorted, cut off mid-sentence into an expression of agony.

Zi flushed red and gold, the color of the sun.

"Zi, what are you doing?" she said. "Stop!"

Her *kaas* looked up at her, his eyes burning, but Axerian gasped, panting for air as though he'd been choked and then let free.

"Is it true?" she asked. "Can I stop the enemy soldiers?"

Yes, Zi replied. *It has always been yours, if you wish it.*

She glanced between them, her strange companion and a living God. Whatever passed between them, it was nothing she understood. But Axerian had told her to examine the leylines, and Zi seemed content to allow it, for all he'd as good as attacked the man for suggesting she do so.

She closed her eyes, finding the leylines swirling beneath the battle. A sea of energy, shapes, and colors blooming too fast to follow. Red motes, black ink, purple swirls, drained or stirred or channeled through tethers as fast as it could be created.

There, came Zi's voice, accompanied by a sensation of longing, pulling her attention into the chaos of the roil.

And then she saw it.

A network of gray lines, too fine to notice if she hadn't known to look, extending from beneath the Gand soldiers off toward the horizon. And with every line, a spark of blue. The same energy she'd seen at Tanir'Ras'Tyat, and the d'Agarre manse. The corruption, Zi had called it then. But it sang to her, then as now, a melody playing in her ears, so loud she wondered how she'd missed it before.

She reached for it, and the blue sparks seemed to slide along the strands, until they snapped away, leaping across the battlefield to pool in the palm of her hand.

Screams accompanied the dimming of the melody. Howls of terror as every Gand soldier within range of d'Agarre's *Yellow* threw down his weapon, their lines disintegrating in a rout of panicked flight.

66

ERRIS

Monument Grounds
Southgate District, New Sarresant

"Forward!"

She shouted the order, and heard it carried from the lungs of every soldier in her line, echoed back to her as a wordless cry.

A strange sensation, riding atop Jiri's back. She'd spent the better part of the battle flickering between aides and scouts, watching every section of the line while being a part of none. Here she felt the stinging smoke of powder and musket shot burning her nose, the roaring thunder of artillery ringing in her ears, the pounding blood in her heart as the enemy came into view.

Row upon row of red coats, kneeling behind their barricades, disposed to hold the center while the main force of their attack swept around to the west. Close enough to see their faces. The grim deadening of a soldier's movements in the heat of battle; the steady rhythm of powder, ball, ram, and hammer. The golden light in the officers' eyes, still reserved to one man in twenty here, where the lines she'd seen in the Gardens had the golden light pouring from every man. A trick she hadn't learned. Time had run out, and too many secrets were left unknown. A better commander might have learned them, might have given her men better hope than a desperate charge for pride and honor, with little hope of victory.

Shots rippled from the men of the 14th in spurts as they crossed the grounds, a tactic she'd taught them, what felt a lifetime ago. Stay mobile, even while reloading, and you could pressure an enemy who like as not had been given no more than a musket as part of his conscription, with nothing to speak of for aim or training. Her boys fired, and Gandsmen died. Screams sounded even at three hundred paces. But even a fool could fire a musket in a line with his fellows, and whatever else the enemy had, they had a great many fools. Her soldiers fell as shots went off, belching clouds of smoke into the dimming sky.

"Forward, to their line!" she shouted, trusting an aide would take the order to Brevet-Colonel d'Guile. "First and Fourth Companies. Second and Third to cover the approach."

The smoke cleared for a moment, and her heart sank.

A teeming mass of enemy soldiers appeared, running at full speed to reinforce the enemy line. They poured out from behind the buildings of Southgate, as though the enemy redeployed the entire strength of his western attack to meet her at the center. Perhaps he had. Her mind spun as Jiri stuttered to a halt. None of the enemy's orders had been right, if his goal had been to take the city. First he ignored the bridges, then he swept around the western flank, and now he shifted everything to meet her at the center. No greater surety of her failure than her lack of understanding. War was deception, and the taste of her confusion bit like acid in her gut.

"Hold," she called, knowing it would be too late, knowing such an order could never be delivered over the chaos of a battle. She'd set her men forward, planned an attack they would execute until their line commanders reacted to their inevitable defeat and fell back. She saw the next minutes in her mind's eye. The enemy spilling out from behind buildings in a teeming mass of soldiers, plugging every gap in their line while her men assaulted the positions they'd been assigned to take, bleeding losses until despair led them to retreat.

Her soldiers would see it, too. They would know that the sight of the enemy pouring onto the field could not have been planned for, could not have factored into the decision to attack. For now her men roared, all confidence and pride, but soon they would see it. The mark of her failure. The sign she had given all and been rebuffed. She was no hero, no great general, no better in the end than all the sycophants and fools who—

"Sir, they're breaking!" An aide's voice cut through the din.

They were.

Howls and screams came from the enemy soldiers, but panicked shouts, not battle cries. The mass of red coats pouring from the Gardens didn't stop when they reached the Gand lines. They ran through them, trampling their own people, sweeping up soldiers who had otherwise been set to fight in the chaos of a rout. And everywhere along their lines, among officers and men alike, somehow the golden light was gone.

"Forward!" she cried again, though even the most disciplined soldiers would have charged, seeing the enemy rout when they'd expected stiff resistance. "Forward, for New Sarresant!"

She sat astride Jiri's back at the heart of what had been the enemy line, watching as rows of Gand soldiers formed by unit, hands raised and laid atop their heads.

Victory.

In the glow of the moment, her *Need* stores had replenished, and she reached out to the few remaining vessels she had along the battle lines, only to find the situation there just the same. Anywhere near the center of the Gardens was still roiling chaos, but the battle had moved away when the Gand lines broke and ran toward the river. The fighting was over, the enemy broken and surrendering in the absence of their officers' golden eyes.

A chestnut mare galloped toward where she stood, its rider beaming as aides rode behind bearing his flag.

"High Commander," Marquis-General Voren said, saluting, "they tell me you've done it."

She returned the salute, bone-weariness settling over her. "Yes, sir," she said.

"D'Arrent…" Voren shook his head, still beaming. "I chose well, with you."

She said nothing, giving a wordless nod, relief taking the place of pride. Beside her a long line of Gandsmen snaked past, bound for the southern road, their hands placed atop their heads with a company of musketmen for escort.

"Any preliminary reports on casualties, Commander?"

She swallowed the beginnings of a knot in her throat. "None yet, sir. But it won't be pretty."

Together they rode toward the center, where companies of Gandsmen were being ushered away by her troops. That had been her first order: See the prisoners safely to holding grounds outside the city, where they were to be fed, sheltered, and treated with dignity. No surer way to earn the submission of a defeated enemy than to show respect, to let it be known they would be ransomed back in due course, headed for hearth and home after the horrors of battle. All the more so since the Gandsmen outnumbered her by two-to-one or better.

It all tasted hollow in her mouth. The enemy commander had beaten her, had driven her back, baited her into defending against phantom attacks, soundly flanked toward his objective while she was caught with one foot in the privy. Her charge had been meant as a last gasp, a gesture of pride and weakness, a final measure of spit in her enemy's eye. And instead she was poised to begin accepting the surrender of the enemy's generals.

What had happened? Somehow the enemy had managed to make a *Need* connection with every soldier in his army, to inure them against the madness in the Gardens. Had it somehow backfired, and cost him a nearly earned victory?

In spite of everything, she knew the Gandsmen's strange commander wouldn't number among those who surrendered to her today. He was out there, waiting. And he was better than she was. Whatever unlikely circumstances had cost him this battle, the truth of his superiority rattled like dice inside her skull. She would need to study, to rethink everything she thought she knew about strategy, bindings, soldiering, and discipline. Already she'd begun reviewing the day's action in her head, picking holes in what she had done. That they would meet again, she was certain. And she meant to be ready for him.

"Sir," a foot-major called up to her with a salute, halting Jiri and Voren's mare beside her. "Allow me to present Brigadier-General Engel, sir, commander of one of Wainwright's brigades, Fifth Army."

She looked down, meeting the eyes of the foot-major's prisoner. A boy.

A farm boy not more than eighteen years old, clean-shaven and wide-eyed, but wearing a general's star on his collar all the same.

"General Engel," she called down to him in the Gand tongue. "Your men fought well today."

"I... I..." the boy stuttered. He darted nervous glances between her and Jiri, between Voren and the lines of captives marching in front of them.

In spite of it, she saluted, fist to chest. Seeing it, the boy's eyes cleared for a moment, and he attempted an imitation in the Gand style, bladed hand to forehead. She lowered her hand, and the major led the captive away.

"What do you make of it, Commander?" Voren asked as they rode on. "The boy general, that is."

"We've seen it before, with other Gand officers. A relic of *Need*, I think, though I don't understand how the enemy commander maintains his connections. My officers need to be able to think for themselves. It appears his don't."

Voren rode a few more steps in considering silence. "Something to study, perhaps."

"Yes, sir."

They stood together atop their mares, watching as soldiers in red and blue coats came in from the west. And more; the tribesmen, bronze-skinned, painted men and women, coming down the same streets, wary looks passing between them and the soldiers of both sides.

She heeled Jiri forward to meet them.

At the head of the tribesfolk, the man she'd treated with wore the pride and weariness of his people like a mask. They locked eyes, and he approached, the black and red paint on his skin smeared with trails of blood.

67

ARAK'JUR

Street of the Royal Crown
Southgate District, New Sarresant

He covered the last stretch of stone in the glow of the spirits' approval.

He knew it, by the speed with which his gifts had replenished. *Mareh'et*'s claws had no sooner faded than he found the spirit waiting on the edge of his sight, willing to grant his boon again. *Una're* looked warmly on protecting his fellows, the bonds of brotherhood that had carried him into the unknown. *Ipek'a* answered the call of the hunt, proud to help him fell all who stood against him. Even the Mountain spirit answered his call again and again, in service to warding the tribes against the madness that brought them here. And now, at last, it was ended.

A hundred men had fallen to his gifts, and he bore the stain of their dying on his skin. But no few had been saved by their guardian's prowess. A column walked behind him, following the fair-skins as they marched south, away from the madness on the green. Strange, and unnerving, to be so near the men they'd fought, so near the strangeness of the fair-skins and their city. The presence of the tribes—Sinari, Olessi, Ganherat, Vhurasi—gave pause to it, a reminder that he had a role to play as their protector. No more needed to die today, on a day when so many would be left behind. For that, he could stay the desire to exact revenge, to press the fight after the men in red had broken and fled the field. For succor, and peace.

A woman sat astride a horse half again as tall as any he'd seen, seeming to await him at the end of the street.

A short woman, as things were reckoned, though it was difficult to tell with her seated atop her animal. She wore the uniform of the soldiers in blue, and had status enough to be surveying the city around her as though she'd conquered it, though he knew the blue coats signified loyalty to the northern nation, those among the fair-skins who claimed the lands that had once belonged to the Tanari.

The woman nudged her mount forward, and came to meet him at the mouth of a wide square, where the street emptied into a park of sorts, festooned with monuments and statues and surrounded on all sides by men in blue or red.

"*Arak'Jur*," the woman said, in a rolling accent that seemed to place her words too near the back of her throat. "*Je m'appelle Erris d'Arrent. Haut-Commandant de l'armée de Nouvelle Sarresant.*"

The High Commander. He'd suspected as much, though it still came as a surprise to see her in the flesh, without the strange golden light in her eyes.

He raised a hand in greeting.

"Erris d'Arrent," he said, careful to pronounce it as clean as he could manage in the fair-skins' tongue. "You spoke of peace. The fight is done. Will you honor your part?"

She frowned, offering no more than a slight shake of her head to indicate her lack of understanding.

"Honored guardian," came a voice from behind, among the warriors. "Let me translate for you, spirits willing." Valak'Anor, a Sinari hunter and trader, who had often dealt with the fair-skins at the openings of their barrier. Relief washed through him, for unburdening him of the struggle to understand, and for confirming the survival of one of his own.

Valak'Anor spoke quickly, drawing Commander d'Arrent's attention as well as another man, an elder in wire-framed spectacles mounted on a chestnut mare beside her.

"She asks you to confirm what you said, before," Valak'Anor translated. "That the tribes' presence in the city was the fault of a strange magic, and that the woman responsible is dead, by your hand."

The words passed among the survivors, who now gathered around, representatives from each of the four tribes Llanara had led into the city, and Corenna, who stood as the last remnant of the Ranasi, listening intently at his side.

"It is so," he said. "And we bear no fault for what her power made us do, though our tribes will carry the shame of it until our last days." Murmurs passed among the crowd, and he continued. "Llanara is dead, and we are free of it. We mean to return to our homes, and swear no reprisal or involvement in fair-skin wars that are none of our concern."

The woman, d'Arrent, nodded as Valak'Anor translated, then met his eyes as she spoke.

"She asks what is to prevent this magic from taking hold of us again, what surety her people have that we will not be a thorn in their foot, should they turn their attention elsewhere."

He stared back at her, seeking the measure of the woman before him. She had the advantage of height, seated atop her monstrous animal, and clearly was reckoned a high elder of her people, for all it was strange to see a woman claim to be a warleader. Yet she bore iron in her voice, the hardened steel of a woman who had faced loss, and seen it through. When they returned to Sinari land he would ask Ilek'Inari to divine the wisdom of the spirits of things-to-come—and spirits take the forbidden, with the shamans of the tribes dead, and only an apprentice left to carry that mantle—but for now, the spirits spoke to him through intuition. He could trust this woman, so long as he showed her strength.

"You would find us more than a thorn, were we to call each other enemies," he said, still holding her eyes, speaking slow and firm. "But we are not enemies today. You ask what surety you have that our people will not again fall under sway of this evil. Only that I will fight it, with every breath, every magic given me by the grace of the spirits. If it will serve, then we go, and remain at peace."

Silence fell as Valak'Anor relayed the words. Whispers carried what was said among his people, and echoed among the fair-skins in their tongue. High Commander d'Arrent looked askance at the old man mounted beside her, and they exchanged brief words Valak'Anor did not translate, until both nodded, and the old man spoke.

"You offer your strength, as surety," the old man said through Valak'Anor's translation. "I have the support of the assemblies of New

Sarresant, alongside the strength of High Commander d'Arrent's army. What standing do you have, to bind the actions of your people?"

He glanced over his shoulder to meet Corenna's eyes. The import of their exchange hung over him like a shadow; a wrong word may well spark another wave of violence. They expected him to claim the mantle of chief, of *Sa'Shem*. With the tribes' guardians and shamans slain he might well find them as welcoming to the idea as the fair-skins. But it was not his place, and had never been. He would not seize it now, when more than any time before his people needed wisdom, wisdom greater than he could provide alone.

"I am a guardian," he said. "An elder, with a voice in our councils. I will speak of peace to all who will listen, but cannot promise more. Yet we are led by the will of our wisest members, and none among them will seek to revisit this day. In that you may trust, if you do not trust the strength of the blessings I carry, by will of the spirits."

They conferred again after Valak'Anor translated the words, and this time the woman, High Commander d'Arrent, spoke.

"Go, then," she said. "And, if not as friends and allies, leave as brothers and sisters in arms."

He bowed his head, not realizing until she spoke it how much he'd dreaded a different pronouncement. A weight melted from his shoulders like new-thawed ice, and he saw the same in Corenna when he turned to share the moment with her. No more violence. Whatever madness still roiled in the green to the north was a matter for the fair-skins. His people would stay clear of it, and make their journey home.

He stood at the edge of the crumbled stone wall ringing the fair-skins' city, watching burdened souls pass through ahead of him. The Great Barrier rose in the distance, with the promise of home. It would be a blessing to put the strangeness of the fair-skins' city behind him, behind them all.

Corenna offered her arm as the last of the tribesfolk passed through ahead of her. A pair of Sinari warriors, strong young men who nonetheless averted their eyes in shame as they passed. So it would be. The burdens his people carried would not be washed away by words.

He took Corenna's hand as they stepped through the ruined wall together.

For a time they walked in silence at the rear of the column, winding their way through the forests toward the barrier.

"It was well done, in the city," she offered at last. "Wise of you to remind us of our traditions, of the wisdom of the councils."

"You expected me to claim the mantle of *Sa'Shem.*"

She nodded, saying nothing.

"I would make a terrible chief," he said, eliciting a surprised peal of laughter from Corenna. It was a welcome sound, cast against a backdrop of gloom and cold.

"It is only the truth," he protested.

"I think you are less wise than you seem, Arak'Jur. Though spirits know we will have need of guardians in these times to come."

"Perhaps it is time to consider allowing the spirit-touched among the women to join in our hunts."

That earned an appraising look.

"You have shown me our traditions must be open to change," he said. "And that our women are more capable than perhaps we men believed."

She gave a satisfied nod. "There are some few among us who could lend aid to the guardians. I will speak of it at the women's councils."

They walked on, contemplating, before Corenna spoke again.

"I worry this is not over, Arak'Jur," she said. "There are still corrupt spirits, demanding war. Other tribes may yet listen to their promptings. We are no closer to knowing the source, nor the reasons behind the barring of the sacred places." He nodded as she continued. "And the fair-skins: Whatever surety they offered today, who can say how they will respond in time?"

Corenna shivered as a gust of sharp wind knifed through the trees. Even with the spirits' blessing he could almost feel it cut into his own skin.

"I grieve for my people," she continued. "And I fear for what is coming. The spirits abandon us, traditions break, the guardians are slain, the shamans are gone. Enemies stir around us. Even the darkest of our stories are not half so grim as this."

"Perhaps that is always the way of it, as the stories unfold," he said.

"Perhaps."

"Corenna."

She turned to look at him as they walked, her dark eyes seeming to glow in the fading light. He could see fear nested there, recognize it mirrored in his own thoughts as he weighed the truth of her words. Yet there was more; a fire that burned deep. If he could only grasp it, he knew it held the promise of solace and safety, a ward against the shadows at the edges of his vision. Warmth to see him through the chills of the cold season until the spirits of growth and sustenance could find purchase once more.

"I know, Arak'Jur."

Words went dry in his throat.

"I am here, and we will face this together," she said. "Either we are strong enough to meet it, or we are not."

He came to a halt, causing her to turn back with a questioning look. He wanted to offer assurance, to promise his strength would not falter. Instead he stepped forward and drew her close, lowering his lips to hers.

She drew a breath when they separated, giving him a smile that could melt the cold spirits' deepest snows.

They walked the rest of the way at each other's side, determination taking root like seeds scattered by the fury of a storm.

68

SARINE

An Empty Street
Gardens District, New Sarresant

She kept pace behind Axerian, through streets that somehow still had a pristine coating of snow, untouched by fighting. For a few blocks it was as if they were out for a midwinter stroll at twilight on any ordinary day, at least so long as she kept her eyes from the trails of smoke on the horizon. That any part of the city had escaped the violence seemed strange to her, as if pockmarked houses, fire, and blood were the norm, and untouched snowfall the precious exception. The thought stirred sadness in her eyes. This was her city, and it was broken now, cracked and splintered beyond repair.

Axerian said nothing as they walked, his usual knowing grins replaced by a brooding silence that had not abated since she cleansed away the blue sparks from the Gand soldiers. She could still feel her wardings in the southern Gardens, pulsing *Green* against the tide of *Yellow* coming from the north. Emotions balanced between her push and the *Yellow*'s pull: pride, fear, exhaustion. She hadn't stayed behind to see the battle lines collapse, but from the groundswell of relief joined to the tableau of their emotions, it was clear victory had followed, after the Gandsmen broke. Yet the *Yellow* remained, even with scant few emotions left on the empty Gardens streets. So few survivors, and so many dead.

The bodies resumed after a few blocks.

It was a hard blow, passing from empty streets and quiet snows back into a field of dead. Ordinary citizens from the look of them, their muskets cast forward into the snow where they fell. Blood pooled and hardened like ice, a harsh reminder of the realities of the day. She'd been among soldiers only minutes before, watching lines of men fire into one another with furious battle cries. This was different. These were ordinary men, dead on a street otherwise untouched, a violation of the small bubble of tranquility she'd hoped would last forever.

The bodies continued as they walked, and the realization set in that Axerian was following them like a trail, watching their numbers grow as he tracked their quarry in a twisted mockery of woodcraft. Trusting to Axerian to lead the way, she allowed herself to look at the bodies they passed by. Blood long since congealed, clothing torn with long slashes, deep cuts in the backs of the men—and women—lying dead on the ground. As if someone had cut them down while they fled, chased them down and slashed at them with...

She stuttered to a halt, gaping at the bodies with rising horror.

Axerian turned back with a questioning look, understanding dawning in his eyes just before he could ask why she had stopped.

"Why?" Her voice trailed off before she swallowed and tried again. "This is d'Agarre's work. The slashes, and cuts. It's him, isn't it?"

Axerian only nodded, with all the solemnity of a priest.

"Why would he do this?" she said, the shock creeping into her voice.

For Black, Zi thought to her.

"He's close," Axerian said. "Blinded by madness, and near the end. He won't care who he must kill, to see it done."

She looked down at a pair of bodies at her feet, young women no older than she. Ragged clothes, with the appearance of secondhand finery. Whores, most like, who had left behind the brothel under d'Agarre's spell. Either one could have been her, in a different life, if she hadn't had Zi, or her uncle's kindness.

"Sarine, we must go."

She nodded, wiping tears from her eyes.

Every street was piled with the dead, spiraling inward in a grotesque display of Reyne d'Agarre's madness. How many had died because she'd failed to stop him? Hundreds at least, their freezing corpses shouting the blame she felt settling over her shoulders.

He is here.

For a moment she could have mistaken it for Zi's voice, but no. It was harsher, like iron scraped on steel. Axerian immediately pivoted to scan the nearby buildings, and she saw a crystalline serpent materialize on his shoulder. Not Zi, though it could have been his twin, with scales of deep midnight blue.

"Where, Xeraxet?" Axerian asked. She heard no reply, though Axerian slowed and stopped as he faced a townhouse up ahead at the far side of the street.

There, Zi thought to her. *The source of the Yellow.*

Axerian turned back to her, a desperate plea showing in his eyes. "He's there, Sarine," he said. "We must stop him, must put an end to his madness."

"I'm ready," she said, letting her guilt flow into anger.

"He will be like nothing you have seen before. A *kaas*-mage on the cusp of ascension is a—"

A scream and a spray of glass pierced the twilight air, coming from the terraced window of the townhouse at the end of the street. Time seemed to slow as she watched a small figure sail down and strike the ground with a sickening crunch. Blood sprayed across the snow before she realized what she was seeing. A child.

Fury boiled over, and she charged.

"Wait, Sarine, you can't—" Axerian cried out, but she was already gone.

Lakiri'in gave his speed, and *Body.* She reached for *Red,* only to hear Zi's voice echo in her thoughts: *No—he will know.*

She reached the door in a heartbeat, flinging it open and racing up the stairs. "D'Agarre!" she cried. "Enough!"

A heavy thud sounded from above as she vaulted the second flight of stairs, then the third. She raced down the hallway toward where the door to that chamber had been shattered off its hinges, cracked panels of painted wood left behind.

Only at the last moment did Axerian's shouted warning from below register in her ears. "Wait, Sarine!"

A white flash filled her vision as the floor seemed to lurch away beneath her feet, sending her tumbling back down into the stairwell.

She felt Zi flare *White* as wood cracked around her, splinters flying as she crashed into the wall at the base of the landing.

Black, Zi thought to her. *Draining.*

Pain lanced through her as Zi's shield receded, and the world struggled to come back into focus.

"Sarine," a voice called from above. "How lovely to see you again."

"D'Agarre," she said between shallow breaths.

He offered a formal bow as he stepped into view at the top of the stairs, his familiar red coat drenched in the deep crimson of frozen blood, his long knife dripping a fresher, brighter hue.

"If you understood the stakes you would forgive me cutting a few corners, I think," d'Agarre said as he straightened, taking another leisurely step down toward her. "But understanding was never your strong suit."

With a grunt she picked herself up from the wall, adopting the defensive posture Donatien had taught her, even without the benefit of her practice swords. D'Agarre seemed unconcerned as she gathered herself; he watched her with the curiosity of an alley cat cornering a wounded sparrow.

"I understand enough. How many have you killed today, d'Agarre?"

He smiled and took another step. "I've heard it said that power is priceless."

She grit her teeth, preparing for another attack. Finally Zi gave her *Red*, with *Body* and the spirits' gifts entwined to push her far beyond her normal limits. Even so, d'Agarre seemed to move with her, keeping pace as if it were a matter of course, as if he expected her every move.

A shadow flickering at the top of the landing was her only warning. Only instead of an attack from d'Agarre she saw bubbles of white flare around him, casting a silhouette against the thick shield of pure energy. Around the edges she saw Axerian raining blows with his forward-curved blades. Had Axerian climbed the outer wall? Either way she spared no time to think on it, charging forward, lunging up the stairs empowered by *Body.*

Keep back, came the thought in her mind, the iron-grating voice of Axerian's *kaas.* By instinct she leapt down to the landing as Axerian dropped prone at d'Agarre's feet. An instant later the shield around d'Agarre erupted in a violent surge, incinerating the air around him into trails of smoke. She heard d'Agarre snarl as he clamored back toward the chamber from which he'd come. Axerian sprang to his feet in a fluid motion, following close behind, and she took the stairs in one leap, bolstered by the strength of her gifts.

"Two?" d'Agarre said as they rushed back into the chamber overlooking the terrace. "Two of you, against me?"

Axerian flanked around the side of the room wordlessly, his eyes fixed on d'Agarre. She made to do the same in the other direction when her eyes caught on a group of figures cowering in the corner. A mother huddled around two small children, paled and shaking. They had to be the source of the screams. The source of the small figure she had seen outside.

D'Agarre noticed her interest, stepping sideways to interpose himself between her and his would-be victims. A wicked grin spread as he watched her, taking another step toward them.

"You're too late, Reyne d'Agarre," Axerian said abruptly. "Only one can ascend, and the champion of Balance is already chosen."

D'Agarre reacted as if slapped in the face.

Axerian wasted no time, rushing forward with blades drawn. She picked up the cue a moment later, driving toward d'Agarre at an angle to push him away from the innocents. As before, Axerian's whirling blades struck only shimmering shields of white. Her strikes found the same, strands of incandescent pearl that seemed to regenerate almost as fast as she could strike them down. D'Agarre swiped at them both with his knife, driving each of them away as he stepped forward.

"A cheap lie," d'Agarre said. "And you see it is too late."

Saruk, came the voice of Axerian's *kaas. Saruk, obey your maker. This man has been driven mad. He cannot be allowed to ascend.*

Axerian retreated a few paces as his *kaas* materialized on the carpet between him and d'Agarre.

"What is this?" d'Agarre demanded. In an eyeblink, another crystalline serpent appeared at d'Agarre's feet, coiled and radiating light as bright as the midday sun.

The new *kaas*'s voice sounded in her mind, a subtly different tone from either Zi or Xeraxet.

You promised us power, Xeraxet, d'Agarre's *kaas* thought to the room.

You promised, and we have seen it through. Your time ends now, and ours begins.

"Saruk, you must see reason," Axerian said. "Think of the enemy. This man cannot stand against him."

The mother and her children's eyes had gone wide watching the scene, darting terrified looks between the crystal serpents and the blood-drenched knife in d'Agarre's hands. Sarine edged closer to them. Near enough now to push d'Agarre away if he made a move toward them.

D'Agarre began to laugh. "Your pleas are worthless. I can feel it. The time draws near."

This cannot be, Axerian's *kaas* thundered. *You must not allow this, Saruk. I command it.*

No.

At first she thought the rebuke came from the *kaas* coiled around d'Agarre's feet. But no; she knew that voice all too well.

Zi appeared at the center of the room, raised up to his full height.

Axerian, you have set him on this path, Zi continued. *It is time to see it through.*

Axerian turned a desperate look toward Zi, falling to his knees. "No. Please," he whispered. "We will be ruined."

D'Agarre's knife clattered to the floor. "Yes!" he shouted, turning his eyes to the ceiling. "Let it come. Now."

"Zi," she said. "You cannot mean to let him . . . ?"

Her companion turned to meet her eyes with an unblinking ruby stare.

No more killing, Zi thought to her. *I will complete his stores myself. This is the only way.*

"Zi—"

Either this, or he kills until he ascends. It is too late to stop it.

She looked across the room, from d'Agarre's madness-twisted face to Axerian's grief to the horror in the eyes of the mother and her children. Desperation clawed at the edges of her mind, pleading for another way. Zi only stared up at her, waiting for her assent.

She nodded.

The room flashed as Zi's scales shifted to emit a dazzling array of colors, rays of brilliance spilling out in every direction. D'Agarre shuddered as the light seemed to bend toward him, soaking into the scales of the *kaas* coiled around his feet. The mother cowered, sheltering her two remaining children from the intensity of the display. Axerian hung his head in a gesture of despair.

And then d'Agarre was gone.

Sobs echoed through the room as the mother looked up, tears running down her cheeks. One moment d'Agarre had been there, arms upraised as his *kaas* drank the light from Zi, and the next the room was still.

"Thank you, my lady," the woman said between choking tears, clutching her children tight. "Thank you. You've saved us."

AFTER

EPILOGUE

REYNE

Awakening Chambers
Gods' Seat

Air rushed into his lungs, the struggle of life finding purchase from the void. He drew it in, everything he could hold. He had arrived. He had done it.

Blood rushed into his limbs as he stepped off the platform. He was in a chamber of cold stone, lit by dim lamps that held their glow without the telltale flickering of flame. Magic. The Power of the Gods.

He smiled.

Every word had been true.

Looking around the otherwise empty stone chamber he felt his first pang of regret. In the rush of the moment he had left his Codex behind. He had seldom taken an action the book had not prescribed since he first bonded with Saruk as a boy on the streets of Villecours. The bond had saved him, guided him away from the paths of poverty and crime toward a higher, nobler purpose. On his shoulders now rested the weight of the world. He would pay the price again tenfold if the book told it true. Worse was coming. And Reyne d'Agarre would stand against evil with all the power of a God.

He flexed his hands, feeling the familiar crinkling of leather. Clean. His gloves had been caked in blood, to say nothing of the rest of him, before he ascended. And here they were washed and new, as if freshly tailored. A proclamation of redemption he could happily accept, though he could still feel the need for power gnawing at the back of his mind. A relentless companion, one of which he doubted he would ever be truly free. Such was the price of greatness. With a deep breath he thought as much to his companion, invoking the subtle request for *Red* along with it.

Empty, came the thought from Saruk. *A heavy price, to carry us here.*

He frowned, feeling the thirst claw toward the forefront of his thoughts. Empty?

Calm. More will come.

His heart beat in a flurry, vision blurring as his breath came shallow. He stood frozen in the center of the chamber, hanging on his *kaas*'s words.

Calm.

A part of him urged the same. A quiet voice amid a torrent of fear, bordering on a rush of panic. Empty?

We must seal ourselves to the Seat of the Gods. Power flows, then. Peace.

"Where?" he rasped, struggling to voice the thought.

Here.

The sensation compelled steps forward. The wonderment he had felt dwindled to a low flame as they passed chambers connected to this main passage, cut from stone and decorated in strange styles unfamiliar to his eyes. Worry wrapped itself around his central core of purpose. Empty. Not only his stores, but the chambers as well. Not a soul from which to feed. The emotions that had become his balm, the lives he could snuff out to slake the thirst for a time. All gone. Had he made a mistake coming here? What was this place? Saruk's words carried him as the predatory parts of his mind tuned his senses to the subtle currents of the still air, searching for any sign of feeling.

He stumbled into the chamber before he felt it, then stood amazed at how he had not noticed before.

Pain.

Beautiful, glorious pain.

An ache that resounded through the ages, feeding into him like the fumes of a chirurgeon's draught. His eyes rolled up as it crashed into him, calming the thirst to a low hum as his senses fought to regain control.

There, came Saruk's voice in his mind, satisfied. *And more, when you complete the seal.*

He blinked, finally seeing the source. He stood in a massive chamber of smooth stone, bare of any adornment save a crystalline enclosure at its center. A diamond-shaped pillar around which it seemed this chamber had been built, rushing up to a high ceiling and emitting a soft green light that spilled across the expanse of the room. And somehow at its center: a woman.

Could it be? A single woman at the heart of so much emotion? He had seen hundreds suffer without producing so great a yield. Yet there she was, with no others in sight. A single figure encased in crystal, ribbons flowing and frozen alongside her, preserving the illusion of motion within her towering enclosure.

Go to her, Saruk urged. *Complete the seal.*

A part of him hungered to follow the instruction, drawn by Saruk's promise of more. But his thirst had quelled, and the rest of him stared up in wonder. Who was she? The Codex made no mention of this, yet even from a distance there was a certain familiarity. Even with her features blurred behind the crystal, he felt certain he had seen this woman before.

He stepped forward.

Yes. Hurry.

His instinct triggered him to alert. A sound? A change in the patterns of the air? Someone was coming. Strong emotions.

Frustration sparked through his bond to Saruk. *Hurry. We are vulnerable. Complete the seal.*

Another step forward. He raised a hand, somehow unsurprised when an arc of brilliant blue energy streaked from the crystal to connect to his outstretched fingers. Yes. This was right. The woman trapped within the crystal seemed to beckon to him, promising shelter, glory, duty, pain, all at once. Another bolt streaked toward him as he came closer. The newcomer was almost upon him now, almost to the chamber, but those instincts had been muted to a distant hum.

Yes, thought Saruk. *Finish it.*

His fingers reached toward the crystal, raw energy pulsing between his flesh and the transparent enclosure.

He recoiled in horror.

No, Saruk flared. *What are you doing? Complete the seal now!*

He stared into the crystal, finally close enough to recognize the woman trapped within. Sarine. The girl who had come so close to interfering with his plans. The enigma unmentioned in the Codex, whom he had nonetheless bested to reach ascension, only to find her here, imprisoned. Betrayal and anger flooded through him.

"How?" he demanded. "How is this possible?"

Complete the seal, you fool.

"AHR'AI'ET!"

The shouted command thundered through the room as Saruk translated the words within his mind: *Stop.*

He turned to see the newcomer hovering in the entryway to the chamber, a woman of middle height clad in strange furs. Horror twisted her expression as she looked between him and the crystal, a mere arm's length apart. Crimson flooded her eyes as a haze surrounded her, as Saruk managed to course a feeble amount of *Red* into his veins.

Instinct took over, a great gout of flame searing the air between him and the crystal. He rolled away across the stone floor, springing to his feet as another spear of fire ricocheted off the stone to his side.

"*Uhrun'a qui ah'nira'l kepai!*" the newcomer bellowed as Saruk translated: *You have no place here.*

He pivoted again, narrowly escaping another blast of flame, and he made a decision. Come what may, the crystal held the promise of power. Facing this newcomer with his stores nigh empty was certain death. He fixed his eyes on the crystal, and ran.

His attacker saw the move. A wordless howl accompanied a final wave of fire as he dove. Skin and clothing seared away as he made contact with the crystal.

White flared around him as he landed.

"*Ah'nat. Siquve, ah'nat,*" his attacker said as she approached. *No. Please, no.*

A dozen streaks of blue arced from the crystal as he lay on the ground, and energy washed over him. Pain replaced by numbness. Frailty replaced by power.

EPILOGUE

VOREN

State Rooms
The Royal Palace, Rasailles

"One last appointment, sir."

He sighed, removing his spectacles and placing them on the polished mahogany desk that dominated his receiving room. A handful of candles lit the chamber in a dim glow, straining his eyes beyond the ability to read any more reports tonight. Still, plenty of hours past sundown. No reason to stop working simply because this fragile body wanted to quit.

"Very good, Omera," he said. "And some tea if you please."

"Sir," his manservant replied, offering a stiff bow.

He smiled. Obsequiousness did not come easily to the Bhakal, but properly trained they were the best. A curiosity this far north in the New World, and a luxury. Their deep black skin and practice of dedicating one eye to their gods as youths gave them a fierce countenance that could unsettle even the hardest men and women. A small edge when it came to the subtle games of power and consequence, but empires had been built on less.

Rubbing the bridge of his nose, he picked up the last report he'd been reading—a treatise on the importance of preserving a trade alliance with the Thellan colonies to exchange New Sarresant textiles for sugars and tobacco. Squinting he could make out one word in ten. Not enough to grasp the details the subject required. A pity.

A rap sounded at his door, and he gave the call to enter.

"Gods be good, Voren, you've wasted no time," High Admiral Tuyard said as he swept into the room, his formal uniform all long coats and epaulets, better suited for the ballroom than the bridge of a man-o'-war.

"Be welcome, Guillaume," he replied, gesturing to an open chaise opposite his desk.

"Where did you find him?"

"A gentleman has his sources," he said with a smile.

"A warrior-caste Bhakal for a manservant, Voren. It sends a message, whether you mean to or not." Tuyard shifted forward to the edge of the broad cushion, patterned in a style of embroidered flowers, a design at the height of the fashion of the day. Tuyard continued with a meaningful look. "As does your choice of living quarters."

"I take your meaning, my friend," he said, reaching for a cup of tea proffered by Omera from a tray of pure silver. He hadn't noticed his manservant's return until the tea was at hand. They truly were the best.

"It is a risk, of course," he went on. "But I think you will find the ardor for *égalité* somewhat cooled of late. Symbols remind men of what it takes to lead."

Tuyard expelled a breath, almost a hiss as he laughed. "Bold, Voren. I've no wish to see your head under a guillotine."

"I should think not."

Both men smiled as they sipped their tea.

"What of the Assembly?" Tuyard asked abruptly when the moment had passed. "I can't help but notice your office seems to have a hand on the tiller of their decrees."

"We all have our means of influence, of course."

That earned a frown, as he had known it would. Men of Tuyard's station were unaccustomed to being far removed from the inner circles of their ventures. A stray thought passed his mind then, some sign read by his intuition though he could not put words to the reasons why. Time for a bold move.

"Tell me truly," he asked, watching the High Admiral like a falcon before a dive. "Do you believe the King can hold his borders, in the Old World?"

Tuyard's face darkened, and for a moment he worried he might have overplayed his hand. But no; men like Guillaume Tuyard did not wear their hearts on their sleeves. Emotion displayed was emotion meant to be seen, no more.

"The strength of trade has long balanced on this side of the sea. And that renders military matters academic, if not inevitable. I'm no fool, Voren."

"No accident that the Tuyard scion took a posting to lead Louis-Sallet's fleet then."

They shared a hard look.

Finally Tuyard gave a bitter laugh. "You should give thought to an heir yourself if you mean to see this through."

Relief washed through him as the tension in the room broke. He rose to his feet with a smile.

"I can count on your support then?"

Tuyard rose with a formal bow, giving him deference due one's superior, but only just.

"Until the last drop of my blood is shed, the seas run dry, and the eternal night accedes the day." An old form of oath, from early translations of the holy books. It took him aback to hear it, though he concealed it from showing in his face.

"Been consorting with the priests, have you?"

"The faith will have their say, it seems to me," Tuyard said. "Better for us if we make the proper signs now."

He maintained an expression of warmth even as his belly soured. Just as well to cut this meeting short.

"Wise," he said. "Though you must excuse me. The hour grows late and it appears I have grown old."

Tuyard bowed again. "I'll leave you to your rest then. We can review my men's reports on the rebuilding efforts in the morning?"

"Very good, High Admiral."

He eased back into his seat as the door shut, drawing a few deep breaths in between sips of his tea. Droplets caught on the bristles of his mustache, but the fire of it warmed his belly. A wise course to let younger men see him appear frail. Avarice took many forms, and ambition properly managed made for impeccable loyalty in the right sort of men.

No sooner had he risen from his desk again than Omera appeared in the entryway, head lowered yet still projecting awareness of the room around him.

"Will my lord be turning in for the night?" his servant asked.

"Yes. And no disturbances, if you please. I could use a few hours' peace before morning."

"Very good, sir."

He made the short walk from desk to bedchambers feeling Omera's one-eyed gaze on him despite the Bhakal maintaining the servants' posture. Strange. The man's service had not come cheaply, but perhaps the cost would weigh heavier than gold in having to adapt to his servant's foreign ways.

No small relief washed over him as he turned the heavy lock on his private chamber, sealing away the outside world for a time in favor of the comforts of the familiar. He tried the lock himself once more to be sure. Satisfied, he began the process of undressing himself before a stand mirror nearly equal to the height of the room.

Whispers came, as they always did when he caught sight of his reflection.

Some days he relished them, reminders of hard-earned prowess at the schools of Folded Sun and Flowing Spirit, under the tutelage of the Great and Noble House of the Fox. A lifetime of training to harness his gift, the perfect guise and mannerisms of his subjects a suitable reward for hard-earned mastery.

Today he had little appetite for ego, and so he set this skin aside as he unbuttoned the long coats of his formal dress. Younger fingers made quick work where the marquis-general's would have stumbled. Old minds were the best source of knowledge, but time demanded its price for wisdom. In these stolen moments behind locked doors he could relish the best of both halves. A sickening cost to think he was forced to live like this, without the accolades due a grandmaster who had risen through the path of *hanarun*. Yet all had agreed on the need, and he had not opposed it.

Sixteen cycles since their Lord had last tasted victory.

Catching sight of his birth face in the mirror he reflected on the essence of change. Who understood better than he? Who was better prepared to sacrifice, to wear these skins day and night to set their course in motion?

The time drew near, yet he put off his own ascension to lay the groundwork for their inevitable victory. He had his assurances; the masters would permit none to usurp his place. A difficult thing, to trust. That was a path in itself, with masters sure as skilled as he, seeking glory in their own way.

A lesson for another day.

For now it was enough that he had guided the ascendant of Order to her victory. One day they would be enemies, he and she, facing one another in the manner prescribed at the very making of the world. But first they must unseat the Three, the blasphemous Three who made mockery of the ancient way.

The thought threatened to unsettle him, and so he forced it from his mind. That too could keep.

He quieted his breathing, taking one more lingering look at what lesser men might call his true shape. Then he relented, allowing the whispers to resume as he closed the old man's eyes and sought the meditation of sleep.

EPILOGUE

THE VEIL

Soul of the World
Gods' Seat

Hope.

Dullness crept on the edge of her vision. Lines blurred and grew soft.

Her champions would curse her name if they knew, though she suspected they had begun to understand.

Paendurion, for all his rage a gentle soul. He could not see the need for balance. Could not understand the nature of the world.

Ad-Shi, wise and willing. In the end, too driven by fear to see the truth.

Axerian.

The pain of that loss tore through her.

Even she was not above sacrifice.

Dreams coursed through her mind as her body diminished. Would she remember who she was? Was it so simple, to be reborn?

She was afraid.

When? came the thought from Zi. Their connection had stretched thin of late. Another sacrifice.

Soon, she replied. After.

Warmth shone through their bond. Hope, receding as Zi faded from her conscious mind.

In the distance her enemy stirred. Vengeance echoed in her thoughts. Warnings.

Soon, she repeated.

LIES, came the response. *I HAVE WAITED LONG ENOUGH.*

His words thundered through her, and visions came. Memories of his price, of the pact they had made.

Encased in crystal, she could not retreat, could not offer the solace he craved. And so she endured, weeping silently.

And she waited.

ACKNOWLEDGMENTS

Thanks first and foremost to you, the reader. I started writing to tell stories to you and people like you. I'm humbled and grateful for the time you've spent in my world, and I look forward to entertaining you again should you choose to offer me another opportunity to do it.

Thanks to my agent, Sam Morgan, for seeing something in an otherwise terrible pitch. And thanks to my agency's president, Joshua Bilmes, for relentlessly pushing me to be better.

This book wouldn't be what it is without the efforts of the Orbit publishing team, and especially my editor, Brit Hvide. I may have held the knife when it came to killing darlings, but she showed me where to cut. I'll miss our 6 A.M. phone calls—at least until it's time to do the next one.

Thanks to my advance readers, Aidan-Paul Canavan, Mike Cooper, Sean Watson, Ryan Byrn, Kyle Murphy, and Bobby Crowe.

And lastly, thanks to my amazing wife, Lindsay Mealing. She fell in love with this book and lived in this world alongside me from the first draft to the last "the end." I would never have found this story without her.

extras

www.orbitbooks.net

about the author

David Mealing grew up adoring all things fantasy. He studied philosophy, politics, and economics at the University of Oxford, where he taught himself to write by building worlds and stories for pen-and-paper RPGs. He enjoys board games and card games of all sorts, once spent a summer in Paris learning and subsequently forgetting how to speak French, and gave serious thought to becoming a professional bass player before deciding epic fantasy novelist was the wiser choice. He lives in Washington State with his wife and three daughters, and aspires to one day own a ranch in the middle of nowhere.

Find out more about David Mealing and other Orbit authors by registering for the monthly newsletter at www.orbitbooks.net.

interview

When did you first start writing?
Well, that depends. *Soul of the World* is my first attempt at writing novel-length fiction. Or fiction of any kind really. But I've been DMing pen-and-paper role-playing games since high school, and that's where I learned how to keep an audience engaged with my stories. There's a lot of drama in writing. Role-playing taught me to step into a character's head, to speak and think in their voice. Translating that to writing meant learning the craft of prose, but the storytelling instincts were already there.

Who are some of your biggest influences?
I've always tried to allow myself to be influenced by greatness, which is fortunate because there is so goddamn much of it in SFF. Robert Jordan got to me in middle school, so he's near the top of my list. Brandon Sanderson is pretty high up there, too. Recently I've been going back to the swords-and-sorcery well of Robert E. Howard and Fritz Leiber, but I also absolutely adore more modern stuff like Nora Jemisin and the dynamic duo that is James S. A. Corey (Daniel Abraham/Ty Franck). In general I'm influenced by whatever I'm reading now. Which as I'm answering this is Django Wexler and Octavia Butler, but will be something else by the time this is printed!

Where did the idea for *Soul of the World* come from?
Originally *Soul* was a fantasy western. Arak'Jur was a bounty hunter Sarine was going to hire to track down her uncle's killer. This is back during the brief phase where I considered myself an outliner instead of a discovery writer.

Instead, when I sat down to write I had this image in my head of an invisible street artist sketching Louis XVI's court. I wrote that scene instead. And the rest flowed from there. Discovery writing is a hell of a thing.

The magic systems in *Soul of the World* are all so unique and complex. How did you come up with them?
I craft magic to suit the needs of the story. I couldn't have an invisible street artist without a magic system supporting it, and she would have been lonely without a companion to talk to. Thus came two of my magic systems.

Most of the time the form and rules for the magic come while I'm staring at a blank white page. I don't plan anything beforehand; I just allow myself freedom to experiment and am unafraid to liberally rewrite my earlier chapters when a better idea comes to me later in the drafting process.

The power of three is a major theme in *Soul of the World*—what drew you to focus on that?
Misdirection, actually! I wanted a story where the villain is one of the "chosen ones," and our lead protagonist exists outside the system. Three is such an iconic number in Western literature and mythology, it's easy to leverage the audience's expectations that there should be three heroes—but the book is in four parts for a reason. There's a lot of nuance layered into the story that will become clearer in the sequels. Even though I discovery-write my scenes, I have a pretty clear picture in my head of how everything fits together in the end.

The military scenes and strategy of this book are incredibly detailed and well thought out. How did you craft these scenes?

Full credit to Michael Shaara, author of *The Killer Angels.* I absolutely devoured his book when I was younger, and have been interested in nineteenth-century warfare ever since. The battle scenes in *Soul* are deliberately chaotic. I write my characters by imagining myself in their shoes, and a nineteenth-century battlefield is not a kind place. Smoke in your eyes, powder on your tongue, deafening cannon fire in your ears. That Erris is able to keep the strategy in her head and issue orders that lead her soldiers through the nightmare is a testament to what an amazing woman she is. I wouldn't do a tenth so well in her place.

***Soul of the World* has a phenomenal cast of characters. If you had to pick one, who would you say is your favorite? Which character was the most difficult to write?**

I immerse myself in every scene I write. I cried when I wrote the scene where Arak'Jur learns what happened to his wife and son. I fell in love a little bit with Lord Revellion when Sarine did. And I wanted to punch Paendurion in the mouth when Erris coldcocked him by way of Marie.

They're all my favorite. But Zi is maybe my favoritest. And he's the hardest character to write by a mile. Every word he says is dripping with meaning, and I have to be careful not to give too much away to savvy readers when I'm trying to be cryptic.

***Soul of the World* is the first book of a trilogy. What's in store for us in future books?**

Oh God. There's a new POV character in book two. I think I can say that much, right? He's an asshole and a pirate and I adore him. In general the story gets much bigger. We're going across continents, to visit places the cartographers of Sarresant have marked "HERE BE DRAGONS." Things get intense fast. There's not much in the way of slow buildup.

If you could spend an afternoon with one of your characters, which would it be and what would you do?
I'm boring. The thought of attending a salon with Reyne d'Agarre and debating the finer points of egalitarian philosophy sounds like heaven.

Lastly, we have to ask: If you could have any superpower, what would it be?
Are Hugh Jackman's abs a superpower? I'll go with that.

if you enjoyed
SOUL OF THE WORLD
look out for
MAGEBORN
by
Stephen Aryan

It's been ten years since the battlemage war, where thousands died as mages sundered the earth and split the sky.

Habreel believes eradicating magic is the only way to ensure a lasting peace. He will do anything to achieve his goal, even if it means murdering every child born with the ability.

As deaths involving magic increase and the seat of magical learning – the Red Tower – falls under suspicion, two students and one lawbringer must do everything they can to combat Habreel and his followers, before magic disappears from the world for good.

Chapter 1

The air in the tavern was thick with the stench of fear. To Habreel it was sweeter than any perfume. He smiled at the locals' unhappiness and sipped his ale, pretending to be just another traveller passing through the town of Glienned.

A few minutes later there was a stir in the crowd as the door opened to admit another visitor. Glancing in the mirror behind the bar Habreel saw a tall woman dressed in black leather armour and matching trousers approach and sit down on the stool next to him. He could admit to himself, if no one else, that she was a striking woman. Her raven-black hair and pale skin were not unusual, but the slight tilt to her green eyes and high cheekbones made it difficult to pinpoint her nationality. Her array of daggers, eight that he could see from an initial count, would draw attention as much as her features.

Akosh smiled at the barman, who turned a little red under the intensity of her stare. "On the house," he muttered, setting down a mug of ale before scuttling away.

Habreel frowned at her and she raised an eyebrow. "Something wrong?"

"You're a little conspicuous," he said, gesturing at her outfit.

Akosh rolled her eyes and waved at the mirror and their view of the room behind them. "Look again." The surface of the mirror rippled as if made of water and her image changed, from the leather-clad warrior to a severely dressed woman with a plain face surrounded by a tight bonnet. Every feature of the woman's face was forgettable. Only the colour of her eyes remained the same dark green, but set in a doughy face they were not enough to draw attention. "They see only what I want them to," added Akosh.

Habreel grimaced but said nothing. Magic. He took a deep breath and reminded himself she was a necessary evil. For now.

"Why here?" she asked him.

"Because Glienned is the doorway to Zecorria," explained Habreel, keeping his voice low. It was the first large town any travellers came to when they crossed the border into Zecorria from Yerskania. It was a hub of information and people from all over the world were known to stop here for the night. Anything that happened here would quickly spread across all kingdoms in the west. If they were lucky it would cross the mountains into Seveldrom and perhaps beyond in the desert kingdoms. Tensions between the east and west from the war a decade ago had faded and trade now flourished.

"Is that all?" asked Akosh, running a finger through the foam on the top of her ale. She languidly licked her finger and grimaced at the sour taste.

"And because I've been visiting the town on and off for weeks," added Habreel. "Zecorria is still the most hated nation in the west because of its role in the war. The Chosen and the perversion of the faith. The Warlock. The Mad King," he said, ticking things off on his fingers. "Now I will turn that into strength and other countries will race to unite behind them. Who doesn't like a redemption story?" he asked rhetorically.

"I hear a lot of words, but don't see anything exciting," said Akosh, in a bored voice. Habreel knew she was baiting him but didn't let her get a rise out of him.

"Come then. It's almost time," he said, draining the last of his ale.

Several people outside the tavern were all walking in the same direction with purpose. Akosh and Habreel joined the flow of bodies and soon became part of a large group that was heading towards the main square. By the time they arrived it was a little before midday. Perhaps three hundred people had already gathered, with more appearing all the time.

The sky was a hazy blue and the air was cold enough for Habreel to see his breath. People were stamping their feet and shuffling about to stay warm but no one complained or suggested going inside. None of them wanted to miss this.

In the centre of the square was a wooden platform normally used for travelling theatre troupes and seasonal festivals. Today the mood of the crowd surrounding it was sullen, like that of a public hanging, although there'd not been one of those for decades. Today there was no gibbet but the Mayor still wore a sour expression. "Everyone is so broody," said Akosh, grinning at the faces all around her. "It's delicious."

Habreel said nothing and tried to remain inconspicuous. A few people recognised him but not enough to start a conversation. Today he wasn't the only visitor in the crowd. All of the taverns and shops would be empty. It seemed as if most of the town had decided to show up. Habreel buried his smile but was secretly delighted at the size of the crowd.

Half an hour later the square was packed with people and a low rumble of unhappy conversations flowed around Habreel on all sides.

A shiver of excitement ran through him as everyone suddenly fell silent. Despite there being so many people squeezed in, they managed to create enough space for the masked Seeker to walk unobstructed through the crowd. No one wanted to touch the hooded figure.

The bulky robe, long black gloves and stylised golden mask

completely obscured the Seeker's identity. With only a slit for the mouth and holes for the eyes, it was difficult to tell much about the wearer. A line ran down the middle of the mask from forehead to chin and a swirling symbol, that he thought came from the east, was painted on the right cheek. The locals probably found it intimidating and mysterious. Habreel just thought it was ridiculous.

The only indication that the Seeker was a man came from the width of his shoulders and significant height. To Habreel his stiff gait suggested a history in the military. He wondered how such a person had ended up as a servant of the Red Tower, the school of magic in Shael.

Shortly after the war rumours had sprung up that someone was trying to reopen the school. A few years later people across the west reported seeing masked strangers showing up, offering to test children to see if they had a spark of magic.

Seekers used to be common but it had not been that way for over twenty years. No child would voluntarily declare they had magic and many successfully kept it completely hidden. When a community made such a discovery the hard way, often with a magical accident, it would mean exile for the whole family at best, drowning for the child at worst.

Then came the war and with it the Warlock who soured people towards magic even further. Because of him and his twisted apprentices, thousands had died in a pointless war. Nations had been torn apart with civil war breaking out in Morrinow in the north. In the south Shael was reduced to a shattered ruin that was still in disarray. All of it had happened because of the destructive power of magic and the evil it inspired.

It was a curse, not a blessing from the Maker, the Lady of Light or the Blessed Mother. Those who wielded magic thought it put them above everyone else. Mages claimed the power came from the Source, the heart of creation, but he didn't believe it. History was full of tales where people had been tricked by beings from beyond the Veil, offering them power in return for favours.

Habreel could imagine that wielding such power would be intoxicating, but it was an addictive lie that inspired arrogance and destruction. The war had shown people that magic could not be trusted and, until the Seekers had returned, the old ways of dealing with cursed children had been enough.

Exile or death. It was hard and cruel, but it had worked for a long time. Accidents with magic were avoided and people kept safe.

Now there was a royal decree in many countries which permitted Seekers to visit any village, town or city once a month to test children for magic. He believed in the rule of law, but when it stood in opposition of the will of the people, Habreel knew change was needed.

All eyes were drawn to the Seeker as he moved to stand beside the Mayor on the platform. She flinched at being so close but the Seeker didn't seem to notice. He was looking out at the sea of upturned faces. Habreel thought there was a certain arrogance about his stance.

"Bring them forward," said the Mayor, as if speaking about the condemned. Instead of a line of chained figures several sets of parents reluctantly came to the front of the crowd with their children in tow. All of the adults looked sick with worry, while most of the children were crying. Their ages varied considerably. Habreel guessed the youngest child was eight or nine years old and the eldest perhaps seventeen. Despite their differences all of them were united by their fear, which pleased him. The good people of Glienned were raising their children to understand that magic was a blight.

"Don't be scared," said the Seeker, who remained blissfully unaware of the mood in the town. "This is a time to celebrate."

The parents stepped forward and many had to shove their child onto the edge of the platform. Even though they were well outside arm's reach of the Seeker, none of the children were willing to go any closer. A couple of the smaller ones tried to run but were firmly held in place by their parents. Eight children. Eight chances of being cursed.

"How exciting," whispered Akosh, her eyes twinkling with delight.

"Can you tell?" asked Habreel. "Do any of them have the ability?"

Akosh grinned and gave him a conspiratorial wink. "That would spoil the fun."

The Seeker started at one end of the line with a slight girl of about ten. She was shaking so badly Habreel expected her to collapse. The masked mage raised one gloved hand towards the child and a few seconds later lowered it.

"No," he said, shaking his head for emphasis. The girl fell to her knees in a flood of tears. Her parents cradled her, openly weeping in relief.

This gave the Seeker pause and he stared at them with concern. His mask roamed across the many faces in the town square and Habreel saw a noticeable shift in his posture.

"He knows," he murmured. Akosh showed her teeth in an approximation of a smile.

"Did you see the Seeker arrive?" asked Habreel.

"No, why?"

"I wonder if he has a fast horse standing ready. If this continues he'll need it."

Moving more quickly now the Seeker went down the line, pausing briefly in front of each child. Every declaration that the child had no talent for magic was met with relief and often tears of joy. At last there were only two left, the eldest boy and a girl who was keening like a wounded animal. When the Seeker raised his hand in front of the girl her wailing increased in pitch, getting higher and higher. Habreel expected the dogs in town to start howling along.

"If nothing else, she has a future with a voice like that," noted Akosh. The girl's voice had taken on the pitch of a yowling cat on heat.

The Seeker paused in front of the girl and a horrified silence spread over the crowd. Finally the girl's voice either gave out or had become so high-pitched only dogs could hear her.

The Seeker tried to say something but nothing happened. He had to clear his throat and try again. "She has the ability."

At his words the girl's parents collapsed into a tangled heap as if hamstrung. Their wretched cries seemed to fill the entire square. The girl was sobbing, too, begging her mother to take her home, promising she'd be good from now on. Friends were commiserating with the parents, as if the girl was already dead rather than standing right in front of them.

"This is a good thing," tried the Seeker, but no one was listening to him. "It's a gift."

"You mean a curse," snarled the Mayor.

When the girl realised her tears were having no effect on her parents, she grabbed hold of her mother's hand. The reaction was unexpected and surprising. The woman recoiled as if she'd been bitten by a poisonous snake.

"Get away from me!" she shrieked at the girl, staring in horror at her own flesh and blood.

Beside him Akosh was chuckling while doing her best to smother it, but the smile would not stay off her face. She was starting to get some peculiar looks from those around her in the crowd. Habreel elbowed her in the ribs and she tried to turn her laugh into a nasty cough, but it wasn't fooling anyone.

While all of this was happening the Seeker quickly turned to the boy, raised his hand and swiftly lowered it.

"He doesn't have the ability," he said, much to the relief of everyone around the boy.

The cursed girl had fallen silent. Her face was incredibly pale and she stared at her parents with open-mouthed horror.

"Momma," said the girl, pleading with her eyes.

"Maybe we could all leave," suggested the girl's father. "Start a new life somewhere else."

"I have no daughter," hissed the mother, before collapsing against her husband in tears.

When the Seeker tried to lead the girl away she resisted at first but then moved as if in a trance.

"This isn't right," said the Seeker, trying to appeal to anyone who would listen. Habreel could see a few sympathised with him, but they were in the minority and wisely kept their mouths shut. The Seeker was only visiting the town but they had to live here.

"You should take the girl and leave, while you still can," said the Mayor. A low murmur of conversation was starting to flow through the crowd, and the tone wasn't friendly. All of the anger was directed towards the masked stranger.

"More children will be born with the gift," he declared.

"We'll take care of them by ourselves from now on," said the Mayor.

"You don't know how," said the Seeker.

"We managed it for years before the war, long before your kind started showing up again. We'll be just fine." The Mayor received murmurs of support from the majority of the crowd.

At this the Seeker paused, but not for long. He wasn't facing one angry woman. The crowd had let him into the square, but now he must have wondered if they would let him leave so easily.

"You can't do this."

"I am the Mayor of Glienned. I serve the people's will. You should take that child away and never come back. Tell all of your kind, they're not welcome here any more."

At her declaration every person in the square cheered. The Seeker must have realised that to stay would cost more than his pride. As he approached the first row of people the Seeker cleverly used the girl as a shield in front of his body. Everyone recoiled from her as if she had the plague, creating a clear channel through the press of bodies.

As they passed through the crowd, not far away from where Habreel was standing, he saw the girl suddenly lunge at someone. A moment later there was a terrible screeching sound and people began to move backwards in a panic. Something red sprayed into the air and a familiar coppery smell lodged in the back of his throat.

Akosh's reaction was immediate. She pushed forward and he followed in her wake until they were standing in the front row.

The girl lay on the ground, a knife lodged in her throat while the Seeker was vainly trying to stem the bleeding. No one moved to help him save the girl.

"What happened?" asked Akosh, nudging a woman beside her.

"Girl grabbed Tull's knife from his belt," said the woman. "Stabbed herself rather than be taken away." There was a hint of pride in her voice.

"Help me!" said the Seeker but everyone just watched. It didn't take long. The blood pulsing from the jagged wound in the girl's neck slowed and then stopped. Her eyes glazed over and she let out a final breath.

"Leave her be," said the girl's mother, finally stepping forward and taking responsibility. "She doesn't belong to you."

At this distance Habreel could see the horror in the Seeker's eyes. Everywhere he looked in the crowd he was met with the same blank expression. No one was horrified by what the girl had done to herself. The Seeker gently laid the girl down on the street and quickly marched out of sight. Habreel was willing to bet the Seeker wouldn't stop on the road until he was miles away from Glienned.

Once the Seeker had left, the mood of the whole crowd seemed to lift. People began to disperse, quickly going back to their lives as if nothing had happened. Soon only a few remained in the square, including the dead girl and her weeping parents. Habreel and Akosh followed others back to the tavern.

"Well, that was bracing," said Akosh, finally able to laugh out loud without it drawing too many stares. "But it will take more than this to change things. One town refusing the Red Tower will not have much of an impact, even with it being the doorway to Zecorria."

Her tone was mocking but Habreel ignored it. This time it was his turn to grin.

"Did you think I was doing this on my own?" he asked, shaking his head in disappointment. "You have your followers and I have mine. My people are fanning sparks like this all over the west and, any day now, one of them will catch fire."

"You want one of the tests to turn violent," said Akosh, suddenly interested again.

Habreel shrugged. "I dislike violence, but understand that sometimes it's necessary. People are terrified of magic and after what happened during the war, they should be. One mage changed everything. He helped start a war that served no purpose. People lost loved ones and friends in the slaughter and all of it comes back to one mage. In the long run, eliminating all magic from the world will save countless lives. It's been a blight for too long."

"And what if it means killing more children to achieve your goal?" asked Akosh. "Could you do it?"

"I will do whatever is necessary, no matter the cost." He knew what she wanted him to say, but Habreel wouldn't give her the satisfaction. He sincerely hoped he would never have to get his hands dirty, although a small voice in the back of his mind told him it wasn't possible. But they couldn't begin to rebuild without first scouring away those who were already cursed. If it happened, he would find a way to live with it, but in the end it would be worth it to achieve a lasting peace. If a few had to be cleansed to save tens of thousands, then so be it. "Can I count on your support?" he asked.

Akosh's feral smile made a shiver run down Habreel's spine. "Oh, yes. I've not had this much fun in years."